A Triple Fix of The Fixer

Jill Amy Rosenblatt

A Triple Fix of The Fixer

Copyright © 2024 by Jill Amy Rosenblatt
All rights reserved. No part of this book may be reproduced in any manner whatsoever without written permission except in the case of brief quotations embodied in critical articles and reviews.
First Printing, 2024

CONTENTS

The Fixer: The Naked Man 1
The Fixer: The Killing Kind 119
The Fixer: The Last Romanov 419

COMING NEXT 851
ABOUT THE AUTHOR 852

The Fixer: The Naked Man

Copyright© 2015 by Jill Amy Rosenblatt No part of this book may be reproduced in any form or by any means without permission of the author, excepting brief quotes used in reviews. *The Fixer: The Naked Man* is a work of fiction. Names, characters, businesses, places, events and incidents are either the products of the author's imagination or used in a fictitious manner. Any resemblance to actual persons, living or dead, or actual events is purely coincidental.

Cover Design and Images: Alan Gaites/Graphic Design

NOTE: The train problem discussed in Chapter 5 is a reference to the Trolley Problem, an ethics problem introduced by Philippa Foot in 1967 and modified by Judith Jarvis Thomson.

For Mrs. Danvers

Acknowledgements

My sincerest thanks goes out to:

Former NYPD Detective Glenn E. Cunningham for his incredible generosity and kindness in sharing his knowledge. His expertise has been invaluable to this book. Thank you Tim Clemente of X-G Productions for making the introduction.

Glenn Franklin, Esq. for graciously sharing his expertise of the workings of the legal profession and his many adventures. Your input sparked an idea for the direction of this series. Thank you.

Jasmine Patel, Esq. for providing information about the education path and requirements to become an attorney.

Jenny Joczik, Director of the Writing Center at Burlington College and my advisor during my Masters Degree program. Your instruction helped me become a better writer. Thank you for sharing about life in Vermont for this book.

Any errors in this manuscript are mine, not theirs.

Ken Sutak, Esq. for his editorial advice.

Dennis Shand for his wealth of knowledge. Whenever I have a question, you have the answer. Thank you.

Alan Gaites/Graphic Design for the amazing e-book cover.

Rebecca Brutus, thank you, younger me, for helping me find my way back to the writing life where I belong. Your encouragement helped make this book happen.

And to my Mom:

Thank you for your never ending support and encouragement, your excellent set of editing eyes, and for passing on to me your love of reading and writing. Best gifts ever.

Chapter 1

"Katrina, I need help." Katerina stumbled out of bed, her cell phone slipping from her hand.

"Damn it," she muttered. Fumbling for the lamp, she snapped it on, blinking several times against the harsh light. She heard the low tone of the man's voice, now coming from under the bed. Even from a distance he sounded frightened and hysterical.

"Katrina? Katrina?"

Bending over the side of the bed, her long chestnut hair cascading onto the floor, she groped for her phone. She grabbed it, bringing it to her ear.

"This is *Katerina*. Who is this?"

"Katr—, it's Joe Lessing. I'm a friend of Phil's. You remember me, right?"

Kat worked to match the voice to a face. After a moment, the film of sleep dropped away. Medium height. Built like a boxer. Strong jaw. Black hair with a widow's peak.

"Yes, Mr. Lessing. How can I help you?"

She listened to Joe Lessing's labored breathing at the other end of the phone; he sounded like he had just come in from a brisk jog. The clock radio read twelve-thirty. It was a little late for a run around the reservoir.

"I can't find Phil. Do you know where he is?"

"No, I'm sorry, I don't."

"He's not answering his cell phone."

"Mr. Lessing, I don't work for Mr. Castle anymore. Maybe his current assistant can help you—"

"Shit! Shit!" Lessing's voice rose. "SHIT!"

"Mr. Lessing—"

"Listen, Katri—Katerina—I need some help. Be a good girl and come over here and I'll make it worth your while. Okay?"

5

Katerina answered with silence. She had met Joe Lessing maybe three times when she worked for Philip. He never struck her as a crazed, rapist murderer…until now. Not a good idea, she thought. *Whatever this is, I don't need it.*

"Look, this is on the level. I'm in some shit here and I need a little help. It's worth a thousand dollars."

That I do need. Desperately. "Okay…twenty minutes."

"Make it ten. It's a matter of life or death."

"Which is it?"

"I'm not sure." He gave his address and hung up.

Kat considered his comment and then threw on a pair of jeans, a sweatshirt, and laced into a pair of ankle boots. She twisted her mass of hair into a sloppy braid. Stuffing some cash, ID, cellphone, and her trusty pepper spray in her pockets, she rushed out into the brisk New York City night. Against her better judgment, she took the subway. But, if there should be a police investigation, a cabbie, overeager to cooperate, would be a liability. In one of his many moments of ego and hubris, Philip had bragged about his golden rule of "fixing" people's problems: get in, get out, get gone. Don't linger. See everything but never be seen.

Keeping alert for drunkards, creepers, and other assorted predators lying in wait, she kept one hand in her pocket, her finger on the button of the palm-sized can of pepper spray.

She found Lessing's building. She glanced up, the bite of the chilly October night air making her give a quick, involuntary shiver. She pushed the call box button.

"Who is it?" Lessing sounded apprehensive.

Who do you think it is? "Katerina."

The buzzer rang. Kat slipped inside.

She found the apartment door ajar. She inched inside. A colorful Persian rug covered most of the foyer. Examining the bright pattern of red, blue, and black and finding no sign of blood, she relaxed. She took tentative steps inside, scanning the living room. Everything was neat and in order.

"Mr. Lessing?" she said.

"In here," he called from the end of the hallway.

Kat hesitated. Move ahead or turn back? She crept down the narrow space lined with modern art consisting of colorful paint splatters. The door was open.

Kat peered inside and saw Joe Lessing, a man in his forties, his overdeveloped muscular build now turning fleshy and soft. He was naked, pacing, and breathing hard. His flaccid penis, dangling like an oversized rotini, bobbed and swayed with every step.

Katerina froze. *Oh shit.*

He turned to look at Kat; she saw the panic in his dark eyes.

"Thank God you're here," he said, turning to the bed. It was a massive four poster with a distressed wooden chest squatting at its foot. A Queen Anne style night stand on each side held a Tiffany lamp. But it was the unconscious, naked blonde woman lying on top of the rumpled covers that grabbed Kat's attention.

"I called someone. She said she would try to get here but I can't wait anymore." He pointed at the bed. "Can you help me, please."

Kat didn't know what to say to him. When he had come to Philip's office he was always calm and relaxed...and fully dressed. He liked perching on the edge of her desk and talking about his motorcycle, his house in the Hamptons, and his wife.

His wife.

"What happened?" she asked.

"I don't know," he said in a shaky voice. "I don't know but I have to do something. *We* have to do something."

He returned to mindless pacing and the penis began dancing again. Kat moved to the bed. The woman had bottle blond hair, a too perfect nose, but her breasts were real, her waist a size zero. Kat leaned over and touched her cheek. Warm.

"I'm fucked, aren't I?" he asked, wiping sweat off his brow. "Am I fucked?"

"She has a pulse," Kat said.

"Thank Christ," Lessing said.

"Have you tried waking her?"

"Of course I did! Nothing works!"

"What happened?"

Joe scratched his head like he was trying to work out a difficult math problem. "We were going at it and it was good—shit, it was great—and then she collapsed. Look, we have to get her the hell out of here."

"When is your wife due, Mr. Lessing?"

Joe gave a short, guilty laugh. "She's taking a night flight from LAX. She'll be here soon."

"What's soon?"

Lessing's eyes met hers. "Less than two hours."

Shit.

"Your —friend needs medical care."

"I can't take her to the hospital. No one can know about this. Her husband would be very upset."

And your wife. "I understand."

"Please, you work for Phil—or you worked for him—whatever. You *know* people. You can work this out for me, right? You have to make this—" he said, pointing in the general direction of the bed, "go away."

Kat mentally tried to construct what Philip, the attorney who considered his oath a suggestion rather than a requirement, would do.

"Just a minute," she said, and pulled out her cell phone. She listened to the ringing on the other end of the line. Finally, there was a click.

"Yeah," the voice said. A chorus of coughing and gurgling noises followed.

Kat waited for him to finish. "Doc, it's Kat," she said when it was quiet. "I need a favor."

"I don't get out of bed for less than a thousand," the raspy voice said, followed by a deep drawing sound for air.

She held the phone away from her ear. "It's going to cost a thousand."

"For both of you?"

"No."

"Will he take Travelers Checques?"

"No."

"Will you take Travelers Checques?"

"No."

"They're American Express," Lessing said.

"I don't care."

Lessing resumed shuffling. Kat averted her eyes so that the penis was dancing in her peripheral vision. *A miniature Slinky.* She was tired of looking at it.

"Mr. Lessing?"

"Yeah?"

"Put your pants on…please."

He looked down at himself and then swiped his pants up off the floor.

Kat got back on the phone. "You need to get out of bed."

"If this needs a cleaner, it's your problem."

Kat glanced over at the unconscious woman. "I don't think so." She recited the address and hung up. *Good God, I hope not.*

***

Doc was known only as that—Doc. He was a licensed physician, or at least that's what Philip always said. He had a black goody bag with the usual items you found in a child's toy doctor set only they were real: a stethoscope, a thermometer, and bottles of brightly colored pills.

Just under six feet, his frame seemed to struggle under the burden of his bulging stomach. His sagging face, the trophy of a dissipated existence, his silver streaked hair and heavy, jowled cheeks made him look more like a veteran porn producer than a doctor.

Only Doc's heavy breathing broke the silence of the bedroom. One knee sunk into the mattress as he arched over the naked, unconscious woman, performing an examination.

Kat and Joe hovered on the other side of the bed, watching.

Doc pressed on the woman's abdomen and ran his fingers in a piano playing motion across the undulating planes of her body, lingering over her breasts.

"Is that necessary?" Kat said.

"A doctor's hands are sexless," Doc wheezed.

"Bullshit," she muttered.

Doc gave a grunt as he pushed his considerable girth off the bed, leaving a deep indent in the mattress. Picking up the woman's purse from the night table, he flicked it open and rooted in the contents.

"So?" Joe said.

"Narcolepsy," Doc said.

"Bullshit," Kat and Joe said in unison.

Doc tossed the tiny flame-red clutch on the bed and placed his stethoscope in his bag. He turned to Joe. "A thousand dollars."

"For that kind of money, aren't you gonna wake her up?" Joe asked.

"Can't. She'll come around on her own."

"What the fuck am I supposed to do with her until then?"

"Wait."

"For how long?"

Doc gathered his bag. "Not long. A thousand dollars."

Joe sputtered in objection.

"Mr. Lessing," Katerina said, "you need to give Doc his money…Mr. Lessing—"

Kat waited for Joe to focus on her. "You need to give Doc his money," Kat said, her voice strong. "I will find a way to get your friend home. Do we know where her husband is?"

Lessing seemed to have trouble focusing.

"Mr. Lessing—where is her husband?"

"He's in Jersey. He's driving back tonight. He could be home already. This was supposed to be a quickie."

Kat nodded. "The money," she said. She had no doubt that amount and much more was somewhere in the apartment. When Joe left the bedroom, Kat considered the unconscious woman in the bed. *How the hell am I going to get this woman home?*

She turned to Doc. "You sure about this?"

Doc opened the clutch and pulled out a medical bracelet with an ID tag.

Kat's face flushed. *Shit! I screwed up.*

Doc tossed her the bracelet and she snapped it out of the air with an easy catch. "You're still young, Miss Kitty. You got a lot to learn."

Kat rubbed the bracelet between her fingers.

"She'll be okay. Most of these cycles are short. She'll have a sense of memory loss. Maybe that's good. She'll forget she was in bed with a schmuck."

"Doc—"

"I don't like him."

Lessing came back into the bedroom with a wad of cash. His lips moved as he counted out the bills. He made two separate piles and handed one to Kat and the other to Doc.

"Okay, so," he said. "What now?"

The call box buzzer sounded.

Kat, Joe, and Doc turned toward the door.

***

Joe Lessing wore blue jeans, a white t-shirt, and a sheepish, cockeyed grin as he opened the apartment door for his wife, Constance, a slender brunette of medium height. She had a hard, unforgiving face and lips that had a generous application of too red lipstick.

"What took you so long?" she snapped.

"Sorry, babe," he said, taking her briefcase. "I fell asleep on the couch."

She grunted at his excuse and brushed past him.

"We need to move out of this place. There's always a bunch of weirdos wandering around."

"Like who?" he asked, vaguely realizing that he usually didn't pay this much attention to her.

Mrs. Lessing let loose a string of complaints as she wandered through the apartment. Joe watched her out of the corner of his eye hoping she wouldn't pick tonight as the night to change her usual habit of tossing her jacket over the chair. She was standing by the closet door.

•••

Kat had one arm wrapped around the waist of the unconscious woman, her other arm across her chest for support. The woman's dress was half on. Kat was sure she would suffocate in the airless closet, trying not to breathe in the acrid odor of the wife's hideous floral perfume. She listened to Mrs. Lessing's robust bitching while straining against the growing dead weight pulling at her arms.

"...then the elevator doors open and this huge fat guy comes waddling out. He's wearing this sickening aftershave, really disgusting. He stunk up the whole elevator."

The blonde stirred, pulling in a deep breath.

"He looked like a pedophile or a pornographer...and he had this wheeze..."

The blonde raised her head, still drowsy. Kat clamped one hand over the woman's mouth. The blonde's eyes flew open as she tensed into fight mode.

"The wife is home," Kat whispered in her ear.

The blonde froze.

Motionless, they listened to Constance Lessing's voice trail down the hall along with her stiletto heels clicking against the hardwood floor.

"Why the hell do you have the window open? It's forty fucking degrees outside. I wondered why the hell it was so damn cold in here."

Kat and the blonde slid out of the closet, shoes and boots in hand. Treading on the balls of their feet, they raced to the front door and slipped out, hustling down the hallway to the stairwell. Kat cast a last glance back at the apartment door as it closed without a sound.

• • •

The limo was waiting at the end of the block. A driver, six foot four with skin the color of almonds, leaned against the car. He had an amused look on his face as if someone had just whispered a joke in his ear.

He flipped the back passenger door open and the blonde jumped in.

Katerina handed him a wad of bills which he tucked in his pocket without counting.

"Thanks for the favor, Luther. The lady will tell you where to go."

"No problem, Miss Katerina. Anything for you," he said. With the smirk firmly in place, Luther walked to the driver's side and slid in behind the wheel; he eased the limo away from the curb.

The gentle whirring noise of the electric window rolling down made Kat look back. The blonde's face peeked out. She mouthed the words "thank you" as the limo pulled into traffic.

Kat dropped her boots to the ground, slipped into them, and kneeled to tie the laces. A pair of tawny, slim legs, feet tucked into Louboutin leopard print stilettos stopped in front of her. Kat straightened up and found herself face to face with an impossibly attractive woman a few years older than herself. A shimmering black wraparound dress accentuated her curves; blond, straight, shoulder length hair fluttered in the light breeze.

"I take it you were Plan B," she said.

"Yes," Kat answered.

"It's taken care of," she said. It wasn't a question.

"Yes," Kat said.

The woman gave Kat the once over from head to toe. "I'm Lisa. You can tell me all about it over a cup of coffee. If I like what you have to say, I have an opportunity that may interest you."

"What kind of opportunity?"

"One where you make a lot of money, doing what you did tonight."

Kat hesitated, and then nodded.

Chapter 2

Someone is in here. Kat froze in the dark entranceway of her apartment. A rush of adrenalin shot through her. Her mind raced. *Get out. Leave. Call the cops.* She saw something on the floor. Ignoring her instincts, she stepped in further, knelt down, and picked it up; a tie. Her eyes had adjusted to the dark and she stood up, placing a hand on a chair; a jacket was draped over the corners. The tension leeched out of her body. She didn't know too many burglars who broke into nondescript, low-rent apartments to strip. The bathroom door opened and a slash of light cut through the darkness.

Philip emerged, naked except for a towel around his waist. Seeing Kat standing with his tie draped over her fingers, he smirked.

"Hi, beautiful," he said, "going to show that on QVC?"

"I hope your apartment is out of hot water," she said, ignoring his remark.

His eyebrows quirked. "No, why?"

"How did you find me, Philip?"

He closed the gap between them. "I'm just back from Boston," he said, caressing her cheek with a feather light touch of his fingers. "And I do have the skills to locate people."

The heat radiating from him made her breath catch in her throat. He was wearing his usual "come hither" smile. Kat knew what that smile meant: a lot of enjoyable moaning and groaning in the night followed by regret and self-loathing in the morning.

"You should've called," she said, walking past him into the bedroom.

The bed had already been turned down. A bottle of wine and two glasses were sitting on the corner of her low dresser.

"We won't be needing those," she said.

"No love for a friend?" he asked, dropping onto the bed.

"No love for an ex-boss."

"But we're still friends, right?"

"You have lots of friends. You won't miss one."

"But you're my best friend." He gave her a slow smile. "Aren't you going to get undressed?"

Kat's lips tightened. She hadn't seen Philip in months. It didn't matter. The college frat boy good looks never changed, the shock of dark hair, the body, lean and fit.

"You don't mind if I do then, do you?" he asked and the towel was off.

He lay on the bed, exposed without shame and she allowed herself to examine him openly. The ripple of muscle across his stomach, his broad shoulders, were an open invitation for exploration with hands, lips, and tongue.

"I would ask how goes the temp gal Friday gigs," he said, "but I can see by your new digs, not well."

"I'm fine."

"Yes, you are. I bet they all tell you how much they love you."

"I'm used to hearing that line," she said. "I don't believe them either."

"You didn't ask how things are for me," Philip said, glossing over her comment.

"You don't look unhappy," she said.

Phil stretched his arms back, lacing his fingers behind his head. "Things are great but I screwed up, you know? I made a big mistake... letting you get away."

"Not interested," she said, but the words had no bite.

She caught the soft expression on his face, the eyes narrowing to dark slits. All she had to do was say the word. His face said he knew she would. So did she. Already, her body was preparing, against her mind, her will, and her reason. The adrenalin of the evening's activities was still pulsing through her veins, every nerve heightened, down to the tingling of her skin. She needed to take the pressure off.

"I don't suppose you'd like to forgive me," he said.

"Naked requests for forgiveness are a little tacky, don't you think?"

Philip rose from the bed and came to her. His eyes held hers as he slowly slid his hands from her shoulders to her waist. He undid the zipper on her jeans, peeling them down, revealing her black bikini panties. Kneeling down, he brushed his lips across her belly. She wanted to run her fingers through his hair, dig in, and hold on for what was coming next. He glanced up with a sly smile. When he stood he caught her sweatshirt within his fingers and slid it over her head, leaving her black lace demi bra in place.

He spent a long moment taking her in with his eyes. "I wasn't a bad boss, was I?"

"I thought lawyers never ask a question they don't have the answer to."

"Who says I don't have the answer?"

"You slept with someone else."

"Hearsay."

"While you were sleeping with me."

"Conjecture."

"I found her panties."

"Circumstantial evidence."

"In your apartment. In *your bed*."

Reaching around, he pulled the elastic band off the end of her braid. He slid his fingers through her thick chestnut hair, untangling the soft waves.

He let out a sigh. "Okay, I was an asshole."

"Your point being?"

"Look at you," Philip said, his lips brushing her neck. "Barely two years ago you were a wide-eyed innocent, a mere foundling. Look how far you've come. But you're not there yet, kid. Not by a long shot. You need me to finish your education."

His arms tightened around her and his lips closed over hers. She could feel her resolve melting as her body heat rose. She would not let him get away with this.

"You know," she said when she was sure her voice would be steady, "I really appreciate this "seduce the secretary" bit but I'm not moved."

He snapped the clasp of her bra, exposing her full, rounded breasts and began slowly caressing her. Involuntarily, she shifted closer to him;

a small sigh escaped her lips. Taking one nipple between his thumb and forefinger, he squeezed. She gave a small gasp and shuddered.

"I'm sure you are," he murmured with a wicked smile. He slid his hand between her legs.

"Forget it," she said. "I'm ready."

•••

The relentless buzz of the alarm woke her. The early morning sun cutting through the cheap, flimsy curtains cast a rectangular pattern on the tangle of blankets. She lay still for a moment, trying to orient herself, listening to Philip's soft, rhythmic breathing.

She stumbled out of bed and into the bathroom. Flipping the light switch, she turned her face away from the glare of the bulbs. After a moment she moved to the sink. She took a long look in the mirror, running her hands through her hair. Her cheeks had a soft, rosy glow. Making a sound of disgust, she bent over the sink, splashing water on her face. But she could still feel last night's warm, languid sensations permeating her body.

"Snap out of it," she muttered.

Reaching into the shower and pulling the top knob, she recited her daily, silent prayer that it wouldn't come off in her hand. She waited for the gurgle and click that would signal a half-hearted spray of water was ready to begin. She hovered under the warm stream, wishing it could wash everything away.

•••

Twenty minutes later, Katerina rushed around the cramped bedroom, dampness still clinging to her body.

"Good morning," Philip said in a lazy voice.

She glanced over to find him propping himself up with both pillows. She continued to rifle through the closet searching for a suitable outfit.

"Wow, now that I get the full view in daylight, you are even more amazing than when I first met you," he said. "Are you into yoga?"

"We are not having sex this morning," she said, pulling out a blouse.

He gave a light chuckle.

She came to the night table and grabbed her earrings. He latched on to her arm and pulled her close.

"Good morning, gorgeous," he said, his voice soft and low.

"What do you want, Philip?"

"What I've wanted since the day you left. Come back to work for me."

She pushed away from him.

Philip swung his legs over the side of the bed and got up; he began pulling on his clothes. "You're gonna drop dead working these crappy temp jobs, Katerina." He glanced around. "This place is barely livable. The only thing you're missing is a colony of roaches you could charge a sublet fee. You're never gonna make rent typing and filing and your father obviously can't pick up the slack."

Kat didn't answer. *He's right. Every day, things are getting tighter. Little by little, I'm going under.* Her parents hadn't sent money in weeks. She couldn't reach them by phone, no answer to her texts or emails; and her father hadn't paid the balance on this semester's tuition. Kat had done the math. To survive, she needed fourteen thousand dollars in two weeks.

"You want to be a lawyer, you need to work for a lawyer," Philip said.

"I won't be practicing your kind of law."

He finished buttoning his shirt. "That's cold, Kitty Kat."

He approached her and gave her a light kiss on the lips and then moved his lips close to her ear. "Can we just take a moment to recognize that you were incredible last night?"

The soft lull of his voice made her close her eyes; the nagging voice in her head kept saying she loved him. *I'm supposed to love him.* Her mindset of deluded innocence had been produced by a small town childhood where the message was unspoken but understood: sex means love. *Love. What is that, exactly? What do twenty-three-year-old girls know about love anyway?*

They stood so close she felt sure that he could hear her heart beating. His fingers sifted through her hair; a small sigh escaped his lips. For a split second he seemed like someone else entirely and then…"I wonder if you could hold on to something for me…"

Kat gave him a shove. Same old Philip.

"It's not dangerous," he said, tightening his hold on her.

"Then you keep it."

"We've done this before."

"That doesn't mean we should do it again. There are lots of things we should never do again. Where's the new secretary?"

Philip gave her his classic bad boy smile. "You were never the secretary. You're someone I trust." Pulling a letter-size envelope from his jacket pocket, he held it out to her. "I'll pick it up in a week or two."

"Fine," she said. "I'll put it in the drawer."

She reached for it and he snapped it back.

He picked up her purse and opened it, slipping the envelope inside. "I'll feel better if it's with you at all times."

Katerina opened her mouth to answer but Philip was already walking out of the bedroom, shrugging into his jacket.

She caught him at the front door.

"You're welcome," she said.

He turned to her. "I meant everything I said to you, kid, everything. Think about coming back. It's a big, bad world out there. You're not ready yet." He winked at her and was gone.

She stared at her purse. He was right. He knew it. So did she.

Tossing the purse onto the chair, she went back inside to finish dressing.

Chapter 3

Three days later, Katerina told the manager at her mindless data entry temp assignment she couldn't work the full day. The woman, in her late fifties with a thick waist and a disgusted expression on her face, shrugged.

"If you have to leave, leave," she said. "Are you planning on coming back tomorrow?"

Kat said yes, just in case.

***

Hanging on to a pole on the R line subway, Katerina mentally reviewed her encounter with the long and lithe Lisa. In less than ten minutes she had decided to interview for a "consulting opportunity" with MJM Consulting. It was part curiosity and part flattered ego. Consultants were considered by invitation only. But what exactly *was* the position? As Kat slipped into a vacated seat, she remembered that Lisa's answer to her question made her both curious and uneasy.

"You're a fixer," Lisa had said, "but the unofficial title is a 'B girl'."

When Kat eyed her curiously, Lisa explained: "You do the bitch work no one else can do."

Katerina had done her due diligence on the internet regarding her potential new employer. She found an address for MJM but no phone number. The description of the company read "goods and services" or "consulting services." Other than that, the company had no website, no listing of clients or customers, and no Mission Statement. For all intents and purposes, MJM was a non-entity; it might as well have not existed at all.

***

Kat trotted off the train, jogging up the steps to civilization. She passed The Plaza, making it to the building with five minutes to spare. She spotted the call box off to the right. She pressed the button and waited.

"Yes," came an edgy female voice, cautious, impatient.

"Katerina Mills. I have a noon app—"

The buzzer sounded. Kat tugged at the door and slipped inside. The open, airy marble lobby exuded elegance. Kat rode the elevator up to the fourth floor. When the doors slid open, she stepped out into the hallway, sinking into the thick ecru carpeting. Every office door was a rich cherry wood, accented with a gold plate etched with a company name. She wandered down the hall until she finally found MJM Consulting. Turning the knob, she stepped inside.

The office waiting room was just that, an anteroom, bare, with dark paneling and a tiled marble floor polished until it resembled glass. There was a short hallway that led to an office. The door was ajar. Kat floundered for a moment, unsure of how to proceed.

"Katerina," a woman's voice called out. "Come in."

•••

Kat entered the office, what little there was of it: plush, burgundy carpeting and a massive ball and claw mahogany desk squatting in front of the window. An oversized black leather chair sat behind the desk. In the chair, a fortysomething woman in black Chanel with pearl teardrop earrings and raven hair swept off her face stared intently at a laptop. There was nothing else on the desk; no pens, paper, or any of the usual items associated with daily business life. Lisa had told Katerina the woman's name was Jasmine.

"Sit down," Jasmine said, gesturing to the one guest chair opposite the desk.

Kat took a seat.

Jasmine turned her attention away from the laptop and focused her laser look on Kat.

"Lisa recommended you. Based on the qualities you've already displayed, you've earned a trial period."

"Thank you," Kat said, folding her hands in her lap to keep from kneading them in anxiety.

"Did Lisa explain what we do here?"

"She said this is an exclusive concierge service."

Jasmine sat back in her chair. "Mmm. We are an introductory service. There are people who need things. We introduce them to you; you provide those things. Requests may range from the workaday to the unusual. But make no mistake. These requests are not for the run-of-the-mill assistant. They require a specialist."

Kat nodded her head.

"We do not, under any circumstances, handle requests that involve body to body contact."

Katerina felt her eyebrows rise. Okay, she thought. That answers that question. This is *not* a high end prostitution ring.

"Here's how it works. I call you and tell you where to report and how much money you are going to receive. When you arrive at the meeting, the first thing you do is collect the envelope."

"You collect payment first?"

Jasmine stared in response. Kat realized she had made her first mistake. Her stomach lurched.

"Once an assignment is accepted, it will be completed. No returns. No refunds. Is that understood?"

Kat nodded.

"The second thing you do is count the money in the envelope. Do not do anything else until that is done. If the money amount is not correct, state that. Do not negotiate. If the correct amount of money is not produced, leave the envelope and leave the premises. Is that understood?"

Kat nodded her head, her mind beginning to race.

"This arrangement requires you to have your own database of contacts to do whatever it takes to complete the assignment. If you cannot complete the assignment, there's no reason for you to be here. Is that understood?"

"Yes. How—how do I get the money to you?"

"The money will be collected. All of it. You'll receive your share after the assignment is completed. Is that understood?"

Kat nodded. This was not Philip territory. This was way beyond Philip.

"There are rules," Jasmine continued, in an even, soft monotone. "You must follow the rules. If you don't, there will be no reason for you to be here."

"Do not share any details of your assignments with anyone. Ever. Any break in confidentiality and there will be no reason for you to be here."

No reason to be working at MJM or no reason to be *alive?* Kat thought.

"Do not book any separate appointments on your own," Jasmine continued.

"You may not accept gratuities."

"You are permitted to decline one assignment per year for an undisclosed reason."

"You may waive an assignment on the basis of illness."

"Do I need to a doctor's note?" Kat asked.

A smile lifted the corners of Jasmine's lips. "We'll know if you're sick."

Kat's breath caught in her throat. She sat mute.

"You are not an employee and no employment contract exists between you and MJM Consulting. You are an independent operative providing exclusive services. We make introductions between you and the people who need your services. We take a fee for this introduction. MJM assumes no responsibilities for your actions. Any legal issues you encounter as a result of providing services are solely your responsibility. MJM will disavow any warranty or relationship between us."

Kat did the mental translation: *if I get arrested, I'm on my own.*

"You may not engage with any other company or entity like MJM while you are using our client introduction service. Doing so is a conflict of interest and there will be no reason for you to be here. You may not place yourself in any outside situation or be involved with any outside person or entity that directly or indirectly jeopardizes MJM."

Kat felt a stab of fear; Philip's envelope burning a hole in her purse.

"You are on probation."

"How long does probation last?"

"For as long as I say it does," Jasmine responded. "You are prohibited from asking for help from other consultants and they are barred from helping you. However, you are permitted to have one meeting with Lisa during which she may advise you. You may decline to use our introductory service at any time. However, once you make that decision, it is final and irreversible. Understood?"

Kat became conscious of the fact that she was staring as she tried to wrap her head around everything she heard. She nodded.

"You're going to Sixty, East Eighty-sixth, between Madison and Park. The envelope is twenty thousand. Your cut is twenty percent. The name is Reynolds."

Kat nodded. *Four thousand dollars. Only ten thousand to go.*

Jasmine returned to staring at the laptop. The meeting was over. Katerina stood up and moved to the door; she had a thought and turned.

"Is the client male or female?"

Jasmine glanced up from her laptop. "It's a man. The client is always a man," she said.

Chapter 4

Katerina exited the taxi at the corner. She rarely ventured uptown. Philip's office was a stripped down affair in the East Village. As she walked she noticed the sidewalks were pristine. She wondered if everyone who came here instinctively knew that the sidewalks were not to be marred by gum and dog shit. Even the birds knew better.

She spied the doorman standing outside the building and headed toward him. The sound of a persistent horn made her stop and turn to see a limousine crawling, keeping pace with her. It eased toward the curb and stopped. The passenger door opened.

Kat glanced at the doorman. He was busy holding the door open for a resident.

She took a step toward the limo and peeked inside.

The man was in his early fifties, wearing a dark suit, white shirt, red tie, and a benign expression. He could have been a teenage girl's favorite uncle.

"Miss Katerina," he said.

She got into the limousine, slamming the door behind her.

"John Reynolds," he said, his voice soft and gentle. "I hope you can forgive me. I'm in a bit of a hurry. You don't mind a meeting on the go, do you?"

"Not at all," she said, her voice sounding small and meek in her ears.

Mr. Reynolds drew an envelope from his pocket and held it out. She reached out to take it and his hand connected with hers and lingered. His eyes held hers; they reminded her of a shark's eyes, cold, careless. Despite his smile, apprehension made her pulse quicken. She pulled her hand back and slid open the lip of the envelope. With a swipe of her thumb across the bills, she knew the money was there.

"How can I help you, Mr. Reynolds," she said.

He disengaged, his hand resting on the seat near her thigh but not touching. She felt compelled to look at him as he spoke, this dapper gentleman with a head full of wavy salt and pepper hair. Despite his easy manner, there was something behind those eyes that made her heart beat fast.

"I'm afraid I've done something terrible where my wife is concerned and I need some assistance to fix it."

Kat nodded. She forced herself to focus, pulling Philip's words of wisdom from her mental file cabinet.

Clients always want to confess.

"I feel awful for having let the situation degenerate this way."

Listen. Nod. Keep your face blank.

"I've been spending all my time in corporate boardrooms and I am out of touch with my partner, my lover, and my best friend. Her birthday is in a matter of weeks and I have no idea what to buy her because I have no idea what she does all day. I don't know my wife."

Katerina gave a quick mental exhale of relief. She nodded but keeping a blank expression was proving difficult when she wanted to pat his shoulder and murmur "poor man." Knock it off, she thought. I didn't just get off the bus. He's either a man in love with his wife who got bitch slapped because he already forgot her birthday, or he cheated on his wife and is trying to smooth it over with an expensive gift.

Either way, not my business. Do the job. Collect your money. End of story.

She met Mr. Reynolds' gaze. She saw none of whatever it was that had frightened her just a few moments earlier.

"I need you to follow my wife. I need to know where she goes and what stores she frequents." Reynolds took her hands in his own. "Most importantly, Miss Katerina, I need to learn her interests and her passions, so I can get to know her again and arrange the perfect gift."

Katerina smiled in response.

Jasmine had said even the work-a-day requests required a specialist. But this? Why did a birthday present require a consultant? Why not give this job to the secretary? She had probably been doing the gift buying for years.

Katerina was about to speak when Philip's most popular mantra played in her head:

DO NOT OFFER ALTERNATIVES. EVER. You put yourself out of work and give someone else the job.

This is a simple job that will net me four thousand dollars. More jobs like this and I'll be out from under.

"I'll take care of it, Mr. Reynolds."

He took her hand in his. "Thank you, Miss Katerina, thank you. She has a spa appointment on Thursday. You can start from there." He nodded toward the driver. "Garrett has the particulars and a number where you can reach me."

The limousine slowed and eased over to the curb.

"Where are we, Garrett?" he asked.

"Thirteenth Street, sir."

It was near her apartment.

"I hope this is all right. You won't be too inconvenienced, will you?"

Kat smiled. "This is just fine, Mr. Reynolds. I'll be in touch."

The passenger door opened and Garrett stood, waiting. She exited the limo taking the paper from his gloved hand. She watched him disappear into the driver's seat and maneuver the limo back into traffic.

Chapter 5

Katerina decided to stop in at her apartment and change before heading to the campus. Her mind was already racing. How to complete this assignment? She needed to shadow Mrs. Reynolds but she had to have transportation.

Kat entered the gloom of her apartment lost in thought, dropping her keys on the table. She opened her purse, bypassing the cash and instead, extracted Philip's envelope. She slid it between her fingers in examination until she felt the thin strip shapes inside. She frowned. So like Philip, she thought. She put it back in her purse. When she looked up, she saw the man sitting in her wing back chair.

She gave a small gasp and took a step backward. For all she knew, he could have been sitting there for hours, patient, waiting. Her eyes had grown accustomed to the dimness and she could see his face was calm, even meditative. He rose and Kat took another step back. Her mind screamed *run* but her body would not obey.

He stood over six feet tall, ramrod straight, his frame chiseled like rock. He was bald with skin the color of mocha; he wore black.

He came to her. "Here for the pickup, baby."

Kat nodded. Her hands shook as she fumbled in the purse. He laid a hand over hers. It was heavy and warm. She froze.

"Shouldn't I—shouldn't I—call to confirm—that you're okay?"

A smile touched his lips. He took out a cell phone, pressed a button, and held it to her ear.

Kat listened and heard a click. "MJM, how can I help you." Jasmine's voice.

He took the phone back. "We're good," he said and hung up.

Kat took the envelope from her purse and held it out. His movements were slow and deliberate as he took it and tucked it into an inside jacket pocket.

He ran a finger the length of her long hair.

"All right, baby," he said. "All right. Now you know."

Katerina nodded. A personal courier and a walking, talking discouragement from even thinking impure thoughts of skimming.

He went for the door.

"How did you know I would be here?" she asked.

He gave a small chuckle but didn't turn around. "If you've got the money, Angel always knows where you are, baby."

He opened the door and was gone.

Kat sank into a chair and forced herself to breathe.

***

The Washington Square Arch loomed overhead, lit up in yellow just as the afternoon sun began to fade. Kat headed to her last class, chiding herself as she always did that she never took a moment to enjoy the experience of being in New York. She had achieved a dream by just getting here.

It was a goal she had willingly pushed back to the far recesses of her mind as she sat by her father's bedside, watching William Mills in a silent struggle, the war waging within him to beat the cancer. After the all clear came, it was another year before his gregarious smile returned along with the faint glow of health as his face and frame filled out once again. She remembered the day her parents called her into the living room. They sat on the couch side by side, Bill and Linda Mills, or Ozzie and Harriet as her brother called them.

"It's time for you to get out of here," her father had said. "You've got an education to get and we have to get back to the Rotary Club and planting the vegetable garden. Everything back to normal."

She had hugged her father but now that she thought back on it, his smile had an odd little twist to it. Maybe that's what had struck her about Mr. Reynolds. He had the same smile.

She made her way to class, coffee in one hand and her cell phone to her ear with the other. This was the time of her weekly phone call with her parents. She would stroll to class hearing all about the big doings in small town Vermont. Her mother would do all the talking but her father would be ever-present in the background, calling out comments until finally her mother handed him the phone.

"How's my girl?" he would say and she could hear the smile in his voice. "Do you need money?"

There had been none of that last week or the week before. Today it was the same. The phone continued to ring. Kat's concern had moved past worry and now her stomach did a familiar somersault as panic rose. She needed to call someone to check on them. Who? The police? It wasn't an emergency. At least she hoped not. Her brother was long gone and far away. She thought of their neighbors, the Taggarts. She clicked off from her parent's number and redialed, her pace increasing with her anxiety as she waited for the connection. She nearly jumped when she heard the click.

"Hello?"

"Hi, Mrs. Taggart. It's Katerina Mills."

"Katerina, how are you dear? How are things in the big city?"

"Uh, big, very big," she said with a nervous laugh. "I'm sorry to bother you but I've been calling my parents and there's never an answer and no answering machine. Have you seen them?"

"Oh, oh, oh," Mrs. Taggart said. "Well, yes, yes, dear. Yes. Yes. They're fine. I have seen them and they have just been very busy and I'm sure they will call you very soon, probably in the next day or so, I'm sure."

Katerina listened to Mrs. Taggart's locomotive speed response. She blurted out the first thing that came to mind. "Mrs. Taggart, is my Dad sick again?"

"Oh, no dear, he's not—sick. He's just—it's just the change of seasons. Everyone's a little off this time of year."

Kat opened her mouth to speak.

"Now dear, I don't mean to rush you but I do have to go. Pies in the oven. Don't you worry about your parents. They are grown-ups after all. They can handle their own lives. You just study hard and be a great, big success. Bye, dear."

Mrs. Taggart rang off, leaving Kat to mull over the strange response she had just received. Who had asked if her parents could handle their own lives? What, exactly, was going on at home?

•••

Kat made it to her Introduction To Ethics class just shy of seven o'clock. She would spend the next ninety minutes discussing ethical behavior, moral compasses, and corporate responsibility with an envelope in her purse that she assumed was of an illegal nature. She had a few minutes to kill before class began and she spent it as she always did: thinking about Philip. She had only worked for him for a couple of weeks when she realized Philip wasn't a trial lawyer or an ambulance chaser. He was a criminal lawyer in every sense of the word. His services included consultation, representation, introductions for the private sale of unadvertised goods, and delivery services utilizing a brown paper bag. On her second day on the job he had said, "We're paperless here, beautiful. You're a smart girl, I can tell. Don't write down my messages or phone numbers, okay?"

"You want it all on the computer?" she had asked.

"I want you to memorize it. I don't do e-mails, texts, or instant messages. I don't want information anywhere but in that pretty little head."

She would have stayed. After all she and Philip had… she thought they would be… Kat shook off the thought. Stupid girl. The man had clients who looked like large blocks of concrete. They would come into the office, give her a smile, and she would almost wet her pants. What kind of man did she think Philip was? The kind of man who had a blonde hiding in the closet when she showed up with Chinese takeout for dinner; and she had just made another mistake sleeping with him again.

Students filed in and the class filled up. She decided she would get in touch with Philip tomorrow, get rid of the envelope, and stop making bad decisions. At least this job was a step in the right direction. She was good at fixing things; she would do what she was good at and make a lot of money doing it. How hard was it to follow around some spoiled rich wife?

•••

The class was a sea of freshman and sophomores. The difference between Kat and everyone else was that they were eighteen and nineteen years old. She was twenty-three with two and a half years more of school to complete. Some students talked of weekend plans and keg parties, while others were already planning for their LSAT's. She lagged behind, plagued by the nagging feeling that she didn't know what everyone else knew and she would always be running to catch up.

***

"YOU'RE ALL LIARS AND HYPOCRITES!"

Professor James, a small, stooped man, with a thatch of unruly, snow-white hair that would have given Einstein a run for his money, was in fine form. Wandering back and forth, at times appearing to talk to himself, wearing an ill fitting jacket, his bow tie slightly askew, he punched his fist into his palm as he spoke.

"I will show you. I WILL PROVE IT TO YOU! There is a runaway train. There are five people strapped to the track. The train will KILL all five. But—there is a switch. With one swipe of your hand, if you flip that switch, you will save the five and the train will take another track. On that track, there is one person strapped down, unable to escape. Do you flip the switch, Mr. Larkin?"

Professor James zeroed in on a male student sprawled in his seat, decked out in his college uniform of jeans, ratty sneakers, plaid shirt, and a sneering attitude of derision.

"Absolutely," he said with an easy smile.

"Ah," Professor James said. "But what if I tell you that the facts have changed. There is still a runaway train. There are still five people strapped to the track. But—there is an overpass and on that overpass there is a very large, one would say, OBESE, man. If you push him off, his...*girth*..." the class tittered at the word, "will stop the train. The five will be saved if you kill the one. Do you push him, Miss Mills?"

The class turned to Katerina.

"No."

Professor James tilted his head down and considered her with narrowed eyes. "And why not?"

"Because it's murder."

Larkin laughed and mumbled something under his breath that caused students around him to chuckle.

"I see Mr. Larkin does not subscribe to your way of thinking," Professor James said. "Why not, Mr. Larkin? Would you do it?"

"Hell, yeah."

"You'd kill a person outright," Katerina said.

"And you're not killing somebody when you pull that switch?"

"It's not the same," she said.

Larkin tilted towards her with a smile. "A push, a flick of the finger, a pull of the trigger. It's *all* the same."

Katerina cast her eyes downward as a flush of heat colored her cheeks.

"Miss Mills, do not be downhearted," Professor James said, his face the picture of understanding. "It should be the same but it is not and that is what we are here to discuss. Morals are about good and bad but ethics is about reason. If you have already deemed that it is better to have one die instead of the five, then reason dictates that you push the fat man as well. Miss Mills? What is your reason why you do not agree?"

Katerina stumbled over her words. "Because... it's just—"

"Different," Professor James finished. "Because you have looked into that man's eyes, seen his face, touched him, and killed him with your own hand. But if you merely flip a switch, something impersonal, it's different. You are not the first to face this quandary, Miss Mills. You will not be the last. Thankfully, the odds of anyone in this room having to wrestle with this particular conundrum are miniscule, so we may discuss in theory as much as we like."

Kat cast her eyes down again onto her notebook. When she glanced up, she found a young man with dark hair, dark eyes, and a fair complexion, staring at her. He was dressed in a blue button down shirt, the tails hanging out over his jeans. He had a Clark Kent quality about him. When their eyes locked, he turned back to the front of the room.

Professor James turned his attention to the class. "Today you will begin to explore your own ethics. You will choose a partner and each will take a side of this case and you will present your findings in a joint paper."

A low murmur of discontent filtered the room. Professor James paid no attention.

***

"Would you like to be partners?"

Kat turned at the sound of the male voice. Clark Kent.

"If you don't have one," he continued.

"Yes." She caught a look of defensive self-preservation cross his face, a mix of anger and disappointment to blunt the blow of rejection.

"No. I mean yes, I don't have a one," she said. "Sure, we can be partners."

He nodded. "Do you want to be for or against?" he asked.

"I'll be against," Kat said.

"Fine," he said, but his brow furrowed.

"If you want to be against, that's okay," she said quickly.

"No, it's okay. You didn't ask me my name," he said. "I do have one."

"I hope so," she said. "You are entitled to one."

The brow smoothed and he smiled. His boy-next-door face reminded Kat of home at this time of year; a vision of evening concerts, the Harvest Festival, and the last Farmer's Markets before the coming of the winter.

"I'm Mark."

"Hi, Mark. I'm—"

"Katerina. Yes, I know."

A slight shiver of anxiety rippled through her. "How do you know?"

"Professor James calls on you every week. And *I* pay attention."

They stood in an awkward silence for a moment. "I think Starbucks would be a good place to meet," he said. "We could have a bite to eat and debate the problem."

"I think a library study room would be a better place," Katerina said, gathering her books and moving toward the stairs to get to the exit. It was a sweet ploy to get her to eat with him. It had been a while since she had a guy try that hard.

"Food is important. We need to keep up our strength."

"I'll bring granola bars."

Mark nodded his head as he kept time with her on the stairs. "Great. But it's extremely dangerous to eat without something to drink."

Katerina stopped short to stare at him.

"Choking hazard," he said. "You're not allowed to bring drinks into the library. I mean, people do, all the time, but they shouldn't and if we get caught, then you're gonna have to give up your water bottle and then you could choke."

Katerina pushed down her smile. She had known someone like Mark back home. She still thought of him sometimes, wondering where he was, and if she had made a mistake letting him go.

"You can give me the Heimlich maneuver," she said, deciding to push a bit further.

"Then, the piece of granola bar will fly out of your mouth and hit the librarian in the eye. Someone will catch it on their phone, it'll go viral, and you'll be all over the Internet."

"Okay," she said. "Starbucks it is."

He stood before her, clearly pleased with his rally to win a meeting that involved a meal. "Great, so I'll call you."

"Sure."

"I need your number."

"Right," Kat said, rattling off her cell number.

He punched it into his phone. "Okay, great...I'll call you and we'll get together... at Starbucks."

"Sounds good. Goodnight, *Mark*," she said.

"Right. Goodnight, *Katerina*."

They went their separate ways; she glanced back over her shoulder to see him striding away with a slight swagger. Katerina turned back. He's a nice boy, she thought. *Remember when you used to date nice boys, Katerina?*

Chapter 6

Katerina woke draped over the kitchen table, her face plastered against her *Introduction to Ethics* text book. Her eyes were dry and sticky and her mouth tasted like last night's coffee. She stumbled to the bathroom, splashed water on her face and brushed her teeth. Then, she rolled out her yoga mat and tried to crowd out her thoughts by concentrating only on the motion of her body stretching, leaning, and lifting. After an hour she settled back into Savasana, the corpse pose, a comforting posture of total relaxation. While her body was supposed to mimic that of the dead, her mind would not cooperate. She still had not spoken to her parents.

The ring of the cell phone jolted her from her thoughts. The number came up as private. It was Jasmine. Another assignment.

•••

When the elevator opened, the door to the penthouse was ajar. Kat hesitated, unsure if she should knock or enter. She heard a man's voice speaking in a low and steady cadence. The voice came closer until the door swung open wide. Kat stood like a schoolgirl, her hands folded in front of her.

The man was dressed in crisp, dark slacks, a tailored white shirt, and a red tie. He had a phone at his ear and motioned with two crooked fingers that she should enter. He turned his back to her and moved back into the apartment. She guessed he was in his forties.

"Look, you tell those assholes that the gross margin has to be set at thirty percent, you understand? It's not worth doing with a margin any smaller. Jesus Christ."

The apartment wasn't a living space so much as an exposition for Rococo furniture. Ornate, asymmetrical pieces with floral designs created a miniature version of eighteenth century France crammed into a New York penthouse apartment. Kat was careful not to touch anything. She didn't dare leave a fingerprint.

"Fine, fine," he said, running a hand through his dark hair. "I have to go into a meeting now. Call me in a half hour."

Obviously, this isn't going to take long, she thought. Judging by the surroundings, Kat guessed he wanted her to track down some hard to find item he saw on *Antiques Roadshow*. She was already mentally making her plan of attack. Who did she know in the antiques world?

Clicking off the phone, he turned to her. He regarded her with a bemused look, and then gave a slight shake of his head as he came forward and made a gesture toward a chair.

Katerina sat and waited.

He drew in a long breath. "Jonathan Cookson. I have a situation. It's delicate and it's time sensitive."

He looked her over again, taking in her face and hair. He gave a short laugh, shook his head and glanced around the room. "My wife is attached to antiques. Not the pieces themselves but the act of hunting them down like prey and acquiring them."

Kat gave a nod, pleased she had been right. However, there was a slight problem.

"Mr. Cookson," she said.

He stared in response, his eyes narrowing at her interruption.

"I'm sorry, sir. The fee."

"Oh yes," he said, moving to the desk. He grabbed a Victoria's Secret gift bag and brought it to her. She accepted the bag and pulled out the box inside. He hovered over her as she counted the packs of bills, never glancing up. When she finished, she replaced the lid and put the box back in the gift bag. Eighty thousand dollars. Twenty-five percent would be hers. Twenty thousand dollars for arranging the purchase of an antique. She realized this was like the diamond merchants she had heard about. Thousands of dollars in gems and they carried them in suitcases like they were marbles, like they were nothing.

"I take it I can continue now?" he asked.

Kat nodded and folded her hands.

As he spoke, his annoyance appeared to wane. He sounded almost bored. "As I said, my wife likes to acquire antiques. Sometimes she changes periods, often without warning, and then sells them. She recently sold a Chippendale Secretaire Cabinet. Two drawers that slide open and two drawers that swing open with a hidden compartment behind a false backing."

He stopped speaking. Kat waited. He responded by sitting down, crossing his legs, and mimicking her folded hands.

Kat finally caught on, shifting in her seat in an attempt to cover her obvious lack of understanding. "What's behind the false backing?" she asked, feeling her face color in embarrassment.

"A VHS tape."

"VHS. This is something from a long time ago."

"Very good, Katerina. The tape showcases a compromising position that must be kept private at all costs."

She nodded. "It would be highly embarrassing to you."

"It would be highly inconvenient to me. It would be highly embarrassing to my wife."

They want to confess.

"My companion in the tape isn't female. I'm not in the mood to go through another divorce."

"Yes, sir," she said, her voice a monotone.

"Indiscretions," he said and he smiled though Kat was sure he was not amused.

"My wife sold the piece at auction. I did not know this until I returned from a business trip. I wasn't concerned until I realized the tape wasn't where I thought it was. It's in the cabinet."

Questions began to float through Kat's mind. Why still have the tape? Why wasn't it destroyed years ago? Maybe he enjoyed watching it, or he enjoyed having it in the house, or he enjoyed the fact that his wife didn't know.

And Philip would say... that's not your problem. Do the job.

"You would like me to arrange a buyback."

Jonathan gave a snort of laughter. "Of course not. Any inquiry to buy it back would require me to speak to my wife and raise suspicion."

Kat's discomfort with her slow performance rose with each tick of the Chateau Chambord clock perched above the fireplace.

"I want you to steal it," he said.

"Steal the piece of furniture."

He shrugged. "You can if you like but I think it would be easier just to steal the tape, don't you?"

"Yes," Kat said. "Yes, I suppose it would."

Chapter 7

There is no way this is going to happen. It had taken a few minutes but Kat's brain had come out of its catatonic stupor. Now an inner monologue sped like a freight train through her head, creating a bullet list of reasons why this had been a mistake from the beginning. What was she thinking? Lisa had told her the straight story: a 'B girl' did the bitch work. But it wasn't work no one else could do. It was work no one else *would* do. Kat chided herself for her foolishness in not connecting the dots: no one paid huge sums of money for a job without risk. What was it Jasmine had said? *Any legal issues you encounter as a result of providing services are solely your responsibility. MJM will disavow any warranty or relationship between us.*

Kat entered the diner and settled on a red stool at the counter, placing the bag on the foot rest to her left. The waitress, a woman in a Pepto Bismol pink outfit, sauntered over.

"What can I get you?"

"Just coffee, thank you."

The waitress, sensing a tip not worth smiling for, set down a saucer and cup and doled out the coffee without bothering to make eye contact.

Kat mumbled a "thank you" and left the coffee untouched. Plans B, C, and D were already forming in her mind. She slipped her phone out of her purse and held it. *Make the call now.* She would tell Jasmine she was heading back to the penthouse to return the bag. No, that was a bad idea. It would make MJM look bad; they had consultants they couldn't control. No, she would go through with the pickup. *Then* she would call Jasmine later or first thing in the morning and decline to consult. Jasmine would get a replacement and Kat would never work there again. *That's fine with me.*

Angel sat down on her left. "You got something for Angel, baby?" he asked, his voice low.

She gave a small nod as a shiver ran through her. She took hold of a sugar packet, compulsively shaking it, listening to the soft, 'flap-flap' sound it made.

He leaned to his right and picked up the bag. He tossed a few bills on the counter.

He regarded her for a moment, then leaned toward her as he slid off the stool. "Go big or go home, baby," he whispered. "It's your choice."

He walked out.

Kat stayed for what seemed like a long time. She would call Jasmine and tell her it was off. Then she would call the employment agency and beg for an assignment. She would do better than that; she would call two or three agencies. She would make sure she was never without an assignment. She was an adult. An adult with ethics. Following someone to make a gift list was one thing. This was something else.

The waitress reappeared. "You want somethin' else?"

Kat shook her head.

***

Exiting the subway, Kat was greeted by a biting chill in the night air. She hugged her coat tight around her as she turned the corner to her block. She hustled up the few stairs and shoved her key in the building door lock. She let out a sigh as she slipped inside, shutting out the cold. Turning the key in her door, she entered the darkened apartment, her eyes adjusting to the gloom. No sign of a man's clothing.

She dumped her purse on the table and shucked off her pumps. She drew Philip's envelope out of the purse, fingering it in her hands. Reaching out, she flipped the light switch. The envelope was closed with the seal glue, no extra tape, no "confidential" stamp across the seal. She could open it, hold the negatives up to the light, then replace the envelope. At least she would know what danger she was in. But if she didn't look, then ignorance was her best defense, wasn't it?

The choral sound of her cell phone made her jump, reminding her she had to make the call to Jasmine. She dropped the envelope back into her purse and grabbed her phone.

"Hello?"

"Hey, kitten, how's my girl?"

"Dad! I've been trying to reach you and Mom for weeks! What's happening? How are you? Is everything okay?"

"I'm fine, Katerina. I'm just fine."

Katerina could see him, that same thin, plastic smile.

"How are you feeling?"

"Fit as a fiddle, precious."

Kat smiled. Fit as a fiddle. Her father was probably one of ten men left in the world who used that expression. That and the word "nifty."

"Daddy, can you put Mom on the phone? There's something I want to talk to you both about."

"I need to talk to you too, kitten."

Kat paced with the phone at her ear. "Daddy, where are you? You sound so close."

"That's because I am close. I'm right outside your building. You want to open up and let your old man in?"

Pulling the phone away from her ear, Kat raced for the door and threw it open, making a beeline for the outside door. She hadn't seen him or her mother when she came in. How had she missed them?

The glass panels of the door made her father appear like a visitor to a house of mirrors, distorting his face and body as well as the person next to him. Katerina threw open the door as he reached the top of the steps. She looked past him at the woman standing next to him.

"Dad...where's Mom?"

•••

Katerina sat at the table, her mind reeling. Her father, William Mills, the father who had carried her on his shoulders, taught her to ride a bicycle, and taken her to pick out her mother's birthday and Christmas presents, sat across the table explaining why he left her mother for a bleached blond, thirty-four D bimbo named Lulu. As he talked, Lulu wandered the apartment, her eyes a vast, vacant lot of boredom.

"You see, honey," her father was saying, "having cancer has taught me a valuable lesson."

"You can never have too much peroxide?" Katerina blurted, fascinated by the immoveable helmet of brassy hair sitting atop Lulu's head.

"Now kitten, don't be ugly. I want you and Lulu to be friends."

Kat stared in response, trying to remember if her father had fallen and hit his head during one of his hospital stays.

Katerina and Lulu exchanged cold, hard glances. *Oh yeah, wicked stepmother, the feeling's mutual.*

"Daddy," Kat said, speaking slowly as if he were a traumatic brain injury patient and not a cancer survivor. "Where's Mom?"

Her father leaned back in the chair, patting his hand against his leg in a rapid, tapping motion, his eyes darting around the room. "She's packing up her few things. By the way, Katerina, change brings downsizing. That includes everything you left in your room. It's all gone to Goodwill."

Kat was on her feet. "Wait a minute. You SOLD the house? You gave away my stuff? For what? For this? For her?"

"Kitten—"

"Don't kitten me! What's gotten into you? Did you take everything? What about Mom? Didn't you give her any money?"

"Don't upset your father," Lulu said.

"Cork it, Rent-A-Slut!"

Lulu's face flushed crimson. With her hands out, she rushed toward Katerina.

"Now, now, girls," her father soothed, jumping up and catching her arm, "let's calm down."

Whispering in Lulu's ear, he handed her a few bills. With an icy glance at Kat, Lulu sashayed out of the apartment.

"Does she have enough singles?"

"Don't be fresh, Katerina. Is this how we raised you to be a young lady? New York City has changed you, that's for sure, and I don't think for the better. Maybe I was wrong to encourage you to come here."

"Daddy, what about your job? Twenty years of your life dedicated to the company. When they transferred you, you set up the plant, you hired everyone personally. Richie can't do what you do. He can't run that business."

William Mills laughed but the sound had no joy. "He thinks he can," he said. "Yeah, my number two...he's his own man...well...life is about change," he said, and gave another short, mirthless chuckle.

What the hell does that mean? "Have you talked to Kevin? Does he know about this?"

"He's still off in the wilds of Costa Rica living in a tree house. We get an email every few months when he gets back to base camp. I tell you Katerina, your brother is a shining example. He's been an inspiration to me."

Inspiration? In what way? Why underwear is not a necessity? Bathing— the pros and cons? Katerina struggled to process the fact that her father had lost his mind.

She stared at the stranger before her, finally taking a long breath and taking her father's hands in her own. "Daddy," she said. "I don't know where you met this woman—"

"Lulu."

"Yes, she is."

"She's a nail technician."

"Uh-hunh. Daddy, you and Mom have had thirty wonderful years together. You two went on romantic cruises. You took her to California, to Yellowstone Park. You had date nights. You're in love with Mom."

He squeezed her hands. "Honey... sweetheart," he said, patting her hand. "Your mother is a lovely woman."

Uh-oh.

"Katerina, if cancer has taught me anything, it's that there's more to life than pleasant trips to Yellowstone Park with a lovely woman."

He sat down and Katerina took her place by his side.

"Daddy, when men survive cancer, they buy a motorcycle or a sports car or a boat. They don't dump the woman who nursed them through their life threatening illness."

He patted her hand, the telltale sign that he was preaching to the congregation but they had neither eyes to see nor ears to hear. "I've been given a second chance, kitten. I need more."

Kat jumped to her feet. "Apparently, you need it all. How is Mom going to live? What is she going to do?"

"Listen to me Katerina," he said, pulling her back down. "This is important. You play the hand you've been dealt, bet and bluff to make the best deal possible, and then cash out when it's time to go. Remember that."

"Mom is not a stake in a poker game," she said, a surge of anger shooting through her. "This is your wife, not a hand of Texas Hold 'Em."

He shrugged.

She forced herself to search for something to say that wouldn't end with her telling him exactly how she felt about him at the moment. "Daddy, are you staying in town for a few days?" she asked through clenched teeth.

"No, kitten, Lulu and I are headed—west. Which reminds me...I'm in a transitional phase, Katerina. As I contemplate where this new path will take me, I won't be able to pay your tuition anymore or help you with rent or expenses."

Kat's mouth dropped open.

"I know, kitten, but look at it this way. You're in the big city. Shouldn't you be spreading your wings and flying solo?"

William Mills gave his daughter a light chuck under the chin and a wink.

Katerina remembered to close her mouth.

•••

It took three hours of calling before Linda Mills finally picked up the phone.

"Mom! Mom! Are you okay?"

"Yes, dear. I'm fine. Why are you yelling?"

Kat adjusted her tone. "Mom, Daddy was here."

"Yes, dear," her mother said. "He said he was going to stop by on his way—out of town. You sound hysterical. Is everything all right?"

Kat stood in her mini kitchenette, tearing open a box of marble pound cake. She hacked off a slice and set to work. "Oh, I don't know, Mom. Do you think everything is all right?"

She heard a sigh from the other end of the phone.

"Mom, I don't understand any of this. When did the house get sold? Where were you when all this was happening?"

"Honey, your father is—going through a change. It's not something you need to concern yourself with."

"Where is Daddy really going?" she finally managed.

"I'm not sure, dear," came her mother's response. "Someplace exotic, like Algeria or Brunei."

Her father, the nice man with the vegetable garden was going to Algeria? She didn't see her father wearing his plaid golf pants and white shoes wandering the streets of Brunei. Her mother had left the realm of reality as well. "Mom, aren't you angry...shocked... hysterical? Why aren't you hysterical?"

"Well, dear," she said. "I never wanted to disturb your fantasy about your father, but he's an ass. He always was. I just didn't have the heart to tell you."

Kat pictured Linda Mills, prim and proper mother, with her shoulder length chestnut hair styled in a perfect bob, wearing her buttoned down dress with a cinched waist, saying the word "ass."

"Sweetheart, what else did he say to you?"

Kat replayed that last moment in her head, her father standing by the door and kissing her forehead. "I'm very proud of you, Katerina. You're going to do something big. I know it."

"Nothing," she said to her mother.

Finishing off the slab of pound cake, Kat opened the fridge door, grabbed the bottle of chocolate sauce, and gave a generous squirt into her mouth. Something Linda Mills would not approve of.

"Mom, how did he manage to take everything?"

"Well, it was all in his name..."

"So what? You're his wife. You're entitled to half."

The question was met with a small, bitter laugh from Linda Mills. "Oh Katerina, my dear girl, what does it matter now? The less you know about all this...unpleasantness, the better for you."

A feeling of helplessness swept through Katerina. *This doesn't make sense.* "Mom, what are you planning to do?"

"I'm moving in with Ethel and Rachel. They have a house together and since I'm... destitute, they've offered to give me a room. They said it'll be our little commune, filled with sisterly support and affection."

"Mom...are Ethel and Rachel lesbians?"

"Yes, dear, but they assured me I don't have to swing that way if I don't want to. It's just until I figure out what to do. Dear, I have to go. It's my turn to prepare dinner. You'll be okay, won't you? You're a smart girl. You always were. Call me Thursday."

Katerina sat with the phone in her lap for a long while. She scanned her small, shabby living space, settling on the pile of mail on the stand near the door. The top envelope bore the insignia of the university. The tuition bill. She thought she only needed fourteen thousand dollars. She was going to need more than that. A whole lot more.

Or what?

No apartment.

No college.

No law school.

Go big or go home, baby.

Home wasn't there anymore.

She got up and flipped off the light. The miniscule living room slipped into darkness.

She would go to bed early and get up early to study.

Then she had to go to work.

She had to begin surveillance on Felicia Reynolds tomorrow.

She had to plan a theft.

She had to.

She needed this job.

Chapter 8

"So, my father has run off with Whore of Babylon Barbie and they're off to happily ever after while my mother is left with nothing."

Kat sucked down the rest of her latte. It was her third of the morning. Studying 18th Century European History at five o'clock in the morning didn't encourage perky wakefulness. The espresso would take care of that.

Her listener, Emma Flynn, nodded, shoving the last oversized wedge of a cinnamon sticky bun into her mouth. She glanced down at her white nursing uniform to see if she was wearing the gooey treat, a usual occurrence at their weekly breakfast-meetings-on-the-go.

The uniform outlined Emma's compact, sturdy, five-foot-five body. Her face, round and plump, held large brown eyes and a no-nonsense ponytail tamed her curly, honey blond hair. Her years in the city had begun to weaken the southern drawl. Kat found the soft lilt comical when Emma let out a string of obscenities at the most unexpected moment.

They had met while rooming with four other girls, a hasty, short-lived arrangement that quickly descended into a pigsty and the occasional pool of puke on the bathroom floor. Together, they fled to a bright, clean, fourth floor walk-up. They went their separate ways when Emma moved in with her boyfriend.

"It happens all the time, hon," Emma said, licking the frosting from her fingers. "A person comes close to death and reacts by doin' a three-sixty. He could have another change of heart."

"He's in the wind and he's not coming back. To top it all off, my mom told me my father's basically been a schmuck my whole life."

How did I not notice this?

Katerina was about to mention her mother's lack of finances but kept silent, the familiar internal alarm warning her to pull back before speaking too freely. This time she feared the conversation would sprawl to her own financial situation and she would makes a mistake and slip something about the new job. When she worked for Philip, Katerina became an expert at redacting and sanitizing information about the job for Emma. The only exception was the affair. Emma knew all about it.

As if reading her mind, Emma looked at her. "Have you seen Philip?"

"A few days ago. He dropped in."

"And?"

Kat took a breath. "I let him drop *in*."

Emma nodded. Katerina guessed it was an occupational habit. So much of what went on in the hospital was out of Emma's control. What else was there to do but nod?

They stopped at the corner across from the hospital emergency room entrance.

"Listen, hon, are you okay for cash?"

Emma's parents were from old money, complete with an aging antebellum plantation housing generations of sins that no one in the family cared to remember. It now functioned as a bed and breakfast to preserve its place in history and prevent it from rupturing into a financial sinkhole.

"I'm fine."

"So, what about this new job? Did you start?"

"Tomorrow. I think it's going to work out fine," she lied.

Emma held her gaze. "What exactly is it that you're doin'?"

"It's like a concierge service for people who only need an assistant once in a while. I do—stuff—that they don't have time for."

Emma nodded. Kat caught the slight lifting of her friend's brows, a signal that Emma's bullshit meter was heading for the red zone. They passed a moment in an awkward silence.

Kat observed people hurry past the hospital, oblivious to the suffering going on inside. *They're not the ones with the problem.* Right, Kat thought. The problem. I'm the one with the problem.

She looked at Emma. "I need to run a bunch of errands for an assignment. I hate to ask but could I borrow your car for a few days?"

Digging around in her purse, Emma pulled out a pack of tissues, a few dollar bills, and a car key on a red, round, Betty Boop key chain.

She dropped the key into Kat's hand. "The car's in the usual spot. Keep your nose clean, sugar. Remember, you're one of those nice girls that don't need to look for trouble. It finds you."

"You're a nice girl."

"Yeah, but I don't look like you, hon. Trouble sees me and walks right on by."

Kat waited for the words of wisdom she knew was coming. In these moments she knew exactly what Emma would look like ten years and two children later. A plump, cherub cheeked face, a mom pixie haircut, a peaches and cream complexion that turned a shade of rose whenever she exerted herself.

"Keep your eyes open and your legs closed, doll. That's my advice."

Kat nodded, concentrating on Betty Boop pushing her white dress down to cover her lady garden.

"I want you to come to dinner tomorrow night," Emma said. "I've got news and a surprise."

"Can't you just tell me the one now because I hate the other."

"Nope. Come tomorrow at nine." Emma pulled her in for a quick hug. "Promise me."

"I promise," Katerina said.

Chapter 9

The next morning, Kat made her way over to Bay Ridge and found the black Honda Civic in its usual spot, two blocks from Emma's apartment. Getting back into Manhattan was the usual snarl of blaring cab horns, endless traffic lights, and people jaywalking at every opportunity. Traffic signals were never an order in New York City, they were more of a suggestion.

At nine o'clock, Kat found Mrs. Felicia Reynolds, or The Wife as Kat called her, where her husband said she would be, in the Elysium Spa. He said it was the only appointment he knew of because the spa had called to confirm and he had happened to answer the phone.

Katerina circled the block like a gerbil on a horizontal wheel and the car's merry-go-round pattern matched her thoughts. Her father was lazing in Shangri-la with his nail technician/prostitute girlfriend. Her mother, à la Blanche Dubois, was living off the kindness of strangers. *And I'm teetering toward the edge of financial and educational ruin, and preparing to remedy my problems by committing a crime.* Suddenly remembering she also had a paper due on Walt Whitman's "Song of Myself" by the end of the week, she cursed silently.

Coming around the block again, she caught sight of The Wife exiting the spa and slipping into the back seat of a Lincoln Town Car.

"Shit!" Kat yelled, slamming on her brakes to avoid being creamed by a taxi. Her excellent driving skills were rewarded with a chorus of angry horns. As the noise blared around her, she realized how ridiculous this was. She didn't know what the hell she was doing and she didn't know a thing about surveillance. I'm not a damned PI, she thought. Why hadn't Reynolds hired one? *Because, genius, if he had, you wouldn't have a job.* The Town Car pulled out into traffic. She had no choice but to follow.

•••

By the end of the morning, it became clear that Mrs. Reynolds had a lot of free time on her hands and she spent most of it shopping. Her morning consisted of climbing in and out of the Town Car carrying packages from Saks, Neiman Marcus, and Louis Vuitton. Kat considered telling Mr. Reynolds to get his wife a generous Amex gift card and be done with it.

At the last stop, Kat lucked into a parking spot and slid in, missing a Buick by an inch. She scanned the storefront signs. The Town Car stood idling in front of a small theatre while The Wife entered the West End Repertory Company. Aha, Kat thought, now we're getting somewhere. Mrs. Reynolds is a patron of the arts.

She kept a sharp eye on the door to the theatre. Her thoughts wandered until one distinct thought popped into her mind. *Turn around. Go back. Don't do this. Don't do any of this.* The clarity of the thought surprised and frightened her. She pushed it away. *No. I can't give up. I won't give up. I need to make this work.*

The Town Car pulled away. Kat shot up in her seat. She had been watching. The Wife hadn't come out of the theatre. The driver had never gotten out of the car. The passenger door had never opened. Just to be sure she sat for another hour even though she knew it was useless. Where was Felicia Reynolds? What had happened to her?

Chapter 10

When the alarm buzzed at five a.m., Katerina jolted upright from her seat at the kitchen table, gasping as a sharp pain shot through her neck and back. Reaching out, she slapped her hand down on the cell phone, cursing as her coffee cup tipped over on its side. A trail of brown liquid snaked a path to the edge of the table and dribbled onto the floor, spreading into a puddle.

Kat sighed as she stretched carefully. Collecting herself, she turned her attention back to the open text book that she had abandoned some time around three a.m. Lying on the open pages was a photocopy from a Sotheby's catalog. She needed to find out who had purchased the cabinet. But how? She didn't know anyone at the auction house. She didn't know anyone who dealt in antiques.

"Shit," she said, slamming the book shut.

She eyed the bursar's letter, still lying on top of the pile of mail. She pushed the chair away from the table and got up. "I need to get a move on," she murmured aloud. "There isn't much time."

•••

"Emma, I'm sorry about last night," Kat said, fighting to be heard against the swell of noise from the recesses of the subway. "It was so late when I got done."

"What happened?"

Katerina bit her lip. Still fuzzy from the late night of studying, she hadn't thought ahead to have her story straight. "I needed to drop off some documents and I got lost. It was hectic."

"How's my car?"

"The car's fine. I just need—Emma, can I keep it for a few more days? I'm sorry. I'll bring it back with a full tank of gas...promise."

"Oh sure, hon, as long as you need to. You know I never drive it."

Kat broke out into a smile. That was the truth. Emma never did drive the car but she would never sell it. Someday she might need it.

"Listen doll, lucky for you Frank had to work late last night or I'd be plum mad at you right now. I'm having a party next Saturday night. You have to promise to be there. Now promise."

"Okay, okay, I promise."

"All right, sugar, I'm gonna hold you to it. Remember, my boyfriend's a cop. I'm gonna send him to get you and the car if you don't show."

"I'll be there," Kat said, her stomach somersaulting at hearing the words "boyfriend" and "cop" in the same sentence. She hoped she wouldn't be seeing Emma's boyfriend for any other reason outside of the party. In the meantime, she was stuck. She needed an expert.

•••

Katerina bolted off the subway, taking the stairs two at a time. She passed a row of bars and tattoo parlors that serviced the area's hipsters and college kids. Steps led down to basements with signs advertising Jägerbombs, Jell-O shots, and music groups that would play and die there, never seeing anything near the big time.

Kat spotted Lisa near the eatery looking like a supermodel as she leaned in to the open window of a limousine. Kat couldn't see the person in the limo. Lisa said a few words, then nodded her head. She wore a black sheath dress gathered at the waist. It hugged every curve of her body, outlining her perfectly proportioned figure.

The darkened electric window rose and closed. As Katerina approached, Lisa stepped back from the limo and straightened. The limo eased away from the curb and pulled into traffic.

"Are you ready for your complimentary coaching session?" Lisa asked.

"I only have one or two questions," Kat said.

"That's fine. There isn't much I can tell you anyway."

•••

Katerina observed her lunch partner with a mixture of admiration and jealousy. Lisa owned everything she did, every movement lithe and fluid, with a class and grace most women only hope to possess. Her hair fell shiny and straight to her shoulders, her complexion one smooth, luminous tone. She never hurried; every move flowed into another with unrehearsed ease.

"You're in law school?" Kat asked, flushing slightly. She had been staring.

"Second year."

"Does that help with the job?"

Lisa smiled but didn't appear pleased. "Not at all. I hope you're not planning to break the rules and discuss the particulars of your assignments."

The server appeared, balancing plates of food. Kat followed Lisa's lead, sitting mute until he left.

Kat, who had been thinking of doing just that, shook her head.

"Good. Don't do that with anyone. It would be a great mistake."

"I don't understand. My contacts know details. Not everything. But I'm sure they can put the pieces together."

"If your contact knows, then he or she was involved. They have no reason to speak up."

"So you're saying there is honor among thieves—not that I'm referring to theft." Kat felt a spike of heat rocket to her face.

Lisa gave the slightest of smiles. "Absolutely not. What I'm saying is that everyone has been paid, in one form or another. Your contact wants you to call again so they can be paid again, in one form or another. Sharing is bad for their business just as much as yours. Most of them aren't even using their real names."

"Is Lisa your real name?"

"Maybe," she said with a slight smile. "Next question."

Katerina tried to process these new facts that she had never even considered. She began to realize that this well ran deeper than she could imagine. "Why did you choose me?"

"Because you thought fast and you were quick on your feet. In this line of work those are valuable commodities." Lisa paused for a moment. "You can still get out if you want to."

Kat gazed at her salad; her appetite had fled. "Is this part of the complimentary coaching session? Giving me another chance to get out?"

Lisa shrugged.

"Or are you doing another evaluation and reporting back to MJM, whoever she is."

"I've never seen MJM, whoever he *or* she is."

"You didn't answer my question."

Lisa met Kat's gaze. "Yes."

They sat in silence for a moment.

"Why only male clients?" Kat asked.

Lisa's eyebrows lifted and then furrowed as if surprised by such a foolish query. She raised a finger as she ticked off each point. "Because men have the perfect trio of traits that make them the ideal client: they enjoy behaving badly, they enjoy confessing their bad behavior, and they always want a Mommy substitute to clean up the mess and make it all better."

Shades of Philip, Kat thought. For all his bloated bragging, he wasn't wrong. *The client always wants to confess.*

"I'm a little—concerned about how to find—contacts."

Lisa nodded. "The common mistake a newbie makes is thinking a contact is only good for the one thing you called them for. Use your present contact to find new contacts. Trust me, your connection knows a lot more than he or she is telling you."

"So my cut really isn't my cut. I'll always be paying out to a third party."

Lisa shook her head and leaned in. "Remember, I said paid *in one form or another*. Katerina, this game is all about pride and ego. Your contact gets off by being the one out of five people on this planet who can deliver what's needed at a moment's notice. Test the fences. See what can be begged, borrowed, or bartered. And if all else fails, don't underestimate the chance of someone being willing to help a damsel in distress."

The lunch crowd was thinning. Lisa checked her phone, a sign that she was finished. I'm on my own, Kat thought. But there was one more question she had to ask.

"Don't you ever—you know—worry?"

Lisa didn't bat an eye. "You're being paid large sums of money. You'd be a fool if you didn't."

"You don't look worried."

"Learn to control it or get out. You have other choices. You can get married and get on the mommy track, drive a computer keyboard for some middle management asshole, or go home. You won't be disappointing me. I don't care."

Kat nodded. They rose from the table.

Lisa shrugged her purse onto her shoulder. "I think you want to be a success. I think you want the power that a successful life brings. I think you're drawn to it and I think you're out of options that will get you there and that's why you're still here."

A tinder of fear rumbled in Kat's belly; she had a vision of a moth, fluttering closer and closer to the flame. The genteel life of summer concerts at the farm and the old fashioned country store with the penny candy belonged to her previous life, even if she had never felt like she belonged there.

"Anything else?" Lisa asked.

"Yes. I have to prove myself to you before I get more than this line of company bullshit, don't I?"

Lisa's face relaxed and her smile, for the first time, was genuine. "I knew I was right when I picked you. Stay alert, Rapunzel, and you'll be okay. Remember, it beats lying on your back for a living."

Lisa laid down a fifty dollar bill on top of the check and walked out; she didn't look back.

When Katerina exited the restaurant, she scanned left and right but Lisa had vanished. A small truck, the name "Exquisite Exports Shipping and Storage" on its side, tooled down the street. Kat watched the truck for a moment and walked in the opposite direction.

Chapter 11

Katerina called Mr. Reynolds with her report to date. He made a slight clucking sound that rang with gravity and surprise. "An interest in the arts. I had no idea," he said. "What's the name of the theater?"

She gave him the details. "I'm trying to wrap this up as quickly as possible for you."

Kat was met with silence on the other end. Oh shit, she thought. He wants to cancel now.

"Take all the time you need, Katerina," he said. "I want to get it right."

With a sigh of relief, Kat decided to see if Mrs. Reynolds was a creature of habit. She parked outside the spa and after two hours, Kat was rewarded for her patience. She should have been pleased but preoccupation with an impending theft that was going nowhere and her part-time occupation as a mule for Philip's less than legal doings prevented her from enjoying her stroke of good fortune.

She allowed herself a tiny smirk of satisfaction as the Town Car pulled up. Mrs. Reynolds emerged, dressed head to toe in beige, and disappeared into the spa. By the time she came out an hour later, Kat had finished formulating a plan.

•••

Katerina waited until Mrs. Reynolds entered the theater. Checking the side view mirror to ensure her open door wouldn't be clipped, Kat scrambled out of the driver's side and hurried across the street and inside.

She was greeted with gloom and silence. Posters from past performances lined the walls. Kat scanned the posters looking for any sign that the wealthy, bored, socialite enjoyed a wild fling as an actress, but Mrs. Reynolds' face was nowhere to be seen.

"Can I help you?"

Kat whirled. She found herself face to face with a tall, muscular man with broad shoulders and a head of long, straight black hair brushing his collar. He stood looking down at her, waiting.

"You startled me," she said with a gasp. She took a deep breath, playing for time. "I'm interested in acting lessons. Do you give acting lessons?"

He broke into a wide smile as he came to Katerina's side.

"Absolutely. Have you studied previously?" he asked, taking her hand.

He had a laser-like focus; Kat found the eye contact disconcerting.

Oh shit. The Wife is in here somewhere but Laurence Olivier isn't going to let me out of his sight.

He continued to study her with expectation.

"I did, but... uh... it was a while ago. I was in a performance of *Oliver* in high school."

"*You* were Oliver?"

"It was a progressive school. The director wanted to reimagine the work."

"Fantastic!" he exclaimed. "Whoever that man was, he was a genius. That's what it's all about, pushing boundaries. And now you're here to push your own boundaries, aren't you?"

Katerina nodded, focusing on the fourteen thousand dollars that was going to keep her from being without the boundaries of apartment walls and doors.

"But I am a bit nervous about this. Could I have a tour?"

"Absolutely," he said.

He chattered as he ushered her through the empty studio rooms, waxing poetic about method and process, Lee Strasberg, Uta Hagen, and Al Pacino.

"Do you have patrons who support the theater?"

"Oh yes, we have several."

"I'd love to meet them, if they're here."

"We'll see who we run into in our travels."

This isn't working, Kat thought. I'm running out of ideas.

As they came out of Studio B, Kat spied a dark haired woman stepping into the elevator, her shoulder length hair and heavy bangs casting deep shadows over her features. She wore a black shirt and slacks and had a black tote slung over her shoulder. As the elevator door closed, Katerina turned away but out of the corner of her eye she caught a sliver of beige.

"Now, when did you want to begin?"

Katerina opened her mouth but didn't respond. Something clicked into place: *beige shoes*.

"Oh," she said, backing up, "this is all so overwhelming for me. I'm sorry but I'll need to call you. I need to process…such a big decision."

Her guide stared at her like he had lost his best friend.

Spinning away, Kat headed for the door. *Sorry Laurence, I have to track a pair of beige shoes.*

She made it out the front door just as The Wife ducked into a cab. There was no time to run for the car. She sprinted to the corner, her arm in the air.

A cab screeched up to the curb. As Kat jumped in, she caught sight of a light, blue Ford behind the cab. The man at the wheel had a crew cut, making his head look like a square box. He had dark eyes. Those eyes were fixed on her. For a split second, they connected and held each other's gaze. Then she ducked inside the cab.

"Lady, where you want to go?" the cabbie asked.

"Follow the taxi up ahead," she said.

"Which taxi?"

Kat faced front. There were four cabs up ahead in the snarl of traffic.

"The one with the *Lion King* ad on top," she said. "Stay close but not too close."

The cabbie mumbled, then said, "You a cop?"

"No."

"Private eye?"

"No."

The cabbie eyed her through the rear view mirror. "What are you?"

"Repossessor of rented goods. The woman in that cab borrowed a Michael Kors bag and never returned it."

"Ahhh," the cabbie said. Gripping the steering wheel, he stepped on the gas.

Only in New York, Kat thought. He's ready to jump into a sting operation for an overpriced handbag.

She had been resisting the urge to turn and check behind her. Now, she turned. The blue Ford, two cars behind, continued to follow. Her pulse began to race.

"Why you look out the back window?"

Kat's hands went cold and clammy; she didn't answer. Damn you Philip, you lousy son of a bitch, she thought.

The cab with The Wife headed to Chinatown.

The cab stopped. Mrs. Reynolds got out.

"Slow down, slow down!" Kat ordered.

The driver eased over to the curb. Kat thrust some crumpled bills at him.

"Can I get a receipt?" she asked, stalling for time to keep an eye on the dark caramel wig as it disappeared inside a building. She glanced behind her. At the end of the block, the blue Ford idled. If she got out of the cab now...

"Never mind," she said to the cabbie. "Let's go back."

"You don't want the bag?"

"Take me back to Midtown. Penn Station."

The cabbie handed the bills back to her with a disgusted sigh. He turned, his large round shoulders hunching over the wheel. As the cab pulled away from the curb, the blue Ford tore past them, nearly sideswiping the taxi and rocketed down the street. Brakes squealing, the cab screeched to a stop. Kat flew back, her head striking the window frame. The cabbie launched into a litany of curses.

Kat closed her eyes; she could see stars behind her eyes.

"Lady, you okay?"

She nodded, fingering the rising lump on her temple.

"Crazy people," the cabbie muttered.

Yes, we are, she thought. Crazy or stupid, and she wasn't sure which category she fit into.

•••

Kat got out at Penn Station and fled down into the subway, the throbbing in her head keeping time with the rhythm of the trains. She switched lines twice on her way back to the theater. Walking to Emma's car, she punched in a number on her cell, holding her breath with each ring. Finally, a click.

"Hi beautiful, how's my bestie?" Philip answered. Kat could imagine his easy smile.

"No bueno, mi amigo," she managed through her ragged breathing. "Someone came around looking for that something you gave me to hold onto. And since they're looking for it, that means they're now looking for me."

"Hold it," he said, his voice wary. "Slow down, kid. Who's looking for it? What did he look like?"

Kat glanced both ways before stepping out to cross the street. "Big, mean, square head, homicidal glint in the eye. Look, I'm working and this is interfering. I can't have this. Come get it. Now."

She tucked the phone between her cheek and her shoulder to fish her keys out of her purse.

"What kind of work are you doing?" he asked.

"Never mind."

"Who are you working for?"

The keys slipped out of her hand, hitting the pavement. "Shit! Philip!" She stopped, forcing herself to slow down and take a breath. "Focus, okay? You have to come and collect your—whatever. I do not wish to have anymore—encounters—with your—business associate."

Silence on the other end of the line.

"Did you look at it?" he asked.

"Seriously?"

"Right, sorry—listen to me, beautiful," he began, his voice silky and seductive. He had used the voice that night, whispering in her ear as he moved inside her. A bolt of heat spiked through her and she cursed under her breath. She shook her head to get the vision out of her mind.

"I don't know what's happening but I wouldn't put you in any danger. I'm out of town but I'll be back soon. Just sit tight. I'll come and get it and I'll make it up to you."

"No, Philip—you need to come—"

"Love you, kid." Click.

Kat yanked the door open, jumped in, slammed the door shut, and jammed the lock. Bastard, she thought. She glanced down at her watch. Seven o'clock. Shit! Starbucks! Mark was waiting. She revved the engine and took off.

Chapter 12

Kat rushed into Starbucks and then stopped on a dime. Leaning against the counter, she forced herself to breathe slowly. She soon became aware of the young women behind the counter observing her with a mix of suspicion and curiosity; she gave them a weak smile.

She ran her fingers through her hair to settle it down, then quickly scanned the tables. Nothing. She craned her neck to check out the second floor. She caught sight of Mark and thought he must have felt her eyes upon him because he looked down at her. She took the stairs two at a time.

"Sorry I'm late," she huffed, dropping her back pack on the table. "Stuck at work." Mark's papers took flight, some fluttering to the floor.

"Sorry, sorry, I'm so sorry," she said, her hands flying in every direction to catch the papers.

Mark shifted his things to make room for her. "It's okay," he said. "No problem. I'm glad you made it."

•••

"There is no difference between pushing a person or flipping a switch, Katerina."

"But that man on the bridge has nothing to do with the train or the people on the track. He's not part of the equation. It's murder."

"You can't look at it that way," Mark said. "Everyone has choices. There are five people versus one person. Both acts are murder. Your reasoning won't change that. If rationalizations were ever acceptable, the jails would be empty. It is what it is. Don't sugarcoat it."

Katerina avoided eye contact, stung by his tone, as if she was still a naive girl from a quaint rural town. They sank into a stalemate of silence, Katerina focusing on their empty coffee cups.

"What kind of law do you want to practice?" he asked, cutting through the silence.

Kat shrugged. "Haven't thought much about it."

"I'm going into environmental law," he said. "Like the PG and E case. Where I can really make a difference."

"I'm sure Erin Brockovich will be happy to have you on her side."

Once again, a stilted silence. A flush of embarrassment rushed to Kat's face, convicting her of her cruel remark.

Mark pulled something out of his bag and held it out to her. It was a granola bar.

She smiled and took it.

"You know, this is a really tough issue, intellectually and emotionally," he said. "I don't mind writing either side of the opinion. It gives me a chance to see it from your perspective, which *is* totally valid. I'm very open to other viewpoints. I want to see the other side."

"Sure, okay," she said, deciding to take the offered olive branch, Mark's version of a left handed mea culpa.

She rose and Mark fumbled to pack up his books and papers. Stalling for time, he cleaned the plates. Then he got up.

"I guess that's it, then," he said.

Kat headed for the stairs. Mark hoisted his backpack on his shoulder and followed her down and out the door.

"Maybe, after the project is over we could catch a movie—or something," he said, his voice tentative.

When Kat glanced over at him, he was staring straight ahead.

"I'd like that," she said. "And...I'm sure you're going to be a successful lawyer."

He nodded, allowing himself a quick glance at her. After a second she caught a smile curving the corners of his mouth.

Kat checked her phone. Eleven o'clock. She had a whole night's worth of study ahead *and* a theft to plan. She still didn't have a contact. She still didn't know where to begin. Realizing she was walking by herself, she stopped and turned to see Mark a few steps behind her, staring again, wearing that same confused expression.

"I'm sorry, did you say something?" she asked. "I was lost in thought."

"I got that," he said with a little shake of his head. "I asked which one was your car. So I could walk you to it—and say goodnight."

"Right," she said.

•••

Katerina stopped at a bodega a block away from her apartment and picked up the necessaries for an all-nighter: soda, Skittles, and coffee. Plenty of students were already popping Modafinil and Adderall. She wouldn't do it. She had only her mind to depend on and she had to stay alert. She was inserting the building door key into the lock when she heard her name.

"Katerina Mills?"

Kat dropped the deli bag, whipping around in the direction of the voice. A young guy, twentysomething, stepped into the light from the street lamp. He was just shy of six feet with a lanky build and an angular face. He had a crooked smile and uncombed hair.

Kat dug her hand into her purse. The mace. Shit, where was the damn mace!

"Are you Katerina Mills?"

She didn't answer but kept kneading deeper into her purse until her fingers closed around the small can. Whipping it out, she thrust it in his direction. He raised his hands.

"Hey...hey...easy!" he cried, backing away. "*You* called me, remember?"

Kat hesitated but kept her arm poised and her finger on the button of the can.

He held out a paper. She could see scribbling on the sheet. She shrugged, giving a shake of her head. He inched closer, still holding out the paper. She stood her ground.

"William, Will Temple. You called me about a part, in a movie?"

"No. You have the wrong person."

He pulled back the paper to reread it, as if it would somehow reveal some new clue. He glanced at her, then eyed the mace.

"I'm not a crazy serial killer. I'm an actor. I have an audition tomorrow morning. I should be in bed now. But this sounded so good I had to come." He held out the paper again. "Please."

Kat took a tentative step toward him and snatched the paper. It listed her name, address, a production company name, Random Girl Films, and the name of the film, *Love's Fury*. She gave him a wary examination. He was adorable in an artistic, scruffy way, with his battered jacket, T-shirt, and worn jeans that fit him like a second skin. Kat caught a whiff of his scent, a pleasing notion of warmth and pheromones.

"Sorry, Will. Someone is playing you. I don't have a production company. I'm not making a movie."

He took the paper back and read it over again. Kat had a moment's regret at being so matter-of-fact. She hazarded a guess that Will Temple was heavy on looks and charm, but perhaps a little light on brains.

"Oh man," he said. "That sucks."

"Do I sound like the woman you spoke to?"

"Actually, a guy called and gave me your info."

Kat stiffened. *Who the hell is giving out my contact information?*

"I'm sorry you came down here for nothing," she said. "I'm sure there must be at least one other Katerina Mills in the city."

He shrugged, the disappointment clouding his face. "I guess. You have to follow every lead, right?"

They stood together for another moment. *He is a cutie.* Under different circumstances...knock it off, she thought.

"Well, good luck to you," she said, dropping the mace back into her purse.

"Yeah, you too. Take it easy."

He turned to walk away but then stopped.

"Katerina."

She was at the door, key in hand. She glanced over her shoulder at him.

"I'm at the Theater For A New Audience, in Brooklyn. I'm in *Hamlet*."

"Are you playing the Prince of Denmark?"

"No…Rosencrantz. Someday I'll be tragic Hamlet, on the stage in Central Park."

"I believe it," she said.

He laughed. "You should come see me."

"I don't know anyone in the business, Will. I'm not a good contact for you."

"Come anyway," he said with a wide, boyish grin.

She smiled in spite of herself. "Maybe."

Pleased with himself, he took off towards the subway.

Goodnight, player, she thought as she let herself into the apartment. The circumstances of their meeting intruded on her pleasant thoughts and she threw the dead bolt on the apartment door. As much as she wanted to worry over this, her brain was overloaded and the circuits were fried, a swirling eddy of times, places, and events. This was a case of mistaken identity, she decided, a screw up…nothing more. She sank onto the loveseat.

She dozed sitting up, her sleep fitful, a whirl of images and thoughts. A half hour later, her eyes opened. She sat still in the dark, remembering the day she met Lisa, remembering the truck passing by the restaurant. Exquisite Exports Shipping and Storage. Suddenly, she realized she shouldn't be looking for a contact at Sotheby's. She should be looking for the transport company that picked up the cabinet at Sotheby's and brought it to the new owner.

I have a contact for that.

Chapter 13

The next morning, Katerina headed into Midtown, a black pencil skirt and crisp white shirt hugging her form, her silky, chestnut hair tumbling down her back. She arrived at Letourneau Transportation and Exports after most of the drivers had left on their runs for the day.

Outside the building, three men stood talking. Judging by the middle-age spread, they were in their fifties with receding hairlines and lines etching their foreheads. She recognized Henri Letourneau's sloping posture and thinning silver hair. A client of Philip's, Kat was betting there wasn't anything he didn't know about tracking the movement of goods, legal and otherwise. He took notice of her right away.

She remembered him as polite with an enigmatic face and a thick French accent that made his English run together like a pleasant melody. He had paid her left handed compliments by congratulating Philip for being clever enough to hire such a smart, capable, pretty girl. She would've bought the kindly gentleman act hook, line, and sinker had Letourneau not been Philip's client. Now, she waited, watching as he left the two men and approached her. Taking her hand, he bowed and gave it a light kiss.

"Bonjour, Mademoiselle Katerina. Always a pleasure to see you."

"And you, Monsieur Letourneau."

"It has been many months. You no longer work for Philip, n'est ce pas?"

Katerina pursed her lips, suddenly realizing how difficult this was going to be. "I've moved on to another opportunity."

"Ah," Letourneau said, nodding his head as if he were a sage who understood all that meant. "But you come to see me."

She stared down at her shoes for a moment. "I need to find the trucking company that moved this item," she said, pulling the photocopy of the catalog page from her purse, "from Sotheby's to its destination. I need the address."

Letourneau looked at the paper but did not take it. "And you think I am able to do this?"

"Yes, I do."

He nodded again. He examined Katerina with a narrow, penetrating gaze. "Katerina, you are a nice girl. But I think your new opportunity is, perhaps...not so very nice. You are sure you want to know this?"

Katerina nodded.

"Philip knows what you are doing?"

"This has nothing to do with him," she said.

Letourneau nodded. His eyes flicked over her, settling on her features. "You are a beautiful girl, Katerina. You should have a nice man to keep you comfortable. I would volunteer, but my wife, she would be very upset."

"I'm sure she wouldn't like you taking a mistress."

"She would not like me taking a new mistress...she has grown used to the one I have now."

Katerina smiled. "Will you help me?"

He hesitated and then took the paper. "Let me make some phone calls. I see what I can do. In the meantime, perhaps you should think about finding a different opportunity. One more suited for a nice girl."

She smiled as he kissed her hand again. He nodded his head and with a quirk of his eyebrows, left her.

Chapter 14

Leaning against the kitchen counter, Kat ate a bowl of cereal. Today was the last day of surveillance on "The Wife." Katerina knew the shops the woman frequented. She had even visited one or two right after Mrs. Reynolds had left, giving the salesperson a line: she had seen a woman buy something and what was the name/brand/color, etc. It had been easy to compile the information.

However, Mr. Reynolds was irritated by the last progress report. He wanted to know his wife's *passions*, not just her purchases. As far as Kat could tell, Felicia Reynold's passions included dressing in disguise and heading out...to do what? Kat had researched the Internet, looking for everything from street theater to female secret societies of the rich and bored in New York City. It had all led to nothing. "You must get closer. Talk to her," he had ordered. It could prove risky, especially if The Wife had spotted her in the theatre. Katerina was uneasy. Once again, she considered turning back but Lisa's words gnawed at her subconscious. *I think you want to be a success. I think you want the power that a successful life brings.* Once again, she pushed her reservations away. It was time to meet and speak with Felicia Reynolds.

•••

Kat shadowed Mrs. Reynolds from the usual starting point at the spa. When the Town Car stopped in front of Saks, Kat maneuvered the Honda around the block to a parking garage and pulled in. She jumped out of the car, tossed the attendant the key, grabbing the ticket out of his hand. Rushing back, she checked for oncoming traffic and a powder blue Ford. Nothing. Despite Philip's protests of innocence, he must have made a phone call.

Kat entered the store. She had prepared for this. She wore Chanel on her back, Louboutins on her feet, and clutched a Prada bag under her arm; all rentals. At least she looked the part. To track The Wife, Kat made a calculated decision. It was either lingerie, jewelry, or perfume.

The shopping trips were not long so she wasn't spending time in the dressing room.

Katerina reminded herself to move at a leisurely pace, careful to assume the appearance of browsing; she didn't want to be mistaken for a shoplifter looking for a quick score. She decided to start with the perfume designer mini boutiques, and found herself in the middle of the floor, surrounded by a swelter of noise and bustling activity.

Great, she thought. I need to find Felicia Reynolds...in the middle of a store event.

Kat squeezed around people, eyes darting from face to face, already perspiring in the closeness of the crowd. *This is impossible. I'm never going to find her.* After fifteen minutes of cramped jostling, Katerina decided to attempt one more rotation and then call it quits and move to another floor. Kat rounded a display case and there she was. Felicia Reynolds was about Kat's height. She wore her ash blond hair in a short, conservative bob. She had a trim, fit, dancer's body.

Kat lingered nearby as Mrs. Reynolds sampled several men's colognes. An associate, a manicured woman with an obsequious expression hovered discreetly. Kat hesitated, unsure of how to proceed. *What will I tell Mr. Reynolds? Congratulations, you're about to receive a lovely gift of cologne.*

Kat decided this was a mistake. She moved to walk past Mrs. Reynolds when a man approached and bumped her.

"Excuse me," he mumbled, moving on without looking back. Kat didn't respond.

She had bumped into The Wife.

She stood face to face with Felicia Reynolds.

Kat froze, her mouth ajar in surprise. "Oh, I'm terribly sorry," she said finally, "that rude man—"

"No harm done," Felicia Reynolds answered with a smile. "These things are always crowded."

Kat watched as her eyes opened wide with wonder. "Oh my God," Felicia Reynolds said. "Your hair is so totally amazing!"

Kat smiled, glad she had decided to leave it loose. "Thanks. I try." Up close, she was surprised to find Felicia Reynolds was so young. *We can't be more than a few years apart*, she thought, *and she certainly doesn't act like a super rich snob. She sounds... a little like me.* She quickly decided that Mrs. Reynolds fit the description of the classic "pretty woman," a perfect combination of features and figure that turn a man's head.

"Sometimes I think I should cut it, you know, be an adult," Katerina confided.

"Don't you dare! It's wild and wonderful. I used to love wearing my hair long and free...well, we can't always have what we want. You must keep it for those of us who can't. Promise?"

"Promise."

They experienced a moment of silence, Kat trying to figure out how to keep the conversation going. *Think fast.* "Your earrings are so beautiful," Kat said, eyeing the delicate quartz shell shapes outlined with diamonds set in yellow gold. "Did you buy them here?"

"No," Felicia said. "I have someone who designs jewelry for me. These are one-of-a-kind."

"Oh...I'm always looking for accessories. I support a small, no-budget theater group...find the props, pay for the props, that kind of thing."

Kat expected a look of surprise, even excitement at a shared interest, but Felicia's expression darkened, her eyes first widening and then narrowing in suspicion. "What theater company is that?"

Oh shit. "The Theater In The Round," Kat blurted, by some miracle remembering the name from a flyer at school. "They're not very good but it's not for lack of trying."

Felicia seemed satisfied and her expression relaxed.

Kat glanced down at the floor. Today's shoes were as always, beige pumps.

"That cologne is so hot," Kat said, nodding towards the bottle. "My boyfriend wears it."

Mrs. Reynolds gave a sly smile. "That's it then. I'm getting it. I've been shopping for something extra special. It's more for me to enjoy than for him."

"Exactly," Katerina said.

They exchanged a smile of gender solidarity. Kat had the sense that in a different time and place, she and Felicia Reynolds would have been friends.

"Good luck with your purchase," Kat said.

"You too," Felicia replied.

Katerina walked away, mentally kicking herself for her obvious failure.

"Wait," Felicia called.

Kat turned. Felicia Reynolds slipped the earrings out of her ears and held them out.

"Oh no, I couldn't—" Katerina began.

"Promise me you'll wear them with your hair down," she said, pressing them into Kat's hand. "Be free. Someone should."

The sentence was final. Mrs. Reynolds was finished.

"Thank you so much," Kat said.

Felicia Reynolds ran her hand over Katerina's hair with a quick, light stroke. Giving Kat a smile, she turned and walked away.

The earrings clutched in her hand, Kat exited the store and walked back to the garage, thinking about their conversation. *We can't always have what we want. Be free.* A shopping spree every day—spa treatments, chauffeurs, limos…a life most women would call perfect. Felicia Reynolds had more freedom than most people could ever dream of. *How could she not be free?*

Katerina settled into the car, examining the earrings in the palm of her hand; a mental tug of war began. She had enough information for Mr. Reynolds and suddenly she wanted to call it a day. She didn't mind the surveillance when she was tailing her but now that she had spoken to Felicia Reynolds; it was… *different.* You're still on the clock, she reminded herself. Mr. Reynolds paid his money, and Mrs. Felicia Reynolds still had stops to make.

Kat was easing the car out of the parking lot when the Town Car came around and idled in front of Saks. Felicia emerged from the store. When the car pulled away from the curb, Kat was certain the next stop was the theater. She pulled out into traffic and checked her rearview mirror. No blue Ford; good to go.

Finding a spot across from the theater, Katerina pulled in to wait. After ten minutes, the Town Car pulled away. That was the signal. Felicia was about to come out. Everything was running on the usual schedule.

Katerina kept an eagle eye on the door. A woman with dark, shoulder length hair, wearing large sunglasses and a gray coat, came out carrying a brown craft shopping bag. Kat relaxed against the seat and then she saw them; the beige shoes.

"Gotcha," she murmured, shooting to attention.

She turned the engine over and slammed the car into gear, easing into traffic as a yellow cab approached. Felicia Reynolds let it go by and headed for the subway entrance.

Shit! Kat was about to roll back into her spot when Felicia veered, stepped into the street, and raised her arm. Kat gave a sigh of relief and settled in for the drive. It was almost over.

•••

Twenty minutes later, Felicia Reynolds exited the cab in Alphabet City. Entering a tall, brick building, she disappeared inside.

Kat circled around, parking at the end of the block. First Chinatown, now here, she thought. What the hell was going on? What next? Go into the lobby? Check the names on the call boxes? Leave? She knew what Philip would say. *Information is power. You need to know everything you can. That's how you stay ahead of the pack.*

Kat decided to sit and wait, keeping her eyes on the windows. Reaching into her purse, she pulled out mini binoculars and gave all the windows a pass. Nothing. She glanced down at her phone. Almost noon. She would give it an hour, no more. She did another check of the windows but the curtains for most of the apartments remained drawn. She checked the mirrors for the Blue Ford. Nothing.

She surveyed her surroundings; a strictly low rent neighborhood. There was a seedy hotel across the street and the usual deli, cleaners, and nail joint. While she waited, a replay of her conversation with Felicia drifted through her mind. She remembered telling Felicia her boyfriend wore the cologne she was about to buy. *It's more for me to enjoy than for him.* That's what Felica Reynolds had said. What hadn't Felicia Reynolds said? She hadn't said *my husband*.

Adrenalin shot through Katerina and the exhaustion fled. *I have to leave. Now.* As she turned the key in the ignition, Felicia Reynolds emerged from the building. Same wig, same coat, same shoes. No bag.

Katerina's stomach roiled with the realization that she had made a terrible mistake. She slammed the car in gear but out of the corner of her eye, she spotted movement at a window on a lower floor. She grabbed the binoculars. A man leaned out the window, naked from shoulder to hip, watching Felicia Reynolds walk to the end of the block. Kat stared at him, her mouth ajar.

Will Temple.

Chapter 15

Driving back to her apartment, a death grip on the steering wheel, Katerina forced herself to breathe normally. *Stupid...stupid...stupid!* Felicia Reynolds wore a disguise because she's a head turner and she didn't want to be noticed. Secret societies? A passion for the theater? STUPID!!! Mr. Reynolds didn't need to worry about buying his wife the perfect gift. She was already getting the gift that keeps on giving, two to three times a week at the very least.

But the affair didn't explain everything. *Why was Will Temple at my apartment? How did he get my name?* In the midst of her mental gymnastics, she raced through a red light and nearly crashed into a car before slamming on the brakes. She sat, heart pounding, feeling the sweat breaking on her forehead. Then the blaring of horns told her she was an idiot and to get moving.

Ten minutes later, she parked and cut the engine. She leaned back against the headrest and took a few deep breaths. *Lisa must have ice in her veins to be untouched by all of the weirdness and garbage she sees every day. How does she do it?* Kat answered her own question with Philip's mantra.

None of this is your problem. Do your job.

Closing her eyes, she allowed herself a few tears. Then she pulled out her cell phone, dialed, and listened to the ringing.

"Hello, darling," her mother said, sounding out of breath.

"Mom, are you okay? What's going on?"

"I'm fine, dear. I'm painting a dresser I moved into my room this morning. I used those handy little slippery things you buy at the store. They're wonderful. If I had known I didn't need your father for heavy lifting, I might have thrown him out ages ago."

"Mom!"

"Well, I'm sorry, darling, but it's all so much more convenient now. I don't have to watch bowling or hear about boring golf and I don't need to burn candles in the bathroom. It's really quite refreshing, literally."

Kat's mouth hung open; she didn't know what to say.

"I went to a sweat lodge last week," her mother continued, "and this weekend we have a fire walk. I asked if it was mandatory and it isn't, so I think I'll just watch. Anyway, Catherine and May have just moved in and they want to do the walk together to symbolize the fusing of their lives."

"Who are Catherine and May?"

"I don't really know, dear, but everyone seems to know everyone else. It's quite a vibrant community, very supportive."

Kat began to cry, being careful not to make any noise.

"They did ask me again if I was interested in a change in lifestyle but I don't think I'm ready to bat for my own team. Not that I have a problem if someone else does. But, I think I still do prefer a penis. I really wish it had been one other than your father's." She gave a heavy sigh. "Well, I guess you work with what you've got."

They shared a moment of silence.

"Are you getting good grades, my Katerina?"

Katerina wanted to tell her mother everything, to let it all pour out. *That is why you called, isn't it?*

"Yes. Mom," she settled for. "Mom...what are you doing for money?"

"I haven't figured that out yet, since my only marketable skill seems to be keeping a vegetable garden. The ladies have been very kind. They've let me have a separate space to plant my own. I was really quite—attached— to what I had. You know, the old saying is true. You never miss something until...it's gone," she said, her voice catching.

Katerina sat, helpless, listening to her mother crying. Hot tears began to run down her cheeks.

"Oh dear," her mother said, pulling in a long breath, "I don't mean to cut you short, darling, but they're calling me. There's a sisterhood ritual starting in ten minutes and I don't want to be late. I'll get stuck next to Lorraine and she has sweaty palms. I'll call you at the end of the week."

Kat clicked off the phone and cried for a few more minutes. She loved her mother but Linda Mills' shy, retiring ways had never agreed with her. The smoke and mirrors of her father's pixie dust dreams had always been more to her taste. Like a pied piper, William Mills had called the tune and she had followed. Katerina suddenly realized she had never really known either of her parents. Now, both of them were gone.

Katerina dried her eyes and set her thoughts in order. Felicia Reynolds was having an affair. Lots of women had affairs. It wasn't the end of the world and it wasn't her business. She would compile the list, give it to Mr. Reynolds, and collect her fee. She had her own business to attend to; she had to help her mother financially as well as take care of her own expenses.

Ironically, she would follow one last piece of her father's advice. She would play the hand she'd been dealt. *I will make this work.*

Chapter 16

Use your present contact to find new contacts. Trust me, your connection knows a lot more than he or she is telling you.

Armed with the delivery address from Henri Letourneau, Kat found Doc in the back of a grim, gray diner. The old checkerboard linoleum floor was dull and scuffed, the vinyl booths faded and worn; the original color was anybody's guess. A prime place for a kitchen-fire-for-an-insurance-check, Kat thought.

Doc was sitting at a small square table. He had a plate of steak and eggs before him, the blood from the rare steak seeping into the eggs. Kat noted that Doc's beard remained impeccable even as his shirt became dotted with stains. His big belly made him dive forward each time he took a bite. He ate between asthmatic wheezes.

Kat sat down across from him. "Morning, Doc. I need to find a thief."

"Have coffee first," he said. He waved a sausage-like finger at the waitress making the rounds with a half empty pot.

A woman with skin like a worn leather bag wearing a name tag that said 'Connie', sauntered over. She upended the cup in front of Katerina, filled it, and walked away.

"What do you want a thief for?" Doc wheezed.

"I need someone who's an expert in gaining residential access—preferably out on Long Island, close to the Hamptons."

Doc swallowed and breathed. His breathing had a frightening cadence: in, out, and wait, every breath sounding final.

"Miss Kitty, if you need money, I can set you up with some very nice loan sharks. Times are tight. The vig rates have really plunged."

"I don't need a loan, Doc."

"Then whatever you're into, get out of it."

Katerina drew in a deep breath. "I'm not 'into' anything. It's not really a—" she leaned in and lowered her voice, "—theft. It's a retrieval."

Doc put his utensils down and wiped his hands on a napkin, giving himself time to chew, swallow, and complete another cycle of breathing.

"Doc, I've wracked my brain trying to find an alternative. I'm the cable girl…my car broke down…I'm a Jehovah's Witness—"

"No one would believe you're a Jehovah's Witness, doll. With that hair, you look like jailbait getting ready for your centerfold spread."

"Thank you, Doc. You're a big help."

"I call it as I see it, gorgeous."

"I can't figure out how to be *invited* into the house, so I need a thief to tell me how to break in."

"My guy isn't gonna do that."

The diner grew louder. Kat glanced around at the booths and tables filling up. The men and women had faces with hard edges and deep lines. She saw defeat and resignation. A sigh escaped her.

She refocused. "Doc, I need the name."

Doc took a moment to suck in a breath. He pushed his plate away.

"Goes by the name of Winter. He's got a loft in the Meatpacking District."

"Thanks, Doc. I owe you."

"Don't bother. I didn't do you a favor."

•••

Kat raced out of her morning class and made it over to Winter's loft space by noon. She rang the bell, laying on the button until the buzzer sounded. Settling into the safety cage of the elevator, she pushed the button for the top floor.

When the lift stopped, she entered a space of luminous hospital white—walls, carpeting, furniture. There were three glass elephant figurines on a wall shelf, placed in perfect alignment, one behind the other, from upturned trunk to tail. She could have sworn they were spaced apart in equal measure. The magazines fanned out on the glass coffee table also appeared to overlap each other by the exact amount.

A man stood in the center of the living space, his black slacks and shirt a sharp contrast to the snow white surroundings. Kat studied him, putting him at a little over six feet, the shirt accenting the muscles of his arms and shoulders. His features were rugged with a strong jaw, and his hair, a closely cropped dark thatch that somehow suited him. She couldn't peg his age but hazarded a guess of late thirties.

He examined her with sharp, blue eyes.

"Mr. Winter." Her voice sounded shy and tentative.

Winter moved to the couch and sat, arms folded across his chest. Kat drew on her social psychology class; to sit while someone stands is the equivalent of ceding power. Winter didn't appear concerned.

Congratulations Katerina, you command no respect whatsoever.

"I assume Winter is not your real name."

"Very good, Miss Mills."

She ignored the condescending tone. "This is an unusual space."

"I'm fond of it."

"Have you lived here long?"

He smirked. "Not long...no...and I'll be leaving tomorrow."

"Why is that?"

"My profession requires me to have residential flexibility, especially when beautiful, foolish young women seek my company."

His voice, a rich mixture of gruff and gravel, had a warm, soft tone.

A voice perfect for telling a bedtime story...one for consenting adults. The thought brought a flush of embarrassment to Kat's cheeks. She caught the glimmer of a smile on his lips.

He finds me amusing. And he's playing with me.

"Did Doc tell you why I wanted to see you?' she asked, channeling her voice from the night at Lessing's apartment.

"He doesn't get involved with details."

"I need to engage your services, Mr. Winter."

The amusement left his eyes.

Pulling a piece of paper from her pocket, she approached him, holding it out. When he didn't take it, she placed it on the coffee table before him. The intensity of his scrutiny made her shift in discomfort.

"Are you familiar with the area where this house is located?"

He leaned forward and glanced at the paper.

"Perhaps."

"Because you've been there before."

"Possibly," he said, his voice indifferent.

He got up and went into the kitchen.

Kat felt rooted to the spot. *Is that it? He's done with me? Great, I'm being dismissed. Why did I come here? Oh right, trying to earn fourteen thousand dollars before the last day of the month to avoid financial disaster. What now?*

He reappeared, carrying a cup and saucer.

Kat exhaled in relief. She pulled another piece of paper out of her purse and thrust it out toward him.

"I'm looking for this piece," she said, thrusting the picture of the cabinet at him.

Winter glanced up after taking a sip of tea. He shrugged. "You want to steal that?"

"I don't want to steal it. I don't want to steal anything. I need to know how I can get into the house to see this piece...I need you to tell me how to do that."

Winter let out a chuckle. "Try the 92nd Street Y. Maybe they've added B and E for Beginners to their course list."

A bolt of anger spiked within her. "Did Doc mention that I'm serious?"

Winter nodded. "He said you were an earnest, intelligent, and enterprising young woman. Where are you from?"

"Somewhere over the rainbow," she snapped. "What does it matter?"

"You're a beautiful girl, Katerina. Surely you can find a less dangerous, more pleasant way to earn a living."

"Not an option," she said.

"Then take my advice, earnest, intelligent, enterprising young woman—pack up Toto and head back to Kansas. This is not the place for you."

"*Not* an option," she repeated.

He nodded at the paper. She swiped it up from the table, crushing it in her fist. Turning away, she headed to the elevator, then stopped and turned back.

"How do you know Doc?"

"I know a lot of people. I'm a very social person."

Bullshit. "I'm sure you are, but Doc isn't. He only deals with people when they have a medical issue. Why aren't you working, Mr. Winter?"

"I work when I need to work."

"How often do you work, Mr. Winter?"

Winter put down the cup and looked her over; his blue eyes were cool. Her pulse quickened.

"You aren't studying law enforcement by any chance, are you Katerina?"

"I'm pre-law. The two have nothing to do with each other."

He got up and closed the gap between them. He stood over her. A hint of cologne filled the space between them, warm and inviting. Her breath caught in her throat as a sudden desire to press her lips against his neck came over her. Her eyes met his; arctic, icy pools.

"You're a thief. You sit outside a house. You watch. You wait; and in that split second, you know you're going to do it."

The low rumble of his voice sent a sensation of heat spreading through her body; She could feel the warmth rising in her face. She fought the urge to close her eyes and lean into him. *How can someone look so cold and give off so much heat?*

"You know that one mistake, one slip, and your life will change. But you enter the house. You get to the box. You bypass the alarm. Then you give yourself five minutes, that's all. You know that every extra minute brings you closer to getting caught. You make a mistake, you don't get out, and it's over. Your life, as you know it, will end."

Katerina realized she was holding her breath.

"You think I can give you a crash course in how to do that?"

She shook her head. "No...you...you'll need to go with me."

The blue eyes laughed at her, then a flicker of interest.

"What's in it for me?"

Kat's mind raced, searching for something, anything to make her case. "The satisfaction of helping a damsel in distress."

Winter chuckled.

Kat let out a sigh of relief.

He bent his head low. "No, really," he whispered, his breath warm on her neck. "What's in it for me?"

At a loss for an answer, she sucked in a ragged breath. *Damn*.

"Is there anything else in that house that would interest me?" he said finally.

"You're not allowed to steal anything."

Winter let out another deep chuckle and walked away.

"I can't have you stealing anything," she said, trotting after him. "I told you, this isn't really a theft. I have to get something out of the cabinet. It belongs to the previous owner."

Settling back on the couch, he smiled. "I see. What are you getting for this—*retrieval*?"

Kat bit her lip. "Twenty thousand."

"I'll take half."

Damn it.

"Twenty-five percent."

"Forty percent." His eyes challenged hers.

Kat imagined she saw amusement in those icy pools. "Listen, I need—" She broke off, mentally cursing herself for the slip.

His eyes slid over her, then held her gaze until she looked away. "I wouldn't want to be thought of as a man who took advantage of a damsel in distress," he said slowly. "Thirty percent...last offer."

Six thousand dollars. She had no choice. "Deal."

They passed a moment in silence, Katerina not wanting to walk away and end the meeting.

"Mr. Winter do you have a first name?"

"Doesn't everyone?"

Kat waited, her annoyance spiking as he remained silent. The smile pulling at the corners of his mouth only served to irk her even more.

"At the moment, I am Alexander."

"Alexander," she repeated softly.

Winter got up from the couch. "Katerina. I'll call you in a few days and let you know."

"But you just said—"

"I said my fee would be thirty percent. I didn't say I would do it. I'll call you in a few days."

She shook her head and turned to leave.

"Katie," Winter said.

Kat stopped on a dime and turned. "That's *not* my name."

"It is now. And the next time someone asks you what your cut is, it would be better if you didn't give the real amount." He paused, giving her a long look. "That's lesson number one."

Kat pursed her lips, forcing herself not to talk back.

On the way down in the elevator, she realized he didn't have her number. She chided herself for her ridiculous concern. There was never a chance she would see or hear from Alexander Winter ever again.

Chapter 17

Using the number he had given her, Katerina called Mr. Reynolds and set up the final meeting. An hour later she stood at the corner of Fifth Avenue and Seventy-ninth Street. The limo pulled up. She opened the passenger door and climbed in.

She found Mr. Reynolds the same as before, legs folded at the ankles, hands in his lap, a benevolent smile on his face. She smiled in return but couldn't maintain eye contact. She couldn't tell him. Maybe he deserved to know but it would not be from her. She recited the list of shops and items, silently hoping he wouldn't bring up her past report about Mrs. Reynolds' interest in the arts. He listened intently, bending his head forward, concentrating to catch every word.

"She seems to enjoy jewelry items that are specialty designs."

Reynolds took her hands in his and held them. "Thank you, Miss Katerina. You have done me a great service. Thank you."

Remembering Philip's Golden Rule of *"less is more,"* Katerina smiled and kept her mouth shut.

The limo eased over to the curb and idled. Mr. Reynolds released her hands. "Until we meet again, Miss Katerina."

Not going to happen. "Good luck," she said and got out of the car. Standing in the middle of the street, people moving around her, she watched the limo pull away. The job was done and over with and she was glad to be rid of it. She would put it out of her mind and move on.

She took out her cell phone and dialed a number.

"MJM," Jasmine's voice came through the phone.

"Assignment one is finished," Kat said. "When can I come in?"

She heard the tapping of keys on the other end.

"Hold one moment," Jasmine said and the line clicked silent. After a few moments, the line clicked back on.

"Assignment completion confirmed," Jasmine said. "Any time after one o'clock."

"Fine," Kat said and hung up. Four thousand dollars; enough for rent, food, and a money order for her mother. She needed to complete the other assignment and she couldn't wait any longer.

***

At noon the next day, Katerina found Luther near his favorite food truck in the East Village. He took a bite of his souvlaki and chewed in thoughtful contemplation while leaning against the limo, one leg crossed in front of the other. Upon seeing her, he gave a smile and a quick, silent chuckle.

"What do you hear, Luther?" she asked.

"Better you don't know, Miss."

Luther owned the limousine and performed all manner of services including door-to-door delivery service for people, items, even small animals. He never said no and he never asked any questions. He understood the two commandments of the service industry: see everything and remember nothing. Luther was very popular.

"I need a car, Luther."

"What kind of car, Miss Katerina?"

Kat thought a moment, unsure of how to answer.

Luther gazed at her with mild eyes. "You don't want that anyone should be able to identify this car after you're done, right, Miss?"

Katerina nodded.

"Maybe a dark color car would be best and the plate numbers temporary?"

Katerina drew in a deep breath to collect herself. *God, I really don't have any idea of what the hell I'm doing. But I've gotten this far. I'll get the car and figure out the rest when I reach the house.*

"It's okay, Miss. A one day rental isn't much. It's the parts and labor that's expensive. My man can do the job for you. It'll cost you ten."

Of course it will. Kat sighed. There was no other way.

"I can only pay him when I get paid."

"That's gonna be a problem, Miss. My man don't do partial payment. Cash. Up front."

"Luther, can you vouch for me? I'm good for it. You know that."

Luther was about to take a bite of his souvlaki but halted with the food near his mouth. "*I* know it, Miss. But that don't count for much with anyone else."

Kat mentally scrambled for a solution. "I can give him two thousand dollars down and the rest after."

Standing up, Luther folded the food back in its wrapping. "Miss, you know what happens if you can't make that payment."

"Make the call, Luther. Please."

Pulling his cell phone from his pocket, Luther tapped a number on the keypad.

Kat's cell phone rang. The screen said "private."

"Hello?"

"You need to go shopping before our little trip," Winter said.

At the sound of his voice Katerina froze; her heart began beating as if she'd been running a marathon.

Winter ticked off a list. "I assume you can remember this without writing it down."

She couldn't answer.

"Katie?"

"I'm making other arrangements," she blurted.

"Cancel them."

Turning to Luther, Kat held up a finger.

"You're sure you're in?"

"I'm in," Winter said and clicked off the line.

Kat took the phone from her ear and shook her head at Luther. Luther said something into his cell phone and clicked off.

"Thanks anyway, Luther."

Tucking his cell phone away, Luther returned to leaning against the limo and began eating his souvlaki. "No problem, Miss. I was just telling Moose all about you. Says anything with a car, he can take care of it for you."

"Tell him I'll catch him on the way back."

Luther gave a light chuckle. "Will do."

Kat turned but then stopped and turned back.

"Did you vouch for me, Luther?"

"Always, Miss Katerina. Always."

She smiled and went on her way. While she was walking, she found herself taking deep, calming breaths.

Okay, she thought. Here we go.

Chapter 18

On a bright and brisk morning, a young woman wearing a pair of jeans, gray turtleneck, gray jacket, and gray sneakers walked down Thirty-fourth Street. She had a backpack slung over her shoulder and her hair tied up tight under a black newsboy cap.

A beige van, the name Lighthouse Electricians painted on its side, idled further down the street.

Across the street, a disheveled man, dressed in army fatigues, made his way down the block. "YOU ALL DON'T KNOW. YOU ALL DON'T KNOW MY LIFE IS IN DANGER," he yelled.

Everyone focused on the man, cutting him a wide berth. No one noticed the girl dressed in gray walking behind the van and never reappearing on the other side. The beige van pulled away from the curb and blended in with the flow of traffic, making its way to the FDR Drive, then the Queensborough Bridge, and onto the Long Island Expressway.

"Why did you bring a backpack?" Winter demanded. "What's in there?"

The sharp tone in his voice made Kat suck in an apprehensive breath. *I just made my first mistake*, she thought.

"Odds and ends, you know. Tissues, money, a bottle of water."

"ID?"

Kat didn't answer.

"A real ID?"

Kat didn't answer.

"Did you bring your house key, too?"

"I've heard of criminals carrying ID, keys, even a library card."

Winter's lips puckered into a smile. "Yes Katie, but only once. You never hear of them again."

Kat could feel the heat rise to her face. She sat, hands folded in her lap, quiet and penitent, Doc's voice still haunting her. *You're still young, Miss Kitty. You've got a lot to learn.*

Winter pulled out a pair of exam gloves and held them out to her. "If you drink from the water bottle, wear these. Stuff the money in your sock and put your ID in the bottom of your shoe."

Kat took the gloves and rummaged around, following his instructions. She pulled out a mass of short black hair from her backpack, shaking out the wig and holding it up for Winter to see. "I remembered this," she said.

Winter glanced over and offered a small smile. "Nice."

•••

Winter turned the van into a pristine neighborhood lined with mini McMansions boasting manicured lawns and colorful gardens. He parked the van diagonally across the street from the target and cut the engine.

Despite her shaking hands, Kat tucked her mass of hair under the wig. Suddenly, the full weight of what she was about to do, with all the possible consequences, hit her. A sickening pain began in the pit of her stomach.

Winter crawled out of the driver's seat and into the back of the van. He removed a plethora of screwdrivers, wrenches, and pliers from a black bag. She watched as he counted the pieces, then repacked the bag.

Kat turned away to survey the house. "It looks clear," she said. "We'd better hurry."

She turned to find him still hovering over the kit, removing the tools one by one.

"Uh...Winter? Are we ready?"

Winter shook his head, continuing his inventory. Kat waited, watching. When he finished, he stayed huddled over the tool kit as if he were in deep thought.

He reached into the bag and removed a tool.

"Oh, no," Kat murmured. Catapulting out of her seat, she lurched into the back, grabbing at his hands. "No...no...NO!" she said. "You're OCD? How could you be OCD?"

He straightened but avoided her gaze. "I am not OCD," he said through clenched teeth. "I'm having some—minor—anxiety issues that manifest themselves in control related behavior."

Kat stared in response. *Like elephant figurines and magazines arranged in perfect order.*

"But you do this kind of thing all the time. What about all those homes you've robbed around here?"

"I never robbed any homes around here," he said. "You assumed I did and I didn't correct you."

"You lied."

"I chose not to elaborate."

Clenching her fists, Kat fought the urge to reach out and pummel him. Instead, she began pounding her thighs until he reached out and grabbed her. Her anger spent, she began to cry. It took a few minutes to get herself under control. She swiped her eyes with her sleeve and looked into his eyes; she was met with fear and uncertainty, a reflection of herself. She pulled in a ragged breath.

"When was the last time you committed a robbery?" she asked.

"It's been almost a year."

"A year!" She bit her lip to keep from shouting. "And... how do you know Doc?"

"He gives me something for the anxiety. It calms me down but—"

"But?"

"The pills take my edge off."

"Did you take the pills today?"

"That would be unfair to you. We'd have no chance at all."

"Uh-huh...well...thank you," Kat said, her stomach sinking. She flashed back to the night at the Lessing apartment. She needed to take charge now; she had to make this work.

She slipped on a pair of gloves and packed the tools in the kit. After the last tool was in, she closed the bag.

"Now listen to me, Bob—"

"Bob? Where did you get Bob? I told you my name is Alexander."

"I don't like Alexander and besides, it's not your name. I like Bob. You're Bob."

"I'd prefer something else."

Where is the cool, confident man from the loft? Kat didn't know but she needed that man. She needed him desperately.

"Listen up, Bob. We're on the move, understand? You need to get your head on straight and get ready to go. *Now*. We're in—and out—in five minutes."

"I need to check one more time."

"No."

"Just a quickie."

"No."

"A visual check?"

Grasping his hands in her own, she stared into his eyes. "Bob, I am in deep shit. I need this to happen. If it doesn't, my life is going to change in all sorts of bad ways. I don't expect you to care but it means an awful lot to me. So, if you could pull yourself together for the next five minutes and help me get through this, I would really appreciate it. Because right now, I have to tell you, I have no idea what else to do."

Kat sucked in a deep breath and closed her eyes. She expected her biggest problem would be an untrustworthy thief. She didn't count on a thief who couldn't function.

When she opened her eyes, she found Winter staring at her. The fear and anxiety in his eyes had melted into an ocean of calm and cool. Now he held *her* hands, his thumbs moving in a gentle massaging motion. Reaching behind him, he pulled out a pair of gray overalls. He held them out to her and she took them.

Shit, Kat thought. This is really happening. *Whatever you do, don't throw up.*

•••

Strolling toward the house, Winter coached her, his tone low and soothing.

"Walk like you're where you're supposed to be."

"Don't keep your head down but don't look anywhere specific."

"After we bypass the alarm, out in five minutes."

They kept an easy pace crossing the street and approaching the front door. Kat followed his lead, holding a clipboard in a vice grip and ducking her head at an angle to shield her face.

Winter knocked on the door and waited.

Nothing.

He turned and headed around the back. Kat followed.

Giving the property a cursory glance, Winter went to the back door. He pulled out two pairs of gloves from the pocket of his overalls. He handed one pair to Katerina and slipped on the other pair. He picked the lock with ease and opened the door.

She held her breath and followed him inside.

He headed down to the basement, took a quick look around and zeroed in on a gray box. He opened the cover, revealing a complicated set of wires and sensors. He put his bag down. Reaching into the pocket of his overalls, he pulled out a piece of tin foil and slipped it into place.

"No shit," she murmured.

He closed the box and gave her a wink. "Five minutes," he said. Picking up the bag, he led the way back up into the house.

•••

Kat moved through to the entrance hall, putting the clipboard on a side table. She made a beeline for the living room, then the den off the kitchen. Where the hell was it?

She checked her watch.

One minute.

She took the stairs two at a time with a light step. Creeping down the hallway, she checked out a bathroom, a bedroom, another bedroom. At the end of the hallway there were stairs.

She went up.

Two minutes.

She found a bonus room. She performed a quick scan, lifting cloth coverings from furniture. Nothing.

She stood still for a moment, allowing for a mental scream. What now? WHAT NOW? Then it hit her. She had missed the master bedroom.

She rushed down the stairs.

Three minutes.

She entered the master bedroom and found Winter standing in front of an open chest of drawers.

"What are you doing?" she whispered.

"This woman has no taste in jewelry. None."

"We talked about you not doing that."

"We talked about a lot of things."

Turning away, Kat found herself staring at the cabinet standing flush against the wall.

She dove as if she were sliding into home plate. On her knees, she tore open the chest doors to find it crammed with magazines and books.

Four minutes.

She threw the books out onto the carpeted floor.

"Uh, first rule of breaking and entering," he murmured at her elbow. "Don't make a mess."

Kat ignored him. With a sigh, he knelt down, making neat piles.

Katerina thrust her arms inside the chest up to the elbow, searching for the latch to the fake panel. Goddamnit, she thought, her inside voice high pitched and hysterical. *Where is it? WHERE IS IT?* Then her fingers found it. She pulled and a panel gave way. She reached behind and her hand touched something square with round loops. The tape. She yanked it out, staring at it. She made a noise, something between a giggle and a cry. She found Winter staring at her, his expression soft, his smile genuine. He chucked her lightly under the chin.

"You did good."

Five minutes.

Kat shoved the books back in, Winter redoing her work behind her. "Don't quit your day job," he said.

A door closed, followed by the sound of running water.

They froze, their eyes locking.

Someone was inside the house.
The water shut off.
Footsteps sounded.
Someone was coming toward the bedroom.
Oh God, Kat thought.
"Time's up," Winter said.

Chapter 19

The bedroom door opened. A teenage boy wearing a rumpled T-shirt and jeans entered. He was all lanky arms and legs and an overgrown mop of hair. Wires dangled from the ear buds in his ears. Grabbing the remote, he pointed it at the TV. The screen spun until settling on a man and woman, both naked, in the throes of copulation.

In the closet, Kat and Winter stood rigid, crushed against each other. Afraid to take a breath, Kat gripped the tape. Peering through a crack in the closet door, she saw the boy hoist himself onto the king sized bed and unzip his pants.

Kat rolled her eyes. I don't believe this, she thought. I'm committing a crime, facing felony charges if I'm caught, and my future is hanging by a thread because some jackass is going to jerk off in his parent's bed.

She felt Winter's body heave against hers in silent laughter. She gave him an elbow. A sudden thought ran screaming through her mind. *We're not going to get out of here.* She tried to draw in a breath but nothing happened. A soft, strangled sound escaped her. Winter froze and then his hand splayed on her chest, just below the base of her neck, the other hand moving to her lower belly. He applied a gentle, warm pressure.

Bending his head low, he placed his lips against her ear. "Easy," he whispered.

Her muscles relaxed, her body released, and she closed her eyes, resting against him.

The ringing of the doorbell made her start in panic; his hand pressed again against her lower belly, keeping her in check. Junior continued his work with enthusiasm, lost in the music from his ear buds, all the while keeping his eyes glued to the television.

Winter maintained a firm grip on her, quelling any urge she might have to bolt and run. She tried to match the cadence of his breathing, steady and calm. After a moment, he took his hand from her belly and curled his fingers around the closet doorknob. Junior's moans grew louder until he tilted his head back and cried out. Winter opened the door and pressed against the small of her back, urging her to move.

Holding her hand, they stole along the hallway. As they crept to the stairs, the static from a police radio broke the silence; a small gasp escaped her. He pointed upward but eyes widening, Kat shook her head, trying to pull away. Winter's grip tightened and she stopped resisting. They went up.

Winter drew her close; they perched near the landing and listened. A deep voice called out on the floor below. "Hey, who are you? What the hell are you doing in here?"

Winter nodded to Katerina and they flew down the stairs. In the entrance hall he scooped up the clipboard and handed it off to her like a baton in a relay race. Before Kat could open her mouth, he opened the door and pulling her after him, strolled out into the sunshine.

Her stomach heaved, expecting drawn guns, capture, and arrest.

No one was there.

Grasping her elbow, he led her across the street. They passed the empty police car and climbed into the van. Winter pulled away, turned the corner and drove out of the neighborhood.

Kat ripped the wig from her head. Throwing her head back onto the seat, she began to tremble.

Pulling to the side of the road, he put his hand on the back of her neck. "Put your head down and breathe," he ordered.

She obeyed. He slid his hand down to her back, moving in a soothing, circular motion. She closed her eyes, surrendering to the warm rhythm of his touch.

***

Back in the city, Winter eased the van to a stop and parked. He turned to look at her.

Reclining in the passenger seat, she glanced over at him. "How did you know to use the front door?"

"Criminals don't use the front door. They come out through the back or the basement."

She nodded. Something else she didn't know. "It'll take me a few days to get you your thirty percent."

"Your fee is yours, in full, free and clear. I couldn't live with myself if I took advantage of a damsel in distress."

Kat looked at him, mouth ajar. She smiled.

"Besides, I owe you. This is the first time in a long time I have truly enjoyed my work. Thanks."

"I aim to please," she said drily.

Winter gave her a wicked smile of delight as he inserted his hand into his overalls and extracted a long thin diamond necklace.

Kat shot up in her seat. "Oh no, oh my God. How could you? You promised!"

"I did not."

"You stole something."

"You normally do when you break into someone's house."

"*I* didn't break in. *You* broke in."

Winter laughed.

"What's so funny?" she asked.

"I find your indignant morality absolutely adorable. *I* broke in?"

"Yes…I don't know how to break into a house."

Winter leaned in. "But you *entered*," he whispered. "A package deal…no?"

"But I only went to get something that belonged to someone else. It's—it's—"

"Different?" He shrugged. "Okay, I stole the necklace because I didn't want to take your money. Does that make a difference?"

"Yes. No. Maybe. No! By taking the necklace, you put us in danger."

"You put yourself in danger by choosing to enter the house. It is what it is, Katie."

Kat clamped her eyes shut in frustration. "I hate that expression. What does that even mean?" she said, sulking against the seat.

"It means that you need to admit the truth. You broke into someone's house. Say it."

"I don't want to."

"Katie. It is what it is. Say it."

Katerina felt her eyes filling and her vision blurring. "I broke into someone's house."

Winter leaned in close, his lips brushing over her cheek. She drew in a long breath, taking in his warm, intoxicating scent.

"You want to dance with the devil in the pale moonlight," he whispered in her ear, "in the morning, don't say it was dark and you didn't see who it was."

He pulled back to look into her eyes. A tear escaped and trickled down her cheek. Winter caught it with a feather touch of his thumb.

"The tin foil was pretty impressive," she said with a sniffle.

He gave her his now familiar smile. "Yes, Katerina, I know."

She exhaled a breath of relief. She got what she came for. The worst was over.

Chapter 20

Standing at opposite podiums, Katerina and Mark argued their ethical positions for and against the imaginary killing of the imaginary fat man to save the imaginary five people on the imaginary track. In the heat of the debate, Kat realized how ridiculous it all was. It was theory and conjecture, a game invented to answer the question: What is ethics? The answer that came to Kat's mind froze her with fear: ethics is whatever you want it to be, as long as you can explain it so that you can sleep nights.

After the debate, Professor James regarded Kat with a long look and a sharp eye. For a moment, she had the uncomfortable thought that perhaps Professor James could see inside her, her thoughts, her past actions. Did he somehow *know* her?

"Well done, Ms. Mills," he said finally. "A very well thought out, well argued position. But a touch of the cynic, I think, don't you? You're a bit young for that. However, even cynics earn an A." And he left it at that.

As Kat and Mark gathered their books, she found him staring at her in much the same manner as Professor James.

"Are you okay?" he asked.

"Oh, yeah, fine," Kat answered.

"You seem—different."

"Do I?"

"Yeah. You did a complete flip. You seemed more for than against. Did something happen?"

Kat shrugged. "I'm glad the assignment worked out," she said. "I've got to go. Errands to run. See you in class."

"Yeah," Mark said, his face pinching.

Kat made a quick exit, fighting the knee jerk reaction to return, to come up with a series of half truths to keep him around while revealing nothing of her real self. She steeled herself and kept walking. Mark was a sweet boy who reminded her of home, of a past that was gone; there was no going back. She took the stairs two at a time down to the main floor and headed into the dark night.

Chapter 21

Katerina delivered the tape to Jonathan Cookson. He took the thick envelope, ripping it open without ceremony. He dismantled the cassette case, pulling out the tape until it coiled, a mass of hopeless tangles. He tossed it into the fireplace.

He spent a moment watching the flames lick the tape. He turned to her, a bemused look on his face. "Are you still here?"

She took her purse and let herself out. She knew the drill; she had never been there.

•••

Kat sat in the guest chair in Jasmine's office, waiting. After several minutes, Jasmine finished tapping the keys on her laptop with a final stroke of the "enter" key. She handed Kat an envelope. Kat gripped it in her hand until her knuckles whitened.

"I have you listed as active and on call," Jasmine said. "Is that correct?"

Kat sucked in a breath. "Yes," she said.

"Fine," Jasmine said and returned to staring at the laptop screen.

The meeting was over.

Chapter 22

At the end of the week, Kat paid the tuition bill and placed a nominal fee into a checking account. Some of the money disappeared into a safety deposit box for law school or an emergency. She made several trips to different post offices, using the rest to purchase money orders, each for two or three hundred dollars. They would go out to her mother, every few weeks, one at a time. She heard Philip's voice in her head as she went through the motions: *don't spend it all at once; dole it out in small amounts; nothing should be obvious.*

She entered Bryant Park, pulling her coat tight around her against the chill; the weak sun offered no warmth. The city had already morphed into a state of cold, gun metal gray for the coming winter. Each day the robbery receded further into the back of her mind. The kinetic energy of panic that had gripped her in those first few days was fading away.

She spied Philip seated on one of the many green chairs, a small bouquet of bright carnations in hand, a newspaper peeking out of his coat pocket. He rose, holding out his arms but she snatched the flowers.

Philip persisted, moving in and snuggling up, gently pressing his crotch against her. "Hello beautiful," he whispered.

"Philip, the penis press, really?"

He stayed close, his lips near her ear. "Why not? You always liked it."

She pulled back to give him a slap, her favorite retort, but he held her fast.

"You have it with you, right?"

She nodded, maneuvering her purse between them. He kissed her cheek and then moved to her lips, all the while snaking his hand into her purse and extracting the envelope. They melded together as he tucked it inside his jacket.

"Too bad we're in a public place," he murmured.

Katerina gave a mental eye roll and pushed him away.

"Playing Candid Camera now," she said, patting his jacket pocket.

Philip gave her a narrow look. "You peeked?"

"I never peek."

"Patted down the envelope, hunh?" he said, slipping his arm around her waist. "That's my girl."

"I'm surprised you didn't use a Polaroid," she said, squirming out of his grasp. "You're into catching cheating husbands now?"

They fell into step.

"Nice try Kitty Kat, but no dice," he said. "However, I will give you a hint. I'm helping to clear up a little real estate dispute."

"Because there's nothing like incriminating negatives to move a negotiation along. Next time, have your secretary be your mule."

"I got rid of my secretary."

"What'd she do? Write something down?" Kat pulled the newspaper out of his pocket and carried it folded. "I'm sure whatever you're into, I'll eventually read about it when the arrests are made." Even as she was riding Philip, her own conscience condemned her. *Hypocrite. You're just like him.*

Philip chuckled. "This was a one-time deal, a show of good faith for a new business associate. I'm on to a new opportunity."

"What's a step up from blackmail? Insurance fraud?"

He grabbed her around her waist and pulled her in to kiss her ear. "*Nyet*. This is big. Helping clients establish their business through offshore company creation."

"Ah-hah," Kat said. "Congratulations. That definitely sounds legitimate."

"Come back to work for me," he said.

"*Nyet*," she echoed. "I'm on to a new opportunity."

"I heard. What have you been up to while I've been gone, jailbait? I met up with Letourneau. He said you came to see him."

"Mmm," she said.

Philip narrowed his gaze but gave up with a nod of his head. "Okay, have it your way. You know, you look different since I last saw you. There's a certain...something about you. More sophisticated, more in control." He leaned in close again. "I find it incredibly sexy," he murmured.

"I bet you do."

Kat unfolded the paper and glanced at the headline.

Manhattan Socialite Murdered

Felicia Reynolds stared back at her from the front page. Opening the paper to the page, Kat felt the blood drain from her face as she scanned the story.

Felicia Reynolds, wife of financier John Reynolds, was found brutally murdered yesterday in the early hours of the morning. She was discovered by a homeless man when he wandered into an alley near Alphabet City. The man, whose name was given as Alvin Burrows, was taken in for questioning but later released.

"Hey, jailbait, what's wrong? Katerina?"

Kat's stomach lurched.

"Nothing...nothing," she said, closing the paper. "I...I hate stories like that."

"That's life in the big city, kid," Philip said.

She could feel her head filling with white noise. Philip was at her elbow, still speaking, but she didn't hear him. She spotted a trash can and ran.

Philip held her hair back while she retched.

•••

When they made it back to her apartment, Philip pressed to stay.

"It's nothing," she said, struggling to keep her tears at bay and find a lie to satisfy him. "I drank too much last night. I should've skipped breakfast this morning."

He looked at her with skepticism, but said nothing and left.

Felicia Reynolds—dead. As the sickening reality set in, Kat had the sudden, overwhelming urge to flee. Instead, she huddled in bed under the blankets in the dark, tears staining her pillow. She thought of Felicia, warm and alive, pressing those delicate shell shaped quartz and diamond earrings into her hand. The man in the blue Ford killed her, Kat thought. Suddenly cold, she curled herself into a ball, drawing her knees up into her chest.

The jingle of the cell phone woke her. She picked up the phone and clicked the green talk button.

"Honey, is that you?' Emma asked. "Honey?"

"Emma...yes...I'm here."

"Well, where are you? My party starts in an hour. I expected you already. Are you feelin' poorly?"

"I was, but, no...now I'm fine," Kat said, struggling to remember the day and time.

"Well, get over here. We can't start without you."

Hanging up, Kat swung her legs over the side of the bed and sat for a few moments. She thought of the phone call from Joe Lessing that had started it all. It all seemed like a dream but asleep or awake, the dream had become a full blown nightmare.

Chapter 23

When Kat arrived she found Emma's postage stamp of an apartment bursting with people. A haze of smoke greeted her as she snaked her way inside. Kat recognized some of the guests as Emma's co-workers. She marveled that people in the business of keeping others alive took no thought for themselves as they drank and puffed away.

Emma had brought a touch of "back home" with her in the bright floral patterns and crocheted lace table coverings. She added a healthy dose of kitsch with travel posters and celebrity photos dotting the walls and entertainment and gossip magazines littering the coffee table.

A football game played on the flat screen, a group of men gathered around. They all wore the same expression: sharp, observant, and alert. The other half of the guest list. Cops.

Seeing her, their eyes sparked with interest, taking in the shiny chestnut hair, the fitted jeans, sweater, boots, and the finishing touch, her brother's battered leather jacket. They offered disarming smiles; she smiled in return but kept moving. She found Emma in the bedroom enjoying a clinch with her boyfriend, Frank Mitchell. A tall, well muscled, New York City detective, he had a head of sandy hair and a high-school-quarterback-handsome face. Emma and Frank had met when Frank was still in uniform; love at first sight over a stabbing victim in the ER.

"Sugar! We've been waiting for you!" Emma cried, throwing her arms around Kat. Kat suppressed the sudden urge to burst into tears and bury her face in Emma's soft, comforting shoulder. Emma held her at arm's length and took a long look.

"Sugar, you look like death warmed over. What kind of job is this that's working you so hard? Did you bring back my car with a full tank of gas?"

Kat held up the key. "Locked and loaded," she said. Sudden fear shot through her like a lightning bolt. *Oh God, Emma's car. The man following me. What if he took down the license plate? What if he comes for Emma?*

She could feel the blood drain from her face.

"You remember Frank, right?" Emma asked.

Kat nodded.

Frank gave Kat a quick peck hello. She thought she spied a flicker of interest in his eyes; the cop trained to identify any sign of distress. After a second, the look was gone.

"Hon, get me a drink, will you?" Emma said, hooking her arm through Kat's.

Frank gave her a smile and left.

"Now, what's with you, doll. Let's have it."

Kat gave her the bad breakfast story. "I'm fine now," she said.

"You better be. I've got the other half of the Dynamic Duo here and he's dying to meet you," Emma said, steering her toward the living room.

Katerina managed a weak smile. The "other half" was Ryan Kellan, an academy buddy of Frank's, and another hot shot detective. Katerina was familiar with their Cinderella story: a spectacular hostage rescue, sustained gunshot wounds, and the reward of writing their own tickets to a gold shield. The story had been splashed all over the newspapers and TV right up to the Commissioner's press conference presenting the Medals of Valor.

Kat took in Ryan's casual navy pullover and blue jeans, dark hair and lean build; a direct contrast to Frank's heavily muscled frame.

She stifled her objections as Emma pulled them both together.

"I'm sure you two will have tons to talk about," Emma said, and then she was gone.

Kat looked up to find Ryan studying her, the pupils of his hazel eyes wide with interest. She watched him perform what must be a cop ritual, the once-over to gather all the pertinent details. He smiled, his expression relaxed and unguarded.

"Emma said you've started a new job. How's that going?"

"Fine," she said.

"Do you like it?"

"So far," Kat said, reminding herself to be careful with her answers. "Making a change is always stressful. No one likes change," she said.

"That's true," he said, his voice pleasant and low. "Where are you from originally?"

"Vermont. Small town outside of Burlington. You?"

"Born and raised on Long Island," he said. "Ever get homesick?"

"All the time," she said.

"Going home for a visit soon?"

Kat glanced around the room. "Can't...new job." She chanced a look at him. He was attractive with a smile that softened his features. With her shredded nerves the questions sounded like an interrogation. She imagined that somehow he could *see* every thought swimming in her head.

Pull yourself together. Act normal. This is first meeting small talk, nothing more.

"Emma says you're off to law school."

"Eventually."

Ryan took a swig of his drink. "So...I'll make the arrests and you'll prosecute. How does that sound?"

"We'll see," Kat said a smile. "What made you decide to join the force?"

"No choice," he said. "It runs in the family—grandfather, father, and Uncle."

"Do you like what you do?"

"I love it," he said without hesitation. "I like the challenge. I like the chase. Although, I don't only chase bad guys."

"What else do you chase?" she asked.

"Sometimes, I chase good girls."

"Do you ever catch one?"

"All the time."

"What if she doesn't want to be caught?"

"Well—" he began with a smile. "If she didn't want to be caught, she would be gone by now." He took a step closer. "You're still here," he said, his voice warming.

"I am."

"Listen up everybody!" Emma called out. Grabbing Frank's hand, she swept her arm out in a semi-circle, carving out a space in the center of the miniscule living room. "Frank and I have an announcement…"

"We're engaged," Frank finished. Whoops, hollers, and applause filled the air as Emma held up her hand with a flourish to show off her diamond ring.

"And…," she continued, "we want our best friends to share our joy so we are asking Katerina and Ryan to be maid of honor and best man!"

The swell of noise rose again. Ryan raised his beer as a yes. Kat smiled, moving through the crowd to congratulate her friend.

Emma crushed Katerina in an embrace, whispering in her ear. "You know what this means, don't you? You and Ryan will be spending a lot of time together."

Kat's heart thumped in her chest.

•••

Hours later, people began saying their goodbyes. By the opening jingle of the eleven o'clock news, it was down to Emma, Kat, Frank and Ryan.

The top news story was the death of socialite Felicia Reynolds. Unable to look away, Kat gravitated toward the television. She watched footage of Mr. Reynolds leaving his apartment and disappearing into a limousine. His head was tilted down, his expression broken.

Oh God, she thought. He has no idea who killed his wife. *But I do.*

"That's just awful," Emma said.

As she helped clean up, Kat listened to Emma with one ear as Frank and Ryan had their own conversation.

"What's the latest?" Frank asked.

Ryan is assigned to the case. He doesn't know about the man in the blue Ford. He doesn't know about me.

"Can't be random. She was staged, left naked, except for a dark wig on her head and beige shoes on her feet."

Oh God, Katerina thought. The beige shoes. And where is Will Temple? He must know what happened… or was he involved?

"We talked to the driver but he wasn't much help."

Frank raised his eyebrows. "The husband?"

Ryan shrugged. "His alibi is airtight...for now. "

Kat continued to stare at the screen as an inner monologue ran through her head. *He doesn't need an alibi. He didn't do it. He just wanted to buy his wife a birthday present.*

"Get this," Ryan said. "He wanted details of the crime."

Frank's eyebrows rose slightly. "Including the sexual assault?"

Ryan nodded.

A lightheaded feeling washed over Katerina. She tried not to imagine what Felicia Reynolds had endured. A ripple of fear surged through her. Emma grabbed her hand, startling her, and pulled her away to the kitchen. Kat was grateful to be led away but her mind kept turning, rationalizing, explaining.

I thought it was safe after the Blue Ford was gone. I thought he was after me, after the envelope.

I had no idea that he was still there all that time, following.

We looked right at each other.

I can identify him. He knows that.

Kat shivered; Emma took no notice.

"So?" Emma said, slicing off two generous slabs of chocolate cake and topping them with whipped cream. "Isn't he yummy?"

Kat forced a smile, straining to act naturally. "He's nice."

"Nice? Oh, honey, come on. You really are hard to please."

"Do they always talk shop like that?" Kat asked, trying to get her friend off the subject.

Emma shrugged. "Frank's not supposed to tell me anything. Sometimes he slips. Sometimes I overhear. Like that socialite that just got killed. The papers didn't report the half of what was done to that poor woman."

Kat's stomach lurched, bile rising in her throat. She picked at the cake with her fork; she wouldn't be able to keep it down.

I could have warned Felicia Reynolds. I should have warned her. But warn her about what? How could I know that man was after her and not Philip's envelope? It wasn't my fault. It wasn't.

But, even as she thought it, Katerina knew that her excuses were just that. *Give a push or flip the switch.* It didn't matter. It was her fault. I'm responsible for Felicia Reynolds' death, she thought.

"Oh, honey," Emma said, covering Kat's hand with her own. "You look pale as a ghost. I didn't mean to scare you. You just be careful out there with this new job you've got, runnin' around at all hours of the day and night. There are crazy people out there, honey."

"I know...I promise...I'll be careful."

Emma nodded and examined her empty plate with disappointment. "So, dinner here, next Sunday night? Ryan's already said yes. What do you say, sugar?"

Kat stared at Emma for a long moment, her mind racing, unable to come up with an excuse. "Sure," she murmured.

Chapter 24

Jasmine scrolled through the data entered into the laptop, checking and rechecking the figures. The money would be moved in small increments systematically through electronic transfers until the final distribution between real estate and investments, completing the cycle. The money would be clean; the cycle would begin again.

The cell phone rang. Jasmine never bothered to check the caller ID. Every number came up as private.

"MJM Consulting," she said.

"This is Gallagher. I need a consultant."

Jasmine adjusted her tone to one of mollified respect. "Yes, sir. We would be happy to make an introduction. What service do you need?"

"Personal services." His said in a calm, pleasant tone. Jasmine knew that tone did not represent the real Thomas Gallagher. The real Thomas Gallagher was a dangerous man. It was best to steer clear of him whenever possible.

"The fee is forty thousand dollars."

"Fine. Her name."

Jasmine scanned her on-call list although she knew it was pointless. Lisa had already called ahead with a warning.

"Anna will be your consultant."

"Anna has already been my consultant."

"Were you not pleased with her service?"

"Her service was fine. Is Anna currently a college student?"

"Yes, she is."

"Does Anna have long, chestnut colored hair?"

"No, sir."

"Has she been on your roster for less than a month?"

Jasmine was silent for a moment. "No, sir."

"I would like a consultant who is a college student, with long, chestnut hair, and has been on your roster for less than a month. Do you have such a consultant?"

"Yes, sir."

"Is she available?"

"Yes, sir."

There was silence on the other end of the line.

"Katerina will be your consultant."

"Fine," he said and the phone clicked off.

Jasmine hit the "end" button on the cell phone. MJM was already well aware of Mr. Gallagher's activities where the consultants were concerned. There had been no objections. The other consultants had gone through the process providing "personal services." Even though they were damaged in their own way with scars not visible to the naked eye, they survived. All except one.

Lisa had lobbied for Katerina to be invited into the inner circle, citing the young woman's intelligence and ingenuity. Jasmine had no doubt Katerina Mills was sharp; but she was not strong. She would not recover from Thomas Gallagher as the others had done. That made her a liability.

Jasmine had received instructions to monitor the new recruit. The Reynolds situation proved inconvenient but no immediate connection to MJM was apparent. The instructions were clear: if there was any hint that Katerina Mills would be a threat, that MJM would be exposed in any way, then she would be dealt with. For now, it was business as usual.

Jasmine sat with the cell phone in her hand. Finally, she dialed the number.

Chapter 25

With every passing day, Katerina's thoughts ricocheted between clarity and panic. Now, she could tick off a mental list of all the little things she hadn't thought of. She had used her own laptop for searches, her own cell phone to make calls. Emma's car could be placed at the apartment. Who had seen her talking to Will? Who had seen her talking to Felicia? What about the killer? Would he find her? Could he find her?

She thought of Will Temple and the "audition" for the film, *Love's Fury*. Then there was the production company, Random Girl Films. Why was the murderer playing this game? To what purpose?

The one-of-a-kind quartz and diamond shell earrings lay tucked away, hidden in the back of a drawer. Katerina knew she should get rid of them. It was dangerous to keep them. But somehow it felt wrong, a desecration to the memory of the dead woman. She should not be able to put away Felicia Reynolds so easily. *I need to remember. I'm responsible.*

The cell phone rang. Switching on the light, Kat squinted to focus.

The screen said private. Kat knew who it was and what she wanted.

Kat hesitated. She had two choices.

Get out. Run away.

I'll be on the outside, with no options, and no contacts.

Go to Emma, tell her everything, tell Ryan everything, talk to the police and answer all their questions.

I'll expose Lisa, Jasmine, and MJM, whoever that is. What will they do to protect their secrets?

And what about the theft on Long Island? It would come out. How would she explain that?

What about Winter?

There was a third choice.

Stay in. Stay alert. Stay one step ahead.

Stay alive.

Katerina picked up the phone and Jasmine's voice came on the line. "I have a client who needs a personal aide. Do you accept?"

Kat opened her mouth to speak. A second's hesitation caught in her throat. A foreboding fell over her, a nameless suspicion that every new assignment would only add to the threat.

She took a breath and pushed the feeling down.

There's no getting out now.

"Yes," Katerina said.

The Fixer: The Killing Kind

Copyright ©2016 Jill Amy Rosenblatt No part of this book may be reproduced in any form or by any means without permission of the author, excepting brief quotes used in reviews. *The Fixer: The Killing Kind* is a work of fiction. Names, characters, businesses, places, events and incidents are either the products of the author's imagination or used in a fictitious manner. Any resemblance to actual persons, living or dead, or actual events is purely coincidental.

Cover Design and Images: Alan Gaites/Graphic Design

Notes:

Chapter 18:

The definition of microeconomics comes from *Principles of Economics* (page 18) available through Saylor University Open Textbooks at: http://www.saylor.org/site/textbooks/Principles%20of%20Microeconomics.pdf

The concept of "Pareto Efficiency" is explained in the "Jargon Alert" section of *Region Focus Magazine,* Winter 2007 issue, written by Megan Martorana.

Poetic License Notes:

As of this writing, the current status of Assembly Bill A7019 - "Prohibits the sale of Salvia Divinorum to persons in New York State" is listed as "in committee."

https://www.nysenate.gov/legislation/bills/2015/a7019

For Mrs. Danvers

Acknowledgements

My sincerest thanks to an amazing group of generous people who make this series possible; any errors in this manuscript are mine, not theirs.

Former NYPD Detective Glenn E. Cunningham for your continuing support for this series. You are always there to answer questions and share your knowledge. Thank you so much.

Former DEA Agent Carson Ulrich for so generously answering all of my questions and giving insight and suggestions as I work through the plotline for this series. Your help has been invaluable.

Former FBI Special Agent Tim Clemente of X-G productions. Thank you for making the introduction to Glenn and Carson and for being so accommodating about answering my questions.

Privacy Expert Frank M. Ahearn, author of the book *How to Disappear*, for his insights into how people "disappear" and how to find them if they do.

Dr. Timothy Westphalen, Program Coordinator of Russian Studies at State University of New York at Stony Brook. Thank you for answering questions and making the introduction to Dr. Geisherik.

Dr. Anna Geisherik of the European Languages Department at Stony Brook University for being so generous with your time, spending hours speaking with me about Russian history and culture.

Jenny Jozcik, my advisor during my Master's Degree program at Burlington College. It was wonderful catching up with you again! Thank you for sharing your experiences and the local culture and folklore of Shelburne, VT, and the surrounding area.

Alan Gaites/Graphic Design for the amazing book covers and teasers. You always take my vision and make something beautiful. I am so happy to be working with you.

Aldo and Jeanette Columbano for sharing their knowledge of New York City and State driving routes. Thank you, Jeanette, for the Italian translations.

Melvin and Doris Aponte for the Spanish translations (and corrections!).

Mary Riley for the great recommendation for the car show. A huge help. Thank you for thinking of me.

Ann Karen for always offering to give me "wads" of material.

Kevin Henderson. I'm so glad we met! Thanks for sharing your student exchange experience in Russia.

To Rebecca, my thanks for your continuing encouragement and for graciously giving an interview for information for an upcoming book in the series.

For Carlos, I tried to bring Mark back but it just didn't work out. Sorry!

To Ellis, wherever you are, your father is right. You are a walking encyclopedia on cars. Thanks for the help, kid. You're cool.

And to my Mom: I can never thank you enough for all of your support. You have read countless drafts, provided amazing insights, excellent editing skills, and thought provoking suggestions. Thank you for being my champion, my editing Yoda. You never let me give up . . . even when I want to.

8 WEEKS BEFORE CHRISTMAS

Chapter 1

"Again?" Katerina asked as a whipping wind whistled around the parked car. "This is the fourth time."

"There's been a delay," Jasmine said.

A few weeks earlier, Jasmine, MJM Consulting's "Iron Maiden" gatekeeper, had called late at night. Thomas Gallagher, one of New York's billionaire one percent, needed an assistant. Except he probably didn't. Katerina Mills had already learned the first rule of a fixer. *The job is never the job.*

"Does he want a consultant or not?" Kat asked, her mouth overruling her mind. *Careful Katerina. Don't antagonize. You have to stay in. It's too dangerous to be on the outside on your own. Not after the last assignment...*

"Yes," Jasmine said. "Any other questions?"

Katerina answered by clicking off the cell phone. Burrowing deeper into her coat, the heavy bangs of her short blond wig brushed her eyebrows as she focused on the apartment building diagonally across the street.

"Bad news?" came a voice behind her.

Katerina didn't bother turning around. On the floor of the backseat, her current client, Lester Callahan, rearranged himself, kicking the back of Kat's seat. She sighed.

"I hear you," Lester said. "It's tough. People are no good, you know? They give their word, it don't mean shit."

Katerina assumed Lester spoke from experience.

A pretty woman, swathed in a fur coat, exited the building and hustled to the corner, her hand in the air to hail a cab.

"Is that her?" Kat asked.

Rustling from the back seat. "Nope."

Katerina crushed herself further into her coat. She didn't want the work but she had to keep her hand in this world, to protect herself. *And I need the money.* But instead of a steady windfall of cash, the jobs had been few and far between. Lester needed an item retrieved; but she didn't know what the item was. From his babbled tale of rambling half-truths, Kat pieced together a picture: Lester had dangerous connections, something had gone wrong, and he needed to disappear. He was about to board a Greyhound bus when he realized he had forgotten something.

"You know it's not easy to get lost."

"So you said," Kat answered.

"Yeah, people don't understand how big their digital footprint is, you know? Take you for instance. You're a young girl. You on social media?"

"No."

"Dating sites? Not that you need one."

"No."

Lester shifted again; Kat's seat lurched forward. She sighed.

"You're smart, you know. There's a lot involved. I hired a professional to help me. Rebel One."

"Yup," Kat said, glossing over the sound of Lester's voice. *Am I smart or did it just work out that way?* she thought, reflecting on her training by her first boss, shady lawyer and ex-lover, Philip Castle. *Stay away from the computer unless it can't be helped. Never leave a trail.* Katerina realized Lester was still talking.

"It's a stupid name but I didn't say that. I didn't want to hurt the kid's feelings. Anyway, Rebel One can make you disappear. You don't realize you do a thousand things every day and leave clues how to find you: the phone, the credit card, the bank account, your magazine subscription to *Cosmo*...everything."

"I don't read *Cosmo*." *My college transcript. My library card. Could I get away clean if I needed to?*

They sat in silence.

"You have a family?" Kat asked.

"Yeah."

"Yeah? And you're just taking off?"

"It's okay, I made arrangements, you know? I left some cash, told the wife we'd get a condo when I got settled."

"Is that what you told your girlfriend?" Kat mumbled.

"I'm sensing judgment coming from the front seat. I don't think you're supposed to do that."

"Sorry," Kat said.

As they fell back into silence, Kat's thoughts turned to her father, William Mills. She had plenty of judgment for him. After walking out on her mother weeks earlier and breezing through the Big Apple with his new bimbo, where was he now? Had he left a digital footprint? Could he be found?

Her father wasn't the only one to pull a Houdini. Where was Lisa, who had brought Kat into this life as a "fixer"? Where had she vanished to? And then there was Alexander Winter. *If it hadn't been for him...*

She relived the robbery in her mind; Winter taking her by the hand, leading her through the break-in to retrieve the client's requested item. He had schooled her, protected her, and brought her home safe. Kat realized that not a day passed without her thinking of him. Except for a post-robbery "all clear" text, he had disappeared. *Where is he now?*

A young woman, rock star groupie attractive, wearing leopard Ugg boots and a winter-white fur coat over black pants exited the apartment building.

"Is that her?" Kat asked.

Rustling from the back seat. "Yeah, yeah, that's her."

Katerina shook her head. *This anemic, two-bit hustler is hooked up with the jailbait leaving the building.* "Let me guess. You bonded over shared interests."

"You know, sarcasm is not attractive in a woman. It shows a lack of self-esteem."

Said the man hiding on the floor of the back seat. "Uh-huh."

"You got the code, the key, and the phone, right?"

"Yes," Kat said, her heart racing like she was on the track waiting for the flag to come down. She slipped on her sunglasses, fussed over the wig hiding her long, chestnut-colored hair, and shrugged a large black bag onto her shoulder.

"Call me as soon as you're in the apartment," Lester said.

Katerina cracked the car door, checking for oncoming traffic. Getting out, she slammed the door and crossed the street. Punching the numbers on the keypad, she slipped into the building.

Remember, keep your head down. There are cameras everywhere. She made a mental note to change out her coat afterwards. The elevator chimed, the doors opened, and Kat ducked inside.

***

Getting out on the fifth floor, Kat stole down the hall. Apartment 512. She slipped the key out of her coat pocket, letting herself in. Taking the phone from the bag, she punched in the number. After two rings, Lester picked up.

"I'm here," Kat said. "What am I getting?"

"Go into the bedroom," he said.

Kat entered a room drowning in feminine pinks. "Okay, what?"

"You don't see it?"

"Obviously not," she said. "Is it a bill, a laptop, a deed to the apartment?"

"Go back into the living room."

Katerina retraced her steps and froze in her tracks. A West Highland white terrier stared at her, its head cocked to one side.

Don't bark. For the love of God and all that's holy, do not bark.

"You didn't tell me there was a dog in the apartment," she whispered. *What I wouldn't give for a Snausage right now.*

"Okay, good. You got it."

"I wouldn't say that—wait ... what? I'm here for the dog? You're leaving—and you want the dog?"

"No, no," Lester said. "The dog has a microchip in it. I need the chip."

"Why?"

"Because if the dog is scanned, the chip has my information. They'll find my wife and then, you know—they find me. Digital footprint."

Katerina blew out a mouthful of air. Still staring, the dog sat down.

"The chip is implanted by the right shoulder blade," he said. "It's the size of a grain of rice. It's nothing to take it out."

"I left my veterinary degree in my other purse." *Moron.* "And what do you suggest I use for a scalpel, a Ginsu knife?"

"If you think that's best. I'm not really attached to the animal. I don't think she is either, truthfully. I mean, look, she doesn't even take it with her when she goes out. I paid a shitload of money for that thing."

Katerina clamped her eyes shut.

"I was told you agency girls are up for anything. *Anything.* I need the chip. Get the chip."

Katerina clicked off the phone. She stared at the dog. It raised a paw as a greeting, then lay down on its back, baring its belly for a scratch.

Unbelievable.

***

Katerina hustled into the car, depositing the bag on the passenger seat. She revved the engine and took off.

"Did you get it?" Lester asked.

"Yup," Katerina answered.

***

Katerina dropped Lester Callahan off at the Greyhound bus terminal. Then, she parked the car and sent a text.

Done. W. 42nd. 8th Ave. Thanks

She got out of the car and walked away. The text had gone to Luther, an entrepreneur with his own limousine service. Luther's clients paid in cash. Luther saw nothing, heard nothing, and asked no questions. Luther had *a lot* of clients. He had gotten the car through Moose, a man Katerina had yet to meet. The car would disappear and turn up somewhere else: different state, different plates, different color. Five thousand of Kat's take had already gone for payment for the service. Contacts liked to be paid up front. That was a problem; she didn't get paid until the job was done.

Kat passed the Plaza and entered an elegant, gleaming office building. A few minutes later, she was standing in the empty, dark paneled anteroom of MJM Consultants.

"Come in, Katerina," she heard Jasmine's hard-edged voice call out.

With her bag slung over her shoulder, Kat entered the small, immaculate office. Jasmine, wearing her signature black Chanel and pearl teardrop earrings, glanced up from her laptop; she didn't bat an eye at the wig on Kat's head.

"The job is finished," Kat said.

"The client called."

I know. I was there. Right before he got on a bus.

"And then he called back again."

Shit.

"You never showed him the item he wanted retrieved."

Katerina caught the hint of a smirk on Jasmine's lips. *Is this part of the 'probation' test? You are not cheating me out of my money. Think fast, Katerina.*

"The client never said he wanted to *see* the item. He just said retrieve it. I retrieved it."

Jasmine was about to speak when Kat's bag moved, a sliver of fur peeking through the top. The smirk vanished. "Is that a dog in that bag?"

"You're not a pet person?" Katerina asked.

"Is that the item?"

"It's the item that contains the item."

Opening a desk drawer, Jasmine removed two rubber banded packets of bills. She held them out to Katerina. "Get it out of here."

Katerina took the money, turned on her heel, and left.

Stepping out of the building into the bright, chilly day, she placed a call.

"Whatever it is, it's gonna cost you a lot of money," the raspy voice said through the line.

"Morning, Doc. I need something removed," Kat said. "But the patient isn't human."

The raspy voice broke out into a low gutteral laugh.

***

Katerina watched over the sleeping Westie. A clean-cut man, wearing surgical gloves and a gown, used a feather touch to perform the procedure. He held up the forceps, showing Kat the tiny chip. Moving to the microwave on the counter, he placed the chip inside, closed the door, and hit a few buttons. Kat watched the plate rotate. A few sparks later, the chip was cooked.

Kat turned to Doc, perched on a stool, his frame struggling under the weight of his bulging stomach. Between wheezes, he puffed on a cigarette.

"Thanks, Doc," she said.

"Don't bother. You still have to pay me."

Kat nodded. *At least he's honest. This little act of benevolent kindness is about to take another healthy bite of my take-home pay.*

A woman entered the room without knocking. Dressed to the nines, she looked to be in her late sixties, a cross between a gracefully aging Audrey Hepburn and Jackie O., complete with swing coat and pillbox hat.

"Miss Kitty, this is Gertie. She provides pet relocation."

"Charmed, I'm sure," Gertie said with a flourish of her hand. "Now darling, time is money. You want a major city or you prefer something rural?"

Thousands of criminals in the city and I get the Dolly Levi of pet theft.
"What do you have?"

"Oh, honey, it's carte blanche. I always have a waiting list for Westies; very popular breed. Lucky you came along. People are so careful these days. Owners almost never leave them unattended."

"You steal to order?"

Gertie's eyes opened wide. "Steal? I beg your pardon," she said. "Darling, I connect pets with loving families. I provide a service. You think Social Security pays enough to live on? A girl's gotta get by. I used to be in the garment business—before they moved everything to China—no disrespect." She gave Kat the once-over. "I can get you a coat at cost. You'd look to die for in a Saint Laurent Chesterfield. You want a coat?"

Kat shook her head. "No thank you. Any location far away from here will be fine." She wanted to apologize. It wasn't judgment. Kat didn't know why, but she never quite felt prepared for the world she found. Even after what she had seen so far, she could be surprised. *Maybe I'm not up for anything. Maybe I just don't have what it takes.*

The man finished scrubbing at the sink. Drying his hands, he turned to Kat.

"How long have you been a veterinarian?" Kat asked.

The man smiled.

Oh shit. Kat turned to Gertie.

"Meet my nephew," she said.

The family that steals together . . . that's one my father missed.

"Still lots to learn, Miss Kitty," Doc said. "Lots to learn."

Katerina glanced over at the sleeping dog. Pulling out the packets of money, she counted out fifteen thousand, half of her cut.

A girl's gotta get by.

She certainly does, Kat thought, watching Gertie and Doc divvy up the cash. And not for the first time, she wondered how she would get by.

4 WEEKS BEFORE CHRISTMAS

Chapter 2

Gazing out the taxi window, Katerina watched the unexpected snow falling on the gray landscape. Glancing down at her red, chapped hands, she mouthed a silent curse. *Another pair of gloves lost.* The cab pulled over to the curb. Bracing herself for the cold, wet wind, she slid out of the taxi and hustled into the restaurant.

"How are you, miss?" Luke, the gushing maître d', gave his familiar, friendly greeting.

"Cold," Kat answered without missing a beat.

Luke laughed as if he had just heard something hilarious. "Let me guess, the wasabi filet mignon, pork spring roll, aaannnd ... the big fortune cookie."

Kat nodded.

Luke let out another raucous laugh. "Our mutual friend must really love that," he said.

Maybe you'd like to deliver it to him. I'll pay you to do it. "He keeps eating it," Kat answered, "so I guess so."

Kat watched Luke glad-hand and schmooze his way through the crush of the lunch crowd until he disappeared into the kitchen.

Katerina felt confident that delivering lunch three times a week to Simon Marcus, the wealthy, obnoxious, hedge fund billionaire holed up in his duplex on Central Park West, was not a job for an MJM consultant. Lester had been right, in a way. Lisa's sales pitch was clear: MJM hired savvy, capable consultants or 'B girls'; girls who do the bitch work no one else can.

"Okay, miss," Luke said when he returned, now serious and subdued. The wide grin was gone, replaced with a controlled impatience, a restrained agitation. He thrust the bag at Kat and ushered her toward the door. "You're all set and you tell Mr. Marcus I got a good fortune in that cookie for him."

Luke hustled her out, his hand on her back, narrowly avoiding people coming in. Turning to peer back into the restaurant, Kat spied the chef, his crimson face a stark contrast to his snow-white uniform. He pointed an accusatory finger at Luke while gesticulating wildly to the manager.

***

Katerina huddled in her coat as she hustled to the corner. She had braved worse winters back home in Vermont, but somehow this one was different. It had started early, eating into her bones, wearing her down in a way the others hadn't. She wondered about the people she passed by. How many of them would vow this was the last season they would endure this? By the time spring arrived, their oaths would be forgotten.

And then it happened again. A woman hurried by. Kat caught a glimpse of the side of her face, a lock of her blond hair peeking from under her hat. Kat skidded to a stop, jolted by a déjà vu as powerful as the relentless gusts of wind. In that instant, Katerina swore she just saw a doppelgänger, or a ghost . . . Felicia Reynolds.

Impossible. Felicia Reynolds, Katerina's first 'B girl' assignment, was dead; the victim of a random act of gruesome violence. The replay button in Kat's head flipped on: following the young socialite, tracking her every move in order to recommend the perfect birthday gift to the husband, John Reynolds. Standing in Bryant Park with Philip days after the job was done, reading the newspaper headline about the murder. Kat knew something no one else did: she had seen the killer face to face; a man in a blue Ford. She relived the assignment again, the fatal misread, mistaking the killer for a player in one of Philip's schemes. A familiar weight settled on her heart. She was responsible for Felicia Reynolds' death; no one could convince her otherwise.

Kat ticked off a mental list of everywhere she had been seen or could be identified. She had spoken to Felicia Reynolds, spoken to Will Temple, the handsome, young actor who turned out to be Felicia's lover. She had used her best friend's car to tail the beautiful socialite; another rookie mistake. Coming to the corner, Kat raised her hand to flag a cab. She glanced around, scanning, a rote habit. She had not seen the killer since that day, but he was still out there, somewhere.

Chapter 3

A simple oval awning protected the walkway to the building entrance. Two evergreens in terra cotta tubs on each side glowed with twinkle lights. The doorman gave a nod as Kat slipped inside one of the wealthiest addresses in the city.

She entered the duplex, listening for Simon Marcus' booming voice. The apartment was one of his multiple real estate holdings. Marcus also had a home in Aspen and an apartment in Miami; and according to him, a wife who wanted them all in the divorce settlement.

Hearing silence, Katerina traversed the rooms, her heels clicking on the polished, gleaming-like-glass floors, the sound cutting out when she crossed the areas covered with Persian rugs. Leaving the takeout bag in the kitchen, she wandered into the "art room." The room had four small paintings lining one wall: Claude Monet's *Bridge over a Pond of Water Lilies*, each one favoring a particular color theme: purple, yellow, green, and red.

She grabbed the issue of *Architectural Times* lying on the coffee table, flipping to the feature on the duplex. The picture of Marcus' smiling face grinned back at her and she picked up where she had left off last time. Thanks to the article, she learned Monet had painted twelve different versions of the bridge and pond on his property in Giverny; none of them were in this apartment. She also learned Marcus had been fleeced on the fakes, the first he had ever bought. He would never sell them, citing sentimental reasons. Katerina let out a small noise of derision. Sentimental and Simon Marcus did not go together … at all. She was about to continue when a bellowing voice interrupted her.

"So where is it? Do you have it?"

Simon Marcus, in his early fifties, sported a full head of thick, black hair, and a round face with a hint of a five o'clock shadow at eleven forty-five in the morning. He was small, compact, and his middle-aged spread oozed over his belt, a round, doughy glob of flesh.

"Yes, sir," she said. "It's in the kitchen."

Glancing around the room, he gave the paintings a once-over with an mirthless laugh. "Stay here," he said.

"Sir, I have another appointment." *With a latte at Starbucks, far away from the sound of your voice.*

"I just need you to wait a minute. Is it a BFD to wait a minute?"

Kat stared at him. "BFD?"

Marcus rolled his eyes. "Big, fucking deal. Is it a big, fucking deal to wait five minutes?"

"No, sir," she said.

"That's better." With a wide grin, he walked out of the room.

Kat examined the fake paintings again, then flipped open the magazine and started reading.

"Hey, kitten, come in here."

Tossing the magazine on the coffee table, Kat followed Marcus' bellow to the galley-style kitchen. The lunch spilled out of the bag; the oversized fortune cookie broken in pieces, the mousse filling sitting in a blob on the counter.

Marcus chomped on a piece of the cookie, his mouth open as he chewed. "Okay, cookie," he said, pleased with his joke. "I got another job for you."

"You need to call in the request," Kat said.

Chuckling, he shoveled in another piece of the cookie. "Already done, pussycat." Taking an envelope out of his pants pocket, he tossed it on the counter, dangerously close to the mound of mousse filling.

Kat's cell phone rang.

"Go ahead," he said. "Answer it."

Kat pulled the phone from her purse. "Yes," she answered.

"It's a retrieval," Jasmine said. "One time. Envelope is sixty. Your cut is thirty percent."

"What about the original request?"

Pulling an envelope out of his other pocket, Marcus waved it at Katerina and threw it down on the counter. The corner of the envelope sank into the mousse.

"Service has been renewed for another two weeks," Jasmine said. "Another fifty thousand. Your cut is thirty percent."

The line went dead.

Kat clicked off the cell phone, already doing a mental calculation. *You said you needed money. Here it is . . . forty-eight thousand when the jobs are done.*

"Okay there, kitten?"

Sure thing, Casanova, she thought. "Yes, sir," Kat said, her voice even and calm. "You'd like an item retrieved."

"My car is in this garage downtown," he said, handing her a ticket. "Pick it up and move it to Unique Auto Storage a few blocks from here. Take care of that this week."

"So you want the car moved from one garage to another garage?"

"That's right, pussycat. You're not gonna screw up this little love affair by asking questions, are you?"

I wouldn't dream of it. "No sir," she said.

Marcus let out a laugh. "You're a good girl. I like you working for me. You want to come work for me all the time?"

"That's a generous offer, Mr. Marcus, but I'm going to have to say no."

Marcus took a piece of the cookie, scooped up a generous helping of the mousse, and shoved it in his mouth. "That's all right," he said with a shrug. "I'd only hire you to fuck you. You know," he said, licking his lips, "you and I should go out together."

"I don't shit where I eat," Kat said. *Not anymore.*

Marcus laughed. "Okay, how about investments? You're making a nice piece of change on this arrangement here. Have you thought about putting that money to work for you? I mean, you don't have the minimum net worth I require but I'd consider it a favor, since we're, you know, friends. We have a *relationship.*"

The investment commercial, wrapped in a come-on, she thought. *Excellent.* "That's very considerate of you," she said drily, "but my portfolio is all taken care of."

"Whatever, kitten. Pick up my car on Wednesday," he said, reading the slip of paper with his fortune, and with a crooked smile, crumpling the paper and tucking it in his pocket. "Actually, no, pick it up on Friday. No wait, pick it up on Thursday. Yeah, Thursday."

"Yes, sir," Kat said. "Thursday pick up."

"You'll remember the name of the garage? Unique Auto Storage."

"Yes, sir." *I remember everything.*

"You know you remind me a little of my wife, you know that?"

Okay, it's time to leave. Now!

"She was always very efficient. Too bad she turned into a human leech, trying to suck out every last dime and flay the skin from my body, the bitch."

"Is there anything else I can do for you, sir?"

He gave her a sharp look, part lecher, part angry husband. "Eleven forty-five on Wednesday," he said. "Don't be late."

Kat nodded and left. Moving a car from one garage to another, a benign workaday request if ever there was one; that's what convinced Kat this was anything but.

Chapter 4

Katerina exited the building, heading for Columbus Circle when her cell phone buzzed. "Hello?"

"Hello back," came the strong, forceful voice of Detective Ryan Kellan.

A jolt of white-hot fear cut through Katerina's cold body. *I'm talking to NYPD's finest with a little over one hundred thousand dollars in cash stuffed in my purse.* "How was your evening?" she asked.

"Not good," he said. "I was alone. I hope you were alone."

"Nope," she said, standing at the curb, waving for a yellow cab to take pity and stop. "I spent my night with a wild crowd. The third floor librarian is a party animal," she said.

"You know, too much studying is bad. Lucky for you, I have a remedy."

"Tell me about it after finals."

"That's not the answer I was looking for."

Katerina fell silent, thinking about Ryan Kellan's dark hair, lean build, and intense nature. When Emma had introduced her to the decorated homicide detective, Ryan had locked onto Kat and began his pursuit. While the attention wasn't entirely unwelcome, she found it nerve wracking—and dangerous. Detective Kellan was working the Felicia Reynolds case.

"Dinner one night this week," she said.

She heard dead air as an answer.

A cab eased its way over, leaving a tire pattern in the slush.

"Better," he finally said. "I'll call you later."

She said goodbye and eased into the cab. The driver eyed her through the rearview mirror.

"Fifth Avenue and fiftieth," she said.

***

Katerina got out of the taxi and into the afternoon wind blustering in the open space. She maneuvered through Rockefeller Center's packed crowd of holiday revelers on the flag-lined promenade. Larger than life-size drummers, decked out in uniforms of red and green, stood between the flags, keeping their watch.

Kat scanned the benches dotting the walkway until she saw him. Angel, MJM's financial courier, got up from a bench and strolled in her direction. He was dressed in his signature leather jacket; no hat, no gloves, no scarf, no problem.

When he reached her, he drew her in, folding her in his arms. Grateful for the moment of warmth, she lingered. While they stayed close, she maneuvered the envelopes out of her purse, slipping them into his jacket pocket.

"Hair smells like strawberries, baby," Angel said, kissing her temple and strolling away.

Katerina moved on, already missing the heat of his embrace. As she turned to head downtown she wondered if he did that with all the consultants.

Chapter 5

Detectives Ryan Kellan and Walter Lashiver wandered the living room, waiting for John Reynolds to grace them with his presence.

Two months investigating the Felicia Reynolds murder had yielded nothing. It was time to start over and interview everyone again.

Ryan took in the intricately designed, brick red area rug under his feet, the fancy dark wood furniture, and the modern paintings of inks and splatters. It wasn't a living room; it was a showroom. The woman who had lived in this house never dreamed she would die a hideous death and be found in an alley in Alphabet City. He gave a small shake of his head. The medical examiner had said she had never seen such a case of sexual abuse; she used the word barbaric.

The sound of approaching footsteps on hardwood flooring drew Ryan's attention to the entrance of the room and John Reynolds. The widower's shocked, stricken expression had been replaced with cold calm. The young detective shot a glance at Lashiver. The older man wore his familiar poker face.

Reynolds went behind the small cherry wood bar, dropped ice into a glass and added a liberal amount of scotch.

"What news do you have for me?" he asked.

"Mr. Reynolds, we'd like to review some details with you," Lashiver said, "and see if perhaps there's anything else you've thought of, no matter how inconsequential it may seem to you."

Reynolds turned to the detectives. "You have no news," he said. "You've made no progress finding the lunatic who killed my wife. Is that correct?"

Ryan flipped open his pad, a pen at the ready. "Mr. Reynolds, we have a number of leads we're working on. We can't discuss them with you while we're looking into it. You mentioned your wife was a patron of the theatre. Can you think of any other charitable causes your wife may have supported, even if she gave her time only once or twice? Something you may have forgotten?"

"Such as . . . ?"

"Handing out blankets to the homeless," Lashiver offered, "working a soup kitchen, visiting a battered women's shelter; something that might explain why your wife was in that area of the city."

Reynolds considered the question. "You think she was the victim of an enraged husband?"

"Anything is possible, sir," Ryan said.

"And since you haven't come up with anything so far . . ." Reynolds let the sentence trail away.

"Excuse me," Lashiver said, "can I use your bathroom?"

Reynolds gave a dismissive wave of his hand. "Ask the maid. She'll show you."

Lashiver shared a look with Ryan and left the room.

Reynolds gestured for the young detective to sit down. The older man took a seat opposite, a glass coffee table between them. He drained his glass and placing it on the table, leaned forward as if taking Ryan into his confidence.

"You've never encountered a case like this before, have you, detective? You've never seen a crime so vicious, so brutal, have you?"

"Sir, please stop pressing for the details of what happened to your wife. It's not going to bring her back," Ryan deflected, discomforted by the fact that John Reynolds seemed to be reading his mind. The case had become a vague, gnawing sensation, always lingering in the back of his mind, even in his dreams.

"I'm going to tell you why I want to know, detective. Because you're going to catch the animal who did this; because he will be the one who convinces this state to repeal the ban on the death penalty; because when it's my turn to stand in court and make my statement, I want to say I know everything that was done to my wife. I want to say I know it as if I had been there. And when I plead for his death, I will know why."

Ryan nodded, watching Reynolds struggle to keep his rage in check. "Mr. Reynolds, we are doing everything possible to catch this person."

"There is no "we", detective—just *you*. The detective on the scene has gone back in the rotation. *You* are shouldering the responsibility for my wife, for justice for my wife. You want justice for my wife, don't you, detective?"

Ryan wasn't surprised. His father and uncle, both cops, had prepared him for this. Family members needed a connection. The detective was the first one to see the loved one as victim. Homicide detectives were the gateway between this life and the next. *I'm the bridge.*

"Absolutely."

"After all, you are a man of selfless bravery and honor. That's what the mayor said at the press conference. The police officer who took on armed men, who stared straight into the face of death. You can find the ... the animal who did this, can't you, detective? Surely, any man who would do such a thing is pure evil, a man with no heart, no soul. Your goodness, your honor, will overcome this evil, will it not, detective?"

Ryan listened to Reynolds, committing his words to memory. "I will not rest until the killer is found. I am a man of honor."

He expected a nod of recognition or a word of thanks. Instead, John Reynolds expression was blank, cold; there was no life behind those eyes.

Lashiver returned, followed by a man in a dark suit with a head of fair hair wound in tight curls; his dark eyes regarded Ryan with arrogance.

"Gerald Manning," the man said, "Mr. Reynolds attorney."

Ryan turned to John Reynolds.

"You may be a man of honor, Detective Kellan, but I need a man of action."

"The Reynolds family has retained a private investigator. He will be dedicated to this case until it is solved," Manning said, holding out a business card. "A reward of two million dollars is being offered for any credible tip which leads to an arrest. If there are any further inquiries, please direct them to my office."

Lashiver accepted the card. "This is an active investigation," he said to Manning, "and all developments have to be turned over. If any information is withheld, that could cause problems."

"If any information comes to light, it will be shared, of course," Manning said.

"Good day, detectives," Reynolds said.

**

Outside, Kellan and Lashiver trudged back to their car, the younger detective chewing on the anger that was working up to a boil inside him.

"I'll try to find out who the investigator is," Ryan said.

Lashiver nodded. "Bathroom cabinet is clean. No sign of a new woman. So, what do you think?"

"I think he enjoys fucking with cops more than finding out who killed his wife."

"Yeah, well, these ultra-rich types. It's all about control with them."

Arriving at the car, they opened their doors to get in.

Ryan shrugged. "Who knows, maybe he loved his wife."

"Yeah, but we don't really know if she loved him, do we?" Lashiver asked with a smirk before he disappeared into the car.

No, Ryan thought. No, we don't.

Chapter 6

In a relentless freezing rain, Katerina finally made it back to her apartment. Evening classes had been hard to sit through. A full semester of ethics, European history, philosophy, microeconomics, and poetry had created a swirling eddy of facts and figures ready to implode within her.

Turning the key in the lock of the building door, Kat flashed back to the night she heard a man calling her name. Will Temple, a young actor and Felicia Reynolds' lover, had her name, address, and wrong information. He thought her apartment was a production company, Random Girl Films, and she, a producer making a movie, *Love's Fury*. Will Temple was still out there, a bit player at a theatre in Brooklyn. The killer was still out there, too.

Hustling inside, Kat slipped into her apartment. Standing in the dark, she listened for squeaking or scratching noises, the telltale sounds of her most recent problem: mice.

Kat flipped a light switch. The postage stamp-sized apartment, painted in various shades of gray, devoid of any holiday decoration, had fallen into the usual end of semester mess of books, papers, and discarded clothing. *No sign of Mickey*. She shook her head. New York City existed in perpetual danger of being overrun by rats the size of feral cats. However, she was sure MJM, whoever she was, and Kat imagined it was a she, did not worry about such things. Neither did Lisa, wherever she was.

***

After lingering under a hot but sluggish spray in the shower to chase the cold away, Katerina took her time combing out her long, chestnut hair. The exercise calmed her, allowing her thoughts to wander. She retraced her first meeting with Lisa, trying to discern any clue that would help find her. *Joe Lessing called me. He said he called another service. They would try to come. He couldn't wait. I came. I fixed the problem. I met Lisa on the street.* Her speculation ended in the usual frustration. She was about to begin again when a loud knock at the door jarred her from her thoughts. Tossing her brush aside, she pulled on a shirt and sweatpants and padded to the front door. Checking the peephole, she spied the stranger. He held up a badge holder.

Cop. Shit.

Keeping the safety chain on, she cracked open the door.

A clean-cut man with straight, sandy-colored hair and a bland face stood looking at her. He wore a rumpled gray overcoat, and a tie loosened at the neck; his entire appearance, down to the brown shoes, vague and forgettable.

He held out the ID for closer inspection. "Miss Mills? Agent Sheridan, may I come in?"

"How can I help you, Agent Sheridan?" Kat asked, glancing at the ID. Agent James Sheridan, DEA.

He gave her a thin-lipped, cold smile. "Miss Mills," he said, his voice genial. "I need to speak to you about your father, Bill Mills."

"What about him?" she asked.

He glanced around. "I think it would be better if we didn't discuss this in the open. May I come in?"

Katerina's antennae shot up. *Simon says no.* "My mother told me never to open the door to strangers," she said, her heart beginning to thump.

"Miss Mills, I need to locate your father."

"*Mazel tov*," she said. "Let me know if you find him."

"You don't know him the way you think you do. Your father is mixed up in some very bad things."

"I don't know the Bill Mills you're looking for. You're knocking on the wrong door."

"He left your mother and ran off with his girlfriend, Lucinda Garvey. I'm looking for that William Mills."

Oh shit. Not a mistake. "Lulu," she corrected.

Sheridan nodded. "When is the last time you saw your father?"

Kat didn't answer.

Sheridan stepped closer, putting his hand on the door. "Miss Mills, your father is involved with very dangerous people. If you cooperate, I can help you."

Katerina kept her eyes glued to Sheridan's hand as the sharp, stabbing pain of a migraine settled at her temple. "Why do you think I need help?"

"You don't want to be on the other side with this. You want to come over to our side, where it's safe."

It's not safe anywhere.

"Why don't you let me in?"

The trembling began inside her; every muscle tightened. "Gee, I'd love to Agent Sheridan but my schedule is booked. I have to wash my hair. I'll try to pencil you in." *Never.*

He chuckled, staring down at his shoes. When he glanced up, the thin-lipped smile had vanished. The cold rage in his eyes sent a jolt of fear through her. He drew a card out of his inside pocket.

As she took it, he grabbed her hand, squeezing until she winced. "There will be others. You need to think about what I said, Katerina. You need to make time to talk to me."

Jerking her hand away, Katerina crumpled the card in her fist. "Goodnight Agent Sheridan."

"Goodnight, Miss Mills."

Katerina closed the door and leaned against it, eyes closed. She could feel him on the other side, waiting. Though only minutes passed, it seemed like hours until she sensed a shift in the air. She checked the peephole. Clear.

Turning away from the door, Kat jumped, letting out a cry of surprise. A small, round, gray mouse darted into a sliver of a crack by a cabinet.

She went for the cabinet door under the sink. A remnant of peanut butter hung from the traps.

"Son of a bitch," she mumbled, slamming the cabinet door shut.

She retreated to the cramped living room and began to pace.

What the hell is this? DEA? That means drugs. What does my father have to do with drugs?

And who the hell is this James Sheridan, she thought, a cold slice of fear cutting through her. And is he who he said he is? She could think of only one person who might be able to find out.

Chapter 7

The next morning, Katerina stopped in at a drugstore, made her purchases, then ducked into a fast food joint next door. Settling into a booth with a breakfast sandwich she didn't want, she took the items out of the bag: two burner phones. Her adventure in dognapping with Lester Callahan had highlighted another of Kat's rookie mistakes: she was using her own cell phone for MJM business. She checked the text messages on her personal cell phone and retrieved the number. Removing one burner phone from its package, she slipped in a SIM card, powered up, punched in the number, and sent the message.

>Bob. Call me

She smiled thinking of the nickname she had given Alexander Winter during their eventful and illegal road trip out to Long Island. The odds were good he had been using a burner phone when he sent the text. The odds were bad he still had that phone. Pulling on her coat to leave, she hoped he would get the message. If he did, she hoped he would call her. *Great. I'm on the hope plan. Not a good plan.*

***

Approaching the subway entrance, she made a second call on the burner.

"Rainbow Farms," her mother's voice came over the line.

Katerina exhaled in relief. "Hi, Mom, how's everything?"

"Oh, right as rain dear," her mother answered.

"Has anyone come by, Mom?" *Like a federal officer serving a search warrant.*

"No, dear, who would be coming by?"

"I don't know. Do you know how things are at the plant?"

She heard her mother sigh on the other end of the line. "I suppose they're fine, Katerina. I'm fine."

Kat closed her eyes. *Stupid.* "I'm sorry, Mom. How's it going?"

"Good, I'm completely in the flow of things now."

"What things?"

"The feeding and care of the animals; I milk the cows."

Katerina held out the phone and stared at it. "Mom, when you chaperoned my school trip to Shelburne Farms you refused to touch the animals. You wouldn't let *me* touch the animals. You hate farm life."

"I think 'hate' is a bit strong."

"Really? You said: 'Don't touch those filthy, disease-ridden creatures. I don't know why your father ever moved us from California.'"

"Did I say that?"

"The whole class heard you. My mother is the only parent who was never asked back as a chaperone."

"Well, then, I did something right, didn't I?"

Katerina gave a silent scream. She could not get a handle on her mother. Just when she was convinced Linda Mills was incoherent of everything that went on, her mother displayed a sly savvy that threw Kat off guard.

"And California was beautiful, absolutely gorgeous . . . a paradise."

"I don't remember, Mom. I was too young."

"Oh, I just remembered, someone did come by."

Katerina's heart skipped. "Who?"

"Sergei."

Katerina let out her breath at the sound of the name. Sergei, the Russian painter who lived like a hermit; Sergei, who did more drinking and smoking than painting; Sergei, her father's friend, an odd couple if ever there was one.

"Uncle" Sergei had crossed the country to be near William Mills in his time of medical crisis. He settled in the secluded solitude of a cabin in the woods, but appeared regularly at her father's bedside. All through her life Sergei had popped in and out, but always sent presents: Russian dolls called *Matryoshka*, for her birthday, bags of candy at Christmas. When she left for college, he came to see her off.

When she was young, Sergei would sing Russian lullabies to her. She remembered a photograph, Sergei holding her while she stared at him in wonder, listening to words she didn't understand. Once, he told her what they meant, 'don't lie on the edge of the bed, otherwise a small gray wolf will come....'

That was back when they lived in the warmer climates out West: California, Arizona, even Mexico. Those times were now no more than snippets of memories.

Mexico.

"Has he heard from Daddy?"

"No, dear, but he's been very kind and supportive."

"What about Kevin? Does he even know? Has he called?"

"No, Katerina."

Super. My dependable older brother; I need him and he's still AWOL in paradise.

"Mom, I want to visit at Christmas."

"That's a lovely idea. Ethel is going to serve a tofurky. It sounds positively disgusting, but everyone assures me it's not. The tofu takes on the taste of whatever it's cooked with."

And my mother has reverted to her former self.

"Okay, Mom. I'm sending you something, a phone."

"Dear, Ethel doesn't mind if I use the phone. I've used some of the money—"

"Mom!" Katerina took pains to remain calm. *Just don't scream. As long as you don't scream, everything is okay.* "This is a special phone and from now on when you talk to me, I'm going to call you on that phone. If you need to talk to me, use the phone I'm sending you, not the house phone. Okay?"

"All right, dear, if that's what you want . . . I love a mystery."

"Mom—"

"I'm sure everything is going to be fine, dear."

Katerina clicked off the line, certain of one thing: everything is *not* going to be fine.

***

Coming up out of the subway, Kat braced herself for the blast of frigid air. Hearing the jingle noise, she shoved a red, chapped hand into her purse and dug out the cell phone. She frowned in annoyance—wrong phone. Not the burner phone. Not Winter.

"Yes," she answered.

"He's ready," Jasmine's voice came over the line.

Katerina skidded to a stop in the middle of the sidewalk. "Now?" she asked.

"Eighty thousand. Your cut is thirty percent. Be there in twenty minutes or forfeit."

The line went dead.

Shit.

Glancing down at herself, Kat took in the battered coat covering a NY Rangers sweatshirt and worn jeans. She had scuffed brown boots on her feet. Not exactly the outfit for meeting one of the most powerful men in the city.

She was supposed to be on her way to school. Classes. Studying for final exams.

Twenty-four thousand dollars.

Twenty minutes or forfeit.

Katerina turned and ran back down into the subway.

Chapter 8

The doorman gave a curious smile as Katerina passed and entered the eye-popping opulence of the limestone and marble lobby. She rode the elevator to the tenth floor. Glancing down, Katerina winced. She had the perfect Chanel outfit. It was hanging in her closet next to the Burberry coat, racking up rental charges. There was nothing to be done about it now. She pulled out the twist that held her long waves in check, allowing them to tumble down around her.

***

An older gentleman wearing a somber black suit, accented by a white shirt, black tie, and a benign expression, met her at the door. She felt her eyebrow give a slight arch at the sight of him. *The butler? He must be in his sixties. What is he thinking? How much has he seen that he was instructed to forget?*

"I have an appointment," she said, but he had already stepped aside in deference, allowing her to enter.

"Of course, miss," he said, closing the door behind her. He took her coat with an easy professional flourish. "Please, follow me."

He led her through the foyer and the living area. Kat had expected something fantastical, a step back into the glorious court of Louis XIV. Instead, she found a staid and sterile gentleman's club decor: dark upholstered leather furniture, wall unit bookcases, and the faint hint of a recently smoked cigar. *If there's a wife, she doesn't come here.*

She wondered if other consultants had been here. *Has Lisa ever been here? I could ask her, if I could find her.*

He stopped at the entrance to a small study and stood off to the side. Katerina peered into the room.

"Thank you, Richard," a man's voice said.

Richard slipped away.

Kat peeked inside. A man, seated in a chair, held a cup in one hand, a saucer in the other. A teapot, a folder, and an envelope sat on the oval table next to him.

"Come in please, Katerina."

Kat approached the smooth voice, her heartbeat quickening. She had done an internet search on Mr. Thomas Gallagher; nothing. Whatever Gallagher did for a living, he did it discreetly.

Presenting herself to him, she found a striking man in his forties, with a face like polished stone, strong and angular. His hair was blond and his eyes, a piercing ice blue. She found his lips inviting and sensual, yet some aura originating from him, something she couldn't describe, made her blood run cold with a nameless trepidation. Whatever he had been, he was now at the full height of his powers. She remained cemented where she stood.

He, on the other hand, remained at ease, a man in no hurry.

"Please sit down, Katerina," he said, the words tipped with a vague hint of an English accent.

She did as instructed, her hands folded in her lap.

"Don't you have something you'd like to ask me, Katerina?"

Kat stared, silent, as a response. "Yes, sir," she finally said, "the envelope, please?"

He put the teacup and saucer down. Standing up, he brought the envelope to her, staying close, hovering over her.

With trembling fingers, she finished her count and raised her head, taking him in from the dark slacks to the black turtleneck, and up to his smooth, pleasing features.

"There now," he said with a smile. "The chore is out of the way."

She breathed a sigh of relief as he returned to his seat. "How can I help you, Mr. Gallagher?" she asked.

"I require a personal assistant for a series of meetings I will not be able to attend. You will attend in my place."

"Is my assignment to see or be seen?"

For a moment, he appeared taken aback by the frankness of the question.

Kat felt the lurch of panic. *Watch your mouth, Katerina. If he wants a toy to display, that's his business.*

"You will do both, Miss Mills," he said with the hint of a smile. "You will be seen and then you will slip into the background to see. You will be asked to take notes of select information but you will remember everything. At a future date, we will have dinner together and you will report your findings to me. Any other questions?"

"No, sir," she said.

Gallagher rose from his chair, his signal the meeting was over. Katerina stood.

When he came to her, she caught the scent of sandalwood. He offered his hand and she took it. The sensation felt strong, almost oppressive.

"Richard will give you the address for the boutique that will provide your wardrobe—yours to keep after the work is completed, of course."

"Mr. Gallagher, I apologize for my appearance. I was called at the last minute. I have an appropriate wardrobe—"

"Think nothing of it," he said. "The outfits are requirements and they are built into the price. I've already paid for them."

Gallagher continued to hold her hand and Katerina realized she had done nothing to escape his grasp; she slipped her hand away.

***

As Kat came out of the study, she found Richard waiting, his enigmatic expression firmly in place.

An assignment requiring that I look pretty, watch, and listen. Oh bullshit, she thought, her head clearing now that there was distance between her and Gallagher's overpowering presence. *I'll have to wait it out until I discover what he really wants. Will I be sorry when I find out?*

***

Gallagher settled back in his chair. He picked up the folder from the stand and flipped it open, scanning the background check of Miss Katerina Mills. He reflected on the meeting. By taking the interview after numerous delays, she had passed the first test. She possessed a stubborn, curious nature. She would not give up. Countless girls before her had shown the same qualities. However, her question indicated a savvy rarely, if ever, seen in a girl of such tender years. She was an exquisite young lady. The plans he made might need an adjustment. Lisa had chosen well this time, very well. He reviewed the file again, wondering if Katerina Mills would turn out to be that rare treat he had been sorely missing: a challenge.

Chapter 9

Katerina arrived for her philosophy class to find it packed as usual. Where her Introduction to Ethics class was taught by Professor James, an earnest idealist, Professor Benjamin Schoeffling was an apathetic realist, and much more entertaining. His teaching style resembled a jaded, cynical comedy schtick. He wandered the front of the classroom, his hands settled in his pockets, declaring his misanthropic distrust of the human race, loud and proud.

"So what do you think?" he said to no one in particular. "Do human beings have free will? We've been talking about it all semester. I guess we should get down to making a decision about it."

The class responded with shuffling of books and papers.

He took another turn, heading back toward the window. "So a wife takes a gun and shoots her husband. It was her free will to do it, right?"

Ashley, a pert, pretty girl, spoke up. "If her husband was an asshole, she didn't really have a choice," she said; muted chuckles followed. "His prior acts of being an asshole determined her course of action. So it was meant to be."

The class broke out in laughter while Katerina fought the urge to get up and leave. Why were these examples always about life and death? *Because a case study on stealing a Krispy Kreme doesn't garner the same excitement. Don't call on me, please. Whatever you do, do not call on me. I don't want to think about this.*

Schoeffling nodded. "Okay, but what if the wife hires someone to do it? She doesn't pull the trigger. She has someone else do it. You know, for the insurance. Is it determinism now? The hit man doesn't know the husband's previous acts so those previous acts don't determine the hit man's actions. So the hit man has free will. He could choose not to do it. Right?"

Katerina shifted in her seat, a threat of a migraine beginning at her temple. *Forget the killer. What about the victim? Don't you want to know if the victim had free will? Could Felicia Reynolds have done something different to avoid death? Did seeing Will Temple set her course? Was it all determined? What about me? What about all the choices I had that could have led to something else? Away from all this . . .*

"Katerina? Something to say?"

She met Schoeffling's laser glance. She shook her head.

"No, he has free will," Ashley said. "He has the capacity to choose otherwise."

"Yeah, but all of his previous actions have been killing people. Isn't that deterministic that he will continue to kill?"

"This was never a good example. He's morally bankrupt," Ashley argued.

"Morality," Schoeffling said with a chuckle. "You've been in the wrong class all semester. Morality and determinism don't mix. We're talking about all acts being the result of previous acts—universal causality. The course is set. You want to talk about morals, go next door to James' class and talk about saving a bunch a people strapped to a train track by sacrificing one poor son of a bitch. Then you can worry if it makes a difference how you kill the poor son of a bitch, flip a switch or push him to his death yourself. Now, let's get back to the hit man. To him, pulling the trigger is meant to be. It's normal. There is no morality. There is no free will. There is no choice. Or is there?"

Katerina felt lightheaded, her nerves making her stomach do somersaults.

"You'll tell me on the final, after I give you twenty points for writing your name on the test."

The class laughed.

"I guess we should talk about your final exam, because who are we kidding, you're only here for the three credits. Please do not regurgitate ad nauseam facts and figures about compatibilism or epicureanism. And don't give me any shit about karma. That's an automatic F. Forget the wife, the husband, and the hit man. All I want to know is this: does man, or woman, have free will, or are you doomed from the day you're born by determinism?"

Katerina slumped down in her seat. *Which is it*?

Chapter 10

Katerina ducked into the garage, the tag for the Porsche in hand. She didn't want to admit it, but a little piece of her could hardly wait to get behind the wheel of the snow-white, eight hundred horsepower machine able to go from zero to sixty in mere seconds. Glancing down at the ticket in her hand, she frowned at her red, chapped hands. *Get a new pair of gloves, Katerina.* She made a mental note to pay more attention to her mental notes, or one day she would get caught short and be shit out of luck.

She found the attendant seated behind the counter reading a magazine. He raised his head, his eyes widening in pleasant surprise. He was Kat's age, maybe, with olive skin, coal black hair, and an easy smile that must have earned him a fair amount of tips.

"How are you today, miss?" he asked, taking the tag she held out. He multi-tasked, searching the key box while half-turning to look at her.

"Fine, thank you, yourself?" Kat said.

"Beautiful. Just beautiful. It's the best time of the year, like the song says. You go see the big tree yet?"

Kat shook her head. Another trick learned. *Never discuss where you've been.*

The attendant frowned in disapproval. "No? C'mon, you got to see the tree, go ice skating. You on ice skates, that hair flying everywhere. That's some dangerous hair, miss."

Katerina smiled. Pegging her as the hired help, he dared her to be sociable. She liked him. "I'll put it on my to-do list, I promise."

"That's all I ask."

Kat watched his expression cloud in confusion as he fingered the keys, glancing down at the tag and back again.

"Miss, are you sure the car is here?"

"My boss left it here. I'm picking it up," Kat said, a sinking feeling opening in the pit of her stomach.

"Mira, joven, venaqua," the attendant called out. A subordinate sauntered over, tall and skinny. His eyes ran over Kat, lingering a minute too long.

"What kind of car, miss?" the attendant asked.

"A white Porsche."

"Mira, ella anda buscando un Porsche blanco."

Kat waited as they talked.

"She was here yesterday for the car," the attendant finally said.

"She?"

The subordinate chattered again without pausing for a breath. The attendant nodded.

"That's right, I remember," he said to Kat. "Dark hair, kind of sour. She wasn't a nice lady."

"Ella dijo que era su esposa," the subordinate said.

"She said she was the wife," the attendant said.

Kat nodded. *Shit.*

Chapter 11

"What the fuck do you mean it wasn't there? You park it in a fucking spot and you fucking pick it up later. It's very simple."

Your wife thought so too. Katerina was about to open her mouth when she hit the pause button.

Simon Marcus stared, waiting for a response.

"Mr. Marcus," Kat said, quiet and careful, "is your wife the owner of the car?"

"What the fuck does that have to do with anything?" Marcus asked.

Kat struggled to take Marcus' outburst, against the backdrop of his paunchy, pugilist stance, seriously. A sudden, intrusive image of the trim, muscular build and calm demeanor of Alexander Winter filled her mind. She hadn't heard from him and it was clear she wasn't going to. Winter was gone.

"If the car is not legally hers, then you have options to get it back."

"Options," Marcus laughed. "You're the option, cookie. You were hired to get the car."

Why am I the option? This is a petty pissing match. Call the divorce lawyer and be done with it.

"The car is no longer there to be gotten. You need to get it from your wife."

Marcus slipped the cell phone from his pocket and dialed a number. "This is Marcus," he said. "You got five minutes to explain to the Little Princess here that she needs to finish the job or it's going to be a problem for her—and you."

He listened, then held out the cell phone.

Kat took it and left the room.

"What's the issue?" Jasmine asked.

"The item wasn't there to be retrieved. The wife took it."

"Retrieve the item."

Kat hesitated.

"You were told the rules. Once you're hired, there is no cancellation and no refund. Retrieve the item or—"

"—there's no reason for me to be here," Kat finished.

"You're still on probation. One more of these calls and you're out. Understand?"

A vibration of panic bloomed in Kat's chest. *I can't be on the outside. I can't. It's too dangerous.* "Understood."

The other end of the line disconnected.

Katerina found Marcus in the painting room staring at his prizes: four fake Monet paintings.

At the sound of her heels clicking on bare floor, he turned. She held out the cell phone and he grabbed it.

"I'll take care of it," she said.

"That's good, cookie. That wasn't such a BFD, now was it?"

"No," Kat said. She cursed silently. Her workaday request had just become complicated.

Chapter 12

In a darkened corner of the pizzeria, Katerina and Ryan sat at a small round table for two. Leftover scraps of a meatball hero littered his plate; Kat ploughed through a heaping plate of spaghetti.

"I love a woman with a healthy appetite," he said, brushing a lock of hair from her face.

"You should be head over heels by now," she said. She had two states: hungry and starving. The wonder of fear, she thought. *It burns off the calories before they get a chance to stick.*

As she brought the fork to her mouth, he took her hand and held it so he could take a kiss. He had just finished his shift and looked every inch of the last ten hours with tousled hair, eyes squinting with fatigue.

Katerina imagined this as a normal scene between two people feeling their way through the start of a relationship. She imagined herself a lucky girl to have stumbled upon a decent man with winning traits she had warmed to. Her conscience wasted no time condemning her. *This isn't normal.*

Seeing Ryan was a kind of addiction: an initial spike of fear like an electric current, then the anesthetic of safety. Every time they met and he *didn't* question her, *didn't* accuse her, *didn't* arrest her, was a confirmation. *I'm safe. He doesn't know. No one knows.* The balance was restored.

As he hovered close, stroking her hair, she held his stare until the thought of Winter flashed into her mind and the eye contact became too much. She leaned back in her chair, twirling her fork in the pasta. She couldn't blame Winter for not calling back. *I'm trouble he doesn't need.*

"Hey," Ryan said softly, "is it nice where you are?"

"Sorry," she said. "You look tired." She never asked direct questions about his work, but she had to say something. It was what normal people did.

Ryan frowned with a shrug. "Just frustrated," he said and left it at that.

The usual gnawing guilt settled over her. *You should tell him. You should have told him already.* "It's not good to live with so much pressure," she said. "Maybe you should talk to someone." *He's supposed to be talking to you, stupid.*

Ryan gave a bitter laugh. "I talk to people. I talk to people all day. Half waste my time, the other half lie, which amounts to the same thing."

You want truth instead of lies? I committed a robbery. Now I'm planning to steal a car. I spoke to Felicia Reynolds. I know who killed her.

"What's with your job?" he asked.

"Same old," she said.

"What was it today? Begging someone to open a shop at two in the morning for face cream? Taking someone's Saint Bernard uptown for a wash and blow dry?"

Following her instincts, Katerina had stuck to the personal assistant angle when explaining her job. It seemed innocuous enough, the upside being no normal person would imagine she was mixed up in anything illegal.

"I'm helping a guy whose wife just left him. He's having trouble navigating his life, you know, getting meals, the usual stuff."

"He doesn't know from Hungry-Man dinners? What agency is this you work for again?"

Keep cool, Katerina. You have to answer the questions. "It's new."

Ryan's eyebrows quirked. He picked up his glass, swirling the red wine a few times before drinking it. "This place is legit, right? You're paying taxes on this money?"

"I filled out a W-4 form."

Ryan leaned in, snaking his arm around her shoulder, nuzzling her ear. "You know, I have a friend and he needs a smart, reliable assistant. Of course, I thought of you. Flex hours, good pay, just what you want."

He snatched her earlobe between his lips, making Katerina's stomach flip. She had the distinct feeling of suffocation. Keep cool, she coached herself. *You can do this.* "Everyone says they have a flex schedule, then I'm working there and it isn't so flex anymore. It'll cause a problem with your friendship."

"We're not *that* close," Ryan said with a laugh. "Don't worry about it."

"This is working well for me. It's really okay."

A small, indented vee knotted between Ryan's eyebrows, the telltale sign of annoyance when he didn't get his way. Kat decided some stroking was in order.

"There is one thing you can do for me," she said, her fingers curling around his wrist.

"What's that?" he whispered into her hair.

"Take me ice skating," she said.

He pulled back and with both hands, swept her hair away from her face. "Your wish is my command," he said.

Katerina let out an internal sigh of relief. *Another bullet dodged.*

***

Opening the door of her apartment, Katerina led Ryan inside. She flipped on a light switch and stopped. The air was different. Something was off. Sudden fear gripped her. *Someone is in the apartment.*

"I'll just be a second," she said, ducking into the bedroom. Nothing. She went to work searching drawers and coat pockets.

"I thought this was a straightforward operation," she heard Ryan call out.

"It is," she said. "I have gloves. I have a scarf." *Somewhere.*

"Didn't you grow up in a cold climate?"

"Yes," she said, her voice pointed. *And my mother always made sure I had these things.* Finding what she needed, she slammed the drawer shut and returned to the living room, discarding the nagging feeling still clinging to her.

Taking her scarf, he arranged it around her neck, sifting her hair through his fingers. "Didn't the Girl Scouts teach you to be prepared for all weather situations?" he murmured, his eyes soft, the pupils an inky black.

"I confess. I flunked out of Brownies."

Ryan shook his head while pulling her in and wrapping his arms around her. "I don't know if I can continue to date a woman without merit badges. What will you do if there's an emergency?"

"Call a cop," she said. *Not.*

Kat enjoyed the fleeting feeling of warm protection. In these moments, she wished she could be normal Katerina.

"To protect and serve," he whispered.

As Kat smiled up at him, her stomach flipped again. The sense of suffocation returned, surrounding her, urging her to run.

The buzzing of a cell phone broke the silence. "Damn," he said, releasing her. She waited as he turned away, the cell phone now at his ear.

"Mmm, hmmm," he said. With his free hand, he searched his pockets until he pulled out a note pad and a pen. "Where was she found? No, it sounds similar."

Kat made a studied effort to stay still. *When you look at him, no change in facial expression. This could be anything. But it's not. It's another one. Another woman murdered. Just like Felicia Reynolds. I know it.*

"I'll meet you there. Thanks."

Ryan clicked off the cell phone and turned back to Katerina. "Sorry," he said, "I have to take off."

Kat nodded. "I understand."

Pulling her into his arms, he rocked her in his embrace and kissed her. "You're a keeper, Katerina Mills, you know that?"

"I do now."

When he kissed her again, she kissed him back, trying to make the moment feel true.

"I'll call you," he said.

She saw him to the door, closing and locking it behind him. Slipping out of her coat, she tossed it on the chair. Shucking off her shoes and peeling out of her clothes as she went into the bedroom, she stopped short, giving a cry of shock.

"Hello, Katerina," Winter said.

Chapter 13

Katerina scrambled to pull her clothes on. Winter approached, slipping off his gloves. She froze as he slid his hands down her arms with a light touch and then pulled her shirt up onto her shoulders. She let him re-do the buttons from the bottom up.

"You still have my number," he said, his voice low and soft.

"You still have your phone," she answered. *You're going the wrong way.*

He smiled. "I see that you're well," he said, finishing the top button.

"Why are you dressed like that?" she asked, nodding at his repairman's uniform of gray coveralls.

"Because it's normal to have a repairman going in and out of a young lady's apartment."

She registered that he was in her life again, his six-foot-one frame filling the cubicle of space. With his wide, muscled shoulders and hard, fit body, he was what her best friend, Emma, called a "climber." A big man you wanted in your bed so you could crawl on top and get to work, the best kind of work.

She felt the familiar flush of heat bloom in her cheeks. He was staring at her, a smile tugging at the corners of his mouth.

Busted.

"By the way," he said, "the burner phone. I'm impressed."

"Thanks, Professor," she said gamely, a competitive impulse to prove to him she could keep up. "How's business?"

"My schedule is packed, thanks to you."

"Don't forget to post a shout-out on your Facebook page," she said.

"I'll tweet it as well."

She was secretly pleased by the cool, confident man standing before her, a marked change from their first meeting. He had been in crisis, gripped by OCD panic attacks that had derailed his career. The robbery on Long Island had helped Alexander Winter get his mojo back. *Leading a criminal back to a life of crime. Where does that go on the résumé?*

"So, what's up?"

Done with the small talk, she thought with a pang of disappointment.

"I had a visitor to my apartment. Official. I need to check him out. I need to know if he is who he says he is."

"Local?"

"Federal."

Winter took the news in silence but his expression darkened. "You need to have someone else do the checking. Not your boyfriend—the police officer."

Katerina broke eye contact. "He's not . . . *technically* . . . my boyfriend."

Winter moved closer. As he loomed over her, she glanced up at him. She had a vision of lifting her hand to touch his cheek, only to have his lips catch her fingers with a kiss.

"Anybody tell him that?" he asked in his low, gravelly voice.

She inhaled his warm, sweet scent as an answer.

He stepped past her into the miniscule living area.

"No Christmas decorations?" he asked.

"Bah humbug," she said, on his heels.

He surveyed the clutter with a shake of his head. Picking up a discarded sweater off the chair, he folded it. "Have you considered tidying up?"

She came to him, palms up. "I know where everything is."

He placed the sweater on her waiting hands. "That wasn't the point. Do you know you have a pest problem?" he asked.

"I have several these days," she said, dropping the sweater back on the chair. "And yes, I know about the mouse."

"That's mice, plural. Would you like me to take care of it?"

"I've got it covered," she said, watching his eyes dart back and forth, a flashback to his discomfort in the van before the robbery. "I'm working on a new living situation."

He took her coat from the chair, hanging it away in the closet. "It's taking a long time. I assumed your cash flow had loosened up."

"It's not that simple. The jobs haven't been coming in like I thought they would. The jobs I have now don't pay until they're done."

Closing the closet door, he turned to her. "I can help you with an apartment."

"I was hoping for something with a lease, with my name on the mailbox. Something normal."

Winter laughed. He came to her and ran a finger along her jaw line. "Katie, if you wanted normal, you'd be in a different line of work. Back home."

Katerina's jaw dropped in response. *How does he know?*

He cupped his hand around her cheek. "That's what I like about you. Your stubborn streak of innocence, it makes you irresistible."

She tried working up to heated annoyance but instead fell into the feeling of his caress. They stood still, a moment of expectant hesitation hanging between them. Winter let his hand drop away.

"About checking out my visitor," she said, glossing over the awkward silence. "If you could just tell me what I need to do and how much I owe you for your time."

"I'm insulted."

Katerina scrambled for a response, the idea that he would be angry with her spinning her into a sudden panic. *None of this is going right.*

"I don't want to take you for granted," she said finally.

"Then you're not doing this right. But if you were going to pay me, what were you planning to pay me with?"

"Most people use cash," she said, a sliver of unease sparking within her.

"Some people prefer more creative methods." Winter pulled on his gloves, reached a hand into his pocket, and pulled out something enclosed in his fist. He uncurled his fingers to reveal the quartz earrings lined with diamonds. *Felicia Reynolds' earrings.*

"You went through my stuff?"

"I go through everyone's stuff. I'm a thief. It's in the job description. I assume you didn't pay for these."

"They were given to me."

Winter's eyebrows lifted at the response. "Not by the boyfriend."

"He's not . . . *technically* . . . my boyfriend."

"It is what it is, Katerina. The truth is the truth. Find it and admit it. These were not given to you by the *boyfriend*."

"No."

"May I ask who this magnificent, generous individual, is?"

"Just—someone...it's not—it wasn't—romantic. It's not what you think."

"I see."

She cupped her hand, and he dropped the earrings into it. "By the way, you know someone else has been in here."

Her eyes widened.

Taking off his gloves, he took her by the hand and led her to the door. She fought the urge to cling to him as he let go, gesturing for her to open the door. He pointed to the lock. Bending down she noted the telltale signs around the keyhole edge.

"It's called bumping," he said. "There shouldn't be any scratches if it's done right."

"You never leave any marks, Professor?" she asked, standing up.

Standing behind her now, he slid one arm around her waist. "Depends on what I'm working on," he whispered in her ear.

A jolt of excitement shot through her from her belly to down deep below.

"Any idea what they were looking for?" he asked. "It wasn't earrings."

She shook her head. "Nothing's missing. Maybe it was a mistake." *Yeah . . . right.*

"You need a better lock. I can help you."

"I've got it covered," she said, the words small and hollow as her mind twisted over this new turn of events.

He slid one hand onto her chest, just below the base of her neck; the other hand slipped down to her lower belly. When he pressed lightly, her stomach fluttered, then relaxed. Turning her head, she rested against him, a comfortable shadow. Katerina flashed back to the break-in in the Hamptons, leaning against him in the dark. It felt like falling; she wanted to fall.

He bent his head low, his lips next to her ear. "Any time you want to tell me," he whispered.

"James Sheridan," she said. "I need to know if he's DEA."

They lingered in the embrace a moment longer. "Give me a few days," he said. Giving her a gentle squeeze, he released her and slipped away.

Chapter 14

Getting out of his car, Ryan was met by the usual barrage of flashing lights from squad cars and an ambulance. He passed by uniforms talking to a homeless man, frazzled, with a filthy beard and a head of matted curly hair.

Lashiver watched the medical examiner, a woman in her mid-forties, examining the body. Ryan could smell the blood as he approached. He steeled himself as he came alongside and looked down on the nude, disfigured victim, just as he had looked upon Felicia Reynolds. He turned his eyes away, fighting the urge to retch as the bile rose in his throat.

"What's the story with that guy?" Ryan asked when he trusted himself to speak, nodding at the vagrant.

"St. Nick over there didn't want to stay in the shelter tonight. He sees the victim in the alley, sees something shiny on her finger, and thinks Christmas came early. Until he gets close to the body."

"This isn't the same as Felicia Reynolds," Ryan said.

"No, not exactly," the medical examiner said, methodically inspecting the body with a detached air. "This one's worse."

I can see that, Ryan thought, still fighting the nausea threatening to overcome him. "Any ID this time?"

"ID, wallet, jewelry, wedding ring," Lashiver said. "Everything. This is Cheryl Penn, wife of hedge fund wunderkind Charles Penn. Whoever did this, wanted us to know exactly who she is."

"Another society lady," Ryan said. "What's your pick? Same guy or a copycat?"

Lashiver shrugged. "Either way, the papers are gonna scream serial killer."

Ryan nodded.

Chapter 15

Banging on the door with her fist, Katerina felt the vibrations of the blaring music coming from the other side. *This is useless. Another morning without studying. Another job that won't pay until it's done. If I ever actually get the job.*

She stepped back, pulling out her cell phone.

"MJM," came Jasmine's voice on the line.

"The client is blasting his stereo," Katerina shouted into the phone. "Do you have another contact?" *And thanks for waiting until the end of the semester to load me up with jobs. Is this another probation test?*

"Just a minute," Jasmine said and with a click, Kat had dead air on the line until it clicked back on. "The editor is coming," Jasmine said. "She'll be there in fifteen minutes."

"Editor?" Kat yelled, pressing her finger against her other ear. "And this is a retrieval?"

"Correct," Jasmine said and clicked off. The bill was fifty thousand. Katerina would take sixty percent. *Thirty thousand dollars. For what? Finding a lost manuscript? Stealing a manuscript? Not again.*

Katerina slipped the phone back into her purse. All the jobs together would pay just over a hundred thousand dollars. *Money for my mother, an apartment, tuition, law school . . . and a partridge in a pear tree. If I complete them all.* Leaning against the wall, she folded her arms, and waited.

***

Twenty minutes later a young woman rushed off the elevator. She kept her dark hair in a short bob and sported black square-framed glasses against the backdrop of a round, soft face. She carried an oversized bag that dwarfed her petite frame. She had a key in hand, at the ready.

"Sorry," she yelled. "I'm Maggie, the editor."

Kat watched her flip the key into the lock and give the sliding door a good pull. Pushing herself off the wall, Katerina followed her inside.

They found celebrated author, Paul Patel, standing in the middle of the loft, staring at a piece of paper in his hands, his head rocking in time to the music.

Kat looked to Maggie.

"Creative crisis," she shouted.

Katerina pointed an ungloved finger at the sound system.

"Sorry," Maggie mouthed, making a beeline to the stereo. Pressing buttons, she finally gave up, leaned over, and yanked out the plug; the earsplitting decibels died.

Paul Patel's head shot up, his eyes zeroing in on Katerina.

"Wow," he said.

"Paulie," Maggie said. "This is the woman we called to help."

"Wow," he said again. In a second, he was in Katerina's personal space. "You are a goddess. You are literary gold. That hair. Can I touch it?"

"No."

He circled her, as if she were on display. "You are a muse, you know that? You inspire," he said, his hands framing her. "There was someone like you for Shakespeare, Tolstoy, and . . . and— "

"Keats . . . Dante?" Katerina finished.

"Yes, yes, yes!" he cried out. "You are Fanny, you are Beatrice, you are the Dark Lady. What I could write with you by my side. " He held out the blank paper for Katerina to see. "But I can't." His eyes squinted shut as if in pain, his body contorting in an invisible struggle. He crushed the paper in his hand. "I can't write you the way you deserve to be written."

Kat felt her eyebrows rise.

"Mr. Patel is working on his follow-up to *The Reckoning,*" Maggie said. "Mr. Patel's work speaks to this generation."

It's speaking to me too, Katerina thought. *It's saying I'm going to get thirty thousand dollars for this.* She settled for nodding. She had heard of the great literary rock star. Last semester, her literature professor had crowned him the next Hemingway.

"Mr. Patel is exploring the misery of the human condition—"

"Mr. Patel," Katerina interrupted. "I need the envelope, sir." Katerina had no issue with Paul Patel exploring the misery of the human condition. But she couldn't take him seriously while he was plumbing those depths wearing four-hundred-dollar jeans, a Gucci polo shirt, and standing in the center of a two-and-a half-million-dollar loft in gentrified Park Slope.

Patel whirled around. "Oh. Yeah. Sure. It's always business first. It's always fucking business first. It's never about the art."

"I'll get it for you," Maggie said, already moving to the desk.

Katerina crossed her arms, waiting. The editor searched a drawer, pulling out two rubber banded packs and brought them to Katerina. Kat took the packs, skimmed them with her thumb, and tucked them away in her purse.

"How can I help you, Mr. Patel?"

"My words," he said, with bent knees and open arms. "I need my words retrieved from in here!" He pointed his forefingers at his head.

"Can you translate that, please?" Kat said to the editor.

Maggie cleared her throat. "Mr. Patel needs certain conditions to stimulate his brilliant visual wordplay. Herbal stimulation."

"I'm guessing ginseng won't do it," Kat said.

"I like her Magpie," Patel said. "I love her vibe. You have amazing vibes. They're honest, they're real. They respect the creative journey."

No, they respect thirty thousand dollars. And I'm transitioning from thief to drug supplier. Excellent. Like father, like daughter?

"What do you want? Antifreeze? Snow? Something else?"

Patel paced, shaking his head. "No, no. Heroin and cocaine for creativity are passé. They don't feed the mind. I need the Diviner's Sage."

Katerina was lost and it showed.

"*Salvia divinorum*," the editor explained. "It's an herb. It's part of the mint family. It's been difficult to procure."

"Since the statewide ban."

"That senator's kid wasn't using it right," Patel interrupted. "He was *unbalanced*."

Tell that to the family of the person whose brains he blew out. I'm sure they'll care.

"The Mazetec Indians. They knew. You use it to see everything. To *feel* everything."

"How long does he have to finish the book?" Kat asked the editor.

"One month. He took an advance of three million dollars."

Bingo.

Throwing himself on the couch, Patel curled into a fetal ball, rocking back and forth. "It's the only way my characters speak to me."

"Get the *Salvia*, please," Maggie said. "Without it the world will be deprived of a genius."

And the genius will be deprived of his three million dollars. "Yes, ma'am," Katerina said. *You wanted a straight up retrieval, Katerina. No hidden agenda, no bullshit. Here it is. Be careful what you wish for. You just got it.*

Chapter 16

Twirling the spoon in her coffee cup, Katerina watched the black liquid lighten to caramel. A dull, vague fear plagued her. She couldn't see her way clear. In these quiet moments, Lester's words came back to her. *I was told you agency girls are up for anything. You agency girls. How many of us are there? What about the others? Are they okay? What are they going through now? Did anyone ever get out?*

Her thoughts shifted again, meandering between Marcus' car and Patel's drugs. She had no idea how to get either. The rest of her life pressed in on her as well: her father, Sheridan, Ryan, and Felicia Reynolds. And of course, Winter, always lingering in her mind, separate, special, apart from the others. The same question circled in her head, like a toy train on an oval track around a Christmas tree. *Can I trust him? God, I want to.*

Angel slid into the opposite seat of the booth, jarring her from her thoughts. He was dressed in his standard black. He took in the cup of coffee and pie on his place setting.

"I thought you might be hungry," she said.

With a smirk, he moved the plate and coffee off to the side. He folded his hands and waited.

"Next to you, under my coat," she said.

Angel glanced at the coat lying in a heap near the window, and quickly transferred the packs into his jacket pocket.

"Later, baby," he said.

"Did you always do this?" she blurted.

Angel stopped, then shifted back into his seat. He folded his hands, resting them on the table.

"I mean, did the ladies, ever take care of this part themselves?" Katerina fixed her gaze on the table. She finally chanced to look at him, finding his expression calm and cool.

"Tick, tock, baby," he said.

"How many are there like me? Like Lisa?"

"Ain't nobody like Lisa. She's all by herself. You could be her. You have the talent."

"But the others—like me. How many are there? How long do they stay?"

"They come and they go, baby."

"Because they want to? Or they have to?"

Angel leaned forward. "Same thing."

His eyes fixed on her. Katerina wondered if his examination was an act of committing her to memory; so he could retain the image of her after she was gone.

"I need to know—are they, were they all—okay?" Katerina leaned in. "Did they all get out okay? Was there ever a girl who . . . didn't?"

Angel's eyes flicked away.

"Oh . . ." she murmured. "Didn't anyone help her?"

"You looking for a confessor, baby, get yourself to a church. Guilt is a luxury no one can afford."

"No one helped her."

Angel leaned in. "This ain't a love-in. This ain't even Manhattan. This is Ancient Greece. The Gods ain't dead, baby. Only they don't look down from the heavens but the penthouse. And they move the people like pieces on the chessboard. You put yourself in this game. So did she. You stay in, you disappear, or you die. And if you disappear, you best make sure everyone thinks you're dead."

Winter's words came back to her. *You want to dance with the devil in the pale moonlight? In the morning, don't say it was dark out and you didn't see who it was.*

"You should have never told me about the envelope until *after* I answered your questions. You got the envelope, I go to the ends of the earth for you. That's why you're not Lisa. Not yet. "

Katerina nodded.

Slipping out of the booth, Angel stood up.

"I don't know what to do," she said.

Angel leaned over. "You'll know, baby," he whispered. "You'll know."

Kat stayed in her seat a long time after he left.

Chapter 17

Bryant Park's Winter Village bloomed with allées of greenhouse-style kiosks selling clothing, food, and trinkets. On the rink, skaters were gliding and swirling as loudspeakers filled the air with music.

Kat had wanted to go home after class. She reminded herself that this yearly shopping tradition with Emma needed to happen. The friendship was straining. *And it's my fault.* Besides, she thought, this is what the normal people do. *I'll shop with my friend, buy a gift for Ryan and be normal.* The familiar, confused feeling soon filled her mind, a cross between a migraine and the sensation of cotton stuffed in her head. Every time she thought of Ryan, the next thought was Winter. She rubbed her hands together for warmth. She had forgotten her gloves again.

Rearranging her backpack on her shoulder, Kat checked around, looking for Emma's curly, honey blond hair. She grabbed her "normal" phone and tapped off a text.

> I'm here. Where are u?

The phone buzzed.

> Running late. On the way. Meet me by Xmas tree

Texting back a confirmation, Kat tucked the phone away in her purse. Stopping at a kiosk, she lingered over a black wool scarf with gray edging. Digging bills from her coat pocket, she handed the scarf to the woman manning the shop. She thought of Ryan wearing the scarf, how it would look against his black coat. She decided he would look very well. *Would Win—*

Katerina closed her eyes to check her thought.

"That's really nice," a man's voice said.

Katerina glanced to her left. A middle-aged man, around five-ten with silver-tinged black hair, a square face, and a sturdy jaw line, stood next to her.

"I wish my girlfriend would buy that for me. Or my wife."

Kat smiled.

"You like that one, hunh?" he asked with a smile.

The seller handed Kat her bag and a few coins of change.

"Have a good day," Kat said to the man as she moved off.

"Yeah, you too, miss," he said.

Making her way toward the Christmas tree, Kat threaded a path through the dense crowd. She smelled warm chocolate and thought to stop and buy whatever it was. People jostled her and she felt a sudden, sharp pain in her right shoulder.

Katerina took a few more steps, suddenly realizing that everyone else was standing still. Why is that? she thought, gazing up at the tree, its festive lights of reds, greens, and golds blurring and blending together.

A powerful arm wrapped around her waist. Her head fell against a shoulder. She heard a voice.

"Boy, you're a pretty girl. C'mon pretty girl, there's someone you need to see."

Katerina heard sounds, people, and music. Then the festive colors faded, disappearing into darkness.

Chapter 18

Katerina woke up to an aching pain in the upper right side of her back. She found herself in an easy chair more suited for flanking a fireplace in a cozy den instead of the dimly lit, frigid warehouse she was in. A folding chair sat opposite her. A man, built like an immovable object, stood nearby.

She struggled to get up.

The man held up one hand, a gesture for her to sit back.

Katerina did as he suggested.

The squealing of metal announced the opening of a door. Carrying a styrofoam cup in one hand, the man from Bryant Park came in.

"How are you, sweet pea, you okay?" he asked as he held out the cup.

"I have a headache," she said.

"Don't worry about that, angel."

"Said the man who doesn't have a headache," Katerina muttered, grasping the cup with both hands.

The man laughed. "You're a good sport." He turned to the enforcer. "Carlo, you could smile you know. You're going to scare the pretty girl. What's the matter with you?"

Carlo settled for taking a step backward and left it at that.

"He means no harm."

Katerina felt certain "means no harm" was a fluid term, subject to change at a moment's notice.

"What's your name?" she asked.

"You can call me Vincent."

The fog in Kat's mind continued to burn off, leaving a growing panic in its wake.

"Vincent, what do you want to talk to me about?"

A man in a black cashmere coat stepped out of the shadows. "*I* want to have a chat," he said.

Carlo snapped to attention, like an NCO whose commanding officer just appeared.

The man sat down on the folding chair. He had a Mediterranean complexion and a full head of black hair. Katerina thought he might be in his fifties. He crossed one leg over the other, laying his hands one over the other on one knee. His nails were manicured, clipped and clean. She caught a scent of aftershave, fresh and cool.

"My name is Anthony Desucci."

He smiled and waited.

It took Kat less than a minute to make the connection. Philip had mentioned that name. More than once. Her blood pressure rose as her heart sank. *Mobbed up Anthony Desucci.* Philip had bragged that the Mob was done. Arrests. Convictions. Competition. They were down and out, a thing of the past. *Not from where I'm sitting.*

He kept smiling.

Katerina said the only thing that came to mind. "How can I help you, Mr. Desucci?"

"That's a good girl," he said, patting her knee. "It's almost time for final exams, right?"

"You broke into my apartment."

"You had your backpack with you at the park."

He nodded toward one side of her chair. Leaning over, Kat found the backpack on the floor.

"You're studying microeconomics. That's a fascinating subject. Most people don't understand it. Do you understand it?"

"I hope so."

"Explain it to me."

"Microeconomics is the branch of economics that focuses on the choices made by individual decision mak—"

"The individual," Desucci interrupted. "It's all about the individual. Exactly. You are a very intelligent young woman. Intelligent and beautiful. Isn't she beautiful, Vincent?"

Vincent agreed with a vigorous nod of his head. "Stunning."

"You are adorable," Desucci said. "Isn't she adorable, Vincent?"

"Absolutely. If I wasn't married—"

"Carlo are you married?"

"I don't think Carlo is in the market for a wife," Katerina offered, the compliments doing nothing to ease the roiling in her stomach.

"Getting back to microeconomics," Desucci said. "As an individual, I have many diversified business interests."

You engage in illegal activity. You're a criminal.

"I make investments and often move my money to keep it liquid."

You launder money, hiding it in legitimate investment vehicles.

"Some of my investments are not earning me any return."

Startled, Katerina froze. This was about her father. Sheridan said there would be others. Dangerous people. A tiny chorus of *Oh God, Oh God, Oh God,* played in her head, never making it to her lips.

Desucci reached for Kat's trembling hand; she recoiled, the cup of water falling to the floor.

"I don't know what you're looking for," she said. "Whatever it is, I don't have it."

"Dear, dear, I know that. Not yet," Desucci answered.

"Would you like more water, sweetheart?" Vincent asked.

"No, I'd like to go home," she said.

Desucci regarded her. "I'll come to the point. You've been hired to deliver Simon Marcus' car."

Katerina's brain did a sharp turn upon hearing Marcus' name.

"I understand his wife has the vehicle. When you get it, bring it to me."

"What does this have to do with microeconomics?" Kat blurted out.

"This is applied microeconomics, my dear. It's all about the Pareto Efficiency. What is the Pareto Efficiency, Katerina?"

"An individual does something for their own benefit without adversely affecting anyone else."

"Correct. I invested my money with Simon Marcus' hedge fund. I have not received the returns I was promised. Mr. Marcus, however, does very well. He benefits while I am adversely affected. This is unacceptable."

"Mr. Desucci, the car's book value will never replace your investment."

Anthony Desucci nodded. "It's a symbolic matter. Mr. Marcus has to know he cannot renege on his promises."

Bullshit, Kat thought. "Sir, my—agency—forbids me to work for anyone else. It would be a breach of ethics."

"Katerina, I'm a student of microeconomics. I don't have much use for ethics. You'll make an exception. It'll be our little secret," he said, patting her hand.

"I'll lose my job. You will benefit while I am adversely affected. This is not Pareto Efficient."

Anthony took her hand and squeezed it. "And you expect me to change my mind."

"I was hoping my adorableness would sway your thinking."

Desucci smiled; after a moment the smile faded. "Retrieve the car and bring it to me." He squeezed her hand again, the pressure sending a ripple of fear through her. He had been patient, tolerating her. That was over now. Katerina nodded her head.

He released her hand and stood.

Coming to Katerina's side, Vincent helped her to her feet. "If you don't mind me asking, a nice girl like you, what are you doing in this line of work?"

"Would you believe I'm just trying to pay for college and save for law school?"

"Of course. Tuition is outrageous," he said, ushering her toward the door of the warehouse. "I don't see how people with a median income of less than a hundred thousand per year can afford to offer the opportunity of a quality education to their children. It's criminal, really."

Katerina gave a weak smile. *I'm discussing economics with someone who is going to break my fingers, and other body parts, if I don't steal a car.*

***

They exited the warehouse. It was night. The wind whistled as it attacked her hair and face. Kat shivered, convinced she would never feel warm again. She stopped at the sight of the black SUV.

Vincent took the backpack from Carlo and handed it over to Kat. "That was a real nice purchase you made for your significant other. He's going to like it."

Carlo slid into the driver's seat.

"Tell Carlo where you want to go and he'll take you there," Vincent said.

Kat shook her head as warm tears began to roll down her cheeks.

"Miss, if we weren't going to give you a ride home, we wouldn't bother with all this, would we?"

Katerina hesitated but Vincent hustled her to the passenger side and settled her in.

"By the way," he said, pulling two items out of his coat pockets, "here's your cell phones and your SIM cards. Mr. Desucci doesn't like to be interrupted when he's in the middle of a discussion."

Katerina took the phones. Vincent slammed the door shut and Carlo eased the SUV away from the building. Katerina remembered to breathe when she realized the car was heading to Midtown.

"Drop me at Penn Station, please," Kat said, huddling up against the door. *Please don't let there be snarled traffic.* She hadn't even thought about the cell phones being disabled. *I could have vanished and no one would have found me.* She closed her eyes, drawing in a shaky breath. *What the hell am I doing?*

Chapter 19

"You scared the shit out of me! What the hell happened to you yesterday?"

Katerina didn't need to press the cell phone against her ear to hear Emma over the city noise. Her friend's voice was loud and clear. Obviously, the after-hours "I'm okay" text hadn't worked.

"I told you. I got a call from a client."

"You should have called me."

Katerina closed her eyes. *I couldn't. I was too busy being drugged, held hostage, and threatened.*

"Have you called Ryan?"

"I'm just about to," Kat said.

Emma's silence condemned her. "He's waitin' on you, hon," she finally said. "Don't keep him waitin'."

"I know. I won't," Kat said and disconnected. She slipped the phone away as a buzzing sounded from her purse. She dug out the burner and hit the green button.

"I gave you the address. I gave you the remote. Where's the car, cookie?"

"I'm working on it." *Not. Not only do I have no idea how to get the car, who do I deliver it to if I get it?*

"I expect to see it with the next lunch delivery," Marcus said and hung up.

Shit.

Katerina went to put the burner away when it buzzed again. She clicked the green button.

"Katie."

Her heart jumped at the sound of Winter's deep, soothing voice.

"Your visitor. He's the real thing."

She took the blunt confirmation in silence. A new problem. James Sheridan, DEA.

"I can help you."

"I've got it covered, but thank you," she said. *Way to go Pinocchio. Why not accept his help? Because I don't want him to think I can't handle this. Not him.*

"Don't lose my number," Winter said and hung up.

***

Katerina arrived downtown for the first of the Gallagher meetings. With no time to visit the boutique, the rented Chanel couture would finally earn its money. Entering the building, she approached the security guard. Before she uttered her name, he admitted her without question.

On the twentieth floor, she found offices and cubicles gleaming in glass contrasted by blood red mahogany furniture. A tall, cadaverous gentleman approached her. *Where's your hooded black robe and sickle?* she thought. With a nod of his head, he gestured for her to follow him. *Is this the part where I'm supposed to beg for a second chance, say I'll change my ways and always keep the spirit of Christmas?*

He didn't lead her to a headstone declaring her untimely death but an ornate conference room with plush executive chairs. A group of young dragon slayers with frat boy haircuts and cocky smiles shifted their attention to her.

"Mr. Gallagher cannot attend," the Grim Reaper announced. "Miss Mills is here to take notes in his absence. If you want something recorded, be sure to cue her."

***

The talk of acquisitions, sales forecasts, fixed and variable costs, swirled around her. Katerina had a realization: if she became a lawyer, this is what she would be doing. Her days would be spent sitting in meetings, wading through endless piles of paperwork. This was the life her father had encouraged her to pursue, a siren's song she had latched onto. *But is this what I want?* She snapped to, realizing she wasn't paying attention. She refocused to take in every word, making note of what she was told to record. The more she tried to quell her thoughts, the more curiosity gnawed at her. *Why do I need to be here? What is the purpose? Any secretary can do this.* She pushed everything out of her mind. *Just do the job.*

Chapter 20

Detectives Kellan and Lashiver conducted the interview in the lobby of the West End Repertory Company. Between questions, the instructor, a man with broad shoulders and a head of long, straight black hair brushing his collar, kept glancing at a studio off to the side. Students were busy with movement exercises, honing their skills as animals, including sound effects.

Ryan glanced over his pad. "You had said you never spoke to Mrs. Reynolds."

"That's right."

"Did she ever address one of your classes? You know, encouraging them in their pursuits?"

The instructor shook his head. "She knew nothing about theatre, detective. She kicked in the line. She gave money and that was about it."

Ryan and Lashiver exchanged looks. "Well, that's not really it," Lashiver said, "we now know she borrowed a wig from this theatre."

"And costumes," the instructor added.

Ryan glanced up from his pad. "Costumes?"

"Yes. She liked to—borrow—and wear the costumes."

"You didn't think to mention this before?" Lashiver asked as the sounds of bleating sheep emanating from the studio grew louder. "Didn't anyone think that was odd enough to mention?"

The instructor gave a small chuckle. "Odd? Detectives, the rich are—"

"Different?" Lashiver finished.

"It was one of the tamer idiosyncrasies of our patrons. She wasn't breaking any laws. She paid for them."

Ryan shook his head as he scribbled in his pad. "Anything else stand out from her visits?"

The instructor shrugged. "There was an interested student on a day Mrs. Reynolds was here. The young woman asked specifically to meet our patrons but then she suddenly left."

"I see," Ryan said with a frown as he took down every word.

"I think that young woman was trying to challenge herself to do something new and it frightened her. Acting can be a frightening experience—"

"Thanks for your help," Lashiver interrupted. "We'll be in touch if we have any further questions. We'll let you get back to the barn."

***

Lashiver and Ryan left the theatre.

Ryan tucked his notebook into his pocket. "So she might not have been in her own clothes the day she died."

"She was found with no clothes," Lashiver said, "just the wig and the shoes. The clothes weren't even a question."

Ryan stopped. "A rich woman comes to a theatre, changes her clothes, puts on a wig, and leaves wearing a costume. Why's she hiding? Who's she hiding from?"

"Maybe she's not hiding. Maybe she has a secret."

"I interviewed everyone in her circle. They *did* talk, they *did* shop, they *did* do lunch. Did. Then, suddenly, she talked to no one. She saw no one." Ryan shook his head. "She was fooling around with someone."

"Maybe. And maybe prostitution isn't the oldest profession," Lashiver said. "These young ladies, they marry these older guys for the money and they find out he can't do the deed, you know. So they go looking for company, while they keep the money. Look, we check out Cheryl Penn, we find out if she had something on the side, too. Maybe whoever this guy is, he doesn't like that kind of behavior. Remember, these women were targeted."

As they walked back to the car, Ryan decided he wasn't convinced that Felicia Reynolds had been targeted by a serial killer. Her death was something else.

***

The instructor wandered back into the studio, standing in the center of his circle of students. As they roared like lions, he gave a fleeting thought to that young woman who had stopped in. He had never forgotten the beautiful girl with long, chestnut-colored hair. She had rushed out so quickly, he hadn't gotten her number. He regretted that there was no way to get in touch with her. She would've been good in live theatre. She would have been sharp and quick. He had a sixth sense about these things.

Chapter 21

Doc was a true concierge physician. He made house calls. He fixed everything from inconvenient STD's to a gunshot wound. His clients appreciated his particular brand of specialized care: no names, no medical records, no police. All the client had to do was pay cash. Thanks to Winter, Kat learned about one other thing Doc provided: pharmaceuticals.

In her most romantic moments, Katerina pitied Doc, an unhappy man living a lonely life. Entering the darkened pub, she found him seated at one end of the bar, a glass and bottle in front of him, watching horse racing on the flat screen television. *Nope, he's pretty happy.*

"What do you know, Doc?" she asked as she slid onto the stool next to him.

"As little as possible, Miss Kitty," he wheezed. "That accounts for my sunny disposition."

"Doc, I need to buy an herbal supplement."

Doc kept his eyes on the screen. "Go to a pharmacy."

"I need *Salvia divinorum*."

"Little girl, you are traveling a path that will leave you older and wiser and you will have the scars to prove it." He stopped to inhale a breath. "Whatever it is, Katerina, walk away."

"You trying to be a father to me, Doc?"

"Nope. No cash value in it."

Katerina sat with him, listening to the sounds from the television. "It's too late, Doc. I have no other way." *Do I believe that?*

He exhaled a breath of resignation. "I don't have it. I know someone who does."

"Where can I find him?"

"The university."

Of course, she thought. Of course.

Chapter 22

The first rule of college life is there are students who do drugs. The second rule is there are drug dealers on college campuses. If you know you have a built-in demand, why not keep the supply close at hand? That's just good logistics.

Entering the student union building, Kat scanned the space until settling on a corner. A man lounged on a couch. He wore an open-necked white shirt, khaki pants, and loafers. With his sun-kissed blond hair, he resembled a California beach bum instead of a freezing New Yorker. *Roger Cole, I presume?*

As she approached, he did a classic double take, lowered his copy of *Inc.* magazine, and jumped to his feet.

"Doc sent me."

"Ciao, Signorina Kat, benvenuti a casa." Sweeping his hand across a couch cushion to shoo away any crumbs, he held out his arms like a maître d', inviting her to sit.

A drug dealer with a touch of panache. Why not? She sat down and he took a seat next to her, close in conference.

"I need to make a purchase."

Roger nodded, his poker face firmly in place. "What can I get for you?"

She lowered her voice. "I need the Diviner's Sage."

Pulling back, Roger shook his head. "Oh man," he said, "Signorina Katerina, mi dispiace molto. Nobody can get Sally-D. That kid, the shooting of that woman—"

"I know, I know, but is there anything you can do? Anything?"

"The well is dry, amica, it really is. Now if you want some weed, I can do that. No one cares about pot anymore. Pot isn't gonna do anything. It'll just make you want a sandwich."

Katerina looked him in the eye. "No. I need this. Really bad."

He thought for a minute. "You come with a very high recommendation. Even though no one's got it, that doesn't mean certain interested parties aren't trying to get it into the city." He leaned in. "I got a guy who can bring it in, but he doesn't know his way around. He'll need transport from the airport. If you took care of it and it was molto bene—"

"So I pick him up and drop him somewhere. And that's it."

"No. He's got stops to make."

Kat's mouth hung open.

"But after it's done, you could take what you needed, no charge. It's a perfect solution."

"Right, because being a drug mule makes everything so much better."

"No no, he's the mule. You're the transportation—an entirely different distinction."

"Not from where I'm sitting," Kat murmured, her mind strangely numb as she considered yet another crime. "How sure is he that he can get it through the airport?"

Roger shrugged. "He says he's got it covered."

"How soon is he coming? I've got a tight window."

"Within a week."

She hesitated even though it was pointless. Before she had walked into the student union, she already knew she would do whatever was necessary. *Does that mean it was determined that I would use my free will to commit another crime?*

"Okay," she said, pulling her purse strap on her shoulder and getting up.

"Molto bene, bella." He handed her a card with a phone number. "Check in with me in a day or so. I'll know more."

Katerina nodded, tapping the card with her finger. As she walked away she flipped the card over. It read: *Roger Cole, Alternative Herbalist.* She reminded herself to check on Roger in another five years. She had a sneaking suspicion he was going to be on the cover of *Inc.*.

Chapter 23

Entering a run-down bodega in the West 30's, Kat took the familiar, narrow aisle to the back. She pressed the button for the elevator, decorated with the number "5" spray-painted large and loud on the door.

Inside the elevator she found the usual sign announcing "no more than 5 people allowed." She always had the same thought: this could be a movie scene where a young woman steps into a dingy building. As the camera pulls back for a street shot, the audience knows something terrible is about to happen to her. The elevator opened, snapping her out of her daydream. Kat stepped out into a dark, gloomy internet café lined with tables of computers and comfortable executive chairs.

Eyeing the gamers huddled in a corner, Kat paid the few dollars to the bored, college-aged girl behind the desk and settled in at a terminal.

Kat did a search on the address Marcus provided, while ticking off the potential problems in her head. One: there was no way to know if the car was at the address. Two: she had no contacts to set up surveillance to make sure. Three: *who exactly am I delivering this car to?*

With a sigh, she clicked the browser closed. Getting up, Kat changed her mind and sat back down. She hesitated, then put her fingers to the keyboard and typed:

Theater for a New Audience

The theater came up first in the search results. Clicking through to the website, she reviewed the cast list for *Hamlet*. Scrolling to the bottom, she expected to find Will Temple's familiar headshot and bio.

She scrolled back up to the top and down again.

No Will Temple.

The familiar panic pulsed through her.

Kat worked to clear her head, get her thoughts straight. There was no reason to think Will Temple not performing meant anything. Maybe he didn't get along with the director and left. Maybe he took a better job. Maybe he got sick or had a family emergency.

Katerina didn't believe any of it. *Something terrible happened.*

Getting up, Kat steadied her legs and stepped back out into the elevator. It lumbered its way down until settling with a heavy thud. The doors opened; Agent James Sheridan stood blocking the exit.

Son of a bitch. She moved to push past him, but he shoved her into the elevator, hitting a button. The door slid shut and the elevator lurched up. Sheridan hit another button; the elevator clunked to a stop.

"I expected to hear from you, Miss Mills. To tell you the truth, I'm a little annoyed that you didn't contact me."

Pinned against the wall, Sheridan pressed in against her.

It's too close in here to use the pepper spray. Damn.

"Did your father come to see you?"

"No. And if you want to talk, Agent Sheridan," she said, mustering the nerve to look him in the eye, "bring me in for questioning."

Sheridan gave a short laugh.

I thought so. She reached for an elevator button but he pushed her back.

"Sure, we can go somewhere to talk," he said, his voice low, controlled, "but not a field office with desks, carpeting, Muzak, a telephone. I have something much better . . . someplace quiet, out of the way, where no one will know where you are. Where no one will find you." He paused, allowing the words to sink in.

Kat could feel the sweat begin to ooze out of her pores.

"Your father came through here. Did you see him?" he said, pushing her against the wall of the elevator, his face inches from hers. "Did you see him!" he yelled.

"Yes, I saw him," Kat blurted.

"And what did you talk about?"

"Infidelity," she said.

Sheridan relaxed. "Very good, Katerina. You see, now, you're telling the truth. That's good, because I can't get done what I need to do alone. I need—assets."

"Invest in a 401k," she snapped, but her voice came out cracked and small.

Sheridan laughed. "Funny girl. No, you're the asset, you can find out things that I can't. Think of yourself as a confidential informant. Or a cooperating witness. Tom-*ay*-to, tom-*ah*-to. Your father is the mastermind of a drug-trafficking operation worth over a billion dollars a year."

Katerina stared at him. Then she laughed. "You're out of your mind," she said.

"That was some cover he created. The plaid pants, the little boat at the yacht club. Mister Middle Class Manager. All the while, shipping millions of dollars in drugs all over the country, hidden in those soft, little plush toys. Clever."

Katerina stopped laughing.

"Have you been reading the news?" he continued. "Heroin addiction is out of control. It's a full-blown epidemic. People are dying because of your father's greed. It's unconscionable, really. Very sad. It's your moral responsibility to find him."

Katerina squirmed against his oppressive presence. "How am I supposed to do that?"

"You're a very smart girl," he said, "and whether you know it or not, your father said something during his visit, something very important. Think about that, while you're making some calls and solving this little mystery."

He slammed his finger on a button and the elevator gave a hard thump and sunk to the first floor. "Call me at the end of the week to report your progress. I'll be waiting to hear from you."

The door slid open. Katerina pushed past him and fled.

Chapter 24

As Katerina walked on Fifth Avenue, it began to snow, the wet flakes clinging to her face and hair. *My father a drug kingpin? Insane. So why doesn't it sound insane?* Glancing up toward the end of the block she found herself staring at the man who drove the blue Ford. Felicia Reynolds' killer.

He wore the same crew cut. His face looked like it had been carved in stone, as if he had no thoughts at all; as if he weren't human.

Their eyes locked; she stopped breathing. She stood frozen, sweat breaking out on her forehead. She could feel the droplets turning icy, clinging to her skin.

Behind her, came the deep, grinding noise of an approaching city bus. The killer took a step toward her. She bolted for the bus as it pulled to the curb. On the steps, she dug for change, feeling the heated annoyance of the passengers waiting behind her. Dropping the last coin in the slot, she slid into the first available window seat. The bus's engine revved and moved on. She saw him; he was still rooted to the same spot.

Their eyes met again.

He smiled.

Her stomach began to churn.

Katerina stayed on the bus, ignoring the stops. She had no idea where to get off. She only knew one thing.

She couldn't go home.

Chapter 25

Katerina slipped into the building after seven o'clock, grateful the answer to her text had come right away. She knocked on the door, stepping back when it gave way under the light touch of her hand. Entering the apartment, she waited for her eyes to adjust to the darkness. She made out the set of furniture in the center of the living room, two couches and two easy chairs arranged in a box formation, each set facing the other. Two side tables held elegant vase-shaped lamps. At the back of the room, a staircase led to a second floor. She went to the couch, letting her purse drop to the floor as she sank into the plush comfort.

Sitting in the silence, she sensed his presence.

"I interrupted your evening," she said.

"No," Winter said.

"I thought you might have a—someone, here," she fished.

"Obviously not," he said. "You had another visit?"

"I didn't come about Sheridan." She couldn't deal with Sheridan now. Every time his words looped in her head, the vision of the killer appeared, crowding them out.

Winter flipped a switch, bathing the room in soft light.

She was surprised to find him in a pair of white cotton pajama bottoms, his eyes soft from sleep, his chest bare and smooth. Her pulse quickened.

"Why did you come?"

"I need a place . . ."

"Katerina, would you like my help?"

"I've got it covered," she said.

"And that's why you need a safe house."

"Isn't that what this is for you?"

"I've chosen to live this way."

Kat felt her lips purse. *Isn't this my choice? Isn't this all my doing? Caused by my free will?*

"Perhaps you should take tonight to consider a career change."

"I'm not a child," she said. "Everyone thinks they should tell me what to do."

"What are you doing, Katerina?"

She looked up at him. "I'm taking care of things because no one else will. Because people say they're dependable. They encourage you to set big goals and take chances. They say they're going to help you. They make you think they're one way and they're not and then they disappear."

"I haven't disappeared, Katie."

Way to go with your daddy issues, Katerina.

"Why didn't you go to your police officer boyfriend?"

Because he never entered my mind. "He's not . . . technically . . . my boyfriend."

"Did you tell him that?" Winter asked.

She examined him openly now, the broad shoulders, the smooth muscles of his arms, the flat, rippled abdomen and narrow hips. Beautiful, she thought. A rush of raw desire to be in his arms, his lips on hers, overcame her. Feeling the heat rising inside her, she glanced away, leaning forward, perching her elbows on her knees. A change of subject was in order. *Stat.*

"What if you need to retrieve something, but two people want it, and you can't say no to either?"

"You need to give them both what appears to be the item."

Great, she thought. *I'll just steal another Porsche.*

"Katerina," he said, his voice gentle, "would you like to share what's really on your mind?"

The urge to speak was like an unbearable weight on her shoulders. She wanted to unload, to have someone else bear the burden. Kat's mind ran through the possible scenarios, the consequences of speaking her secrets aloud.

"I'm just worried about getting into law school."

"Mmmm," he said as an answer, what Katerina took to be a polite way of saying *liar, liar, pants on fire.*

A sudden wave of exhaustion swept over her, the urge to lie down and close her eyes. "Why is it so warm in here?" she asked.

"Because it's so cold outside," he said.

"Is Alexander Winter renting this apartment?"

"Patrick Hayes is renting this apartment."

She nodded. "I prefer Bob."

He smiled.

"I just need a place to spend the night, Bob," she said. "Just tonight."

"Go right ahead," he said, flicking the light switch off.

"Where should I sleep?" she asked in the darkness.

"Anywhere you like," he said. "You're not a child, Katerina. You've made that clear."

She listened to his catlike footsteps moving away from her. She wanted to call him back. But she didn't want to call him Bob. She wanted to call him by his name, the only name she knew. Alexander. Alex. She wanted to ask him to come to her, comfort her, but her mouth wouldn't open and her body wouldn't move. Her eyes fluttered, heavy with sleep. The last thing she remembered were images, blending, bleeding into each other. Winter's image faded, superimposed by the face of a killer.

Chapter 26

Opening her eyes the next morning, Katerina knew he had gone. Lying still, she waited for the film of sleep to fade away. Sitting up, she spied the note, a lighter, and an ashtray next to the paper.

She marked the small, neat printing.
Towels in the upstairs hall closet.
Breakfast in the fridge.
Something for you in the bedroom.
Something more for you in the coat closet.
Take as much time as you need.
Don't bother about cleaning up.
Text if you need me.
Remember to burn this.
W.

Getting up, she padded into the kitchen. Opening the refrigerator, her eyebrows lifted at the sight of the stocked shelves. For some reason she had the idea that Winter never ate. He seemed to her an otherworldly creature who didn't require any of the basic necessities that everyone else did. Pulling out a fruit platter, she brought it back into the living room.

She munched on slices of ruby-red strawberries, kiwi, and grapes while considering her temporary oasis, a refuge that she wished she never needed to leave. Now awake and alert, her mind lingered over all that could have been the night before. She got up and went upstairs.

She found the bedroom bathed in hospital white. The sterile room had no personal items, no sign a person lived there. Winter could disappear tomorrow; no one would know he had existed.

Her attention zeroed in on the long-sleeved Chanel winter-white dress with an optical illusion waist hanging on the door. A shoe box sat on the floor. Crouching down and removing the lid, she found a pair of white Louboutin peep-toe leather shoes. Turning to the bed, she stared at the Victoria's Secret box. With one finger, she flicked off the cover, removing a snow-white, lace-trimmed demi cup bra attached to a floral patterned garter slip with cutouts. Hidden under layers of tissue paper, she found a lacy, white bikini panty and nude stockings.

He didn't run out and buy a wardrobe overnight. The realization that he had been thinking about her, stockpiling the gifts, brought a smile to her lips. Running her fingers under the filmy lingerie made the familiar warm, languid feeling release within her. She had a vision of herself wearing the outfit and Winter peeling it from her, one piece at a time. Her desire for his touch assaulted her, her body making her pay for last night's lost opportunity. Squeezing her eyes closed to chase the images away, she left everything and went into the bathroom, finding a supply of expensive makeup, brands she didn't know, from foundation to lipstick.

***

An hour later, showered and dressed she went downstairs, ready to leave. In the closet she found a black, three-quarter-length Armani coat that screamed warmth with its rabbit fur-lined neck and cuffs. A black silk scarf lay around the shoulders. She shrugged into the coat and her hands found a leather glove tucked into each sleeve. She smiled. *He thought of everything.*

Shopping bags emblazoned with brand names crowded the closet floor. She needed to get moving, but a girlish notion, immature and foolish, gripped her; she wanted to see what he had bought her.

Piling the boxes on the couch, she opened the lids one after the other, revealing a treasure trove: elegant eveningwear, stylish ensembles for work, warm and comfy winter-white separates for relaxing, along with matching shoes and boots. She left the Victoria's Secret boxes untouched. Better not to know.

Repacking everything, she read over the note again. She wanted to write "thank you" on the bottom and leave it for him but he had been specific in his instructions. She wouldn't dare disobey him. This wasn't a game.

She flicked on the lighter, watching the flame catch and consume the paper. Dropping it into the ashtray, it curled and turned to ash. The fantasy was over. She had to go back out into the real world; and stay one step ahead of everyone.

Chapter 27

Racing up the steps to her building, Katerina had the pepper spray in one hand as she shoved the key in the lock with the other. *The lock you need to upgrade. Way to take care of things, Katerina.* Tomorrow, she thought, glancing around as she pushed the door open and rushed inside. In the apartment, she stowed the bags on the closet floor and rushed to get out.

Back out on the street, she had the burner at her ear as she made her way to the corner. He had a right to know. He had to be warned.

"Sir, this is Katerina—yes, sir, thank you. I'm calling because I have to see you. It's urgent. Today, please. It really can't wait. Yes, sir, thank you. I'll be at the corner of Seventy-ninth and Lexington. Yes, sir, three o'clock. Thank you."

Clicking off the phone, she peered into the traffic, looking for the limousine on its way for her. Right now, she had to find a car for the airport run. It was time to meet Moose.

***

Sitting in the front passenger seat, Katerina closed her eyes, taking a few precious moments to think. Outside, a misting wet snow began to fall. Even though the limo heater blasted, she felt she would be cold forever. She missed the warmth of Winter's apartment. She missed Winter.

"You should let me do my job, Miss Katerina," Luther said. "You're the client. The client sits in the back seat."

"This is above and beyond your job, Luther. I appreciate it."

"It's all good, Miss Katerina. Moose has been looking forward to meeting you."

"Any idea what this is going to cost me?"

"Not my area, miss."

Kat nodded. She shouldn't have asked. Luther was much too smart to get into that discussion. Whatever the cost, he already knew the price and had negotiated his cut with Moose.

***

They made it to Queens in good time. Luther pulled the limo onto a side street in a dingy, worn-out neighborhood past its prime. Making a turn, he stopped in front of a chop shop hidden behind apartment buildings.

"I was expecting something bigger," Kat said.

"Moose likes to keep it on the low-low."

As they got out of the limo, a man, wearing oil and dirt-stained gray coveralls came out of the small office on the side. Medium height with a slender frame, he had a face of sharp angles, a nose a tad too large for his features, and dark hair, cut short. A teardrop tattoo sat below his left eye. *He's killed someone.* Moose, the neighborhood rental agent of stolen cars, obviously had no problem with the occasional wet work.

He looked her up and down then greeted Luther with a handshake. "Que lo que?" he asked.

"*Ta to,*" Luther said. "Miss Katerina, this is Moose."

Moose greeted her with a nod and a smile. "How you doin', miss?" he asked, mixing the familiar with the formal.

"I do fine, thank you," Katerina said.

Moose nodded. "Good to know. You need a car. I got a beauty for you," he said, motioning for her to follow.

***

In the shop, Moose flipped a light switch, revealing a red Camaro with clean lines and sparkling hubcaps. Next to it sat a slick, sleek silver sports car. Kat noticed the insignia, a backwards "E" connected to a "B". Her mouth fell open. *Bugatti Veyron. A car worth over two million dollars sitting in a garage in Queens. Why not?* She caught Moose watching her, wearing a sly smile.

He moved and Kat noticed the bulge under the bottom cuff of his right pant leg. *Gun. No one will be stealing the Bugatti. If they do, they'll die trying.*

"I think this vehicle will suit your needs," Moose announced, nodding at the Camaro. "This is a recent addition to my fleet."

This car is stolen.

Katerina gave Luther a sideways glance. He stood at rest, hands folded over each other, face impassive.

"So, miss, what do you think?" Moose asked.

"I'm looking for something a little more low-key," she said. "Something that says, 'I'm here to pick up my Uncle,' not, 'I'm the trophy wife of a man in the midst of a midlife crisis.'"

Moose chuckled. "I see, I see, okay, all right. But this will require another vehicle. Each vehicle requires custom work, entiendes? You understand what I'm sayin'?"

Yes. You're saying this is going to cost a fortune.

"The price is ten thousand."

"For one day?"

"Ten thousand, mami. And those are friend rates. Non-negotiable."

Oh, bullshit. And I'm getting held up without the gun.

"Everything is negotiable," she said.

Moose's expression relaxed and he smiled. "Yo, man, Luther, I like this girl." He took a step closer to Katerina. "Okay, mami, what you want to give me for *a discount*."

"It ain't like that Moose," Luther said, his voice cold. "And it won't be like that."

"Yo, am I talkin' to a *loca*? No. You think I can't tell a lady when I see one? Not that you wouldn't be happy if the Moose was loose, you know what I'm sayin'?"

Katerina didn't answer.

"I like doin' business. I believe in—cómo se dice—when you take care of the neighborhood?"

"Good will," Kat said.

"Yeah, yeah, good will. The Moose can have a lot of that good will for the right person."

Katerina circled the Bugatti. "Is this car part of your fleet?" she asked, already suspecting the answer.

"This is my personal vehicle. Over two hundred and fifty miles per hour, zero to sixty in under three seconds."

"And you love this car," she said.

"Don't it look like it's loved?"

"No dirt on the tires. For something you love so much, you don't spend much time in it."

"Yo mami, this car is special. You don't just take it out. I mean, you want to give it the full treatment, you know what I'm sayin'? You want to make an entrance."

Katerina examined the angular face, the nose that was just a bit too long and a smidge too sharp for the rest of the features. Moose never had the looks to make the big entrance. Not in high school, not in his twenties, and not now.

"You want the car and the girl," she said.

Moose approached Kat. She steeled herself, her heart beginning to thump in her chest. *What the hell am I doing?*

His face screwed up in contemplation. "I gotta go to my cousin's wedding. It's the weekend before Christmas."

"Fine," Kat said. "Wedding and reception. That's it."

"We dance a little merengue, get our picture taken—"

"Fine," Kat interrupted. "No charge for the car."

He nodded. "*Ta to*. But I rig up you and me gettin' picked for the garter bit, you keep the car for a week."

"No."

"You let me take a little peek, I *build* you a car. Any make, any model, hood to hubcaps."

"No. Wedding, reception, dance, and picture," Kat said, folding her arms across her chest.

He stared at her then threw up his hands. "All right, mami, all right. A man's got to try."

Luther took Katerina by the elbow, leading her out of the garage. He shot a glance back at Moose over his shoulder.

"What?" Moose asked. "What?"

Chapter 28

The relentless ringing of the burner told Katerina that Marcus had found his lunch on the kitchen counter. She dug around in her purse, pulling out the phone.

"That was clever, cookie," Marcus' voice boomed over the line.

"I'm working on it," she said.

"You know, you got a great ass. Better keep it nice and tight. You don't bring me my car, bending that ass over is the only way you're gonna make a living."

Katerina listened to the click then threw the phone back in her purse. *Enjoy your lunch looking at your fake paintings, jerk off.* Katerina looked behind her and spied the limousine approaching. She stiffened as it pulled over to the curb, idling long enough for her to open the back passenger door and duck inside, the welcome heat washing over her.

"Mr. Reynolds, thank you for seeing me." Katerina had expected to find John Reynolds still in mourning, wearing an expression of inconsolable grief. Instead, he appeared calm, even meditative.

"Of course, Miss Katerina," he said, taking her hands in his own. "We aren't client and consultant anymore. We're friends. What's on your mind?"

"I'm so . . . so . . . terribly sorry about your wife," she said, struggling through the words.

He nodded.

"Mr. Reynolds, I know—I know who killed her."

He took the news in silence, her hands still in his iron grip. Then he spoke, his voice careful, controlled. "How did you discover this?"

"When I was on the assignment, I thought—I saw someone, and—"

Reynolds fixed his gaze upon her, his dark eyes unreadable.

"I thought he was following me. I never dreamed it had anything to do with your wife."

"Why do you think this man had been following my wife?"

Katerina shook her head. "I have no idea," she said. "Mr. Reynolds, I saw him again yesterday. I don't know if he'll come after you. I wanted to warn you."

John Reynolds nodded. "You did well, Katerina. You could have gone to the police. But then, details would come out, wouldn't they? Private things would become public ... so inconvenient for so many people."

Tears sprang to Kat's eyes. "Mr. Reynolds, I feel responsible for your wife. If I had known ..."

"Miss Katerina, we make a thousand decisions every day and must bear the consequences for them."

The words hit her like a slap. What had she expected? *Absolution. Isn't that why I came? I want to be forgiven.* Instead, with a few simple words, Reynolds had indicted and convicted her, even as he held her hands and smiled upon her.

"Is there anything more I should know?" he asked.

Katerina pressed her lips together, weighing the words that sat on the tip of her tongue, straining to break out. *There's no way to spare him now.*

"Mr. Reynolds, when I was following your wife ... I saw ... Mr. Reynolds, your wife had a friend ... a man ... a young man ..."

"You didn't tell me about this," he said, his soft, even voice condemning her again.

Glancing away, Katerina shook her head.

"What about this man?"

"I think something terrible has happened to him. Not that you should care. I think it has something to do with your wife ... and that other poor woman who was killed ..." She let her words trail off, lost in her own miasma of confusion.

John Reynolds nodded. "Is that what the police think? That my wife and that other woman are connected?"

"I don't know what the police think."

"Is there no way for you to find out? In your business, you know people."

Kat hesitated.

John Reynolds waited, patient.

I owe it to you. "I may be able to find out," she said. "But you need protection."

He squeezed her hands. "Don't worry, Miss Katerina. I have plenty of protection. I have you. You are keeping me out of harm's way. Because of you, no one can get to me. Investigate and then we'll talk again."

Chapter 29

Kat rounded the block to her apartment, the wind whistling in her ears and a pain circulating in her head. She held the burner to her ear with one hand, the other curled around the tiny can of pepper spray in her pocket.

"Are you making progress?" Maggie, Paul Patel's editor, asked. "He's very anxious."

"Yes, ma'am," Kat said in breathless bursts. "I'm working on it. I will have something for you shortly." *And I'm so glad you're not Simon Marcus calling.*

"I hope so. You could call with updates. That would help."

"Yes, ma'am," Kat said and ended the call.

Looking up, she saw a vehicle idling in front of her building. Without thinking, instinct kicked in; she drew out the pepper spray. As the engine cut out and the driver's side door opened, she recognized the car. Detective Ryan Kellan got out.

Shit. I never made the phone call. She shoved her hand back into her pocket.

"Where the hell have you been? I've been calling you. Don't you check your messages? You have been home, right?"

"Yes. No. It's been—I've been up at the school."

He grabbed her arm, pulling her hand out of her pocket. He slipped the bottle from her grasp and gave a mirthless laugh. "Where did you get the coat?"

"It's a rental," she said.

He shook his head. "A twenty-three-year-old girl, wearing an expensive-looking coat, is wandering the city at all hours of the night while some lunatic is out killing women." He held up the bottle. "And you think this is going to save you. What's wrong with you?"

She opened her mouth but nothing came out.

"I was worried about you," he said, his tone tamping down as he took her bare hand in his own. "You've lost your gloves again, haven't you?"

No. I have the expensive leather gloves Winter gave me in my pockets. She settled for nodding.

Ryan shook his head. "I swear to God, Katerina, you need a minder."

As they started for the stairs, Katerina's thoughts ran wild. *What if Sheridan is in there? What if the killer is in there?* She slipped on a step; Ryan caught her arm in a vise grip, steadying her.

Her hand shook as she tried to jam the key in the lock. Reaching in, Ryan took the key away. Opening the door, he hustled her into the building. Entering the apartment, Kat gave an audible gasp.

Ryan moved in front of her, drawing his weapon. "Don't move," he ordered.

"Jesus Christ, dial it back. I'm an officer of the court," Philip said, throwing up his arms. "Kitty Kat, c'mon, call off the nice policeman."

Ryan looked to Kat.

Katerina, her heart still pounding in her chest, placed a hand on Ryan's arm. "I used to work for him."

Ryan kept his stance. "What are you doing in here?"

"Kat had lent me a key so I could crash here when the current . . . whoever . . ." he said with a chuckle, "gets tired of me and throws me out."

"Try a hotel."

Philip nodded. "Right. I'm returning the key." He made a show of laying the key on the table. "Here you go, Katerina. I'm sorry. Thank you."

Ryan lowered his gun.

"I'll see myself out," Philip said.

"No, *I'll* see you out," Katerina said, swiping the key off the table as Philip headed for the door.

She motioned to Ryan to give her a minute and followed Philip out.

***

Katerina and Philip navigated down the stairs and out to the sidewalk, checking for black ice.

"What the hell, Philip? You can't just show up."

"Forgive me, I was thinking about you," he said with a sarcastic clip. "I've been enjoying a windfall of riches from my little business venture and I came to offer a little *glasnos*t, you know, a little *perestroika*."

"Philip, *nyet*, okay?"

"Since when are you dating Columbo?"

Closing her eyes, Katerina stifled the urge to scream. "Did you leave anything in my apartment?"

"No," he said, "but I found something." Fishing around in his pocket, he pulled out a newspaper clipping. He tapped the picture of Felicia Reynolds. "I remembered this. My newspaper, when we met that day in the park. You threw up after seeing it."

She glanced over her shoulder at the building. *Was Ryan searching her things? What was he looking at? Oh God, what if he finds the earrings?* Turning back, Katerina snatched the page out of Philip's hand. "You shouldn't be looking through people's stuff."

"You shouldn't be saving articles about murdered socialites. You don't want Serpico to find it since he's working the case."

"How do you know that?"

"The world is a lot smaller than you think, kid. Didn't I teach you that? You'd be amazed at what gets around. Now, what the hell is going on with you?"

Kat didn't answer.

Philip lowered his voice. "I know you didn't kill anybody."

"It's complicated," she finally said.

"Shit," Philip said, shaking his head. "He's not going to tell you anything, Katerina. He can't even if he wants to."

He just did. He thinks it's a serial killer. I'm not convinced.

"You still have that PI on the payroll?" she asked.

"Who do you need to find?"

"An actor. Will Temple. I don't need any contact. I just need to know if he's around."

"You mean alive."

"I need to know if he's okay. And if he's not okay—I need to know what the police think happened to him."

Staring at the ground, Philip shook his head.

A spike of anger shot through Katerina like a bullet. She glanced over her shoulder again. Still clear. Grabbing Philip by the arm, she tugged him further down the street. "No? I seem to recall acting as a safety deposit box for you. This is a little more important than an envelope with some damn negatives. This is—"

"What? His life? Your life?"

Tears threatened behind Kat's eyes. "I need your help," she said.

"I'll see what I can do. Remember, kid, the longer you don't tell him what you know, the more you can be charged with, after the fact."

Philip glanced past Katerina. She turned to see Ryan standing on the top step. Philip walked away. Kat made her way back to Ryan.

"I'm here," she said, as she came up the steps.

Ryan held open the door for her, his expression somber, unsmiling.

***

Ryan closed the apartment door behind them. Katerina slid out of her coat and kicked off her shoes, feeling him watching her, the thick silence filling the room.

"What's his name?"

"Philip Castle. He's a defense attorney."

"So he gets guilty people off."

"What happened to innocent until proven guilty?"

"Did he give you all that stuff in your closet?"

Katerina whirled around to face him. "Why the hell are you snooping in my closet?"

They stared at each other, a wordless standoff.

"They're all rentals," she said. "Lisa gets the bags, sticks in the stuff. She wants us to project a certain image."

Turning away, she flipped the kitchen light switch and let out a yelp. A small, gray mouse darted across the floor and disappeared into a sliver of a crack between the cabinets. She stood there, her breathing ragged, her hand on her chest.

Ryan was at her side. "Is that part of the image, too?"

Kat blinked fast, chasing away the urge to cry. She wanted him to go away; she wanted to run away.

"Get your rented coat," he said. "You're staying with me."

He was already gathering up her purse when she said, "I can't."

He threw the purse on the chair. "What the hell, Katerina? You're a smart girl but you're acting pretty stupid. Rented designer clothes? You live in a shithole. What the hell are you doing?"

"Taking care of myself!"

"Bullshit! You're taking care of nothing. I'm here with my hand out and you keep biting it off. Why are you acting like a reckless, stubborn child?"

Kat's eyes welled, smarting from the insult.

Ryan came to her, placing heavy hands on her shoulders; he kissed her forehead. "Hey, I'm worried about you," he said, his voice soft. "I care about you."

"Ryan, I got burned by a bad guy."

"Yeah, I know. I just met him."

Kat started.

"As soon as I saw him, I knew he was a bad guy. But not every guy is a bad guy. Some of us are good ones."

"I'm not ready."

He wrapped her in his arms. "You know, you're making a lot of assumptions. You're assuming if you stay at my apartment and put the moves on me, that I'm easy. I'm insulted."

Katerina smiled but his choice of words reminded her. *Winter.* Her brain began throbbing again in that familiar confusion.

"I have a comfy couch and warm blankets."

I should love you. I should. "No," she said, "but I'll call Emma."

He took a deep breath. "Not exactly my plan," he said, "but I can be patient. Now, get Emma on the phone."

Katerina bristled, a knee-jerk reaction at being told what to do. With the earrings in the apartment and the newspaper article in her coat pocket, she wasn't going to argue. She had to get him out as fast as possible.

As she threw a few items into her purse, she made sure to bury the burner all the way in the bottom.

Chapter 30

Katerina woke up to the sound of whispering. She lay still, listening to Frank and Emma's hushed conversation, the rustling of keys, and the muted opening and closing of the apartment door.

Turning to lie on her back, Kat waited. Emma padded over in her robe, carrying two cups of coffee. Pulling herself up, Katerina leaned back against the couch. Emma handed off one cup and planted herself at the other end. They sipped their coffee in a stilted silence.

"You're back with Philip?"

"Emma, *no*."

"Good, so now that you've got a good guy, you wanna give me one reason why you were sleepin' on my couch when Ryan had a warm bed for you?"

Katerina went to open her mouth when a thought intruded upon her; a name that made her freeze.

"Honey, what are you doin'?" Emma asked.

"I'm trying to do the right thing. I don't want to hurt him."

"How on earth would you do that?"

Getting up, Katerina deposited the coffee cup on the table and started folding the blanket.

"Hon, I lived with you, remember? By this point in the semester, the last thing you would ever be doin' is cleanin' up. Is this about your parents? I know the split threw you."

"No. Look, I don't have to please everyone else."

Leaning over, Emma grabbed Katerina by the hand, pulling at her to sit down. "I'm your friend. And I'm tellin' you straight, this is crap. You don't talk to me, we don't hang out anymore. Why are you cuttin' yourself off from everyone?"

The buzz of a cell phone broke the silence. Fishing in her bag, she saw the burner vibrating. *Shit.* She took it out.

"Hello?"

"Katerina, ciao bella!" came the voice of Roger Cole. "We're a go, bellina."

"Okay," Kat said, her nerves lighting up like fireworks at the sound of the words. *You knew this was coming,* She committed the flight information to memory, all the while knowing Emma's watchful eyes were on her.

"I've got it," Kat said and clicked off. Turning her attention back to Emma, she found her friend viewing her with a mixture of sadness and suspicion.

"You don't want to talk to me, don't. You want to sleep on my couch, doll, go ahead," Emma said, "for as long as you want. But you can believe me. Ryan loves you. No one's going to love you more than he does."

Chapter 31

Alexander Winter placed his eye against the scope and focused on the object of his interest: a library in the apartment across the street. Nothing yet. His own darkened surroundings were just as plush, with a jackpot inventory: a Hockney, a Klimt, and a Renoir. He wasn't here for any of them.

Instead, he kept his eye fixed on his target. Weeks of observation had finally yielded the opportunity to get eyes—and ears—on the apartment. To his right, a table held the night's supplies, lined up like good soldiers at attention: laptop, speaker, cell phone, and a bottle of water. The computer screen glowed, showing flat lines waiting for sound to be born.

Winter entered the building every evening and slipped away before dawn. He didn't like keeping a routine; it was dangerous. The tenants had fled to South Beach, escaping the miserable New York weather. Winter was more than a little jealous. He should have been long gone himself. He always went south once the cold weather came. Not this year. Not since a beautiful, young woman had insinuated herself into his life.

Katerina Mills had found him drowning in a crippling anxiety, with nameless fears plaguing him. There had been no warning the first time. He had been in the middle of a job, a perfect job going off without a hitch, when the fear had struck. Winter knew the groundwork had been laid years before, a lifetime ago. Ghosts of his past, waiting for their moment of haunting; the methodical habits, the orderly precision, hallmarks of his work, the only things that soothed him, had turned against him and become his enemies. Finally, he stopped working. Nothing could break the spell. Until her.

The anxious torments were a luxury he could no longer afford. Katerina Mills was clearly in the wrong place with the wrong people, including himself. Ever since the job in the Hamptons, he fought to stay away. Yet he took foolish risks, sending her that text, keeping the burner phone in case she called, in case she needed him again. Each time he saw her, her lovely face, the sharp, quick mind, that streak of sweet innocence, his plans fell apart all over again. There were no choices; he wasn't leaving her.

Ambient noise from the apartment registered as spiked lines on the computer. The man Winter had been waiting for, the mark, entered the room. A night owl, the mark preferred to spend his time alone in his study while the rest of New York slept. Winter watched through the scope as the mark settled at his desk for another evening of reviewing documents, checking, or perhaps cooking, the books.

Take the painting off the wall. Open the safe. Winter had entered the apartment weeks earlier and planted a microphone chip to pick up the distinct chirp of each button of the combination. Two other professionals had attempted to crack the safe before him; only Winter had done his homework. The mark favored a safe lock programmed to booby-trap when attacked. With good behavior, the professionals would earn their parole early. Winter's favorite mantra crossed his mind. Keep it simple. Simple is always best. *Record the combination. Enter at leisure. Make the pickup. Simple.*

The mark half turned, as if he were going to rise.

C'mon. Show me the prize.

The mark turned back to his desk.

Shit.

Winter sat back, grabbed the water bottle from the table, and took a swallow. He glanced over the table. No food. In the middle of a bustling city of restaurants and delis, he still experienced a stab of anxiety that he would be cut off without food for eight hours. He put the bottle down and then fingered the items, making sure they were in perfect alignment.

He returned to observing the mark. The middle man was worried. The client was antsy. They were not the only ones. A spike of anxiety nagged at Winter, but of a different kind. He wanted to finish the job and return to his primary responsibility, a beautiful girl with long chestnut-colored hair. She needed some looking after.

Chapter 32

Staring out of the train window, Katerina watched New York City fade away replaced by the sprawl of Long Island. She thought of students hunkering down for the university study days, prepping for finals by poring over textbooks until falling asleep over them.

I should be doing that.

Kat fingered the cord of her earbuds, listening to one of Professor Schoeffling's lectures. It would have to do for now. Hearing a muffled voice overhead, she pulled out an earbud to listen.

This was her stop.

***

The cab eased to a standstill four blocks away from Kat's true destination. She didn't like using a taxi but with no connection in the area, she had no choice. Besides, she had a strong feeling Mrs. Marcus wouldn't be filing a police report for the stolen Porsche.

If the car is even here.

Exiting the cab, a frigid wind curled around her. With an oversized brown scarf wrapped around her head and neck, her brother's beat-up leather bomber jacket on her back, and North Face boots on her feet, she felt comforted and warm. She congratulated herself; she remembered her gloves.

Stopping at the corner, she scanned the upscale neighborhood until she spotted the house, a colonial sitting atop an incline driveway.

The driveway was empty.

She trudged ahead against the driving wind. Flashing back to the break-in with Winter in the Hamptons, she heard his voice in her head, schooling her, coaching her.

Walk like you're where you're supposed to be.

Don't keep your head down but don't look anywhere specific.

Crossing the threshold of the driveway, she pulled out the remote and pressed the button. After a hesitation, the garage door clicked to life and rose.

You used the remote so you're not breaking and entering.

Her hand was already in her pocket, her fingers curled around the key.

Touch the door handle.
The car will read the access code on the key.
If she hasn't changed it.
The door opens.
Get in.
Start the car.
Back the car out.
Don't bother to close the garage door.
One hour drive back to the city.
Done.
If the car is even here.

As she reached the top of the driveway, the garage door clicked to a stop. She stared at the pristine space, empty except for the sleek white Porsche. Approaching the car door, she reached out her hand and touched the handle. She gave a slight tug and felt the door give and open.

She remembered to breathe.

Easy in. Easy out. Almost there.

Sliding into the driver's seat, she inserted the key into the ignition. The engine turned over and ran silent.

Katerina heard the clicking noise before she felt the cold metal of the gun up against her temple. She raised her hands.

"Turn off the engine," a female voice said.

Chapter 33

Katerina turned the key. The car went silent.

"Where did my bastard husband find you?"

"I'm the hired help," Katerina said, her voice trembling along with her body.

"What happened to Ellen?"

"I don't know any Ellen. I'm hired to pick up the car and his lunch. That's all."

The woman gave a disgusted laugh. "Does that schmuck still use that Thai place? The one with the big fortune cookie?"

"Yes."

Another chuckle.

In a state of stunned fascination, Katerina watched her own hands shaking.

"You cold?"

"Scared shitless," Kat said. "Can I leave now?"

The woman stepped back, gesturing with the gun for Katerina to get out of the car. "No. But *I'm* cold. I'm Betsy Marcus. We're going inside. I want to finish my tea."

Katerina got out of the car and walked up the three small steps into the house. Mrs. Marcus followed.

***

The country-style kitchen boasted a blue monochrome color scheme, lacy curtains, colorful cookie jars, and a yellow accented tile backsplash. Definitely not the kitchen of people who live in a cold, sterile Central Park West apartment with four fake Monet *Bridge over a Pond of Water Lilies* paintings in purple, yellow, green, and red.

Betsy Marcus wasn't the prototypical wife of a hedge fund magnate, rail thin and peroxide blond. Mrs. Simon Marcus wore plus-sizes. She had dark, short hair, sharp eyes, and a pinched mouth.

Katerina stood in the kitchen, observing a seated Mrs. Marcus take it in as if she were seeing it for the first time.

"The article in *Architectural Times* doesn't mention this house," Kat said.

"That's because Simon never appreciated this house." Betsy Marcus took a sip of her tea. "Schmuck," she said.

Silence followed, leaving Katerina feeling like a serf, waiting to be dismissed by the well-fed landed gentry. *You've got the gun. It's your party. What do you want?*

Betsy regarded Kat with a flicker of interest. "So, you rent yourself out for repo?"

"I rent myself out for whatever needs doing. Mrs. Marcus, do you mind if I ask why you're so attached to the car. It doesn't fit with the image of this house."

Betsy Marcus drained her cup and picked up the gun. Katerina took a step back.

"I feel better now," Betsy said. "Back out into the garage."

Katerina, reluctantly, went out first, Betsy Marcus and her gun behind her.

***

Kat stepped into the garage as Betsy Marcus threw the light switch.

"My husband doesn't just love this car," she said, making a circular inspection of the vehicle and running her fingers over the exterior. "He covets it. Right now, it's his most prized and cherished possession." She looked at Kat. "I want you to take pictures of this car."

Katerina hesitated, unsure of where this was going.

"Go ahead," Betsy said, waving the gun in Kat's direction. "Take out your phone and take pictures of the car. Better yet, take video."

Slipping the burner out of her pocket, Kat flipped on the video function. Taking a slow turn around the car, she zeroed in, capturing every angle.

"My husband has had many objects of his affection. The last one must have had a pussy made of gold, because he gave her an apartment in the same building."

Katerina pursed her lips, staring straight ahead, concentrating on the video.

"He would get in the elevator and ride it down to the fifth floor so he could get it up with his little whore. You know that kind of thing is bad karma. You believe in karma?"

Katerina didn't want to answer but she sensed Mrs. Marcus would take offense at her silence. She settled for nodding. *Yes, I do. Oh, God, yes I do.*

Betsy followed Katerina, droning on in a monotone monologue as Kat kept filming. "Yeah, me too. Funny thing, karma," she went on, "your life is great and then you do one thing, and all of a sudden," she snapped her fingers, "your life starts falling to shit. That's how it happens, you know. That one wrong thing. Bad karma, that's what my husband's got. A nice big, fat, fucking case of bad karma. Focus on that scratch on the right rear bumper. That scratch is *very* important to him."

Then why the hell didn't he have it fixed? Katerina thought. *Why don't you have it fixed since you're keeping the car?*

Betsy Marcus positioned herself in the frame, standing next to the scratch. "Hello, darling," she said, her voice dripping venom. "Take a good look. This is *your* car. This is as close as you're ever going to get to it. You will *never* get your paws on this car. Merry Christmas, shithead."

Katerina shut off the phone and slipped it into her purse. "I'm sorry I disturbed you."

"Save it. Get out."

Mrs. Marcus hit a button on a panel. The garage door lurched and began to descend. Katerina scurried out, turning to look back as the door closed behind her with a thud.

Katerina wrapped her scarf around her neck and mouth, the white puffs of her breath suddenly extinguished. She dialed a number on her cell.

"Taxi," the voice on the phone answered.

Katerina gave the name of a crossroad she remembered passing and clicked off. She started walking.

Chapter 34

"Un-fucking-believable!" Marcus yelled. Watching the video, he smacked the burner on the counter and gave it a shove, sending it sailing Kat's way. Standing at the end of the island, she slammed her hand down over the phone before it could drop onto the floor.

"How did you fuck up something so simple?" he asked.

Un—believable. "She held a gun to my head," Kat said.

"What's your point?" he asked.

Katerina counted to five before answering. "I don't have one."

"You're gonna get the car from that bitch, right?"

"Yes, sir," she said.

"You're gonna get my car from that bitch no later than close of business, two weeks from today, right? *Before* Christmas. Or should I write a fuckin' letter to Santa Claus and ask him to bring it."

Kat nodded. "Two weeks, max."

She grabbed her purse and let herself out.

Two weeks.

Or there's no reason for me to be here.

***

The frigid temperatures had eased, making way for the light snow falling. Katerina spotted Vincent heading toward her. She ducked into the maze of holiday shops at Columbus Circle, disappearing among the kiosks decorated in festive candy cane colored stripes. Positioning herself where she could see him coming, she fingered a fine silk scarf in a deep, rich shade of purple and waited. After a moment, Vincent sidled over.

"Tell your boss I didn't get it," she said. *And I'm not really sorry because I have no idea how to solve this little conundrum of one car for two people.*

"He knows that, honey."

"So why are you here?"

"Because you didn't get it."

Katerina turned to him. "She held a gun to my head. Not that anyone cares."

"That's terrible. Very upsetting. But you're all right, thank God."

Katerina walked away to exit the makeshift shopping village. Vincent came alongside.

"I'm working on it," she said.

Vincent grabbed her arm. "He says to work faster, honey," he said. "Or next time, I may have to bring Carlo. No one wants that."

Vincent walked away, leaving Katerina standing in the middle of the crowd moving around her. She had no idea what to do. She needed help. Taking out the burner, she sent a text.

> Need advice. Can we meet, Professor?

Slipping the phone back into her purse, she headed for the subway.

Chapter 35

The twinkling of the restaurant's delicate icicle lights greeted Katerina when she stepped out of the limousine. Making her way to the entrance, a sudden wave of dizzying nausea gripped her, then faded.

Katerina was struck by the surreal scene surrounding her. These shiny, sparkling people knew nothing of how it felt to be out of breath, out of options, out of time. They didn't worry about Vincent and Carlo. *I'll never be one of them. The best I can do is pull an Eliza Doolittle, the imposter trained to play the part.*

Once inside, Katerina handed the elegant black mink shawl coat Alexander Winter had provided for her to the coat check. The maître d' appeared.

"I'm meeting—"

"Yes, Miss Mills," he said. "We've been expecting you. Please follow me."

She could feel all eyes on her. She had pulled up her hair in intricate swirls and anchored it with crystal clips, highlighting the daring teardrop opening in the back of her black beaded silk dress. Winter and his impeccable taste, she thought. She heard the rustling of patrons turning to gaze after her.

***

Katerina did a quick sweep of the dimly lit, intimate dining room. A crystal vase holding a single rose sat in the center of each ecru linen-covered table. Male wait staff moved in silence to and from the kitchen.

Kat settled in at the oval table for two, prepared for a long wait. Powerful men enjoyed being fashionably late, a reminder to everyone that they are in charge. No sooner had the thought crossed her mind, she sensed someone next to her. Gazing upward, she found Thomas Gallagher standing over her.

He wore a black suit and shirt accented with a red tie. The icy pools of his eyes contradicted his warm smile.

Katerina moved to rise but Gallagher placed a hand on her shoulder.

"No, my dear," he said, settling in next to her. "I'm looking forward to your report, Miss Mills," he said, slipping open the button of his jacket.

A rush of fatigue coupled with a feverish wave swept over her. Again it passed. Katerina wished she could lie down and sleep. If she did, there would be no reports to give.

***

A low hum of conversation filled the room. Katerina pushed her Salmon à la Grecque around the plate, her stomach too unsettled to enjoy the meal. Gallagher, on the other hand, sat in easy comfort, savoring each bite.

She finished rattling off the details of each meeting, verbatim and unredacted.

"Interesting," he said, putting his fork down and dabbing the corners of his mouth with his napkin. "Now, Katerina, what did they *really* talk about?"

"Fishing and drinking, not necessarily in that order," Kat said, flashing back to the coma-inducing male chatter of catching, gutting, and cleaning fish. Glancing down at the salmon, she laid her fork down.

"One final question. One of these men has broken their confidentiality agreement, betrayed me, and approached my competitor. Who is it?"

Kat's mouth fell open. She heard the conversations around her, the clinking of glasses, and tinkling of silverware.

With a pleasant smile, Gallagher picked up his fork and returned to eating.

Katerina did a quick mental calculation of the money she would *not* be collecting, the money she would *not* be sending to her mother, and the money for law school she would *not* be saving.

"Mr. Gallagher, I wouldn't dare answer that question."

"Are you reluctant to answer because you don't know or you don't wish to bear the responsibility for your answer."

"I absolutely do not wish to bear the responsibility."

Gallagher sat back in his chair, twisting the stem of his wine glass between thumb and forefinger. "Why should that concern you?" he asked.

"One careless word and I ruin a man's life. Why shouldn't it concern me?"

He nodded. "A thoughtful viewpoint," he said.

Katerina folded her napkin, placing it on the edge of the table. "I'm very sorry I could not complete the assignment to your satisfaction. I will let the agency know immediately."

"On the contrary," he said, laying his hand over hers, "I'm quite satisfied. In fact, I have an additional assignment for you. I will contact the agency first thing in the morning to submit my request, as per protocol."

"Mr. Gallagher, I don't understand," she said, a wave of dizziness threatening to overwhelm her. "I didn't make a choice."

"That wasn't the assignment. I hired you to gather information. I chose to ask you a question. You gave a sound reason why you will not answer. I'm satisfied."

Katerina wasn't sure what was happening. A kaleidoscope of colors suddenly swirled before her eyes. She felt Gallagher's hand on her arm; she heard his voice.

"Miss Mills, I think some fresh air is in order."

Katerina tried to answer, but the words kept slipping away. The room began to swim. Then everything went dark.

Chapter 36

Katerina awoke in a bedroom with cream-colored walls and white and gold French provincial furniture. She remembered the restaurant, the sickness, Gallagher. Peeking under the soft down comforter, she found she was in a blood-red, spaghetti strap nightgown. *When did this happen?*

Sitting up, Kat swung her legs over the side of the bed, testing for any sign of illness. Nothing happened. A breakfast tray sat on a stand, waiting. She lifted the lid from a plate and found warm toast and a bowl of oatmeal; a slick of steam rose. She poured out hot water from the teapot into the mug. Amid the silence, she munched on the toast, her mind clear.

Silence.

Katerina listened. No blaring taxis, no hum of traffic, not even the muted noise of an active household. *No windows. If I screamed, no one would hear me.* Her pulse began to race, a sudden need to be gone gripped her. Dropping the toast on the plate, she ran to the door. Grasping the door knob, she hesitated, then turned it; it twisted under her hand. Exhaling in relief, she left the door latched and went to the closet.

She found her purse but not her dress. In its place were jeans, a thick blue sweater, and suede boots. She pulled them from the closet and got dressed.

***

Katerina found Gallagher seated in a breakfast nook off the kitchen. As she entered, he rose.

"I'm terribly sorry," she began.

"Not at all," he answered, reaching out and taking her hand in his own. She found his eyes benign, a disarming smile curving his lips. "I hope you are feeling better."

"Yes, thank you. You're very kind."

Hearing movement, Kat turned to see a woman, mid-forties, prim, proper, and professional, coming out of the kitchen.

"Mrs. Shields attended to you."

The woman nodded, moving off before Katerina could say thank you.

Still holding Kat's hand, Gallagher's eyes flicked over her. "The clothing suits you. Do you agree?"

"Yes, thank you."

"But not the other clothing I provided you?"

"I . . . I didn't have time to go to the boutique," she stumbled. "My schedule . . . I apologize."

"There's no need. The dress was lovely, quite appropriate. You chose it yourself?"

"It was a gift from a friend."

"Your friend has excellent taste," Gallagher said. "The dress has been sent for cleaning. Leave an address with Richard and he'll have it messengered. We wouldn't want your friend wondering what happened to it."

He let go of her hand, the benign smile now forced, cool with displeasure, sending a ripple of unease through Kat's stomach.

***

Gallagher sipped his tea and reviewed the previous evening's events. He had been through the "assignment" drill before with the others. Same task. Same executives. There was no traitor. Every one of the young ladies had given a name. They pronounced a career death sentence without so much as a second thought, their greed driving them for the benefits and perks they craved, except for Lisa. She had called him on his little game. They had negotiated and Lisa had done well for herself; a generous compensation package for her "visit" to the apartment. The same room Katerina had slept in. But even Lisa had to admit defeat and it had been a painful, unforgiving lesson he had taught her.

Katerina Mills was different. She possessed a glorious innocence, the mark of the ingénue. Her sense of fairness was an unsustainable commodity in her line of work. Scrolling through his phone, he checked the spyware installed on both her phones. A few of the phone numbers had already been traced. Miss Mills, you lead an interesting life, Gallagher thought. *Simon Marcus. John Reynolds. Interesting, indeed.* But he was most interested in one number. She had called him "Bob" and "Professor", no doubt, the provider of the dress. He mulled over this other man, someone of obvious refined tastes and means. If "Bob" became an impediment, he would have to be dealt with. Gallagher wanted Katerina Mills for himself. *And I will have her.*

Chapter 37

Hours later on Eighth Avenue, Katerina passed the predators keeping a vigilant watch on the fresh-faced girls coming off the buses at the Port Authority terminal across the street. Go home, she thought. *Would I go back? If I could, would I give up? Would I get out?*

Entering the dive of a diner, she spotted Philip hunched over his food.

When she slid into the booth, Philip didn't acknowledge her; instead he continued to wolf down a plate of eggs and potatoes. She fingered the newspaper on the table, the front page headlining yet another skirmish in the ongoing bloody verbal battle between the mayor and the governor over the fate of Gotham City. She shoved the paper aside.

"Nobu was booked?"

Philip didn't answer. With every second of silence, Kat's anxiety doubled. "Okay, Philip, what's the word?" she asked.

When he raised his head, Kat had expected the usual cocky arrogance, the mischievous twinkle in his eyes. Instead, the windows to Philip Castle's soul, if he had one, were filled with fear.

"The word is shit and I think you're in a pile of it."

Katerina licked her lips, bracing for the bad news.

"There's no movement at Will Temple's apartment. No activity on his cell phone. No purchases on his debit card. He's vanished."

No. He's dead. "Are the police investigating?"

He nodded. "A few friends reported him missing."

"Does anyone mention Felicia Reynolds when they talk about him?"

Philip gave a short, disgusted laugh. "The cops are too busy worrying that there might be a serial killer hunting rich women. So far, there's no connection."

They sat in silence. Katerina knew Philip wouldn't ask questions. Not about Will Temple. Not about Felicia Reynolds. He was too smart for that.

"You need to disappear, kid," he said.

"Nobody knows about me."

"Are you sure?"

"I'm not directly involved."

"If—when—the cops get around to you, and they will, explain it to them. I'm sure they'll believe you."

Katerina closed her eyes for a moment. "Jesus Christ, Katerina," she heard him say, "what the hell kind of trouble are you in?"

She opened her eyes. The frat boy good looks appeared strained, like Philip had just finished a marathon of hard partying. In the beginning, she had seen him as exciting, handsome, and worldly. That was gone now. Had it ever been? *How could I ever have seen those qualities? Why was I attracted to him to begin with?*

"Thanks, Philip," she said. "You did me a real favor."

He didn't answer. No promises of protection and rescue. No declarations of love and devotion. She hadn't expected it. She slid out of the booth.

He grabbed her wrist. "I'll check in on you at the end of the week."

"No, you won't. You'll keep your distance like a smart lawyer would. That's what you taught me, remember? Protect the client but protect yourself first."

"Let me give you some money. Get out of town for a while."

"It's too late for that. It's okay, Philip. I know an envelope of photo negatives only buys so much."

Philip let go.

As Katerina walked out, it was coming on dinner time; the sun was already setting. She remembered her first days working for Philip. It wasn't a few weeks before she realized he was dirty. *Why didn't I leave? If I could do it over again, would I get out? Would I go home? Or am I my father's daughter?* She glanced around, scanning the street for Sheridan and a cold-eyed killer.

Pulling out the burner, she placed a call to John Reynolds, her impatience growing with every ring. Finally, the annoying beep so she could leave her message. She made it quick and vague, asking only for a return call. Just as she was about to tuck the burner back in her purse, she saw it, a missed text from hours earlier.

     429 Kent Avenue, Brooklyn. W.

 Kat took off for the subway, hoping it wasn't too late.

Chapter 38

Entering the building, Katerina ducked into the elevator, instinctively knowing to press the button for the top floor.

When the door opened, she stepped into another space bathed in hospital white; the clean, comforting minimalism she had come to expect. She was greeted by a wave of warm air and Alexander Winter, outfitted in black. *Why are you dressed,* she thought with a stab of disappointment.

He reached for her coat.

"I'm cold," she said, pulling it close.

"Shhh," he soothed. "It'll be all right. Sit down."

Relinquishing the coat, she settled on the couch. The coffee table held a plate of fresh fruit, small squares of dark bread, and various cheese wedges, symmetrically cut. Next to them, a small plate of whole strawberries dipped in glistening chocolate and a white teapot with matching square cups and saucers.

She watched him open a closet door, revealing an empty space except for his coat, a briefcase on the floor, a fleece throw and a spare pillow on the shelf. Once again, Winter would come and go and no one would ever know he had been here. He wasn't, really. She realized that now. He was a ghost.

He brought the fleece and wrapped it around her shoulders. Sitting down diagonal to her, he prepared a plate of food and a cup of tea. She accepted the steaming mug, inhaling the rich apple scent. When he set the plate before her, she dug in without ceremony. As he took a bite of a chocolate-covered strawberry, she stopped in mid-chew, staring.

His eyebrows lifted.

"Sorry," she said. "I—I never imagine you—actually eating."

He smirked. "I perform all the functions necessary for survival, Katie. Eating, drinking, making love . . ."

She could feel the heat rising in her face.

She saw the amusement in his eyes.

They ate in a comfortable silence. When she dared meet his gaze, she found him considering her, his eyes soft, the icy blue having melted to a warm azure. She fidgeted. When he looked at her that way, it made her feel shy and unsure. That didn't dampen her desire to move closer, to slip her hand under his shirt and feel the warmth of his bare skin under her fingers.

"Did the clothes work out for you?"

"Yes," she said. "Very much. Thank you."

He reached out, fingering the sleeve of her sweater. "Are you sure?"

Glancing down at the outfit Gallagher had provided, she gave herself a mental kick for her stupidity. *I should've stopped at home to change. You're afraid to go home, remember? And you still didn't change the lock on the front door. Tomorrow.*

"I was with a client and I became ill." She rattled off a muddled explanation until with a shrug, she gave up. "It's complicated."

His brows pinched in response.

"You're angry with me," she said.

He cupped his hand around her cheek. "Are you feeling better?"

She nodded. Her eyes wandered the room as she searched to find a way to break the awkward silence. "Is Alexander Winter renting this apartment?"

He smiled. "Steven Bartholomew is renting this apartment."

"I like Alex Winter better," she said.

"Then we'll stick with what's comfortable. You wanted to talk to me."

"I . . . I want your advice . . . I need your advice. My assignments . . . I've got them covered—"

"Yes, Katerina, I know," he said. He sipped his tea, waiting.

"I just wanted to make sure."

"A second pair of eyes never hurts."

Kat nodded. "Last time I saw you, I asked about a retrieval, two people wanting the same thing, but there's only one item."

He nodded. "Did you go to Sunday school?"

Katerina made a face. "Yes," she said. *I think we can all agree that was a waste of time.*

"Do you remember the story of the judgment of Solomon?"

"Two women. They both claimed to be a baby's mother and Solomon called for a sword. I can't cut this item in half either."

Winter smiled. "That wasn't the point of the story. Each woman said the child was hers. But only one woman *really* cared about the baby. The other just wanted to have it for the sake of having it, to win."

She nodded.

"What's the item?"

"A Porsche," she said without hesitation.

"There are ways to get two of something without spending a fortune, including a car, even if one is a replica," he said. "The trick is deciding who gets what."

"Figure out which person just wants to possess the item to win."

He nodded. "That person gets the replica. I can help you."

"I don't want you to get caught up in this."

"No one's caught me yet," he said.

"I've got it covered," she said. *Not.*

"Anything else?"

Kat hesitated for a split second. *You wanted someone to confide in. Here he is. This is your chance.* "I have a pick up at JFK."

She watched for a reaction but Winter's poker face remained firmly in place.

"Animal, vegetable, or mineral?"

"Herbal."

"You're in the herb business now?"

"Temporarily."

"Mmm." Putting down his tea cup, he leaned forward.

She inhaled his scent, warm and pleasing. *This is business. Treat it that way.*

"How were you going to do it?"

He turned to her, his knees brushing against hers.

He's so beautiful.

"Katie," he said softly, resting his hands on her arms.

She could feel the heat burning through her sweater. She drew in a shaky breath. *This is business. You're here for business.* "I go in, wait at the baggage claim, and pick him up. Out and gone. Quick and clean."

He took her hands in his. "The first rule of the job, keep your transportation accessible and available. If the car is in short-term parking, you're stuck."

She nodded, feeling herself trembling inside in anticipation, watching her fingers entwine with his.

"You need to be mobile and you need to blend in. No one should notice you," he said. "How will you do that?"

Kat's mind raced through her options. She wanted to be smarter, sharper, to show him she could hold her own. *Who goes to the airport often and is usually invisible?* "I'm a driver, there to collect him."

"Smart. Good. Stay with your car at the curbside pickup. You'll need a uniform. Wear a hat." He swept a tendril of hair away from her face. "Wear a wig. Keep your head at a slight angle when you get out of the car. That will help obscure your features. The cameras aren't that great anyway. Remember, Katerina, the best solutions are the simplest. Don't over think it. Keep it simple."

She gave a shiver and he pulled the fleece tighter around her shoulders.

"Now, have you seen Sheridan?"

"It's been a few days." *And I've been trying to ignore the situation hoping it would go away.* "He told me my father, the mild-mannered factory manager, the man who thought plaid pants were a sophisticated style choice, has been living a double life as a drug trafficker."

"I don't think his lack of fashion sense influenced his alleged criminal activity," Winter said drily.

"Sheridan has to be wrong. He has to be."

"Do you want me to look into this?"

"Yes, please."

Getting up, he went to the closet and retrieved her coat.

No offer to stay the night?

Katerina stood as he came to her.

"It's late," she said.

"Yes, it is. I've got work. I'm on the clock."

He held up the coat, the signal for her to turn around.

"Kiss me goodnight," she said.

He gave her a long look, then tossed the coat over a chair. Reaching for her, he drew her into his arms. Sliding her hands over his shoulders, her heart began to pound at the thought of what might happen next, what she hoped might happen.

"If I kiss you good night, I'll be kissing you good morning," he whispered into her hair.

Her heart jumped and a spike of heat flared down deep inside her. "I like the sound of that."

He kissed her forehead and her temple, his lips settling by her ear. "What would the boyfriend say?" he asked.

"He's not . . . *technically* . . . my boyfriend."

"Did you tell him that?"

She answered with silence.

"I assume there's a reason you continue to see a police officer who's *not* your boyfriend."

"It's complicated," she said.

"Mmmm."

"You think I'm bad," she said, casting her eyes downward.

He pulled back, lifting her chin with a light touch of his finger. "I think you're scared. This play you're making, keeping him close—it's dangerous. One slip—"

"And life as I know it will end," she finished, remembering his pep talk from their first meeting. She knew it was all true, but she didn't want to hear it. Not tonight. "Kiss me goodnight," she said.

"It's complicated," he said, his voice gentle.

The disappointment seeped in, choking out the moment as it slipped away. "And you're on the clock."

"That's right," he said. "You're welcome to stay here," he said, kissing her cheek. He hesitated, finally releasing her. He took her coat back to the closet, exchanging it out for his own. He took a briefcase from the floor.

She settled on the couch as Winter moved to the door. He stopped, turning back to her.

"Katie, why did you think I was mad at you over the clothes?"

"The client. He purchased outfits for me at a boutique. I didn't pick them up. At the dinner, I wore the dress you gave me, the one with the cutout in the back. He wasn't pleased."

Winter's face turned cool; he didn't answer. After a few moments, he gave her a warm smile. With a last look, he exited the apartment.

Katerina leaned back on the couch, her bed for the night. Then she remembered. *He said I could sleep anywhere I wanted.*

***

She crawled into his bed, his pajamas swimming on her slender frame. Burrowing deep under the blankets and snuggling into his pillow, she inhaled his scent, her desire for him so strong she could almost feel his hands caressing her skin. She wanted to lose herself in the fantasy but nagging anxieties mixed with annoyed confusion pulled her back. To be with him would be complicated. *But not impossible. Why buy me presents and then do nothing? Why get close and then put me off? I'm ready to choose him. But he has to choose me. And he doesn't.*

Exhausted from the endless mental merry-go-round, she slipped in and out of sleep. Her thoughts drifted between Winter and Gallagher, both light years away from Philip and his blustering bravado and bullshit. No, these were serious men, strong, precise, and successful. Gallagher almost certainly knew as much or maybe more about criminal activity as Winter did.

While they shared similarities, Kat had detected the differences. Gallagher oozed polish and finesse. She imagined him at home on the Côte d'Azur or in Monaco. Although Winter could slip into the role of the wealthy man of leisure, she had seen the rugged, working man persona; the version she suspected was closer to the truth. Gallagher should have generated heat, but any warmth dissipated under his withering, icy gaze. Winter, despite his name and the sometimes frosty blue of his eyes, was not made of ice and steel. He rejected the persona as surely as he rejected the frigid temperatures he obviously hated. He was blood and bone, muscle and sinew, heat and flame. She had seen his weakness. Winter was human. And the only one she trusted.

Chapter 39

The garage on Ninth Avenue blended in with the surrounding blue-collar businesses of scrap metal, trucking, and construction.

"A Town Car by tomorrow? No se puede. The Moose is not a miracle worker."

Mechanics ignored the vehicles up on lifts to stare at Katerina until Moose shot them the evil eye. Kat took note as Moose spun on a dime from affable charmer to alpha male. The ever-present bulge at his ankle signaled protection and a warning. Kat had no doubt that wasn't the only gun he was carrying. The mechanics returned to their work.

"It's a Town Car, not a Hummer," she snapped. "The city is loaded with them." The previous night's lost opportunity with Winter and the question mark looming over the future was eating away at her patience.

"Muy difícil, mami. This will require a lot of, cómo se dice, various moving pieces falling into place, you know what I'm sayin'?"

Katerina folded her arms across her chest. "What do you want?"

"I'm thinking we could do the introduction at the reception, you know. They're gonna play the theme from *Rocky*. You and me, you know, we could come out, do a little dance . . ."

"Fine, whatever. Keep your hands to yourself."

"I got you, mami. Yo, did you get your dress yet?"

"Moose, I have to commit—I'm working on it."

Moose raised his hands. "Hey, the Moose is down. You got *business*. I like a serious woman."

"Can you do it?"

He nodded. "I got you covered. You leaving the hair, like, you know . . . frothy . . . for the wedding, right?"

Frothy? "Right."

***

As she made it to the campus, Katerina dialed a number on the burner. "I'm calling with an update," she said.

"Do you have it?" came Maggie's voice, breathless with excitement.

"I expect to have it tomorrow."

"Expect? You will or you won't?"

"Barring any unforeseen event, I expect to have it tomorrow."

Kat heard a heavy sigh from the other end of the phone.

"You should be a lawyer," Maggie said, and hung up.

Tell me about it.

Chapter 40

The midmorning crowd rushed in and out of the eatery. Every time the door opened a fresh blast of cold air assaulted the patrons. Katerina hurried in, already mentally at JFK, rehearsing in her head how it would all go. That was the secret, wasn't it? First visualize doing the job and then make it happen. *I'm applying positive thinking principles to crime. Excellent.*

"Shouldn't you be at work? What's up?" Kat asked, shucking off her coat and sliding into the seat.

Emma sipped her tea as an answer.

The door to the café opened. Emma glanced beyond Kat. Turning, Kat watched as Ryan scanned the room and found them. She froze. *Set up. Shit. I won't get to the airport. I must get to the airport.* She turned back to Emma.

"Desperate times, sugar. He's got it bad and it ain't right what you're doin'. I'm spendin' my time defendin' you and I've never had to do that before. Get in or get out, but don't torment him like this."

"Emma, you had no right—"

"No lectures, doll. Take care of it."

Katerina lapsed into silence as Ryan approached the table. He stood there, as if he were waiting for permission to take a seat, unsure if he was welcome.

"Ladies," he said.

Rising from her seat, Emma shrugged into her bulky, pink jacket. "Here, hon, I've got to go."

Giving Kat a sharp, parental look, Emma grabbed her purse and took off as Ryan took her place.

They both watched her go, and then turned to each other, sitting in a stilted silence.

"I'm sorry," Katerina said, giving voice to her subconscious guilt.

"Did you do something?"

Where do I start?

"Katerina?"

"You're a good man, Ryan. You really are."

He nodded, his face revealing his emotions: anxiety, anger, even fear. "You know, I don't mind you being gun shy, but it takes two people in the same room, at the same time, to try to make a go of this."

"It's school, and work—"

"I've given you fixes for those things."

No, you haven't.

"You keep leaving me out in the cold, and that shit's not working for me anymore."

"Ryan—"

"Do you want me around or not?"

Katerina's heart flipped. She stared him, knowing how to answer, the words on the tip of her tongue. *Maybe this is my way out. Maybe I don't need to stay one step ahead. Maybe he won't catch me. I don't have to keep on with this. I don't have to hurt him. I don't have to be this . . . bad person.*

"I *know* what I want," he said.

Katerina's mind raced, then faltered, whispering unknown disasters yet to come. *If he gets on to me, I'll never see it coming.*

Ryan leaned forward, jumping on her hesitation. "I want you. I want you in my life." His voice shifted now, turning forceful. "I want to see you for dinner three nights a week. I want you out of that rat trap apartment and sleeping at my place for those three nights. I'll take the couch or the bed I don't care. I want to see you when I'm off. You know this is right, Katerina. You know I'm the right person for you. You're not giving yourself a chance. You're not giving *us* a chance. It's unfair of you to do this, to give up on us like this. You know it is."

He kept talking, an endless monologue of pushing, forcing, and cajoling, and then back all over again. She felt like a suspect, slowly wearing down. I don't know what you'll do, she thought. *I have to get out of here. I have to pick up the car. I have to get to the airport.*

Sinking into a quicksand of confusion, Kat found herself nodding. "Yes," she blurted, even as she felt the blood draining from her face. "I want this to work." *What the hell did I just do?*

Exhaling, Ryan sat back with a relieved smile. "Okay then," he said. "Good. Now, where are you going today?"

"I'm . . . I'm going to school." *Another lie.*

"I'll give you a ride."

And I can't say no.

He stood up, holding out his hand. She took it and got up. He gave her a quick kiss on her lips. At the door, they bundled up, braced for the cold, and went out.

***

Ryan pulled the car to the curb near the Washington Square Arch. Leaning over, he gave Katerina another kiss. She kissed him back, her brain numb.

"I'll see you tonight," he said.

She got out of the car, waving as he drove away. Kat waited until he was out of sight before racing for the subway station. If she didn't fly, she wouldn't make it.

Chapter 41

Katerina baked in the blasting heat of the idling Town Car. Tapping the steering wheel in a rapid staccato, she fidgeted in her uniform of black slacks, white turtleneck, and black jacket. Watching weary travelers weave in and out of the sliding doors of the terminal, she kept her eyes peeled for a man of medium height with short, straight, fair hair and non-descript, round, gold-rimmed glasses. A man no one would pay any attention to. A man who would fade into the background and be forgotten. The Town Car had a white sign taped to the right rear window. One word—SMITH. That's who she was waiting for. Mr. Smith. She followed her ritual, turning, scanning around her, checking the rearview mirror, checking the sliding doors.

She straightened the bangs of her wig while giving herself a mental pep talk. *Focus on the job. Get the herb. Make the delivery. Then worry about a DEA agent, a crazed killer, and a mobster. And Ryan. And Winter.*

Glancing into the rearview mirror, she caught a glimpse of slivers of dark blue. She snapped to attention as the crowd parted like the Red Sea. *Shit.* It wasn't slivers of blue; it was NYPD blue. Two of them, one with a German Shepherd on a leash. The sliding doors parted and they disappeared inside the terminal.

Katerina's stomach did a handspring and her heart thudded in her chest. Mr. Smith was about to be detained and taken into custody. Katerina remembered to breathe when she saw the officers exit the terminal. They were looking for her man, she knew it. She glanced again at the sign, SMITH, taped onto the window. *Where the hell are you, Mr. Smith?*

They moved toward the Town Car. Kat froze, staring straight ahead, her hands gripping the wheel, then sliding off from the sweat.

They passed the Town Car.

Katerina held her breath.

The sliding doors opened. The officers ducked back inside, the German Shepherd in step beside them.

Katerina blew out a mouthful of air. She could feel the perspiration trickling down her sides, soaking her shirt. She glanced over to see the terminal doors open again. A man, wearing a tan coat, jeans, and scuffed, black, rubber-soled shoes emerged. He had fine, light brown hair, and wore small oval glasses. He carried a battered brown backpack.

That's him. The Invisible Man.

Jumping out of the Town Car, she maneuvered around to the front end.

"Mr. Smith, sir, I'm your driver," she said.

The man considered her with a bemused smile as she rushed to open the passenger door. He slipped into the back. Slamming the door, Katerina hustled around and slid behind the wheel. With a sigh of relief, she put the car in gear and pulled out into the flow of traffic. She checked the rearview mirror just as a man exited the terminal and stood at the curb, looking, searching.

Fair haired, round oval glasses, a non-descript face. Her heart somersaulted, her knuckles going white as she gripped the wheel.

No. No. No. It can't be.

"Mr. Smith?" she said, her voice cracking.

The passenger shifted forward to the edge of his seat. A cold, sharp object pressed against her neck.

Gun.

"*Nyet*. Not Mr. Smith," he said in a thick, Russian accent. "Drive."

Chapter 42

"I'm sorry about this . . . misunderstanding," she said. "My mistake, obviously. I can drop you somewhere, anywhere, and give you money for a cab." *Please just take your gun away from my neck.*

"I don't need money for cab," he said. "I got transportation. I got you. You are driver."

The cold metal object shifted to the back of her skull.

Suddenly lightheaded, she gripped the wheel, forcing herself to take a deep, slow breath.

"Where do you want to go?" she asked, her voice a whisper.

"Drive. I tell you."

***

"She's not getting the car."

Holding the cell phone to his ear, Anthony Desucci's lips pursed. "Where is she and what is she doing?"

"She just left the airport," Vincent said. "Our guys didn't pick up the—uh—guest— because he got into the wrong car."

"What car did he get into?" Desucci asked, but he had a sneaking suspicion he already knew the answer.

"She's in a Town Car. She's got a uniform and everything. Then another guy came out of the terminal, and he looked like, you know, our guy. So, our guys thought that the other guy, maybe he was the right guy."

"Don't tell me what I think you're going to tell me."

"Our guys got the wrong guy in their car. She's got the wrong guy in her car. What are the odds, you know?"

"I'll call you back." Desucci clicked off the cell phone and shook his head. *Young girls.*

***

Katerina drove on autopilot, watching her knuckles turn white as she gripped the wheel.

"Ease up on gas pedal," he said. "You have lead foot. It will attract police."

"Look, I have no idea why you're here, and I don't want to know—"

"Christmas shopping," he deadpanned. "You are driver all the time?"

"No. I'm not really a driver. I'm a fixer. I—fix—people's problems."

He laughed. "Me too. But I am not fixer. I am cleaner."

Katerina's stomach lurched. *Shit.* "What's your name?"

"That is joke, right?"

"No. What should I call you?"

"Ivan. What I call you?"

Mud. "Katerina."

"Yekaterina. Good Russian name. Your mother is Russian?"

"No."

"Your father?"

"No."

"Why you named Katerina?"

"I don't know."

They rode in silence.

"Someone in family read Russian books?"

"I don't think so."

"Good. Very depressing. Lot of poverty . . . love on rocks . . . you read *Anna Karenina*?"

"No."

"Good. Don't. She dies. Throws herself under train."

"I really just need to drop you off and be on my way."

"*Nyet*, Yekaterina. You are driver. You drive me."

They rode in silence.

The cell phone buzzed.

Katerina jumped at the sound.

The buzzing filled the silent car. "It's not good if I don't answer the phone," she said.

"*Da.* So answer phone." The gun pressed harder against her skull. "Watch step, Yekaterina."

She hit the connect button. A voice came over the speaker.

"Mia cara, what happened?" Only Roger Cole could sound incredulous and yet not really worried at the same time.

Katerina stole a look at Ivan. She found his eyes trained on her like a laser.

"There was a bit of a mix-up. Where is he?"

"He had to fly, bella. The place was crawling with cops. They had the dogs out. You didn't see that?"

"Uh, yeah, well, there was a lot of activity."

She felt the gun jam in harder.

"Am I on speaker phone?"

Katerina struggled to steer, talk, and not shit her pants. "Yes, it's fine. Where is he now?"

"Not sure. He's gone dark."

"Shit!"

"Watch language, please," Ivan whispered. "You look like nice girl."

"Who's that?"

"The radio. I'll call you back." Katerina pressed the end button.

Somewhere between mind-numbing fright and the urge to throw up, Katerina found her voice. "Look, this was a little mix-up."

"I hear, *myschka*. This is big mix-up. And now you are in mix."

Oh, what the hell. "Look, I have to get to my supplier for a drug buy or I forfeit the job and if I do you might as well kill me because I'm as good as dead."

Ivan clucked his tongue in disapproval. "What do you buy?"

"*Salvia divinorum.*"

"What this? New word for heroin?"

"No. It's an herb. It's a member of the mint family."

Ivan took in this information with raised eyebrows. "Mint? That is not drug. That is good for drink. You seem like nice girl. Why you do this?"

"Would you believe I'm just trying to earn money to pay for college and go to law school?"

"Higher education. It is prohibitively expensive. It is crime, really. But, I have to make stop. You drive."

"You mean you have to kill someone."

Ivan shrugged. "I thought you prefer I not say that. Keep eyes on road, please."

The cell phone buzzed again.

Ivan let out a heavy sigh. "Eight million people in New York City, I get social butterfly."

Katerina answered the phone.

"I want to talk to your passenger," Anthony Desucci's voice came over the line. "Off the speaker."

She tapped the speaker button and handed the cell phone to Ivan.

Katerina watched Ivan in the rearview mirror as he listened. He said "da" a few times, all the while examining her.

He held the phone out. "He wants you."

Katerina took the phone.

"Why is he in the wrong car?" Desucci asked. "Why are you in the wrong car?"

"I'm juggling multiple assignments," she said, maneuvering a turn toward Midtown.

Kat imagined Anthony Desucci sitting comfortably in his study, pinching the bridge of his nose between his thumb and forefinger in an exaggerated expression of strained patience.

"My staff has your man," Desucci said, "so we're going to make an adjustment. He's going to visit with us for a while. You're going to take your passenger where he needs to go and once he's done, you're going to help him get on his way. Then you and your man can be on your way."

Adjustment my ass. As soon as Boris Badenov finishes his wet work, we're both going to die. Starting with me.

"No," she said.

"Excuse me?" Desucci's voice came over the line with a hint of amusement, as if someone had just told a joke. "You don't have a choice, sweetheart."

Yes, I do. "Here's what we're going to do. We're going to go to a nice crowded place, the Manhattan Mall, and we're going to make a swap. You're going to have Huey and Dewey bring my man right now."

Desucci chuckled into the phone.

"Because I'm heading toward Times Square," she said. "You *know* what they have in Times Square. That nice big NYPD sign. Maybe I'll drive right up. Or maybe, I'll just crash the car and they can come to investigate. Either way, your man is screwed. You're screwed. I'm screwed."

Katerina heard her own voice, shrill, hysterical. She didn't care. She met Ivan's eyes in the rearview mirror. "And you, Boris, finger off the trigger!"

The gun vanished from the back of her neck, leaving behind hot, clammy sweat clinging to her skin.

"O-kay," Desucci said in a soft, drawn out, monotone. "Let's calm down and not lose control."

"Who's losing control?" she yelled, glancing in the rearview mirror. Ivan was reclining in the back seat, a smirk planted firmly on his face.

"Sit tight, young lady," Desucci said. "I will make the arrangements. Manhattan Mall in a half hour. They'll be there. Everything will be settled. Everyone will be happy."

Kat clicked off the phone.

"You sure you are not man?" Ivan asked.

"What?"

"I think when we pull over, you check pants. I think you have large set of balls in panties. When this is over, you come to my home, teach my daughter to be like you."

"You have children?"

"What? I should not have family?" Ivan said, sounding hurt. "I am nice man. I am married to nice Russian girl."

"Does the nice Russian girl know what you do for a living?"

Ivan gave a snort of derision. "You think I visit, how you say, boys who sing in choir? If someone sees me, *myshka*, there is reason. They are not Boy Scouts, Yekaterina. But I have son. He will do better than me. He will go to university."

"You want him to be a doctor or a lawyer."

He made another noise. "MBA. Computer programmer. Money is much better in white-collar crime. He will make fortune."

"Good for him."

"Who are these Huey and Dewey?"

"Nephews of Donald Duck."

"Ah, cartoons. My children, they like them."

"That's nice. Now give me the gun," she said. "Pass it forward. Carefully."

Ivan smiled. "Okay, *myshka*, okay."

Katerina took the gun, curling her hand around the butt. "Now the backpack."

Ivan let out a small chuckle and passed it forward.

"What does '*myshka*' mean?"

"It is term of endearment. It means little mouse."

"Knock it off," she snapped. "No mice."

"You have pest problem?"

"You have no idea," she said.

***

Katerina tapped her fingers against the wheel, anxious for the call to connect.

"Yo," Moose said.

"I have to ditch the car."

"Where are you, mami?"

"Midtown, the Manhattan Mall."

"Leave it on Thirty-second. I'll send a crew."

"I need a replacement."

"You're going through a lot of my cars, you know?"

"I am not sleeping with you."

"Hey, nobody said sleeping, okay? I was just gonna say, if you was a bridesmaid, that would be better, because the bridal party, we're thinking we want to do a dance number, you know, like a musical thing, at the reception, you know what I'm sayin'?"

Turning on West Thirty-second, Katerina spied an empty spot and quickly maneuvered into the space.

"You don't think your cousin will find it odd to have a bridesmaid she doesn't know?"

"Nah—mami, my cousin's a bitch. She can't get nobody to be a bridesmaid. She's like one of them bridezillas, you know, she got the girls cryin' and shit. I'd be doin' her a favor."

Katerina let out a sigh of exhaustion. "Okay, *papi*, I tell you what, bridesmaid, dance number, photographs, no sex."

"Hey, the Moose is cool. I'm sending a crew with a replacement."

Katerina clicked off. She checked her wig, grabbed the backpack, and got out of the car, holding the gun concealed behind her jacket. Opening the back passenger door, she leaned in, showing the gun and shaking it at Ivan.

"Get out of the car."

Ivan shifted toward the door and climbed out of the vehicle, shaking his head. "I think you are not *myshka*. I think you are *mishka*."

"What's the diffcrence?" she asked, slipping the gun into her inside coat pocket.

"One is little mouse. The other is little bear. I think you more bear than mouse."

"Then be a good boy, *Boris,* and do what I say."

Chapter 43

Crossing Herald Square, Kat held onto Ivan's arm as they took the Thirty-second street entrance into the mall. With the blood pounding in her ears, Katerina found the song "Jingle Bells" looping through her head, only the words were different.

Dashing through the mall, with a man who likes to slay, O'er the shops I go, shaking all the way...

***

Entering, they were greeted by the swelling noise of the throng of holiday shoppers. As they passed the sparkling Christmas tree decorated in elegant red and white ornaments, a text buzzed onto Kat's burner.

2nd Floor

***

Taking the escalator up, they found the mall bathed in white except for the black and white checkerboard marble flooring, and the columns dotted with green wreaths bedecked with silver bows.

Ivan and Katerina walked the perimeter. She spotted Carlo lingering by the entrance to an optical store. Standing next to Carlo was Mr. Smith. Carlo whispered something in Smith's ear; Smith looked straight at Katerina.

Kat's phone rang.

"Okay, honey?" Vincent asked.

"Fine," she said. "We meet at the head of the escalator, make the switch, and ride down and go our separate ways. Don't get cute. If your boss still wants the car, I'm the best way to get it."

"Sure, sweetheart, you don't have to be nervous. Let's just have calm, okay?"

Katerina clicked off the phone. *Calm, my ass.* She and Ivan strolled toward the escalator when Ivan put his arm around her.

"What the—"

"I think it better we look like lovebirds, yes?" He snuggled in close and whispered in her ear. "You still have gun."

Katerina sucked in a breath. *How the hell am I going to give it back?* As they gazed into each other's eyes, she caught a snatch of something blue in her peripheral vision. A very familiar blue.

Turning, she saw four blue uniforms with Mall security. Vincent, Carlos, and Smith slowed down in hesitation as the officers stopped people, asking them to open their bags and jackets. *There must have been a theft. Shit!*

As her knees buckled, Ivan's grip tightened.

"Not now, *myshka*, not now."

She was out of ideas when Winter's words floated through her fast collapsing mind. *Keep it simple. The simplest solutions are best.*

What's the simplest thing to do?

She noticed something red out of the corner of her eye.

Katerina tugged Ivan into a recessed cubby housing a fire extinguisher box. Ivan removed his glasses while Kat pulled off the wig and jacket, stuffing them into the backpack. As the police passed the cubby, Ivan kicked the backpack behind them and yanked Katerina into his arms, his mouth closing over hers.

Katerina gripped his coat as she let her resistance go. She heard the police officers whisper, chuckle, and move on.

Ivan extracted his gun from her pocket.

He pulled away, smiling at her, a playful twinkle in his eye. "Maybe you are not such nice girl. Maybe we are good match, *Natasha*."

"Let's go," Kat said through clenched teeth. They slipped out of the cubby and got on the escalator. She spotted Vincent, Carlo, and Smith six or seven steps below.

As they reached bottom, Vincent and Carlo got off and headed left, Vincent shoving Smith off to the right.

Without a word, Ivan got off the escalator and followed the two men.

Katerina came up behind Smith, hooking her arm in his and exiting with him into the gray afternoon. She hustled him back to the spot where the Town Car had been to find a black Audi in its place.

Spotting the keypad on the driver's side door, Kat took out her burner and checked the latest text message.

691034 door
78341 ignition

She punched in the numbers and they got into the car.

"I'm sorry about the confusion, Mr. Smith," she said.

"No problem," he said, as he snapped his seatbelt. "At least no one threatened to cut off my fingers or electrify my balls."

She punched in the key code on the front panel and the car hummed to life.

"That's comforting," she said, pulling out into traffic.

Chapter 44

A few hours later, Katerina dropped Mr. Smith at Penn Station and headed back out to Brooklyn. By the time she arrived at the loft, the sun was beginning its descent.

Finding the loft door open, Kat entered to find Maggie seated on the couch, reading a magazine, and Paul Patel, hands stuffed into his pockets, pacing in a small oval pattern. His head jerked up at the sound of Kat's footsteps.

Katerina pulled a large baggie from her purse. Patel rushed to her, skidding to a stop, holding his hands out as if ready to receive a newborn. She dropped the baggie into his palms.

He stared at the bag, mesmerized. "You have set me free, Dark Lady," he whispered, shifting his laser gaze to Kat. "But you, you are enslaved. You must escape."

Stunned at his words, Katerina suppressed a sudden urge to cry.

"Okay, Paulie," Maggie said. "You need to take your medicine now."

Giving Kat a slight smile, he made a beeline for the bathroom, slamming the door behind him.

"Do you need anything else from me?" she asked.

"Call the office and let them know it's done."

As Katerina left the apartment, she heard Maggie on the phone. When she got down to the street, she pulled out the vibrating burner.

"You can come in," Jasmine said and clicked off the line.

Kat dropped the phone into her purse and fought the gusting winds back to the car. Back to Manhattan.

***

With thirty thousand dollars cash in hand, Katerina made her stops at three post offices for money orders and the bank for the safety deposit box. As she stepped out of the bank, she stopped short as the driver's side door of a car opened. Carlo got out.

***

Anthony Desucci sat in the warmth of the back seat, wearing a beige coat and an annoyed expression. She watched him with the familiar feeling of not being able to breathe.

"I take it we can get back to business now?"

Katerina nodded and moved to open the car door. Desucci grabbed her arm, pulling her to stay.

"I expect you to concentrate on this little favor for me. If you don't give this the attention it deserves, I'm going to think you're not taking me seriously." He increased the pressure of his hold. "You are taking me seriously, right?"

"Yes."

"You have a very important job here, Katerina. You're a buffer."

"A buffer." *I already don't like where this is going.*

"A layer of protection between the end objective and myself."

I take the fall if anything goes wrong.

"You shouldn't have a problem with this. You've done "favors" for people before. I'm a little more important than a two-bit, low-life lawyer past his expiration date, wouldn't you say?"

Katerina winced as his grip tightened. She nodded.

Desucci let go. "Good girl. Keep me posted, Katerina."

Katerina got out of the car.

Philip and his photo negatives. Now he's loaning me out.
Great.

Chapter 45

Katerina dumped the Audi on Tenth Avenue. She sent a text with the word "thanks" and the address. She entered her building after dark, pepper spray at the ready. Opening the apartment door, she flipped on the lights, reciting a silent prayer that there would be no unwanted visitors, rodent or human. Satisfied after a sweep of opening closet doors and peeking behind the shower curtain, she tossed the pepper spray in her purse and dumped the purse on the table.

Kicking off her shoes and peeling off her coat, she wanted only to lie down, close her eyes, and shut out the day's events. She marveled that her reaction, after everything, was no reaction at all; as if this was expected, the new normal. Part of her secretly hoped there was a nervous breakdown in her future. *That* would be normal. Lost in thought, her mind slid from one thought to the next, like the horses rising up and down on a carousel: Will Temple, who was probably dead, and John Reynolds, who had gone off the grid. How to find him? What would Lisa do? *I can't even figure out how to find Lisa.* She went over the Lessing job in her head again. *Joe Lessing calls me. He said he called someone else. They said they would try to come. I go to the apartment. I do the job. I meet Lisa on the street after it's done. What am I missing?* She turned away from the front door toward the bedroom. *Shit. The door lock. I'll change it first thing in the morning.*

She let out a stunned cry.

Sheridan.

"You're not studying for finals," he said, nodding toward the books littering the tiny kitchen table. His tone was matter-of-fact.

Glancing around the apartment, he made a "tut-tut" sound. "This is a real shitbox. But I guess you know that. I'm surprised. A pretty girl like you. All those wealthy men you visit, all those naughty things you must do."

"Were you absent the day they taught breaking and entering is illegal?" she said, attempting to sound flip, but the raw fear in her voice betrayed her.

Sheridan stepped forward; Katerina stepped back, eyeing her purse on the table. *Reach for the spray or run for the door?*

"Not for us, not when we're after criminals. We can do anything we want. You were supposed to call me with an update, weren't you, Katerina."

Get out. She bolted.

Catching her by the hair, he yanked her backward; she cried out, trying to twist out of his grasp. Shoving her against the wall, he pinned her in a vise grip.

"What do you call them? Uncles?" he leered, his face inches from hers.

"Let me go," she said.

"Maybe *we* should do those naughty things," he said, ignoring her as if she had never spoken. "Maybe I should do those things to you whether you want to or not because I have to tell you, Katerina, I've been trying to be nice, but it just isn't working. You were supposed to call me."

"I'm working on it," she said, straining against his grasp, "I don't know anything."

He pressed her against the wall, holding fast, digging his fingers deeper into her arms. "Now, there you go, lying again. That's very wrong, Katerina. A young woman, with no job and no bank account manages to go to school full time, yet doesn't know anything about the ten million dollars that her father took off with."

He crushed his body weight against her, wedging himself between her legs. She fought for breath, pushing back with all her strength, but he held her pinned, helpless.

"Get off me," she gasped.

"You know what really troubles me, Katerina? The trips to those post offices to get the money orders that you send to your mother. Do you know what money laundering is Katerina?" he asked, his fingers groping at the button on her pants.

A rush of fresh fear shot through her. Bringing one knee up, she made contact. He grunted, his grip loosened. Tearing one hand free, she raked her nails across his cheek.

"Bitch," he said, slapping her face so hard, her head thudded against the wall. Dazed, she went limp.

Spinning her around, he shoved her face against the wall, pinning her hands behind her back. "Money laundering is the process of passing illegally obtained funds through legitimate enterprises in order to "clean" the money," he said, his voice raw with anger.

He jerked her around again, slamming her back against the wall, keeping one arm across her neck as he unzipped her pants with his other hand. "You can get up to ten years in prison for money laundering. They're going to love you in general population. Especially that hair."

Numb and disoriented, she fought for breath, struggling to focus.

"You know what happens when you go to prison, Katerina? First, they make you strip for a body cavity search," he said, yanking her pants down below her hips. "Then, some strange woman puts a glove on and searches you for contraband."

Shoving his hand down her panties, he inserted two fingers, rough and hard. Katerina cried out as he pushed his full body weight against her, thrusting his fingers in a deep rhythmic motion.

She stared past him, barely able to draw breath from the pressure on her neck and the stink of his sharp, pungent sweat in her nose. It was as if she had been sucked into a vacuum, without time, space, and sound except for Sheridan's heavy, labored breathing in her ear. His fingers kept moving inside her, probing her, hurting her. He gave a hard final thrust. Katerina cried out.

"Awww, you didn't come. Too bad." He withdrew his hand from her panties and released her. He sucked on his fingers and chuckled. "Mmm, you do taste good. I knew you would."

She stood frozen, unable to move.

Taking a handkerchief from his pocket, he wiped the side of his cheek, smiling at the red smear on the cloth. "You work for me now. You're my asset. Find your father. Or you *and* your mother are going to prison. If you think it's going be bad for you, just think of your mom. She's not built for that, Katerina. It could kill her."

Katerina stayed rooted to the spot, her body now shaking.

"When I contact you, you have answers for me. Understand?"

Katerina nodded.

He gave a playful tap to the tip of her nose. "Remember to lock up after I go. You can't be too careful these days. You know someone else has been in here, right? There are some bad people out there. You're lucky you have me to look after you." He left, closing the door behind him.

Katerina slid to the floor. She didn't know how long she sat there, numb. The sudden jangle of a cell phone startled her. Struggling to stand, she faltered, her legs unable to hold her. Sinking back down, she crawled to her purse, dumping the contents out onto the floor. The pepper spray fell out, rolling out of her grasp. The sight of it brought fresh tears to her eyes. The burner was quiet. The other phone kept ringing, Ryan's name on the caller ID.

Not now. Not now.

She clicked to connect.

"Hey good lookin'," came Ryan's voice, "what's cookin'? You ready?"

Sound normal. If he finds out, he will destroy everything. He will destroy me.

"Getting ready now," she said, forcing her voice to sound calm. *Please don't let your cop instinct kick in.* "Give me an hour and I'm all yours."

She heard his laugh from the other end of the phone. "I'll take that challenge," he said. "See you soon."

She clicked off and put the phone down. Staring at the pepper spray, she picked it up and threw it. It made a cracking sound as it hit the wall. She began to cry again.

***

She stood in a hot shower, scalding and scrubbing herself, trying to wash away the stink of Sheridan from her body and mind.

Sitting on the bed, wrapped in a towel, she tried over and over to control her breathing but every attempt ended in tears. She held out her hands, watching them shake. Her mind spiraled into a panic. *How will I hide this? I have to.*

***

Katerina, pulling on fresh jeans and sliding a heavy turtleneck sweater over her bruised neck, honed her story while she dressed. She packed only what Katerina, the college student, would need for a stay at her boyfriend's apartment. *This assignment is going to be the most dangerous of all.*

Chapter 46

I'm fine.
Remember. Nothing happened.
I got hit in the face with an ice ball at school.
He believed me.
Nothing happened.
Do not speak. If I speak, he will destroy everything.
He will destroy me.
Do. Not. Cry.

Kat's inner monologue raged as she stood behind Ryan, watching him turn the key in the lock of his apartment door. Every nerve in her body continued to scream in protest. A deep, aching pain inside her and the nausea in the pit of her stomach told her she would have to run for the bathroom the minute she entered the apartment; if she could hold out that long.

Please open the door.
Open the fucking door.

The deadbolt gave and Ryan stood aside with a flourish to allow her to enter the typical male setup: bulky furniture in shades of brown and black, coffee table, a dining table for four, small enough to avoid overpowering the compact space. A flat screen TV was bolted to the wall, situated for optimal viewing from the overstuffed couch.

I'm normal.
Nothing happened.
Act like it.

Turning to him, she smiled. "What's for dinner?"

He gave her a kiss.

Winter. Tears burned behind her eyes as she headed for the bathroom.

***

A discarded ice pack lay off to the side on the coffee table. In the center were two plates with crumpled napkins and silverware. One plate was wiped clean, the other dotted with the remains of ziti and meat sauce. Kat had forced herself to eat something, enough to convince him there was nothing wrong. The food had settled in her stomach like a rock and she wished she could find a neat and quiet way to throw up. She ducked into the bathroom, muzzling the urge to cry as she sat on the closed toilet seat, the painful, raw feeling inside her bringing tears to her eyes.

I can't hide in here.
He'll be knocking on the door.
He'll ask questions.
He'll want answers.

Her heart skipped a beat.

When she came out, Kat found two glasses of wine on the coffee table. Ryan lounged on the couch, an open textbook in his lap. Kat's focus shot to her backpack, the zipper undone, the mouth hanging open. A sudden rush of anger came over her, a high pitched scream in her head. *Who Are You To Go Through My Things?* Her purse, sitting on a chair, was closed.

Hold your tongue. You have to.

He flipped the pages of the textbook. "How are you doing with all this?"

She settled in next to him, forcing herself to act normally, even though the pain made her want to put her hand to her abdomen.

Don't cry.

"Good enough to pass, I hope," she said, forcing a light tone.

He nodded. Leaning forward, he took a glass of wine from the coffee table and handed it to her.

"You didn't like philosophy?" she asked.

"No. It's just a way to make excuses. All the bullshit about determinism and the 'I don't really have a choice' crap. Everybody has a choice between right and wrong. There's no in-between," he said.

"People don't fit into neat little boxes. There are circumstances. There are reasons why people do the things they do."

Ryan laughed. "Sure, criminals have reasons. They're breaking the law because they want something and they don't think they should have to work to get it. There's no such thing as a good criminal, Katerina."

Kat felt the sting of his comment. *I'm a criminal.* "I'm just saying life isn't black and white. There's a lot of gray."

"Not in my world. The guy who shot me wasn't operating in the gray."

They sat for a long moment; a standoff of silence. He gave her a sideways glance with a sly grin. "Wanna see my scar?"

"That all depends. I'm a nice girl. What do you have to take off to show it to me?"

That's right. Act normal. Like nothing happened.

He gave an evil laugh and leaned in, taking a kiss. Getting up, he pulled up the side of his sweater to reveal a raised, thin line running down his side.

Kat nodded. *You can't see my scars.*

Sitting back down, he opened his arms for her to lean into his embrace. She settled in, momentarily grateful for the sudden rush of his body heat.

"Man, you're cold all the time," he said. "That's not good, Kat. That's not healthy."

She ignored him. "What were you thinking, when it happened?"

He was silent for a minute. "Afterwards, I realized I wasn't thinking. So much of the job is instinct. You're dealing with an enemy that's unpredictable, violent, psychotic. That's a bad combination. You try to talk to them, but you don't know what you're going to get. You realize you're sweating, your heart's pounding. You know you could die. One mistake and it's over and not just for you. So you have to be ready to react in a second and hope to God you make the right decision. One wrong move and they're grabbing a hostage to execute."

Katerina hung on every word. "You weren't responsible for those hostages. You can only do the best you can."

Ryan gave a bitter laugh. "Yeah, you can say that. But it's bullshit. Those people are helpless, they can't defend themselves. Whatever move

I make, it's going to free them or take their life away. I'm responsible. That's the oath I took."

Katerina couldn't argue with that. *Wasn't I responsible for Felicia Reynolds? Aren't I responsible for John Reynolds, wherever he is?* "What was the one wrong move?"

"Me and Frank, we were getting the job done. They were going to let the hostages out and keep us. And then, all I said was, 'You're doing the smart thing.' And that was it. Something went off in the guy's head and he started shooting. Then Frank was shooting and I was shooting. The hostages were screaming, running for the doors. For a minute I didn't even realize I got shot. It's just a blur of pain and blood. And I knew it would be the one guy that would be the problem. My instincts are never wrong. Then I'm down but I'm covering a hostage. And I hear the guy coming. So I turn my head. I look at him. I know he's going to do it. He's lifting his gun to take aim. He's smiling, the bastard. He's fucking smiling. He's going to kill me, then he's going to do the hostage, and I can't do a fucking thing about it. Then a pop and he fell. Frank got him from behind. I still dream about it. That moment when everything stops, even the fear, and you can't believe it's happening to you."

Kat stared at him.

It doesn't matter that he might understand. Don't say a word. Don't tell him. Don't confess.

Don't cry.

Ryan leaned in for a deep kiss. His lips were warm; he tasted like red wine. She kissed him back, faking the enthusiasm. *Why wouldn't I want this honest, law abiding man? What's wrong with me? Am I my father's daughter?*

"I'm glad you're okay," she said, when they parted.

"Yeah, me too. But I'm worried about you." He shook his head. "You're always on the run, you're exhausted, and now getting hit in the face. It's a sign, babe. Trouble is finding you. You need to make some big changes after the semester is over, like getting out of this job, like moving in with me."

"Ryan, please—"

"You need a change. There's a bunch of crazy, out of control people out there."

"I know, I read the newspaper. I read about the murder. Another socialite. Did the two women know each other?"

Ryan reached for his glass and drained the wine with one swallow. He hesitated, then shook his head.

"Is it a serial killer, like the papers are saying?"

Ryan kissed her forehead. "Don't believe everything you read. But that doesn't mean you shouldn't be careful."

Katerina processed Ryan's words. "Why do you think it's not a serial killer?"

"Instinct," he said.

"And you're never wrong," she said, more to herself.

He took a look at the clock and frowned. Picking up the textbook, he held it out to her. "As much as it hurts me to admit this, you need to study, even though I can think of much better things for us to do."

Kat took the book from him. *He still has no idea who did it. He doesn't know about the man in the blue Ford.*

Hours later, Katerina lay on the couch, the book open across her stomach. She felt the book being lifted away and a heavy blanket draped over her. *Winter.* From somewhere in her haze she remembered where she was. *Not Winter. Ryan.* She shifted, the deep pain inside stabbing at her, a dead weight of fear pressing on her heart and mind.

Being with Winter will have to wait.

Chapter 47

When Ryan eased the car over to the curb, Katerina pulled her backpack from the floor. He leaned over and kissed her. Hearing his breath near her ear, Katerina jolted in panic, willing herself to hold her tears in check. When they parted, he swept her hair away from her face.

"You could use more ice on that cheek, babe."

"I'm fine."

He frowned.

"I'll get some, I promise."

"Do I pick you up here or are you going into the office?"

Office. Right. I'm supposed to have a normal, legal job. One that requires an office.

"I've got study sessions on campus for the next two days. It would be easier if we caught up tomorrow night."

"Okay," he said, his tight frown broadcasting his displeasure. "You on campus all day?"

"Yes," she said, suppressing her annoyance, making a mental note that she would have to remember this as well.

"Call me later when you're taking a break."

She gave him a nod and a quick kiss and got out, slamming the door shut. Waving goodbye, she watched the car blend into traffic. When it turned the corner, she pulled out the burner and tapped off a text.

Bob, I need you

She hit send and kept the phone clutched in her hand. Seconds later, the phone began to vibrate.

Where are you?

She typed.

School

She waited.

Northeast corner, University/Waverly Place.

Katerina dropped the burner in her purse and started walking.

***

The pub was a dimly lit, oblong space outfitted with a bar and booths with dark, leather seats. Winter sat beside her; she pressed against him. The car ride had been quick and silent. Now, he examined the tears staining her face, caressing her swollen cheek with a feather touch.

"Tell me," he said, his voice tight.

"Sheridan came back," she said. "Last night . . . he . . ." she couldn't finish.

His benign expression morphed into one of cold, fierce anger, even as he tenderly stroked her hair. "Do you need Doc?"

"I'll be okay," she said.

"That wasn't the question."

"No," she said, her voice cracking.

Putting an arm around her, he drew her close.

"When the DEA uses a person as a confidential informant—"

Winter moved to quiet her but she shook her head in defiance.

"—or a cooperating witness, what does that mean?"

"It means you function to feed him information to help him make his case."

"And after?"

"After, you get a reduced sentence. Maybe. I don't think you need to worry about that."

"Why?"

"Because the DEA isn't looking for your father. They have an active operation in Vermont for the toy factory. In the past few years, they've run several sting operations on the trucks transporting the toys. There's only one problem."

"They never find anything?"

Winter caressed her cheek. "That's right. Every time they raid a truck, the toys are clean. No drugs."

Katerina nodded. "So why is Sheridan running his own operation here?"

"Sheridan isn't running anything. He's not on active duty. He got shot a couple of months ago. Side wound, no major organ damage. The bullet went through muscle. A relatively short recovery time."

Katerina took the news in silence until she asked, "Who did it?"

"He says he doesn't know. It was dark out. He didn't see who it was."

Katerina met Winter's eye. She knew they were both thinking the exact same thing. *Bullshit.*

The server appeared. Katerina could feel the woman's curious glance and gave a hurried swipe across her cheeks, whisking any tears away. The server set out two coffees and a plate of bread pudding and disappeared. Winter took a forkful of the pudding, drizzled in a caramel sauce, and handed it to Kat. She tasted it, finding the sugared confection sweet and comforting.

"Katie, what exactly does Sheridan want from you?"

She swallowed. "He wants me to find my father. How should I know where he is? I don't even know why he bothered to visit me."

"Maybe he left something behind in the apartment. Maybe that's why you've been having visitors."

Kat shook her head. "I was with him the whole time. He didn't even use the bathroom." She stopped, pulling in a convulsive breath heavy with tears. "I can't get my job done if Sheridan's following me . . ."

Winter hovered over her, rubbing her back. "Katie, the only way to know who's following you is if I follow you."

"But you're busy."

"I'm off the clock now," he soothed.

The immediate thought that he would be there, watching over her, lifted her spirits at once.

"Do you want me to take care of everything?" he asked.

"Yes," she said without hesitation.

Reaching into his jacket, Winter pulled out a cell phone and held it out to her. "Tracking software is installed."

She nodded as she took the "Winter" phone. Her breath caught in her throat and she coughed as a stab of panic gripped her. *If he follows me, he'll know everywhere I go. Everywhere.*

"When you're following me, you might see me spend time with—"

"The boyfriend who's not your boyfriend," he said. "Any time you don't want to be found, turn off the phone."

She clamped her eyes shut as the words tumbled out. "It's not what it looks like—because—I'm not—we aren't—nothing is happening—-nothing is happening."

Oh God, Katerina, shut up. Shut. Up.

"Never mind," she said. "If I wanted to show that I worked for a company, how could I do that?"

"Is this a real company?"

"No," she said.

"So you want to create a dummy corporation with a paper trail. You'll need business cards, stationary, and a working telephone for an answering machine or a live person to answer."

"How do I do that?"

"You don't. You have someone do it for you. I'll help you. Katie, you can't keep this up, whatever this is, indefinitely."

"You live under false pretenses."

"Yes, but that's all I do. The lie is who I am. You can't live two lives. One will destroy the other. Do you understand?"

As he drew her close, she shifted and flinched, a cry of pain escaping her lips. He examined her features with fresh concern. With a light touch, he shifted the fabric away from her neck, baring the bruised skin. His eyes darkened in fresh anger. "Tell me what happened."

She closed her eyes, whispering in his ear as her tears fell. His arms tightened around her and she buried her face in his neck, desperate to replace the memory of Sheridan's stale sweat with Winter's warm, pleasing scent. A sudden surge of frustrated rage rose within her; her hands balled into tight fists as she cried in silence, her mouth and eyes clamped closed. Winter's embrace tightened, his lips pressing against her temple. Suddenly, all her muscles relaxed, the rush of relief mixing with the pain as she melted into his embrace.

After a long while, they shifted apart. He dried her eyes and face with a studied, gentle touch. Then he got up to allow her to slip out of the booth.

"I'm right behind you," he whispered.

***

Alexander Winter kept Katerina Mills in his sights as she moved to the corner and raised her hand to signal a taxi. His mind shifted like a pendulum between guilt and rage. *I wasn't there.* He wanted to take care of James Sheridan immediately but the cost of vengeance in the heat of moment would prove too great. Such a move would put Katerina at risk; and that was out of the question.

Now in his car, Winter observed her getting into the cab. As it pulled into the flow of traffic, he eased his car out to follow.

As he kept the taxi in his sights, he took a silent oath. *No matter how long it takes, James Sheridan is going to pay for what he did.*

Chapter 48

Ryan and Lashiver walked toward the Theater for a New Audience. "What's the story here?" Lashiver asked.

"Felicia Reynolds made out a check to this theater. I missed it."

"How big was the check?"

Ryan pulled open the front door for Lashiver to walk inside. "Big enough to deserve an interview."

Lashiver nodded.

***

"I met Mrs. Reynolds, of course," said Madeline Wilcox, the theater's manager. A stylish woman in her early fifties, she dressed considerably younger than her age.

Ryan scribbled in his pad.

Lashiver stood off to the side, his coat slung over his arm. "Did she spend a lot of time here?"

"No, no," she said. "She really had no interest in the arts. She had been a chorus girl, I think. This was just something for the society résumé. You know, the trophy wife of a rich man seen doing things that are culturally enriching for the community, that kind of thing."

Ryan nodded his head as he kept writing. "When was the last time she was here?"

"Last summer, for an exhibition; not the usual event our patrons attend. Most of them prefer the annual gala."

"Can you think of anything else about Mrs. Reynolds," Lashiver asked, "like, perhaps, did she ever borrow the costumes and take them home for a few days?"

Madeline Wilcox's face twisted into a quizzical expression. "No, of course not. What would she do with a sixteenth century frock?"

"Was Cheryl Penn a patron of this theater?"

"The other woman who was killed? No, she wasn't. You think the two women are connected?"

"Just routine questions," Ryan said, closing his notebook.

"Thank you for your time," Lashiver said as he pulled on his coat.

"Not at all. You caught me a bit off-guard. I thought you were here to question me about Will Temple."

The detectives stopped in their tracks.

"Will Temple?" Lashiver asked.

"One of our actors. He was in our current production but suddenly he disappeared. Someone from one of the precincts called saying they needed to come and ask questions. I thought that was why you were here."

Ryan and Lashiver exchanged a look.

"Do you know if Mrs. Reynolds provided any extra help, sponsorship, to any of the actors?" Ryan asked. "Such as Mr. Temple?"

"I have no idea. Will did quite well in the supporting roles. He had aspirations of playing the lead in *Macbeth* or *Hamlet*." She shook her head. "Every actor longs to be the next Olivier or Branagh, holding up the skull and moaning about "Poor Yorick," if you know what I mean."

The detectives nodded as if they understood.

"Of course, in the end he wanted the quick buck."

"Quick buck?"

"The last I heard, he got a call from a local production company on the East Side, in the teens somewhere. Something about a part in a movie. For all I know he's up in the wilds of Canada, filming."

"Did he mention the name of the film company?" Lashiver asked.

"I think it was something Girl Films. Like I said, it was downtown, around Fourth or Fifth Avenue, maybe."

Ryan flipped open his pad and scribbled the information.

"Would you happen to have any pictures of Will Temple?" Lashiver asked.

"Yes, of course." Madeline Wilcox went to her computer and clicked the mouse several times. "Here we go. This was the exhibition."

Ryan and Lashiver came up behind her as the photo loaded on the flat screen monitor. She pointed a finger at a handsome, young man.

"That's Will," she said.

Ryan held out his hand and pointed to another person in the crowded picture, a petite, pretty young woman smiling for the camera. "And that's Felicia Reynolds," he said.

Lashiver took a card from his pocket and held it out to Madeline. "If you think of anything else, please give us a call. Remember to give all these details about Will Temple to the investigating detective."

"Of course," she said. "Oh, I remember now. The film company. Random Girl . . . Random Girl Films."

***

As they pushed open the front door, the cold curled around the two men.

"I want to talk to the detective assigned to the Will Temple case," Ryan said.

Lashiver nodded. "I think you should. But this doesn't mean that we don't have a serial killer."

"But what's the connection? There's nothing linking Cheryl Penn and Felicia Reynolds. They didn't even know each other. And Cheryl Penn came from money, she didn't kick in the line and marry into it."

"They both had money when they were killed," Lashiver said. "That's enough of a connection. Besides, maybe if we dig into Temple, we'll find the boy toy had two patrons. Maybe we got a nasty little trio here that went wrong."

Ryan stopped at the driver's side door, looking over the top of the car at his mentor. "Or maybe this guy was involved with just Felicia Reynolds, killed her, killed himself, and the second killing is a copycat."

"Maybe this guy wasn't involved with Felicia Reynolds, she was killed randomly, and the second killing is a copycat."

"Maybe Felicia Reynolds was involved with Will Temple and her husband found out and killed her while Will Temple went off to make a movie," Ryan said.

Lashiver shrugged. "The husband's alibi is airtight. Maybe Will Temple is the serial killer of both women and Random Girl Films is his sick little clue of a calling card."

"It's not a serial killer," Ryan said.

"We keep interviewing. We have no idea what this is," Lashiver said. Lowering his head, he ducked into the car.

Chapter 49

Katerina returned to her building after dark. She stood outside the apartment door, feeling as if she were outside herself, watching herself in a flashback, watching herself turn the key in the lock, ignorant of what was about to happen next. A tremor, deep inside, shook her. *Winter is close. He won't let anything happen.* Letting herself in, she flipped the light switch. The discarded clothes left strewn around the apartment had disappeared. Her schoolbooks sat stacked neatly on the kitchen table. Colorful Christmas decorations along with a touch of garland and nutcracker figurines lightened the drab apartment. In the corner of the postage stamp living room sat a tree trimmed with sparkling bows, wrapped presents dotting its base. A new, plush recliner and a daybed covered with a bright quilted comforter filled the space.

Moving into the kitchen, she opened the refrigerator to find fully stocked shelves and a packed freezer. Listening for scratching sounds, she was greeted with silence. She gave a sigh.

Entering the bedroom, she found a new pale blue down comforter on the bed. Opening the closet, she discovered her clothing hanging neatly, items grouped together, organized. She grinned as she fingered the note on the nightstand.

> Locksmith coming tomorrow morning.
> Call me anytime.
> Please eat something.
> You know what to do with this. Bob

Flicking the lighter on, she watched the paper burn. *Safe. For now.*

***

Except for the "Winter" burner, Katerina turned off her phones and dropped out, venturing from the apartment only to complete Marcus' lunch drops. He took in the bruise on her cheek with a look of mild curiosity. He made no comment, settling for a cockeyed smile.

Enjoying thoughts of my misfortune. Prick.

After slapping the bag on the island counter, she would go home, anxious for a hot bath and then curling up under the comforter to sleep. Her physical pain had stopped after several days, leaving other scars in its wake. Nightmares woke her, damp with sweat, from a dead sleep. Even during the day, thoughts of Sheridan drifted into her mind without warning and she would dissolve into tears.

Still, his words rang in her head. *Whether you know it or not, your father said something during his visit, something very important.* Katerina had gone over the visit a thousand times. Only one thing stood out. *Listen to me Katerina. This is important. You play the hand you've been dealt, bet and bluff to make the best deal possible, and then cash out when it's time to go. Remember that.*

What if I wanted out? Could it work?

Kat found her thoughts meandering, wondering about Lisa. Had she been through anything like this? Had she ever considered cashing out? *I could ask her. If I could find her.*

Her nights all ended in the same way, in exhaustion, falling back to sleep in search of escape. Except for the nights when she had to force herself from her comfortable refuge and join Ryan after his shift. They would grab dinner and camp out at his place, watching a little TV before she studied. Ryan talked; all the little things couples talk about: tickets to a Rangers game, going to Long Island for Christmas to meet his family. She zoned out, except for the occasional nod and cursory comment. One morning, Ryan let her out by the Washington Square Arch. She gave him a kiss and went to open the door.

"See you tonight?" he asked.

"I should stay in the city, close to the school."

He nodded. "I've really enjoyed the last few days. I think we're in a good place."

She smiled. "Me too."

As he pulled the car away, Kat waved goodbye. Somewhere Winter was watching. She thought to send a text, telling him to get ready. She couldn't put it off any longer. She had to return to her life.

Chapter 50

A light snow began to fall as Katerina left her apartment building. Hailing a cab at the corner, she gave the driver an address. The "Winter" phone buzzed.

"You've got company," he said.

"How many?"

"At least one. This is what I want you to do."

Katerina gave the driver the change of address. At the stop, she told him to wait, dashed out of the cab and into the jewelry store, the life-sized diamond adorning the building looming overhead. She collected the small package waiting for her and headed out, ducking back into the cab. The "Winter" phone buzzed.

"Where to?" she asked.

He told her.

Next, Katerina visited a tiny art deco perfume boutique. The woman smiled at her, handing her another small package. Kat thanked her, left, and a hailed another cab.

"What's next?" she asked when Winter called.

"This is what I want you to do."

Ten minutes later, Katerina got out of the cab, the burner phone at her ear.

"The black Infiniti on the corner," he said. "That's your car."

***

Katerina belted herself in, the "Winter" burner resting on the passenger seat, the speaker on. "Do I still have company?"

"Yes," he said, his voice calm and steady.

"What now, Professor? Should I drive to the corner? I can jump the light and make a left."

"Do *not* shoot the gap."

"You're afraid I'll get a ticket?"

"I'm afraid you'll get into an accident. Go up to the light. Make a left, when it's time. Go around three times. Keep checking your rearview. I'll call back in ten minutes."

***

Ten minutes later, Winter was back on the line. "Did you spot them?"

"Yes. The one car is Huey and Dewey. The second car is—him."

"I've seen the dynamic duo for the last few days."

"I've got stops to make."

"You'll make them. Head downtown."

Without question, Katerina followed his instructions.

***

She was near Chatham Square. Katerina parked the car and wiped her damp hands on her coat. She spotted a pair of police officers standing on a corner.

A tan car drove past her.

"You lost the duo," Winter said. "But not the other one."

Kat checked the rearview mirror. She could see Sheridan, parked four cars back.

"He's not going to leave," she said.

"Get out of the car," Winter said, his voice stern and tight.

"What?"

"Go over to the cops."

Kat stared at the uniformed officers. "No."

"Look in the glove compartment," Winter said.

Katerina flipped open the compartment lid and brought out business cards for Gal Friday, Inc., the fake company for her fake job.

"Take a business card and the packages. Get out of the car. Go to the officers and tell them you're on an assignment. You noticed you've been followed ever since you were at the jewelry store and point to Sheridan's car."

Katerina shook her head. "I can't. What if they question me?"

"There are receipts in those bags. If they call the number on the card, they'll get a recording."

Kat checked the rearview mirror again. Sheridan had opened his driver's side door.

"He's coming over here," she said, her voice shaking. Paralyzed, all thought fled as the panic rushed in, flooding her body. She couldn't move.

"Do you trust me?"

"I can't do this. Please. Bob, I can't."

She spotted Sheridan in the side mirror, walking toward the Infiniti, a wide smile on his face.

"Katie, *Trust me*. Lean on the horn," Winter yelled. "Do it! Now!"

Katerina pressed on the car horn, letting it blare until the officers zeroed in on her. She watched them approach. In the side mirror, she caught Sheridan beating a retreat to his car.

Katerina rolled the down the window as the officers approached. She recited the story just as Winter told her to. Sheridan drove past, disappearing around a corner. The officers, easy and open, chatted with her for a few minutes. She thanked them and they left her.

"Are you still there?" she said.

"Yes, I'm here," Winter's voice came through the phone. "This is where I want you to go."

***

Katerina parked the car and cut the engine.

"Now," Winter said, his voice softer now. "Tell me what you learned."

Keep up with him. "He doesn't want me talking to the police."

"True, but more important, *he* doesn't want to talk to the police. Why?"

Kat tried to clear her head and follow Winter's line of thinking. He was right, of course. Why wouldn't Sheridan just flash a badge?

"Wait a minute," she said. "You've been following me for days. Wasn't he following me all this time?"

"Smart. Good. Work it through, Katerina. It is what it is. Find the truth. We know there's no active investigation here. We know Sheridan's not in charge. We know he got shot but he conveniently doesn't know who did it. We know he's not following you all the time and he wants *you* to find your father. Tell me why."

"Because . . . no one is supposed to know he's here."

"Good. Why?"

"Because . . ." her mind was moving faster now, putting it all together, "he's not supposed to be here."

"Good. Why isn't he supposed to be here?"

"Because . . . no one's looking for my father, some guy who ran off and left his wife." *Except Sheridan. Ten million dollars.* "Because he's a dirty agent."

"You get an A," Winter said. "My thought is, he was your father's business partner, whether your father wanted a partner or not. And something went very wrong."

That's a polite way of saying my father shot him.

They sat in a shared moment of silence, until she said, "Thanks for teaching me to spot a tail. Does it always work?"

"No. Sometimes they have a Plan B. You have to be able to spot that too."

She checked her mirrors. "How come I can't spot you?"

"Because I'm exceptionally good at what I do."

Yes, you are. "What about these packages?"

"Open them."

Katerina flipped open the jewelry box first, revealing a delicate necklace dotted with diamond teardrops; she sucked in a breath of appreciation. Next, she pulled out the oval perfume bottle and sniffed the warm, vanilla scent.

"Do you like them?" he asked.

"Very much. Do I return them now?"

"No, Katie. You enjoy them," he said.

"Thank you," she said, her joy suddenly marred by a stab of frustration. *You'll give me presents but go no further. Why?*

"You're welcome. Look across the street."

Katerina spotted an idling limousine. The driver's side door opened and Luther got out.

"Leave the car. You're free and clear," Winter said. "Enjoy the ride."
Before she could say anything, the line went dead.

Chapter 51

"*M*ierda, mami, this is a special, *special* order," Moose said, watching the video of Simon Marcus' car on Katerina's burner. "Aww ... mierda!" Throwing up his arms in frustration, he looked at Katerina. "He scratched the car. What's wrong with him? That's a deep scratch, man. That shit's not easy to fix."

They were standing in a garage near the West Side Highway. A brisk business was going on, a parade of men bypassing the garage for the stairs leading to the second floor. Kat heard footsteps overhead, women's laughter, and the faint noise of music. A girl's gotta get by, she thought.

"Moose, I need another one of this car. It's critical."

"I got sympathy, mami, I do, but I'd have to send out for this job, entiendes? You know like when you want to buy a new car and you send your specs to the dealer, like I want standard shift, not automatic, right, and the dealership, they want to make the sale, you know, but they don't have that car, so they have to contact another dealership and see if they have it and then they have to get it shipped over and the customer, he don't know—"

"Moose, I get it." She did understand. She understood there was no way Moose could get this car. She knew it from the beginning. She had set this up. She would make her play and hope it worked.

"Look . . . I'm sorry about the wedding."

"Yo, yo, yo, yo, yo. What's with the wedding?"

"I won't be able to make it."

"Yo! Woman! That is cold. I thought you was a person of your word. That shit's important to me."

"*Papi*, two people want this car. I have only one. Whoever doesn't get this car is going to kill me or get me killed. I have to get out of town."

Moose stared at the ground, rubbing his chin in thought. "I see you have one of them . . . cómo se dice . . . ?"

"No-win situations."

"Yeah, yeah, the no-win situation." He gave her a long look. "The Moose can be very sensitive to the no-win situation."

"I don't want to welch on our deal," she said. "I do have one other idea."

"Tell me, mami. What can the Moose do for you?"

"If another car can't be—acquired," she said. "Can it be duplicated?"

Moose broke out into a slow smile. "You wear one of them spaghetti strap slinky numbers."

"Yes."

"And you leave the hair down."

"I told you I would."

Moose nodded his head. "Okay, mami, only for you, I build a car."

"Don't forget the scratch."

With a wink of his eye, Moose wagged a finger at her. "Eres muy inteligente."

Katerina caught Luther's smirk as she settled into the front passenger seat. Somehow his approval didn't make her feel any better about herself. She had used her free will to make a decision. Desucci wanted the car as a matter of principle, just to deprive Marcus of his prized possession. She was going to give a member of the Mob a replica car; if he found out, she didn't see any way that it wouldn't get her killed.

Chapter 52

Katerina got out of the limo near the building. While Luther went to circle the block, she clutched Simon Marcus' bagged lunch with one hand as she dug into her purse with the other for the buzzing cell phone. *I'd like to dump this crap in the garbage,* she thought. She pulled out the "Ryan" phone. Nothing. With a curse, she dropped it back in and rooted around, pulling out the burner, her eyes stinging from the frigid wind.

"Yes," she snapped.

"Our mutual friend is very concerned. You don't follow instructions," Vincent said.

"I'm working on it—I'm working on it."

"That's not what he's talking about. You've been spending a lot of time with or near law enforcement. He says that's not productive to our working together. This is very disturbing to our mutual friend."

"Well, if our mutual friend doesn't want any problems, tell him to give me my space and be a little nicer to me, since I'm doing him a favor," she said and disconnected. *Stupid, Katerina. Really stupid. Desucci doesn't need a buffer that badly. When is your mind going to catch up to your mouth?*

***

Simon Marcus paced with the phone, shouting at ear-splitting decibels about his missing fortune cookie. Katerina imagined Luke standing in the restaurant, holding the phone at arm's length. As his complexion grew increasingly florid, Marcus stopped to take a breath. Whatever Luke was saying, it wasn't right; Marcus exploded into yet another bout of cursing and swearing. *Jackass.*

Katerina left him to hide out in the painting room, examining each of the fake Monet *Bridge over a Pond of Water Lilies*: purple, yellow, green, and red. She picked up the copy of *Architectural Times* and opened to the article on the Marcus apartment. She attempted to read a few more sentences but against the background of Marcus' bellowing, she finally gave up.

I have to finish this job and get rid of this moron. She had seen men who didn't just talk and bluster. Winter. Moose. Sheridan's face flashed into her mind, making tears spring to her eyes. She had seen a killer face to face. Simon Marcus wasn't like any of them.

Katerina heard heavy footsteps coming in her direction.

"I don't see my car here, doll face," he said. "Do you see my car here?"

"I still have time," she said.

Marcus laughed, shaking his head. He withdrew a slim, rubber banded wad of cash and tossed it at her. Kat caught it just as the bills brushed against her face.

"Lunch deliveries will be daily from now on," he said. "We'll talk about my car, every day, until the deadline comes. Then you won't have to worry about my lunch, or anyone else's lunch, ever again."

Katerina walked out of the apartment.

Chapter 53

Luther protested but Katerina insisted he go off the clock for the rest of the day. She got off the subway, absently thinking she was adopting Winter's expressions. Heading into Madison Square Park, she spotted Angel coming from the opposite direction. She readied for the embrace and hand off. But there was something else she needed to do.

Sliding into Angel's clinch, he picked the packet clean out of her open purse. As he moved to leave, she held fast. He stopped.

"I need to find Lisa," she whispered.

"Not the social secretary, baby," he said.

"But you know where she is," Kat pressed.

"You want to find her, you can. That's how you become her," he said, and his lips brushed against her cheek as he left her.

***

Katerina walked on, her breathing heavy, her mind spinning. That's how she pictured herself now, always running, always out of breath, always something bearing down on her from behind. In her dreams, she was fleeing from someone behind her. Every time she turned to look back, there he was, nameless, faceless, always the same distance behind. She couldn't outrun him; she couldn't get away.

Katerina ducked into a fast food joint for comfort food and coffee. She took her tray and slid into a booth. *Focus. You have to find Lisa. What would Winter do? He would keep it simple. He would find the truth.*

I get a call from Joe Lessing. He needs help. I go. What did he say? Be exact. He said, "I called someone. She said she would try to get here but I can't wait anymore." I helped. I meet Lisa coming in as I'm going out. That's it.

Katerina twisted and turned the coffee cup between her hands.

No... that's not it, she thought. Joe Lessing said, "I called someone. She said she would try to get here." *She* said *she* would try. Katerina closed her eyes. It was right there all the time, I just didn't see it. Joe Lessing didn't call a service. He didn't call Jasmine. He called Lisa. Direct.

Keep it simple.

Pulling out her normal "Ryan" phone, Kat searched, pressing buttons until she hit the green button. "Mr. Lessing, it's Katerina," she said. "I need to see you."

She hung up the phone. *God I hope I'm right.*

Chapter 54

Entering the hotel, Katerina passed one of the glass-paneled columns to check her look, admiring the simple backless, black bondage dress highlighting her every curve. Something Lisa would choose. *Imitation is the sincerest form of flattery. Lisa should be very pleased.*

She found the darkened hotel bar sparsely populated. There were a few banking wizards, young turks who had chucked the revolution for tailored suits and Rolex watches. A suit at the end of the bar, thin with an angular face, slicked back hair and a shit-eating grin, tried to make time with a long and lithe blonde. The blonde wore a wraparound red sheath dress above a pair of tawny, impossibly gorgeous legs. Lisa. The suit leaned in, invested.

Lisa made no move, not a nod, not a facial tic, not even a raised eyebrow to indicate she had seen Katerina.

Kat lingered; then left. Taking a seat in one of the rich, elegant chairs in a discreet corner of the lobby, she waited

"I'm impressed," Lisa said, throwing her purse onto a chair and sitting down.

"You're not going to ask me how I found you, are you."

"Of course not," Lisa said. "It'll be more fun to figure it out on my own. Since I don't need help, I assume you're here because you do. I'm already disappointed."

"Don't be. You don't have the time for it. You're going to be busy arranging a contact for surveillance on Long Island. One week, maybe more."

"Camping out in a freezing car does sound tempting," Lisa said drily. "What does he get out of it?"

"Whatever it is, you'll need to provide it to him."

Lisa answered with a laugh.

"That's not all. You'll be a point of contact for a dummy corporation. Someone calls, you answer the phone. You're running a personal administrative assistant service."

"Keep the lie close to the truth. Clever." Lisa leaned forward. "Now, why would I do any of this?"

"Because Joe Lessing called you, personally, the night we met. Because you told him you would try to get there. Because Jasmine had no idea where you were that night and she has no idea where you are tonight. Because you're not working for MJM right now . . . and that's against the rules."

Lisa sat back in her chair. "My, my," she said at last, "how the world does turn."

"I don't give a damn about what you're doing," Kat said.

Lisa shook her head. "No, no, princess, you want to do this, you go all in. Don't apologize for playing the high hand. Don't disappoint me that way." She regarded Kat with new interest. "Fine. Deal."

They rose from their seats, turning to the bar. Another suit had joined Lisa's mark. Katerina stared at the unfolding scene. *Shit.*

"I'm not into threesomes," Lisa said, slipping her hand into her purse. "I don't finish this, you don't get your Christmas presents. That means you keep Tweedledum busy so I can get my work done."

Leaning over to give Katerina a kiss on the cheek, Lisa slipped something small and round into Kat's hand.

Kat closed her hand around the vial.

"Lucky for you, Eliza, I'm feeling a little Henry Higgins tonight," Lisa said. "A touch of kitty flipping should keep him busy."

Katerina didn't answer.

"Ketamine and Ecstasy combo," Lisa said. "Don't give him too much. You don't want him to drop dead."

Katerina stood immobile, her brain in full flight mode.

"If you're not up to this," Lisa said, "walk away and we're done."

"I've got it covered," Kat said.

Lisa left for the bar.

Is that the mistake the other fixer made? Walking into a hotel room with a stranger?

The buzzing of the cell phone broke her thoughts. Winter's phone. She clicked to answer.

"Anytime you want to tell me," Winter said.

Without hesitation, she gave him the Cliffs Notes version; a beat of silence on the other end. But when she entered the bar five minutes later, she had a plan and a partner.

***

He was taller than Lisa's mark, with textured hair, and a wolfish smile. Perching on a stool at the end of the bar, Katerina gave him time to check her out. She waited for the familiar warmth that indicated a body had come up next to her.

"How can someone so beautiful be sitting alone? Whoever he is, he should be ashamed of himself."

Out of the corner of her eye, Kat caught Lisa and her mark slipping out of the bar. She gave her own mark a smile. His smirk made her stomach turn. *At least I don't have to do this alone.*

"His loss, someone else's gain," Kat said with her sweetest smile.

***

The mark pawed over Kat as they stumbled into the hotel room, planting wet, sloppy kisses on her neck, moving down her chest. She clamped her eyes shut, clenching her jaw, assaulted by flashbacks of Sheridan.

"You are gorgeous," he whispered, his whiskey breath overpowering her as his hands slid down, grabbing her backside. "How much?"

Kat froze. *Prostitution. Terrific.*

"What do you want?" Kat whispered.

Laughing, he lunged in for a kiss.

She dodged her head to the side. "Sorry, that's never on the menu."

"Let's start with half and half and finish with around the world," he slurred.

Kat gave her sweetest smile. "Five hundred," she said, thinking his fumbling for cash would waste more time.

He broke out in a laugh and stumbled to the bed. Pulling out his wallet, he counted out a pile of bills as a knock broke the silence.

Kat opened the door. Winter, dressed in a uniform, pushed a cart with a champagne bottle tucked into an ice bucket and two glasses into the room.

The mark gave a laugh. "Fuck, yeah! Let's do it. Bring on the bubbly!"

Winter popped the bottle's cork while Katerina stood in front of the mark, blocking his view. As Winter picked up a glass, she noticed his hands. *White glove service. No prints.*

"Something for your trouble," she said, getting her clutch purse and pulling out a bill. She handed the bill to Winter and put the open purse down on the cart, the top of the vial peeking out.

He fixed the other glass, his hands slipping in and out of her purse. When he handed her the glass, she saw his eyes, dark with disapproval and concern.

"That will be all," she said.

Winter hesitated, a pregnant pause between them, his eyes boring into hers like a laser.

"Thank you," she said. "That's all."

With a last look, he left.

"Give me your bag," the mark said.

With the glass from the cart in one hand, her purse in the other, she approached him.

He stuffed the money into the clutch bag and then flung it on the low dresser.

"Drink this," she said, holding out the glass. "You'll like it."

He yanked her down on his lap, burying his face in her chest, his hands everywhere. He knocked the glass out of her hand, sending it sailing to the floor.

Shit!

Pulling her down on the bed, he rolled his weight on top of her. He slobbered on her neck, a stink of sweat and booze permeating her nostrils. As his hands forced their way under the fabric of her dress, panic cascaded over her like a waterfall.

No. No. Not again.

"When we're done, we'll find my friend," he whispered. "You girls can have fun while we watch. Or is that extra?"

As he pressed his crotch against her, an adrenalin rush of fear cut through her. *He's hard. He won't take no for an answer.* He clawed at the fabric of her dress, yanking the straps off her shoulders. She searched the room. *For what?* Then she spotted her open purse, the tip of the vial peeking out. *He left it. Thank God.*

"You could have an extra special time," she purred, "if you drink the magic potion."

He stopped.

"I have some candy," she said. She pushed him off, backing up so he could keep his eyes on the soft, round flesh of her breasts bursting over the fabric of her dress. Gaping at her, he watched as she slowly peeled off the dress, revealing a black lace strapless adhesive bra with matching panty and garter. He let out a long breath.

Taking the other glass, she tapped in a dash of powder. Bringing it to him, she knelt down on her knees, wedging herself between his legs. "Now be a good boy and drink up."

She held the glass up to him like an offering. He downed the liquid in one swallow. Dropping the glass, he placed his hands on her head.

"Do me," he said, his voice thick.

She took her time opening the buttons of his shirt, making a slow trail of kisses from his chest to his stomach. She slid the zipper on his pants down.

"Why don't you lie back," she whispered.

He answered by grabbing her shoulder with one hand and her head with the other. "Do me," he said. "I wanna watch."

Shit! Why isn't this stuff working? Where is Winter?

Pulling down his shorts, she took him in one hand, working him with long, slow strokes.

He shook he head. "Nooo, not that way . . . this way . . ."

His hand pressed against her head. She clamped her lips closed, resisting. Suddenly, he let go. She straightened to find him weaving from side to side, his eyes half-open. She gave him a shove; he fell back onto the bed.

Jumping up, she grabbed her dress as the door clicked open. She turned as Winter entered. He took in her bra and panties with a raised eyebrow.

"Nothing happened," she said, feeling her face coloring as she pulled on her dress.

"Don't tell me," he said.

***

They worked in silent tandem, wiping down surfaces, cleaning the glasses. Katerina returned the money to the nightstand. She waited, watching as Winter performed a methodical check, once, then twice, making sure nothing had been missed. For once, she appreciated a little OCD. It could save your life.

Satisfied, Winter took her hand and led her out.

Chapter 55

Kat and Winter sat side by side in a booth in the back of the diner, sharing a large slice of black forest cake.

Katerina devoured her side, while Winter worked through his with methodical precision.

"You didn't give me the whole story," he said.

"There wasn't time." Feeling his eyes fixed on her, she concentrated on the cake. "This sort of thing doesn't fit your 'under the radar' profile."

"You'd be surprised," he said. "I could've made arrangements for you."

She looked up, her eyes betraying her anxiety. "I don't want you to get caught."

"No one's caught me yet," he said. "How do you know your friend will keep her end of the deal?"

"She's not my friend and she doesn't have a choice."

The fork stopped halfway to his mouth. "Blackmail?"

"I presented a compelling incentive," Kat said.

He considered her, the cool blue eyes widening as if discovering a new side of her. "Very good," he said.

Katerina suppressed a smile of secret pleasure at his approval. "You know you're not all that mysterious," she said, wanting to change the subject. "I know something about you."

"Like what?"

She met his gaze. "Like, you have a sweet tooth."

"Sherlock," he said with an indulgent chuckle.

"Tonight reminded me of our field trip to the Hamptons," she said. "We work well together."

"Butch and Sundance, together again."

She stared at her empty side of the plate, searching for what she wanted to say. Too many thoughts were fighting for supremacy. "If

I—wasn't in New York," she began, "would that make a difference with Sheridan? I mean, what could he do?"

Winter sat back, lining up his fork next to the plate. "Where would you be?"

Kat shrugged. "I don't know. Home. Maybe. What could he do?"

Winter considered the question. "He's limited. He could shift the investigation to you, but that's dangerous for him."

"He could shift the investigation to me and my mother, to try to draw my father out."

"Katie, your father has made it clear he's not moved by you or your mother's needs. It could end in a stalemate. Nothing will happen. Remember, there are always unknown factors. You're taking your best guess. That's all you can do. It's your decision."

Go big or go home, baby.

"You should see the apartment," she said. "It's still neat."

Winter didn't answer.

"I guess that would be complicated," she said.

Slipping his arm around her, he pulled her close. She melted into his embrace. After a few moments, he kissed her forehead. "Let's get you home, Sundance," he said.

Katerina pursed her lips and swallowed her disappointment, coated with a thin layer of anger. *Turned down again.*

Chapter 56

Entering the boutique, Katerina found herself sucked into a vacuum of quiet elegance.

A woman Kat could only describe as perfect, approached. She wore a tailored suit, her thick, blond hair cut short at the nape of her neck, the front falling in a straight blunt cut that ended at her chin. Her eyes were cool and detached.

"I have an appointment—"

The woman took Kat's hand in a firm, non-threatening grasp. "Miss Mills, I am Evelina; it is a pleasure to meet you. We were beginning to despair of ever seeing you. Mr. Gallagher informed us your schedule had changed rather suddenly."

Katerina nodded. *Is she battery-operated?* "Thank you for your patience."

"Not at all. We are at Mr. Gallagher's disposal. And yours, of course."

Katerina answered with a smile. *How many other women has Thomas Gallagher sent here?*

"If you will follow me please, I have quite a few things for you."

Kat nodded and obeyed.

***

The smiling Stepford Wife, Evelina, didn't work alone. She had a tag team of three ladies in waiting, all with names from Regency romance novels: Patience, Frederica, and Sophia. For the next hour they doted and hovered, hanging on her every word, bringing in one outfit after another until Kat wanted to flee.

She noticed the difference between this selection and the clothes from Winter. The winter-whites, soft beiges, and ecru pieces were signature selections that spoke of Winter's neatness and order. Gallagher's pieces ran the gamut, from pinks and grays to sudden bursts of purple and red.

At the end of the session, she changed into one of the outfits, the red and black Versace sweater with the signature Greek key motif, and black pants. Gathering the bags, Kat gave her profuse thanks to the ladies for their kind hospitality and exited the boutique with a sigh of relief.

Chapter 57

The pre-war apartment boasted crown molding, a Georgian style fireplace, three bedrooms, a kitchen, a bath-and-a-half, and natural hardwood floors.

Gallagher stood off to the side. Katerina could feel his eyes on her, watching her every reaction. She was mired in an inner monologue, attempting to figure out why a wealthy, powerful, successful man would hire a college student with no interior design background to decorate a four million dollar apartment. *The job is never the job. So what is the job?*

"Mr. Gallagher, if you could tell me who will be living here and why, that would help me."

Gallagher strolled the living room. "This apartment is for visiting executives. I don't want them to stay in hotels. An accommodation with creature comforts is always preferable."

Katerina nodded.

"Miss Mills, you don't care for the assignment?"

The question was polite, without anger or annoyance.

She turned to him. "Mr. Gallagher, I have no experience in this field," she said, breaking Philip's first rule. *Do Not Offer Alternatives. Ever. You put yourself out of work and give someone else the job. But what is the job? And where is the advice maven? I still have a score to settle over his renting me out to a mobster.* Gallagher's voice jolted her out of her thoughts.

"I didn't explain myself. You will have an entire team of designers to direct."

"Then, what do you need me for?" Katerina blurted, a tinge of hostility in her tone. *What is this?*

"Because this project needs a vision," Gallagher said. "If I hire a crew of designers and tell them I want a home away from home, they will give me something that looks like a high-end hotel suite. I trust your instincts, Miss Mills, to guide you to the right choices. The crew will make it happen."

"I may pick a style that you don't like."

"Katerina," he said with a smile, "if I don't like something I'll let you know."

"All right, Mr. Gallagher. I'll take care of it."

He came to her and took her hand. "That pleases me," he said.

***

Extraordinary, he thought. *Dangle the keys to the kingdom and she's not interested. I give her carte blanche and she doesn't want it. She has no aspirations that she can or will ever be in this apartment as an occupant.*

With every temptation he placed before her, she rejected them all. *She rejects me for "Bob."*

He reigned in his annoyance, noting her choice of outfit for their meeting. She chose the red: a power color. He would have to be careful with her. Though he had ignored it, he had caught the edge in her voice. *She has a temper.*

The next assignment had to happen quickly. It would provide crucial information; picking items for someone else always reveals the giver. People don't choose for others; they choose for themselves. When she decorated, she would reveal her personality, her likes and dislikes. He needed to know that information before he could implement his plans. He had directed the first room for decoration would be the bedroom. She's a tough one, Miss Katerina Mills, he thought, a sly smile tugging at the corners of his mouth. *She will have to be conquered.*

Thinking of "Bob's" clever maneuver to meet her on a street corner when she had texted for help, made his smile fade. He had dispatched his people, knowing it was useless. They had disappeared. The Brooklyn address had been checked but it had already been vacated and scrubbed. "Bob" was a professional. For now, he remained a ghost. If he continued to present a problem, "Bob" would be dealt with. Gallagher almost hoped he would.

Chapter 58

Ten minutes after Winter parked the car and cut the engine, the cold cut him to the bone. The frigid temperature brought back the nightmare memories, as if they had just happened, as if they could happen again: the cold, the hunger, the pain. Memories belonging to another time, another name, his true name, long dead; a name he hadn't uttered in years.

He waited. Finally, Katerina exited the building and ducked back into the idling limousine. Winter watched her long, luxurious hair swirling around her. *Fragile beauty.*

He had been losing the battle and it hadn't been chivalry holding him in check. He wanted her. He knew that one word, one move from him, and she would give in, she would be his. But that would forever alter the course of her future and she would have to live with the consequences. Confused and overwhelmed, she was primed to be easily swayed by passion; but clearly not ready to make or understand such a life-changing decision. He had held back.

The limousine pulled away. Winter switched his focus to the man seated on the bench outside the park, across the street from the building; the third time this week. The man rose from the bench and walked away. Winter got out of the car and followed.

***

Stepping into the warmth of the coffee shop, Winter spotted the man at a table in the back, next to a window. He was in his early thirties with a wiry build, a runner's body. Sporting a face with baby smooth skin and an aquiline nose, his features came together to make an unusual, attractive face complemented by a full head of short, thick, coal-black curly hair.

Winter sat down in the chair across from him.

"How can I help you, officer?" the younger man asked, wearing an amused smile.

"That *is* funny," Winter said. "What do you call yourself?"

The younger man sat back in his chair. "Daniel Clay."

"Well, Daniel, you've been spending a lot of time watching the building facing the park and I can't help but wonder why."

"I'm fascinated with architecture."

"I'm sure you are. I'll bet it's right up there with your other passions, trainspotting and bird watching. What's so fascinating about the building?"

"Well, it's not exactly the building..." Clay said.

Winter gave a hard stare.

Clay shifted in his seat.

Winter leaned in. "Let me help you. The young lady is off limits."

Clay's eyes sparked with interest. "You've seen her? Oh . . . is she yours?"

"Women are not objects to be owned."

Clay laughed. "Okay, she's yours. No problem. I understand. She's unbelievable. And that hair. I'll bet she keeps you happy all night."

Winter leaned in, his expression dark and dangerous.

Clay held up his hands. "No . . . hey . . . I'm sorry, no offense. She is beautiful. But trust me, she's not the object of my attention."

"What is the object of your attention, Daniel?"

Clay hesitated, shifting in his chair. "The object of my attention is an object, so, you see, no problem."

"What business are you in, Daniel?"

"Acquisitions."

"Of what?"

"Whatever. As long as it has value."

"Who do you work for, Daniel?"

"Whoever can pay. You can ask around about me but you won't find anything. I keep my private business private."

Winter nodded. "The young lady is off limits."

Clay nodded. "I got it. But her client is not. There's a risk she might get caught in-between."

"That would upset me, Daniel."

"Collateral damage, my friend. It happens. Maybe you should pay closer attention to what your girlfriend is doing." He raised his hands. "Not that it's any of my business. You know, I didn't catch your name."

"Bob. Remember what we talked about, Daniel," Winter said, and left the table.

"I certainly will, *Bob*," Daniel Clay muttered. "I certainly will."

***

Winter stepped out into the cold, his breath expelling into the air like brief bursts of white smoke. He had already done his due diligence on this new player days ago. It had been risky to expose himself but Winter had to hear Daniel Clay's story for himself, a clever piece of half-fact and half-fiction. Daniel Clay was more dangerous than whatever Katerina was already into. More dangerous than Sheridan.

Winter ingested this new set of circumstances, chiding himself for his stupidity. He had delayed too long. The last time he had done that, the mistake had been fatal. *I won't make that mistake again.* Giving Katerina time and space to make life-changing choices had just become a luxury neither of them could afford.

In a split second, Winter made his decision and his plans. He would make his move. She would give in. Then he would get her out and Katerina Mills would leave her life, everything and everyone, behind. She no longer had a choice. As the thought of being with her floated through his mind, he couldn't say he was sorry.

Chapter 59

When the text came, Katerina dismissed Luther for the rest of the day, despite his protests that this was becoming a habit. What she needed to do now, had to be done alone. She decided to keep the "Winter" phone with her. It was a chance she would have to take. Whatever he witnessed he could figure out. She didn't know where he was, but she didn't want to be without him.

She headed uptown, cold even in her heavy sweater and coat. Amazing how little it takes to get used to being pampered and cared for, she thought, already missing the comfort of Luther's limousine.

A different limousine tooled down the street, slowly easing over to the curb. The door opened and Katerina climbed in, welcoming the warmth.

"Mr. Reynolds, are you all right?" she blurted, overcome with a tidal wave of relief upon seeing him.

He grasped both her hands as a greeting.

"I was so worried about you, so afraid something had happened."

"Miss Katerina," he began, "I am sorry for your alarm. What is it? Have you seen that man again since we last met?"

Katerina shook her head. "No, sir."

"Well then, my dear, what is the cause of this distress?"

"Mr. Reynolds, I believe the police don't necessarily think your wife's death is the result of a serial killer."

His face folded into a frown that dissolved in the next moment. "Could it have been this—friend—of hers that has gone missing?"

"Will Temple. I don't know. I know only that the police have not settled on any one theory and they're still looking."

Deep in thought, Reynolds held her hands captive. "The police still don't know about this man you saw?"

"No, sir."

"Can you find out more, Miss Katerina? I need to know what the police have been doing, who they have been interviewing. Do you have connections inside the police department?"

She hesitated, considering what she would have to do to fulfill this request. She would need to question Ryan, carefully probing for information. *I don't love him. And now I'm just using him.* Guilt began to gnaw at her.

John Reynolds' earnest expression weighed on her as well. *What if he's in danger? I'm responsible for this.* "Yes, I have a contact. I'll take care of it, Mr. Reynolds."

He squeezed her hands. "I know you will, Miss Katerina, I know you will."

Chapter 60

Katerina headed back downtown. Entering the student union, she found Roger Cole reclining in his usual spot, reading a magazine. Looking up, he tossed the magazine aside and springing up, began smoothing his hair and rumpled shirt.

"Hey," he said, a flush creeping up his neck, "what can I do for the extraordinary Katerina Mills. I heard all about your little adventure. You are Wonder Woman, you know that?"

Sure, too bad my magic bracelets are in the shop. "I haven't come about that."

He gestured for her to sit down. "What can I do for you?"

"I need to find out more about a certain distribution channel for a very specific substance."

Roger glanced around. Then his gaze returned to Katerina with a combination of interest and suspicion.

"Uh . . . Kat . . . uh . . . I don't know anything . . . about anything . . ."

Getting up, Katerina shrugged off her coat and stripped off her sweater, revealing a form fitting, long-sleeved shirt underneath. She began to tug off the shirt but Roger's hand on her wrist stopped her.

"Hey, okay, I get it, you're not wearing a wire."

"You can frisk me if you want to," she said as she sank back down.

He leaned in. "Why do you want to know?"

"It's personal. Do you have any idea where your supply of Antifreeze comes from?"

"Si, señorita," Roger said in a low voice. "The product comes from only one place. You do not want to mess with those hombres, comprende? You don't want them to know your name."

"But isn't it possible that it could be coming from somewhere else, someone else? Look, I'm trying to find someone. I think he was moving—product."

Roger thought for a minute. "There's one source for the US. But, in the past, there was talk that there was someone on the East Coast who was buying large amounts of product from the source and taking it from there. If there was such a person, once he bought the product, then he assumed all the risk and all the profit."

"What is *all* the risk?"

"The whole enchilada. Transportation, distribution channels, middle-men. He's responsible for it all. It's his money. Anything goes wrong, it's on him. He loses a shipment, it's on him. He gets held up, it's on him. And he could be out *a lot* of money."

"How much?"

"A few million a shipment."

"Is there any way to find out if this person is still in the business or if someone else is running the operation?"

"Kat, I'm not that high up in the food chain. There's a lot of buffers in-between. You know about buffers?"

"Yeah," Kat said with a tinge of bitterness. "I know all about buffers."

"If it's any consolation, there's been no interruption in service. The transportation is running smoothly like always. Everything is exactly the same."

They sat together, Roger giving her space as she lapsed into silence.

So, what does it all mean? I have no idea if my father is in business, out of business, or just on the run. Why did I even come here? What did I hope to accomplish anyway?

Katerina realized Roger was staring at her, his face a mix of curiosity, even concern.

"Thanks Roger. It's a real favor."

"Anytime, bellina, any time."

Kat pulled on her sweater and her coat and walked away. As she did, she answered her own question. *I came because I need something, anything, that will give me leverage against Sheridan. To do what? Stay in? Get out?* Her thoughts turned to Winter; the urge to go to him, tell him everything, ask for help, pressed in on her. *And what if he did help? I would be putting him at risk. He could get caught. Nothing can happen to him. Nothing. It's not his problem.*

Her phone buzzed. She dug down into her purse and pulled out the burner. She dropped it back in with a curse. Three damn phones. She rooted around and pulled out her normal "Ryan" phone and checked the text.

It's late. Where are you? When will you be here? R

A spike of annoyance shot through her as she typed.

On the way. Be there soon. K.

It was time to gear up, be the normal girlfriend. And get the information John Reynolds needed. She decided she would have to get it from Ryan without his knowledge.

It had to be done.

Chapter 61

When Katerina got off the subway, she checked the "Winter" phone. The text said "all clear." Heading toward the apartment, she spied Ryan, Emma, and Frank waiting outside the building.

Right. Dinner with friends. This is what the normal people do.

She greeted Ryan with an embrace and a kiss. Winter's face drifted into her consciousness. She pulled back.

"All right," Emma said. "Let's get on to the important stuff. Where are we gonna eat?"

They walked in a line, the guys holding their girls close.

"Missed you today," Ryan whispered in her ear.

Kat managed a smile.

***

"Now listen, hon, we need to do some serious Christmas and wedding shopping. As my maid of honor, you have a lot of responsibility."

Will I even be here for that?

"I am all over it," Kat said. Emma gave her a wide-eyed look and Kat doubled down. "Seriously, I've got it covered. I know exactly what to do for the bridal shower."

"No male strippers," Frank said.

"Geese and ganders," Kat retorted.

"I solemnly swear," Frank said, holding up his right hand, "there will be no strippers at my bachelor party."

"Right," Ryan chimed in. "Just a few female police officers."

Emma gave Frank a playful slap on his shoulder.

"You two will have plenty of time over the holidays to make plans," Ryan said. "I promise I'll bring her back into the city as often as you like."

Kat responded with a questioning look.

"We'll be close, out on the Island, with my parents."

"I'm going home to visit my mother."

The conversation dropped as if it had gone over the side of a cliff.

Ryan gave a tiny chuckle. "We talked about this."

"Yes," Kat said. "And I assumed we would be alone when we finished talking about it."

Emma put her hand on Kat's arm. "Plenty of time for everything, sugar. It's getting late anyway."

***

Twisting the key in the lock of the apartment, Ryan entered the darkened space in silence, standing aside for Kat to follow.

Careful Katerina. Mind your mouth. You have to stay here tonight.

When Ryan flicked on the light, Kat did a quick reconnoiter. The briefcase was in its usual spot—on a kitchen chair. She braced herself. She knew him. He wasn't going to waste any time. He was going to dive right in.

"I thought we decided to spend Christmas with my parents."

"No, *you* wanted me to spend Christmas with your parents and *I* need to spend Christmas with my mother."

Ryan kept his distance, his body tense.

To Katerina, it looked as if he were preparing to do battle with a criminal. *You already are.*

"I want everyone to meet you. I need everyone to see you. I keep talking about you. They're starting to think I'm making you up."

"I need to see my mother and make sure that she's okay."

Ryan smacked his hand on the back of a kitchen chair. "I want to show you off. Is that a crime?"

Her nerves tightened, struck by the déjà vu of her position near the door. *Do I stay or run? Will he let me get out the door?*

"I want to meet everyone. I do," she said, trying to control the mix of anger and fear spreading through her. She took a slow breath. "Can't we figure out something where we do both?"

"Sure," he said, his voice clipped. "No problem."

"I'm going home," she said, making a move toward the door.

He darted in front of her, blocking her way. Kat drew back, crossing her arms over herself to stave off an expected attack.

"Hey," he said, eyes widening with surprise. He raised his arms in surrender. "I'm sorry. I want you to stay. I like having you here. I like the way you look in the morning when you're still sleepy. I like the way the place still has the scent of vanilla after you've gone."

He stood, hesitant, until she dropped her arms. Then he leaned in, his mouth finding hers. She kissed him back, wishing he was Winter.

***

In the dark, Katerina sprawled on the couch above the covers, eyes wide open, heart pounding. Ryan had fallen asleep; of all nights, he had left the bedroom door open.

Get up and do it.

But she didn't move, continuing to lie there, trying to conjure an excuse if he caught her. *I tripped into your briefcase, it popped open, and your private case notes fell out?*

What would Winter do?

He would keep it simple.

Get off the couch. Close his door. Take the notebook from the briefcase. Read it by the refrigerator light. Put it back.

No, the bathroom is better. If I get caught, I chuck the notepad in the hamper and then go back for it later.

Get up.

Do it.

Like the break-in with Winter in the Hamptons.

Like Philip used to tell you. Get in. Get out. Get gone.

She stood motionless in the dark, her pulse racing, listening for Ryan's deep rhythmic breathing. Tiptoeing to his bedroom door, she grasped the knob. She began to ease the door toward her, leaving it open a crack.

Turning, she crept to the table. She opened the briefcase.

She searched for the spiral running across the top of the pad.

Sudden rustling sounds came from the bedroom.

She froze.

She waited, holding her breath; quiet returned. Feeling around, her fingers found the spiral. Sliding out the pad, she stole into the bathroom, locking herself in and turning on the light.

Katerina winced as she read the notes on Felicia Reynolds, the facts of her life, the details of her brutal death. Fighting tears, her stomach sickened as she scanned the notes, looking for a pattern between the murders of the two women, looking for a serial killer. She flipped through more pages.

Will Temple. Missing.
Production Company.
 Random Girl Films.
Film Love's Fury.
Theater for a New Audience.
Will Temple.
Felicia Reynolds.
Same picture.

Katerina's breathing turned shallow, leaving her lightheaded.

He's closer than I thought.
He'll continue to dig.
He'll find a witness.
He'll make the connection to me.

Closing the pad, she tiptoed out of the bathroom and slipped it back into the briefcase. Slowly, with a feather touch, she closed the case.

Katerina crawled back onto the couch, numb with fear.

She lay awake in the dark, shivering in spite of the blanket, wondering who would get to her first, the killer out there or the detective sleeping in the next room.

Chapter 62

The next morning, Katerina waited for the bomb to drop. Ryan sipped his coffee in silence; she wolfed down a breakfast of cereal as if it were her last meal. He got up from the table and shrugged into his coat.

Kat dumped the dishes in the sink and put on her coat. She fumbled in her purse and then held out a business card to him.

"I want you to have this. If I don't answer my phone, call this number. They can find me anytime, anywhere. You can always get in touch with me. Always."

He considered the card and then took it, turning it over, examining the name. *Gal Friday, Incorporated.* He tucked the card into his inside pocket. He gave her a kiss on the lips and they left.

***

Entering her apartment, Katerina dropped her backpack on the floor, a smile of surprise curving her lips at the sight of Alexander Winter sitting in her living room.

"Good morning," he said.

"Good morning back," she said. "So much for the super, new door lock. Was I followed?"

"Sheridan's been out of town. You lost your other two fans after you hit Manhattan."

The Vincent and Carlo show. At least it's not a killer in a Blue Ford.

Katerina went into the kitchen and opened the fridge door.

Suddenly, the air changed; a flush of heat came over her. *He's behind me.* A spike of adrenalin, a flashback of Sheridan pinning her against the wall from behind made her jump. Then Winter slid his arms around her, gently placing one hand just below the base of her neck, his other hand resting on her lower belly.

"Shhh," he soothed.

He's right, she thought, working to let the excitement overpower the fear. *You're safe. It's Winter.*

"I've been thinking," he began, his lips nuzzling her ear lobe.

"Uh-hunh," she said, melting against him.

"It's time you drop this line of work." His lips found her neck with soft kisses.

"Uh-hunh," she answered, breathing in his scent and beginning to feel senseless as his mouth moved over her skin. *It's happening*, she thought, her body trembling. *It's okay. This is what you wanted. It's here. Don't let the other one win. Just let it happen. He won't hurt you.*

She tried to turn around but Winter snuggled her closer.

Her mind raced, desperate to enjoy the moment. He slipped his hands under her sweater; her heart thudded in her chest, her skin on fire from his touch.

He wants to play. It'll be good. Let it happen.

"If I do that, what happens with . . . everything?"

"I'll take care of it. I'll take care of you," he whispered, as his hands slid lower down below her belly and lingered.

She let out a moan, thinking of what he would do next.

He switched to nibbling at the shell of her earlobe. "You need to tell me everything."

"Uh-hunh."

"Let's start with your daily trips across from the park. Who's your client?"

"Simon Marcus. Hedge fund manager. He's the one with the Porsche problem."

"Did you ever decide who gets the replica?" he asked, his hands snaking their way back up, resting just below her breasts.

"Yes," she murmured, the sudden desire to see him naked, to touch him, mixing with an unwanted apprehension she couldn't shake.

"Anything else special about Mr. Marcus?"

Her body stiffened in response to the questioning. "His wife hates him," she said, her voice sharp. "And he's got some fake Monet paintings in his apartment that he's in love with. Four of them. They're all the same. A bridge, a pond and some flowers."

Winter caressed her skin as he peppered her cheek with soft kisses. "*Nympheas*," he whispered. "One of those real "flower paintings" once fetched fifty-four million at auction. How do you know they're fakes?"

Turning cool, she turned to face him. "They're the wrong size. You're in the business of stealing fakes now? Or do you want me to get an inventory of the entire apartment."

"That would be generous of you," Winter said, his voice curt but calm. "But you're on the wrong track, Katie."

"Why don't you set me straight, *Professor*."

"Now is not the time to be stubborn. You've already got more than you can handle—"

"That's my call to make."

He took a deep breath. "Okay. You have a new groupie. This player thinks Marcus has something of great value. He thinks you know what it is. This man is dangerous. And you're in the mix. I don't need to know *just* about Marcus. I need to know *everything* you're into so I can get you out."

Katerina stepped back, folding her arms across her chest; she walked out of the kitchen.

He followed her into the living room. "Katie—"

"*Katerina*," she said, beginning to shake with anger as she turned to face him. "A new player watching Marcus' apartment; how convenient. This is about a fifty-four million dollar payday? That's what this . . . the clothes, the food, the comfort, the kissing, is about?"

"Not even close," he said.

"Bullshit," she said, her temper spiking. "All this time you've been putting me off, turning me out. Now, all of a sudden, you want to turn me on."

"There's no time for this. I had my reasons. It's complicated."

"Bullshit! I wasn't *useful*. But now that you're looking for a score, now I'm useful. This is just like the Hamptons."

"This is *nothing* like the Hamptons. This is different."

"It doesn't feel any different," she said. "I can't believe I was so stupid. That's some cool con you pulled. What an angle. Being honest."

"About what?"

"The lie is who you are."

"This is different," he said.

She ignored the statement as if he had never spoken. "It never even occurred to me that you would screw me—oh wait, we didn't get to that." She gave a humorless laugh. "But I guess we were going to get to that, so you could get everything you wanted."

"*Katerina*," he said, his jaw set in anger. "You don't want to be anywhere near this man."

"Of course not. Because thieves are dangerous. You have to watch them."

He came to her. "I am the last person you should be afraid of. You need to get out."

"I've got it covered," she said.

"Not even close. You're vulnerable."

She held her ground as he looked down at her. "I'm sure I am, *Bob*. Because now, you know all my business."

"No, some of your secrets are still safe. You never told me why you need to date a policeman who's *not* your boyfriend. You never told me about the earrings you're hiding in this apartment."

Caught without a ready response, she opened her mouth to retort, then shut it again.

"You are not thinking clearly, Katerina. You're going to miss something."

"I see what I need to," she said. "Please leave."

"Katie . . . you need to trust me."

"Out," she answered.

He held her gaze for another moment and then grabbing his coat, he walked past her and out the door, shutting it silently behind him.

She stood rooted to the spot for a long moment, then began to dig around in her purse. She found Winter's tracking phone, turned it off, removed the battery, and threw it back inside. All at once, her knees went weak; she sank down onto a chair. How will I make it without him? she thought, closing her eyes. *The same way you used to. Put your big girl panties on. No more fantasies about a criminal with a heart of gold.*

I thought he loved me.

What do twenty-three year old girls know about love anyway?

***

Anger and tears spiked in rollercoaster waves all day and late into the night, rising, receding, then back again. *Complicated, my ass.* She finally decided Winter *had* been right about one thing. She needed to get out. But Winter was also wrong. This new thief, if this person even exists, she thought, is not the priority; and Marcus is just a blowhard. *The real problem is Sheridan.* She needed to find a way to get clear of him. Ditching Sheridan was her way out.

Roger Cole had said the drug business was running smoothly, no changes. Katerina ran through her choices.

Option One: William Mills was still running his drug business remotely. But if Sheridan had been her father's partner, he would know all the details of the business. So wouldn't her father have changed everything: transportation, delivery, distribution; anything and everything in order to keep Sheridan off his trail?

Option Two: William Mills cashed out after shooting, and failing to kill, a DEA agent. That would mean someone new had taken over her father's business. Someone who had no idea James Sheridan had been the silent partner of William Mills.

As far as Kat was concerned, Option Two was more likely.

She played out the scenarios in her head, wincing as Winter's words came back to her. *You're taking your best guess. That's all you can do.*

And I have no Alexander Winter to talk me through and tell me if I get an A. The thought made her stomach queasy with anxiety.

She went to bed in the small hours of the morning, exhausted from her anger and fear. *I'm all alone out here.* But she had managed to formulate a plan and felt ready to make her play. She would follow her father's advice: *you play the hand you've been dealt, bet and bluff to make the best deal possible, and then cash out when it's time to go.* She would do this backwards, first the bluff, then the bet, and then cash out.

And she would do it alone.
There's no one I can trust now.

Chapter 63

As Katerina came out of her building, she stopped at the sight of the limousine. Luther got out and opened the passenger door.

"It's okay, Luther," she said. "You can go."

"The man paid me, Miss Katerina. You're my only client, twenty-four-seven."

"The job's been cancelled. Don't worry, he won't ask for a refund."

"Miss Katerina, it's cold."

"I'll catch you on the way back, Luther," she said.

Luther, frowning, closed the door. "You take care of yourself, miss."

"Will do," she said. Feeling a pang of regret, she picked her way carefully down the icy sidewalk toward the corner.

***

Katerina sat in the miniscule café, crammed with tired, harried New Yorkers, the air punctuated by coughs and intermittent sneezes. People pulled off layers of clothing, struggling in the constant purgatory between bitter cold and dry heat. She squeezed into a corner table, ordered a coffee, and let it grow cold, untouched.

She sat, watching the door, every muscle tensed as she braced herself. He entered, scanning the room. Her stomach somersaulted at the sight of him; rage, her new companion, washed over her.

Sheridan squeezed into the chair opposite her, a cockeyed smile on his face. "Our first official meeting. I'm very excited."

The urge to lunge at him, scratch, claw, and kick, flooded over her. Her eyes began to smart.

"Aww, what's the matter?" he asked, as if she was a five-year-old.

She bit back the urge to cry. *Grow up. There's no guardian angel anymore.*

"Business is still running without a hitch. Nothing has changed."

Sheridan took the news quietly. "When did you see him?"

Keep calm. Keep cool. You can do this.

"*You* could have seen him. I guess you weren't looking hard enough. He saw you."

Sheridan nodded, his mouth tightening. "Your little shopping trip. Cute."

Katerina smiled. *Let him do it. Let him draw his own conclusions.* "The real question is, how come you don't know that everything is the same? Don't you have confidential informants in the factory? Or are they cooperating witnesses. I get confused."

She observed his silence, watching his pupils turn an inky black. "You probably missed a few meetings while you were in the recovery room," she needled. "Tough being on the outside."

He gave a chuckle and leaned in. "You know that's some smart mouth you have."

He took her wrist, bringing it down on the table and squeezing. Her eyes squinted from the pain and she held her breath, pressing her lips closed.

"I'll bet I can stuff something in that mouth to get you to shut up." He lowered his voice to a whisper. "Something big and hard."

Kat's chest vibrated in panic and her stomach turned as the pain bore down deep in her wrist. "You're after ten million. He's making a hundred times that—every day. You want to find him, you can. I'm sure you can think of a way to get his attention, since his transportation is running nice and smooth, without a hitch. Or do you want me to do everything for you."

C'mon, you bastard, take the bait.

He gave a harsh laugh. "Daddy's little girl. Ready to sell out the old man."

Katerina shrugged. "I don't see enough cash coming my way." *Keep the lie as close to the truth.* "I want immunity and a walk. For me *and* my mother."

She watched him turn the information over in his head. He nodded. "Your get-out-of-jail-free cards are only good with me, understand? I'm the only one who can help you and your mother. Once I rattle your old man's cage, you're going to say what I tell you and get him out where I can see him, face to face. Understand?"

"Understood." *On the hook. Done.*

You look good," he said, releasing her wrist. "You look very good."

When he walked out, she watched him go, the familiar pain in her chest rising into her throat as she rubbed at her wrist.

Keeping her head down, she swiped the tears away from her cheeks. She had set things in motion. There was no going back now.

It was time to make her bet.

Chapter 64

In the corner of the library reading room, Winter flipped the pages of a magazine with a gloved hand. He studied the article several times, poring over the paintings in the photographs. As Katerina had said, the Monet paintings were unmistakable reproductions. Each one had its own color scheme: purple, yellow, green, and blue. The article explained that many considered Marcus a fake as well: a fake genius, a fake aristocrat, a crass 'new money' charlatan with questionable business practices. The next Madoff. Marcus laughed it off. He was proud of his fakes; they showed how he had risen above being conned. Now he was the sharp one; no one put one over on him anymore.

Winter sat back, considering the article, considering Daniel Clay. Why fixate on an apartment that only had four fakes to show for itself?

After making color photocopies, he stole away down the hall and around the corner to the massive vestibule. His light step contradicted his heavy, troubled mind.

Exiting through the revolving door, he stepped into the wintry December air, chewing on Katerina's comments.

It never even occurred to me that you would screw me.

I wouldn't. The job in the Hamptons, taking that necklace, wasn't what she thought. Could I do it? That's what it was about.

I see everything I need to.

He shook his head. Headstrong and stubborn. She had already missed something. It never occurred to her that when he arranged for the new front door lock, he had a second key made . . . for himself. Slipping into the apartment while she slept, he had inserted the tiny tracking device into the lining of her coat sleeve. But even that didn't ease his mind. *What the hell was she doing meeting with Sheridan?*

A storm is coming, he thought.

And she's the eye.

Chapter 65

When Katerina entered the office, Henri Letourneau gave her a wary look. She sat down to wait, coaching herself up to the last minute. She found herself thinking about Angel. *Go big or go home, baby.* To do one, she needed the other.

Henri spoke softly in French. It reminded her of how kind he had been when he came to Philip's office. Sometimes, he would talk a little with her, complimenting her on how well she spoke his language, listening to her chatter of plans to visit Paris. There was no time for any such niceties today. He said *a demain*, followed by *ciao* and hung up the phone.

"Katerina, the cold in your cheeks makes you even more beautiful."

"Thank you for seeing me on short notice, Monsieur Letourneau."

He nodded. "I assume that if you had called me and told me what you wanted to talk about, I would have said this meeting was not a good idea, hmm?"

Katerina smiled. Henri Letourneau had a face weathered from age. Still, his accent made him seem more attractive than perhaps he had a right to be.

"What opportunity do you work on now?" he asked.

"Trucking routes. Deliveries from Vermont to New York."

"For what?"

"Toys."

Letourneau's head tilted to one side. "What kind of toys?"

"Special toys with a surprise packet inside. I'm looking for the people who own the packets inside the toys, and take care of transporting them."

Letourneau considered her for a long moment, his expression unreadable. "The people in the business of supplying toys with a surprise packet inside prefer to remain anonymous. These people . . . you do not want to know them. You do not want them to know you."

Katerina forgot to breathe. "Pass a message through channels. Someone came to see you ... someone bearing the gift of a DEA agent."

Something flickered behind Letourneau's eyes. "They will want more than your word."

"Their operation is in danger. Their transportation is compromised. One of their runs is going to get hit. Soon. If this agent finds something, he'll have what he needs to make his case, enough to bring it to a grand jury."

"Katerina, once I do this—"

"I know. Keep my name out of it."

"What is your price for this magnificent gift?"

Katerina found herself caught with no answer. Her tunnel vision had been solely focused on removing Sheridan from the equation. Once he showed himself in the raid, the new dealer would take care of the rest. *But this could be my exit strategy. I won't need my father's money.* The sudden option of taking money from these people set off fireworks of fear within her, frightening her even more than a corrupt DEA agent. "Right now, I want them to know I'm acting in good faith. That's what's most important."

She got up.

Letourneau rose. He took her hand and held it for a long moment. "Katerina, please, find a safe place and go there. Hide there."

"Merci, Monsieur Letourneau. I will try," she said.

***

Katerina left the office with a strange, hollow feeling in her heart and mind. She hadn't pulled a trigger but she had flipped a switch and set things in motion. *It is what it is. Find the truth and admit it.*

I just murdered James Sheridan.

Chapter 66

"Mom, how are you?"

"I'm fine, dear. Why do you sound hysterical?"

Taking a deep breath, Katerina forced herself to calm down. "I am not hysterical, Mom. I'm just out of breath."

Katerina was, in fact, out of breath. She had made it to the campus with minutes to spare. It was time for her first final.

"Mom, are you using the phone I sent?" she asked, struggling to hear over the noise in the crowded hallway.

"Yes, dear, I'm talking to you on it right now. *You* called me. Are you sure you're okay?"

"Yes, Mom, are you using the phone to talk with other people?"

"What other people, dear? Since your father left, no one talks to me anymore."

"Why not? Why don't they talk to you?"

"There's never any room at the table for an extra woman, dear," she said, "not that it's any great loss," she added, her voice dropping to a mutter.

"What did you say?"

"Nothing, dear. Nothing at all."

Katerina let it drop. *I can't think about that now. I have more pressing business. Digital footprints.*

"Mom, do you still have any of Daddy's mail? Bills? Anything?"

"No, he shredded everything."

Katerina closed her eyes. *Damn. Dead end.*

"Wait . . . I think I have a few old subscription receipts for one of his boating magazines."

"Don't throw them out! Okay? Just promise me you'll keep them. I want to look at them when I come home."

"All right, but why in the world do you need them?"

Katerina heard a deep, rasping voice with a thick accent in the background.

"Mom, is that Uncle Sergei?"

"Yes, dear. Talk to him. He'd love to talk to you."

She waited.

"Katya," came the low, familiar voice. "How are you?"

"I'm well, uncle."

"You are running around big city now, becoming very important person, yes?"

"Not so important, uncle."

"Katya, I will look after your mother. You have someone to look after you?"

"I'm okay."

"You are coming home soon?"

"Yes, very soon."

"Watch out for the wolf, Katya," he said, his voice dropping to a whisper, "like I used to sing to you ... remember?"

The hair prickled on the back of her neck. Hearing voices and rustling behind her, she glanced around. The lecture hall doors were open and students were beginning to file inside.

"I remember," she murmured. "I need to go now. Say goodbye to Mom for me."

She clicked off the burner and tucked it away in her purse.

It's too late. The wolves are here.

Chapter 67

Winter strolled into the coffee shop and took the seat opposite Daniel Clay. Clay had a cup in his hand; he paused as he brought it to his lips. With a smirk, he put the cup down.

"I just read a fascinating article," Winter said. Still wearing his gloves, he opened his coat and drew out the color photocopies, spreading the sheets out on the table. "It's about a man who has millions and yet he's attached to four fake Monet paintings."

Clay gazed out of the coffee shop window.

Winter took his gloves off. "You see, it's not about the money for Mr. Marcus. It's all about the sentimental value—because he's a sentimental guy."

"You went through the whole thing, hunh?" Clay said.

"I'm thinking those paintings are like door number one, two, three or four. Tell me, Daniel, which one has the prize?"

Clay gave a tight laugh. "Okay, what do you want?"

"What we discussed. Leave her out of it."

"She's been in the apartment. She's the only one who knows."

"Knows what?"

"If all the paintings are still there."

"You know which one has the prize."

"Yes."

"And why wouldn't it be in the apartment?"

"Let's just say I hear things, okay?"

Winter leaned in. "What things?"

"Your girlfriend's client may be facing some legal trouble. The kind of legal trouble that makes one take a long vacation in a country without a US extradition treaty. The kind of trouble that might induce one to sell off stolen artwork." Clay lowered his voice. "Stolen artwork that is hidden behind the lining of a painting." He tapped a finger on a page. "Behind that painting."

Winter took note of the painting Clay pointed to. "What's the surprise?"

Clay took a piece of paper from of his pocket and placed it on the table.

Winter glanced over the color photocopy; a vase of poppies. By any standard, a small masterpiece. The actual painting was only one foot by one foot. No one had seen it since it was stolen from a museum in Kuwait over ten years earlier.

"I've been chasing this thing down for a long time," Clay said. "I've put a lot of man hours into this. I have an interested party."

Winter kept his eyes on the photocopy.

"How much do you want?" Clay asked.

"We'll get to that in a minute. Surely, Marcus has a lonely maid who can give you access."

"He does. I tried. It was a no-go. That building is like Fort Knox."

No building is like Fort Knox.

Winter indicated that Clay should take the paper away. A painting of a bouquet of flowers, he thought, that could be worth fifty million dollars at auction. Marcus would only get ten percent of that price selling it on the black market. He shook his head at the absurdity of it all.

"You see why I need to talk to her," Clay said.

Winter fixed his eyes on the younger man.

Clay sat back. "No problem. I'll find another way."

"*We'll* find another way."

"Right," Clay said, tucking the photocopy into his pocket. "Of course."

The odds of Van Gogh's *Poppy Flowers* being hidden behind the lining of a cheap copy of Monet's *Bridge over a Pond of Water Lilies* is a million to one, Winter thought.

But that doesn't mean it isn't possible.

Chapter 68

Don't call. Please, just give me a few more hours and don't call. The burner buzzed.

Shit.

Katerina hesitated, steeling herself for the daily abuse.

"Yes," she said.

"You're getting to be like *The Shadow*," Marcus said.

Katerina could hear him chomping on the fortune cookie from the lunch she had just dumped on his counter fifteen minutes earlier. *Before I ran out the door.*

"Mr. Marcus, I'm making progress—"

"Oh, cookie, you're funny. Where do you think you'll go after this? You know the high class houses don't make you see more than ten johns a night ... if you get lucky. Otherwise, that pussy of yours is gonna be pretty sore, unless you prefer to take it up the—"

"Mr. Marcus, I will have your car in a few days."

This is the man I'm going to make a deal with? I'm sure he'll appreciate that I did him a favor. Anthony Desucci wanted your car but I took care of it, Mr. Marcus. So please don't take it out for a spin or I'll be dead. Yeah, that'll work. If I even get the car.

She waited for his laugh and usual vulgar insults. "Yeah, well, you put all your efforts into that, cookie," he said, his voice calm, "because Luke sent me a good fortune today. I don't need any more lunch deliveries."

Finally, some good news.

"Deliver my car," he said, his voice sliding from calm to menacing. "If you don't, I finger the agency and I let everyone know it came from you. I'm gonna burn the house down, bitch, and you're the human sacrifice. You go up in flames first. Understand?"

Katerina stopped, frozen to her spot on the sidewalk, shivering from fright rather than the bitter cold. Before she could open her mouth to speak, he hung up.

After a few minutes she started walking again, her mind racing.

The sudden buzz of the burner phone jolted Katerina from her stupor. She checked the message.

>*Katie. The 4 paintings. All still there?*
>*Call me. Urgent. W.*

In a sudden surge of anger, she deleted the message, throwing the phone back into her purse. *Never again. I will never trust you again.*

***

Katerina's nerves had settled by the time she neared Gallagher's apartment. Pulling out the burner, she punched in a number, and waited.

"What's up, Buttercup?" Lisa's voice came over the line.

"I need an update," Katerina said.

"There's no pattern to her movements," Lisa said. "Yesterday, she took a day trip to the city. Billionaire's Row. West Fifty-seventh Street. He said the Porsche is sweet."

Kat clamped her eyes closed. *Stupid.* The car was out in the open. *And I should have had your contact steal it.* She shook her head at the thought. *No. Too dangerous. More than enough people know way too much about me. So where the hell is this going? What am I doing?*

"Is he done?"

"Not yet," Kat said. "Tell him to hang in a few more days."

"That's going to be extra," Lisa said.

"No it isn't," Katerina said.

"You're using up all your wishes, Cinderella. After this, the footmen turn back into mice."

Katerina winced at the analogy. "Got it," she said. "Tell him to stay on it."

"Understood," Lisa said. "By the way, I got a call from someone interested in booking Gal Friday for services. He asked a lot of questions. Don't worry, I gave all the right answers to the nice policeman." She clicked off the line.

Katerina clicked off the phone. *This has to come to an end. It's too close.* The addiction had turned on her. The anesthetic of escape wasn't enough. Only risk remained. *And I'm going to get caught.*

Chapter 69

As soon as she entered the apartment, Katerina noticed the change in the design crew. They raced around, feverish and frenetic, overflowing with nervous energy.

He's here. Damn.

In the bathroom, Kat untangled the wrap at the nape of her neck, letting her hair spill out. She checked her makeup and straightened her outfit: an apple red knit dress accented by black Louboutin stiletto pumps. The dress had a v-neck with long sleeves, and buttons down one side, the soft, gathered fabric creating a fitted silhouette; another item from the boutique. Slathering her hands with a generous helping of lotion, she gave herself a final onceover. Leaving the bathroom, she ran into Thomas Gallagher.

"Good afternoon, Miss Mills," he said. "How are you today?"

"Very well, Mr. Gallagher. I hope you will be pleased with the progress."

Making a sweeping arc with one arm, Gallagher stepped aside to let her pass. "Let's see your creative vision," he said with a smile.

If hyenas could smile, she thought as she preceded him, they would look like that—right before they tore into their prey.

***

Katerina crossed the bedroom in the darkness. She swept aside one of the rich, black satin curtains, tucking it behind an ornate gold hook, allowing a swath of daylight to flood the room.

It revealed a dramatic study in black: from the walls to the luxurious, decadent, smoky silk sheets and pillowcases. The armoires were accented with mirrors on the sides, tops, and doors. Glass crystals, painstakingly applied to the walls, sparkled in the sunlight.

Gallagher wandered the room, the silence broken only by the breathless arrival of the designer, a tall whip-thin man with a penchant for stating the obvious. "Ah, you're here . . . excellent . . . well, I believe Miss

Mills imagined a retreat for the weary traveler," the designer babbled. "Something like a dark oasis of quiet in the tumult of the city."

"I see exactly what Miss Mills imagined," Gallagher snapped. The designer fell silent.

Gallagher turned to Katerina. "Did you enjoy this assignment, Miss Mills?"

A slight blush bloomed in her cheeks. "Yes, Mr. Gallagher," Kat said, blinking back an unexpected threat of sudden emotion.

His eyes narrowed and he examined her for a long moment. "I'm glad, and . . . I approve," he said. "On to the rest of the apartment, I am curious to see what you will do next."

Wearing the same serene smile, he walked past her and out of the room.

Katerina unhooked the curtain, letting it fall, allowing the darkness to envelop her.

***

After Katerina had gone, Gallagher returned to the bedroom. He didn't bother opening the curtains. He had seen everything he needed to. Katerina Mills was a passionate young woman, a curious combination of heady romance and raw sexuality. She wanted something sensual with just a hint of danger. A few more assignments like this and he would draw her out completely. The joy of the impending conquest didn't hold the usual high. The young detective she was currently keeping company with was of no concern. No, it was the text from "W" that interested him. *Bob, I presume?* He had used a different alias, but the same phone number. *Careless, Bob, very careless.* Katerina had deleted the text regarding the paintings. Gallagher took another glance around the room. Judging by her emotional response, the interloper was gone for the moment, but certainly not forgotten. Katerina Mills still had set her heart on this man. She had been thinking of him when she designed the bedroom.

Chapter 70

In the library, Katerina threw her coat over a chair behind her. Keeping her purse close, she sat down at the computer terminal and did a quick search. She gave a silent curse. No luck getting a list of companies at Nine West Fifty-seventh Street. Who would Betsy Marcus be going to see?

What would Winter tell you?
He would say it is what it is. Find the truth and admit it.
And keep it simple.
Simple is always best.

If you want to hurt your husband, what do you do? *You throw in with someone who hates him. Who hates Simon Marcus?* Kat typed.

Simon Marcus + enemies

Katerina clicked on the top result, an article detailing a pissing contest for the ages between Simon Marcus and a Harold Wesley. Lawsuits and counter lawsuits, all over a property dispute as neighbors. Katerina searched again. Harold Wesley owned the hedge fund Kana Capital Management. He had a net worth of over three billion dollars. He owned New York apartments, Connecticut mansions, private islands, yachts, and cars. Very expensive cars. Katerina entered Kana Capital Management into the search toolbar. The page popped up. The hedge fund had an office at Nine West Fifty-seventh Street. *Bingo.*

Betsy Marcus is going to sell her husband's prized Porsche to the one man her husband hates more than anyone else in this world, she thought. *And he's going to buy the car even with the scratch on it? Take your best guess.* It had to be. It was all she had to go on.

Turning around to grab her coat, Katerina found the chair empty. *Shit.*

***

"Lucky you called your Aunt Gertie, darling. I knew you'd be back."

They were inside a makeshift office in the back of a tchotchke shop in Chinatown. Still shivering, Katerina curled into the blanket wrapped around her shoulders. Gertie pulled a Saint Laurent Chesterfield off a rack next to the desk. "Here sweetheart, put this on. You're going to love it."

Katerina did as she was told, her head throbbing with a migraine. Struggling into the coat, her hair falling into her face, she couldn't get it to sit right on her frame.

Gertie came over, pulling the coat up around her, fussing with her hair. Katerina stared at herself in the mirror, Gertie nodding her approval next to her.

The older woman turned, taking Kat by the shoulders. "Honey, what's the matter?" she asked, seeing Kat's tears.

Katerina shook her head.

"I know those tears. I've seen them on a thousand girls. What did he do? Step out with someone else?"

Katerina shook her head.

"Take your money?"

Katerina shook her head.

"If he wasn't unfaithful and he didn't steal from you, what could he possibly have done?"

"He wasn't who I thought he was," she said.

"Oh honey, they *never* are." The older woman put a motherly arm around her. "Listen to your Aunt Gertie, sweetheart. You should think about getting out of this line of work. It's not for you. Go find a nice, stable man who sells insurance and comes home every night at five o'clock. 'Cause that's what you really want, right?"

Katerina bit her lip so she wouldn't blurt out what was on her tongue. *No.*

"That's what I thought," Gertie said. "You'll be all right. Next time you see him, give him a big kiss on the lips and a good kick in the balls. And then you take him back." She held out her hand. "A thousand dollars for the coat."

Katerina opened her purse. "No discounts for a repeat customer?"

"This isn't Groupon, sweetheart. A girl's gotta get by."

Katerina couldn't argue with that.

***

As Katerina stepped back out into a freezing rain, the burner rang.

"There's movement at the house," Lisa said. "The Porsche is getting a wash and wax. Does that help you?"

"The minute she leaves in the car, no matter when or what time, you have to call me right away."

"Got it," Lisa said and hung up.

Katerina made a call.

"I need the vehicle ready. Now," she said.

"Yo, mami, these things usually take six weeks to build. At least give me six days."

"You've got sixteen hours, maybe," Katerina said. Clicking off, she headed for the subway, careful to check around her, although she knew it wouldn't do any good. Without Winter watching her back, she'd never see anyone coming.

***

Winter drove the icy streets as a slushy, freezing rain came down. "What the hell is she doing wandering the Upper West Side?" he muttered. Pushing the Range Rover as fast as he dared, he cursed the heavy stop and go traffic hemming him in, holding him prisoner, keeping him from getting to her. His phone rested on the passenger seat, taunting him, the beacon blinking, stationary, at Grant's Tomb.

***

As the dusk faded into evening, Winter fought the wet, frigid wind on foot as he approached the monument. Squinting against the icy rain, he stumbled around until he saw her, wrapped in her coat, lying on the ground. A strangled sound escaped him.

He rushed forward, slipping and sliding; seizing her coat, he turned her over. He froze, finding himself staring into the face of a homeless man, mumbling in his sleep. Winter's shoulders sagged, the air rushing out of his lungs as a wave of relief washed through him. He released the coat, letting the man fall back.

Winter stood there for a long moment, raw fear beginning to churn in his stomach.

I've lost her.

She's out there all alone.

Chapter 71

"Tell me, Miss Katerina. Tell me everything."

After switching taxis three times, Katerina had barely settled into the limousine when John Reynolds captured her hands in his own.

"My source is not convinced this is the work of a serial killer. He's made the connection between your wife and her friend."

"Her lover," Reynolds corrected. "I see. What do they think happened to him?"

"The police are still investigating," Katerina said. "Looking into Will Temple and your wife might lead the police to make other connections."

"What would those be, Katerina?"

How do I explain this? "For some reason, during the assignment, Will Temple showed up at my apartment. I don't know why. This was before I realized who he was. I spoke to him. He was looking for something, someone. He was looking for me but he had wrong information. Mr. Reynolds, the killer is playing some kind of game."

Reynolds stared at her. "You think this is a game?"

The sound of his voice, low, cold, even brittle, sent a sudden shock to her nerves. "I—I think you're in danger. Do you have any idea how someone could know you hired me? Or why someone would want to hurt your wife? Or you?"

He shook his head. "No, Miss Mills, I don't know why anyone would want to hurt me. Why would my wife want to hurt me by taking a lover? Why would you want to hurt me, by keeping it from me?"

"Mr. Reynolds—," she began, suddenly lightheaded. It was too hot in the car; her throat, dry and raw, hurt every time she swallowed. "That's why I didn't tell you. I . . . I *didn't* want to hurt you."

Reynolds stared out of the window as if he was suddenly bored with the conversation. "Does your detective boyfriend think Will Temple may have committed the murder?"

"Sir, I don't know. I'm telling you Will Temple didn't do this. He didn't kill your wife. He didn't kill Cheryl Penn. The police are not even sure the same man killed both women."

Reynolds began to stroke Kat's hands, caressing them, holding them hostage. "It doesn't matter what they're sure of."

"Mr. Reynolds, someone has targeted your wife, Will Temple, even me..."

Her voice trailed off.

I never said I had a boyfriend who was a cop.

She stared at her hands, captive in his grasp.

"Katerina," Reynolds said, "look at me."

She lifted her head.

"When you have a cancer, you have two choices. You can do nothing. The cancer is in situ, it is contained. Or you can be aggressive and cut it out... destroy it. My marriage was a cancer. I chose to be aggressive. I destroyed the tumor but you must take the surrounding tissue. You must be sure. Hence the removal of Mr. Temple."

Katerina stared at him, unable to move.

"It was you who convinced me, Katerina Mills. You were the "random girl" I chose. I thought you would be special, you would be different. Once you found out about *him,* you would tell me. If only she's honest with me, I told myself, it will be the sign. We had our meeting. You gave your report. But you hid the truth from me, the same way she hid things from me. That was when I knew you weren't special. You were the same. All of you are the same. Such a disappointment, but I knew what I had to do." He paused, looking at her out of narrowed eyes. "Since you are the reason this happened, Katerina, you are the one who is going to help me."

Shrinking back, she shook her head, tearing her hands from his grasp. He gripped her coat, pulling her close, his face inches from hers.

"Don't make the mistake of trying to break free of me," he said in a harsh whisper. "We are all connected now, Miss Katerina. You, me, my wife... Cheryl Penn..."

Her mouth opened but no sound came out.

He chuckled, his eyes glinting with amusement. "Oh yes, the diversion created to lead the police on a merry chase for an imaginary serial killer . . ." he sighed, "well, not every plan works. Your boyfriend is a little smarter than I thought. I find that stunning, but no matter. We will come up with something else."

We?

He's insane.

She gave a violent twist as Reynolds suddenly let go, crashing backwards against the door. Grabbing the handle, she began yanking it back and forth.

"If you behave yourself," Reynolds said, "you won't see the man in the blue Ford again. He's there to make sure you don't become forgetful and say something you shouldn't to your policeman boyfriend . . . and to make sure you complete the assignments *I* will give you. We still have a lot of work to do together, Miss Katerina."

The limo eased to a stop. The locks popped open.

Throwing open the door, she bolted from the limousine and ran.

Reynolds chuckled; Garrett appeared and closed the door. A moment later, he slipped back behind the wheel.

"Home, Mr. Reynolds?" came his voice over the intercom.

"Yes, Garrett, thank you," Reynolds said. "It has been a long day."

Chapter 72

Plates dotted with scraps of leftover food, empty wine bottles, and crumpled, discarded napkins littered the dining room table.

As Emma told her story, her blond hair bounced, brushing her shoulders, her cheeks rosy after two glasses of wine.

Frank and Ryan, both smiling, looked at her expectantly.

"So he's sittin' there, doubled over, sayin' he's fine, he wants to go home. Me, the doctor, and the officer are staring at the x-ray. He swallowed a ring and two diamond-studded penguin earrings. So I say to him, 'How is it you have a jewelry box in your belly?'"

They chuckled, then quieted down, waiting for the punch line.

"So he says, 'I got 'em for my girlfriend for Christmas but I didn't know where else to hide them.'"

Peals of laughter broke out around the table; Katerina, laughing along, tears rolling down her cheeks, clenched her fists at her sides, her nails pressing deep into her palms.

"That's nothing," Ryan said, jumping in. "Tell 'em about the guy and Bellevue," he said to Frank. "Never mind, I'll tell it."

"Go ahead, you tell it," Frank said, still chuckling.

"So we're taking a guy to Bellevue. He's screaming and crying, right?"

Kat stared in mock interest, as if hanging on Ryan's every word.

"So we say, 'Sir, please calm down. Can you tell us what happened?' But he just keeps screaming, 'My briefcase, my briefcase, I left my briefcase.'"

"So he asks," Frank says, jerking his thumb at Ryan, "'Where did you leave it?' And the guy says—"

"—and the guy says, 'Bed Stuy,'" Ryan finished.

Frank shook his head.

"So I tell the guy, 'Sir, the case might have been there but there's no way it's there now.' So the guy says, 'No, no, no, you don't understand, there's ten thousand dollars in the case. You gotta help me. You gotta help me.'"

Ryan took a moment to catch his breath.

Katerina's heart thudded in her chest, a wave of dizziness washing over her.

"Did you go?" Emma asked.

"Yeah," Ryan said. "We went. The guy gives us directions. We get there. The case is still there. No shit, it really is. We can't believe it. We get out of the car and the guy runs over to the case. He grabs it and he's hugging it. I thought he was gonna kiss it. He turns to us, right, and says 'Thank you, thank you.' So we look at him and I say, 'You're welcome, now where did you get the ten thousand dollars?'"

Frank, still smiling, started to laugh.

"And then," Ryan said, "he drops the case and runs like hell!"

In the midst of the laughter, Katerina wondered what her story would sound like. *I broke into a house to steal a sex tape. I smuggle illegal drugs. I worked for a man who killed his wife. I'm responsible for her death.*

***

"And what have you been up to, darlin'?" Emma asked Kat.

Katerina had worked the cover story down to the last detail. "Sitting in meetings, taking notes," she said.

"Why doesn't the guy have his own secretary go to the meeting?" Frank asked. A jolt passed through Kat, every nerve raw and exposed. She met his pointed look; his eyes were filled with antagonism. And distrust. *He doesn't believe me.*

Katerina shrugged. "I guess he needed her to do something else. We didn't chat while getting our nails done."

The room lapsed into a dead, uncomfortable silence.

Keep looking. You won't find anything.

"So you sit in meetings all the time? That's it?"

"Nope," Kat said. "Sometimes I pick up lunch."

"Hey, there is no shame in picking up the lunch," Ryan said. "I do it all the time for Lashiver."

"Oh yeah?" Kat said, turning her attention to Ryan. "What lunch do you pick up?"

He leaned over. "Number ten with a medium drink. You want fries with that?" he asked.

"Supersize me," she said, and he took a kiss.

When they parted, she noticed Frank still watching her, his eyes cold and calculating.

You're going to be trouble, aren't you?

***

In the kitchen, the remnants of the meal preparation were everywhere: pots, pans, spoons and spice bottles dotted the counter tops.

Standing at the sink, the faucet running full blast, Katerina watched the bubbles rise, the water cascading over her hands. She washed plates and glasses, sloughing the soap away under the running water and stacking them in the drainer, while her thoughts held her captive in a limousine with a mad man.

She heard a cracking sound. Gazing down into the sink, she saw the swath of red cutting through the soap suds as a sharp pain made her cry out. Picking up her hands, she saw the blood oozing from her palm. Turning at a noise behind her, she found Ryan, his face a study in concern.

"I'm okay," she said, reaching for a dish towel.

***

Katerina sat on the toilet lid while Emma worked, quiet and efficient, cleaning the cut. When she swabbed the antibiotic across her skin, Katerina jerked her hand away. Emma held fast.

"I'm sorry about the glass, Em," she said. "I know it was part of a set."

"Not to worry, doll," Emma said. "They were an early, early wedding present from Frank's mother." She leaned in confidentially. "I hate 'em. Ugly as sin. You're lucky, it didn't go too deep. You'll get away without stitches but it's gonna hurt like hell."

Katerina nodded. It was on the tip of her tongue. *Say it. Say, I have something to tell you. Say, Emma I need help. Say, Emma, I'm in trouble.*

Say it. It is what it is. That's what Winter taught you, right? Admit the truth. Say it. I'm in trouble. I need help.

"Emma—"

The jangle of a cell phone stopped her.

"What is it, hon?" Emma said, winding the last piece of surgical tape around Kat's hand.

"That's my phone, I have to get it."

Emma let go and Katerina bolted off the lid, following the noise to her purse. She pulled out her "Ryan" phone and pressed the green button.

"Hello?"

"Hello, myshka."

Katerina froze. *Don't look around. Don't check to see who's close to you. Don't call him by name.*

"How are you?" she asked, maneuvering out of earshot, making sure to keep Frank and Ryan in her sights.

"Natasha Fatale, we have little problem." Ivan's voice came through calm, unperturbed. "I finish work here but I need to arrange transportation."

"Call Enterprise, they'll pick you up," she said, aware of the throbbing in her palm, pounding like a heartbeat, keeping time with her own.

"Nyet. I need you."

"I can call someone to pick you up and help you with tickets."

"Nyet. You come."

"I can't help you."

"Myshka, I still have wig and jacket."

Katerina forgot to breathe.

"You put them in backpack. Now you come get them. You are driver. My driver."

She said the first thing that came to mind. "Meet me at the Chelsea Savoy."

"Da." The phone clicked off.

Ryan came to her. "What's going on, babe?"

"I have to meet a client."

"At this hour?"

Shrugging into her coat, she nodded. "I have to meet him."

Ryan took her by the shoulders. "You just hurt yourself. You're not going anywhere."

"A client," Frank muttered.

Ryan turned, shooting Frank a sharp look.

It was then Katerina noticed that Emma had her head down, staring at the floor. Her eyes shifted to Frank; he didn't bother to conceal his hostility—and judgment.

They think I'm a prostitute, she thought. *This is your chance. Make it work for you. Get out now.*

"Oh . . . I get it. You think I'm a hooker?" she said with a laugh. "That's great. Fantastic. I am so lucky to have such good friends."

"Hon," Emma began, moving towards her.

Katerina whirled around, advancing on Frank. "I am meeting a client, a fully clothed client." She turned to Ryan. "I thought I would do my normal, fully-clothed job, and then we could go back to your apartment for some alone time. But I've rr my appetite for that and everything else," she said.

Wrapping her scarf around her neck, she headed for the door. Ryan caught her arm. "Kat."

Katerina wrenched her arm out of his grasp.

"Okay, okay," he said, edging between her and the door. "We are way, way, off base," Ryan said.

Kat's eyes opened wide. "We . . .?"

Ryan's face turned red. "No, I . . . no, I didn't think—"

"Save it."

"Baby, I can explain. Just let me go with you—"

"I don't do threesomes," she snapped.

"Okay. Okay. We go. You help your client. Then we go back to my place and I apologize for myself and these horrible people," he said with a sheepish smile.

"I'm a big girl. I work alone. And I'm done . . . we're done."

The color drained from Ryan's face.

I'm sorry, she thought. *Trust me. I'm doing you a favor.* Pushing past him, she threw open the door and ran out. As she raced down the stairs, she heard Emma's voice calling after her . . . then heavy footsteps.

Don't look back. Don't let him catch up.
Run.

Chapter 73

When she entered the Chelsea Savoy hotel, Katerina didn't see him. She searched the small lobby but only a man with dark eyes and a stony expression lounged on a couch in a secluded corner. He wore a buzz cut and the beginnings of a beard. Then the solemn expression melted into a sly smile. Remembering Ivan's relaxed posture in the back of the Town Car, Katerina made the connection. He got up and approached her.

"Natasha, it is good to see you again," Ivan said. His eyes went to her bandaged hand. "How you hurt yourself?"

"Save it, Boris. Where's my stuff?"

"Soon, little bear, soon. We make stops first. You have car?"

"Let's get going," she said.

As they went for the exit, she caught him giving her a sideways glance, the sly smirk still firmly in place.

"I like our kiss. You like our kiss?"

"The earth moved," she snapped, annoyed at the rush of heat in her face. She put the burner to her ear. "*Papi*, I need a car. How much?"

***

Two hours later, Ivan had collected his new, fake passport and train tickets. The only thing Katerina had collected was another headache: Moose placing the garter on her thigh at the wedding.

Outside the Amtrak waiting room, Ivan and Kat lingered, checking the big board.

"Okay, Boris, happy trails. Now give me the key."

"What key?"

Out of patience, Katerina's anger spiked along with the pain pulsing in her palm. "The key to the locker that has my stuff," she snapped, holding out her good hand.

"No locker, no key. I give wig and jacket to our Uncle Tony."

"Son of a bitch," Kat said, her voice rising. Grabbing his arm, she pulled him into a corner. "What the fuck did you give them to Desucci for?"

Ivan held up his hands. "Such words from nice girl. He say he want them. He pay me. I work for him. I give them to him."

Katerina released her grip. Blowing out a mouthful of air, she stood, her body stiff, impotent with anger. She nodded her head, conceding defeat.

"Okay, Boris. Thanks a lot. Safe trip."

Katerina walked away.

"Wait. I need money."

Katerina whirled around, her mouth open. *Un—believable.* Walking back, she dug her good hand into her pocket, pulled out a few bills, and slapped them into Ivan's open hand. Taking the money, he tucked it away without counting it. As Kat turned to leave again, he pulled her in, giving her a soft kiss on each cheek and then one on her lips.

"Now, I work for you," he whispered.

"I don't need you for anything," she said.

"Someday, Yekaterina Karenina, you will. You will have despair. You will think to end everything. Do not despair. You paid me. I work for you."

He released her and walked away.

She stood for a long moment, staring after him, feeling as if the air had been sucked out of her lungs. Finally, she started for the exit, holding her throbbing hand up against her body, her shoulders sagging under an invisible weight, a weight that had become her constant companion. A cell phone buzzed in her purse. She dug out the normal "Ryan" phone. Five text messages, three from Emma, two from Ryan.

No more, she thought. *I'm out. I'm not getting back in.*

Chapter 74

"What the—hell was that?" Katerina demanded as she entered the warehouse, Carlo on her heels.

Anthony Desucci responded with a smile. Vincent flanked his boss, ready to serve.

"A necessary exercise to keep you invested. I find that people are more motivated when they have some skin in the game, you know, a direct liability. Your adventure with Ivan, the cleaner, takes care of any temptation you might have to confide in your boyfriend in exchange for immunity."

No chance of that. "I want my stuff."

"I want the car."

"I'll have Marcus' car shortly and then I want my stuff."

"How many days in a shortly?"

"I'm working on the wife's schedule. When she moves, I move. There are signs she's getting ready to move."

"Vincent and Carlo will assist you."

"I've got it covered."

"That wasn't a request. They will follow you. They will assist. And no more trips downtown to talk to law enforcement. Understand?"

Katerina curbed her mouth and nodded her head.

Chapter 75

Katerina sat in her coat while taking her microeconomics exam, her bandaged hand resting in her lap. As she scribbled feverishly with her right hand, she noticed the red, raw knuckles. She stopped writing, watching the pencil shaking in her grasp. Sitting in the midst of the hushed, packed lecture hall, her mind spoke loud and clear, the words looping in her head.

John Reynolds killed his wife.
He had her murdered.
He had her mutilated.

They hadn't seemed real; words resting on the surface, never quite sinking in . . . until now. A cool sweat broke over her body and she shivered, her stomach queasy, nausea rising. Gathering her exam and her purse, Kat walked down the steps and handed in her test. Exiting the auditorium, she stole into the bathroom. Barricading herself in a stall, she retched into the toilet.

"You okay in there?" a female voice asked.

"Yeah," Kat managed, her voice thick. Swiping hot tears from her face, she stayed in the stall, vomiting twice more until only dry heaves were left.

I could run now.
Reynolds will come after me.
Sheridan will come after me.
They will find me.
They'll track my digital footprint.
I can't run. Not now. Not yet. Not without a plan.
Like Angel said. If you disappear, you best make sure everyone thinks you're dead.

Katerina eased out of the stall. At the sink, she splashed water on her face and rinsed her mouth. Trudging out into the cold, night air, the same question that she had been asking for weeks, gnawed at her. *Is my life fate? Karma? Determinism? Free will? Did I have no choice?*

Am I my father's daughter?
It doesn't matter anymore.
I can't do anything but finish this.

Chapter 76

Alexander Winter sat in a corner booth in the back of a darkened pub. The slight man across from him was in his fifties with an angular face, a pair of thin-rimmed glasses resting on a sharp nose. Winter knew him only as Durant.

"Have you ever visited Russia?" the man asked, his French accent soft and smooth.

Winter shook his head, studying a piece of paper on the table, a color photocopy of an icon of the Madonna and child. He was certain it wasn't even close to doing the item justice.

"The White Nights are beautiful," the man said, almost as if he were talking to himself. "You should see them."

"I'm not traveling outside the U.S. now."

"But you have."

"But not now."

"The item is not in Russia. It is in this country."

Winter took the news in silence.

"My client wants this and only this. No substitutions. If you take the job, he expects it will be completed."

"It's pay-or-play," Winter said. "No guarantees."

Durant shrugged.

"Five million. Two and a half up front. The money is to be wired into an account number I give you. Nothing happens until the deposit is confirmed."

The older man nodded. "He would expect you to leave right away."

"Then he should get someone else. I have business here that must be concluded. I'm not leaving until it's done."

Durant thought and then nodded.

Winter took the paper, folding it and tucking it into his inside coat pocket. He slid out of the booth.

"Mr. Bartholomew," Durant said, "my client is very particular. He wants you because you're the best. He expects you to fulfill the order, no matter what. He is a man of honor above business. It is a matter of honor that you deliver."

"Pay-or-play."

Winter got up and walked out of the pub. A finicky client was not his problem. Katerina hadn't answered his texts or turned on the tracking phone. He couldn't leave her. Not yet.

Chapter 77

Katerina pulled on long johns, jeans, and a sweater. She stopped, cursing silently. After the final, she had an appointment at Gallagher's apartment. She did the mental calculation.

Run to school. Run back to apartment. Change. Run uptown to Gallagher.

Shit. Forget it.

In a fit of impatience, she threw off her outfit and went for the elegant black slip dress and heels. The coat would have to do.

I'll be warm tomorrow.

***

Hustling out of her building, Katerina zeroed in on navigating her stilettos on the icy steps down to the sidewalk. When she looked up, she ran smack into Philip.

"What the hell, Philip?" she cried, giving him a shove.

He grabbed her arm. "We have to talk. Now. Let's go back inside."

"I don't think so," she said, wrenching herself out of his grasp. "And by the way, thanks for loaning me out to your posse of criminals, asshole."

"What are you talking about? I'm here because there's a little problem," he said, "with that thing that I asked you to hold on to for me."

"I never opened it. I never took anything out."

Philip held up his hands. "I know that. That's not why I'm here."

"I'm late for my final," Katerina said, brushing past him. He caught up to her, gripping her arm, falling into step.

"Hey, you're going to be early for a funeral—yours. The photographer is dead."

"Who?"

"The photographer who took the pictures is dead."

"How?"

"Suicide. It's bullshit. Trust me. He was a happy guy. He *didn't* kill himself."

Katerina stopped, all attention now.

"Listen, kid, you know how sometimes there are two bullies living on the same block? Well, this is kind of like that. I was hired by one bully to get the pictures and that's pissing off the other bully."

Katerina clamped her eyes shut. "Philip, I am cold. No, I am freezing. I am tired, my head hurts, my hand hurts, and I want all of this to be over. I am sorry he's dead. You're not going to make this my problem."

"Kiddo, this is already your problem."

"Screw you! You told me you're a brilliant lawyer, smarter than all the others. Then you fix this. I've got all I can handle."

Shaking free, she headed for the subway station. She didn't look back.

Chapter 78

As Katerina stepped on campus, a cell phone buzzed. She pulled out the "normal" phone. Silent. With a curse, she dropped it back in her purse and dug out the burner and clicked to connect.

"The wife is on the move," Lisa said. "She left the house about fifteen minutes ago. My guy is following. He'll text updates. I'll send them on to you. Give her about an hour or so to get in here. Then you're on."

Katerina glanced toward the building. *The philosophy final*. "Got it," she said.

"Good. Don't screw it up," Lisa said. "If I'm going to be blackmailed, I don't want it to go to waste."

Lisa clicked off.

Katerina took one last look at the building. Then she turned, heading for the subway.

Chapter 79

Katerina walked toward West Fifty-seventh Street, the burner at her ear.

"What's shakin', mami," Moose's voice came over the line. "Are we in go mode?"

"Yes," she said. "Are you ready?"

"Ready to roll. You see the big mami?"

"I'm not there yet. Almost. Once I get the car, where am I going?"

Moose gave her the address.

"If I don't ditch Huey and Dewey, this doesn't work. Have you got the plan down?"

Moose laughed. "No sweat. Once you're in the car, you call me, tell me where you are. My posse will take care of traffic control, know what I'm sayin'?"

"Moose, delay, not destroy, right?"

"Hey, I know how to display . . . cómo se dice . . . ?"

"Self-control?"

"Yeah, yeah. I got a lot of that self-control. I got you mami, don't worry. You get your dress yet?"

"Moose, business first, wedding second," she said through gritted teeth.

"Yo, no worries. You know we should go into business. I need a partner. I need structure—"

"Moose!"

"Okay, *ta-to*, we talk later."

One last thing. I just have to get through this one last thing. And then do what?

Kat decided she couldn't think about it now. She was going into this with no backup, flying blind. She went over everything Winter had taught her. She was sure of only one thing. Winter would not approve of the plan.

Chapter 80

"She's hit the city, heading toward the park," Lisa said. "You good?"

"Yup," Kat said and hung up.

Simple, elegant decorations of giant red and black striped candy canes adorned the building on West Fifty-seventh street. Trees lining the sidewalk sparkled with tiny twinkling lights.

While she shivered in the cold, she killed time calling Gallagher's office and left word she had to postpone the appointment until tomorrow. As the wind bit at her bare legs, Katerina imagined Vincent and Carlo circling the block in a heated car. Remembering the warm outfit she had on that morning, discarded on her bed, she cursed silently. She couldn't go into any stores; she could be identified. She would have to wait it out.

***

Katerina ducked around the corner. The Porsche came down the block, darting into an open parking spot. Betsy Marcus got out and strode into the building.

***

Out on the street, traffic continued to ebb and flow in both directions. Katerina eyed the car, hesitating.

She could have changed the lock.
She could have changed the key fob combination.
No time to worry about that now.
Katerina crossed the street.
She passed the trees with the twinkling lights.
The car loomed larger as she came closer.
The key was out and in her hand.
Look like you're where you belong.
She reached the car.
Step off the curb.
Pull on the door handle.

The door gave under the weight of her hand.

Get in the car.

Key in the ignition.

The car engine purred to life.

Check over your left shoulder.

Pull out into traffic.

Katerina checked the rearview mirror. Vincent and Carlo were back there, somewhere, following her.

Chapter 81

Remember what he taught you. Katerina fought the stop-and-go traffic for blocks. She turned left at a traffic light, checking her mirrors. It was the gray Lexus. It had to be. Two more times around and she was sure. The car kept its distance, never too fast or slow.

Katerina called Moose on the burner. "I'm at Fortieth Street."

"Okay, mami, wh- y- g-t . . . ma- a --ght."

The call dropped.

"Moose! Moose!"

Katerina slammed her hand on the steering wheel.

What now? What now? Damn it!

The dynamic duo in the gray Lexus were still back there.

Easy. Calm down. Moose knows where you are. Watch Huey and Dewey. As soon as they're out of the picture, make a right. Then try to call again.

Coming out of her thoughts, Katerina saw the red light just in time to slam on the breaks. Heart thudding in her chest, she gripped the wheel, her palm pulsating with pain. At the green, she stepped on the gas.

A chorus of car horns broke out behind her.

In the mirror she saw the gray Lexus pulling over to the curb, the emergency lights blinking, another car pulling in behind it. Car doors began opening.

That's my cue.

She made a right turn as the burner buzzed.

"Yo," Moose's voice came through the static, "where you at?"

"Twenty-ninth, crossing Sixth."

"You golden, mami. The Moose is gonna talk you in."

Katerina gave her mirrors a quick check. A sea of cars and taxis, and another gray Lexus. Ignoring it, she focused on the traffic in front of her. *This whole thing is crazy. Is it even possible it's working? Don't think about it now. Just follow it to the end. Finish this.* Following Moose's voice through the static, Kat spied the open garage door and pulled in.

Jumping out of the Porsche, she went for the replica. Moose hovered over the original, peering inside the open car door.

"Mierda. Man, she's beautiful. This is a piece of work."

Katerina left the replica to slam and lock the Porsche's door.

"Cold, mami. That is frigid."

Kat ducked into the replica. "I don't want the Moose to get loose. Back in twenty," she said through chattering teeth.

Katerina slammed the door shut, revved the engine and drove the replica out of the garage.

Almost there.

Chapter 82

Katerina turned down Ninth Avenue. The sun was disappearing, making the warehouse buildings look like a prison compound. The wind whistled against the car windows. Katerina shook her head to clear out the anxious whisperings and imagined premonitions.

An enforcer motioned her to ease the replica into the warehouse, parking next to an idling Town Car. She cut the engine and got out. Desucci got out of the Town Car along with two hulking enforcers. For a moment, Kat missed Vincent and Carlo.

Approaching Desucci, she dropped the key in his hand.

"No problems?" he asked.

"None," she said through chattering teeth. "I'd like my things, please."

He smiled.

Hearing a car engine behind her, she turned. A pristine Lexus pulled in. A gray Lexus. *Sometimes there's a Plan B.* A man in a dark overcoat got out, six feet, built like the Terminator with a face to match. No mercy. The air rushed out of Katerina's lungs. She backed up into Desucci. When she turned, he was in her face.

"Meet Louie. Donald Duck had three nephews. Now take out your cell phone and call your friend to bring the real Porsche. Now."

Fumbling in her purse, Katerina brought out a phone. The normal phone. With trembling hands, she dropped it back in her purse, rooting around until she put her hands on the burner. She dialed.

"Yo."

"Bring the car to Thirty-six, Ninth Avenue."

"Tell him to wait outside," Desucci whispered.

"You locked the car. The Moose can't get loose."

"Bring the car now," she said, her voice hoarse and cracking. "Wait outside. You understand me?"

There was a moment of silence.

"I got you, *chica*. On the way."

Katerina clicked off the phone. With a gloved hand, Desucci brushed the tear from her cheek.

"He's coming," she said.

"That's good, Katerina. That's very good."

***

Desucci ushered Katerina outside as a cold, wintry mix started to fall.

A Lexus came around the corner. As it drove past and rolled to a stop, Katerina spied the crumpled right rear bumper. Vincent and Carlo got out of the car.

"Not very nice, miss," Vincent said as he and Carlos approached.

Katerina shrank back.

"I don't think he's coming," Desucci said.

"Give him a minute."

"Katerina—"

"One more minute!" she cried.

At the sound of an engine and squealing tires, they all watched the end of the block. The white Porsche rounded the corner, the engine roaring as it sped toward them; it stopped on a dime with inches to spare.

The driver's door opened and Moose stepped out.

"Zero to sixty in three seconds, motherfuckers," he said, a self-satisfied smirk on his face as he tossed the key. Vincent snatched it out of the air.

"Wait here," Desucci said, handing Kat off to Moose. Vincent drove the Porsche into the warehouse and jumped out of the car to slide the warehouse door closed. Carlo and the enforcers remained where they were, impervious to the weather.

Kat shivered in the wet, cold whipping wind.

"I'm sorry," she said to Moose.

He pulled her close. As her arm snaked around his waist, she felt the gun. "No worries, mami," Moose whispered. When she gazed up at him, his eyes were black and cold, fixed on the enforcers. "If we goin' out, we ain't goin' alone."

Moose's hand slid inside his jacket.

"Please . . ." she started.

An enforcer gave a disarming smile.

The warehouse door rolled open and the enforcers hustled to do their assigned jobs. The real Porsche rolled out of the warehouse first, followed by the Town Car, and the Lexus. The vehicles all stopped and idled. Vincent got out of the real Porsche. Desucci strolled out of the warehouse. The replica rolled out last.

As Desucci approached her, Katerina let go of Moose. "You really are adorable," Desucci said and then ducked into the Town Car. The enforcers followed and the Town Car pulled away.

Katerina still in shock, hadn't moved.

"Okay, miss. You're good to go," Vincent said, bringing her the key and a plastic bag, the jacket and wig peeking through the top. "Mr. Desucci will be taking the replica."

"Mr. Desucci gonna pay for the replica?" Moose asked.

Kat looked at Moose, her eyes a mix of desperation and pleading.

"No problem," Moose said, pulling her closer, "we'll call it good will."

"That's the spirit," Vincent said with a smile.

Katerina looked from the replica to the Porsche to Vincent and back again, her head throbbing in confusion.

"What's the matter?" Vincent asked with a chuckle. "We're giving you the real thing. What are you afraid of? You think we installed a bomb in two minutes? Do I look like I could do that? Don't worry," he said.

Katerina stared at the key in her hand, finally closing her fingers around it.

"Good luck, miss," Vincent said. "Mr. Desucci is very impressed with you. Very impressed."

Vincent gave Moose a nod. He and Carlo got into the replica and drove away.

"Yo, shit, woman. You deal with some heavy players. That is some crazy shit." Moose inspected the Porsche. "This one's the real one. Can I drive?"

"No," she said.

In the driver's seat, Kat inserted the key in the ignition. She took a breath. With a twist of her fingers, the car came to life.

Moose settled into his seatbelt. "Let's ride, mami," he said with a smile.

Putting her foot to the gas pedal, Katerina remembered to breathe. *Still alive.* Pulling out the burner, she made a call.

"What?" Marcus's voice boomed through the phone.

"I've got it," she said. "I'm bringing it now."

She hung up.

Chapter 83

Katerina arrived at Marcus's building just shy of five o'clock. The city lights were sparkling in the night. She thought to call Jasmine that the job was done. *Later.*

***

Entering the apartment, Kat noticed an overnight bag in the foyer. *Great. Can't wait to take it out for a spin.* Marcus came out wearing a thick, gray cable sweater and corduroy pants. He had heavy, brown work boots on his feet.

Katerina held up the key and placed it on the table.

"Fan-fucking-tastic cookie, really," he said.

"Mr. Marcus, I need you to call in that the job's done."

"We'll get to that in a minute, cookie," he said.

"No, we'll get to it now. Call it in, let them know that the job's done. And I wouldn't plan on going out for a joyride," she said, nodding at the bag.

"Why's that?"

"Anthony Desucci is not pleased by the lack of return on investments in your hedge fund. He wants your car instead."

"Hunh," Marcus said, falling into an unusual silence. "That's quite a BFD, isn't it?" he finally said.

"Yeah, it is. For you. For me, it's NMFP."

Marcus furrowed his brows. "NMFP?"

"Not my fucking problem," she said. "Now call in that the job is done."

Marcus nodded with a smile. "Okay, cookie," he said. "Wait here a minute."

He left Katerina in a state of annoyance. She already had her evening planned and she wanted to get to it: a boiling hot shower, a hot chocolate, and a long sleep under the heavy, quilted comforter. Taking off her coat, she wandered into the painting room.

Examining the paintings made her think of Winter, the familiar mix of anger and sadness surging within her. Grabbing the magazine from the coffee table, she flipped the pages to the article. She glanced over the photo of the four fake Monet paintings of *Bridge over a Pond of Water Lilies*: purple, yellow, green, and blue.

She flipped the page and started reading where she had left off.

She froze.

Blue?

She flipped back to the photo. Looking up, the four fakes on the wall stared back at her. Purple. Yellow. Green. *Red.*

No blue.

Winter's text. The 4 pics. All still there? No. No they are not.

Why would anyone want a fake?

Keep it simple. They wouldn't. No one wants a fake.

The job is never the job.

There's something hidden under the fake.

If the blue fake wasn't on the wall, where was it?

A wave of dizziness swept over her.

The painting is in the car.

Only it's not in the car.

Desucci has it.

Shoving her hand into the bottom of her purse, Kat fished around, desperate to find the two things she needed as she beat a path to the door.

***

"Where do you think you're going, cookie?"

Katerina stopped, the soft tone of his voice making her heart skip a beat. "You made the call. Our business is finished."

"Not quite," Marcus said. "I told you. Luke sent me a good fortune. Time for me to take a trip, cookie. You're going to drive me," he said.

"You didn't hire me for that."

"I'm adding services." He had his right hand in his pocket.

Kat glanced back at the front door.

The battery was in and the "Winter" phone was on. *It had to be giving off the signal now. Winter would see it. What if he didn't? What was Plan B? Think!*

"I'm off the clock," she said.

Marcus took his hand out of his pocket, revealing a gun.

Kat legs turned to jelly. She sucked in a slow breath.

"That's okay. I'm thinking this one's on the house, like comping a room for a high roller."

"The agency doesn't do comping. And they keep track of their consultants. Call it in or you'll never make it out of the city. I guarantee it."

A heavy moment of silence lingered between them.

"Sure, cookie. Whatever. I don't need any bullshit while I'm trying to get on my way." He took out his cell phone and placed a call, giving the job details. "No, it's only for a few hours. Yes, she's here. She's fine."

Please ask to speak to me. Please.

"Are we good or what? Fine."

He hung up the phone, the gun still trained on her. "Take out your phone."

Katerina put her hand in her purse. *For once, for God's sake, pull out the right phone.*

She pulled out the normal phone.

Marcus waved the gun at her. "Take out the SIM card."

Kat did as she was told. He waved the gun at her. "Now the other phone."

"What other phone?"

"Cut the crap. I know you've got another one."

Katerina dug into her purse. She pulled out the burner.

"Same thing." He watched as she repeated the process. "Now put everything in my bag."

Kat bent down and unzipped the bag, finding it crammed with clothes, socks, underwear, and rubber banded packs of cash. She dropped in the phones and SIM cards and zipped it closed.

Keeping an eye on her, Marcus slipped into his wool pea coat. With a wave of the gun, he indicated she should take up the bag and head toward the door.

She went to put her coat on.

"Forget it. Just take it. And your purse. And your plastic bag. Let's go."

Glancing down at her slip of a dress and stiletto pumps she turned to him, "Please," she said.

"Now it's please. NMFP cookie. Get moving."

As Katerina walked ahead of him, she prayed that the Winter phone, still stashed in the bottom of her purse, was giving off a clear tracking signal. If it wasn't, she hoped to God Plan B would work.

Chapter 84

After Jasmine's call, Angel moved into position. He spotted Kat exiting the building. He hadn't expected to see the client with her. Once the Porsche pulled out into traffic, Angel kept a safe distance. He hit the speed dial on his phone for Jasmine. Something wasn't right.

***

Crossing the street, Winter heard the chime of his phone. Checking it, he saw the notification. The tracking phone was on; the software was working. She was crossing Amsterdam Avenue and moving fast. He doubled back, sidestepping shoppers and the dirty, leftover piles of snow getting a makeover from the fresh coat coming down.

He rushed for the Range Rover and revved the engine. Punching a number into his cell phone, he waited for the connection.

"You want the painting? I know where it is. Be outside, I'm on my way."

Winter clicked off, slammed the car into gear, and pulled out into traffic.

It is what it is. Find the truth. Katie was a smart girl. She found out the truth. He was afraid she had figured it out too late.

***

After Jasmine hung up with Angel, she made another phone call. She reported Katerina's status to MJM. Jasmine was told to wait and placed on hold.

***

Katerina drove north on the Henry Hudson Parkway. She didn't understand. Something was off, way off. Before they got into the car, Marcus had thrown his bag into the front end trunk, along with her coat, purse, and the bag with the jacket and wig. The *empty* trunk. Marcus didn't bat an eye. *Where else would you keep a painting? Where the hell is it?*

"Maybe if you told me where you're going—"

"Where we're going, cookie."

"Where we're going."

"Where we're going is a surprise. Now shut the fuck up and take the upper level of the GW Bridge. Can you do that without asking anymore fucking annoying questions?"

Katerina bit her lip and kept her eyes on the road. In her purse, she imagined the tracking signal still going strong. *Did Winter see it?*

She checked out the sea of traffic behind her. She had to believe Angel was back there somewhere, following.

You got the envelope, baby, I go to the ends of the earth for you.

I hope so, she thought. *God, I hope so*. She eyed the heat settings in the car, wishing she could turn them up to full blast. She shivered.

***

The heat cranked on high in the car.

"You sure about all this?" Clay asked. "If that painting is still in the apartment—"

"It isn't," Winter said.

"And I'm getting the painting," Clay said.

"You ever done this before?" Winter asked, ignoring the question.

"Shit, man, I've done everything before," Clay said.

Winter gave a disgusted laugh. He didn't like playing this game. It was dangerous. But he had no choice. Two against one made for better odds. Besides, he needed someone to cover him. He had a feeling Katerina needed someone to look after her.

"You have a gun?" Winter asked.

"At this moment?"

"Never mind. I'll give you one."

"You want to give it to me now?"

"I don't want to give it to you later."

They rode in silence.

"And you don't want the painting?" Clay asked.

"No."

"And you don't want a cut?"

"No."

They rode in silence.

"She's really worth all this?"

Winter didn't bother to answer. It wasn't even a question.

***

The wipers went back and forth like a frenetic metronome, barely repelling the onslaught as the snow switched over to a wet, freezing rain. She slowed the car, tapping the brakes.

A fender bender...

A sharp, metallic edge poked in her side.

"Don't be thinking of aborting this little trip, cookie. Not a good idea. If I'm not getting out, neither are you."

The car edged toward the bridge.

***

"Gal Friday Incorporated," Lisa said, sounding every bit the dedicated receptionist of a reputable high-end temp agency. "How may I help you?"

"I'm trying to reach Katerina Mills," the male voice said.

The cop boyfriend. "I'm sorry, sir, she's not in at the moment. May I please take a message?"

"Yeah, look, this is her—this is *Detective* Kellan. Her cell phone isn't working. Do you have any idea where she is?"

"She's out on assignment but I do expect her to call in shortly. I'd be happy to pass along a message."

She heard a sigh of disapproval from the other end of the line. "Ask her to call me."

The line clicked off.

Lisa called Kat's burner, listening to the computerized message saying the number is not in service. She hung up and dialed another number.

"You've got a problem," Lisa said when the line connected. "I think your interior decorator is in some shit. You might want to check it out."

She hung up the phone.

***

The overhead lights on the upper level of the GW Bridge highlighted the freezing rain dancing its way down onto the cars. They were approaching the end of the bridge and the Palisades Parkway.

"Can I please turn up the heat?" she asked.

"No," he said.

***

"You want to repeat that, please?" Angel said. He was on the upper level of the GW Bridge, still keeping the Porsche in his sights.

"Discontinue the follow," Jasmine repeated.

"Payment has not been collected," he said.

"This comes from the top. You are relieved of this collection. Discontinue the follow."

Angel clicked off. He hadn't bothered to ask why this consultant just got a pass to keep an entire fee. Katerina Mills wouldn't live to spend the money. He knew the drill. He'd been through this once before. MJM had made a decision. Katerina Mills had been cut loose.

***

Katerina struggled to keep pressure on the gas pedal as a numbness settled in her feet. She followed Marcus's instructions and maneuvered the car onto the New York State Thruway, Route 87.

They were heading upstate.

We're going to Canada.

No. He's going to Canada.

Chapter 85

The city had faded away behind them, the crowded mass of gray rectangles and squares long gone. Gripping the steering wheel, Katerina struggled to drive as sleep threatened to overtake her. They had pulled off the Thruway and were on Route 28, a winding, hilly, two-lane road that had turned slick and treacherous under the onslaught of freezing rain. She slowed the car to a crawl, her bandaged hand throbbing as she fought to keep the vehicle steady.

Simon craned his neck to look skyward out the window. "Shit," he said, as the tires continued to grind, slide, and skid.

Katerina had no idea where they were, only a vague notion that they had been on the road for hours and they weren't getting very far. She had nodded off a few times, jerking awake to Marcus cursing at her as the car drifted off the road.

He suddenly flipped on the radio, flooding the car with a holiday carol, Karen Carpenter singing about being home for Christmas.

"We used to do Christmas big at the house every year," he said.

What if I did swerve off the road, just a little. It might be enough. Enough to relax his grip on the gun ... to give me a chance to grab for it.

"We had lights everywhere, inside and out, holly around the fireplace, wrapped around the banisters. It was beautiful. I always liked Christmas the best."

"Betsy said you never appreciated the house," Katerina said.

"*I* didn't appreciate it?" he said, shaking his head in disbelief. "She doesn't know anything. I gave her everything. And what does she do? She sics the Feds on me. I know it was her. I have to leave everything now. My whole life gone. I won't have a home. I won't have friends. I won't even have my name. I can't use my real name ever again. I won't even exist. You believe that?"

Katerina listened in silence.

"They're probably in the apartment now, fucking Feds. Executing their fucking search warrants. Let 'em. Fuck 'em. There's nothing there.

Just a computer tower beat to shit with a hammer. I beat 'em all, cookie. I beat 'em all."

Suddenly the Porsche went into a skid. A gasp escaped her as the car began a rapid, out of control slide. Pumping the brakes, she turned the car into the skid and then back; the car slowed and held the road. A feeling of weakness came over her, her hands and arms aching.

"We need to stop," she said, her voice trembling. "If we spin out, we'll be stuck. Then we'll need to call someone."

He shoved the gun in her side. "Call who? We're in a dead zone, cookie. There's no cell service here. Just keep driving."

Kat blinked back tears. There was no one out there. Winter wasn't coming. No one was coming.

***

The bare branches of the mammoth trees hovered over the road, bending under the weight of the ice and snow clinging to them.

"Stop here," Marcus said.

The wheels crunched as they slid to a stop.

He leaned in closer to her. "We're getting out, cookie, nice and slow."

Kat's thoughts jumbled together, bleeding into each other.

I'm responsible for Felicia Reynolds' death.

I deserve this.

It's karma. It's fate.

It's determined.

"Please," was all she could manage.

"One shot to the head, cookie. You won't feel a thing. Run, and once I catch you, and I will catch you, I'll put one in your stomach and let you bleed out and die of frostbite. Now get the hell out of the car."

Katerina opened the car door. A blast of frigid air engulfed her. She slid out, her shoes filling with icy slush. Pellets of freezing, wet snow rained down on her, clinging to her wraparound dress, the waves of her hair, her eyelashes. The wind tore through her, at her face and hands; she gasped, stumbling.

Marcus waved the gun at her, motioning her to walk toward the woods.

If I run . . .
I'll hide in the woods.
He won't find me.
If I can survive until morning . . .
"Let's go, cookie, I don't have all day."

Katerina, her body numb, began walking. She tripped out of her shoes and went down, breaking her fall with her hands and knees. She cried out, struggling to her feet, as the gun jammed into her shoulder.

Her feet were moving but she didn't know how. As they entered the woods, she gazed into the darkness. *I'll go in there and be lost. No one will find me. Is this what happened to the other fixer? Is this how she went out?*

Stumbling to her knees, she lingered there, digging her hands into the hard, wet snow.

"Let's go, cookie. Don't make this a BFD."

He was coming up close behind her.

Struggling to rise, Katerina spun around, hurling a fistful of wet, icy snow into his face with all the strength she had left.

Then she ran.

The gun went off.

Chapter 86

"Bitch!" Lurching out blindly in the dark, the adrenalin rush of fear driving her forward through the snow, Katerina ran for her life. Pitching and stumbling, she didn't feel the ice-laden branches striking her face and body as she ran.

The wind spoke to her, whispering in her ear to give up. She thought to listen, to stop, to hide in the dark.

No. Keep moving.

Her pace began to slow; she couldn't feel her feet and could no longer will herself to speed up. Was she going straight or in a circle? She didn't hear him. Where was he?

A dull, aching pain throbbed in her left arm.

She heard noise.

She tried to run.

Moving forward, she looked over her shoulder. Nothing. She crashed into something solid. She cried out, flailing to get away. Hands gripped her arms. She began to twist and writhe to free herself. The hands pulled her closer.

Lips brushed against her ear.

"Katie."

She lifted her face toward the voice in the darkness.

Winter.

He had come.

Chapter 87

Winter had Katerina clasped against his chest with one arm, pointing the gun with the other.

He caught sight of movement.

"FBI. Stay where you are," Winter said.

Marcus stopped. He cursed and raised his hands.

"Turn around," Winter said. "Back to the road. Real slow. Any sudden move, I kill you."

***

They came out of the woods near the car.

Marcus looked off to Winter's right. A Range Rover, idling.

Winter hesitated. *Where the hell is Clay? Is he going to come up beside me or double-cross me?* No, not until he has the painting, Winter thought. Not until then.

"Put your hands where I can see them," Clay said, coming into view, his gun trained on Marcus.

Marcus cursed as he raised his hands.

"Now put the gun down and move away from it," Winter said.

With Katerina crushed against his chest, Winter forced himself to keep his mind on the moment. She had no coat, no gloves. He glanced down. Bare feet. *Shit.* He had felt a sticky wetness when he grabbed her arm. He hazarded a glance at her dress; a red stain on the sleeve.

"Look guys, we can make a deal," Marcus said. "I've got something in the car—"

"We know, Simon," Clay said.

"Great, so, fuck it, let's make a deal."

"No deals," a voice said.

Winter, Clay, and Marcus squinted as a pair of blinding headlights flashed on. A man stood in silhouette.

"FBI. Hands up."

The man shifted into the light. He had a gun in one hand, a badge in the other. His thin, brown hair whipped in the wind. Another agent, gun drawn, stood a few steps behind.

"Agent Thompson," he said, holding up a badge.

"I've got one of those too," Winter said, taking aim at the agent's heart. "Don't move."

"Or we're going to blow your brains out," Clay chimed in.

Winter heard Katerina crying. He wanted to kiss her, comfort her, but he couldn't give himself away.

"I'll make you a rich man," Marcus said to Thompson. "All you have to do is kill them so we can stop freezing our balls off." He glanced at Katerina. "Kill the bitch first."

Thompson smiled. "What do you wanna do, chief?" he asked Winter. "Have a Mexican standoff in the middle of a fuckin' blizzard? Let's play nice, okay? He's wanted for securities and exchange fraud, mail fraud, wire fraud, and a partridge in a pear tree. I'm not greedy. You take the collar. Just give me the girl, and we can all go home. I won't hurt her. I promise."

Katerina cried, curling deeper into Winter's embrace.

Winter kept the gun trained on Thompson. *Who the hell are you? And who's paying you?* "Not happening," he said, as his finger tightened on the trigger.

The sound of two quick, muted shots rang out.

Chapter 88

Winter and Clay turned in unison. The man was tall, with skin the color of mocha, a tight wool cap on his head. He walked past them to lean over the bodies of Agent Thompson and his partner.

"What the fuck?" Marcus said, lowering his arms and raising them up again as Winter waved the gun at him.

"Good for five minutes," Angel said to Winter. "Maybe a few more."

"Do what you need to," Winter said to Clay.

Clay headed straight for Marcus, bringing the butt of his gun down on his forehead. Marcus gave a yelp, covering his head with his hands. Clay grabbed his arm, hauling him over to the two inert bodies. Angel took a pair of cuffs off Thompson and tossed them to Clay, who handcuffed Marcus to Thompson.

Winter, desperate to get Katerina into the car, still delayed, keeping this new player in his sights, even as he had a creeping suspicion he wasn't the enemy.

"Hang on," Winter whispered in Katerina's ear. "One more minute."

Clay slid into the driver's seat of the Porsche as everyone watched.

He started the engine, flipped on the wipers, and finally, after a second's hesitation, pressed the driver's window switch.

There was a popping sound; the passenger airbag panel gave way. Only there was no airbag.

"Oh shit, c'mon man, don't do this," Marcus whined. "Who the hell are you guys anyway? You're sure as hell not FBI. Once these other guys wake up, they're gonna find you. They're gonna hunt you down like fuckin' dogs. There's nothing in the car. I swear. Nothing."

Clay scrambled out and got into the passenger seat. He pulled the panel away and like a surgeon, slipped out a small package wrapped in brown craft paper. He got out of the car and gave Winter a wide smile.

Winter turned to Angel. "You got a taser?"

"I do."

"Do these guys," Winter said, nodding at Marcus and the two unconscious men.

"Done."

Winter motioned for Clay to walk ahead of him, back to the car.

"The bags," Katerina mumbled, "the phones . . . the money."

"Clean the car," Winter said.

Angel raised his hand.

Winter heard Marcus yell "Son of a bitch!" Then a buzzing sound. Then silence.

Chapter 89

At the back of the SUV, Clay fussed over the package. Winter had Katerina plastered against him while he grabbed a blanket and a first aid kit.

Without ceremony, Winter tore away Kat's soaked slip of a dress and checked the wound on her arm; a graze, not serious. Wrapping the blanket underneath her arms, he pulled it snug around her from her chest down to her hips. Angel approached, carrying Kat's coat, purse, the wig and jacket, and Marcus' bag. Winter took the coat and bundled Katerina into the car, reclining the passenger seat and sweeping her soaked and matted hair away from her face and neck.

Taking off his own gloves, Winter forced her frozen hands into each glove in turn, taking notice of the tattered, wet bandage on her hand. He then set to work wrapping his scarf around her feet. Her head lolled back and forth as she alternated between mumbling and crying.

"It's okay," he said, in a voice soft as velvet, "you're safe now."

Moving around to the driver's side he turned over the engine, cranking out a low, moderate heat, forcing himself not to overcompensate by turning it up high and hot. *Remember, better to warm the trunk first, not the extremities.*

Angel leaned into the car, passing each item over to Winter, ending with Marcus's bag.

"Money . . . take the money," Katerina whispered, her voice hoarse.

Angel ran a gentle finger over her reddened cheek. "Not here for the pickup, baby."

Getting out of the car, Winter went around to the back, his gun out of his coat pocket. He found Clay still fretting over the painting.

"We need to move," he said.

"Yeah," Clay said, distracted.

"Give me the gun," Winter said.

Clay straightened. "Why?" he said, his voice shaky.

Winter held his hand out. "You don't need it anymore."

Clay nodded toward the front of the car. "What about him?"

"He's not here for this," Winter said, nodding toward the package. "Give me the gun."

Clay took the gun from his pocket, holding it as if he were unsure what to do with it. "Okay," he said, "but, you're going to give me a ride home, right?"

"Hand it over. You'll be riding in the back seat. You don't need a gun."

Clay nodded, holding it out. "Sure, okay, but you're going to be a stand-up guy about this, right? You're not going to leave me here. It's cold."

Winter shoved the weapon in his coat pocket. "Get in the car," he said.

Clay went for the passenger side. Grabbing him by the collar, Winter shoved him towards the driver side.

"Hey, beautiful," Clay said as he climbed in the back. "Feeling better?" Leaning forward, he popped open the first aid kit and smoothed Kat's hair away from her face to tend to her cheek.

"Don't touch her," Winter ordered.

Clay raised his hands in surrender. "No worries, man. I got this. Let me help."

Winter hesitated. "Check her arm," he said and slammed the door to trap the heat inside the car.

***

Winter and Angel surveyed the three men lying on the ground.

"You want 'em just like that?" Angel asked.

"No," Winter said.

***

Clay worked with a delicate touch, dabbing antiseptic on Kat's arm and cheek.

"Winter," Katerina mumbled.

"It certainly is, beautiful. It certainly is. But you're warm in here."

"Alex," she murmured.

Clay leaned in close by Kat's ear. "Hey, beautiful," he whispered, "is that who that is, Alexander Winter?"

"Yes, Alex," she mumbled and faded out.

Daniel Clay stared out the window at the man standing in the storm. "So that's who that is," he said aloud.

***

Thompson was the first to come to. He registered snow falling on his face, flakes landing on his eyelids. There was dried drool on his cheek; his head ached and his muscles twitched. A sick feeling permeated his whole body and he had a vague urge to vomit. He attempted to lift his hand to his face but a dead weight prevented him.

He found his wrist in a handcuff; the other half of the cuff clasped around the wrist of Simon Marcus.

"Shit."

Hearing a moan from his other side, Thompson gave a disgusted sigh as he lifted his other arm and found himself shackled to his partner. He'd have a word with the client about this mess.

Chapter 90

She saw shapes, floating, drifting. They were squares or rectangles, all white. The shapes mixed with visions, memories: darkness, freezing cold, the sound of an engine, doors opening and closing, someone leaning over her, touching her face.

She remembered a hot, sweet drink. Had she imagined it? She tried to open her eyes but her lids, heavy as lead, refused to move. She gave up then tried again. The floating shapes of white became clearer . . . furniture. She let out a sigh of relief. *Winter.*

Katerina tried to move her hands and found them wrapped in flannel. She tried wiggling her toes, they were wrapped as well. Under layers of soft down, she felt warm and dry.

She found Winter seated in a chair next to the foot of the couch, watching her, his face impassive. Only his eyes, dark with concern, gave him away. He came to sit next to her on the edge of the couch. Leaning over, he stroked her hair. Placing her swathed hands on his shoulders, she pulled him close. He held her in a gentle embrace, kissing her temple.

Safe.

He took a mug from the coffee table. "Drink this, it's good for you," he said, sliding his hand across her back and lifting her.

She did as she was told. The hot chocolate flowed down her throat, the warmth filling her stomach, sweet and soothing. She drank slowly as he held her in a tight embrace. After, she sank back onto the pillows.

"Good," she murmured.

Putting down the mug, he settled the covers around her.

She tried to build a mental bridge between the present and the events that had passed.

"Thank you," she said. "I'm sorry."

Winter smiled. "Which is it?"

"Both."

Leaning over, he kissed her cheek.

She noticed the tubes of creams and bandage rolls on the coffee table. "Doc was here?" she asked.

Winter nodded. "You're going to be all right."

"Who was the man with the painting?"

"Just a man who wanted a painting."

"He's the new player, isn't he? He was watching Marcus' apartment."

He kissed her forehead.

"You didn't want the painting?"

"I got what I wanted," he said, kissing her forehead.

"Why didn't you want the painting?"

He didn't answer.

"You only steal to order," she said.

He traced her cheek with a feather touch. "I got what I wanted."

Her eyes flew open in sudden panic. "The FBI."

"Those two men were not FBI."

She took a deep breath, settling down again. "The player, he pulled the painting from inside the car," she said.

"The car had a compartment tied to the electrical system," he said. "It's called a trap."

"You know all these things. I don't know any of these things. I didn't see," she said.

He leaned over. "Anything you need to know, you can learn," he said, brushing her cheek with his lips, "if that's what you want."

She lifted her head to look at him. "I know one thing now, about us being complicated. I'd have to leave it all, wouldn't I? Even my name. I couldn't ever go back."

He pulled her in, held her, and kissed the top of her head. "You get an A," he whispered.

A heavy moment of silence hung between them.

"I'm going to go home," she said.

His eyes closed. Then he pulled back, and lifting her chin with a gentle touch of his hand, he kissed her. A delicious spike of warmth surged through her as the tip of his tongue gently touched hers. A sigh escaped her. Snaking her arms around the wide expanse of his back, she surrendered into his embrace, falling into the deep kiss.

When they parted, he whispered, "Don't go back to your apartment. You stay here until you leave."

She nodded, kissing his cheek, then his neck, tasting his skin as she inhaled the scent of him.

He pulled back again, peppering her lips with kisses, running his fingers through the mass of her hair. He finally forced himself to settle her back down under the covers. Her eyelids soon fluttered, heavy with sleep.

"Could you help me with one more thing?" she said, already drowsing.

She told him and his concerned expression relaxed. "I'll take care of it," he said.

Katerina nestled further beneath the comforter. The furniture retreated to vague shapes of squares and rectangles, first clear, then fuzzy, then fading to black.

Chapter 91

When she opened her eyes, she knew he had gone. She pressed her lips together, still feeling the tingling sensation from his kisses.

She fluttered her fingers and toes, and found the wrapping gone. Drawing her arms out from under the blankets, she sat up, glancing down at the white, silk pajamas. Grabbing the "Winter" phone from the coffee table, she oriented herself to the date and time. It was five o'clock, the time she had left with Marcus. Two *days* earlier. Her phones were on the coffee table. There was a text waiting on the burner. Her heart quickened as she tapped it open.

> Passed along your message.
> Anonymous as you asked.
> No response. H.L.

She put the phone down, the familiar weight of her worries, like a creeping poison, seeping through the portal of Letourneau's text. For a moment, she didn't know what to feel, relief or disappointment. Kat noticed the familiar trio: paper, lighter, and ashtray, next to the serving tray. Lifting the lids from the plates she found muffins and fresh fruit. Realizing she was hungry, she munched while she read the note.

> Everything in the upstairs bedroom.
> Text me if you need anything.
> You know what to do with this.
> W.

She lit the paper, tossing it in the ashtray when the flame licked her fingers. She glanced around. Marcus' bag was gone. Opening her purse, the rubber banded packs of money tumbled out.

***

She lined up the packs in a neat row on the coffee table. Sinking onto the couch, she stared at the sight.

One hundred thousand dollars.

She did a quick calculation of all the jobs, the money she had been paid, what MJM owed her. All together she would have close to two hundred thousand.

Was it enough to outrun Sheridan? Reynolds? A killer? Was it enough to keep her mother safe? For how long? She couldn't keep all of it. She had a debt to pay; she didn't welch on her debts.

She decided it wasn't enough for a new lifetime, not yet. But this money was the start of the exit strategy. She needed more and she would get it. She found it ironic. She had realized what a life with Winter would mean, the sacrifice it would entail, just as she was about to go home, see her mother, and make plans to leave everything behind. *To leave Winter behind.* Without warning, tears threatened. *Text me if you need anything.*

No. I can't do that. I can't involve you.

I don't want you to get caught.

Nothing can happen to you.

Standing up, she stretched her body, testing its condition. After a few steps, she realized she was all right. She checked her hand; the cut was finally healing. She tested her arm, inspecting the bandage.

Stripping off the pajamas, she headed upstairs to shower and get ready, knowing everything she needed would be waiting for her.

Chapter 92

Gallagher sat straight and stiff in his chair, sipping his tea, waiting for the phone call. The situation was not at all to his satisfaction.

The cell phone rang. "Yes," Gallagher said.

"It's me," Thompson said. "We ran into an issue."

"Obviously. I don't have the package. Where is the package?"

"You weren't the only interested party. The girl knew him. She chose *him*."

Gallagher pursed his lips. "Do you have any information on this other interested party?"

"No. It was a little dark out," he said drily, "and this mess was more than what I was hired for."

"You will be well compensated."

"That's nice," Thompson said, his voice ringing with sarcasm. "That doesn't help me with my problem. I have an unwanted guest. He can't stay with me any longer. Understand?"

"Send me an address where the guest is to be picked up and I'll have someone there within a two-hour window. Is this acceptable?"

"Is this someone bringing a bonus payment for my trouble?"

"Of course," Gallagher said. "You will assist him, won't you?"

A disgusted sigh came over the line. "If it's reflected in the envelope, yeah."

Gallagher clicked off. She chose *him*. A rush of heated annoyance spiked Gallagher's blood pressure. The spyware had been disabled; her phones had been cleaned. *Clever, Bob. Very clever.*

The thought that Katerina was well and cared for subdued his anger. It would suffice, for the moment. A cleaner would be dispatched to close out this unfortunate situation. Three people would be disposed of. Marcus would require a plausible story. The two contractors would disappear as if they had never existed.

Chapter 93

When Katerina announced herself over the building intercom, there was a distinct moment of silence.

"Come up," Jasmine said.

Kat presented herself in front of Jasmine a few minutes later; by then, the raven-haired gatekeeper had her facial expression under control, unreadable. She handed over packs of money. Katerina tucked them in her purse but didn't move. *We're not done yet.*

"I don't have any assignments for you," Jasmine said.

"I'm not here for one," Kat said, forcing her nerves in check. Katerina had remembered Angel's words. *Not here for the pickup, baby.* MJM had given her up for dead. Just like the other girl. Whoever she was. That wasn't all Katerina had figured out.

"I completed driving Mr. Marcus. The payout," Kat said.

Jasmine's eyebrows quirked. "I don't have confirmation the job was finished."

No, no, Wicked Witch of the West. Not going to work.

"So? Verbal confirmation from the client was never stipulated in the orientation. It's *not* one of the rules."

How many of the girls had gotten so caught up, they never figured it out? What did Angel say? Ain't nobody like Lisa. She's all by herself. You could be her.

Jasmine maintained a hard stare. Katerina knew she was doing the math.

That's right. Now tell me Angel never made the pickup from me so I can ask you why.

With a deliberate motion, Jasmine opened a desk drawer and withdrew two additional rubber banded packs. She placed them on the desk. Katerina deposited them in her purse.

Consider it my hazard pay, bitch. Now you go tell MJM I'm not dead.

"Graduation day is here. You're off probation," Jasmine said.

Katerina walked out.

Jasmine sat still behind the desk. Then she picked up her cell phone and made a call.

Chapter 94

Lashiver found Ryan at his desk, engrossed in paperwork. He took note of the drawn, tired expression on the young detective's face.

"Hey, how about going home?" the older man asked. "How about sleep?"

Ryan shook his head. "I'm fine.

Lashiver lowered his voice. "Hey, Frankie M. told me."

Ryan nodded but wouldn't make eye contact. He had been about to file a missing person's report when Emma called. Katerina had sent a text; she was okay, that was it.

"I'm sorry about your girl. These things happen."

"I'm fine," he insisted. "I've got plenty of work to do."

Lashiver nodded at the files. "What have you got?"

"I've got a lot. A lot that doesn't make sense. I spoke to the detectives on the Will Temple disappearance. This Random Girl Films doesn't exist. But he went somewhere. He had an address but they can't find anything on paper."

"What does this have to do with Felicia Reynolds?"

Ryan shook his head. "I don't know yet. But it does. What about those shopping trips she took? Who was she buying for? Will Temple? Had to be. Maybe she had a favorite store, favorite salesperson. She must have been talking to somebody about lover boy, or about her husband. I got a lead on one of her friends from the kick line. She's out on a road tour but I'm tracking her down."

"Where does Cheryl Penn fit into this?"

"I don't know that she does." He spread his hands over the papers littering his desk. "There has to be something, or someone, that ties all this together. All of these pieces have to fit. I've got all day and all night to work on it."

Lashiver nodded. "Do what you have to do. But get some sleep first. I promised your father I'd look after you."

"I'm fine."

Lashiver hesitated. "Look, maybe you want to talk to someone, for a little extra help, like you did after the shooting. You know, it doesn't hurt."

A sudden flash of anger made Ryan scowl but it ebbed as quickly as it appeared. "I told you, I'm fine."

Lashiver continued to stand at the desk; Ryan took the hint. He got up and grabbed his coat. The older man put a hand on his shoulder. He hated to see the kid this way. If he thought it was the right time he would have told him. The beautiful ones; they were always trouble.

"Whoever this guy is," Ryan said. "I'm gonna get him. There's somebody out there who's the key to this. I'll find him or her. I will."

"I know you will," Lashiver said. "I know you will."

Chapter 95

Katerina approached the security desk with halting steps.

"Miss Mills," the bouncer-built guard said, his cold, impassive face morphing into that of a kindly gentleman. "Mr. Gallagher is expecting you. Please, allow me to escort you personally."

"Thank you," Katerina said.

***

Katerina was shown into the executive suite. Thomas Gallagher stood behind a desk of glass, a panoramic view of the city stretched out behind him. He came forward, holding out a hand to her, indicating she should be seated in one of the sleek, silver guest chairs. She held her faux fur-lined coat, her snow-white scarf and mittens in her hands.

Kat had been unsure of what to make of the phone call, the request for the meeting. *Be direct and to the point. Apologize. No begging. No bullshit.*

"I'm terribly sorry, Mr. Gallagher. I apologize for inconveniencing you." she said, working to keep her voice even and confident.

Gallagher positioned himself in front of her, leaning against the desk. His contemplative study of her made her shift in her seat.

"Not at all, Katerina," he said. She held her breath as he reached forward, shifting a tendril of her hair from her face, revealing the healing cut. "I don't require any explanation. I can see it for myself."

"You have been sent a replacement consultant, I hope?" she asked.

"I didn't ask for one," he said, "and I believe you are not ready to return to your assignment yet, yes?"

"I'm going home for the holiday. I'm sure another consultant can help you—"

"I'm sure, if I had any interest in one. I called you to suggest we reconvene in the New Year, shall we?"

She nodded her head. "Yes, thank you," she said, even as she had no idea if she would be coming back.

Gallagher took her hand as she rose to leave, holding it in a light grip. She met his gaze. His eyes were still cold but not as impenetrable as before.

"You will take care of yourself, Katerina, won't you?"

"Yes, sir," she said. "I'll try."

He held her hand for another moment, finally releasing her.

***

After she left the office, Gallagher brought up the security monitor for the lobby. He watched Katerina Mills slip into her new coat, scarf, and mittens. The Ugg boots were a nice touch. He kept watching until she left the building, disappearing from view. He found it odd, disconcerting, that he had not only wanted to see her but *needed* to see her. He entertained thoughts of what it would be like, taking her for the first time, that lovely face, the soft, baby smooth skin the color of cream. His tongue flicked over his lips. Like a first bite into a perfect, ripe peach, soft, sweet, and luscious. She would be a delight he would never tire of. Plans were already in motion. *Soon enough, she will belong to me.*

And as for you, Bob, he thought with a smile . . . *your part of the operation has been put into motion. You will be found—and removed.*

Chapter 96

The canvas was on the table.

Daniel Clay watched as the radiographer pored over the x-ray of the painting. The negative highlighted the darker areas around the vibrant flowers. The technician stepped back. He shook his head. "It's not his style," the expert said. "Sorry, no go."

Clay shook his head. A fake. Disappointment welled within him until he turned and picked up the painting, bringing it down over the corner of the table.

There's always next time, Danny," the expert said. "It's the way it goes."

Clay stood with hands on his hips, waiting for his anger to abate. *There won't be a next time*. The Van Gogh had vanished, purchased by a Dr. No-type collector everyone insisted didn't exist. Even though there were always exceptions, none of that mattered now. He had to move on. Besides, he had a new direction to go in. He was onto something big. Something very big: Alexander Winter.

Chapter 97

The sun had been long gone by six-thirty. People braved the bitter evening, arms full with packages as they tackled the final round of Christmas shopping.

The garage bay door was open; the Bugatti, lights on, idled. Moose, scrubbed, groomed, and dressed in a black suit, waited. A limousine tooled down the street and pulled up to a stop. Luther exited the vehicle, opening the back passenger door. Taking Luther's hand, Kat stepped out.

Sparkling in a long, slinky, silver spaghetti strap number with a long slit in the front, and matching shoes, Katerina struck a pose.

Taking her in from head to toe, Moose gave a soft whistle. "*Mami*," he said. "I wasn't sure. I heard things—"

"I keep my word," she said. "I always keep my word."

Moose took her hand. "Okay, I have a night planned for you. It's gonna be beautiful."

Luther draped Kat's faux fur coat over her shoulders. "I'll be back at two to pick up my passenger," he said.

"Understood," Moose said.

Luther nodded at Katerina and eased into the limousine. He backed out and moved off.

Moose led Katerina to the Bugatti, opening the door with a flourish, and settling her in. When he slid into the driver's seat, he found Katerina holding out a pack of bills.

"Good will," she said.

He tucked the packet in his inside jacket pocket. He took her hand and kissed it. "All right. It's time for the Moose to get loose. You ready for a good time?"

Katerina smiled in spite of herself. Yes, I am, she thought. *Yes, I am.*

Chapter 98

Katerina found Professor Schoeffling in his office, leaning back in his chair, his feet up on his desk, crossed at the ankles, reading *The Stranger* by Camus. She hadn't wanted to come, but without an exit plan in place everything had to appear normal.

She knocked on the open door.

Putting down the book, he said, "What can I do for you, Miss Mills?"

"Did you get my message?" she asked.

"Yes, I did. Your car wasn't available and you were stuck outside the city."

"Yes."

"What'd you do, have it stolen for the insurance money?"

"No," she said. "Is there any way I can take a makeup final?"

"Sit down," he said.

She slipped out of her coat and took a seat.

"You're holding a gun. You point it at someone. You fire the gun. Is it free will or determinism?"

"That's the final?"

Schoeffling nodded. "You never spoke up in class the whole semester. I'd like to know your answer."

Katerina scrambled for a response. "Why so drastic? Why does it have to be a gun?"

"What do you suggest?"

"A person spends all day, every day, doing a thousand different things that society deems unsuitable. What if I break into someone's home or I help a thief steal something? What if I help someone import illegal drugs?"

Professor Schoeffling gave a smile, leaned back, and put his hands behind his head. "But that's not what I asked you. You don't have free will over the question."

Now on the spot to think about what she had avoided at all costs, Katerina stewed in rising panic. "What are the circumstances? What did this man do to me?"

Schoeffling shook his head. "We've been through all this. We're not talking about justifiable homicide, self-defense, or biblical justice. No morals. Give me an answer."

Katerina thought of the men in her life: Moose, Carlo, Vincent, her own father. They had all done it. They would do it again. Pull the trigger. Take away that last breath, like it was nothing. *Even Winter would have done it. For me.*

And what about me? Didn't I flip the switch on James Sheridan? I meant to. And I slept at night, no problem. Am I my father's daughter? Is that why I told Ivan I didn't need him? Because I can pull the trigger myself?

We are all the killing kind.

"You're right," she said.

"I usually am," Schoeffling said. "But be more specific."

"It's a waste of time arguing over a story about five men tied to a track and whether it's different killing one man to save the five by flipping a switch or by pulling a trigger. It's the same."

"That's gratifying, Miss Mills. Last chance. What's your answer?"

"You're asking me if I have free will to do it. Of course I do. Any choice I make, I could have done otherwise, therefore I have free will. What you didn't ask me, is do I have enough of a desire to use my free will to face this man, hold the gun, and shoot."

Professor Schoeffling took his feet off the desk and sat up. "So you're saying it depends on desire? I'll grant you that. But is it possible in a world ruled by determinism, where you have no control over the countless things that can and do happen to you, that you can still have free will?"

Katerina realized her mind was still and quiet. "Yes. Maybe this man I point the gun at did something terrible to me. Maybe he's in my life through no fault of my own. Maybe his presence is a culmination of prior events that led up to the moment he entered my life. But it's bullshit to say any of that matters. I can use my free will to fire the gun if my desire is strong enough. And then I am subject to Marley's Law."

Professor Schoeffling gave her a quizzical look. "Marley's Law? We didn't cover that."

Kat nodded. "Jacob Marley . . . *A Christmas Carol*, 'I wear the chains I forged in life.' Whatever I choose to do, I'm going to have the balls to take responsibility for it. The decision is mine and mine alone."

Schoeffling nodded. "Interesting. But hold on a minute. Aren't the gods responsible for any of this? Or are you opting for the Nietzche defense? 'All Gods are dead.' You don't give yourself a pass at all?"

Kat smiled. "The gods? There are no gods in the heavens, Professor. They're living here. And they look down from the penthouse. And they move the people like pieces on the chessboard."

Schoeffling laughed. "So, you *do* give yourself a pass. You're suffering under coercion, manipulation. *They* are making your decisions, determining your future. Where does that leave your precious free will?"

"I have the desire and the power to use my free will to fight their decisions."

"You think so?" he said with a laugh. "Be careful, Miss Mills. Aren't you afraid you'll make the gods angry?"

"Not anymore," Katerina said.

Professor Schoeffling nodded his head. "This is a very interesting viewpoint, Miss Mills. You passed."

She managed a mumbled "thank you" and left.

Chapter 99

Katerina stood in the country kitchen, watching Betsy Marcus sit comfortably at the table, pouring out hot water from a blue flower-patterned teapot into a square, yellow cup. Kat had been more than a little surprised by the summons. She wasn't surprised by the front page of the newspaper lying on the table. A picture of Simon Marcus' face under a bold headline reporting his unexpected suicide; the body had been found near the border, on the American side.

"I asked you here for a specific reason," Betsy said, "to give you a piece of information. Something you need to know." She spooned sugar in her tea, letting her words sink in.

Katerina stiffened, glancing around, on the alert.

"You thought it was about the car. That's the problem with people your age. Tunnel vision. You missed the big picture, actually, the little picture."

Katerina didn't argue the point. "When did you know?"

Betsy smiled. "Over a year ago. When I agreed to the magazine feature, he went crazy over the photo of the paintings. Then the blue fake disappeared. I figured he was up to something. So I looked into it. It would have been easier to just swap out the car but he outmaneuvered me and put that damn scratch in it. Tough to duplicate that."

Not if you have a Moose you can set loose.

"So I had a copy of the painting made." She looked Kat in the eye. "Did you ever see it?"

Katerina shook her head.

"I'm sure I wasn't the only one after it. Who else was there?"

The enemy of my enemy is not my friend. I'm not telling you shit.

Betsy shrugged. "Have it your way," she said, with a small, mirthless laugh. "But whoever it was, they stole a fake."

Katerina swallowed hard, her imagination running wild, wondering who Betsy Marcus was working for, and if there was a recording device somewhere in the country kitchen.

"You made a deal with the Feds for immunity?" she asked.

Betsy leaned forward, her face flushing. "Listen to me, you stupid bimbo," she began, "I don't need any deal with the Feds. I set up my finances a long time ago. I even sold the painting for a few million, extra pocket change. I had you come here, you little brat, so I can tell you to your face that you're out of your league. I beat you. I beat him. I beat all of you. My husband got exactly what he deserved. Now get the hell out of my house."

Katerina nodded. She slipped out, closing the door with a soft "click" behind her, making her way down the driveway to the idling limousine waiting at the curb. The warmth welcomed her as she climbed in.

"Thanks for this, Luther," she said, even though she knew Luther had been well paid. "I appreciate it. Any problem retrieving the few things from my apartment?"

Luther glanced back at her through the rearview mirror. "No, Miss Katerina. All taken care of. No problem at all. Your business is done now?"

"Yes," she said. "Please take me to the Amtrak Station."

Chapter 100

In the Amtrak waiting room, Katerina sipped her tea and indulged in a carb fest: a double chocolate chip muffin and a giant salted pretzel. Her thoughts wandered aimless and unchecked, half-formed plans and ideas dangling with no foundation. With the money tucked away in the safety deposit box, next steps had to be addressed. She would defy the gods. She would disappear. How to leverage the money to get more? Doing what? How long would it take before there was enough to disappear? Thoughts of her father and ten million dollars floated through her mind. *Can I find him? Did he leave a digital footprint? Can I erase mine?* Sheridan, Reynolds, even Ryan lurked as dangers in her mind. She wondered if another name needed to be added to the list. Anthony Desucci. He should have killed her for lying to him, for trying to cheat him. Why didn't he? And to what purpose?

And then there were the earrings, Felicia Reynolds' earrings. She should have moved them, but to where? The risk of getting caught in the process had immobilized her. For now, they stayed hidden away in the apartment, like Dorian Gray's picture buried behind the locked door, an ever-present peril never far from her mind.

She focused on the Christmas gift bag that Luther had brought with her things. Another gift from Winter, she thought with a smile. She put her hand into the bag, feeling something soft. Peeling away the tissue paper, she pulled out a plush toy. A kangaroo. As she fingered the familiar tag of the toy factory, her excitement evaporated. A piece of paper stuck out from the slit for the pouch for the baby kangaroo.

Kat slipped out the note, staring at the writing, neat, legible.

> Thank you for the warning and the advice.
> We appreciate your good faith.
> We will contact you, Katerina.

Panic gripped her. *Oh God. They know me. They know my name.* In her desperation to escape, she had opened another front. She threw the plush toy back in the gift bag. Instinctively, she dug in her purse until she pulled out the "Winter" phone. It was still on, giving off a signal. She put the phone back in her purse. At least he knew where she was. She wasn't lost. If she needed him . . .

Katerina indulged herself in the familiar daydream, disappearing with Winter. They would go off, slip away to a quiet, quaint little village in France. No one would find them. They would be safe. They would have each other.

Pulling herself back to the present, she noted the time on her phone; time to go. She got up, swinging her long braid over her shoulder, and raised the handle on her case. She did another scan of the waiting area. For the moment, she was nobody and happy to be so.

***

Lingering in the crush of the crowd outside the waiting room, Alexander Winter kept a sharp eye on Katerina. *Fragile beauty.*

He had questions for her, about spyware infected phones, dangerous clients . . . and a pair of expensive earrings still hidden away. For now, the questions would have to keep. She had been pushed too far. She couldn't handle anymore.

Winter watched Katerina exit the waiting area, his premonition of uneasy anxiety justified as he picked up on a man parallel to him, loitering by a Dunkin' Donuts. The man, his eyes dark and cold, also had Katerina Mills in his sight. The man moved out into the crowd to follow her, pulling a ticket out of his coat pocket. Who are you working for? Winter thought. A painful knot twisted in the pit of his stomach as he remembered Thompson's words. *Just give me the girl.*

A few moments earlier, Winter had seen the gift bag, the stuffed animal, the panic wash over Katerina's lovely face. Trouble waited for her at home. Sheridan would be waiting as well. Winter's teeth clenched at the thought. That item of business would always occupy a special place in his mind. Sheridan had to answer for what he did. *And he will.* Winter knew all about keeping a score; and settling it.

Winter scanned the area until he found a man with the forgettable look of a bland businessman. The man wore a gray flannel suit with a matching color coat; he went by the name of Carter. Winter had used Carter's services before. Since Katerina's return to the city, Carter had been on the job as her new guardian angel. Winter watched the guardian head for the train, Katerina's train. Carter would shadow her, day and night, ready to do whatever necessary to keep her safe.

Watching her walk away, an ache burgeoned inside Winter, its strength blindsiding him. He checked his watch. Out of time. *Pay-or-play*. The client had wired the money and he had no choice: he had to get to JFK. He was back on the clock.

Still, Winter delayed, watching until the crowd swallowed the last glimpse of her. He had convinced himself that it would be best if Katerina went home; a foolish delusion of wishful thinking.

Katerina Mills has nowhere to hide.

The Fixer: The Last Romanov

Copyright© 2019 by Jill Amy Rosenblatt No part of this book may be reproduced in any form or by any means without permission of the author, excepting brief quotes used in reviews. *The Fixer: The Last Romanov* is a work of fiction. Names, characters, businesses, places, events and incidents are either the products of the author's imagination or used in a fictitious manner. Any resemblance to actual persons, living or dead, or actual events is purely coincidental.

Cover Design and Images: Alan Gaites/Graphic Design

Notes: Masha and the Bear is a Russian folk tale. The version of the tale referenced can be found at:

https://russian-crafts.com/russian-folk-tales/masha-bear-tale.html

.

For Mrs. Danvers

Acknowledgements

I am so fortunate to have met these amazing experts in my research travels. Any errors in this book are mine and not theirs. My sincerest thanks go out to:

Former NYPD Detective Glenn E. Cunningham for his incredible generosity and kindness in sharing his knowledge. You are amazing! You have been so helpful with your insights and expertise. I can't thank you enough. There would be no series without you.

Phil Mortillaro of Greenwich Locksmiths. Thank you so much for being so kind to meet with me and sharing your knowledge of safes (and safecracking). And thank you to Phil Jr. for your suggestions and input as well.

Elaad and Dov Israeli of Precision Lock & Safe, Inc. Thank you Elaad for spending hours introducing me to the mystery of lock manipulation. Your help has been invaluable to this story. One plot line in this book would not have been possible without you. Thank you to Dov for being so patient and helpful with directions!!

D.P. Lyle, MD, author of the book *Forensics: A Guide For Writers*. Thank you for your time and expertise, answering questions about specific scenarios, and reviewing scenes.

Dr. Anna Geisherik for her assistance with Russian translation and cultural information.

Frank Ahearn, author of the book, *How To Disappear,* for his insightful information and suggestions.

Greg Harkins, for talking with me about LA freeways and drive times and sharing your insights into Balboa Island. Thanks for reading scenes and making corrections and suggestions.

Jeanette Columbano for Italian translation.

Mel and Doris Aponte for your continued help with Spanish translation.

Myra Alperson of Noshwalks for the fantastic tour of Washington Heights. You are a wealth of information and it was a wonderful visit to this vibrant area of the city.

Philippe Lacarriere, thank you, my friend, for helping with French translation.

Alan Gaites/Graphic Design for the amazing book cover and the awesome Book 4 cover reveal. Thank you for taking my vision and making something beautiful.

Edwin Villarreal and Chris Miller of the City of Newport Beach, Harbor Resources Division, for information on sailing vessels and Balboa Island.

And to my Mom . . . my reader, my editor, my champion. Thank you for the hours and hours of your time that you've given in support of this dream. Thank you.

"I am in blood
　Stepp'd in so far that, should I wade no more
　Returning were as tedious as go o'er."
Macbeth, 3.4. 142-144
William Shakespeare
"this young girl, who stands so grave and quiet
at the mouth of hell, looking collectedly
at the gambols of a demon."
Jane Eyre
Charlotte Brontë

CHAPTER 1

Katerina Mills sat in the silver Honda Civic, peering through the lenses of the binoculars. The factory parking lot loomed larger as she watched the first shift employees filing out, heads bowing to brace against the frigid Vermont winds, and dashing to their cars.

Katerina knew every inch of the toy factory her father had managed. In high school, she had helped out after classes, typing, filing, and bookkeeping. Following graduation and while caring for William Mills through his bout of cancer, Kat worked a few hours a day and carried paperwork back and forth to her father at home.

Can you keep an eye on things for your old man?

Bullshit, Kat thought. It was time to find out the truth.

Kat snapped out of her thoughts as Richie Calico emerged. She watched him turn up the collar of his jacket as he hustled toward a shiny, red Dodge Durango. Kat knew Richie as a third-generation, blue-collar working stiff, always looking for an angle and an easy buck.

That looks new, Kat thought as she sharpened the binoculars on the Durango.

Richie's head swiveled back and forth as he hurried to the SUV.

That's not the confident man I remember strolling up to my desk with a singsong "Kat-a-reeena."

As if we shared a secret.

Richie slid into the Durango, revved the engine, and took off, speeding out of the lot.

Time to spill your secrets, Richie.

Kat put the Civic in gear.

***

Katerina watched Richie pull into a strip mall, park in front of a run-down pub, and get out. She followed, parking in the back of the lot and cutting the engine.

Leaning forward, Kat wrapped her arms around the wheel. *I have to go in. I need him to fill in the blanks. How do I get in and out without being noticed? Steal in and out. Like a thief.*

She sighed. It had been a little more than two months since her first B and E. Alexander Winter, "Bob," and "Professor," to Kat, a good man and an expert thief, had walked her through it and brought her out. *He would know what to do.* She closed her eyes, the familiar ache of missing him threatening to overwhelm her.

Not now, Katerina thought, opening her eyes and forcing herself to return to the business at hand. *There's a reason Richie is looking over his shoulder.* Remember what Winter taught you, she thought. Once you go in, you give yourself five minutes. Every minute you linger, your risk of getting caught rises.

Scanning the lot one more time, she flipped the fur lined hood over her chestnut hair, opened the door, and got out.

***

Slipping in through the back door, Katerina stepped into the shrouded gloom of the deserted dive bar. She came up behind Richie as he slouched in a booth, drinking alone.

Suddenly, Richie's eyes shot up from his Coors and he jolted at the presence of a person looming over him. Shifting to face him, Kat brushed her hood back and watched his eyes grow wide. He gaped at her as she slid into the booth.

"Katerina," Richie said, his Adam's apple bobbing as he swallowed hard. "Uh . . . Merry Christmas, Happy New Year . . . when did you get home?"

"Hi Richie," Kat said. "How's the heroin business?"

Chapter 2

Katerina did a quick inventory of the bundle of nerves opposite her; the twitchy, restless hands, the fidgeting arms and legs. Beads of sweat began to bloom on Richie's brow; he drained his bottle of Coors and licked his lips. A man dying of thirst, Kat thought. Or a man afraid of dying.

He shook his head. "I—I don't know what you're talkin' about," Richie said, his eyes darting around. "I don't—"

"Sure you do, Richie. The way I figure it, you were in on it from the beginning. When my dad got sick, you just put your hand all the way into the toy stuffing to sell a little junk on the side. And my father just didn't need to know, right?"

Richie shifted in his seat. "Hey, *he* asked me, okay? I just followed orders."

"Three months ago, my father stopped off in New York before he pulled his Houdini. He mentioned your name. 'Richie, my number two. He's his own man.' He sounded a little bitter. Try again."

Richie threw himself against the back of the booth, one leg bobbing up and down like a frenetic yo-yo. "I made one little change. I saved the operation a lot of money."

"More for you to buy your shiny, new little red wagon?"

Richie's tennis match scanning continued between the bar in the front and the back door.

"Expecting company?" Kat said, feeling perspiration break out beneath her clothing.

"You . . . you haven't seen anybody . . . like, you know . . . like . . . cops . . ."

"What kind of cops? Uniform cops or special cops, with a special name, like DEA?"

Like a corrupt DEA agent who showed up at my apartment demanding I find my drug-dealing father? Why yes, Richie, I have. I wouldn't be here if I hadn't.

This is what happens when you're desperate.

"Hey, I told that guy—"

"What guy?" Kat asked, her heart giving a thump in her chest. "The guy who wants his ten-million-dollar drug money payoff? The guy with brown hair, brown shoes, and a gunshot scar on his side? *Agent* James Sheridan? That guy?"

Richie leaned in. "How do *you* know him?" he asked in a choked whisper.

Katerina wondered if her expression betrayed her thoughts as the memories attacked like a battering ram at a crumbling fortress. Her shock at finding Sheridan in her New York apartment, her useless mad dash for the door, being crushed against a wall, pinned . . .

You work for me now. Find your father. Or you and your mother are going to prison.

"We went for a mani-pedi," Kat snapped, pushing the images down like an overstuffed suitcase she was desperate to close. "What about the shooting, Richie?"

"That was your dad," Richie said. "*He* pulled the trigger."

***

This is taking too long, Katerina thought as Richie grabbed a napkin and wiped the sweat from his forehead.

"I don't know where the money is, Kat. I swear on my mother's grave."

"Bullshit and your mother is alive. She lives in Jersey."

"So I bought a fuckin' truck, so what? I got stiffed on the real money," he whined.

Katerina did a quick mental estimate of the percentage of lies in Richie's story. At least half. Probably more.

"How did it work?" Kat asked.

Richie shook his head. "It was in the paperwork, the bookkeeping. Some of the bills you paid for supplies, materials, toy stuffing? That wasn't toy stuffing. Those weren't real suppliers. That was product coming in."

"What about sending the product out?" Kat asked.

"You didn't know you were typing phony invoices? Lost shipments weren't lost, there were no damaged or stolen boxes of toys, sometimes the whole distribution company was a fake," he babbled. "They were distributing, just not plush toys. Everything you were doing mixed in the drug money with the regular money."

Great. Just what I needed. Another felony.

"And then the money kept moving around until it was okay. I really thought you knew. Your dad had it all figured out. It was perfect."

"How did something so perfect blow up? What was that one little change?"

"After you left, you know your dad was better but not a hundred percent. Everything was going great, like always, so, he trusted me, and then I saw an opportunity so . . . I changed the trucking."

And I wasn't here to tell him, Kat thought. "You just cut out the first trucking company, just like that?"

"They got pissed. But the new company was cheaper. They didn't need to know anything. Just deliver the boxes. I think a box must have opened, or a seam on one of the toys ripped, maybe one of the packets fell out. Somebody made a phone call. All of sudden Sheridan shows up and he wants money."

Kat marveled at the depth and breadth of Richie's stupidity even as she hung on his every word, desperate for an angle that could hold off a dirty DEA agent.

"What about the laptop my dad gave you? You were using it to move the money?"

Richie nodded. "He had a bunch of accounts. He took it back."

Kat felt her blood pressure surge in frustration. Searching for her next move, she made a snap decision to play dumb.

"Who's in charge at the plant now?" she asked, even as the hair on the back of her neck prickled, even though she had a feeling she knew the answer.

Richie sat poised like a runner ready to push off the block. "*They* are," he said. "They've got people on the inside. They took back the trucking; they took control of the product. They took everything."

They have a name and I need it. Before Christmas, Katerina had sent *them* a gift through an intermediary, a tip. Their operation was at risk from a DEA agent. She had provided just enough details, without a name, gambling *they* would remove corrupt DEA agent James Sheridan, alleviating her problem. She lost. They didn't.

"Who was your contact? What's their name?" she pressed.

Richie's eyes darted around in another sweep of the pub. "No real names. I just dealt with a middleman."

A big man, with dark hair and bovine features, crossed the threshold from the bar into the back room, a glass of beer in his hand. He sported the popular lumberjack look: jeans, checkered plaid flannel shirt, down jacket, and Doc Martens construction boots. He set the beer down on a table out of earshot. He pulled out the chair and sat parallel to the table, facing the flat screen television.

Kat watched Richie's complexion blanch, his eyes fill with fear.

You didn't follow Winter's advice, Katerina thought. You stayed too long. Now you're out of time.

***

Richie grabbed his coat, keeping watch on the man staring at the television. He made a move to bolt.

Katerina took hold of Richie's arm, squeezing with everything she had. Faced with an exercise in failure, she tried one last time.

"What about Lulu?"

"Who?" Richie asked, snapping to attention.

Katerina rolled her eyes. "Don't give me the bullshit that you don't know about my father's cuddle bunny hooker."

Richie shook his head, his eyes still on the lumberjack. "I don't know why he took up with that skank," he said, sweat gathering again at his temples and on his upper lip. "Kat, I gotta go."

"Where did the skank live?"

"She rented a studio in a private house," Richie mumbled. He rattled off the address, his eyes darting to the interloper still nursing his beer.

"Give me your cell number," Kat said, wishing she had left five minutes earlier.

"Why?" he asked.

"Because I said so."

Richie whispered the number. He looked over her, as if seeing her for the first time. "Your dad always bragged about your memory, how you never forgot anything." He leaned in. "If you see him, put in a good word for me, okay? Tell him I didn't try to hurt him. I was just tryin' to make a little money, something just for me."

Sure thing Fredo, Kat thought.

Richie hustled out of the booth, shoved his hands into the pockets of his coat, and rushed out the back like a man trying to outrun flames licking at his heels.

Katerina stayed in the booth, waiting to see which way the lumberjack would head out before deciding her exit route.

He didn't move.

Kat thought maybe Richie's paranoia had leeched into her, warping her judgment.

Her eyes took in the glass of beer sitting untouched, the man's eyes staring at the screen, his fingers drumming on the table.

Katerina could feel the flop sweat break out over her body.

He's been playing a waiting game.

And he's not waiting for Richie.

***

Kat bolted out the back door, running around the back of the building. As she came through the parking lot, she watched the taillights of the Durango grow smaller as it tore down the road. She jumped into the Honda, her heart racing.

The lumberjack exited the bar and stood still, skimming the lot.

Katerina's breath came fast and shallow as she slid down in the seat, feeling like a duck in a shooting gallery, hoping he couldn't set his sights on her.

He stopped scanning. Katerina followed his gaze to an idling gray Altima parked across the street. The lumberjack went to a dark sedan and climbed in. He gunned the engine and drove off. The Altima didn't follow.

Katerina started the car and pulled out of the lot, checking the rearview. Nothing. When she checked again her heart thudded in her chest at the sight of the Altima, following behind.

Who the hell are these guys?

Chapter 3

Kat zigzagged around town until the Altima vanished and she felt clear to return to the farm. When she stepped into the kitchen, a New York newspaper tucked under one arm, the sweet scent of sugar mixed with a hint of incense greeted her. The warm, welcoming space was a jarring juxtaposition of blue and white country style mixed with hanging crystals and a small Buddha on a shelf, sporting an enigmatic smile.

Kat's mother, Linda Mills, standing next to the deep, double-wide copper farmhouse sink, didn't look up from slicing vegetables for the evening dinner.

Katerina couldn't quite absorb the new Linda Mills. For as long as Kat could remember, her mother had kept her hair in a neat bob and favored conservative dresses cinched at the waist. Now, her mother's shiny, abundant chestnut hair swung about her shoulders and she sported the BoHo chic of long, flowing dresses, paisley maxi skirts, and puffy, peasant style blouses. Even her cream complexion had taken on a youthful glow. Being dumped by her husband and left destitute had worked wonders for Linda Mills.

"You were out early today," her mother said. "Did you drive by the house again?"

"Yup," Kat said. After her mother had asked the question the first time, she settled on the lie of frequent drives past their former home as expedient and easiest to explain her absences.

Katerina's gaze zeroed in on the pile of newspapers on the trestle table. Newspapers she had been buying at the bookstore every day since she came back.

"Are you done with those?" her mother asked, turning to Katerina and frowning at the sight of the paper under her daughter's arm. "Katerina, we are guests in this house. They recycle. You shouldn't let these things pile up and buy more. Why do you need them?"

Because I have to know if there's been a break in a murder case.

I have to know if I'm going to be arrested as an accessory after the fact.

"Just keeping up with current events," Kat mumbled.

"You can do that on the internet."

Web searches can be tracked. And presented as evidence at trial.

Katerina suffered through yet another of her mother's sudden silences. When she lived in New York, Kat had found the light, flippant, and sometimes ditsy tone of her mother's phone calls exasperating. Upon Kat's return, Linda Mills had reverted to her "Minnesota Nice" upbringing of constrained politeness. Katerina didn't need to wonder why.

William Mills had been Kat's Pied Piper, filling her head with grand dreams of an exciting career as a high-powered lawyer in New York City. William Mills had turned out to be a man neither she nor anyone else could know or trust. The blinders had been torn away too late; gravitating to him had been a betrayal, one that couldn't be forgiven. Linda Mills no longer saw a reason to hide her displeasure with her only daughter.

"How are you, love," Rachel said, gliding in and breaking Kat's purgatory.

"Everything's Gucci," Kat said, suppressing the urge to open the paper and start scanning.

Rachel eyed the papers. "Anxious to go back already? We would hate to lose you so soon."

"No. I have a few more weeks," Kat said. "I'm enjoying the break." *From cops, criminals, and a crazed, sadistic client...*

"I hope they don't work you too hard," Rachel said.

"No, it's standard, personal assistant stuff, taking care of the family car..." *Stealing a car for Simon Marcus—from his wife.* "...running errands..." *Getting an exotic, illegal drug for Paul Patel's writer's block.* "...decorating an apartment..." *Why does Thomas Gallagher call MJM Consulting, an agency that supplies consultants to do the dirty work no one else can, for decorating his apartment?* "...recommending a birthday gift..." she added, almost to herself.

"Your clients must love you," Rachel said.

Simon Marcus tried to kill me. "I get the job done," Kat said.

"I'm sure your agency appreciates you," Rachel said.

They helped Simon Marcus try to kill me. "They're always thinking of me."

Katerina caught her mother giving her a sideways glance, but Linda Mills remained silent.

Rachel took a warm cider doughnut from an overflowing plate and handed it to her. "Sometimes we spend so much time caring for others, we forget to nourish ourselves."

Katerina nodded. Rachel's wisdom came from her lifelong spiritual journey, a mix of transpersonal psychology and shamanism, seeking the bridge between states of consciousness and forging connections between this world and other unseen and unknown worlds.

"Don't forget there's a gathering ceremony tonight, my love," Rachel said.

"What's it for?" Kat asked.

"Finding your spirit animal," Rachel said. "Your mother is coming."

"Interesting," Kat said, looking to her mother. Linda Mills had turned back to the sink.

Rachel gave Kat a motherly pat on her shoulder. "You stay as long as you like. This will always be a safe haven, a home . . . for both of you," she said with a gentle smile as she slipped from the room.

Without Rachel, the tense silence returned. Katerina sat at the table, turning the pages of the newspaper in a slow, methodic cadence, her heart skipping in trepidation.

Searching for the perfect birthday gift. Katerina remembered the day John Reynolds, her first client, had hired her to follow his wife, Felicia, and discover her preferences and passions.

When Katerina had crossed paths with the kind and impulsive socialite, Felicia had pressed a gift of her own earrings upon Katerina, a one-of-a-kind pair, shell-shaped quartz encrusted with diamonds, in exchange for a promise. Katerina should never cut her long, flowing, chestnut hair, a symbol of freedom. *Be free. Someone should*, Felicia had said. Now, the earrings were hidden away in Kat's apartment, a talisman of capture and imprisonment.

As Katerina turned another page, her heart surged again with grief and guilt at her naiveté; Reynolds had used her as a canary to discover his wife's true preference and passion—a handsome, second-string theater actor, Will Temple—and he had already set the real assignment in motion.

He unleashed the man in the blue Ford, a man Katerina could identify. This man had brutally murdered Felicia Reynolds and a second victim, Cheryl Penn, a copycat killing to throw police off the scent. John Reynolds had confessed it all to her. *Why? For what purpose?*

Katerina turned the page, wondering if she would see a story on Will Temple. She could close her eyes and see him standing in front of her apartment building, a charming young man with careless hair. He had come to audition for a film, *Love's Fury*, for a production company called Random Girl Films. He had her name. The case of mistaken identity was hardly a coincidence.

Will Temple had disappeared before Christmas. Maybe he ran, Kat thought. Maybe he escaped. *I hope you did.*

When Kat reached the sports section, she closed the paper. *Another day's reprieve.* The relief vanished in the next breath, as it always did. Back in New York City, Detective Ryan Kellan was on the hunt to find the killer. Kat knew the dark-haired, intense, decorated young detective from their brief dating stint last year. *The closer he gets to the truth, the closer he gets to the one link that connects to John Reynolds, Felicia Reynolds, Will Temple, Cheryl Penn, and a killer in a blue Ford . . . me.*

Katerina looked up to find Linda Mills studying her only daughter.

I should never have come back here. How do I tell you any of this, all of this?

"I think I'll go out and help Ethel," Katerina said, avoiding her gaze.

"That's nice, dear," her mother said.

Katerina dumped the newspaper in the recycle bin and fled the kitchen.

Chapter 4

New York City detectives Ryan Kellan and Walter Lashiver got out of the car as a man exited a diner, still chewing on the last bite of his lunch and carrying a Styrofoam cup. In his early forties with a short, neat haircut, he wore a black coat over a dark suit and tie.

"Detective Tom Morse," Lashiver said.

Morse's eyes sparked with recognition. "No shit," he said, thrusting out his hand. "You *are* still alive."

Lashiver chuckled and nodded in Ryan's direction. "You spoke with my partner, Ryan Kellan."

Morse nodded. "I remember. What can I do for you?"

"Just checking if anything turned up on Will Temple," Ryan said.

Morse shook his head. "Guy fell off the map. No one's seen him. But no sign of foul play."

The two detectives nodded.

"Nothing yet on the dead socialite?" Morse said.

"Two dead socialites," Lashiver said. "We're looking for a break on the Cheryl Penn murder, too."

"You think the kid did it and ran?"

"We don't know," Lashiver said.

"We think he's a possible victim," Ryan cut in.

Lashiver shot Ryan a look but the younger detective remained undeterred. "What about the airports, trains . . . morgue?"

Morse shook his head. "Everything is clean. Look, he could be off doing a movie, lost his cell phone, broke his iPad, or maybe he just got a better deal as someone else's boy toy."

"Maybe. Did you try again on Random Girl Films?" Lashiver asked.

Morse nodded. "There's no such company."

"What about his friends?" Ryan asked. "Did he mention Random Girl to anyone?"

"A couple of people knew he had an audition. He told them it was a bust, but he met a pretty girl. That's it."

Lashiver and Ryan processed the dead end in a moment of silence.

"You think we could see his apartment before everything is tagged and bagged and put into storage?" Ryan asked.

Morse glanced between the two and shrugged again. "Sure, I can get over there this week."

Ryan offered his hand and Morse took it.

As Ryan headed back to the car, Morse and Lashiver shook hands.

"Your partner's got a hard-on over this."

"Yeah. He's a little—he's not himself. Trouble with the girlfriend."

Morse nodded. "Girlfriend or ex-girlfriend?"

"Right," Lashiver said.

"So he's sniffing in the wrong place?"

Lashiver hesitated. "Maybe."

Chapter 5

Taking one of the horse-drawn wagons, Katerina rode over the rough hills of Rainbow Farms, stopping near a large copse of trees. Hidden away behind them, Kat found the half shell of a tiny house and Ethel, Rachel's other half, dressed in overalls and layers of flannel, working on the build.

Since her arrival for the Christmas holiday, Katerina had forgone her usual yoga routine, finding herself drawn to this most unlikely exercise. With the lingering specter of Agent James Sheridan always on the periphery of her thoughts, Kat preferred being outside, a knee-jerk reaction to the fear of being trapped in a small space. The older woman had shown patience, allowing Kat to work on the project, a gracious yet distant host.

The cold quickly fled as Kat's body heat rose from the exertion of drilling holes for the steel studs in the framing. She had never done the taxing work before; in the beginning, the drill had felt strange and difficult to control.

Ethel no longer needed to stand over her, instead leaving her to herself. With the whirring of the drill, Kat's mind turned, searching for a way to extricate herself from the web of MJM, John Reynolds, drug dealers, and James Sheridan. She was on the clock to find a way to keep the corrupt DEA agent at bay.

I'm running out of time.

The thought of him unleashed a sudden firestorm of images. Sheridan shoving her against the wall, striking her, restraining her . . . forcing his fingers inside her . . . In her rage, Katerina wasn't drilling the frame anymore; she was driving the bit into Sheridan, inflicting pain on him as he had done to her. A sudden wave of exhaustion washed over her and she set the power tool down.

Pulling off her gloves and safety glasses, Kat wiped her sleeve across her face and tested the sore muscles in her shoulders, back, and neck.

Ethel inspected her work. "I think you've found your calling," she said. "Let's take a break."

***

Ethel broke out a thermos of coffee and filled two Styrofoam cups. They leaned against the truck, drinking in a comfortable silence, Ethel's trusty .17 HMR rifle close by.

"How did you meet my mother?" Kat asked, curious to know how Linda Mills had found this refuge among strangers.

Ethel took another swig of coffee. "I didn't. Rachel did. Your mom went to one of the Reiki circles."

My mother. Linda Mills. At a Reiki circle.

Bullshit.

Katerina kept her thoughts to herself and switched the subject. "How did you and Rachel get together? What was it about her?"

Ethel gave Katerina a sideways glance; a prolonged silence followed. Ethel pulled out a cigarette from the pack stashed in her pocket and lit up.

Katerina realized that her question could be misconstrued as prying—or a prelude to judgment. "I mean, how did you know you were meant to be with this one person out of everyone in the world?"

Ethel took a long drag on her cigarette, examining Katerina through narrowed eyes. "Are we talking about me?"

Busted.

"Who is he?"

Kat looked out at the expanse of property, the mental image of Alexander Winter causing a sudden flush to rush through her. *How do I explain a steal-to-order thief who lives in the shadows?* "He's a—he's self-employed."

Ethel shrugged. "Sometimes you don't know," she said. "But with Rachel, one look at her and—"

"And what?" she asked, turning to the older woman, impatient for the answer.

"Beats me," Ethel grinned, her weathered skin crinkling around her blue-gray eyes. "I just knew."

"Knew what?" Kat pressed.

Ethel took another drag on her cigarette. "It had to be her. I didn't want to be without her. It would never be right." She looked into Kat's eyes. "Make sense?"

Katerina nodded.

"How old are you, twenty-five?"

"Twenty-three."

"Shit, girl, don't even worry about it. You've got years of bad decisions ahead of you," she said. "You going to find your spirit animal tonight?"

Katerina registered the slight snark in the question. "The vision quests, the fire ceremonies, the sacred stones . . . you don't believe in any of it, do you?"

"Hell, no," Ethel said, flashing a broad smile. "But it's important to Rachel, and I wouldn't want her to be any other way."

"Maybe that's how you know," Kat said.

Ethel held out her cup and Katerina tipped her cup against it. "I'll drink to that," Ethel said.

Katerina worked for another hour until tiny pinpricks of cold wormed their way into her thighs, her fingers tingling in the heavy gloves. She put down the drill and left. Ethel continued on with no word of thanks. Katerina didn't need it. As she headed back to the house, Katerina took in the silence and seclusion of the property, remembering Rachel's words. *A safe haven.* She had no idea what Rachel and Ethel had suffered in order to be together. She wondered at the coincidence of her mother going to a Reiki circle and meeting a woman who happened to own an isolated farm, making it easy to drop out and stay hidden.

Why does my mother need to hide?

***

Up in her room, Katerina showered and curled up in bed under the earth-toned patchwork quilt. She glanced up at the dream catcher hanging on the wall above her. A simple wooden hoop with threads woven into a web, it entangled bad dreams, binding them until they burned away in the morning sunlight. Not all of them. The guilt over Felicia's death, Cheryl's death, and Will's disappearance held fast, clinging companions never further away than a stray thought.

She would buy the newspaper tomorrow, addicted to the ritual, needing to know if she had escaped for one more day. But in the back of her mind, the words of John Reynolds at their last meeting twisted knots of terror inside her. *We still have a lot of work left to do together, Miss Katerina.*

She had remained with MJM Consulting to stay one step ahead of the game, but the idea that had been forming in her mind before Christmas mushroomed, like a new shoot on a plant, unfurling, stretching out, growing larger each day. *What if I can find a way to leave, escape everything MJM and my father has brought into my world.*

Katerina let the exhaustion overtake her and settled her head on the pillow. As she dozed, another memory intruded: the dead of night in Upstate New York, a raging snowstorm, and two men, FBI agents, demanding to take possession of her.

Except they were not the FBI.

Katerina remembered the words one had spoken.

Just give me the girl.

To take me where?

For what?

And Alexander Winter, gun in hand, standing in their way.

She hadn't seen or heard from Winter since he brought her back into the city, safe and sound. She wanted to reach out to him but didn't dare. She had put him in enough jeopardy. *And it had been my choice to come home.*

If I disappear where John Reynolds, MJM, Detective Ryan Kellan, James Sheridan, and drug dealers won't find me . . . *Alexander Winter won't find me either.*

Right before she fell asleep, Katerina wished her only problem was decorating Thomas Gallagher's apartment.

In your next life, be an interior decorator.

It's safer.

Chapter 6

On New York's Upper East Side, Thomas Gallagher feigned relaxation as he sat in his favorite chair sipping his tea, listening to the gentleman seated across from him deliver his report.

Joseph Smith made a trim, dapper appearance, dressed in a suit, vest, and tie. If Thomas Gallagher exuded an icy chill, Joseph Smith, with his square jaw, short, blond hair, and cold eyes, could only be described as glacial. He spoke with quiet authority, secure in his abilities, confidence oozing from every word he uttered.

Smith finished his recitation and waited.

"I'm disappointed in the turn of events," Thomas Gallagher said.

Smith nodded. "You thought this man she calls "professor" would follow her to Vermont, a logical assumption."

"Perhaps a few more days," Gallagher suggested.

"Someone is shadowing her. This—bodyguard—has picked up on our surveillance—"

"Then your man was sloppy," Gallagher snapped.

Smith shrugged off the comment, ceding the point. "This could work to our advantage. If my operative makes contact with the girl—"

"No. Your man was sent only to remove the professor, not to contact Miss Mills."

"A slight adjustment. If my operative removes the bodyguard and takes hold of the girl, the professor will come to her aid. I assure you my man will act with restraint and self-control."

Gallagher mentally ticked off the inconveniences this would cause: the mother would contact the police, the John Reynolds connection could come to light, the detective would come back into the picture. "Absolutely not."

Joseph Smith suppressed a sigh of annoyance. "Then, this changes to a fact-finding exercise. I need to learn more about this professor. A look inside the girl's apartment will—"

"*Miss Mills'* apartment is off-limits," Gallagher said.

Though surprised at Gallagher's response, Joseph Smith opted for a dulcet tone of reassurance. "You know any information I uncover about—Miss Mills—will be held in the strictest confidence. I've already demonstrated my client confidentiality in dealing with the Simon Marcus issue and the two contractors upstate—"

"I have no qualms regarding your ability to keep secrets," Gallagher said. "It's been your business for over twenty years, but you will handle this within the parameters I set. If the professor will not go to Vermont, then search for him. I gave you the Brooklyn address. Start there."

Smith maintained his poker face. He'd had countless clients who fancied themselves back seat drivers. "This might cause a further delay," he offered.

"I have faith in your expertise," Gallagher said.

Smith nodded. He would participate in the charade and the subsequent waste of time. It was Gallagher's time. These men were all the same: powerful and yet pussy whipped and pining. The myopic obsession would only grow worse over time as the blurring lens of reason continued to degrade; it would eventually drive Gallagher to come around. After he left the apartment, Smith sent a text to his operative: if the opportunity presented itself, take possession of Katerina Mills.

***

Mrs. Shields, carrying a Spode Blue Italian teapot of hot water, entered the study silent as a cat. Thomas Gallagher watched his housekeeper as she prepared a fresh cup of tea. When he had first seen her, she had been a thin, delicate sprite with heavy bangs just brushing the fringe of lashes framing her deep blue doe-eyes. She had belonged to one of his business partners, catering to his every whim without question or protest.

She set the cup down on the stand and waited.

"Thank you, Mrs. Shields. You anticipate my every need."

The woman nodded and left.

Gallagher took the cup in hand, considering the polite flattery he had just bestowed on Mrs. Shields. Flattery . . . so easy to dispense. Plans for Katerina Mills twisted like threads in his mind; he ruminated on how best to bring her under his wing and resolve this situation once and for all. A sudden surge of anger spiked within him at the thought of Katerina in love with her "professor," choosing him over all others. *Choosing him over me.* Gallagher had been privy to their written communications until the professor had discovered and removed the spyware installed on Katerina's phone.

He had signed his texts "W."

She had called him "Bob," no doubt a pet name for him, a private joke only they shared. His lips pinched in distaste at the thought, and he sucked in a deep breath to cool his ire and focus on the task at hand. Destroying "Bob" would have to be done with care, leaving Katerina Mills vulnerable and in need of a place of safety. A comforting, protective cage she wouldn't want to leave, even if the door of escape stood wide open. He forced his anger into submission. I will not punish her for choosing the professor, he told himself. *No, I will forgive her and speak to her with—flattery.*

Chapter 7

Katerina shivered in the frigid car in spite of the bright noon sun. The used Civic blended in with the few parked cars scattered up and down the street. She had done several rounds of surveillance on the well-worn pale blue clapboard house at the end of the block. She observed the owner's schedule of comings and goings, taking note of any activity in or around Lulu's apartment on the side of the house. The owner, a woman, had shown the place a few times.

Kat had considered presenting herself as a potential renter but decided it would open up a host of new problems. *I won't be left alone so I can't search for... whatever. I can be identified.*

I have to break in.

Katerina thought back on her experience with Winter, breaking into the house in the Hamptons and found herself at a loss. She doubted there would be an alarm but if a lock needed picking...

She continued to watch the apartment, the sparse bushes and the ground on either side of the door still covered in snow and ice. Kat ruminated over Alexander Winter's golden rule. *Keep it simple.* What do people do just in case they get locked out of their house or forget their key? *They keep a spare hidden nearby.*

Twisting her hair into a coil, Kat pinned it up, then tugged a cap down over her head. Zipping up her North Face parka, she opened the car door and got out, pulling in a long breath of icy air. As she walked, Winter's voice whispered in her head.

Walk like you're where you're supposed to be.

She plodded forward, her breath coming in puffy, white bursts.

Don't keep your head down, but don't look anywhere specific.

The wind plucked at her clothing as she approached the house. A beat-up gray Nissan, dented and scraped with the beginnings of body rot, sat in the driveway. No sign of activity.

Crouching down by the door of the apartment, Kat thrust her hands in the snow, checking for an overturned flowerpot or fake rocks. The action triggered a sudden flashback: Upstate New York, the dead of night, in the woods, on her knees, numb with cold, a gun pointed at the back of her head. Determined not to go out without a fight, she pawed in the icy snow with her bare hands, forming a rock-hard ball.

Katerina forced her mind back to the present as her fingers closed over a hard, round object. A sense of satisfaction shot through her as she found two other objects of the same shape but different sizes.

She glanced around; no signs of life. Pulling the objects out, she held three rocks, small, medium, and large. Poppa rock, Momma rock, and baby rock, she thought as she examined each piece. Under her prodding, the baby-sized rock gave way and a key fell out.

***

Katerina surveyed the shabby, run-down apartment. Most of what Lulu owned had been moved out; only a few boxes and some yellowing newspapers remained. Kat wondered how many times William Mills had come here to see little Lulu, betraying her mother. Kat's stomach turned at the thought. She forced herself to put it aside.

Once again, the clock was ticking.

***

Kat made short work of searching the boxes and then moved on to the cabinets. She hit pay dirt in a junk drawer. Lulu must have been in a rush to leave, forgetting the few phone bills and deposit slips stuffed in the back.

"What the hell are you doing in here?"

Kat's heart lurched. Shoving the papers in her coat pocket, she whirled around.

The woman had a round, lined face, gray, disheveled hair, and an overweight body underneath a rumpled yellow housecoat and an old ratty sweater. She blinked several times, as if attempting to focus.

"I'm here about renting the apartment," Kat managed, as the familiar nervous perspiration broke out under her clothing. "The door was open."

"I told you, you'll have to wait," the woman slurred, staring at Katerina with glassy eyes.

Completely shitfaced. Still, Kat knew she needed to be careful.

"I need the place now," Kat said. "I can clear this stuff out."

The woman's eyes narrowed. "Nothin's goin' nowhere. Tenant still owes me for two months."

"That doesn't help me."

The woman put her hands on her hips. "Watch your tone."

"Whatever," Kat said, breezing past her.

"Hey! Hey!" the woman called out. "You wait just a minute, girlie."

Afraid the woman might make a scene and take it outside the apartment, Katerina stopped and turned around.

The woman shuffled up to her. Kat flinched as she caught the stale smell of alcohol and cigarettes.

"Little wiseasses, both of you. You tell little Lulu if she wants her stuff, she can come back with my money." The woman stuck out her hand; Katerina dropped the key in her upturned palm.

***

Katerina beat a hasty retreat to the car. Sliding into the Civic, she gripped the wheel with shaking hands, willing herself to calm down. She turned the key in the ignition and took off.

Close. Too close.

Alexander Winter would not be pleased.

Glancing in her rearview mirror, her stomach somersaulted at the sight of the gray Altima following.

***

Katerina drove at a measured pace, threading her way through the downtown area and into the picturesque heart of the UV campus. She kept checking her mirrors; the gray Altima still followed at a steady distance. She scanned the other vehicles, looking for the dark sedan the lumberjack drove. *What if he switched cars? What if they're working together?*

Her mind raced with every compulsive check in the rearview mirror as she tried to figure out who was behind this.

Sheridan wouldn't play this game.

Cops would have already pulled her over and made an arrest.

Felicia's killer? Her stomach sliced again. No, Reynolds wouldn't let him off the leash to wander this far.

Then who?

Katerina spotted a busy corner and made a split-second decision to jerk the Civic over to the curb. She jammed the gear into park and checked the rearview mirror, waiting to see if the Altima would step on the gas and move on.

The Altima passed the Civic. Katerina watched the red taillights shine as the driver hit the brakes and then maneuvered into an open spot.

Katerina sat stunned, the ragged, shallow sound of her breathing in her head as she flashed back. Last month, sitting in a parked car in Manhattan, her eyes glued to the rearview mirror, watching Sheridan get out of his car, watching his every step as he came closer . . . A fit of anger washed over Katerina. Not again, she thought, and she threw open her door and got out.

Her eyes shifted between the car and the crowded street in the seconds it took her to reach the Altima. The driver held a cell phone to his ear as she knocked on the window. He said a few words and clicked off the phone. With a soft whirring sound, the window descended. He wore a short, neat haircut and dark coat; he looked like a middle management businessman.

"You and your partner suck at surveillance," Katerina said, sneaking a glance at the pedestrians, her insurance policy.

"I work alone," he said. "And who said you're under surveillance?"

"Who are you working for?"

He gave a kind smile. "A friend."

"I have enough friends. Unless someone drops dead, I can't have anymore," she quipped.

His eyebrows rose and he gave a smile. "Everyone can use another friend, especially you, Katie."

Katerina's heart skipped at the sound of her nickname. Only one person called her by that name.

"Alexander Winter says hello."

Katerina felt the relief flood in as her breath escaped. Winter who had been there, upstate, in the snowstorm, in the dark woods, when she had run out of strength, out of options, out of time.

"What about the other guy? The lumberjack in the Doc Martens?"

"Don't worry about him," he said. "He's gone now."

Katerina nodded, not wanting to know the exact definition of "gone."

"What do I call you?" she asked.

"Carter."

Katerina, heart thudding in her chest at yet another escape from disaster, said, "Please tell Winter I said thank you."

Carter held out the burner phone. "Tell him yourself."

Kat accepted the phone with a nod.

***

When she slipped back into the Civic, Kat sat behind the wheel, cradling the phone and considering Carter's words, wrestling with the urge to make the call. She shoved the phone in her purse, refusing to put Winter at further risk.

The Altima sat idling, waiting on her to pull out.

As she maneuvered back out into traffic, Kat decided she needed to drop out of sight for a few hours. She needed a warm, welcoming place to decompress and get her head together.

She knew where she needed to go.

Uncle Sergei.

Chapter 8

"Everyone wants a prime piece of real estate, right?" the retired executive said. "Every millennial with, what do you call them, the haircuts, you know, short in the back and long in the front? Jesus Christ, what is that? Anyway, everyone wants a big high-rise or a loft—a fade, that's what it's called, yeah, it's called a fade. Damn kids. They're spending the check before they even cash it. Anyway, everyone wants an apartment that's not a fuckin' closet where you eat, sleep, and shit all in the same room. But where can you find that? So, I'm thinking, you know, commercial. Commercial real estate is where to be now. You pay a few million, have it renovated, hang up a lamp, and call it chic. Before you know it, some snot making a mint at a tech startup can't wait to buy up what used to be part of a meat packing plant." He took another swig of his scotch and shook his head. "I should have done this years ago. I could have retired at forty."

As the retired executive talked, Joseph Smith sat across from him, nursed his drink, and listened. "You only have space in Manhattan?" he asked.

"No, no," the executive said, shaking his head. "Two years ago, I bought a building in Brooklyn. What a bitch to fix up, a fucking nightmare. But it's earning its money. I sold some of the units."

"So you only sell."

"No, I mean, yeah, I sell, but if it doesn't sell, you know, I don't want to carry the cost." He knocked back the last of his scotch and raised the glass to catch the bartender's eye. He examined the stranger again, confirming he had an okay look about him. He looked like he had money; and that's all that mattered.

"I heard you have a penthouse available. Cash. No credit checks."

The retired executive went quiet. "Oh yeah? Where'd you hear that?"

Smith smiled. "Relax, friend. I was given your name by a former tenant."

"Who?"

"He rented the penthouse in December. Quiet. Professional."

The retired executive went silent. Sure, he remembered the guy who had rented from him. That guy didn't strike him as a person who made referrals. Or had friends. *What the hell do I give a shit? That's his problem.*

"Oh yeah, sure."

Smith leaned in confidentially. "Which name did he use? Burton Johnson?"

The retired executive laughed. "Jesus Christ, what a name. Where did he come up with that? No. Steven Bartholomew."

Smith laughed. "Well, friend, don't worry. I can pay better than Steven Bartholomew. Is he still wearing the beard?"

"No, no, clean shaven, short haircut. Good looking guy. Bet he does well for himself, hunh?"

"The ladies love him," Smith said. "You have a business card?"

The retired executive pulled out his card and slid it over to him.

Smith picked it up and slipped it into his pocket. He got up, peeled off several bills, and placed them on the bar. "I'll be in touch."

The retired executive lifted his glass. "No problem. I can get you something in Midtown too, if you need it."

He watched the stranger stroll out of the bar, a vague uneasiness washing over him. Maybe he had said something he shouldn't. He knocked back the last of his drink. So what? he thought. *Not my fucking problem.*

***

After exiting the bar, Joseph Smith took out his cell phone and placed a call to his team. He gave instructions to locate and dissect Katerina Mills' "professor," one Steven Bartholomew.

Chapter 9

Katerina drove the Civic down a paved, two-lane road, taking the twists and turns at a measured, cautious pace. Each fall, tourists flooded the area. Armed with maps, they searched out the artisan workshops that were hidden away in the landscape. Katerina slowed the car, easing off the paved road and onto a narrow dirt path; thick, sloping tree limbs encased in ice and snow created an arch above her. Exiting into a frost-covered clearing, the familiar birchwood cabin greeted her, a spiral of smoke puffing out of the chimney. The smaller structure next to the cabin, the artist's studio, appeared deserted. *This workshop isn't on any map*, Kat thought. *It isn't meant to be found.*

Katerina eased the Civic to a stop and cut the engine. Two young men she had come to recognize, Sergei's nephews, came around from the back of the cabin. They had dark hair and solemn faces, and they wore their usual thick denim jackets, wool caps, jeans, and sturdy boots. They eyed her, as always, with a curious deference.

The cabin door opened and Sergei Grigorievitch Volkov emerged from the house. In his younger years, Sergei had been strapping and handsome with a head of black hair, a full, neat beard, and piercing dark eyes. Time had treated him well; he still had a solid, sturdy build. His hair and beard were now salted with gray and there were lines etched into his forehead and around his eyes. He waited at the door while the young men approached Katerina, faithful footmen flanking her, ready to catch her if she should slip.

As she approached, Sergei held out his hands to her. Kat responded, slipping into his paternal embrace, breathing in the sharp, familiar scent of cigarette smoke clinging to his clothing.

"My little Katya," he said, kissing her on both cheeks.

***

The cabin, clean and comfortable, had a welcoming living area with an overstuffed sofa, heavy pine coffee table, and a well-stocked bookcase. In the compact kitchen, Katerina stood at the stove in front of a large fry pan. Using a spatula to loosen the thin pancake, *blini,* she turned it out onto a growing stack. Taking each one in turn, she used a light touch and folded twice. After arranging them on a plate, she spooned a generous helping of strawberry jam and sour cream on top. She brought the plate to the round oak table where Sergei sat and placed it before him; he gave her a wide smile of approval.

***

They ate in a comfortable silence. The man she knew as "Uncle" was neither gregarious nor taciturn; he had a quiet, gentle way about him that appealed to her and eased her mind.

"Thank you for the use of the car," Kat said.

Sergei gave a wave of his hand, dismissing the thanks as unnecessary.

"Are you going to stay here in your *dacha*?" Kat asked, glancing around.

Sergei shook his head as he dropped a dollop of honey into her steaming mug of tea. "This is not dacha. *Dacha* is summer house. You do not have your good things in dacha because you are always outside, in garden, taking fresh air."

He motioned with a wave of his hand that she should drink her tea. "I am happy you visit your Uncle Sergei many times, since you will soon leave. I would have liked it to see you more."

"You could have come to the farm," she said.

He made a noise of disgust. "*Kuriatnik*," he said.

Katerina gave him a questioning look.

"How you say . . . chicken coop."

Kat smiled. "Hen house, Uncle, hen house."

"*Da, da,*" he said. "But you don't say "Uncle" in Russian. *Dyadya.* You need to study."

"I will. How are the nephews?" she asked even though she had seen them on several occasions, in the marketplace or at the supermarket. They nodded in acknowledgment but never approached.

He grunted. "Evgeny is foolish. Pavel is the more foolish. But they do like they are told."

Sergei took up a bottle of vodka, pouring out two fingers into his glass. "So, you come to visit, we talk, you say many things but tell me little. About this, I am not happy."

"What do you mean, Uncle?" she said, suddenly cautious.

"You don't talk about your life in Big Apple . . . if you see someone."

Katerina felt a flush rise to her cheeks.

"Ah," he said. "A man. I knew this. Now you *talk* and say something."

"There is a man. I like him very much."

"This I see, in the face, in the eyes. So . . .?"

Katerina caught herself before she spoke. She held the mug between her hands, enjoying the surge of warmth. "Sometimes you can't be with the one you want. It's not possible."

When Kat glanced over at him, she found warm understanding in his eyes. "You are wise girl. You have learned much already about man, about the foolishness of the married man."

Katerina straightened, anxious to rush through the door Sergei had unexpectedly opened, the subject that had lingered between them, unspoken. *Now, we talk.* She put her mug on the table. "Did you know, Uncle? Did you know what my father was going to do?" *Do you have any idea who my father really is?*

Sergei's face pinched in disapproval. "No one knows this. Always he is like this. Hiding things. Sometimes, Katya, it is loudest man who has the most secrets."

"But you stayed his friend?"

"When I first meet him, many years ago, I see him. I see your mother. I think, this man, he knows beauty. He values the beauty. But I am wrong in this." He patted her hand. "We must trust everything will be as it should," he said, "if we take care to always do right thing, yes? You talk with your mother, spend time with her?"

Katerina stared at her plate. "It's—hard."

"The hard things, Katya, they are most important. We never know how much time we have with someone. We must take the moment and not waste. One day, there is no more time."

Sergei took hold of her hand and she felt the comfort of his grasp, appreciating his efforts to step into her father's shoes.

"Did you finish book I give you?" he asked.

Katerina shifted in her chair. "Yes," she said, chiding herself for forgetting this subject would come up.

"But you say nothing. You do not like this book?"

Katerina averted her eyes. "I don't understand why it's called *The Captain's Daughter*. Most of the time Marya Ivanovna—"

"Masha," Sergei interrupted.

"*Masha*, just stood around looking petrified."

"Ah, but in face of evil, still she stood. This is very brave thing, to stand. Do not think silence is weakness, Katya."

"But a woman should be able to do something," Katerina said, warmth flooding her face as she thought of the night in Upstate New York. In the thick of the storm, sick and wounded, Alexander Winter held her close in his arms, gun in hand, ready to kill to save her. "If she can; maybe even save the man."

"Masha does this," Sergei objected. "She saves this man she loves from execution."

"By spilling her problems to a stranger who just happens to be Empress Catherine the Great, who fixes everything and pardons Masha's beloved. That's convenient."

"Now you don't believe miracles? You don't think you can talk to person, not know who they are, what they can do? Powerful things that change destiny."

"No, I believe in that," Katerina said.

They sat in a strained silence until Sergei gave a deep sigh and said, "Perhaps you are right. But it is the job of man to do these things," he added.

"You're old-fashioned, Uncle—and a romantic."

Sergei gave a snort of displeasure. "What is wrong with romance? Romance is in heart of every Russian. How can you say you do not like this book? You say you don't like Pushkin, the great writer, the heart and soul of Russia? He believed in love. He challenged a man to a duel over the one he loved. This was brave man."

"A brave man with bad aim," Katerina said. "He wasn't there to love her anymore. He died."

"It was noble death."

"Dead is dead," Katerina said, shocking herself with the bluntness of her statement. "And they were separated, forever." Kat worked to stifle the emotions threatening to surge to the surface.

Sergei shrugged. "He had to do it. Believe me, there is nothing worse for man than to be helpless to save one he loves."

"I take it back, Uncle. You're a *hopeless* romantic."

"So was Pushkin," Sergei said.

Katerina, discomfited that she had disappointed her host, rose from the table and wandered to the bookcase. Tilting her head and running her finger across the spines, she stopped, slipped a book off the shelf, and turned to him. "Uncle, why do you have a Bible?"

"I should not have Bible?"

Katerina brought the book to the kitchen table. Sinking into her chair, she placed it on the table between them.

"You're an atheist."

"An atheist does not believe in God," he said. "I am not this. Of course, God exists. We know this. He has made man in his image." Sergei tapped his fingers on the book. "What do you see man doing?"

A sudden chill ran through her, making her shudder. *Spilling blood. Killing.* "Some are doing good, others not."

"And so, I already know God. Sometime he does good, sometime not. So man is same, like God. This is not book about only God, but book about men."

"Some men are like God."

"No, Katya, this is not true."

"Some men . . . they might as well be gods," she said.

"You take this book. Read it. You will know what men have in their hearts, what they will do. And you will find how to defeat men, the ones who are like gods."

She nodded.

"You don't believe your *Dyadya* Sergei tells truth?"

"I do, Uncle," Kat said, Winter's words of wisdom whispering in her head. *Did you go to Sunday school?* "I've heard this before. The man I—like, he believes, like you."

"This is smart man. I like this man." He patted her hand. "You are good girl, *moya malyshka,* my little Katya. It is not easy to do right. It is not you. It is the world. The world does not deserve you. You should stay home with your mother."

"I want to help her, Uncle, not be a burden to her."

Katerina stopped herself; not wanting to say more. She didn't want to hear her own confession out loud.

"Katya, your mother loves you. You must talk with her. Before your time here ends, you must begin. You will do this?"

"Yes, Uncle."

"This is all I ask."

The nephews entered the cabin. Evgeny hung back while Pavel came forward, hovering near Sergei's ear, whispering in Russian.

"*Da, da,*" Sergei said with a wave of his hand. The young men stole away.

"Now, is time for you to go," Sergei said and behind his kind words Katerina detected the familiar, firm tone. The visit was over.

***

They walked outside arm in arm, Katerina leaning her head on his shoulder, the Bible in her hand. The sun, a vibrant blue-orange ball, would begin its descent in a few short hours.

The nephews waited; smoke billowed from the tailpipe of her idling car.

"Good for something," Sergei said, nodding in their direction.

"Again you didn't show me your paintings," Kat said.

"My work is for important men, Katya, rich men. They do not like for anyone to see their prize before them. They pay much money; they can have what they like. No one sees the work."

"I won't ever see what you do?" she asked.

"When time is right, you will see everything," Sergei said, kissing her forehead.

As Katerina turned from him, the young men came to her, walking with her to the car; a comforting flow of heat greeted her as Evgeny opened her door.

As she backed the car up to turn it around, Sergei gave a wave of his hand. She lifted her hand, realizing her nerves had settled, her heartbeat returning to its slow, normal rhythm.

Heading back down the road, she glanced into the rearview mirror to see the Currier and Ives scene of the quaint cabin nestled in the snow-covered woods and Sergei with his nephews. The man she called Uncle retreated into the cabin and closed the door as the young men went inside the studio.

I thought no one sees the work?

A twinge of anxiety rumbled inside her as she thought of Sergei's words.

When time is right, you will see everything.

Chapter 10

Will Temple's apartment could have been a photo exposé on what makes New York City renters lose their minds. The miniscule living space contained a few sticks of beat up furniture, a kitchen crevice with a microwave and a hot plate, and a nook pretending to be a bedroom. The empty space posing as a closet could hold maybe a dozen items. Stacked plastic containers with the mouths facing out held extra clothing, books, whatever could be crammed inside. A narrow table holding a small lamp took up the sliver of space between the wall and the head of the bed.

Detective Morse stood at the door while Detectives Kellan and Lashiver, wearing exam gloves, searched the space. Ryan studied the wall filled with photos in cheap plastic frames documenting Will Temple's stage performances. In every shot, he stood just off to the side of the principals, the perpetual wingman, never at center stage.

"A legend in his broom closet," Ryan said.

"He's not a bad looking guy," Morse offered. "He could be in a weekly show. You know, playing the cop or the PI?"

"You'd want him to play you?" Ryan asked.

"Why not?" Morse said.

"I don't see him as the lead in a show," Ryan said.

"How come?" Lashiver asked.

Ryan shook his head. "Too pretty. He's not damaged enough."

Morse shrugged. "Whatever."

Ryan motioned to the barren closet. "So Barrymore decided to take a trip."

"That's what it looks like," Morse said.

Ryan glanced over the bed. "You found it like this? All the sheets and blankets gone?"

Morse nodded. "Must have been laundry day."

Ryan opened the night table drawer.

"Nothing," Morse said. "No papers, no notes, no Random Girl Films."

Examining the items in the plastic bins, Ryan spotted a bottle of cologne; expensive and way beyond Will Temple's budget. He dug a baggie out of his pocket and placed the bottle inside.

***

The trio of detectives exited the building.

"The area canvas didn't turn up anything?" Ryan asked.

The older detective regarded the younger man with amused impatience. "That's right," Morse said.

Lashiver shot Ryan a look. Ryan laughed. "Yeah, sorry, what I meant was, when you did the interviews, did anyone mention seeing a woman wearing a dark wig and beige shoes? If it didn't come up, maybe you could canvas again."

"Yeah, sure, we could do that," Morse said. "Maybe we could ask if anyone saw him carrying out all those dirty sheets and pillowcases. 'Cause they didn't cover that in detective school so we wouldn't know to ask that."

Lashiver placed a hand on Morse's shoulder. "Hey, Tommy M., you're helping us out and we appreciate it. Just looking for a break on this one. The LT is up our ass and the pressure's on. You know how it is."

"I didn't mean anything by it," Ryan said.

Morse gave him a long look. "I'll send you what we got from the canvassing. You want to interview again, be my guest. There's nothing here. He took off. It happens."

They shook hands in turn, Morse giving Ryan a hard stare. The two detectives stood by as Morse got into his car and took off.

"Take it down a notch," Lashiver said as they made their way to the car.

"Yeah, yeah, I know," Ryan said. "I want to run the bottle for prints and take a look at the receipts again."

"Uh-hunh," Lashiver said, his tone clipped.

"What?"

"You're not going to ask John Reynolds about his wife's purchases for her lover."

"No, of course not," Ryan said.

"And we don't know if that cologne was purchased for him by Felicia Reynolds or Cheryl Penn. There's a second victim. Don't forget that."

Lashiver held out his hand and Ryan tossed him the keys.

"Admit it, you think he's Felicia's boy toy," Ryan said.

Lashiver opened the driver's side door, leaning on its frame. "He's somebody's boy toy."

"You know who's usually responsible for a murdered wife when there was an affair."

"Yeah, I do. They covered that in detective school," Lashiver said. He got into the car and slammed the door.

Chapter 11

"Good afternoon, Miss Mills," Thomas Gallagher's voice came through the cell phone.

Katerina froze at the sound of the smooth voice with a hint of an accent. She could picture him exuding the Big-Apple-I-can-have-any-woman-I-want playboy vibe. "Mr. Gallagher," was all she could muster.

"Please, call me Thomas," he said.

"I don't think I'm allowed to do that," she said.

"I see," he said, his amusement humming through the line. "I can contact the agency and have use of my first name stipulated in the assignment—"

"No!" Kat blurted. "That won't be necessary—Thomas."

Gallagher took the outburst in stride. "Very well, Katerina. I'm sorry to disturb your time with your family. I'm afraid I'm rather anxious about the project. May I ask when you are scheduled to return?"

Katerina struggled to come up with an answer to a question she had never expected. "Mr. Gall—Thomas, it's going to be a few more weeks."

"I see," he said.

She hesitated, weighing her words. "Sir—Thomas, I'm sorry to ask, would you consider waiting for me to return?"

"Why?"

Katerina spoke freely, letting her concern slip out. "If I don't complete an assignment, the agency will take action and—"

"You will lose your place at the agency," he finished.

"Yes," she said.

Her heart pounding, Katerina listened to the silence from the other end of the line. The agency was the enemy, but everything had to continue without disruption, like saucers spinning on sticks. Being on the outside would leave her defenseless against any onslaught; she would be taken by surprise.

"Have no anxiety about this, Katerina. It is my pleasure to perform this little service for you. I wouldn't have anyone else complete this assignment. I think we work well together. We make a good team, don't you think?"

"Yes," Katerina said.

"Now, I want to ask you to perform a little service for me."

A sliver of fear shot through Katerina. "Yes?" she said.

"When you return to the city, contact me first, as soon as you arrive. Will you do that, Katerina?"

Kat let out a sigh of relief at the simple request. "Yes, Thomas, I will," she said.

Katerina hung up the phone, taking a moment to force her nerves to calm down. She had no idea if she would be returning to New York City.

***

After Thomas Gallagher clicked off his cell phone, he reviewed the call several times, considering Katerina's words. She was a clever young lady, clever indeed. It was the clever move to keep her hand in with the agency. However, he had no illusions that Katerina would be returning to New York City. He decided that she must be persuaded to come back as soon as possible. The situation required an escalation, a parallel operation Smith didn't need to know about. He took out his cell phone and made a call.

"Lisa, how is your current assignment progressing?" Gallagher listened. "I think you're going to need some assistance. I have the perfect option for you."

Chapter 12

Katerina, encased in her insulated parka and boots, braced against the frigid cold. Struggling to keep the New York newspaper tucked under her arm, she trudged through the fresh snow up to the farmhouse.

Entering the kitchen through the side door, she found Linda Mills sitting at the trestle table. Across from her, a man turned his head and gave Katerina a wide smile.

Agent James Sheridan.

Katerina's heart thudded in her chest as a silent string of profanity ran wild in her head, cursing the drug dealers who had failed to do the one thing she had hoped for.

"Katerina, this is James Shamus. He was—is your father's investment advisor."

"I didn't know Daddy had an investment advisor," Katerina said, her laser gaze zeroing in on Sheridan. "We didn't see you when he was sick . . . or at any other time."

"He didn't want to worry you both with financial concerns. He was always investing with an eye to the future. You'd be amazed at his tenacity for building for a brighter tomorrow."

When Kat didn't answer, he grinned at her, the smile making her stomach turn.

Katerina searched her mother's face for any sign of confusion, even fear, but a blank look had settled over Linda Mills' features as if a curtain had descended. "I'm afraid my husband never mentioned you."

"No problem," Sheridan said. "We can straighten this out. Is there a number where he can be reached?"

"She doesn't have one," Kat broke in. She looked at her mother, who now appeared stricken.

"I—I'm afraid I don't have one," Linda Mills parroted.

Katerina took in her mother's sudden turn as the tearful, devastated wife, a stark contrast to her pronouncement of William Mills only last year. *I never wanted to disturb your fantasy about your father, but he's an ass. He always was. I just didn't have the heart to tell you.*

What the hell is this?

"Why don't you and I talk outside, Mr. *Shamus*," Kat said.

Sheridan didn't move.

"Unless you want to review my father's portfolio right now. You did bring a copy of the portfolio?"

Sheridan got up and offered his hand to Linda Mills. "It's been a pleasure meeting you. I'm so sorry to hear about your difficult situation. Believe me, I'm going to do everything I can to see you get what's coming to you."

Katerina's teeth clenched, radiating pain through her jaw.

"Thank you," Linda whispered, "you're very kind."

As Sheridan walked out, Kat followed him, wondering how she would contain the rage building within her.

***

"Smooth move, *Shamus*," Kat said. "Get lost."

"Is that a way to speak to your lifeline?" Sheridan asked with a chuckle. "I don't think so, especially since that bum tip on the trucking route is still in your debit column. You fucked up."

No, I didn't. They were supposed to get rid of you. They screwed up.

"I don't know what happened with that," she said. Her hand, shoved in the pocket of the parka, damp with perspiration, crushed the deposit slips and phone bills in her iron grip.

What do I do now?

Sheridan took her by the arm, as if helping her traverse the ice on the way to his car. She winced from the iron grip.

"Cut the crap," Sheridan said. "You think you're clever playing both sides. We can go about this another way. I'm a pretty good judge of character, if I say so myself. I just can't shake the feeling that Mom knows more than she's saying."

Katerina started. "Bullshit!" she said.

Sheridan shook his head. "No, I think little Linda is in this up to her very attractive ass."

Katerina jerked away from him. "She doesn't know jack shit," Kat said, hoping she sounded sincere, hoping the inkling of doubt about her own mother wasn't seeping through.

"Ah, I don't know, she could just be a good actress." They stopped at Sheridan's car and faced each other. His eyes ran the length of her. "Like mother, like daughter," he said. "What have you got for me? Where's the old man?"

Think fast, Katerina. Think of something. Keep the lie as close to the truth as you can.

"He's gone dark again. If it was that easy to find drug lords, everyone would be doing it. *You* would be doing it."

"Not good enough."

"I still have time," Kat said.

Sheridan's eyes moved over her face. He gave her a tiny smile that made her want to run inside and take a shower to wash him away. "The clock runs out at one on Thursday. Show up and have something solid for me, or I pay your mother another visit." He leaned in. "You're not the only one I can make wet," he whispered.

Katerina's eyes narrowed. "Touch my mother and I'll kill you."

Sheridan laughed. "Just like the old man. Bet you're a lousy shot, too." He went to open the car door and she stepped back. "Don't be stupid and skip. Remember what happened last time. It can happen again—but not to you."

Sheridan got into the car and drove off, leaving Katerina shivering in the cold. Gazing out at the expanse of the farm, she felt it shrinking around her, closing in on her. The threat had been the reason for the visit. James Sheridan could get to Linda Mills any time he wanted. Katerina decided that dropping out was now the top priority. But she wouldn't do it alone. Linda Mills needed to disappear as well.

Chapter 13

Thomas Gallagher strode into his office, his assistant closing the door noiselessly behind him. He sat behind his desk in quiet contemplation, fingertips pressed against each other, listening to Mr. Smith's report.

"We pinpointed the second penthouse he used in December after bringing the gi—Miss Mills, back into the city. The "professor" used the same name, Steven Bartholomew."

Gallagher's eyes narrowed. *Steven Bartholomew. Where did the "W" fit in?*

"And what can you tell me about Mr. Bartholomew?"

Joseph Smith smiled. He leaned forward in the guest chair and held out a sheet of paper.

Thomas Gallagher took the page, looked up, and gave Smith a wry smile. "Perhaps you would be kind enough to fill in the gap," he said, lifting the blank page.

"I would, if there was anything."

Gallagher's smile melted away.

"Steven Bartholomew has no assets, no bank accounts, and no credit history. For all intents and purposes, Steven Bartholomew does not exist." Smith let that sink in before continuing. "I'm sure your "professor" has other aliases. They will lead to the same place, a dead end. If I'm right, and I usually am, this man is special."

Thomas Gallagher's icy blue eyes zeroed in on Smith. "A special man," he repeated, "how so?"

"The identification is synthetic. He creates an identity using a mix of real and false information. In my opinion, Mr. Bartholomew has been doing this a long time."

"How can you be certain?" Gallagher asked.

"*I've* been doing this a long time," Joseph Smith said. "To find him, an examination of her personal belongings will yield a clue. It never fails. I guarantee it."

Gallagher contemplated his consultant's advice. His consideration was contaminated by the phone call with Katerina. It roiled him. His urge, no, his *need* to hear her voice. *She should be calling me, coming to me.*

Smith observed his client's silent struggle.

Gallagher shook his head. "No. Keep digging," he said.

"I understand," Smith said. He tried another tack, the trusted advisor imparting the necessary pearl of wisdom, while searching for the magic bullet that would push his employer over the line. "Mr. Gallagher, if you wish to be with Miss Mills, you must remove this professor; and you will never remove the professor without Miss Mills."

Gallagher nodded. "Thank you, Mr. Smith. I appreciate your frank advice. I will take it into consideration."

***

Alone, Gallagher wrestled with Smith's advice, an innate instinct telling him it was wrong. But the urge, the impatience, the *need*, returned with a vengeance, going to war within him. The professor, Bob, "W," the clichéd thorn in his side, had to be removed. He tapped out a text on his phone.

Go ahead

Gallagher rose from his chair as his assistant entered. He tucked the cell phone into a pocket and thanked her as she handed him a file for his meeting. As he left his office, he tried to compartmentalize the situation into the back of his mind in order to make room for other business but found his anxiety increasing rather than decreasing. There would be no return to normal until Katerina Mills was safely within his grasp.

***

Joseph Smith greeted the text with a satisfied smile that soon faded as he considered the challenge to come. This "professor" would not be easy to locate—or erase. Smith had already learned something about him. The professor would not hesitate to take whatever steps necessary to protect Katerina Mills.

Smith's operative had learned that painful lesson firsthand; he wouldn't be putting on his Doc Martens for a long while. He had barely escaped with his life.

Chapter 14

The trestle table vanished under the serving trays and place settings. The women's chattering played like a white noise in Kat's head as she took her seat across from her mother. Catherine and May had brought a book on spirit animals to the table and the gathering ceremony was on everyone's lips.

"I saw a lion in the fire and then it came to me in a dream," May said as she passed the book to Katerina.

Lions, tigers and bears, oh my, Kat thought as she took the oversized volume and flipped the pages.

"At least it didn't show up on the doorstep," Ethel mumbled.

Katerina handed the book back, pursing her lips to suppress a smile. "What does the lion symbolize?" she asked.

"Strength and courage," Rachel said as she placed a platter of crisp vegetables, seasoned with garlic and oil, on the table.

"I've felt a change," May said. "What did you see, Kat?"

"Nothing," Kat said.

"It will come," Rachel said, "in its own time."

"Maybe you already saw it," Catherine offered, "before you came home."

"Then it's probably a mouse or a rat," Kat said. "In that case, the entire island of Manhattan has found their spirit animal." She chanced a glance at her mother to find Linda Mills considering her.

"You don't have to physically see it, do you?" her mother asked.

"No, not at all," Rachel said. "Sometimes it's a sense, or a dream."

"It could be anything," May said. "A horse, a tiger—"

"A fox," Linda Mills said.

Kat locked eyes with her mother.

Rachel came up behind Katerina, laying a hand on her shoulder. "The fox is known to be cunning and sly, but its quick thinking provides luck and opportunity for escape in the nick of time."

May turned to a page in the book and read aloud. "The fox is nocturnal and a hunter and has a heightened sense of hearing and smell."

As she took her seat at the head of the table, Rachel gave Kat a smile. "Remember, the spirit animal is not a reflection of who you are, it is medicine for what you need. You may see it several times," she said with a nod toward May, "or only once and never again. It will still be within reach, but you must stay in contact, always seeking to establish connection so it will come to you in your hour of need."

The ladies resumed their conversation, but Katerina remained silent as the serving plates passed around family style. Without looking, she could feel her mother's censure, and a wave of relief washed over her as her cell phone vibrated in her pocket. Katerina slipped the phone out and checked the number. What about a snake, she thought. Is that a spirit animal?

"I have to take this," Kat said, rising from her seat. She grabbed her coat from the rack and slipped outside, knowing her mother's gaze followed her.

***

"Rapunzel, Rapunzel," Lisa's voice came over the line, "let down your hair. I've got an opportunity. Where are you?"

"Iowa," Katerina said, huddling deeper into her coat, watching the puffy clouds of her breath disintegrate into the cold air.

Lisa gave a harsh laugh. "I'll bet. I've got a retrieval."

"I'm still on vacation," Katerina answered and then said, "animal, vegetable, or mineral?"

"Human. It's a two-person job."

"Since when?" Kat shot back. "Take your own advice from our last field trip. Try a little kitty flipping to keep him quiet."

"Her," Lisa answered.

Kat went silent. The thought of a woman mixed up in something that needed Lisa's exceptional skills and abilities didn't sit well with her. And why did her sire, the woman who had brought her into MJM Consulting, need her? "The clients are always men," Kat said. "Is this outside the agency again?"

"No, it's in," Lisa said, the usual bite missing from her voice. "The client is a man. The retrieval is a woman."

Kat searched in vain for a quip or a comeback.

"Not getting squeamish on me, are you, princess?"

Go to hell. "Why isn't Jasmine calling?"

Katerina listened to the labored sigh from the other end of the line. "Because it's my assignment and I'm not on probation and neither are you. Who I cut in is my choice."

"How much?"

"Your take is fifty."

"How much is the job?"

"And let me repeat myself because you know how much I love to do that. Your cut is fifty," Lisa said.

Kat listened to Lisa rattle off a hotel name and address located close by. Convenient, she thought, her antennae up and alert. Fifty thousand dollars. A plan formed in Kat's mind, like clay on a potter's wheel. Take this job, get the fifty thousand, go back to New York, and collect the stash in the safety deposit box. *Move my mother out. We disappear.* A slash of anxious caution flashed in Kat's mind, the fear she was moving too fast without thinking it through. "Do you need an answer now?"

"I'll be checked in at the hotel the latter half of the week. If I don't hear from you by Thursday night at eight, I'll take that as a no. See ya around, Cinderella."

The cell phone clicked off.

Katerina slipped the phone into her pocket and turned to go back inside. After dinner, it was time for that talk with her mother.

Chapter 15

Katerina found Linda Mills out by the goat shed. Of all the places, Kat thought. Linda Mills stood inside the small enclosure staring at the animals, as if she were waiting. *For what?*

Katerina hovered just at the edge of the entrance, the frigid wind biting at her back. "Mom, why are you out here? It's freezing."

"I needed a little fresh air," she said. "It's good for you."

You hate the cold. You always hated it. Another lie. *Forget it. Move on.*

"Mom, why haven't you moved off the farm?" Katerina asked, taking a tentative step inside. "With the money I sent, you have enough to move away."

"It's your money, Katerina. You may want it back some day."

"I *gave* it to you," Kat said.

Katerina watched her mother observing the animals with a curious mix of fascination and disdain. *That's right. You hate goats. You hate farm animals. What are you doing out here?*

"Mom, you could have gone to stay with Kevin."

Linda Mills let out a bitter laugh. The animals cast surreptitious side eye glances at the two interlopers.

"Mom, I'm sure he would be fine with it."

"I haven't spoken to Kevin since before your father left."

"You can call him now. I think a change of scenery—"

"Katerina, under no circumstances am I going to visit your brother in Costa Rica."

"Fine, Mom, don't go to see Kevin," Kat snapped as she stepped back. What to say? How much to reveal? "But I think you need to start over. I could come with you . . . we'll go together."

Linda Mills turned to her daughter. "New York didn't turn out so well?"

Kat shook her head, struggling to choose her words. "I wasn't ready."

"Even when you are," she said. "Sometimes you never see it coming." She lapsed into silence for a few moments and then, "Katerina, what did your father tell you when he visited you in New York?"

Linda Mills had asked that question before. Katerina remembered her original answer.

Nothing.

Kat took a breath. "He said the cancer made him realize that he had a second chance and he needed more. He said he knew I was going to do something big."

Linda Mills nodded. "Are you doing something big?"

Convicted by Sergei's directive, Kat searched to strike a balance between the need to bridge the chasm and the danger of revealing the truth. Katerina gave her mother a weak smile. "No. Mom, I'm—not. I didn't realize—all that time growing up—I should have done things differently, with—everything." She faltered as her mother looked at her, her face a cipher. "I should have realized what you were going through. You were unhappy. I should have seen things the way they were—with you—and Daddy."

"It's over," her mother said, turning her attention back to the goats. "You can't change the past."

Katerina's heart lurched. "But we can make a new future," she said. "Have our own adventure."

Linda Mills shook her head. "I'm staying here," she said.

Katerina walked away from the goat shed, tears stinging her eyes. She knew the reason for Linda Mills' refusal to leave this place with her only daughter.

My mother doesn't trust me, she thought.

Chapter 16

Detectives Kellan and Lashiver entered the familiar sitting room to find John Reynolds waiting. The widower said nothing, nor indicated that the detectives should be seated.

"Mr. Reynolds," Lashiver began, "we have a few more questions."

"More questions," Reynolds said, shaking his head. "But no solutions. Perhaps you would like me to solve my wife's murder for you. When I see the Police Commissioner at dinner tomorrow night, I'll suggest that to him."

"We apologize for disturbing you, but we feel it could help the case. We're trying to pin down additional details of your wife's schedule during her last weeks."

Reynolds shook his head again, and with an exaggerated sigh, sat down.

Ryan kept his eyes on his notepad, flipping the pages. "We know Mrs. Reynolds shopped at several high-end department stores, sometimes every day."

"Brilliant deductive reasoning, Detective . . . or perhaps you gleaned that information from the receipts and the credit card bills."

Ryan glanced up, cocking his head in sheepish penitence. "Yes, we know that she purchased a bottle of cologne, men's cologne, Clive Christian. Would you have that cologne available, sir?"

Ryan took in Reynolds' practiced blank stare. The detective watched for random eye movements, body tics; even the slightest twitch could tell the tale.

The silence mushroomed, filling the room until John Reynolds said, "I don't wear that particular cologne."

"I see," Ryan said.

"Perhaps there was a nephew or a cousin, an uncle, a male relative who had a birthday?" Lashiver added.

Reynolds shook his head, an expression of confusion now on his face.

"Mr. Reynolds, we know that your wife was a patron of the Theatre for a New Audience. This is the same company where an actor, Will Temple, had been appearing, until he disappeared without warning," Ryan said.

Reynolds didn't answer.

"Our canvassing near his apartment confirmed that someone matching your wife's description was seen in the area."

Lashiver's jaw set as he stared down at his shoes.

"A bottle of the cologne was found in his apartment. Your wife's fingerprints were on the bottle."

John Reynolds stood up, his face flushing. "What are you saying, Detective?"

Nice performance, asshole, Ryan thought.

"Sir, we're just trying to ascertain if your wife had been taken in," Lashiver said. "Will Temple may have been looking to take advantage of your wife, for gifts, financial support—"

"Sir, were you aware that your wife was having an affair with Will Temple?" Ryan asked.

Lashiver shot his partner a look. Ryan ignored him, continuing to stare at Reynolds.

Reynolds' face folded as if he had been struck. He groped for a chair and sank down. Ryan took the seat opposite the older man.

"You must be mistaken," Reynolds said, his voice soft. "She was incapable of such a thing."

"We're investigating every theory—" Lashiver started.

"We're sure," Ryan cut in.

Shaking his head, Reynolds turned away from both men to stare out of the window. "My God," he uttered. "My God." He turned back to the detectives. "Are you saying this man—killed my wife?"

"We're pursuing every lead," Lashiver said.

"We need to have a look at Mrs. Reynolds' wardrobe," Ryan said, "to check for hairs and fibers."

Then Ryan saw it; the slight cock of the head. John Reynolds had come up against something he hadn't counted on or expected.

"Unfortunately, my wife's clothing has been donated," Reynolds said.

"I thought you said her belongings were in storage," Ryan countered, flipping through his notebook.

"Yes, yes I did," Reynolds said. "And they were. But I decided they could be put to better use by someone who needed them. So I had them delivered to Goodwill."

"Did you donate all the clothes?" Ryan pressed.

"Yes . . . well," Reynolds said slowly, "I gave instructions—"

"We can take care of checking for you," Ryan said.

"I don't think so, Detective, no," Reynolds said.

A beat of silence followed.

"I'm sure Mr. Reynolds can confirm this," Lashiver said.

"Yes," Reynolds recovered. "I'll speak to my housekeeper right away."

"Thank you, sir. We're sorry to have disturbed you," Lashiver said.

The detectives turned to leave.

"This doesn't change anything, you know," Reynolds called after them.

The detectives stopped and turned back.

"She loved me. And I loved her. Nothing changes that. Nothing."

Lashiver nodded and he and Ryan walked out.

***

"What the fuck was that?" Lashiver demanded as soon as they were back in the car.

"He's lying," Ryan said.

"That doesn't answer my question," Lashiver said, his anger inching up with every word. "Since when are we lying to a victim's spouse?"

"I didn't lie to a victim's spouse. I lied to a suspect."

"His alibi is airtight, remember? He was in his office."

"Did you see his reaction?"

"His secretary was sitting right outside his office door."

Ryan gave a short laugh. "He didn't know about the affair, what bullshit."

"He was on a video conference call, live, in real time. He makes a few calls and we're back walking a foot post, you hear me? He's not a suspect. Yet."

Ryan's eyes narrowed at his partner's statement. He could understand Lashiver's reluctance. One wrong move and the case could torpedo both their careers.

"You tipped your hand by trying to muscle us in to get a look at her stuff. That was a stupid-ass careless move. Next time, you better think before you talk. Spend less time on your little stakeouts at night and more time concentrating on the case."

Ryan made a face and glanced away.

"You don't go off script and not talk to me first, understand?" Lashiver said.

"Walt, he's wrong. I'm telling you, he's wrong."

"I know what you're telling me and if the evidence says he's the guy, we'll get him. But, let me tell you kid, you go fuckin' rogue again, we're going to have a problem, a big one, understand?"

"Yeah, I get it. I'm sorry," Ryan said.

Lashiver turned over the engine and eased the car out into traffic.

Chapter 17

Katerina spent the early morning working with Ethel on the tiny house, hoping her subconscious mind would come up with an idea of what to do. The only word that came to mind was Winter. The urge to call him gnawed at her, testing and tempting her. *He'll know what to do.* She overcame the pressure in her head, pushing the impulse down until she couldn't hear it anymore.

She left the work and retreated to the house to calm her complaining muscles with a hot shower. She stepped out, toweled off, and wrapped herself in her robe. She went to her coat and emptied her pockets. Spreading the deposit slips and phone bills on the bedspread, she placed them next to her father's boating magazine subscription receipts, the ones she had asked her mother to save.

She fingered the deposit slips, noting the dates from a few months ago, the bank names, and the small amounts.

Katerina thought of Philip Castle, a lawyer with a lowercase "l," her former lover and first boss after she had moved to New York City. *My first mistake.* Philip had one other area of expertise besides the law: crime. He'd had clients accused of money laundering.

What's another way to launder dirty money, Katerina?

Make small deposits, using different banks, in order to wash the money.

And what did Philip call the people who made these deposits?

Smurfs.

Katerina put the slips of paper down. Lulu had been smurfing for dear old Dad. *Big surprise. So what? How does that help?* She picked up the phone bill, searching for her father's cell phone number, shaking her head in frustration. Another dead end. *And the clock keeps ticking. What the hell am I going to do?*

Katerina tossed the phone bill aside but after a moment, she grabbed it again. Scanning one more time, she stopped at one phone number. She knew it. It had just been given to her.

Richie Calico's cell phone.
Kat checked the date.
Richie had spoken to Lulu in the last three weeks.
Lulu had been *Richie's* smurf.
Richie got stiffed?
Bullshit.
Richie had skimmed for himself.
Or maybe Richie was still in touch with dear old Dad.
Katerina got up and pulled together clothing to get dressed.
Either way, it didn't matter.
Richie lied to me.

Chapter 18

Another weather-beaten clapboard house, this one a pale gray. The Durango sat in the driveway.

I've seen this movie.

If I approach from the front, I can be seen, and Richie gets a heads-up.

She eyed the side of the house, steps leading up to a door.

Probably the kitchen.

The path had been shoveled clear.

So what's it going to be Katerina? What do you want to do?

What would Winter do?

Winter would be smart enough not to get himself into this steaming shit pile I'm standing in.

She had thought about how best to confront Richie. She knew him well. He would deny everything and lie about the rest. The best approach would be to play on his fears and present herself as his only solution. Tell him she could help him but only if he helped her.

Katerina rooted around in the glove compartment, took what she needed, and slammed it shut. She pulled on gloves and got out of the car; the wind bit at her cheeks, tugging at her hair. She pulled her cap down low.

When she reached the door, she grasped the doorknob and gave a twist. Locked.

Kat gave the door a once-over: old, worn, paint peeling around the edges.

Not Fort Knox.

Glancing around, she pulled a screwdriver out of her pocket, wedging it between the door and the jamb. Richie calling the police for a breaking and entering was not something to be concerned with. She leaned her weight on the screwdriver until she felt the door give way. Slipping inside, she noted the patches of splintered wood. With a grimace, she closed the door. *If I ever do see Winter again, I need to ask him how to properly pick a lock.*

She listened for the sound of footsteps, a sign of Richie coming downstairs. Nothing.

Standing in the center of the small, mean living room, Kat took in the worn couch, nicked coffee table, beat up leather recliner, and flat screen television. She watched the TV flicker and play.

He's in here somewhere.

Her eyes moved over a closed door, probably the basement, and stopped at the stairs. She listened for movement but heard only silence.

Well, Katerina? Which way? Up or down?

Go up.

***

In the bedroom, she found the bed with rumpled sheets and blankets, clothing strewn over a chair, and an overnight bag sitting open in the middle of the floor.

Crouching down, Kat ran gloved hands over the bag and rifled its contents: underwear, socks, and a change of clothes. Pushing the clothes aside, she found five packs of bills lining the bottom. Fifty thousand dollars.

Katerina rocked back on her heels, considering the money.

He's getting ready to run. Shit.

He wouldn't leave without his stash. Where the hell is he?

And what about the laptop?

Getting to her feet, Kat stood with her hands on her hips. Her eyes wandered over to the bed.

She went to one side of the bed, pulling back blankets, pressing her hands down on top of the mattress, then lifting it up, checking underneath. Nothing. She picked up one pillow, crushing it, and threw it back down. She grabbed the other pillow, struck by the weight in her hands.

Must be industrial strength goose down. At least three extra pounds worth.

She lay the pillow down, placed her hands on top and pressed, feeling something square and solid inside. Unzipping the pillow, she inserted her hands and extracted a laptop.

Right. You spend your time shoving packets of drugs inside stuffed animals, you stick with what you know.

Katerina unzipped her coat, shoving the packets of money into the inside pockets. Grabbing the laptop, she stuffed it between her turtleneck and her sweatshirt, and zipped up her coat.

I won't have to worry about finding Richie.

He'll come to me.

Kat exited the bedroom, taking the stairs with tentative, light steps. She headed for the door.

A sudden pungent smell assaulted her nostrils.

She stopped.

Bleach.

Katerina turned to find a man standing in front of the wide-open basement doorway.

She forgot to breathe.

A cold sweat broke out of her pores.

He stood about five-foot-ten, thin, wiry, with an angular face, his black hair pulled back in a ponytail. His t-shirt clung to him in damp patches and his arms glistened with perspiration. He stared at her with a cold, calm gaze while wiping his pale hands with a towel.

"Looking for something?"

Katerina struggled to speak. "Richie," she said.

"Richie's not here anymore."

Katerina's body tensed even as she began to tremble.

"Don't you want to know who I am?" he asked.

Kat stared at him, at the rhythmic rubbing of his hands.

I already know.

"I'm the housekeeper. I'm here to straighten up, keep everything in order."

Katerina's throat had gone dry. She tried to find enough saliva to swallow but tasted only the acrid smell of the bleach. "You're the cleaner," she whispered.

He smiled and kept wiping his hands. "That's right. The cleaner. That's right, Katerina."

Katerina's heart pounded in her chest. She shook her head. "I'm not . . ."

His eyes widened in mock surprise. "You're not her? My mistake. But you know her, right? You're a friend of hers?"

She nodded.

"When you see her, give her a message. Tell her she needs to finish what she started."

"I thought . . . she gave—you—what you needed. That's what she told me."

He chuckled and stepped closer. Katerina flinched, staring past him at the open basement door.

"She promised to "deliver" an agent, that's what she said. She can "deliver" a DEA agent. Did she think we were going to go out and do something that would bring a lot of attention? That's not how this works. And how could we be sure? She only gave a hint. Hints are no good. We need a name."

Katerina's back ached from the weight of the laptop. She didn't dare move, convinced it would shift and hit the floor right there between them. "She has to be careful," Kat said, her voice cracking from strain. "She has to do it her own way."

The man nodded as he examined his hands. "Your friend is waiting for you," he said, jerking his head toward the street. "He must be a real good friend, following you around all the time. Tell Katerina that she should be a good friend. She has to come to us and give us that name."

You'll kill me as soon as I tell you.

"Tell her it needs to be soon . . . real soon. We're not gonna wait forever." He glanced up at her. "Goodbye, friend of Katerina."

Katerina forced her gaze from him and began to inch over to the kitchen door. As she exited the house, she spotted Carter getting out of the Altima. When he saw her, he slid back behind the wheel.

Katerina slipped into the Honda, gunned the engine, and took off, the bile rising in her throat, tears filling her eyes.

Richie is in the basement.

What's left of Richie is in the basement.

There's nothing left of Richie.

Richie's dead.

And I just stole fifty thousand dollars from the drug dealers who killed him.

Chapter 19

Joseph Smith made a methodical sweep of Katerina's compact New York City apartment. He followed his set routine of searching through desk drawers and cabinets, poking and prodding like a physician until the space gave up all its secrets.

Using his phone, he snapped pictures of items of interest: a credit card bill, a spring semester class schedule, a business card for Gal Friday Inc., and newspaper articles reporting the murder of socialite Felicia Reynolds.

Moving to the bedroom, Smith discovered designer clothing hanging in the closet. A twentysomething college girl able to purchase an expensive wardrobe? No. These items had been bought for her.

He examined the contents of each dresser drawer. When he slid the top drawer in, it resisted. He tried again, then peered underneath, spying something taped to the bottom. He pulled the drawer out and peeled away the tape with care. Straightening, he ran a gloved finger over a pair of yellow gold, shell-shaped quartz and diamond encrusted earrings in the palm of his hand. He snapped a picture with his phone, then taped the earrings securely back in their spot. Slipping the drawer closed, he stepped back, surveying the bedroom. Identifying a discreet spot, Smith placed a tiny camera, as he had in the tiny living room and the kitchen. Gallagher had not requested it, but he found most clients didn't think through what they wanted. Smith had no doubt his thoroughness would be rewarded.

Joseph Smith made one last visual sweep and headed for the front door. The vibration of his cell phone caused him to halt. Pulling out the phone, he swiped to connect the call.

"Hold for a moment," the voice said.

"Why?" Smith asked.

"Unmarked police car."

Smith stood in the center of the living room, prepared for a long wait. During surveillance, the unmarked police car had been spotted several times. It had been a calculated risk that tonight would not be one of those nights. He had been wrong.

***

Detective Ryan Kellan alternated between running the engine to generate heat and turning it off, counting down how long it would take for the warmth to evaporate.

He took a sip of his coffee, wincing at the now cold, bitter liquid. Five more minutes, that's what he always told himself. Five more minutes and then he would head home.

Ryan pulled out his cell and punched in a number, his impatience rising with every ring,

"Gal Friday, how may I help you?"

"Yes, I'm still trying to reach Katerina Mills," he said.

"I'm sorry, Detective. Katerina is still on school break. She's not expected back for another few weeks."

"Do you have the exact date of her return?"

"No, Detective, I'm sorry, I don't. I'm sure she'll be back for the first day of class."

Ryan sat silent, for once, at a loss for a follow-up question.

"Do you want to leave a message?"

"No, thank you. I'll call back."

"Have a good night, Detective," the silky voice said; the line disconnected.

Ryan clicked off, staring at the phone in his hand. He started at the rapping on his window. Detective Frank Mitchell held up a Styrofoam cup. Ryan popped the lock. Frank walked around and climbed into the passenger seat. He held out the cup and Ryan took it with a nod of appreciation.

The two friends sat in silence while Ryan took a deep swallow of the hot coffee.

"How's the case?" Frank asked.

"Stalled," Ryan said. "Still trying to find a link between the two victims. I don't think there is one."

Frank nodded. "And the husband?"

Ryan kept his focus on the apartment building. "Can't budge the alibi." He shook his head. "With the boy toy off the grid, we've got a piece missing."

"You won't find it sitting here," Frank said, giving his friend a pointed look.

Ryan stared down into his coffee, considering it. "I screwed it up," he said.

"Some combinations just don't fit together," Frank said. "Maybe you tried to force something that wasn't meant to be."

"I wasn't forcing—"

"Okay, fine. If it was supposed to work out, it would have. Some women—they take a lot of energy. They drain you."

"She wasn't like that."

"What was she like?"

Ryan turned to the man who had saved his life. "Everything would've been fine but she . . . I don't know, I always felt like I couldn't reach her."

"Exactly. Look where you're sitting. *Outside* her apartment. She *is* out of reach."

Ryan moved to object, but Frank cut him off. "This is what I'm talkin' about. Let it go. You've got the case to think about. Keep your eye on what you need to be doing right now. Don't fuck this up because you're not paying attention."

Ryan sat back. "Lashiver called you."

"He's worried about you. You're pushing the husband too hard and too fast. Be careful, man. That's all I'm saying. Be careful."

"You trying to save me again?"

"My fucking life's work. Go home," Frank said. "Get some sleep."

Opening the car door, Frank got out. Using the rearview mirror, Ryan watched his friend get into his own car. He waited for the headlights to cut through the darkness, for Frank to pull away, but the car sat, idling. Ryan let out a short laugh of disgust, stowed the cup in the holder, started the car, and drove off. Frank's car pulled out and followed.

Ten minutes later, Smith exited the apartment building, his face obscured by the upturned collar on his coat and a hat pulled down low over his forehead.

Chapter 20

Katerina hustled across the brick and cobblestone Church Street Marketplace. Seeing the pizza joint, she pushed down the anxiety over what she was about to do. In her mind, this meeting was already over and she was back at the farm, sitting her mother down for an eye-opening chat followed by hasty packing before getting the hell out of town.

Ducking inside she found a cramped space with a short counter. Beyond that, a dining nook crammed with tables. Business was slow; a bunch of boisterous college kids consuming pizza and cokes. Her eyes went to a booth where Sheridan sat, working his way through a hero.

Kat slid into the booth opposite him. She watched Sheridan hunch over his plate, chewing with his mouth open. *Choke on it, you SOB.*

"So?" Sheridan asked.

Katerina reluctantly gave up her fantasy to concentrate on the enemy at hand. "Richie has the money," she said.

Sheridan stopped in mid-chew. His lips curled in a hint of a smile as he resumed eating.

"That little dumbshit has nothing," he said, swiping at the sauce running down his chin.

Pig. Katerina leaned back. "If you say so."

Sheridan eyed her. "What makes you so sure?"

"He has my father's laptop. He and the laptop are gone. That means he's still working for my father. You're welcome."

She watched Sheridan take in this nugget of information. The next words out of his mouth would tell her if he'd been shadowing her, seen her with Richie, seen her at Richie's house.

"I want both," he said.

She stared past him, past the table with the college kids, to an alcove in the back; a small sign indicated the restrooms. She noticed a slash of daylight peeking through the slit of an open back door.

"Both?"

"The laptop and your old man. Find the dumbshit. Understand?"

"No, I don't understand. You have the resources. You find Richie."

Sheridan put down the hero and took up a napkin, wiping his mouth. "Nice try," he said. "Richie Calico isn't wanted in connection with a crime."

"Unless he's a suspect in the shooting of a DEA agent."

Sheridan pushed his plate away. "I'll think about it. But you and your mother don't get off the hook until I get the money *and* your old man."

Katerina nodded. *Knock yourself out, asshole. My mother and I will be long gone before you realize we're in the wind.*

The waitress came to the table, check in hand. "Anytime you're ready," she said, setting down the slip of paper between them. "No rush."

Sheridan eyed the check, then gave Kat a smile. "Thanks for lunch," he said. He got up and grabbed his coat. Extracting a card from his pocket, he threw it down on the table. "You can reach me at that number." He glanced past her toward the counter. "And next time, don't bring any company."

Katerina gave a half-turn as if watching Sheridan leave, expecting to see Carter loitering at the counter.

Shit. It's not him.

***

Antennae up, Katerina fingered the check, her mind racing. The man, medium height with brown hair, held a cell phone to his ear.

The college kids began to pull on coats and file past her, clogging the area between her table and the front counter. A fleeting thought of slipping out among them dissolved in panic; he could tail her in the open marketplace. *I'll be a sitting duck in plain sight.* She stared ahead at the crack of light breaking through the darkened alcove. *Back door.* Adrenalin shooting through her, she shoved the business card in her jacket pocket and tossed a few bills on the table. She rushed out the back door, smack into a solid block of a man. Hand clamping over her mouth, he pushed her back inside and into the bathroom.

***

Katerina flailed as he shoved her up against the bathroom door. Making a fist, she aimed for his nose. A noise escaped him as blood spurted from both nostrils. Grabbing the sink with one hand and bracing against the wall with the other, she kicked out with both feet. He fell back; Kat turned, seizing the door handle and yanking it open. She had one foot in the alcove when he pulled her back inside. Spinning her around, his hands closed around her throat, squeezing.

Katerina's eyes flew open.

Can't breathe.

She struck out, clawing at his eyes; he grunted as she hit her mark; his grip slackened. Coughing, she reached for the door as if in slow motion. Grabbing her by her coat, he yanked it down, pinning her arms at her sides. He twisted her around like a rag doll, shoving her body against the sink; one hand gripping the back of her neck.

Kat heard the sound of gushing water. Both of his hands slid around her neck as he pushed his body against hers, forcing her over the sink; the water splashed against her face, sloshing over the side, and spilling onto the floor.

Katerina, straightjacketed in her coat, struggled to plant her feet, but they skidded on the wet floor, sliding out from underneath her. His hands, like lead weight, pressed against the back of her neck.

Her face plunged under the water.

Katerina clamped her eyes closed and pressed her lips together, her lungs screaming for air. The sound of the water muted, and a blackness began to descend, seeping into her consciousness.

All at once, the pressure vanished; Katerina came up out of the water with a strangled gasp. Coughing and sputtering, she slid to the floor.

Unable to move, she listened to the sound of her own labored breathing. She turned her head; through the sodden mass of her hair, she saw the man lying motionless on the floor, Carter looming over him.

Then Carter had her by the coat, pulling it up to free her arms as he hoisted her to her feet. He swiped her hair away from her face. "Can you walk?" he asked.

Katerina gaped up at him.

"Can you walk?" Carter asked again.

Dazed, Katerina looked into his eyes. Dumb, she nodded.

He pulled the hood up around her face. "Go now. Out the back door."

"There was another . . . at the counter" Kat whispered.

"Don't worry about the lookout," Carter said. "Go. Now."

Nodding, she obeyed.

***

Coughing as the frigid air rushed into her lungs, Kat staggered back to the car, managed to get the key in the ignition, and drove away from the downtown on auto pilot.

Shivering even as heat filled the car, she gripped the wheel, her knuckles white. She became aware of a relentless buzzing. It stopped for a few beats and then began again. From somewhere in her mind she thought *cell phone*. Katerina edged the car over to the side of the road; it jerked to a stop.

Fumbling in her purse with trembling hands, Kat struggled to grip the burner phone and click on the call.

"Katie."

Alexander Winter's voice came across deep and controlled.

"He . . . tried to—" she stammered, her voice hoarse.

"Where are you hurt besides your throat?" he asked.

"He . . . he . . . was going to—"

"Katie," Winter persisted. "Where did he hurt you?"

She could hear the panic coming through the line.

"Doc isn't here," she said, feeling warm tears trickle down her cheeks.

"I will get you to someone. Tell me."

Katerina shook her head as if he could see her. She began to cough again, suddenly aware of her running nose and blurry eyes. "No—don't send anyone. How is Carter going to—?"

"Don't worry about that," Winter said, his voice tight.

Like Richie, she thought. Another body will disappear. Another person gone. As if he never existed.

"I'll be there in a few hours," Winter said.

Through the fog of her thoughts, Katerina found a seed of clarity. "I'm leaving here," she blurted.

"Katie, stay where you are," he ordered. "I'm coming."

Katerina could hear the anxiety in his voice. The urgent need to be in his arms went to war with the need to protect him, to keep him away from all this.

"No—don't—"

"Dammit, Katerina," Winter said, his voice rising, "this is not the time to be stubborn!"

The silence hung between them, broken only by Katerina's soft weeping. She heard him let out a ragged breath.

"Katie, shhh," he soothed, his voice cracking. "I'll send you an e-ticket," he said. "Come to me."

"I have it covered." She heard the sharp intake of his breath. "I'm getting out under another name. Please, stay on the phone with me for a little while? Please, just talk to me and I'll be okay."

She waited through the beat of silence.

"Carter will be right behind you when you go."

Katerina glanced out at her surroundings, realizing she had stopped by Shelburne Farms. She had a sudden vision of herself as a child on a school field trip with her mother, remembering the fleeting expression of sadness and misery on her mother's face; an unguarded moment when her mother thought no one had been watching. *Now I have to leave her behind.*

Katerina jolted up in her seat. "No. He has to stay—Bob—please," she pleaded. "He has to stay here and watch over my mother."

"Nothing will happen to your mother," Winter said. "He won't leave her, I promise. Keep your phone on at all times so I can track you. I will meet you wherever you are."

"I'm too hot," she said.

I can run but not you. I will never see you running for your life because of me.

"You're warning me off?" Winter asked.

"Yes," she said.

"How will you do that?"

"I just told you, I'm too hot," she repeated.

"What if you're in a situation where you can't tell me that," he pressed.

"Then—then, I'll give you a sign, a code."

"What will you say?"

"I'll talk about things we would never talk about, so you'll know something is wrong."

"Like what?"

"Like . . . I'll ask you, 'How was your day, dear?'" she said, her throat aching with each swallow, tears trickling down her cheeks.

He gave a tight chuckle. "I'll say 'Swell.' Then what should I say?"

"You should ask 'What's for dinner, chicken or fish?'"

"And if you say chicken?"

"That means it's all clear," Kat said, wiping her eyes.

"And if you say fish?"

"I hope I never say that. You never eat the fish."

"Why's that?" he asked.

"It's from a movie, *Airplane,* a spoof of all those cheesy airport movies from the seventies. The joke was anyone who ate the fish dinner died. I watched that movie all the time with my Dad, when he was sick." *Tons of movies. Over and over again. Because he never wanted my mom. He only wanted me or the nurse. Why had I remembered it differently?*

"What do I do if you say fish is for dinner?" Winter asked.

"Get out. Don't even think of coming near me . . . run."

"Katie, I won't ever be far from you."

"Yes, Bob," she said, blinking back fresh tears. "I know."

She sat for a long time on the side of the road. Alexander Winter stayed on the line, his presence as close as if he sat next to her.

"This is the second time you saved my life," she said.

"Yes, Katie. I know."

Chapter 21

Katerina pulled up to the farmhouse to find it shrouded in darkness except for a pale moon struggling to break through the shreds of cloud cover. *You want to dance with the devil in the pale moonlight...* She cut the engine and waited, her heart pounding in her chest. At last, the buzz of the cell phone. She exhaled as she read the text.

All clear. C.

***

In the semi-darkness of her room, Katerina packed, slowed by the aching muscles and throbbing pain in her throat. Exhaustion blanketed her with an overwhelming desire to lie down and sleep. She stuffed Lulu's phone bills, the deposit slips, the subscription receipts for her father's boating magazine, and the money packs among her clothes in the overnight bag. Knowing that Carter stood watch gave some comfort but the longer she lingered, the greater the risk for her mother.

A sudden shard of light sent Katerina spinning around. Linda Mills stood in the bedroom doorway, her hair curling around her shoulders, her nightgown smooth and fresh, as if she had not yet been to bed.

"No lights," Kat said, her voice a hoarse rasp.

Her mother closed the door and rushed to her daughter, her hand reaching for Katerina's swollen cheek, her eyes on the blooming bruises covering her neck. "My God... who did this?" she whispered.

Katerina shook her head. Her mother grasped her hand and pulled Kat down onto the edge of the bed.

"You need a doctor."

"No—no doctor," Katerina said. "I'll be okay."

Linda Mills eyed the open bag, the packs of money.

"Now what are you into for your father?" Linda Mills asked.

"Mom—no," she said. "I've never—*worked* for Daddy."

"Then, why did he come to you in New York?"

"To tell me he was running off with his . . ." Kat shrugged. "I don't know why he bothered," Kat said. "Did you know about the factory . . . the drugs?"

Linda Mills ran her fingers through her daughter's hair, sweeping it away from her face. She nodded and got up and went to the bathroom.

Katerina shuddered at the sound of the water running in the bathroom sink. It stopped and her mother reappeared. Kat gave an involuntary shiver as her mother placed the hot, wet cloth against her neck.

"Richie Calico's dead," Kat blurted out. "I didn't kill him. The money belongs to the people who did."

"How did you get the money you've been sending me?"

"You don't want to know." Katerina said, catching the shades of dismay clouding her mother's face. "I'm not a prostitute."

"I didn't think so. I thought you were an escort."

Kat decided not to split hairs over sex trade nomenclature. "Mom, James Shamus isn't an investment counselor."

Linda Mills gave a soft laugh. "Of course, he isn't, dear."

Katerina gave her mother a long look. "He's a DEA agent and a dirty one. He's after Daddy and ten million dollars. Mom, this money, the money I have in a safety deposit box in New York, and the payoff for the last job I'm about to do should be enough for us to get away, disappear."

Her mother stroked her cheek. "I wanted you to go away to school when he first got sick. I begged you to go."

"He begged me to stay."

"And just once, I hoped you would say no."

Stung by her mother's words, Katerina felt a stab of fresh guilt, a new wound on top of the old ones.

"And then I wondered, what in God's name he was asking you to do now."

Katerina absorbed the words quietly, turning them over in her mind. William Mills had never asked her to do anything. *He never intended to. His visit was the point. He wanted James Sheridan to land on my doorstep and linger, giving him more time to make his getaway.*

I was the buffer.

My own father sold me out.

When Kat looked at her mother, she found understanding, rather than condemnation, in her eyes.

"You were always a sweet girl," her mother said. "Even as a baby, you were always smiling, always happy. I would come into your room every morning and open the lid of a music box on your dresser. The tune would wake you and then I would say, 'Good morning Katie,' and you would lift your head, look at me, and smile."

Katerina's heart lurched at the name. *Katie. She called me Katie, too.*

"I don't want to leave you here," Kat said.

"I'll be safe. Ethel has the shotgun. If anyone comes, she'll take care of them and we'll bury them in one of the back pastures. No one will ever know."

Katerina's jaw dropped at her mother's matter-of-fact pronouncement.

"Um—well—there is a man who will be close by. His name is Carter, and his job is to keep you safe." Katerina provided a complete description adding, "So please tell Ethel not to shoot *him*."

"How much are you paying him?"

"I'm not. He's doing it as a favor for a friend."

"The lawyer?" Linda Mills said.

Katerina shook her head. "Philip is out of the picture. Someone else. His name is—Bob. He's a good man, a very special man."

"Do you trust him?"

"With my life, and yours," Kat said without hesitation.

"Then you should be going off with him."

"That's not going to happen. Mom, *we* have to go. And when we go, you won't be able to tell anyone where, not even Uncle Sergei. I'm sorry, you'll have to say goodbye to him."

"We've done it before," Linda Mills said, stroking her daughter's hair. "Old friends always find a way back again."

***

Katerina crept down the stairs, her overnight bag in hand. She had insisted her mother stay upstairs, away from the front door and out of sight. A rustling caused Katerina to jump and spin around. Rachel stood before her, an ethereal figure in a white, silky robe, her dark hair a contrast against her shoulders. The moonlight filtered through the curtains, throwing lacy shadows across her delicate features.

Rachel came to her, placing a small bag of leaves in the palm of Kat's hand. "One teaspoon in a cup of boiling water. It's good medicine," she said.

Katerina nodded. "Thank you."

As Katerina turned to go, Rachel took hold of her arm in a firm grasp. She extracted a necklace from the pocket of her robe, a dark, smooth stone in the shape of a teardrop on a twisted cord. She slipped it around Katerina's neck. "Protection for the journey. And it will help you to connect, spirit to spirit, to see and hear what others cannot," she said, pulling Katerina into a comforting embrace.

When they separated, Rachel caressed the blooming blue-black mosaic of bruises on Kat's neck with a gentle touch. "Do not fear the Shaman's Death," Rachel murmured. "What is burning away must die in order for you to regenerate, to become what you are meant to be. There will be other deaths. Do not be afraid," she repeated, "your spirit animal will come to you. Its medicine will help you on your journey and guide you to your destination."

"How will I recognize it?" Katerina whispered.

A small smile touched Rachel's lips. "You'll know," she said.

Chapter 22

Two figures stood in the doorway of the cabin as light snow fell; Katerina, shivering in her coat, Sergei appearing comfortable in his turtleneck, robust in the cold air.

"Katya, come inside, warm yourself," he said, his hand on her upper arm, a firm but gentle guide.

She resisted. "No, Uncle, I can't."

The moonlight's reflection in his eyes revealed him, calm, unreadable, as always.

He held out his arms and she melted into his embrace. She breathed in the sharp scent of his cigarette smoke, basking in the warm, fleeting feeling of safety.

"Katya, tell me," he whispered, "what has happened?"

"I picked up the phone," Kat said, remembering that first desperate call from Joe Lessing three months before. *Katerina, I need some help. Be a good girl and come over here and I'll make it worth your while.*

If I hadn't gone, I wouldn't have met Lisa. I wouldn't have taken the job at MJM. Maybe, somehow, all this wouldn't have happened.

But I wouldn't have met Winter.

Sergei nodded as if he understood everything her words meant. "Remember, Katya, I am always your friend. If you need some place, you come here. I have room here. It is safe for you. No one will find you."

Thank you, Uncle," Katerina said. "I'll call you and let you know where I'm leaving the car. It would be best if you didn't use it again."

Sergei looked at her for a long moment, nodded, and then kissed each of her cheeks in turn.

Katerina hustled back to the car. When she settled behind the wheel, she glanced up at the cabin and found the man she called Uncle standing there, watching her, the same enigmatic expression on his face.

Chapter 23

At dawn, Katerina turned onto Route 2. She tooled along until coming to the hotel, a low to mid-priced affair, the typical triangle-shaped overhang out front, a shuttle bus idling and ready. Kat drove around to the deserted back parking lot. At this time of year, tourists wouldn't be found in this part of the state; they were strapping on skis in Ludlow or Stowe.

Glancing in the rearview mirror, she stared at the stranger with the swollen, puffy eyes looking back at her. Her body ached and with every swallow her throat complained, bringing back the attack once again, the scene circling afresh in her head, her own private horror movie. Still, she steadied herself and eased out of the car. Reaching a side door, she pulled out an access key card and slipped it in and out of the card reader box. The green light flashed, and she ducked inside.

The hotel had a bland, utilitarian quality, nondescript beige wallpaper and an orange and brown patterned carpet. Katerina took the stairs; the hallway stretched out, empty, in front of her. She moved soundlessly, checking the numbers on the doors. When she found the room, she knocked twice, waited, and then slipped her card in and out of the key card reader. Twisting the door handle, she stepped inside.

The suite was brown everywhere except for the pale forest green couch. Lisa sat at the desk littered with discarded protein bar wrappers.

"Of all the gin joints and two-star hotels in all the world . . ." Kat quipped, her voice hoarse and cracked.

"Cute," Lisa shot back, holding out her hand and snapping her fingers for the key card.

Katerina handed it over. A few years older than Kat, Lisa presented as a double threat: attractive and intelligent. In her burgundy corduroy pants and bulky sweater, blond shoulder length hair curling over her collar, she looked like an ad for a weekend winter getaway for the rich and playful.

Lisa gave Kat the onceover. "Are you sick?"

"Do you care?"

Lisa smiled. "As long as you're up for the job—no."

"What's so important that you need me?"

Lisa ignored the question. "We're booked into a spa this morning for a reflexology appointment."

"What, no massage?"

"We'll be making a quick exit. Are you packed to go back to the city?"

"I did everything you told me, as you told me," Kat said.

Lisa answered by offering an envelope. Katerina took it and examined the contents: driver's license, passport, and a flight confirmation for JFK under the name of Catherine McFee.

"You know how I love to repeat myself," Katerina mimicked her mentor. "What's the big deal that you need me?"

Lisa got up and shrugged into her coat. "I told you. It's a retrieval. A young woman is running wild with Daddy's credit card. He'd like his card, and his daughter, returned to him."

Lisa pulled her purse strap onto her shoulder, took hold of the handle on her rolling suitcase and headed for the door. Katerina sat down.

Giving an exaggerated sigh, Lisa turned around. "The esteemed Governor of New York, the Honorable Richard Haley, is upset. His daughter, Destiny, has taken up with a man deemed unsuitable. We go to the spa, collect little Destiny, and provide door-to-door service, delivering her to the Governor's handlers."

Katerina had seen frequent pictures of Destiny Haley on Page Six.

"She's a handful," Katerina said.

"She's a hell bitch," Lisa answered. "I thought if I told you, you'd back out."

No chance. I stay here, I die.

***

They rode in silence on Interstate 89N heading toward Winooski/St. Albans, Katerina behind the wheel. She glanced at the craggy, snow-covered mountains. It would be months before the scene would become a panorama of greens, burnished reds, and golds.

"Pretty," she murmured.

Lisa shrugged. "You've seen one backwater state you've seen them all."

Katerina took Route 15 and headed east. A few turns and they pulled into the spa parking lot. Katerina noted the elegant structure, the enclosed walkways snaking a path between the buildings.

Kat turned to Lisa and caught the hard, sour expression, her game face, firmly in place.

They got out of the car.

As they crossed the parking lot, Katerina glanced back over her shoulder, her anxiety over leaving fifty thousand dollars sitting in a bag in the trunk tormenting her.

"Something special back there?" Lisa asked.

Kat blanched mentally at her screw-up. "Nope," she said.

"You ready?" Lisa asked.

"Yup," Kat answered.

"Good, because if anything goes wrong, we're blown, understand?"

"No shit, no bullshit," Kat said. "I'm ready."

***

They stepped into a soothing oasis of earth-toned ambiance, complemented by the gentle trickling of the water feature on the wall. Two receptionists, young women with flawless skin and obsequious smiles, manned the check-in desk.

Lisa ignored the blonde on the left, speaking to the curly-haired brunette on the right.

"We have eight o'clock appointments. Smith and Jones."

The brunette nodded, clicking a few keys on the computer. She went to a closet, pulled out white fluffy robes and rubber slippers, and handed them over.

"This way," she said.

Kat and Lisa followed the girl through a room with soothing sand-colored walls, large glass bowl sinks, and water closets, to a smaller room with curtained changing cubbies on one side and a wall of lockers on the other. The brunette explained the process for setting the locker code.

While she spoke, she cast a watchful glance toward a spa guest to their left, fresh from the shower.

"After you change, please relax in our lounge until you're called for your appointment," she said.

The guest took out a hair dryer, closed her locker, and slipped into the next room.

Katerina, Lisa, and the brunette stood in silence, waiting until they heard the whirring noise of the hair dryer.

"The codes are six, one, two, nine," she whispered.

Lisa drew an envelope out of her coat pocket.

The brunette snatched the envelope. "It's the room at the top of the stairs," she said. "Make it fast."

The girl hustled away.

With military precision, Katerina and Lisa opened their lockers and extracted spa uniforms. Without thinking, Katerina shucked off her turtleneck. Lisa stopped short, staring at Kat's neck. Katerina pulled it back over her head and arranged the uniform top over it. They shoved their clothes, along with the robe and slippers, in the lockers and closed them.

Casually walking through the lounge area, they exited into a stairwell. Taking the carpeted staircase with light, noiseless steps, they slipped into a room at the top of the stairs.

A young woman was lying face down, her cheeks and forehead in the headrest, her short, ash blond hair in disarray. A blanket covered her from the waist down, exposing a soft back and arms.

"Wakey, wakey, Sleeping Beauty," Lisa whispered in Destiny's ear. "Daddy says it's time to come home."

Destiny Haley lifted her head and eyed Lisa. She turned her head, giving Katerina the once-over.

"Who are you two supposed to be? The lesbian secret police? Fuck off."

"Get up and get dressed," Kat said. Three seconds and thirteen words and already she didn't like this Paris Hilton wannabe.

Destiny Haley pushed off the blanket and slid off the table. She stood about five eight, her short chop of hair with baby bangs giving her a sixties mod look. She was small breasted and doughy from lack of exercise. She looked tired and worn out, like a party girl at five a.m. after another night of mistakes. She stood before them, naked and unashamed.

Destiny approached Katerina. Placing her hands on Kat's shoulders, she massaged them.

"Not even a little foreplay?" Destiny said, her voice silky and low. "Awww, you're a newbie, aren't you? Don't worry, I'll be gentle."

Katerina realized she was standing toe-to-toe with a naked woman, and completely outmatched. Destiny Haley understood the basic principle of power. You have to act like you own it.

And she pegged me as the weak one.

Destiny's hands slid down to caress Kat's breasts with a light touch. Katerina grabbed Destiny's wrists. "Cut the crap. Your boyfriend bailed and he took all the money."

"Nice try, bitch," Destiny said, wrenching free of Kat's grasp.

"It beats facing felony drug charges," Lisa said. "He's in the wind. You've got five minutes."

"Or what?" Destiny demanded, but her shoulders had sagged.

"The credit card is burned," Kat said. "The hotel will call the police for nonpayment of your very large, outstanding bill."

Destiny went for the white robe on the wall hook, brushing against Katerina as she passed. "You didn't think this through, did you," Destiny said, tying the robe's belt and turning back to them, a smug smirk on her lips. "There is no way my father would suffer the public humiliation of my arrest."

"Who said you'll make it to the police station?" Lisa asked.

Katerina controlled herself, maintaining eye contact. *Something else not discussed during the pregame warm up. Another test. I should know the drill by now. Maybe it is a good thing I never get used to it. Maybe that's the only thing that will save me.*

Kat watched Destiny go through a similar mental struggle, until she finally said, "Let's do it."

"Good answer," Lisa said.

**

Peering out into the empty, silent hallway, Kat and Lisa crept out and padded down the spiral staircase, keeping a firm grip on their charge. Passing through the lounge area to the lockers, they took turns getting changed. When they finished, Lisa pulled out a third set of clothes and tossed them at Destiny.

"Hurry it up," Lisa said.

They stowed the uniforms and Destiny's robe in the linen bin and together, the trio walked past the empty front desk and out of the spa.

When they reached the parking lot, Kat slid behind the wheel while Lisa piled into the back seat with Destiny.

Lisa's cell phone whistled. She answered, listened, said "mmm" a few times until she ended with, "I understand. It'll be taken care of."

She clicked off the phone.

"Your boyfriend's an asshole," Lisa said to Destiny.

Destiny laughed.

Lisa met Kat's eyes in the rearview mirror. "Plan B. No airport. There's a reporter sniffing around. Drive to the Amtrak station."

Kat put the car in gear and headed out.

Back to New York.

Chapter 24

Three women, a blonde, a brunette, and a redhead, dressed in simple business attire, rode the train.

"Keep an eye on her," Lisa said. "I'm going to the bathroom." She got up, tossed a magazine on her seat and walked down the aisle of the car.

Katerina watched Destiny for any sudden movements, although where she would go on a moving train, Kat couldn't imagine. Still, with fifty thousand dollars in drug money sitting in the overnight bag next to her, Kat stayed alert. The situation was ripe for disaster. Kat kept one arm leaning on the case at all times.

"I want something to drink," Destiny said.

"Nope," Kat said.

"You know, it's unhealthy to be without fluids. I could dehydrate."

"When you get back to the city, we'll get you an IV drip."

"You don't look so good. You sound like you're losing your voice."

"Shut up," Kat said. "Nope, it still works."

Silence.

Kat didn't look up as Destiny leaned forward, glancing over the top of Kat's newspaper. Katerina worked to keep a neutral expression, even as she knew the next page could announce a break in the Felicia Reynolds or Cheryl Penn murder case—or the death of Will Temple. For the moment, she read an article announcing the creation of a special New York City police task force to root out organized crime, a pet project of the Mayor. For a fleeting moment, Katerina wondered how Anthony Desucci would react to that. *You won't be seeing him again, so you'll never have to know.*

Destiny's voice broke her thoughts.

"Wow, Hizzoner is fighting the good fight. What a fine, upstanding moral citizen. I bet my dad loves that."

"Maybe he'll buy him a cape," Kat said.

Destiny let out a laugh. "My dad would go for you. You're spunky."

"I don't really give a damn what your dad goes for. I won't be meeting him any time soon."

Destiny's chuckle turned sly. "You never know, the world's a lot smaller than you think. You're a little old for him, but you'll do. You've got good cheek bones. Dad loves a good pair of cheeks."

Katerina ignored the comment. She sensed Destiny studying her, no, examining her. *Testing the fences.*

Kat wanted to turn around and check if Lisa was on her way back but didn't dare take her eyes off the spawn of Satan sitting across from her. *What the hell is taking so long?*

On top of the danger in front of her, what of the dangers she left behind?

Who tried to kill me? The drug dealers? Sheridan? What about MJM? They already tried to get rid of me through Simon Marcus. The only reason he didn't succeed was Winter.

If I asked, he would leave everything and come.

Katerina pushed the thought of Alexander Winter from her mind. He couldn't save her, and it was selfish to think he should. This was not his burden to bear. *I have to do this myself. I have to save myself.*

"Awww, you look sad," Destiny said, a hint of venom in her voice. "Wanna talk about it?"

Kat raised her head and found Destiny's attention settled on the overnight bag. When she glanced back to Kat, she had a wide grin on her face.

"Sure," Kat said. "You first. What's the problem with a nice cushy life, an expensive education, and every little thing your heart desires?"

Destiny gave Kat a hard stare in response but sat back and crossed her arms. "The problem is you have to pay," she said. "It isn't free."

Free. The same word Felicia Reynolds had used. *Be free. Someone should.* Katerina controlled the urge to answer. The thought that the conversation might continue made her uncomfortable.

"You look like shit. I bet you could use a vacation. Have you ever been to the Seychelles? Grand Cayman?" Destiny asked.

"Nope, and if I wanted to go, you wouldn't be my travel agent. Especially since all of your accounts have been closed."

"It's easy to open accounts, especially offshore. You wake up and you have money in those accounts. A lot of money."

Katerina fought to suppress even the slightest raise of an eyebrow that a twenty-year-old brat knew a hell of a lot more than she did. "You don't have any money, remember?"

"That's what you think," Destiny taunted.

"If you did, you wouldn't be sitting here with me, up to your ass in shit."

Destiny laughed and leaned forward, moving to slide her hands inside Kat's thighs. Katerina shifted her legs to the side, crossing them. She pursed her lips, feeling her blood pressure spike. It was Simon Marcus all over again with this little witch gnawing at her last nerve.

Destiny gave a sigh. "It's too bad you're so uptight. We could have a lot of fun." She lowered her voice to a whisper. "I've seen plenty of you before. My father has his own private club of women like you—his own little pussy parade. I tried out a few of them. Just another piece of—"

"Save it," Kat said.

Destiny shrugged. Katerina went back to the newspaper. Suddenly, Destiny reached for the overnight bag. "I want some gum," she said.

Stunned by Destiny's sudden move, Katerina yanked the bag back. "I'm all out of Trident," she said through gritted teeth.

Destiny laughed, holding fast, managing to pull down the zipper. "Oh boy, what have we here," she said, pulling out a short, blunt cut, jet black wig. She was diving in again when she spied the small EpiPen-sized needle hovering close to her skin. She froze and glanced up; Lisa sat down next to her and leaned in.

"You can go back to your father conscious or unconscious. Makes no difference to me," Lisa said.

Katerina took the bag, stuffed the wig inside and pulled the zipper closed, telling herself that the money packs were buried, telling herself they hadn't shifted, and Destiny had seen nothing.

Destiny sat back, a blank expression on her face.

***

Three ladies got off the Amtrak train, walking side by side in the station. Lisa checked a text message on her phone.

"Downstairs to the LIRR," she said.

Katerina wanted to protest and ask why, but she held her tongue. She glanced over, noticing the calm in Destiny's eyes, as if this was just another day. *Bullshit.*

They took the stairs and blended in with the crush of the crowd; they walked the long concourse three abreast, Destiny sandwiched in the middle.

Katerina tensed as she spotted a cluster of NYPD cops up ahead on her right.

As the three women moved closer, Katerina panicked, shifting the bag from her right hand to her left.

Just before they reached the police officers, Destiny placed her hand over Katerina's, sliding it down and grasping the bag's handle. They were directly in view of the officers. Katerina didn't dare protest or pull to reclaim the bag; she didn't even breathe.

In an instant, Destiny slid the bag out of Kat's hand. She pulled ahead of Kat and Lisa, leaving Kat to watch, helpless, as her bag with fifty thousand dollars disappeared in the sea of foot traffic.

***

In Penn Station, Lisa and Katerina stood at the bar of an eatery. Katerina's glance darted back and forth, spying NYPD blue out of the corner of her eye. Every nerve in her body vibrated within her; a scream inside her head kept building, growing louder with every passing second.

"Easy, Cinderella," Lisa said with a smirk. "Worried she'll swipe your panties?"

"Easy my ass," Katerina muttered. "What the hell do we do now?"

Lisa said, "Go to the bathroom," and she nodded toward the restrooms next to the LIRR waiting area.

"I don't have to pee."

"Do what I tell you, Cinderella," Lisa said, her tone calm and measured. "Go to the bathroom."

***

Katerina passed the officer manning the MTA Police help desk and entered the restroom just off the LIRR waiting area. She wandered down the line of stalls, checking the floor for a sign of Destiny's outfit. In a corner stall against the wall, Kat spotted familiar looking pants. *My pants.*

The stall door opened, and Katerina came face to face with Destiny now wearing Kat's jet black wig. Kat shoved her back into the stall and twisted the lock closed.

The girl chuckled as Katerina frisked her with shaking hands.

"A little to the left," Destiny said. "Oh yeah, that's my spot."

Kat found some of the money packs stuffed into the waistband of the pants. As she tore them out, Destiny laughed. In a burst of visceral rage, Kat ripped at the girl's shirt, pants, and pockets, searching for the rest until she grabbed Destiny by the shoulders, shaking her with a fevered frenzy.

When Katerina locked eyes with Destiny, the girl's smirk had disappeared into anxious fear. The fever broke and Kat loosened her grip.

"Keep it," she said. Aware of an acute exhaustion washing over her, Kat took up the bag with one hand, popping the stall lock with the other. She grabbed Destiny by the arm. "Let's go."

***

They exited the bathroom. A stairway off to the left led to a short walk, another set of stairs, and freedom. Katerina moved to pull Destiny back into the depths of the station and found Lisa leaning against a column, relaxed but ready. Kat scanned the area and spotted three men dressed in business casual, each in a strategic spot, reading a newspaper, swiping a phone, waiting for a train.

Waiting for Destiny.

Kat threw a glance at Destiny and found her watching them, too.

Kat realized Lisa had seen it all in her head. Ever since Kat's slip in the spa parking lot, Lisa had run with the idea of the bag as a carrot for Destiny; and a trap. Lisa had calculated all of the scenarios and risks before they ever got off the train: Destiny stealing the bag, changing her look, and hiding out in the bathroom closest to the exit until the opportune moment to run.

Katerina watched Destiny glance at the MTA Police help desk. Empty. The girl gave a tiny laugh as Lisa sidled over. Together, they all headed to the stairs.

When they reached the landing, they found the Amtrak Police help desk empty. They kept moving with the crowd. Destiny's gaze darted left, right, and over her shoulders to the men behind them, blocking them in.

Katerina sensed the metamorphosis; Destiny became someone else right before her eyes. Philip always said you never really saw the real person until they were stripped of everything. Destiny Haley had morphed into her true self: a frightened young girl.

The noise of the city burgeoned as they took the stairs up to the street, then exploded as they exited Penn Station.

"See you on the other side," Destiny said.

Of what, Kat thought. *Of what.*

A man stepped forward to flank Destiny Haley on Kat's side, forcing her to step away. They moved off with Lisa through the crowd to a town car idling at the corner.

Destiny glanced back over her shoulder and her eyes met Kat's.

Katerina realized Destiny wasn't just frightened.

She was terrified.

Oh God, I should have helped her run.

Chapter 25

Katerina purchased a burner phone and made a call.

"Mom," she said. "I'm here. Safe and sound."

"My girl, what now?"

"I'll pull the finances together, head back, and then we're gone."

I did what I had to do.

"All right, dear."

I didn't have a choice.

"You still sound so hoarse. You need to see a doctor."

"I'm okay," Katerina said.

Yes, I did have a choice. Instead of helping her escape, I turned her over.

"You'll tell me everything when we see each other?" her mother asked.

Kat swallowed hard. "Yes, as soon as I get back. I promise. Mom, is he there, watching?"

"Yes, of course he is. I spoke to Ethel. She has promised not to pop a cap in him."

Katerina breathed a sigh of relief that Carter remained on the job, at the ready.

"His partner is here as well."

Katerina stopped in the middle of the sidewalk. "Partner?"

"The other man who's been watching."

Katerina froze, a swathe of colors swirling before her eyes as sudden, suffocating hot fear surged through her. "What does he look like?"

"Medium height, very thin. Sickly looking. He has black hair, in a ponytail."

The cleaner.

"Are you there? Katerina?"

Katerina, shaking, searched for words that would caution her mother without causing panic. "Mom, he's not the partner. He's . . . he's not . . . one of the good guys. Did he talk to you?"

"No, no. I've seen him but he doesn't come near me."

Don't go anywhere by yourself, okay? Please."

"Katerina, tell me what is happening."

"Just promise me you won't go out alone. If you have to, make sure Carter is close, okay?"

"Yes, I see," her mother said.

"Mom, I'm coming back. And then we're leaving right away."

"Maybe if you talked to Sergei about this—"

"Uncle Sergei can't help with any of this. Just wait and I'll be there tonight, tomorrow at the latest."

"Yes, my girl. You be careful."

Katerina clicked off the phone and dashed off a text on the Winter burner phone.

> Bob. Please alert C.
> Thin, dark hair, in a pony.
> Watching Mom.
> NOT FRIENDLY.

She started moving, the phone in her hand. She stopped short when the phone buzzed.

> Understood.
> Taken care of.
> Nothing will happen.
> NOTHING.
> W.

Katerina stuffed the phone in her purse. His assurance soothed her as no other could. She had to get the drug dealers back on track to remove James Sheridan; and keep them far away from her mother.

Chapter 26

Katerina found Henri Letourneau in his stripped down, serviceable office, speaking a low, melodious French into the phone. Even discussing business, he sounded as if he were making love to the other party.

Kat took note of the secretary, a pretty girl with long, silky straight blond hair rippling down her back, an aline dress highlighting her slender figure and small hips. She sized up Katerina, then glanced to Letourneau for instruction. Letourneau nodded at the worn guest chair even as his eyes never strayed from Katerina, taking in the blond wig on her head.

The secretary gestured toward the seat. Kat settled into the chair as the secretary continued with her filing.

Letourneau hung up the phone. He rose from his seat and took Kat's hand as a greeting. He surveyed Kat's ensemble with distinct disapproval. "*Bon jour Mademoiselle,*" he said. "*Que s'est-il passé?*"

What happened? Where do I begin?

Katerina, thrown by the French, called upon her memory. "*J'ai un petit probleme, Monsieur. J'ai besoin de votre aide encore une fois.*"

Letourneau's expression darkened. "*Quel genre d'aide?*"

"*S'il vous plait, je dois envoyer un autre message—*" Katerina stopped, searching for a word until she said, "*Monsieur, pourquoi avons-nous besoin de parler français?*"

Letourneau looked to his secretary. "Jeanine, a moment, please."

The secretary nodded and left the room, closing the door behind her. Henri sat down at his desk.

"Why were we speaking French?" Kat asked.

"Because my new secretary speaks only English."

"Why would the head of an international transport company want a secretary who speaks only English?"

"Because there are times I want to speak only French."

Katerina smiled.

Henri studied her. "What is this about sending a message? How can this help you? I told you those people are not interested."

"Circumstances have changed," Kat said, extracting a slip of paper from her purse, the note she had received from the drug dealers before Christmas. She handed it over; Letourneau fingered the note, read it, then tossed it back on the desk.

"Did they contact you?" he asked.

"We've crossed paths," she said.

Letourneau rose from his chair and paced in agitation. "I begged you to go someplace to hide. I should have sent you away myself," he went on, "yes, I should have taken you down to the pier, put you on a boat to somewhere, *et voila*, you disappear, no one would find you."

"Another message is necessary," Kat said.

Letourneau let out a sound of disgust as he leaned against the edge of his desk, hovering over her. "You must give these people what they want. And the moment you do, they will kill you."

Maybe they already tried. "I know," Kat said.

Letourneau bolted off the desk, pacing again, waving one hand as if to conjure a solution. "You know." He turned to her. "Then what to do? What to do? There is nothing to do. There is nothing to appease them. *Rien!*"

"Monsieur," she began.

He stopped. "I will not do this. I will not send you to your death."

Katerina sat in silence. She had already gone over this in her mind and made her decision. She had calculated her choice on one criterion only. *What would Winter do?*

She had imagined his voice in her head, counseling her as if he stood before her.

Did you go to Sunday school?

Yes. And I've been reading Uncle Sergei's Bible.

Then you know the story of Saul and David?

David is chosen to be King and Saul isn't ready to cash in the crown. David pulls a Grizzly Adams and hides out. Saul pulls a Mad Max and goes in pursuit.

That wasn't the point of the story, he whispered in her mind. *David has a chance to kill Saul . . .*

But he doesn't. If you want to neutralize your enemy . . . save his life.

And you will find how to defeat men, the ones who are like gods.

"Monsieur Letourneau, I'm going to give them a name, but not the one they're expecting."

Letourneau tilted his head in confusion.

"Send a message through channels. Tell them Richie Calico is about to become a suspect in a drug trafficking and money laundering ring. The DEA will be seizing his accounts. They need to clean their books and the books of any front companies they are continuing to use," she said, reciting company names and invoice amounts from memory. "And tell them I didn't have to do this since they acted in violence against me."

Letourneau stared at her.

"Tell them I have acted in good faith and they should remember that and act in kind."

Letourneau sat down behind his desk, gripping the arms of the chair.

"*Monsieur, j'ai besoin de votre aide,*" she said, noting that even French could make desperation sound beautiful.

Letourneau stared at the note on his desk.

"Will you help me?" she repeated.

He met her gaze and nodded his head.

***

Katerina left Letourneau. One down, the next one to go, she thought, like ticking off the items on a mental shopping list. *Bread, milk, eggs, kidnapping, money laundering . . . murder.*

She kept moving while she took out her cell phone and dialed a number. When the call connected, Katerina asked, "Where and when do you want to meet?"

"For what?" Lisa asked.

"Hilarious. You know how I love to repeat myself. Where and when do we meet for you to make payment?"

"In order for you to receive payment, Rapunzel, I have to know where to send it."

Katerina stopped cold. "What do you mean, you don't have my money?" she said, a rocket of anger shooting through her.

"That's not what I said," Lisa said. "I need payment instructions to make the transfer."

"I want my payment in cash, is that instruction clear enough?" Kat said, but she found her gait off kilter, weaving around people as she walked.

"You're not on probation anymore, Cinderella. You graduated, remember? It's non-cash transactions now. We use wire transfers. I get a transfer from the agency. You give me instructions. I transfer your share to you."

"How do I—" Kat stopped, already sorry the words had left her mouth. *Another game. Another test.*

"Don't worry, princess, I'll hold your payment until you get it straightened out."

Translation: figure it out or fuck off.

"By the way, the nice detective keeps calling Gal Friday, Incorporated. He misses you," Lisa said. The call clicked off.

Katerina dug out her regular phone and checked her voice mail. She listened to Detective Ryan Kellan's impassioned, sheepish pleadings of 'getting past their rocky start' and trying again. Her posture stiffened at the next batch of messages, Philip Castle, cajoling, pleading for her to meet him, just for a few minutes, even though 'I know I jammed you up a little' and 'Yeah, I boned you a little on the negatives' but he needed to talk to her as soon as possible. Philip would know how to set up the bank account, but she wouldn't dare risk a meeting to get the information. Katerina deleted the messages.

Both men would be looking for her.

I can't go back to my apartment.

Katerina did a mental calculation. Almost two hundred thousand dollars sat in a safe deposit box. Her mother still had the stash of money orders she sent last year. Richie's fifty—forty— thousand was tucked in her overnight bag. It was a good start but not good enough to disappear. She needed Lisa's fifty thousand—and had no idea how to get it.

Faced with her own inadequacy to manage the situation, Katerina was forced to admit she had not thought this through. How to get new sets of identification? If she couldn't get a new name how would she pay for hotels and housing when she and her mother reached wherever they were going? Could they even stay in the country? Probably not. That opened a whole host of new problems.

Katerina pulled out the "Winter" burner phone, the urge so strong to reach out to him, lean on him for help. The dull ache in her throat held her back. *Keep him out of it.*

Use your head, Katerina. How do people pay for things without cash, checks, debit, or credit cards?

Pre-paid credit cards.

Gift cards.

And how does one buy a large amount of pre-paid credit cards and gift cards for cash without attracting attention?

Katerina found herself wandering past Macy's Herald Square, the scene of another crime in her young career. Through a case of mistaken identity, she had crossed paths with Ivan, the out-of-town contract killer. Chauffeuring him at gunpoint, she had needed to dump her car and get another vehicle, so she called . . . Moose.

Katerina remembered Lisa's advice. *The common mistake a newbie makes is thinking a contact is only good for the one thing you called them for.*

Maybe Moose, the stolen car rental agent, had other business interests? Maybe he was in the pre-paid credit card or gift card business? *And the temporary housing business.*

She needed a place off her usual path.

Somewhere Philip Castle wouldn't find her.

Somewhere Detective Ryan Kellan wouldn't find her.

Somewhere John Reynolds wouldn't find her.

Somewhere a killer in a blue Ford won't find me.

Chapter 27

Detectives Kellan and Lashiver found widower Charles Penn at home, hanging by a fraying thread of composure. The detectives exchanged a flash of silent communication, a shared understanding of the need to tread with a light touch. A man in acute emotional pain, Charles Penn exhibited a palpable grief, one that could not be simulated. In his late fifties, his hair salted, he appeared to have aged twenty years since the last interview less than a month ago. He fidgeted as if every nerve ending in his body could implode like a stick of dynamite, scattering him around the apartment.

"Don't you have anything yet? Why haven't you found this—this animal?"

"Mr. Penn—" Lashiver began.

"I don't understand this . . . I just don't."

Ryan stayed silent, allowing his partner to take the lead.

"Mr. Penn, we are still trying to find a connection between your wife and the first victim, Felicia Reynolds."

"I have already told you, my wife and I were not friendly with John and Felicia Reynolds. My wife did not know her."

"Sir, you said your wife graduated with a degree in art history. During her studies or recently, did she show any interest in, or spend any time in the theater, even amateur theater as a hobby?"

"No."

"Did you or she support the theater in any way, particularly the Theater for a New Audience in Brooklyn? They perform Shakespeare."

"No, Detective. We are—were—I—am a supporter of the Metropolitan Museum of Art, The Frick, and MOMA. My wife is—was—devoted to the study and appreciation of art."

Lashiver nodded, giving Charles Penn a moment to catch his breath.

Ryan Kellan thought Penn looked like a man about to crawl out of his skin.

"Did your wife know a Will Temple?"

"No. Who is that?"

"Mr. Penn," Lashiver said, with slow and measured precision, "is it possible your wife had friends you didn't know about."

Charles Penn's face flushed. "My wife and I were planning a trip to Anguilla, to celebrate our wedding anniversary. We went to the office together every morning. My wife was redecorating the offices that didn't need redecorating because I encouraged her to do so. She didn't understand why I wanted it done." He gave a choked laugh. "I wanted my wife in the office, with me. I enjoyed having her there." He stopped, taking a ragged breath before forcing himself to continue.

"She had picked out chairs and the interior designer couldn't get them. If she had . . . if she had, Cheryl wouldn't have had to go to that other showroom. She would still have been in the office." He looked away.

"I should have told her to forget about the chairs," he said, his voice breaking, "do you understand? I should have told her they didn't matter."

Charles Penn stopped, unable to continue.

"Mr. Penn," Lashiver said after a moment, "we're sorry to have to ask these questions. We're trying to determine if we missed anything, anything at all. If we could take another look at your wife's credit card bills and receipts . . ."

"We also might need to see her personal effects, such as clothing. Would you still have any items?" Ryan asked.

Charles Penn sighed. He appeared small and deflated, shrinking in breadth and depth. "Yes, of course," he said, sinking into his chair behind his desk. "I have everything. Our assistant—my assistant, Mary Ellen, will provide you with whatever you need."

Lashiver excused himself to speak with the assistant, leaving Ryan to sit with the grieving man. Ryan knew his job. He understood that with each passing day, the shock of the death had worn away and the reality of Charles Penn's loss settled in. Once again, Ryan would be the keeper of the confessions, the regrets, the unfulfilled promise of a life destroyed.

Once again, he functioned as the gateway, as if he could somehow take these last testaments and send them from this life to the next.

"Five years," Charles Penn said, speaking as if to himself, "that's all we had. I had hoped for fifteen, perhaps twenty, if she would have kept me that long. It was always there, in the back of my mind. What if she became bored with me? I never worried about the future. If she had stayed, I always assumed I would go first. Then she would have everything. She would be taken care of. She would be safe."

Ryan gave a small nod of empathic commiseration.

John Reynolds killed your wife.
But how did he do it?
And why?

Chapter 28

Katerina slipped out to Queens on the Long Island Railroad. Arriving at the garage, she picked her way around the patches of black ice scattered across the parking lot. Reaching the door, she found it unlocked. *Not concerned about intruders. The whole neighborhood knows you enter at your own risk.*

Stepping into the gloom of the building, she left the daylight behind. Ducking into an empty bay, she listened. A faint wisp of a noise beckoned her to go through to the back.

Kat approached a door cracked open an inch. The noise crystallized. She heard a familiar voice followed by the sound of a fist hitting flesh, a grunt, and a fit of coughing.

At the sounds, a slice of fear cut through Katerina. She knew the element of surprise would be a grave mistake. Eyeing a worktable, she swept her hand across the surface, knocking tools to the floor. The clattering noise reverberated, followed by a sudden, sharp silence.

She positioned herself directly in front of the door, bracing herself as heavy footsteps approached. The door swung open in a slow arc; Katerina saw the gun first. Tilting her head, Kat looked into Moose's dark eyes.

He registered her presence and his eyebrows, knotted in suspicion, relaxed. He broke into a sly smile as his eyes swept up and down, taking her in.

"Mami," he said, lowering the gun to his side.

He held out his arms and she accepted the invitation by stepping into his embrace. She lingered, breathing in the deep musky scent of his adrenalin.

"You look good, mami," he said.

She glanced up at the teardrop tattoo under his left eye, watching him scan behind her.

"Luther didn't bring me," she said. "I came alone."

Moose glanced back over his shoulder. "Yo, chica, always a pleasure, but the Moose is, cómo se dice . . ."

"Occupied with business?" she finished, shifting to peek around him, already calculating what to say to convince him to let the "business" go.

Moose blocked her, spiriting her away from the door while avoiding eye contact. "Yeah, yeah, I got business right now. Some people don't understand, just because it ain't discussed specifically, there are things you don't do. It's like a . . ."

"Implied contract?" Kat offered.

"That's right. The Moose takes the implied contract very seriously, especially when it comes to timely payments, if you know what I'm sayin'."

Katerina nodded. *I should have you talk to Lisa.*

He touched Kat's elbow. "So, tell the Moose, *que lo que*, mami. *Dimelo*. Talk to me."

Katerina found herself at a loss and fell silent. She didn't know where to begin. She sensed the slight change in his stance, the tension in his posture.

'You seen those players again?" he asked. "You playin' with Desucci?"

She shook her head. "I need to make a purchase of pre-paid credit cards and gift cards. A large purchase."

Moose nodded his head. "I got you. The Moose has associates that can assist you."

Kat nodded. "And I have a little housing issue." She felt his eyes on her and she met his gaze in return. "I need to stay off the grid. I can pay, if we can work something out."

"No te preocupes, mami," he said. "You got some credit from your last payment."

"Thank you."

Putting his arm around her, he pulled her close. "The Moose is gonna take care of everything."

The embrace brought memories flooding back of shivering in the cold outside a warehouse, facing Desucci and his men. Moose had a gun then, too. *He would have used it in a heartbeat.* The sounds of footfalls at the door broke the moment.

A young guy in his twenties appeared. He had sharp, chiseled features as if he had been fashioned from stone with rudimentary tools. He eyed Katerina with a mix of attraction and curiosity.

"*Que quieres hacer con él?*"

Katerina stared at Moose intently, even as he avoided her gaze. "*Papi*, I'm sure he understands the implied contract now," she whispered.

Moose gave Kat a sideways glance and then a tiny shrug. "Tell him this is a gift," he said. "Tell him to say his prayers tonight and give thanks an angel saved his life. And tell him I want my money by tomorrow. *Mañana.*"

With a smirk in Kat's direction, the young guy turned and disappeared into the back room.

"*Vamo*, mami. I got the perfect place for you."

"Moose, I'm not staying at your apartment."

"Hey, nobody said," Moose protested, holding the gun against his chest. "I know how it is. The Moose is a gentleman."

Katerina nodded.

Moose slipped his arm around her shoulder. "Implied contract," he repeated. "Chica, you should be a lawyer."

Katerina blew out a mouthful of air. *Tell me about it.*

***

The cramped apartment pulsed with the sounds of bachata music and arguing. Mouthwatering scents of warm spices coming from the kitchen reminded Katerina she hadn't eaten. She sat on the couch listening to Moose plead his case.

"Aw, c'mon *prima*, don't be like that," Moose said, then lowering his voice. "She's a good girl. She did a good job with the garter and shit. Everyone had a good time. *Mira*, she did you a solid."

Gabriela Colon had a plate of food in one hand and a drink in the other. She let out a string of obscenities before switching to English. "A favor! You didn't bring this *blanquita* to my wedding for me, but for you, you want to make time with her."

"No, prima—"

"Qué piensas? You think I'm stupid? You didn't even tell her to dress down so she don't show me up. What's her problem, anyway? How come Miss Blancanieves over there can't take herself to a hotel."

"*Mira*," Moose said, "Gigi, she needs to stay on the lo-lo, you know what I'm saying? Problems con la policia."

Gabriela threw the plate down on the table, pieces of mofongo scattering onto the table. "And you bring her into my house!"

"Aw, like they never been here before. *Donde esta tu marido*?"

"*Caillete, boca de trapo*!"

What Katerina assumed to be a string of insults went on for another few minutes. She listened to the melee with her eyes closed. When she realized the room had fallen into silence, she opened her eyes to find Gabriela staring at her while Moose hovered behind.

"Blancanieves, *cuál es tu historia*, hunh? What'd you do?"

"I answered the phone," Kat said.

Gabriela regarded Katerina with equal parts mistrust and curiosity.

"So, what, like, someone tryin' to kill you?"

Katerina pulled the collar of her turtleneck down, revealing the black and blue marks on her neck. "Someone already tried."

Gabriela raised an eyebrow while she considered her visitor. "Bienvenido a mi casa. Welcome to my house."

Gabriela left the room. Moose came to her and took a seat next to her. She felt his anger, alive and palpable.

"You tell me who did this to you, mami," he said.

"It's taken care of," Kat said.

Moose nodded.

***

Katerina took a last swallow of Rachel's tea, exhaling as she burrowed under the covers and gave in to the pain. It had only been a little over a day since the restaurant, yet she felt as if she had been awake for a week. The cramped bedroom doubled as storage for Gabriela's business, clothing that had, tragically, fallen off the back of a truck. A girl's gotta get by, Kat thought. She considered the absurdity of forty thousand dollars buried with the laptop deep in the closet, like money stuffed in a mattress. *Or drugs hidden in toys.* The money is safe, she reassured herself; no one in their right mind would break into this apartment. Everyone knew better.

In the quiet, Kat took her thoughts and disbursed them, arranging them in an order she could understand and digest.

She had called her mother to explain the delay; Linda Mills had taken the news calmly, more concerned for Katerina than herself.

The droning buzz of the cell phone interrupted the silence. With a groan, she forced herself to get up and fish through her purse. She grabbed the Winter burner phone and clicked it on.

"How was your day, dear?" the low, graveled voice came through the line.

Katerina's heart skipped at the sound of his voice. "Swell."

"What's for dinner, chicken or fish?"

"Tonight will be chicken," she said, and a relieved sigh came out before she could stop it.

"Sounds good. I can be there before breakfast."

Katerina hesitated, the thought of seeing him, being in his arms . . .

"I have business here."

"That's far uptown for business."

"It's okay. I'm with Moose."

"Do I want to know who that is?" Winter asked, his voice going tight.

"I met him through Luther. I trust him."

"Katie, that's not a word we use."

"He supplied the Porsche replica. He came through for me last time."

Winter gave a sigh. "That stubborn streak of innocence. It makes you irresistible."

Katerina's stomach tumbled at his words.

"Katie," he said. "Come to me."

Kat's emotions surged within her. Twice, her mouth opened to say "no," but she couldn't bear to hear her own voice reject him. "I have to finish my business here," she said finally.

Katerina held the phone in her hand, her heart pounding, knowing she had said the wrong thing, knowing that every word other than "yes" was the wrong thing. *I'm sorry. I will never have you running for your life because of me.*

"Keep the phone on at all times," Winter said.

"Always," she said.

"Sleep well," he said and hung up.

Not a chance.

Tucking the phone into her bag, she fell back into bed. She closed her eyes, hoping she would be too exhausted to dream. Maybe for tonight, just one night, the nightmares born of her guilt would let her rest. If not, the specters of Felicia Reynolds, Cheryl Penn, and Will Temple would have a new companion: Destiny Haley.

Chapter 29

Lisa dressed with slow and deliberate movements, slipping on bra, panties, and stockings, attaching the garters like a ritual. She turned toward the bed. Thomas Gallagher sat up, the rumpled silk coverlet across his waist. He breathed in a heavy, labored cadence, his face still flushed. She smirked; the powerful Thomas Gallagher in a weakened condition, a prisoner of his detumescent state. One wrong move, one wrong touch, and the pain could be crippling.

"How did she sound?" he asked.

"Rapunzel is very unhappy she's not getting her money," Lisa said, slipping into her wraparound dress. "I'm unhappy I had to go off schedule and waste time herding that little brat into Vermont just to pick up Rapunzel."

"You were reimbursed for the inconvenience," Gallagher answered with an easy smile. "Now, how did she sound?"

Lisa didn't bother to conceal her amusement. "Don't you know?" She gave a pantomime of surprise. "You haven't heard from her. Oh, don't tell me. Your consultant was supposed to keep in contact—and she didn't?"

"We had an informal arrangement," Gallagher answered with a calm, but sharpened gaze.

Lisa made a *tsk tsk* sound as she came to the night table on his side of the bed, scooping up her earrings sitting next to his cell phone. "You can't get good help these days," she said. "So disappointing for you. After entertaining yourself with all those greedy, disingenuous, gold-digging recruits, you thought you had found a unicorn of purity. And then she turns out to be just like the others."

"Not quite," he said.

Lisa wandered away from the bed and sat down on a chair, looking over at Thomas Gallagher. He did have one peculiar talent, knowing what would cut to the heart of a woman. Each time she brought a new consultant into MJM, Thomas Gallagher would decide whether to hire the novice for an assignment. Each time, one look at his face, his apartment, his obvious wealth, and lo and behold, the girl was in love. Gallagher toyed with each one, studying, waiting, and with cold calculation, adjusted his approach. If a girl craved something sweet and romantic, he gave her pain and degradation. If she wanted something wild, he allowed her to degrade herself before rejection, removing her from his presence with a wave of dismissive boredom. Some stayed with MJM, others moved on. In his own way, he destroyed them all.

Until a small-time college student crawled under his skin, Lisa thought.

"You're still convinced she's different from the rest of them."

"Them? Don't you mean us? I remember our first agreement and *your* visit here."

Lisa tucked her feet into her stilettos. "By my choice. And I survived. Maybe your powers are waning."

Gallagher gave a smile; it didn't fit with his icy expression. "I'm touched by your concern but I'm in no danger."

That's unfortunate, Lisa thought.

"My sources tell me she's gone off the radar," he said. "She's in Washington Heights. Going there is not an option."

"Why don't you just call her? See if she can squeeze you in."

Gallagher's calm, meditative expression remained even as hostility tinged the air.

Lisa gazed at him with ingénue innocence, a smirk twitching at the corner of her lips, the tell of pleasure at his discomfort. "Relax. She won't skip town without her money."

"What makes you think she's leaving?" Gallagher asked.

"I forgot to mention that someone did a number on her. She had bruises all over her neck."

Lisa watched for any sign of emotion, but Gallagher remained stoic.

"You have an ample supply of my cash at your disposal," he said. "You could have spirited her to me with a promise of payment."

"I could have. But I can't help but wonder, how much is she really worth to you?"

"Ah, the negotiation," Gallagher said. "Planning for life beyond law school. Practical."

"I want a transition," Lisa said, "out of MJM."

"I don't have any sway with MJM, whoever that is."

"I want a seat at the table and a share. No more hotel rooms. No more fetch and carry. I negotiate on your behalf. I take a percentage of the spoils. Twenty-five percent."

"Ten."

"Seventeen."

"Twelve," Gallagher said.

Lisa hesitated and then: "Done."

He smiled. "Now, what do you intend to do?"

"She's looking for an exit strategy. I'm going to feed her the ugly stepsisters as a business opportunity, one that would take her overseas—with the money I owe her," Lisa said. "The sisters don't need to be disturbed for this. Using them as bait will be enough."

"Clever as always," Gallagher said. "Bring her to the estate."

"Why not here?"

"This is different."

Lisa took up her purse and headed for the bedroom door.

"Fail and you forfeit everything," Gallagher said.

Lisa stopped and turned to him.

"Everything that is yours, your work, your body, your life, becomes mine. Do we have a deal?"

Lisa smirked. "Be ready for delivery."

***

Crossing through the dining room, Lisa found the dutiful, aphonic Mrs. Shields laying out Thomas Gallagher's breakfast. Lisa moved on, making no attempt to speak to the gatekeeper.

Francine Shields had more than one task and Lisa knew it well. After Gallagher finished with each of his pretty victims, it fell to Mrs. Shields to tend to the destruction he left behind. *Including me.* She considered it a point of pride that she had never given him the satisfaction of crying out loud.

***

Lisa exited the building and the driver hustled up the front steps and offered his hand. She accepted and he shepherded her down and into the waiting car. She glanced out the window and up at the building.

Katerina Mills would fall victim to Thomas Gallagher.

She would never escape him.

Better her than me.

Chapter 30

Long after dark, Katerina and Moose rounded the corner of St. Nicholas Avenue and 181st Street. She heard the sound of an idling engine. Out of the corner of her eye, she caught a glimpse of a parked car. She didn't dare turn around. Moose's expression was set as if cast in stone, as if he were back in the garage.

Kat felt the emptiness in her pocket where the Winter burner and tracking phones should have been. They were back in the apartment. She would not cause him anxiety by her movements—or put him in jeopardy by prompting him to check up on her. Underneath Katerina's layers of turtleneck and heavy coat, Rachel's stone necklace felt cool against her skin. Katerina found herself wishing its intuitive and protective properties were as real as Rachel believed. *I can use all the help I can get.*

They approached a building; a lookout at his post, sucking on a cigarette, gave them a cursory glance. He continued to scan up and down the block, like a security camera in a scheduled rotation.

Moose and the lookout shook hands and spoke in their own language. The lookout nodded at Katerina. She shivered, though not from the cold. Katerina's attention snapped to as the lookout stepped aside and opened the building door. Moose took the lead, motioning for her to come inside.

In the hallway, two men sidestepped, allowing them to pass. A third came forward, leading them into the gloom of the stairwell and up to the third floor. When they stopped at a door, Katerina realized she had stopped breathing. He opened the door, stepping aside to let them pass through. Moose nodded, indicating that she should enter.

The stripped-down apartment functioned as a mini warehouse with electronics, appliances, and computers coming and going. Glancing down the hallway into a vacant room, Kat saw three men standing over a small floor safe, engaging in an animated discussion. She turned her attention to the other side of the room, a desk situated against the wall, a vantage point for watching everyone else, and the older man seated behind it. In his late forties, his round face held playful eyes, a friendly expression, and a goatee consisting of a small, razor thin line of facial hair. Katerina nicknamed him The Entrepreneur. He considered her for a moment and rattled off something at Moose.

Moose ushered Katerina over to the desk and answered. The Entrepreneur, satisfied, leaned forward to shake hands. The sound of conversation and the clanking of tools drifted in from the trio working down the hall. Kat registered the noise of a drill.

Moose turned aside. "My pleasure to introduce Miss Katerina. She's looking to see your selection in prepaid credit and gift cards."

"Bienvenido," the Entrepreneur said without a smile.

Katerina didn't see the gun but knew he had one. Everyone in the room had a gun.

He opened a desk drawer and set several packs of plastic cards on his desk. He drew out a gun, holding it in his lap. "So, what you need?"

Katerina had done a calculation of expenses. *I'll take Visa or Master-Card for ten thousand, Alex.* "I'll take a mix, five cards, a thousand each, ten cards, five hundred each."

The Entrepreneur's eyes widened.

"I'm a shoe addict. I can't help myself," Kat said, the drone of the drill in her head.

The Entrepreneur laughed. He culled two small piles and put the rest away.

"They have to work for internet purchases, prepaid hotel rooms, and airline tickets."

He opened his arms. "You can use for anything, hotel, car, whatever you want. You don't worry about nothing."

The drilling came to an abrupt stop. Chatter rose as the trio came up the hall, one carrying the drill. They continued their heated discussion while trooping single file out of the apartment.

Katerina tried to block out the distraction as The Entrepreneur spoke.

"I give you twenty cards, five hundred each. Cost you eight thousand."

Kat pursed her lips. Moose hung back, waiting.

"I heard the discount is forty percent," Kat said. "That's six thousand. What's the extra two thousand for?"

"Activation fees," he said. "Chica, these are friend rates."

"These are bank rates," Kat said.

He swept his arms open, the gun waving in the air. "What you think you got here? This is the bank of Pablo. I got clocks and toasters, too."

The words "forty percent discount, straight up," sat on her lips.

Katerina heard noise behind her; others were filing into the apartment. *Don't turn around. Don't look behind you.* She couldn't know how many there were but every single person in the room had a gun. Guaranteed. *Except me.* Moose had his hand at his side, alert, ready.

"Deal," Kat said.

With slow, methodical movements she opened her coat, just as Moose had instructed, extracting the money.

As she completed the transaction, the drilling trio returned, one with safety glasses dangling on a band around his neck, a blow torch in his hand. They disappeared back down the hall. Katerina's head pounded with a migraine and the insistent urge to be somewhere else.

Pablo took the cash, counted out the cards, and handed them over." You like shoes? I got shoes. I got the real shit. I got the Gucci, the Louboutins. I got good shit."

"I already have a connection, thanks."

"Phone, computer, laptop?"

"Not today," Kat said, her face flushing at the mention of a laptop, thinking of the one burning a hole in her overnight bag stuffed in the back of Gabriela's closet. "I'll keep it in mind," she said as she packed the cards away.

***

They turned the corner, leaving the building behind. Moose drew Kat in for a hug. "Bueno, mami," he whispered in her ear. "Bueno. That could have been some wild shit, chica. *Mucha sangre*. Lot of blood. It's all good, though. He takes all the risk with the credit card numbers to get the prepaid and gift cards; you get the discount. *Ta to*, mami."

When Katerina didn't answer, Moose gave her a squeeze. "What you worried about, some little old lady in Hoboken gettin' stuck for the bill? Nah. She reports the fraud, the credit card company pays."

Katerina sucked in a deep breath. While she appreciated Moose's breezy primer on victimless crime, it did nothing to make her feel better. Mentally moving on to her next order of business—an alternate identity—she realized her moral compass had already veered off into a healthy case of amnesia. *If Professor Schoeffling could see me now.*

Lost in thought, Katerina heard the sound of the tires before she saw the car. By then it was too late. The SUV had pulled up alongside; the men were out of the car, their guns glinting under the streetlamps. They grabbed Moose, manhandling him toward the car. With a gun stuck in her side, Katerina found herself forced inside the vehicle after him.

Chapter 31

Katerina sat on a cold metal chair in a frigid warehouse. Crates and boxes surrounded the open patch of space. She twisted her wrists against the cords tethering her to the chair's steel frame, shivering as she stared at her coat a few feet away, laying in a heap on the floor. Off to the side, several well-built men, dressed in dark clothes, stood with guns in hand, keeping watch. Soldiers, Katerina thought. She didn't recognize them. Moose was flanked on either side by personal enforcers; his eyes stayed fixed on her.

Two men entered, one middle-aged, five-ten, with silver-tinged hair and a square face. The younger man, built like an immovable object, served as enforcer. Katerina pursed her lips. *It's the Vincent and Carlo show*. No, she thought. It's the Anthony Desucci show. A spike of terror went through her. *The Van Gogh. It's payback.* She stared at Vincent, waiting for him to acknowledge her. He stood with his head down, eyes focused on the ground.

Oh shit.

She snapped to attention at the sound of movement. A man stepped into the space. He wore a leather jacket, black turtleneck, and slacks. He had a full head of dark hair and looked to be ten to fifteen years younger than Anthony Desucci. Katerina guessed this man was a boss. Not the big boss, but the boss of a crew. This crew. The soldiers, with the exception of Vincent and Carlo, answered to him.

He came right to Katerina and stood over her.

"Where's the envelope?" he asked her.

Katerina's mind jerked in confusion, then annoyance. "In the mail? Where's Desucci?"

The man answered her with an openhanded smack across the side of her face.

Kat floated in momentary shock, her cheek vibrating from the burning pain. She felt a thin line of wetness running down her cheek. She noted the ring on the fourth finger of his hand.

He leaned over. "That's *Mister* Desucci. My name is *Mister* Massone. Where is the envelope?"

Katerina answered in a slow, deliberate cadence. "I don't have any envelope."

Massone administered another backhanded slap. Tears sprang to Kat's eyes as the cut on her cheek stung deeper. The corner of her mouth burned; she tasted blood.

She heard a brief cough; Vincent clearing his throat. Massone shot a look in Vincent's direction but said nothing.

Massone administered another slap. Katerina gave a cry and tears ran down her face.

With one finger, Massone lifted Kat's chin. "I know other people have been asking about it. I know I'm not the only one. I explained that to Mister Desucci. He hasn't made this a priority. He will. I hope you didn't give it to someone else. That's gonna be a problem."

Envelope.

No. It couldn't be.

A soldier brought the butt of his gun down on Moose's forehead; Moose fell to his knees.

"Philip has it," Katerina blurted.

Philip Castle," Massone said with a chuckle. "Philip Four Fingers. That's what we call him now. That fifth finger don't work so good anymore. Funny, he said you had it. We checked your apartment. We didn't find it. You must have hid it real good."

Massone leaned over Katerina; she shrunk away on instinct. He grabbed a hank of her hair, yanking it backwards, forcing her face skyward.

"Where is the envelope?"

"I don't have it," Kat said, her neck throbbing from the strain.

An enforcer brought the butt of his gun down on Moose's forehead.

"I'll get it," Kat said. "He's not involved in this. Just me. I'll get it."

A nod from Massone and the enforcer brought the gun down again, administering a third blow. Moose let out a guttural grunt.

"Mister Massone," Vincent said.

Kat's neck vibrated in pain; she strained against the ropes, her whole body shaking "I said I'll get it. I told you."

"Uh, Mister Massone," Vincent repeated.

Massone turned his head. "What?" His eyes caught the red beam; following its path to his shirt, Massone stared down at the dot lingering over his heart.

"Put 'em down," a man ordered.

Massone let go of Katerina.

The soldiers laid their guns down on the floor. Moose got off his knees and collected the firearms.

Through watery eyes, Katerina noticed men swarming the space. The man leading the charge came to her. Flicking open a knife, he cut away the rope. She recognized him. Enrique. Ricky. Gabriela's husband.

"*Vamo*, chica," he said.

Katerina stumbled off the chair and grabbed her coat.

Moose, now holding a gun, pushed the soldiers down to the floor. Kat watched them collapse to their knees one by one, like marionettes. Moose went down the line, cracking each one over the top of the head, eliciting grunts of pain. When he reached Vincent he heard, "Not those two. Leave them. Plus Massone."

Moose turned; his eyes locked with Katerina in a wordless standoff. He stepped back, holding out his hand for her to come to him.

"*Mas tarde*, motherfuckers," Moose said.

Katerina gave Massone a last look.

"Remember, we know where to find him. You too," Massone said.

Outside the warehouse, Enrique closed the door and slapped on a padlock. As Moose hustled Kat into the back seat of an idling car, Enrique shot out the tires of the SUV.

Katerina pulled tissues from her pocket. Pressing them to Moose's forehead, she watched the red color stain and spread. He brushed them away and pulled Kat into his arms. She laid her head on his chest and closed her eyes.

Chapter 32

The sharp sting of the Brugal went down dry and lingered in her mouth. The warm vanilla and oak-scented rum snaked down her throat and back up into her face, dulling the pulsing heartbeat of the swollen, bruised skin. The bleeding at the corner of her mouth had stopped and her cheekbone sported an angry, purple gash.

Her mind grew thick and a woozy, unsteady feeling settled over her even as she reclined in bed.

The door to the bedroom opened. Gabriela came to Katerina, repositioning the ice pack so it lay squarely across her cheek. Then she flopped onto the edge of the bed.

"It's not safe here anymore," Katerina said.

Gabriela shrugged her shoulders. "Why? Blancanieves, it ain't no accident they picked you up on the street. They wouldn't be stupid enough to come here. Lines of demarcation, you know?" She let her words settle before she said, "So, what's in the envelope?"

"Photo negatives," Katerina said, her words coming out slow and labored. "I don't know who's in them. I never asked. I held onto the envelope and then gave it back. That's it."

Gabriela nodded. "Who's this Philip guy?"

Katerina fought through the haze of the rum to answer. "Old boss, old boyfriend . . . a shitty gift that keeps on giving." Kat adjusted the ice pack with a wince. "Thank you. Enrique, too."

"*De nada*. When Moose got business, Ricky helps out. He had a sick time. By tomorrow, he'll be thanking you." They sat in silence until Gabriela said, "So, you know, Moose, like, has a hard on for you, right?"

Katerina didn't answer.

"What? He's not good enough for you?"

"I'm in love with someone else," Katerina blurted.

Gabriela crooked her arm at the elbow, her head resting on her hand. "No, shit, how come you ain't hiding out with him?"

"I can't."

"He inside?"

Kat shook her head. "He's never been in prison. At least, I don't think so."

Gabriela laughed. "Shit, *blanquita,* you don't know? Not that they tell you, 'cause they don't. They don't tell you shit. But you can find out."

They sat in a moment of silence.

"What's he do?" Gabriela asked.

Katerina hesitated. "He's . . . a personal shopper for rich people. They want something, he gets it for them."

Gabriela smiled. "Oh yeah? How's he do that?"

"However."

Gabriela nodded. "Yeah, okay. What's he look like? Let's see."

"I don't have a picture."

"*En serio*? Why not?"

"He doesn't like having his picture taken."

Gabriela shook her head. "Sounds like a vampire, or a ghost. You sure he's real?"

Katerina had occasionally wondered the same thing. The thought of their last kiss brought a flush to her face. "Yup. Pretty sure."

"I don't know, chica. I don't see why you can't be with him."

"Because someone tried to kill me. Because tonight is a perfect example of why not."

Gabriela made a clucking sound. "Shit. He's a big boy. He can take care of himself. They don't care about that danger shit. If you told him that, he'd be like, 'Fuck that shit.'"

They fell to silence again.

"Thanks for taking me in," Kat said.

"*Con mucho gusto*, Blancanieves," Gabriela said, getting off the bed. "But I tell you straight, you ain't doing the right thing. The men, you know, they play, that's what they do, but when they're done, they want to come home."

"He doesn't have a fixed address," Katerina said.

Gabriela came to Katerina, rearranging the ice pack back on her cheek. "Blancanieves, don't leave him out there." She pointed a finger at Katerina's chest. "You gotta let your man come *home*."

Moose came in carrying a glass in one hand and a bottle in the other. The bruising around the cuts on his forehead had fully bloomed. He sank onto the edge of the bed; Gabriela left without a word.

Moose poured a few fingers of the liquid from the bottle into her glass. They took a swallow of their drinks in silence.

Katerina spoke first. "I'm so sorry about tonight."

"All in a day, mami, just another day," he said and knocked back the rest of his drink.

Moose stared at the floor. Katerina watched his expression turn and she saw the man in the garage, a dangerous man. "That's the second time you asked me to back down," he said. "Next time, chica, I take care of my business."

"It doesn't help your business to kill a capo of Anthony Desucci," Kat said. "All that does is get you, and the people you love, killed."

A silent standoff passed between them. Katerina felt the stress pounding in her head, her heart, and her cheek. She searched in desperation for a change of subject.

"Why couldn't those guys drill through the safe?" she asked suddenly.

"Yo, what?"

"At the bank of Pablo. What happened that they couldn't drill the safe?"

Moose shrugged. "They hit a relocker," he said. He watched her brows knit in confusion. "A plate of glass with bolts attached. People do all kinds of shit to booby trap a safe, relocker, explosive, gas. With the relocker, once the drill hits the glass, the bolts click in and then you fucked."

"Guess the owner really wanted to hide something," Kat said.

Moose studied her. "Talk to the Moose, mami. I always got a lot of that good will for the right person."

Katerina hesitated. "What if you need to move money, but you can't do it all by gift and prepaid cards. Is there a way to do it without sending it through a bank?"

Moose nodded. "The Moose is very sensitive to cash flow issues. You want private, *private* banking."

"Exactly."

"No te preocupes, mami. You call the *hawaladar*."

Katerina blinked twice to focus her eyes and clear her head. "The what?"

Moose leaned in. "A private broker. So, like, you want to go to Paris. You need ten thousand dollars to be there when you get off the plane. You give ten thousand dollars to the *hawaladar* here in New York. You tell him, 'I want to pick up my ten thousand dollars in Paris in two days.' He gives you the password. You go to Paris. You meet another *hawaladar*. You give him the password, you collect your money."

Katerina stared. "No shit," she said when she found her voice.

Moose laughed. "*Ta to*, chica. It's easy."

"How does the second broker get paid?"

"That ain't your problem. That's between the brokers. Mami, you don't want to know what goes on in the dark."

I believe you. "Can you make an introduction?" Kat asked.

"I got you, the Moose has got you." He fell to studying her again for a few minutes. "Not sure that good will you showed Massone and those two players is gonna be worth it."

"I know," she said.

It was a calculated risk. *You want to disarm your enemy, save his life.* She had an unpleasant premonition that the theory would only get her so far. She glanced above her head, thinking of the dream catcher, the delicate threads joining together to weave a trap for nightmares. Now she feared the threads of her life were weaving tighter to imprison her.

One day I won't escape.

Chapter 33

Detectives Lashiver and Kellan sat at their desks wading through piles of credit card statements and receipts. Ryan checked a receipt against an inventory list and then let it drop onto the desk. He sat back in his chair and ran his hands through his hair.

"So?" Lashiver asked.

Ryan shook his head. "Everything Cheryl Penn bought has been accounted for. It was either for her, her husband, her brother, or her father. Every item. They have them."

"What about the rest of the interviews?"

Ryan flipped the pages of his notebook. "The chorus girl friend of Felicia Reynolds is still traveling around on a twenty-city tour. Cheryl Penn's former roommate, Amelia Kensington, is still in Europe on her honeymoon. I got her on the phone as they were boarding the Eurostar. She said Cheryl and Felicia didn't know each other." He tossed the notebook down. "I don't get it. The wounds were similar on both victims."

Lashiver sat back, thoughtful, flipping a pencil between his fingers. "There was a difference between the two murders."

"They were both vicious."

Lashiver nodded. "The Reynolds murder was more methodical, more personal, like it was orchestrated. Everything was done to the victim in just that way, for a reason. Even the way the body was arranged. Cheryl Penn was different. Like the killer was feeding a need or getting it out of his system. There was no rhyme or reason."

"A rage killing," Ryan said. "You're thinking two killers, one copycat?"

Lashiver shrugged. "Possible. The murders took place about a month or so apart," he said. "It's been about that time. No next victim."

Ryan sat back in his chair. "Unless it is one killer and he has a new victim we haven't found yet."

"Will Temple," Lashiver said.

Ryan nodded his head. He fiddled with the files on his desk. "We go back to Felicia's driver."

"He dropped her at the theater. The car was ID'd at another location by an area camera. Right where he said he was. He wasn't anywhere near Will Temple's apartment or where she was found."

"Reynolds' secretary—"

"She was in and out of the office right before the conference call. She brought him his coffee. There is no other exit out of the office. He was in the car with his driver coming to the office before the call. He was on the conference call during the estimated time of death. He was in the office after the conference call. She brought in papers to sign after the call ended. He was right where she left him."

Ryan sat, fingering one of the receipts. "There is one person."

"You still on that?" Lashiver asked.

"Absolutely. There is one person who connects Felicia Reynolds, John Reynolds, Will Temple, Cheryl Penn, everyone. One person solves this case."

"John Reynolds' private investigator never returned my call," Lashiver said. "Maybe it's time to check in with him."

Ryan nodded though he wasn't convinced.

Chapter 34

"It's your lucky day, Rapunzel. I've got something for you."

"I didn't get what was coming to me last time," Katerina shot back, annoyed at Lisa's smug tone of assured confidence.

"I've been thinking about that. Sometimes I forget you're still a foundling," Lisa said. "I might be willing to help you "fix" your little problem of setting up an account."

Katerina gave a hollow chuckle at the pun, but her need for fast cash had her paying attention. "What's it gonna cost me?" she asked.

"I'm feeling generous."

"Bullshit," Kat said.

"I've got another opportunity for you," Lisa said. "I've got some people for you to meet. Two ladies. Two very special ladies."

Katerina took the news with a stab of anxiety pricking her heart. Finally, she said, "Where, when, and how much?"

"It's worth more than you'd ever see through the agency. Not local either. This is the real graduation. You'd be going global."

Katerina did the mental arithmetic. MJM wasn't involved, a definite plus. The odds were promising the job would come with a fake passport and a way out of the country. *This could be the exit plan. The hawaladar can move the money. The extra money I earn would be a cushion after disappearing. I'll be able to take care of all my mother's needs.*

"How soon would I be leaving?" Kat asked.

"Hold on, Cinderella. You didn't pass the audition yet. You have to interview before you get to go to never-never land."

"How do I know you're not full of shit?"

"You don't. You won't know unless you meet me. Trust me, you want to sit at the grown-ups table. You want to take the meeting."

"I'll think about it," Kat said.

"This deal is on a timer."

Kat held her tongue and her temper, keeping a smart-ass comeback in check. "Fine. I'll meet you."

After making the appointment to go out to Long Island, Kat hung up. If this worked . . . *if* this worked. Dealing with Lisa didn't give her a shred of confidence. Katerina turned over the same question in her head. *What would Winter do?* He would keep it simple. And he would stay under the radar where he couldn't be found. Getting out of the country wouldn't be enough. *I have to erase any trace of myself so no one can follow me. Who can do that? Rebel One, the computer wunderkind who erased Lester, the idiot bagman. To find Rebel One, I need to find Lester.* Katerina knew where to start.

Chapter 35

Katerina sat in the car, the day's newspapers folded on the passenger seat. She had scoured them for the trio of names and found nothing. She stared out the window at the apartment building diagonally across the street, overwhelmed with a sense of *déjà vu*. Same spot, same vantage point. *I've seen this movie.*

She checked her phone again, her new compulsive habit. Carter sent regular text updates with short confirmations that her mother was safe. Nothing from Letourneau.

Kat slipped a gray wool hat down over her short brown wig. She wore a plain brown coat, faded blue jeans, and sneakers. She slipped on black-rimmed glasses, obscuring her fresh face, bare of any makeup.

When she checked the rearview mirror, Katerina Mills had been replaced by Tina James, animal lover and ASPCA activist.

The bruises under the Band-Aid strip would be put to use as war wounds, an attack by a skittish rescue dog. Another rule of the game: use everything you have and make it work for you.

She recalled Philip boasting about how he pled down a charge for a guy impersonating a police officer.

"He knew the secret. You have to own the part, not just look it. Like you know every inch of the life you're playing because you do. You live it. Every day."

Katerina took one last look. *Okay, Tina. It's now or never.* She grabbed a folder hidden under the newspapers, opened the door, and put one sneaker on the ground.

***

At the first rap on the door, Katerina heard the high-pitched barking.

Oh shit, she got another dog. I hope it's as friendly as the last one.

Kat knocked on the door several more times until she heard the locks twist. The door opened and Katerina stood face to face with Lester's girlfriend, a pretty blonde wearing a white silk robe and a bad attitude.

"Yeah," she said.

"Tina James, ASPCA," Katerina said, and she slipped her ID holder open and closed, an expert sleight of hand. The girlfriend continued staring, a bland, bored expression on her face.

"Tell the neighbors to piss off about the barking," the girlfriend said and moved to slam the door.

Katerina wedged her foot into the door jamb. "I'm here about a West Highland white terrier in your possession. We've received an anonymous report of abuse."

The high-pitched yipping continued. The girlfriend went to turn her head and yell something but thought better of it. "The dog's fine," she said. "Don't you hear it?"

Katerina pushed her glasses up on the bridge of her nose with her forefinger. "Ma'am, I can't take your word for it. I'm going to have to see the animal for myself."

Kat saw stars as the girlfriend smashed the apartment door against her foot. Channeling every ounce of activist outrage, she said, "If you don't let me in to see the animal, I'm going to make a formal report. Do you want me to do that?"

The girlfriend glanced over her shoulder, then back at Kat.

"Whatever," she said, opening the door. "Make it fast."

***

Katerina entered the apartment but hung back to let the girlfriend go ahead of her. *Remember, Katerina, you've never been in this apartment before.*

She regretted that she wouldn't have a chance to say, "Now about that pink vomit of a color on the bedroom walls," because the dog, another Westie, sat on her shoes, clawing at her pants.

Katerina crouched to her knees, cooing as if she were an expert in animal care and behavior. Pulling the chip scanner out of her purse, Kat silently cursed her own stupidity for not having practiced with the prop, just in case. The girlfriend hovering behind her didn't help, either. She pressed the button and the device beeped.

"So," the girlfriend said. "Are we good here?"

Katerina scooped the squirming ball of fur into her arms and stood. "No, ma'am, we are not good," she announced. "This is not your dog."

The girlfriend crossed her arms and thrust one leg out from her white silk robe. "Of course, it is. Who the hell else would be the owner?"

Katerina let the fidgeting animal down and it scooted around the apartment in a fit of excitement. She opened her folder and flipped up the sheets of a pad. "Ma'am, our records—"

"Miss," the girlfriend interrupted. Tapping her foot, she kept glancing toward the bedroom.

Great. Another anemic, small-time hustler boyfriend behind Door Number One.

Kat didn't bother to turn around. "Miss, we understand that a terrier, serial number four, six, nine, two, seven, three, zero, eight, registered to a Lester Callahan, was residing at this address and this is not that animal. Where is the animal?"

Katerina watched the girlfriend's eyes dart back and forth. "How the hell should I know? I don't know any Lester, and this is my only dog."

Liar, liar, pants on fire.

Katerina took a step forward into the girlfriend's space, simulating a full steam of indignation. "Oh, I think you do know Lester Callahan. If you are harboring an abuser of animals—"

"Shhh," the girlfriend said. "Okay, sure, I know Lester, but I don't know where he is."

Lie numero dos. C'mon, tell me what I want to know.

"Miss, if I don't locate the animal—"

"Look," the girlfriend said in a whisper, "he isn't here. I don't know where he is. He probably has the dog with him."

"I'm going to have to call in the authorities."

Katerina went so far as to pull her cell phone from her purse even as a small inkling of anxiety bloomed in her chest. She didn't like the way the girlfriend kept glancing toward the bedroom. *What have you got in there?*

"Okay, okay! Fine," the girlfriend said, crossing to the kitchen table and scribbling on a pad. Tearing off the paper, she handed it over to Kat.

"He's at this number." Her voice dropped to a whisper. "Go call him and ask him about his damn dog."

"This number could be disconnected."

"I just talked to him last week."

Bingo. But not good enough.

Katerina held her pen to the pad. "Last known address."

The bedroom door opened. Katerina watched the girlfriend's eyes widen.

Katerina turned her head; she felt the blood rush out of her face.

Oh shit.

Lester Callahan's replacement stood at about five-ten. Built like a linebacker, he had a square, mean face, dark eyes, and coal black hair in a receding widow's peak. Wearing a white t-shirt, his right arm sported a tattoo of a black dagger wrapped in a red snake with drops of blood dotted underneath. Her eyes followed the tattoo down to his meaty hands. Good for crushing things, Kat thought. When he talked, his voice came out hard and unfriendly. Even the dog stopped barking.

"What the hell is this?" he asked as he gave Kat the once-over. "What do you want?"

The girlfriend took on the persona of docile sex kitten.

"I'm here about a complaint related to the family pet," Katerina said, gamely thrusting her face toward the man she nicknamed Brutus.

The girlfriend chimed in and ran with it. "Neighbors complaining about the barking," she said, taking Kat by the arm. "I fixed it, baby."

The boyfriend shifted, blocking Kat's path. "Which one of those pricks called, hunh?"

"Confidentiality forbids me to give out any information on calls of concern," Kat babbled.

The boyfriend lurched forward, forcing Katerina back until she hit the wall. Her face flushed and her chest vibrated at the sudden flashback of Sheridan cornering her.

Kat pushed her glasses up on the bridge of her nose and jutted out her chin, but her knees knocked as she gave her best indignant enthusiasm required for the part. "Sir, I am a duly authorized investigator responsible to root out animal abuse. If I think for one moment any harm has come to this animal, I will notify the authorities to take possession of this animal and hold you criminally responsible."

The girlfriend stared, a mix of confusion and wonder on her face. Brutus held up his hands. "No one's touching the dog," he said.

The girlfriend grabbed Kat by the arm and hustled her to the door.

"Coconut Motel, Boca," she whispered as she shoved Kat out the door.

Katerina didn't stop to catch her breath until she had slammed the car door shut. She shoved the key in the ignition and started the car. *Keep moving. Whatever you do, keep moving.*

Chapter 36

Thomas Gallagher entered the study. Dressed in Armani for his dinner engagement, he shot the cuff of each shirt sleeve in turn. Smith stood at his employer's entrance and held out his cell phone. Gallagher took it, listening to Smith's report as he swiped through the pictures.

"Miss Mills possesses an extensive wardrobe and an exquisite pair of shell-shaped quartz, diamond encrusted earrings, none of which she can afford."

"Provided by the professor," Gallagher said.

"Some of the items."

"Really, why not all?"

"The earrings were taped underneath one of the dresser drawers."

Gallagher folded the information into his train of thought.

"She has news clippings about a murdered socialite, Felicia Reynolds."

Gallagher shook his head to dismiss the comment and handed the phone back to Smith. "Anything else?"

A smile curved at the edges of Smith's lips. "She's moonlighting," he said. "She's working for Gal Friday, Incorporated. They offer personal assistants. I called. The young lady on the phone was quite professional but somehow, I can't help but think she never expected an actual client to call."

He paused, enjoying Gallagher's anxious impatience, like Pavlov's dog, his appetite whetted; he wanted more.

"Gal Friday is owned by a shell company, IGS Capital. My team is digging into it as we speak."

"Excellent, Mr. Smith," Gallagher said. "As for the earrings, don't trouble yourself. I will be seeing Miss Mills shortly. I'm sure we'll discuss them."

Gallagher smirked at Smith's expression of surprise. "When she is safely in my care, I will transfer her cell phones to you. Use them, and whatever you discover about IGS, to draw the professor out of his hiding place, and remove him."

Smith nodded. "Understood. Mr. Gallagher, I should also mention, the detective we spoke about is still staking out her building. He's waiting for her. If your intention is to hold her, he could complicate that."

"I can handle a New York City detective without issue, thank you, Mr. Smith," Gallagher said with an icy smile. "One more item. After this matter is taken care of, I want the contents of Miss Mills' apartment removed and destroyed. All of it. Is that understood?"

Mr. Smith folded his hands one over the other. "Yes, sir."

"I trust you can see yourself out," Gallagher said.

***

In the limousine, Gallagher considered the situation. Once in his possession, he expected Katerina would tell him everything. He would listen and offer kind words of comfort. He would assure her that no harm would come to "Bob," while Smith acted as his hand, removing the impediment permanently.

Gallagher took out his cell phone and placed a call.

"Mrs. Shields," he said, "please have the house on Long Island prepared. I will be going there shortly. Yes, with a guest. Yes, we will be there for some time."

Chapter 37

Detective Ryan Kellan buttoned into his coat, a Styrofoam cup in one hand, approached the tan Sebring parked across from a sleazebag, one-star roach motel on Tenth Avenue.

The driver of the car rolled his eyes and rolled down the window. He held up an ID holder. "Licensed private investigator, Detective."

Ryan laughed. "Retired Detective Timothy Green." He held out the Styrofoam cup as an offering. "Detective Ryan Kellan. Pleasure."

Green accepted the cup with a shrug.

"Can I talk to you?" Ryan asked.

Green nodded his head but avoided eye contact.

Ryan picked his way around the landmines of ice and snow, opened the passenger side door, and ducked inside.

"What's the case?" Ryan asked.

Green took a swallow of the hot liquid. "Some little wife screwing around on the old man. Lucky for me he doesn't need audio or video. He just wants a shot of them coming out of the hotel. I get my snap on the phone, I'm good to go."

"No audio or video?" Ryan said. "Where's the fun in that?"

Green gave a sour laugh. "He'll want it, eventually. They say they don't, but they always do. They like to watch, you know?" Green lapsed into a sudden silence and took another swallow of the coffee.

"What do you care? More money for you to retire to Florida," Ryan said.

Green chuckled. "Fuckin' A. Soon."

Ryan nodded. "Once the Reynolds job is done."

Green stared out the window.

"Bet that's a sweet job, hunh? What? He told you not to play nice in the sandbox with us, me, Lashiver, right? He doesn't get how it works. You can do a favor for a Brother in Blue, can't you?"

Green took his eyes off the fleabag hotel. He turned to Ryan.

"I'd help you out, but you know how it is, client confidentiality and besides, I don't have anything that would help the investigation, so, there it is."

"Did he tell you the wife was banging some pretty boy, an actor? Did he tell you the actor disappeared?"

"So, the boyfriend is good for it," Green said, his jaw set. "It's always the boyfriend."

"You forget your training already?" Ryan said. "It's always the husband."

Green opened his door and poured the coffee out, a blast of cold air assaulting them both. He slammed the door shut. "Oh, look, I'm finished. Nice talkin' to you."

"You know what I don't get," Ryan continued as if Green had never spoken, "a cop on the job all those years, and now, you don't give a shit this woman was killed. What's he paying you to sit on your ass and do nothing?"

Green turned his body toward Ryan, his eyes dark with anger. "Fuck off and do your own job, hotshot. I'm not going do it for you so you can meet the Mayor and get your picture taken again."

"This is how you end your career—"

"Fuck you. I retired."

"You got out before they threw you out," Ryan said.

"IAB cleared me. One hundred percent. I got my pension. You do your fuckin' job. Interview the witnesses, look at the evidence, peek under the bed, check under the desk—get the fuck out of my car. You're stinking up my seats."

Ryan nodded toward the fleabag motel. "You missed your shot."

Green snapped his attention back to the hotel and spotted a man and a woman walking away from each other. He cursed under his breath.

Ryan got out of the car and hustled back to his own vehicle. He had uncovered one important piece of information: retired NYPD Detective Timothy Green feared his client more than the cops.

***

Green cursed, sorry he had dumped the coffee. Fuckin' hotshot kid, he thought. He's gonna be a fuckin' problem. The whole thing's a fuck up. He chided himself again; he should never have taken the job. But the money; he had wanted that money.

Green shuddered thinking about that pretty girl, the college student with the hair down her back. *Man, what a prize. I could do her all day and night, no problem.* He had bumped into her in Saks, sending her right into the wife's path; he was proud of that move. *Poor kid. Maybe she got out.* If she had, she should run and keep running. If Reynolds sent his monster . . . *Fuckin' Frankenstein.* If he got his hands on her . . . *God help her.*

He felt the sweat break out on his forehead, caught the stale scent of his own fear.

Time to get my money and get the hell out.

Chapter 38

Katerina spent the subway ride reviewing the plan. *Go to the bank first, then out to Long Island to see Lisa. Get the assignment. Get back to Moose. Make the transfer to the hawaladar. Pick up my stuff, make arrangements for Mom, and then we're gone.* She repeated the items in her head, as though it were a normal shopping list: milk, eggs, butter, bread, laundered money— escape.

Katerina entered the bank carrying a shopping bag from a high-end department store, a shoe box stashed inside. After being shown into the safety deposit box vault, the stoic bank associate took Katerina's key from her and inserted it into the slot next to her own in the tiny door. Kat caught the sidelong glance of the bank employee, taking in the oversized sunglasses and the hint of the purple bruise peeking out. Katerina had prepared, dressed to the nines, playing the part of a sharp, stylish woman emptying the safety deposit box to escape a lousy husband or a bad boyfriend.

Pulling out the long, large box, the associate ushered Kat into a privacy cubicle. Katerina worked fast, arranging the packs of bills neatly into the shoebox. The money from her jobs and the money Simon Marcus had packed for a getaway. When she finished, she stood there, staring at it, as if trying to convince herself the packs of money were real.

Katerina knew the stash wouldn't outrun the growing list of people looking for her. Even Simon Marcus had known the cash wouldn't be enough. *That's why he had planned to sell a stolen Van Gogh hidden in his Porsche to finance his disappearance. That's something I could use right about now.*

Kat closed up the shoe box, then on second thought, opened it again. Taking out a few packs, she distributed them between her purse and an inside pocket in her coat. She closed up the box and placed it inside the shopping bag. Opening the cubicle door, she called the woman to return the empty safety deposit box to its place. Thanking her, Kat exited the bank. In her mind, Katerina already imagined herself five steps ahead, past her meeting with Lisa, packed up and gone from Washington Heights, on a plane leaving the country.

Making her way to the corner, the door to a limousine flew open, blocking Katerina's path. She stopped short and turned to stare into the smiling face of John Reynolds.

Backing away, she hit the brick wall of someone behind her. *No, no, not again.* On instinct, she twisted away, shifting the shopping bag from one hand to another to keep it clear. In one sweeping motion, Reynolds' driver caught her above the elbow, yanking her back. Katerina attempted to twist in the other direction, hoping to force her way out through the sliver of a space between the car and the open door but he stepped in, blocking her maneuver and shoving her down into the limo. He wrenched the shopping bag out of her hand.

Heart thudding, Kat scrambled for the door as it slammed in her face.

She whirled around to find Reynolds inches from her. "Miss Katerina, we have so much to talk about," he said.

Chapter 39

Reynolds reached out and removed her sunglasses. Katerina flinched, raising her hands to smack him away. He handed her the glasses with a glint of amusement in his eyes. "I'll make this very simple," he said. "You will begin your assignments for me immediately."

Katerina struggled against the spiraling panic racing into every pore. Her brain fractured as she split her focus between Reynolds and staring out the back window. The sound of the heavy thud of the trunk slamming shut reverberated in her ears. The money was out of reach; it might as well have been in another country.

"Miss Katerina, did you hear me?"

Kat brought her attention back to him. "Our business is done," she said dumbly, at a loss for anything else.

Reynolds' fleshy hand encircled around her wrist. The sudden vise grip made her wince and she struggled, grunting in pain as she tried to wrench her wrist out of his grasp before it broke.

"This game of hide and seek is useless," Reynolds said, still wearing the cockeyed grin.

Lunatic, she thought, as she kept struggling. As the limousine pulled out into traffic, he let her go. Her eyes darted to the window. *Oh God, where are we going?*

"We're not going to see *him*," Reynolds said. "I have another project for him. How that project progresses depends entirely on you."

Another socialite? Will Temple? Don't say anything. Don't answer him.

Katerina watched with a mix of fascination and horror as John Reynolds rambled in a slow, measured drone.

"*His* loyalty is absolute. I understand him. It's an urge. Not something he can control. But I provide an outlet, a structure. He has a sense of belonging. He's happy." The sickening smile widened. "Miss Katerina, you're running from where you belong. It's time to stop and accept your role."

You're insane.

Words began to tumble out of Katerina's mouth, spewing forth of their own volition. "I will not do anything for you at any time. My movements are being monitored. I am being watched. If I don't appear when I'm expected, the interested parties will come for you."

John Reynolds chuckled in response. "Miss Katerina, you know how I abhor dishonesty. You are lying. Poorly."

"Are you willing to risk that? If you contact me again, I will notify the police that a suspicious man, a man with a crew cut, driving a blue Ford, has been following me."

Reynolds continued to laugh. "And where did you see this man?"

"When I made purchases in my capacity as a legitimate, professional, personal assistant. Because that's what I am—and I have the documents to prove it. A man in a blue Ford followed me after a routine pickup at a jewelry store on 5th Avenue. I have the receipts."

Reynolds' smile disappeared. "I see," he said, studying her with cold eyes.

"I will give a description to the police and they will bring him in," she said, struggling to keep her tone low and calm, even as the urge to scream raged within her. "They will question him, ask him about his routine, his whereabouts. How do you think he'll hold up under questioning? Do you think he'll go to prison to protect you? Does his loyalty go that far?"

Reynolds eyes seemed to grow larger as he continued to stare at her.

"Stay away from me and anyone connected to me. I don't want to hear or see of you again. Now tell him to pull over and let me out."

Reynolds pressed a button. "Garrett, pull over, please."

Katerina's heart pumped in her chest as the limousine slowed and pulled over to idle at the curb.

Thrusting open the door, she tumbled from the car. She spun around to find no driver, no bag.

"The spoils of war, Miss Katerina," Reynolds said, his lip curling. "Whatever you brought out of that bank, is now mine."

Unbridled rage rushed through Kat; she primed to lunge at him.

"Come ahead," Reynolds said with a wide grin. "Make a scene. The police will come. We can show them the package in the trunk, together."

Katerina halted, frozen, impotent.

"Savor your small victory, Miss Katerina," Reynolds said. "All wars are made up of many battles."

As Kat opened her mouth, Reynolds pulled the door closed. The limousine inched away from the curb.

***

Katerina hurried away down the sidewalk, fighting against the wind, desperate to create distance, a barrier between herself and the place where she had just been. Out of breath, she stopped in the middle of the sidewalk, her chest heaving, choking back the sobs rising in her throat.

She had held off Reynolds . . . temporarily . . . the money, the money. Her hands, shoved in her pockets, curled into fists. She had forty, maybe fifty thousand dollars of the money in her purse and coat pocket, but the rest of it? Gone.

Always half measures. Always not good enough. Always two steps forward and four steps back.

Her stomach roiled as she fought a silent battle not to give in to the pandemonium in her head. An insistent buzzing cut through the noise of her mental screams. The buzzing stopped, then started again. She dug the phone out of her pocket and clicked it on.

"Yes," she said.

The voice of Jasmine, MJM's iron maiden gatekeeper said, "I have an assignment. A retrieval."

"No," Katerina blurted. "Get someone else."

"You're listed as available."

"I can't," Kat said.

"This is urgent. The client is willing to pay a premium for a consultant to leave New York and come to him immediately."

Katerina stopped. "Where?"

"California."

In a sea of confusion, Katerina said, "How much?"

"The assignment is two hundred thousand," Jasmine said. "Your take is fifty percent."

Katerina closed her eyes. When she opened them, everything appeared to be floating, even the people milling past her, as if she had stepped out of the normal continuum of time, and she existed alone. *Get out. You have to get out. Now.*

"Cash payment only," Katerina said.

She heard a beat of silence.

"Agreed," Jasmine said.

"I'll take it," Kat said.

Katerina heard Jasmine's fingers clicking across the keyboard. "You leave tonight. You'll get more instructions after you land. I'll text you where to pick up your travel documents."

"No, I'll give you the pickup point," Kat said.

"Fine," Jasmine said.

Kat disconnected the call only to hear the ring of her burner phone. Pulling out the cell, she saw Lisa's number. She pressed the button to reject the call. *Sorry, Professor Higgins. I can't take any chances. I need a sure thing.*

***

Jasmine placed a call and waited for it to connect. "He just made contact," she reported. "I placed the call after she left him." She listened. "Yes, she took the assignment." She listened again. "Yes, I will advise as soon as she arrives."

Jasmine hung up the phone.

Chapter 40

In the bedroom, Katerina packed the overnight bag with clothes, cash, prepaid cards, Lulu's deposit slips, the phone bills, the renewal receipts for her father's boating magazine, and Richie's laptop. She zipped up her bag.

"Shit, *chica*, we was just gettin' to the good part," Gabriela said.

Kat smiled.

They both turned at the opening of the door. Moose entered. He gave Katerina the once-over, taking in her swollen eyes and flushed complexion.

"*Que lo que?*" he asked quietly.

Katerina shook her head.

Moose shot Gabriela a look. She got off the bed and walked out, closing the door behind her.

He came to Katerina. "*Dimelo*, mami," he said.

"I need to keep this bag where it's safe. Some place where I can get to it at a moment's notice. Where I know it will be there if I need it."

"What about the *hawaladar*?"

Katerina shook her head again as an answer.

Moose nodded his head. "I got a place for you."

Moose took the bag off the bed and pulled her in for a hug. Kat curled into his embrace as a few hot tears fell. He kissed the top of her head. "I got you, mami. The Moose has got you."

When they came out of the bedroom, they found Gabriela sitting at the table, a plume of smoke rising from the cigarette between her fingers.

"Catch you on the way back," Kat said to her.

Gabriela took a drag on her cigarette. As Kat and Moose were halfway out the door, Gabriela's voice called after her.

"*Cuidate*, Blancanieves. Be careful."

Katerina nodded and walked out.

***

They went through the garage to a storage shed squatting behind the building. Following Moose inside, Katerina watched as he kneeled down to remove a portion of the floorboards, revealing an oversized metal box nestled in the soft earth. He unlocked the box. She placed the bag inside. He closed up the box and buried it in the ground, putting the floorboards back in place.

Moose stood up and pulling a key off his ring, handed it to her.

"You come back any time, day or night. It's here for you."

Katerina nodded. If something went wrong, plan B would be here.

Chapter 41

"Sony Building, one hour. Send Angel," Katerina said into the cell phone.

"He only handles pick up," Jasmine said.

"It's him or it's off," she bluffed.

"One hour," Jasmine said and hung up.

Katerina clicked off the cell phone and headed toward Fifty-sixth Street and Fifth Avenue. MJM was much too anxious for her to take the job.

With no other avenue for cash, at least she would see it coming.

I hope so.

***

The atrium served as one of several public spaces the city had decreed for New Yorkers to escape their claustrophobic cubicle apartments without freezing their ass off in winter or sweltering in summer.

The sterile, modern space was outfitted with matching silver chairs and tables spaced far enough apart to afford a modicum of privacy.

Kat spotted Angel, MJM's designated courier, right away. Once a consultant on probation visited the client and picked up the cash fee, Angel stepped in to collect the envelope. The consultant received their share only after completing the job. Angel, six feet tall, sported a bald head and a rock-hard body. He existed as a walking, talking deterrent to skimming.

Right before Christmas, sleazy hedge fund manager and white-collar criminal Simon Marcus had called in one last job; he wanted to make a run for the Canadian border and he wanted Kat to drive. Angel had been on call to make the pickup. Simon Marcus had no intention of paying for the service; and he had no intention of letting her live.

As Kat took a seat at the table, she remembered that Alexander Winter had not been the only one to come to her aid.

Not here for the pickup, baby, Angel had said.

She watched his eyes skim over her as they always did, watched them linger over the bruises on her cheek.

He extracted a manila envelope from his inside jacket pocket. Placing it on the table, he slid it over to her.

Kat accepted it and peered inside. The driver's license had her picture and the name Beth Miller. She shoved the envelope into her purse.

"I don't do delivery, baby," Angel said without malice.

"I don't trust anyone else," she said.

One eyebrow quirked upward.

"Did she ever go out of town for MJM?" Katerina asked, a sudden urge to know if a previous fixer, before her time, the one who didn't live to transition out of this life, had walked the same path.

Angel stared out at the people shucking off their coats and sweaters, removing layers as they switched from frozen to overheated. "Not the travel agent, baby," he said.

"*You* would know," Kat said.

"She only took a bite out of the Big Apple, until it bit her back."

Kat stared down into her open purse at the manila envelope that contained a new name and a ticket. "Do you know where she's buried?"

Angel turned to her. "I don't dig, baby," he said, rising out of his seat, "and you're asking the wrong questions." He stopped by her chair and leaned over her, lingering to catch the scent of her hair as he kissed her temple.

"Something's coming," Kat said. "I don't know what it is."

Angel ran a finger over her bruised cheek with a tender touch.

"See as they see, baby. That's the only way."

Chapter 42

"Thanks for the chip scanner, Gertie," Kat said, as she handed it over.

"Your Aunt Gertie always has what you need."

In her late sixties, Gertie favored Chanel creations and looked like she should be meeting Audrey Hepburn for breakfast at Tiffany's. They were holed up in a back room of a restaurant doubling as a black-market couture showroom.

"What happened to pure breed pet relocation, Gertie?"

"It's there. A girl's gotta get by, darling. It's always best to diversify."

Katerina watched the older woman pick through a rack of recently "liberated" clothing for the discerning young female. Kat couldn't take her eyes off a sheer, deep V-neck mermaid dress with enough strategically placed lace applique to avoid a charge of indecent exposure.

"You have good taste," Gertie said.

Feeling her cheeks color at the thought of wearing the dress for Alexander Winter, Katerina shook her head.

"So where are we off to?"

"Iowa," Kat deadpanned.

"Smart girl," Gertie said. "And you remembered the most important rule, that's why you came to see your Aunt Gertie." She pulled a pale blush ensemble off the rack, tags still on, and held it up against Katerina. "A girl always makes time to be fashionable. So tell me, is it warm or cold in Iowa?"

***

Katerina, stripped down to bra and panties, slipped into the outfit.

"Oh, absolutely," Gertie pronounced. "You need a jacket and a belt."

"Thanks for being available on short notice, Gertie. I didn't know if you'd have stock."

Gertie laughed. "Darling, I can get you couture right off the runway. There's always another odd lot around the corner."

Odd Lot. Katerina had never heard stolen designer goods referred to that way. Crime had its own unique language and syntax. *Like a personal shopper for wealthy individuals, otherwise known as a steal-to-order thief.* Like any foreign language, one only learned by total immersion.

"Try this on," Gertie said, thrusting an asymmetrical wraparound in royal purple and black against Kat.

"I don't like this one, Gertie."

The older woman put her hands on her hips. "You know this how? You haven't seen it on. It's not the same when it's on the hanger."

Kat did as instructed.

"Now let me see you."

Katerina turned and Gertie set to work fussing and primping as if Kat were about to hit the catwalk.

"How's Doc?" Kat asked.

"He's around," Gertie said, eyeing the bruised cheek and neck. "You need him?"

"No. I just wanted to know if he's okay."

Gertie patted Kat's cheek. "You're a good girl," she said with a sigh of resignation. She backed up and studied Katerina with a critical eye. "Stunning. See for yourself."

Katerina turned around. The dress clung to her figure, flattering every curve from firm, rounded breasts to slim waist, slender hips, the smooth curve of her backside, and down to shapely calves.

"Oh," Kat uttered.

"You're forgiven," Gertie said. "You young girls, you don't see the big picture, not like an old broad like me. You have to think outside the box, whether we're talking about a dress or something else. You can't be so stubborn."

The rebuke brought back the argument with Winter last year and his angry exasperation on the phone. Staring at the mermaid dress, Katerina's heart squeezed at the thought of him and tears sprung to her eyes.

"Oh honey, not again," Gertie said. "What did Prince Charming do this time?"

Katerina shook her head. "Not a thing."

"Now he's Mr. Perfect, of course," Gertie said. "You're sure you only want three outfits?"

"Yup." *Especially, since I just lost more than half my money.*

Gertie sighed. "Four thousand for the trio. It's a song."

That's one hell of a tune. "Will you take gift cards?"

"What, I'm a shopping mall now?" Gertie considered Kat and gave a wave of her hand. "I'll take half in cash, the rest in cards. A girl's gotta get by."

Katerina divided up the cash and cards and handed it over.

"I'll see you when I see you, Gertie," Kat said.

Gertie nodded as she counted the bills. "Now you're learning," she said.

***

As Katerina hustled out of the restaurant, she pulled out her burner phone and connected the call.

"You're late, Rapunzel," Lisa's said. "Are you lost?"

"I'll catch you on the way back," Kat said, "and you still owe me my money."

Katerina heard a pregnant pause from the other end of the line.

"This is not something you want to miss out on," Lisa said.

"Change of plans."

"I told you I would set you up for the wire transfer," Lisa said. "No shit, no bullshit."

"I'll be in touch."

Katerina hung up. One last piece of business left, she thought. *One stop I have to make.*

Chapter 43

Katerina waited in the outer office. Vincent, her attentive escort, chatted as he took her coat. "It's good to see you, miss. I mean, you're okay, thank God. I'm real sorry about the misunderstanding," he said, gesturing his own cheek.

"Which one? The first one, the second one, or the third one," Katerina asked.

"Mister Massone can get a little carried away," Vincent said. He lowered his voice. "That was a very nice thing you did."

Let's see how nice.

Carlo, one hand folded over the other, stood at attention, although Kat detected a softer texture in his usual stone-faced expression. It did nothing to lessen her anxiety.

"Come in, Katerina."

Kat's body tensed at the sound of Desucci's voice.

Carlo stepped aside.

***

Anthony Desucci sat behind his large oak desk viewing Katerina with bemused interest. He looked every bit the older, dapper gentleman in his dark suit, his full head of slicked-back, black hair.

Katerina sat on the plush, upholstered guest chair across from him. She was beginning to think she had been overly optimistic in calculating how much her act of benevolence would be worth.

She felt Vincent and Carlo standing behind her. *What about Massone?* She shifted in her seat, giving a half-turn.

"Mister Massone isn't coming," Desucci said, reading her mind. "Now, what did you want to talk about, Katerina? Economics? Literature?"

"Photography," she said.

Desucci nodded.

"The man who was with me. The man Massone tracked to find me."

"Yes, I met him right before Christmas. Moose."

"He doesn't have anything to do with photo negatives. I'm asking that he and his family be left out of this."

Desucci considered her statement. He glanced behind her to Carlo and Vincent. "He would have killed my men."

"He had his skull cracked three times. That can upset a person."

Desucci chuckled in Vincent's direction. "Done," he said. "Anything else?"

Katerina steeled herself. "I don't have the negatives. I don't know where they are."

Desucci drummed his fingers on the desk. "You gave assurances you would find them."

"Because I didn't want his skull cracked a fourth time."

"You're very good at finding things. We both know that."

Katerina felt her nerves shredding at the seams. "I fulfilled your request."

"After you attempted to deceive me."

"You received the Porsche. And now I returned your staff to you unharmed."

Desucci raised his eyebrows. "You want me to interfere in this matter on your behalf and cancel your commitment."

"Yes. And since you don't support this exercise to begin with, it's in your best interest as well. Mister Massone can concentrate on important business."

Desucci leaned back, considering her. After a moment, he adjusted and sat forward. "I can tell Mister Massone to drop this. I can tell him that you don't work for him."

Katerina felt the air rush out of her lungs in relief. "Thank you," she said.

"Because you work for me."

Kat froze. "For you?"

"Yes," Desucci said. "In exchange for this consideration you're asking for."

"You'd be looking for the hole your men were buried in if not for me. That should be consideration enough."

"It's your choice, Katerina," Desucci said.

Katerina searched but found nothing to grasp. She knew he wouldn't ask about the Van Gogh. He knew that she would lie and deny any knowledge. This was payback, pure and simple. "No, thank you. I'll handle this with Massone myself. Would you be willing to give some breathing room, at no cost?"

Desucci sat back in his chair. "Let's say, until the start of the semester," he said.

"Thank you," Kat said. Without ceremony, she rose out of her chair and left.

Carlo followed her out.

***

Anthony Desucci sat lost in his own thoughts. Vincent approached the desk and waited until Desucci registered his presence.

"What do I tell Mister Massone?" Vincent asked.

"Tell him she's been granted a temporary pass," Desucci said.

"What about the Dominican?"

"Tell Mr. Massone to keep his distance."

Vincent nodded. "She's got a knack for this kind of thing."

Desucci gave a sigh. "Runs in the family."

"She's a nice girl," Vincent said.

"Yes, she is."

"I think her father will be expecting a little more leeway for her."

"Her father has his own problems. He can't help her. She's going to have to manage on her own," Desucci said.

Chapter 44

The limousine pulled up curbside at the terminal. A tall man, his skin the color of almonds, exited the driver's side at the same time the trunk popped. He stopped at the rear passenger door; opening it, he took the hand of the young woman, helping her out with a careful, gallant flourish. She wore a full-length coat over a sleeveless dress, a hybrid outfit between the cold Northeast and her destination, the balmy West Coast.

Katerina reached into her purse and pulled out a hundred-dollar bill.

"You already paid me, Miss Katerina. In full."

"It was last minute, Luther."

"Always got time for you, Miss Katerina."

Katerina stood on the curb while Luther drew out her bag from the trunk.

"You have someone out where you're headed, someone you can call?" he asked.

"I'll catch you on the way back, Luther," Kat said.

Luther watched until she disappeared behind the terminal sliding doors. He extracted his cell phone from his pocket as he got back in the limousine.

Chapter 45

Lisa sat in the guest chair in the sterile, intimidating office. She heard the twist of the doorknob, the familiar footsteps as Thomas Gallagher entered and sat down across from her.

"Something spooked her," she said.

Gallagher's expression remained fixed, like smooth stone, unsmiling. "You miscalculated," he said. "Or perhaps she's better than you give her credit for. Could she be better than you?"

Lisa smarted at the dig. "I still have her on the hook for the wire transfer."

Gallagher nodded. "All or nothing, my dear. Bring her to me or you forfeit."

**

After Lisa left, Thomas Gallagher sat, stewing in his thoughts. Katerina Mills had been in his sights and had slipped through his fingers. He had a sneaking suspicion of how and why.

Gallagher sent a text.

> You breached our agreement.

His anger boiled as he received no answer. He sent another text.

> Where is she?

He hit send and waited.

> She is on her way to meet the Romanov.

Gallagher pursed his lips and typed again.

> The assignment is unnecessary.
> I already gave assurances that I would cover

> the issue with "JR." Call her back and release her to me. I will assume risk and responsibility to close out the matter
> .

Gallagher waited.

> No.

Gallagher tapped a button to exit the text conversation and placed the cell phone on the table. He ruminated on the delicacy of the Reynolds matter, the police involvement. It would only grow worse. He would not deal with Reynolds directly. He would not lower himself to negotiate with someone so unstable, so unworthy of his attention.

He placed a phone call, his anger rising with each ring.

"Yes," Smith's voice came over the line.

"She's gone off the radar," Gallagher said shortly. "I suspect she has left the area."

"May I ask how you know this?" Smith asked.

"She is on her way to meet a client," Gallagher answered, ignoring the question. "I will forward information on his last known whereabouts and aliases. Locate him and you will locate her. Understand?"

"Understood," Smith said and clicked off the call.

Thomas Gallagher sat, holding his cell phone in his hand.

Katerina Mills could be lost.

He would not allow that to happen.

Chapter 46

Huddled in a dark corner, he coughed and sputtered. He listened for the footsteps, for any hint of sound that told him the kidnapper had returned. He strained at the shackles on his wrists and ankles, even as they dug into his skin. He cried again, the salt stinging his eyes. He rubbed at his face, scratched at his matted hair, sickened by his own stench. He didn't know how long he'd been laying in his own filth.

His stomach howled and his mouth was so dry he couldn't make saliva. He put his hand to his stomach, feeling the bone underneath the flimsy covering of skin. The meager scraps of food had stopped coming. He didn't remember when they had stopped.

The metallic screech of a door opening somewhere, and he curled up tighter, pressing himself into the corner, waiting for the kidnapper to come in. After a gap of silence, his captor entered the space, silent as always. No matter how he begged, the kidnapper wouldn't utter a word.

Now, the kidnapper busied himself with a tangle of cords, equipment, and a compact box that resembled a computer tower. Suddenly, a blare of lights cut into the gloom; on a table he arranged a laptop with a webcam. Then he took out a black bag, laying it on the table and taking out tools.

"Please," the captive begged. "I didn't do anything to you," he cried. "I didn't do anything to anybody."

"Oh, but you did, Mr. Temple."

A voice from the monitor. The kidnapper grabbed Will by his chains, hauling him to the spot directly in front of the webcam. Will looked at the face on the screen and his hands came up, pressed together, a prayer and a pleading.

"No, please, you got it all wrong. I didn't hurt her. I didn't do that. We were friends. We liked each other."

"Yes, I know."

Will Temple, on his knees, pleaded before the webcam. "We weren't trying to hurt anybody."

"I'm sure," John Reynolds said, his voice soft and empathetic. "But the fact of the matter is you penetrated my wife without my permission."

Reynolds' face filled the screen except for a glimpse of plain paneling behind him.

"Please," Will cried. "Please let me go. You'll never hear from me again. I'll disappear."

Reynolds laughed. "My God," he said, almost to himself. "She had no taste. An imbecile every time."

Will yanked at the chains attached to the pipe. They rattled and shook but held fast. "That's right. I'm just an actor. I'm nothing to you. Let me go," he said, pulling harder even as his shoulders felt like they would dislocate from the sockets.

The kidnapper moved with a calm precision, snatching one of Will's feet.

Will Temple struggled as his foot was attached to a spreader bar. He twisted in vain, and the kidnapper caught the other foot. Will found himself on his knees, his legs forced apart. A hysteria overtook him, and he flailed, uselessly yanking at the chains, emitting deep rhythmic grunting sounds. He heard Reynolds chuckling.

Exhausted, Will Temple stopped struggling and whimpered, "Please, please I'm sorry. I'm just an actor."

"I'm sure this will be your most lifelike performance," Reynolds said.

Will Temple didn't hear the chuckling anymore. He only heard his own screams.

Chapter 47

Be free. Someone should.

Katerina jerked awake, her hands at her throat, fighting an invisible threat. She coughed, then pulled in a deep gulp of air. One hand went to the sacred stone around her neck. She oriented herself, trying to remember the dream. In her head she had heard Felicia's voice, but she had seen Will Temple, a fleeting glimpse, a momentary sensation of inexplicable, painful connection,

Katerina glanced over at her seatmate, a man dressed in business casual. Her eyes still filmy with sleep, she mistook him for Carter; she thought he bore a slight resemblance around the eyes and chin.

His eyes flicked over at her with the flash of a warm smile. "Bad dream?"

She nodded. "The kind where you know all you have to do is open your eyes, but you can't."

He nodded. "Hate those." He handed her his packet of peanuts. "You're okay."

She smiled her thanks as she took the little gift. While she munched on the snack, Kat stared out the window and waited for her head to clear.

She tried again to piece together a recollection of her dream, but it had fled. I didn't even see a spirit animal, she thought wistfully. Rachel had said sometimes it comes in a dream. She didn't remember seeing any lions, tigers, or bears. Oh my, she thought. *You're on your own. Figure it out.*

She knew her play would not hold off Reynolds for long. She didn't understand how it had worked. *All that matters is that it did work . . . for now.* She could finish this job, replace some of the money Reynolds took, collect her mother, and get on the move, outrunning Reynolds, Sheridan, Massone, and the drug dealers.

And what about the drug dealers? *If they had planned to kill me all along, why did the cleaner in Richie's house let me walk? Because of*

Carter? Never. They could have taken care of him, too. A sickening realization of fear rushed through her. What if the attacker in the restaurant wasn't connected to the drug dealers? *What if they try again? Will I see it coming?*

Katerina shivered in the stale, recirculating air, thick with the effluence of everyone's coughs and sneezes. She realized she never thought about finishing college and going to law school anymore. *Because that's over now.*

This is what happens when you're desperate.

***

Katerina had fled New York in the middle of a biting, vicious winter and deplaned in the California sunshine. Carrying her overnight bag, she walked through the open sliding doors of the terminal and into the delicious warmth of a balmy seventy-five-degree day. *I love LA.*

***

Katerina followed the herd onto the shuttle bus for the ride to the rental car company, her seatmate still with her. Even though he appeared preoccupied with his cell phone, Kat's antennae stayed up, an uneasy feeling prickling at the hairs on the back of her neck.

Thirty minutes later, Katerina itched for the smiling, obsequious rental representative to finish touting the freshly washed car and reviewing its pristine condition. She signed the papers as Beth Miller and handed the pen and clipboard over. He opened the door for her to take possession of the vehicle.

"I hope you sleep better tonight," she heard from behind and turned to see her traveling companion moving off to his own car. She kept an eye on him until he pulled out of the lot and disappeared. Kat's attention broke away at the buzz of an incoming text.

Delano
Laguna. Wed. 5 p.m.
Zilinsky

Katerina texted back "ok" and shoved the phone back in her purse. *Shit.* She would be stuck at the hotel for at least two nights, if not more.

Pulling out of the rental lot, she headed for the 405. She wouldn't stay in Laguna; a reasonable distance, like Irvine, would do.

Settled in for the drive, she made a call, her heart pounding in her chest until she heard the familiar voice say, "Katerina, what's happening with you?"

"Hi, Mom," Kat said, letting out a relieved breath.

"Are you all right, my girl?" her mother asked.

"I'm still here, Mom."

They spoke a few minutes and then Kat heard a voice in the background.

"Rachel wanted me to ask if you've had a vision of your spirit animal yet," her mother said.

The only animals I've seen are a pack of wolves and a Tasmanian devil. "Tell her not yet, Mom. I'm still looking."

Chapter 48

"Where the fuck are you?"

"Iowa," Katerina shot back, checking to see if the hotel guest next to her in the breakfast buffet line had heard James Sheridan's question through the phone.

"Get your ass back here," Sheridan said.

Katerina carried her tray to a table at the furthest edge of the dining area. "I'm working remotely," Kat said. *Working on getting the hell away from you as fast as possible.*

"I don't give a shit what you're doing," he said. "Get back here and find the dumbshit."

Sorry Shamus, that's your job.

"Why haven't *you* found him yet?" she baited. "You know, with all the technology you have at your disposal."

Sheridan laughed. "His car was found at the airport. It's bullshit. He's too fuckin' stupid to skip town."

"Hmm," Kat said. "Maybe he's with my dad. Maybe you should look a little harder. You know, since you're a trained investigator and all. This is me hanging up."

"You can't get out, you know."

Katerina had just pulled the phone from her ear when she heard it. She drew the phone back.

"You still there? Good," Sheridan said. "You know, I've had this job for a while. I've met a lot of people in your position."

"What position?" Kat asked.

He ignored her. "They get a bright idea that they can make a getaway but that's just a fantasy. You know there's no escape, right?"

Katerina searched for an answer but found no smart-ass remark ready to trip off her tongue.

"Wow, maybe you do belong out in the cornfields. Who would've thought you'd be so naïve?" Sheridan gave a mirthless chuckle. "Okay, Iowa. Keep your armed guard standing watch out at the farm. The longer I wait, the bigger your tab. When the time is right, you pay up. One way or another."

The cell phone clicked off.

Katerina tucked the phone away in her purse. She picked at her eggs until discarding the tray and heading back upstairs to her room. After ten minutes of flipping channels, she grabbed her purse and keys and went out.

***

She drove down the PCH toward Laguna with the windows open, basking in the balmy breeze coming off the Pacific. She took a deep breath, loving the freedom of flying down the highway. Katerina remembered little of her time as a toddler in California. *Does this bring anything back? Can you see them? Your mother? Your father? What happened here?*

She spotted a beach nestled against a towering rock wall. Pirate's Cove, she thought, watching the tide roll onto the sandy beach, then ebb away. Driving on, she gazed up at the homes cut into the rock of the high cliffs, multi-colored monopoly houses appearing deceptively safe and sound. A West Coast Positano, she thought, wondering if that might be a suitable place to hide.

***

She left the car in a parking garage and walked toward Main Beach. Abandoning the self-talk, she opted for a stroll along a row of art galleries. Lingering in each one, she took in the beach scenes and seascapes with pallets of soft, muted blues and greens. Katerina thought of an exhibit back in New York, a stark white space with hardwood flooring that creaked under her every footstep. On the walls, installations of boxes with tiny buttons, insistent blinking lights that formed frenetic traffic patterns.

Yes, Dorothy. You are not in Gotham anymore.

The change of scenery, the physical distance from New York, the sunshine, even the palm trees began to work its anesthetizing magic. For the first time, her problems were *out there*, somewhere far away.

Exiting the gallery, Kat stepped out into the dazzling light, the warm sunshine caressing her skin. She strolled along, coming to an archway leading into a plaza. She discovered a set of shops nestled within, with stairs in the center, leading up to a second level. A young boy manned a makeshift stand selling pure oils outside a perfume shop. She judged him to be around twelve, blond with an angelic face. Her interest piqued, Katerina inched closer. As she began to examine the products, he disappeared inside the shop.

Suddenly sensing someone behind her, she stiffened, a surge of panic seizing her. She made to bolt but a strong arm snaked around her; she couldn't move.

"Easy," a voice whispered in her ear.

Her breath expelled out of her lungs, eyes closing as she sagged against him. He had whispered in her ear and held her this way before; she didn't know whether to laugh or cry.

Turning around, Katerina opened her eyes to look into the face of Alexander Winter.

Chapter 49

Under the shaded seclusion of the stairs, Katerina sank into the comforting strength of Winter's embrace as they kissed. His lips were warm and insistent, releasing a flood of desire within her; she could feel the flush of heat blooming in her cheeks. She closed her eyes, giving a small sigh as he drew her closer, running his fingers through her hair. Wrapping her arms around his body, she strained against him.

"Alex," she murmured, as his lips barely brushed the bruised skin, trailing tender kisses over her cheek and neck.

When the boy came out of the shop, they slid apart under his curious glance.

Katerina took a moment to examine Winter, fit and healthy in his black slacks and crisp white shirt. As always, he was clean shaven, his usual trim thatch of hair grown a bit longer; she decided she liked it.

With his arm around her waist, they moved to leave. As they passed the table in front of the shop, the boy wordlessly offered a tester strip. They stopped and Kat took the strip, running it over her wrist; she held out her arm. Winter leaned in, catching the vanilla scent. He glanced up, smiling at the rosy blush in her cheeks. Withdrawing a roll of cash from his pocket, he peeled off a few bills and handed it over as the boy put a small, delicate bottle in a bag.

Chapter 50

In the car, Katerina held Winter's hand, feeling his warm strength seeping through her, simultaneously stirring serenity and excitement within her. This is how we're supposed to be, she thought, looking over at him. His eyes were hidden behind his mirror sunglasses. Sensing her scrutiny, he brought her hand to his lips, kissing her palm; she sucked in a breath.

He pulled the car into the lot of the Ritz-Carlton and parked. Taking off his glasses, he turned to her, the inky black of his eyes sending ripples of exhilaration tumbling deep in her belly. Drawing her close, he kissed her, long and deep; she let out a sigh of satisfaction.

When they parted, he drew his key card from his pocket and said, "Executive suite, fourth floor. Go in first and head straight for the elevator. I'll be right behind you."

She nodded and slid out of the car.

***

The hotel lobby was spare yet elegant, gleaming white, accented with pink floral touches. Katerina glided across to the elevators.

Keeping an eye on the floor numbers above the closed doors, she fidgeted, each number lighting in its turn, seeming like a small eternity. She waited, consumed by thoughts of what would be coming next . . . when they entered the room, when he closed the door, when he came to her . . .

The doors opened.

"Hi, beautiful."

Katerina's heart lurched at the sight of Daniel Clay standing before her.

"Imagine running into you," he said, then glanced behind her.

Katerina turned to see a stone-faced Alexander Winter.

"Oh, sure," Clay said with a laugh. "Of course. Are you two staying here?"

Katerina waited for Winter to answer.

"We're having lunch here," Winter said, his voice low and cold.

"Great," Daniel Clay said, clapping his hands together as he stepped out of the elevator. "I'm hungry. Let's eat."

Chapter 51

The displeasure in Alexander Winter's face had burgeoned into outright hostility, tinged with an implied violence toward Daniel Clay.

Clay seemed to take no notice, chattering as he dug into his eggs Benedict. He took up a napkin and dabbed at his mouth. "You don't look happy to see me."

"I'm not," Winter said.

Clay gave a snort of a laugh and turned his attention to Katerina. "So how are you, beautiful?" He nodded toward her cheek. "You look a little worse for wear."

"Everything's Gucci," Kat said.

"Good. Glad to hear it, because, you know, you didn't look so good when I saw you last."

"How did the Van Gogh work out?" Winter asked.

"Excellent," he said.

Kat let out a small sound of derision.

Clay narrowed his gaze at her. "Surprised? Why?"

Immediately aware of her mistake, Kat cleared her throat and settled for a shake of her head. "Surprised to see you," she mumbled.

She glanced over to Winter, hoping he hadn't registered her screw up. He sat stilted, uncomfortable, as if he couldn't find a place for himself. It reminded her of their first robbery together, his OCD attack in the van. Now, he still hadn't touched his plate or silverware. *Shouldn't he be rearranging everything? Moving the fork from the left side of his plate to the right and then back again?* An urge to help him without knowing how occupied her. She broke off a piece of bread, holding it out toward him. He nodded with a soft smile and accepted it, eating it plain.

"You shouldn't be," Clay said to her. "Haven't you heard of synchronicity?"

Katerina caught the slight flick of Winter's attention directed away from the table.

Kat came back to Clay and shook her head as an answer.

"What is one of the most enduring, basic principles of human existence, a building block of natural law?"

"Always brush after meals," she said.

Clay chuckled. "Synchronicity is all about repeating patterns, meaningful coincidences. Believe or not, life really is all about meeting the same person over and over again."

"Until when?" she asked, suddenly discomfited by the thought.

"Until you learn what you're supposed to learn," Winter said. "What are you supposed to learn, Daniel?"

Daniel Clay smiled. "Me? I'm learning patience, and persistence. You don't realize how much you need me."

"Don't you have that backwards, Daniel? You wouldn't have your prize without me, without us," Winter said, nodding toward Katerina.

Clay pointed a finger toward Winter. "Exactly, if Bonnie and Clyde are getting back together, I'm thinking you need the whole gang."

"Doesn't that make you Clyde's unfortunate brother, Buck, who gets wasted?" Kat asked.

Daniel Clay clasped his hands to his heart, feigning an injury. "Beautiful—harsh. And after I took care of you."

"You mean, after *he* took care of me," Kat said, nodding toward Winter.

"Hey, I helped, didn't I help, Mr. Winter?" Clay didn't wait for an answer and shrugged off the discussion. "So, what are you crazy kids doing out here?"

"It's ten degrees in New York. Do you need to ask?" Kat offered even as a flush of guilt vibrated in her chest. *Winter. He knows Winter's name. Because of me. I'm responsible. This is why you should disappear and stay far away from him.*

"It's a vacation? Mr. Winter doesn't take vacations. Mr. Winter is a workaholic, aren't you, *Bob*? As a matter of fact, I think you're on the job now."

***

Daniel Clay did most of the talking but Winter still did not eat or drink. His tight smile and the hard glint in his eyes increased Kat's growing panic. She wondered if Winter was angry only with Daniel.

She drifted back to the conversation. ". . . so, I've been catching a little culture, visiting a museum," he was saying, "I bet you've been to a lot of museums, haven't you, *Bob*."

"I don't like museums," Winter said.

"That's like a kid saying he doesn't like the candy store."

Winter's lips twitched.

"As a matter of fact, you've been to several museums, Bob. The Getty, the Huntington Library, the Hammer—"

"I got a deal on Groupon," Winter said.

Clay leaned in, lowering his voice and pleading his case to Katerina as if they were alone. "Do you know some of the biggest museum heists have never been solved?"

"That doesn't mean they were a good idea," Winter said.

Clay continued his attention to Katerina. "You see, the thing about museums, believe it or not, is more of them than you think have lousy security systems. There's no way to afford an insurance policy that would ever cover the true dollar amount of the loss."

"That's why a museum is a waste of time. You're stuck with something you can't sell," Winter said.

"Unless you have a private buyer," Clay pointed his fork at Winter to emphasize his point. "You can always find a buyer." He turned his attention back to Katerina. "The barter system is not dead in twenty-first century economics. It is alive and well. Artwork is very popular these days as payment."

"Who accepts artwork in place of cash?" Kat said.

Clay smiled and looked at Winter. "She's cute."

Katerina felt the sting of embarrassment at the put-down.

Winter caressed her back. "Your salmon is getting cold," he said softly.

Kat took his correction. *Translation: keep your mouth shut. You're out of your league.*

"Art can be used to pay for anything, pharmaceuticals, weapons, people—"

"She doesn't need to know about any of that," Winter said.

Clay shrugged. "The point is, *Bob,* I'm willing to be an open book."

"Because you're a stand-up guy," Winter said.

"Exactly. I am out here to acquire something for a client. I think you're here for the same reason, and I'm wondering if it's the same item."

"Daniel, you have a one-track mind. I'm here on vacation. I don't have any clients."

A buzzing noise sounded and everyone at the table checked their phone. Winter hesitated as he took out the vibrating cell phone.

Clay gave him a wide smile. "Please, take it," he said. "Clients don't like to be kept waiting."

Winter excused himself, getting up and stepping out of the dining room.

Daniel Clay turned to Katerina with a smile. "I know what Mr. Winter is doing here," he said. When he leaned in, the smile slipped from his face. "So tell me, beautiful, what are *you* doing here?"

***

"Disneyland," she said. "I'm a sucker for the princess makeover."

"Cute," he said, hovering in Kat's space. "I see someone has already worked you over, Snow White. Didn't you have enough fun in the forest? Don't you learn?"

"I guess not. Why don't you educate me," Kat said.

"Everything," he said, running a finger around the curve of her shoulder, "is a commodity, even a pretty girl who's where she doesn't belong. She could get into trouble."

"Or she could be fine," Katerina said, but her voice came out small and insecure.

"Or she could disappear, put on a private flight, taken by car, or better yet, by boat. Then they'll decide where to sell you." He sat back.

"The world is a big place, beautiful. He won't find you," Clay said, nodding toward the restaurant's entrance.

Katerina followed his sight line, glancing back behind her. At the sound of rustling, she turned back to find Daniel with his hand in her purse. She grabbed it back, but he already had the driver's licenses out and in his hand.

"Hello Beth," Daniel Clay said. He held up the second license. "Or should I call you Catherine?"

He leaned toward her and Kat snatched the licenses from him with one hand while shoving him away with the other. Clay grasped her wrist and held fast, pulling her in close. "Don't think you'll be able to do that. That'll get you a beating. One of many. The slightest infraction will bring punishment. Day after day, you'll lie down, stand up, get on your knees, bend over. And every day you'll think, 'I can survive one more day.' Prince Charming is not going to come for you and wake you from your nightmare with a kiss. Go home, beautiful. Get out now and go home."

He released her. The air shifted as Winter returned and took his seat. His eyes locked on the driver's licenses shaking in her hand.

"Who would like to tell me what I missed," Winter said.

Chapter 52

In the parking garage, Winter pulled the car in next to Katerina's rental. He cut the engine and she curled into his embrace.

Kat breathed a contented sigh as his mouth closed over hers for a slow kiss.

When they parted, she said, "You have to change hotels."

Winter nodded. "So do you. What was Daniel telling you when I stepped away from the table?"

"Scary stories about the future," she said. "Nightmares."

"Like what?"

"He said I could get—taken. No one would know where I was."

Winter's expression darkened with anger even as he ran a gentle finger along her jaw. "I know where you are."

"Why did we even have lunch with him? You told me he's dangerous."

"Yes, I did."

"More dangerous than a corrupt DEA agent?"

"Yes."

Katerina shrugged in annoyance. "He lied to you." she said.

"Yes, he did," Winter said, leaning in for another kiss, soft but insistent. "But you already told me that," he whispered when they broke away.

Katerina avoided his gaze, her cheeks burning with fresh embarrassment. She nodded.

Winter pulled back. "Simon Marcus wasn't driving to Canada in a snowstorm to sell a fake Van Gogh."

"He didn't know," Katerina said, burying her lips in the crook of his neck, listening to the quick, heavy sound of his breathing.

"Who pulled the switch?"

"Marcus' wife. She changed out the original painting for a fake before I ever picked up the car."

"What else did our Daniel tell you?" Winter asked.

"He warned me to leave." She hesitated. "I screwed up back there."

"Yes, Katerina, I know," Winter said. "You'll learn."

She lifted her head. "Will I be as good as you?"

"You'll be better than me." He kissed her forehead. "Do you want to tell me the rest of what happened in Vermont?"

Katerina gave Winter a recap, ending with, "and then I broke into Richie's house and stole his laptop and fifty thousand dollars that belonged to the drug dealers who moved in on my father's business. I'm sure they'll want it back."

"And Richie?"

"Dead," Katerina said, her voice matter of fact. "When I came downstairs, I . . . uh . . . found the cleaner."

Winter squeezed her tighter into his embrace. While she gazed at him, he stared out the window, the muscles of his jaw working.

"Do you know why he let you walk?"

"Carter was outside the house . . . and . . . before Christmas, I contacted the dealers through an intermediary. I said I could deliver Sheridan, but I didn't give his name. I sent a clue where to find him, but they didn't take the bait. They're still waiting."

She took his expression as both surprise and condemnation. "I screwed up again."

"I didn't say that," Winter said. "I didn't say that at all. Did you see Sheridan?"

Kat nodded. "He showed up at the farm."

"Don't let him rattle you. If he could do something, he would have done it already. When are you going to tell me the rest?"

"You know what happened in the restaurant."

Winter caressed the bluish tinge of a bruise on her cheek. "What happened in New York?"

Katerina didn't answer.

"Does it have something to do with the break in at your apartment? Or the earrings?"

Kat shook her head. "You're—you're very special to me."

He smiled, a touch of amusement in his eyes. "Go on," he said.

"I can't have you caught up in this."

"No one's caught me yet."

"I'm the one who screwed up, when we were upstate. I mentioned your name to Daniel."

"You were in shock."

"I'm responsible."

He kissed her forehead. "He would've found out eventually."

"He knows your name."

"It's not my name," Winter said.

"It is to me. When are you going to tell me who Daniel Clay really is?"

"When you can lie to everyone."

She took his correction in silence.

"Katie, what made you come here?'

The answer sat on the tip of her tongue. *Because I need money, a lot of money, to get away, to disappear. That's what I was going to do. Until I saw you.*

"Work," she said. "I have an appointment with the client tomorrow. Why are you here?"

"Work," he said, "in LA."

Sliding his hand into the mass of her silky hair, he kissed her.

A burst of heat flowed through her; she fumbled with the buttons of his shirt, moving to press her mouth against the warmth of his bare skin. She heard the ragged intake of his breath and raised her head to find his eyes half-closed. A rush of pleasure filled her at being able to affect him that way, that he could be content with her.

Long, deep kisses followed by soft caresses made Katerina surrender herself to a delicious senselessness until the slamming of a car door broke the moment. They jolted at the noise, staring at the fogged windows, breathing in a shared cadence. Winter leaned back on the head rest. Katerina slipped her hand in his; his grip tightened. They sat in silence.

After a few minutes, he sat up and pulling an envelope from his jacket pocket, he handed it to her. She slipped open the lip to find a driver's license, social security card, and a credit card.

"Prepaid. For whatever you need."

She lifted her wallet out of her purse and opened it, revealing the prepaid credit and gift cards.

His eyebrows quirked. "Well done." He plucked the card out of the envelope. "It has ten thousand."

"Thank you, but I can't take what's yours."

"I don't mind sharing."

"I won't be a burden. You're not John Robie."

Winter answered her with a bemused expression.

"Cary Grant," Kat said. "*To Catch A Thief*? John Robie, the wealthy retired thief, living in his hilltop villa in the French Riviera."

"Not yet," Winter said. "In the meantime, there's enough for two." He placed the card in her hand and folded her fingers over it. "Keep it, just in case."

She shifted the card between her fingers. "Wait a minute. How did you know you needed to have this ready for me? Who told you I was coming out here?" She stopped. "Luther."

"B plus," he said. "It took you a while to figure it out."

Her brows furrowed. "You distracted me," she said—and then another realization dawned. "The guy sitting next to me on the plane."

"A minus," Winter said. "He said you look cute while you sleep. He said you had a nightmare."

"He looked like Carter."

"He should. They share the same mother. His name is Keyes."

"How do you know them?"

"Work," Winter said. "Years ago."

Katerina's impatience wanted the whole story, but she decided to be happy with what he gave. Winter would not reveal anything until she proved to be a trustworthy keeper of his secrets. She placed her hand on his arm. "We could go somewhere else?" she offered.

"I have to make other arrangements now—for both of us. That's going to take time."

"Tonight?"

"I have to work," he said.

"I don't suppose you can skip a night," Kat whispered.

"No, I can't."

A toxic mix of frustration and disappointment hung between them as they sat in silence.

"I have to get rid of the car, too?" she asked.

"Yes. When you get back to your hotel, pack up and check out. Return the rental car. I'll arrange for another car and text you your new hotel reservation."

Katerina nodded. "Why didn't you eat?" she asked. "You must be hungry."

"Hungry for something else. It will have to wait."

She tucked the envelope into her purse.

They came together for a last kiss. He forced himself away from her, got out of the car, and went around to the passenger side. Holding open the door, he offered his hand to help her out. Settling her into the driver's seat, he closed the door and stood back as Kat started the car and maneuvered out of the garage.

***

A few hours later, Alexander Winter checked into another hotel. Another name; another identity. He wrestled with the lost opportunity to be with Katerina. His mind looped over every planned moment, down to the soft breeze coming off the ocean and fluttering through the curtains of an open window. His hands in the silky waves of her hair as he rocked her back and forth, her lips close to his ear, her sighs filling his head.

Another sensation intruded, choking the thoughts away, breaking the moment. Hunger. He hadn't eaten. A familiar flash to his childhood, surrounded by food, but unable to eat. Starving in the midst of plenty.

Why did we even have lunch with him?

Because I need to keep an eye on Daniel Clay. Because Daniel Clay is dangerous, much more dangerous than a corrupt DEA agent. I needed to have lunch with Daniel to find out what Mr. Clay is after, and now I know.

Winter had buried himself so deep for so long; with each passing year, he tried to convince himself the chance of discovery became more remote.

He never believed it.

At least one of the servers in the restaurant belonged to Daniel.

A drink of water, a taste of food from a fork, a wipe of his mouth on a napkin.

Daniel Clay with a DNA sample would be a deadly combination.

And life as I know it could end.

Chapter 53

Katerina chose a dark blue, conservative skirt and jacket ensemble, complimented by a straight, brunette shoulder-length wig for the meeting. She entered the restaurant and surveyed the formal, elegant, pristine, white dining room. Winter would approve, she thought.

The maître d' led her to an alcove tucked away behind a low, decorative gate. A man sat alone at a table next to the window. She nodded her thanks and sat down.

The man took no notice of her, continuing to dig into his filet mignon. He motioned toward her place setting with his knife.

"No, thank you," she said, studying him. He was in his fifties, soft, with abundant, wavy salt and pepper hair, and a square, full face. *Mr. Zilinsky, I presume?*

Katerina knew the drill; forget the small talk and get down to business. "How can I help you, Mr. Zilinsky?"

"I am denied my rightful place in my family," Zilinsky said, his accent thick and hard to place.

Kat's lips pursed. *Okay, here we go.*

"You're having a dispute with a family member?" she asked.

"I am in dispute with the whole world," he said, the knife pointing outward as he gesticulated.

"Why don't you start from the beginning," Kat said.

Zilinsky continued to eat as he spoke, appearing lax, almost bored, hovering between ennui and disgust. "The beginning, the beginning is the Revolution."

The Revolution?

Katerina asked a question but had a sinking feeling that she knew the answer. "Which revolution are we talking about, Mr. Zilinsky?"

When he leaned in, a small piece of meat clung to the corner of his mouth. It moved, dancing as he went on.

"When they destroyed the *Rodina*, they destroyed the motherland. What other Revolution is there?" he asked, waving the knife.

Kat worked to keep a blank expression, but she was sure she wasn't getting it right. She gave herself a pat on the back for paying attention to Uncle Sergei's stories of the history of his homeland, ensuring every word would be committed to memory. "There were two, Mr. Zilinsky. Are you referring to the February Revolution and the abdication of the Tsar or the October Revolution where Vladimir Lenin overthrew the provisional government?"

Zilinsky gaped at her in silence. Suddenly, he lunged forward, the words tumbling out in a hoarse whisper almost faster than he could form them. Even his unkempt mass of hair seemed to rise. "I am talking of the death of my great-grandfather, Tsar Nicholas the Second, Nikolay Aleksandrovich, and his family. They were taken, all of them, marched like dogs into the basement of Ipatiev House and shot."

He stopped speaking when the server appeared with a bottle. He motioned toward his empty glass. "Yes, fill up, please."

Once the server disappeared, Zilinsky continued. "They raped my beloved country, the stinking Bolsheviks. They wanted it for themselves. But it belongs to me. They said the whole family was dead, but it was not true. Not true at all. Lies. There were survivors. I am the proof. I am the rightful ruler of Mother Russia. Retrieve it for me."

Katerina could only stare. *What the hell is this?* "I'm sorry, Mr. Zilinsky, you're saying the children were not killed and you are a direct descendant of the last Tsar of Russia."

"*Da,*" Zilinsky said, returning his attention to his plate.

"I see," Kat said. "Which one of the children are you a descendant of?"

"Alexei."

Oh bullshit. "I'm sorry?"

Zilinsky sat back, his eyes narrowing in annoyance. "I am the grandson of Alexei Nikolaevich, Tsarevich of Russia, and only son of the Tsar."

"How, exactly, did Alexei, a hemophiliac, survive and live to have a child?"

Zilinsky viewed her with his chin raised in indignation, his mouth pinched. "Secret medicine from Rasputin," he said.

Oh, bullshit!

Katerina placed her hands on the table and took a breath. "Mr. Zilinsky—are you saying Rasputin wasn't dead, either?"

Zilinsky tossed back another swallow of wine. "No, no, no, dead like a doorknob. But he left special medicine for Alexei, my grandfather."

Is this after your grandfather settled in a secluded cottage in an enchanted wood with seven dwarves? Katerina, you moron. You never expected this.

"Mr. Zilinsky, everyone knows the family died," Kat said. "The remains were found. DNA tests were done—"

"No!" he said, slapping his hand on the table. "The church did not accept the results. It was never conclusive!"

"There are other descendants with lineage all the way back to Emperor Nicholas the First. What about the surviving branches of the family—the Alexandrovichi, the Nikolaevichi, the Mikhailovichi—"

Zilinsky choked on his food, his face flushing red. He gulped water, coughed, then mopped his face with his napkin. "Imposters!" he said finally. "You are talking about frauds. I am the only true heir. I am the last Romanov." Zilinsky held up his wine glass, considering it. He emptied it and placed it down on the table. "I want my—birthright."

Katerina considered the cost of getting up and walking out.

How the hell am I supposed to do this?

You can't. That's the point.

Katerina's blood began to boil. *MJM sent me all the way across the country to fire me when the job can't be done. How did Jasmine know I would take the job?*

Katerina took a breath as the answer dawned on her. *Of course. MJM knows all about Reynolds. And they were watching.*

Like a jackass, I panicked and gave up the job with Lisa. How am I going to get the money? How am I going to get out? How am I going to get my mother out?

The waiter appeared and refilled Zilinsky's glass. He took a long drink, gazing at Katerina over the rim, considering her for a long, pregnant moment.

When the server left the table, Zilinsky said, "There is a man. Viktor Mikhailovich, of the Mikhailovichi, descendant of the Grand Duke Michael Nicolaevich."

"What about him?"

"He has a house on Balboa Island. He has it."

"Your birthright," Kat said.

"*Da*. Retrieve it for me."

Katerina weighed her words as she restrained the angry tirade ready to burst forth.

How much is MJM paying you to get rid of me?

"I'll take care of it, Mr. Zilinsky," Katerina said.

Chapter 54

Katerina grabbed her cell phone, checked the time, and then tossed it down on the bed. Stumbling into the bathroom, she looked in the mirror at the tired and drawn face staring back at her, as if she had spent a long night making bad decisions.

Letting out a groan of disgust, she went into the living area and found Alexander Winter sitting on the couch, two cups of coffee on the table in front of him, Uncle Sergei's bible open on his lap.

"Good morning," he said, taking in the rumpled t-shirt, tousled hair, and strained expression. She sank down next to him. He clapped the book closed and placed on the table. Picking up one of the steaming cups, he held it out to her.

"Mmm," she said, grasping the cup with both hands and inhaling the rich aroma. She closed her eyes.

"You didn't sleep well?" he asked.

"Did you?"

"I didn't sleep," he said.

"How was work?"

"Uneventful," Winter said.

"Is that good?" she asked.

"In my profession, that can be good or bad."

Katerina shrugged. "Why are you here?"

"Attempting to train your senses to realize when someone is in your hotel room," Winter said. He held up his hand to reveal a cord entwined in his fingers, a burnished, ebony stone dangling at the end, flickering green, blue, and gold as it caught the light. "Pretty," he said. "Where did you get it?"

"It was a gift. It's a sacred stone. It's supposed to give me heightened insight and awareness."

"Ironic," he said.

Katerina felt the warmth in her cheeks. "Why are you going through my stuff?" she demanded.

"I'm a thief. I go through everyone's stuff."

"That would be the only reason for you to be here," Kat said, the Zilinsky meeting still festering, leaving her spoiling for a fight.

"I can't read your mind, Katie."

"Do you think I'm stupid?" she blurted.

"I wouldn't be here if I did," Winter said.

Kat gave a disgusted laugh. "Everyone is smarter than me," she said.

"Statistically, that's impossible," he said.

Kat shook her head in objection. "Everyone is getting one over on me. Everyone knows more than I do. I never know enough." Kat slumped back on the couch, as if the battle had already been fought and lost.

Winter took the cup out of her hand and placed it on the coffee table. He slid the necklace over her head, resting the stone on her chest.

"The assignment is bullshit," she said. "There's no way I can complete it. Some idiot says he's a direct descendant of the Romanovs. You know the Romanovs?"

Winter smiled. "I've heard the name."

Kat shot him a sullen look. "This jackass is as Romanov as I'm Russian—and he is definitely not the grandson of the young Tsarevich."

"He's the grandson of Alexei Romanov? Interesting. What exactly did the "jackass" ask you to do?"

"Bring him the proof, his birthright."

Winter pulled her close. She sank against him, her body relaxing. "The problem isn't that everyone is smarter than you," he said, his voice gentle. "The problem is your temper. You're letting your temper get the best of you. If the agency knew the assignment is bullshit, why would they give you the job?"

Katerina remained silent, floundering for a lie she knew she couldn't tell. "It's complicated," she said for lack of anything better.

"Mmm," Winter said, and left it at that. "Did he suggest where to start?"

Katerina nodded. "Viktor Mikhailovich. He's a supposed member of one of the remaining branches of the family. He has a house on Balboa, and he has what my client needs to reclaim Russia. And I'm out a hundred thousand dollars."

"Not yet," he said, kissing her temple. "What do you do first?"

Kat thought about it. "I learn all about Viktor Mikhailovich."

Winter squeezed her tighter. "No, first you lose that stubborn attitude. Then, you drop all your preconceived notions. If you don't, you will miss something."

Winter rocked her in his arms, and she fell into the rhythm until he whispered in her ear, "Anytime you want to tell me why you took this job."

She hesitated. "I rode shotgun for Lisa, an assignment from Vermont to New York worth fifty thousand. She screwed me. She refused to pay in cash. To collect, I need to set up an account to hide the money offshore... I don't know how."

Winter swept her hair behind her ears with a studied attention. "Katie, that wasn't my question. What happened to Simon Marcus' money?"

Katerina cast her eyes downward. "I don't have—most of it, anymore," she said.

With the lightest touch of his finger under her chin, he raised her face so she had to look at him. "Sheridan?"

Katerina shook her head.

"Katie, did you go to Sunday school?" Winter asked.

Kat smiled in spite of herself, happy to have the real conversation, not just imagine it in her head. "Yes."

"Do you remember the story of Daniel and the King's dream?"

"The King had a funky dream about the future that no one could interpret. He was about to 'off with everyone's head' when Daniel saved the day. I left my crystal ball in my other purse."

"That wasn't the point of the story."

"And what is the point of the story?"

"No one knows everything. Even doctors need a doctor. I told you that anything you need to know you can learn, if that's what you want. You need to open a shell company and an offshore account so the money can't be found. It's not complicated. All you need is an application, five hundred dollars, a driver's license or passport, and a fax machine. I have someone who will act as the agent."

Katerina stared at Winter, her mouth open.

He smiled.

"Just like that?" she asked.

"Just like that. We'll do it together the first time. Then you'll be able to take care of it yourself. It would be best to set up more than one shell company and then create different accounts to pass the money through."

Kat rested her hand on his chest. "Do we have to go right now?"

"No," he said.

"Did you have any plans for today?" she asked.

Winter smiled. "I'm going to a museum."

Katerina lifted her head. "I thought you don't like museum jobs."

"I don't."

"So, why are you going to a museum?"

"Because I don't like museum jobs."

Katerina tried to parse out the logic from Winter's statement but her thought process got lost in the warmth of his hands stroking her back.

"You realize that doesn't make sense," she said.

"Like a man who wants you to prove he's a Romanov."

Katerina made a face. Winter was right, of course. Everyone was lying. Everyone gave their performance, played their part. *What part do I play? I can't figure out my own situation. Why? Because I can't lie to everyone.* She wound her arms around his torso.

I never want to let you go.

"It would be better if you went with someone, someone who could take attention away from you, leaving you free to do what you need to."

His embrace tightened. "Absolutely not."

"I'd be a diversion."

"You'd be a shill and in harm's way."

"I would be helping. Let me help you." She squeezed her grip to match his. "It would be a perfect opportunity to spend quality time together."

"We could do that right now," he said.

Katerina looked up at him, watching his eyes turn an inky black. "I like the sound of that," she said.

His hand snaked under her nightshirt, the sudden warmth of his touch causing her to sigh.

As he leaned in to kiss her, a rapping at the door intruded. Winter cursed under his breath.

"Housekeeping," a female voice said.

"Come back later, please," Kat called out.

They heard the sound of the key card being inserted into the reader.

"Come back later, please," Katerina called louder.

They listened to jostling noises of the door handle.

The key card reader clicked.

The door handle shifted.

"Just a minute," Winter called out.

A beat of silence.

Kat's heart lurched as Winter broke away from the embrace and bounded off the couch. As he stole to the door, he reached around, extracting a gun from the waistband of his pants.

Kat hurried to the other side of the door.

Winter reached for the door handle, shifting it open.

***

Katerina waited in the eternity of the passing seconds until the door opened and Winter slipped back into the room.

Winter shook his head.

"It could be nothing," Kat said.

"Is that likely?" Winter asked.

"No," she said.

"Katie, why did your agency send you out here?" Winter asked.

The words popped into her mind, perching dangerously on the tip of her tongue.

To kill me.

"It's complicated," Kat said.

Winter nodded. "When I brought you back into the city last month, your phone had spyware installed, gathering phone numbers, text messages, and email addresses."

She went to react, but he cut her off. "I had them cleaned," he said. "I want to check again."

Katerina grabbed her purse, opening the zipper.

"You'll come to the museum with me," Winter said.

Katerina nodded, handing over her phones.

Winter took them, tucking them away in his pocket. "For now, I want you to go shopping."

"I brought clothes with me," Katerina said.

"Head over to Fashion Island while I make arrangements for you."

Katerina didn't question. If Winter wanted her in a public place, that was her best bet right now. Trouble had just knocked on her door and she had no idea who was responsible. What if her visitor had *not* been sent by MJM? Katerina thought of the cleaner in Richie's house. *We're not going to wait forever.* She thought of two FBI imposters upstate in a snowstorm. *Just give us the girl.*

Kat glanced down at the stone dangling from the cord around her neck. Rachel had said it would provide protection. She thought Winter needed it more now. Someone had his burner number, his text messages. *His jeopardy keeps rising. Because of me.*

"Alex, maybe you should go to the museum alone," Katerina said.

Winter wrapped Katerina in a warm embrace. "Why is that?"

"Did you ever go to Sunday school?" she asked.

"Go on," he said with a smile.

"Remember what happened to Daniel because he was loyal, because he was faithful?"

Winter gave Kat a tender kiss on her lips. "I'm not worried about getting thrown into the lion's den. No one's caught me yet."

Chapter 55

"My little Katya, tell me how your Uncle Sergei can help you." Katerina smiled at Sergei's slow, smooth voice coming through the line. She had stopped at a coffee shop for a quick internet search on Viktor Mikhailovich. Pictures revealed a round face, a distinctly European look. He wore his hair in a short chop, flat on his scalp, as if his hairstyle betrayed his manner, blunt, with no time for pleasantries. The oligarch specialized in being a billionaire and staying on the good side of the current Russian government. *Glasnost* had been very good to Viktor. After the Soviet Union fell apart in the early 1990's, Viktor Mikhailovich had been one of the lucky ones to swoop in on the fire sale, devouring oil, mineral, and natural gas companies, former state-owned industries. Viktor possessed a mega yacht, a private island, a seat on the board of the Los Angeles County Museum of Art, and a wife who gleefully tormented him through a nasty divorce that never finalized. Viktor took comfort in an endless supply of young, nubile beauties which only enraged his wife to file further motions to delay the divorce and extort more rubles.

Synchronicity, Katerina thought. If Simon Marcus was here, he and Viktor could have their own club. *If Simon Marcus was alive.*

Katerina shuddered at the thought and threw it off for the business at hand. The biography had one item missing.

"Uncle, can we talk about the Romanovs?"

"You want more history lesson?" he asked.

"Modern history. I'm trying to find out if a Viktor Mikhailovich belongs to the house of the Mikhailovici, one of the branches of the Romanovs."

A long beat of silence followed. "Katya, may I know why you ask this?"

"It's a bit complicated, Uncle."

More silence and then, "I see. No, Viktor Mikhailovich is not member of descendant house of Romanov. He is very wealthy businessman."

"Did he ever buy one of your paintings?"

"I do not share my work with this man."

"Thank you for your help, Uncle."

"Katya, I warned you, watch out for the wolf. You remember I tell you this?"

"Yes, Uncle, I remember."

"This is a wolf. Very dangerous. Forget about Viktor Mikhailovich."

***

By late morning, Katerina pulled into the parking lot at Fashion Island. She ruminated on Zilinsky while she wandered into Neiman Marcus. Winter had been right, of course. She had lost her temper and she would have missed something if not for his guidance. Mikhailovich had nothing to do with the Romanovs; Zilinsky was full of shit. So why pick Mikhailovich as the object of the exercise? Because the name was a convenient fit for Zilinsky's story. *Is that the only reason?*

As her Uncle's warning repeated in her head, Katerina spotted the sign for lingerie. The girlish impulse beat within her like a pounding drum. She followed the arrow.

Watched over by the scantily clad mannequins in barely-there lace, she lingered over the La Perla offerings: silk thongs, garter belts, and bras. She imagined wearing each outfit for Winter, imagining what he would do. Kat glanced around, embarrassed the pink flush of desire could be seen on her face. All of a sudden, a familiar wisp of anxiety intruded. Winter's dark, dangerous look, the inky black pupils of his desire had excited her. But after what she had suffered last year at Sheridan's hands, a specter of fear, unwelcome, unwanted, placed a foot in the door of her mind, holding fast.

"I prefer it in black."

Katerina started at the male voice close to her ear. As she found her breath, she gave a sideways glance at Daniel Clay.

"Good for you," she said, recovering.

Clay laughed and hung by her side, even as she moved away to another table. "You know, I don't think you're considering your options."

Kat kept her eyes on the lingerie. "You're a personal shopper now?"

"No, no," he said, glancing over the items. "I wasn't referring to *clothing* options. I meant companion options."

She stopped to turn and face him. "You've got to be kidding."

He raised his eyebrows in surprise.

"Weren't you the one schooling me on the horrors of human trafficking and forced prostitution? If that's your idea of foreplay, you must be a fun date," Katerina said, walking away.

She kept her eyes fixed on the undergarments and then he was back at her side again. *What the hell is this?*

"Listen," Daniel said, placing his hand lightly at her elbow. "Yeah, I played it a little rough. I was trying to warn you off because I'm concerned about you."

"You're concerned about your fake Van Gogh scam."

Daniel Clay narrowed his eyes.

"Relax, your secret is safe. I don't tell him *everything*. You want to pawn off a copy, be my guest. He wouldn't care—if he knew."

"How did you know?"

Katerina leaned in. "I don't tell *you* everything, either."

Clay searched her expression and ended his examination with a smile. "I like you, kid. I really do."

Katerina bristled at the nickname; the same put-down Philip favored.

"What's wrong with giving me a shot? I'm a nice guy."

Kat laughed.

"Hear me out," Daniel said. His voice held a sharper tone, one that told Kat she should turn around and listen. She faced him, her arms folded across her chest. Daniel approached, the easy-going smile back on his face.

"I bet I can tell you your life, right now," he said.

"Knock yourself out, Nostradamus."

Clay scanned the area for anyone nearby before coming back to her. "I think you're in the middle of something. I think you're looking not for a white horse, but a racehorse, one that's gonna outrun whatever you're into and get you clear."

Katerina worked to keep her expression soft, even bored. She glanced at the mirror behind him, hoping to catch a look at herself, hoping she was playing her part.

"But here's the thing about horse racing. You have to choose the horse that can go the distance, not some worn-out nag ready for the glue factory."

Katerina laughed. "Wow, thanks for the on-the-nose explanation. This has been more fun than a barrel of monkeys. Catch you on the way back, Danny."

Katerina walked away. She pursed her lips in annoyance as he came up alongside her. "Look, I get it," Daniel said, keeping step with her. "The older man, knowledgeable, worldly . . . it's like that movie with Cary Grant."

"*Charade*," Kat said, "with Audrey Hepburn."

"Exactly. I know why you're doing this."

She stopped to face him. "You know what my favorite part is? When Audrey says to Cary, 'You know what's wrong with you?' and he answers, 'No, what?' and then she puts her face right up to his and says, 'Nothing.' That's how I feel about Winter."

Katerina moved off again.

"I was gonna say you're doing this with Bob because you've done it before."

Katerina halted. *How the hell does he know about Philip?*

Clay wandered around her until he stood in front of her, that same, satisfied smile back on his lips. "If I like someone, I want to get to know everything about them," he said. "I mean it's normal for a young woman to become infatuated with her older boss, especially when he's an attorney—"

"What do you want?" Kat asked. *What else do you know?*

"I told you. I like you, Katerina. I think you're a great girl. I think we could have something. But I think you're in a destructive relationship pattern. You're making the same mistake you made last time. Didn't Cary Grant's character use an alias in that movie?"

"He used several," Katerina said.

Clay nodded. "Right. Yeah, I remember now. *Alexander* Dyle. See? Meaningful coincidences. Do you even know *Bob*? What do you know? Don't make the mistake of trusting him, Katerina."

Daniel Clay took his wallet from his pocket and held it open. "You want to check into me? Go ahead. I have a real name, a real childhood, a real everything. Can you say the same for Bob? How many aliases is he using? Yeah, I warned you to go home. For your own good. Because I don't think Alexander Winter is good for you. It's important you remember that."

Katerina searched for a smart-ass comment, something to get on top of the situation. "I did you a favor. I kept your secret. It's important you remember *that*," she said.

He nodded. "I'm ready to show my appreciation. I'm worthy of your trust, Katerina. I'm the real thing." Daniel leaned forward and kissed her cheek. "He wasn't the only one willing to fire a gun. Think about that," he whispered in her ear. When he pulled back, he gave her a cockeyed smile. "Go with the black. Definitely," he said with a wink and walked away.

Katerina tried to blow off the encounter and return to shopping but one of her problems she thought she had left behind in New York had inched its way back into her consciousness. She had no idea what game Daniel Clay was playing; she only knew she didn't want Alexander Winter caught in the middle of something he couldn't escape.

Chapter 56

Retired NYPD detective Timothy Green paced the room.

"Sit down, Mr. Green," Reynolds said.

"I don't want to sit down. Listen, the cop came around. The younger one. I knew he would. I told you, you can't do anything with this one."

"Yes," Reynolds said, "I know."

"I'm out. I want my money and I'm gone. Now."

John Reynolds folded his hands in his lap. "I'm sorry to hear this, but the assignment isn't finished yet. I will be very disappointed if you don't fulfill your obligation. Bruce will be devastated. I don't think he would be able to get past it."

"Don't threaten me," Green said.

John Reynolds held out his hands. "Detective, I merely expressed my disappointment."

"Can the shit. Keep your homicidal houseboy to yourself."

Reynolds' lips twitched.

"Yeah, that's right," Green said. "I know all about you, so don't pull any crap with me. This cop is going to keep coming."

"Yes, well, we'll see," Reynolds said. He rose from his seat and went to the window, gazing at the frozen paradise outside, delicate icicles clinging to the tree branches.

"I want my money," Green repeated, this time the words sounded hollow, without bite.

"I can't possibly pay you when you haven't provided everything to me."

"I told you there's nothing on Cheryl Penn. No nude photos, no secret lesbian lovers, no S and M lifestyle. Nothing. *She* didn't fuck around on her husband."

Timothy Green didn't see the thin-lipped smile on Reynolds' face as he gazed out the window.

"I wasn't referring to Cheryl Penn," Reynolds said.

"I sent you the pictures."

Reynolds turned around, a flash of anger darkening his face. "Not everything, *Mr.* Green. You followed Miss Mills late last year. You followed her when her detective boyfriend picked her up and took her to his apartment in Brooklyn. You followed her when the detective dropped her off at school the next morning. There are no photos after that, yet you billed for the full day. Where are the rest of the pictures?"

"What happened to your wife's little fuck puppy?" Green pivoted. "The actor, the pretty boy. I'm not going to be an accessory to anything you and your little sicko helper pull off, you hear me?"

Reynolds turned back to the window. "If you want to leave, no one is stopping you, *Mr.* Green. But there will be no payment without the full dossier. You should think about tomorrow. You never know what a new day will bring. That investigation at Internal Affairs could come up again. New evidence could be found. It happens all the time. You have two days to produce the rest of the pictures. Make up your mind quickly, *Mr.* Green. Time is running short. After all, it's going to rain."

Green stormed out.

Reynolds shook his head. Everyone wanted to leave. *Oh Katerina, if you had only stayed where you belonged. All this would have been unnecessary.* He gave a small sigh. Katerina Mills would have to be brought back into line.

He glanced out the window. *It's going to rain.*

Chapter 57

Katerina, wearing an Aidan Mattox scuba crepe plunging halter dress, exited her hotel. At the curb, a black BMW idled; the driver's side door opened. Winter got out to open the passenger door for her. As Kat went to slip into the car, she lingered long enough for him to breathe in her vanilla scented skin and place a soft kiss on her neck; her legs went weak and she was glad to settle into the seat.

Closing the door, Winter circled the car and slid behind the wheel. He handed her cell phones back to her. "They were clean," he said.

She nodded as she tucked them into her purse. "You look dapper," she said. "Or is the correct expression natty?"

He raised his eyebrows. "Neither," he said.

And I was right. No silver spoon upbringing. Definitely a working man. "Who are you today?" she asked, filing her piece of intel away.

"Frederick Mason."

"Why?" she asked, shaking her head in disapproval.

He gave a laugh. "Because he's convenient."

"Does he know this?" Kat asked. As he reached over, she lifted her arms, allowing him to take hold of her seat belt and snap it in place.

"Only if he's had a sudden resurrection."

Katerina went quiet.

"Tragically, Frederick died at the age of four. It's one of the many things not to be proud of in this line of work. Assuming the identity of a deceased child who had a social security number avoids a lot of potential issues."

"How many times have you died?" she asked.

"More than I can count, Katie."

Winter eased the car toward the exit ramp.

Kat studied him as he drove; his eyes stayed fixed on the road. "We have time. We should put it to good use."

Winter smiled. "What do you propose?"

"Twenty questions," Kat said. "Are you game?"

Winter gave a laugh, but his fingers tapped on the gear shift in a rhythmic pattern.

***

When they arrived at the Los Angeles County Museum of Art, Winter pulled the Beamer into a parking spot and cut the engine. The ride had been more quiet and thoughtful than Katerina had expected. She had found the simple exercise of probing for information complicated and frustrating. So far, she had only confirmed Alexander Winter had, in fact, been born, but not much else.

"Do you have a father?"

"Yes," he said, his stilted tone telling her she had made a mistake.

"Do you have a mother?" Kat said, pushing ahead.

"Mmm," he said.

"That's not a yes or a no."

"Yes," Winter said.

He stared at her, his gaze sharp and focused.

"What did I do wrong now?"

He took her hand in his own. "You do realize I'm offering you the benefit of my years of experience."

"Yes," Kat said, sporting a pronounced pout.

He leaned in and gave her a kiss. "It would be helpful if you didn't shit all over that."

She pursed her lips until she answered, "Yes, I want your help, Professor, thank you."

"You asked me if I had a mother and a father. Those are two questions you wasted because the answer is obvious. Unless someone is created through cloning, everyone has a mother and a father. You didn't learn anything more about me than you knew before you got into the car." He leaned over, his lips close to her ear. "Remember, Katerina, you are looking for useful information so you can draw conclusions and plan your next move. Every question should contribute to your goal, whatever that is. If it doesn't, it's the wrong question. Now, what is your goal?"

"To learn everything I can about Frederick Mason slash Steven Bartholomew slash Patrick Hayes slash Alexander Winter."

"Last two questions for today. Make them count."

Katerina thought. "Did you know your father?"

"No," Winter said with a nod of approval.

"Did you know your mother?"

"Yes."

Katerina appealed to him with exaggerated, imploring eyes.

A mischievous grin came across his face. "Okay, one more."

"Have you ever been married?"

"No," Winter said.

"Do you have a girlfriend?"

His eyebrows quirked. "No."

"Have you ever had a girlfriend?"

"No."

Katerina took in this new item of information. "But you—"

"Yes, Katerina, I do."

She thought how to choose her next words. "Then—so—you . . ."

"Make an appointment with a discreet, professional, lady."

"Oh—yes," Kat stumbled, staring at the steering wheel as if it had just become an item of fascination. "Are you nice?"

Winter crooked his head down to meet her eyes.

"With her," Kat said, glancing up at him. "Are you nice?"

"You weren't concerned about my being 'nice' at the hotel."

"I've had time to think about it."

He smiled, his eyes soft and warm. "I'm very nice."

"Always?"

Winter kissed her forehead. "Yes, Katerina. Always."

Katerina gave a nod and sat back. "Now, are we here to see or be seen?"

Winter stared at her, taken aback by the astute question. "Both," he said.

Chapter 58

Heather freshened up and changed the sheets for her next client, a new client. She had covered the ground rules prior to accepting the booking, strict rules that kept her clean and healthy. No fetishes, no S and M, no perversion, golden showering, or defecating. She didn't do role playing or violence; she'd been slapped around enough when she got into this business. She didn't do the girlfriend experience. No psycho-emotional babble or bullshit. She offered a bed, not a couch. She sometimes marveled at it all, realizing she had come a long way from hustling at fifteen. She had at least another ten years, easy. But what then?

It hadn't taken long to notice how clients enjoyed boasting of their conquests. Their words flew in one ear and out the other. She'd heard it all and it all sounded the same. Until one day, an idea for a retirement plan had come to her. After that, she had installed the recording system. The clients kept talking. She kept listening—and taping.

Her blood-red silk robe swirled around her ankles as she strolled to answer the knock at the door. She undid the belt a touch so the black lace teddy and garter belt peeked through. Clients liked a teaser, the sign of things to come.

When she opened the door, she found a clean-cut man with a short, neat haircut, wearing a dark three-piece suit, a solid, navy tie; his coat draped over his arm. He appeared fit, solid and imposing, with a stance like a boxer. This didn't surprise her; most of these men had a competitive nature and a healthy ego. They enjoyed keeping their bodies and their businesses in top form.

Heather moved aside to allow him to enter the apartment. In the living room, he placed his coat on a chair and unbuttoned his jacket.

"Would you like a drink?" she asked, stepping behind the bar.

He turned to her. "No, thank you," he said, still standing.

"Why don't you tell me what you do like?"

He smiled. "I like what Steven Bartholomew likes. He gave me your name."

Heather prepared her drink, her hands concealed behind the counter. "I have no idea who that is."

"I apologize. The client who pays from PSL Select Limited. PSL is part of a web of shell companies that includes IGS Capital. Is that better?"

"No, Mr. *Smith,* it isn't," she said, stalling, hoping to buy a few precious seconds. She knew she was in deep shit; the man in her living room had crawled into the bank accounts. *Cop? Maybe once, but not now.*

Wearing a patient, plastic smile, Joseph Smith said, "I'm going to need a description and his other names," Smith said.

"He has a dick and a pair of balls and I have no idea what else he calls himself."

Smith gave a sigh. "Evasive answers are going to cause a problem," he said.

Heather darted out from behind the bar and made for the door, but Smith grabbed her arm, jerking her backward off her feet. His hand clamped on her forearm and twisted; she gasped.

"You are unnecessary," he whispered in her ear. "If this is a vacant space tomorrow, no one will notice. Let's try again. Description and name. He calls himself something with a "W." What is it?"

Heather squirmed. He twisted her arm again and she let out a moan.

"This will go on as long as necessary. What is W's name?" he asked.

"I—"

Smith gave a sudden grunt and pitching forward, fell against her; they tumbled to the floor, Heather pinned beneath his dead weight.

"Get this asshole off me," Heather said, the break in her voice betraying her fear.

Her fixer, well over six feet with a beefy, thick body, had come when she pressed the panic button concealed under the bar. He hauled Smith off, dropping him in a heap to her left. Reaching out his hand, he helped her to her feet.

Heather crouched over Smith's inert body and rifled his pockets. Pulling out his wallet, she scanned the credit cards and counted the cash. Examining the driver's license, she rose to her feet and went to her purse. Taking out her phone, she took a snapshot. She returned to the unconscious man and took a snap of his face.

Heather put everything back and gave instructions. "Dump him somewhere. I need at least three hours to take care of my business here. This place is burned. I'll let you know where to find me."

He nodded. They both went to work.

Chapter 59

On the third floor of the Ahmanson Building, Alexander Winter and Katerina Mills strolled the rooms arm in arm, stopping at each painting in rapt examination. Katerina had been to museums before, but this was different. She peppered him with questions about an artist's background or the period, and his answers came with the unrehearsed ease of one familiar with the subject. It didn't take her long to realize that Alexander Winter not only stole fine art, he possessed a great deal of knowledge about it.

"Why don't you go on ahead," he whispered in her ear, "and I'll catch up."

With a smile and a kiss, she wandered away on a self-tour of discovery, admiring masterpieces by Manet, Tissot, Van Gogh, and others.

As Katerina moved toward the next painting, she encountered a wisp of a man in his late fifties, maybe close to sixty, wearing John Lennon spectacles and a brown tweed suit under a beige overcoat. A yellow bowtie peeked out from under a brown knit scarf wrapped around what she imagined to be a scrawny neck; he clutched an oversized umbrella with a duck head handle. Kat suppressed a smile. *If I blow on him, I bet he'd do a Mary Poppins and float away.*

Curious about this gnome of a man, Katerina inched over. The man suddenly turned his head and peered at her. She smiled and watched his expression morph from surprised to open and artless as he registered her.

He indicated the canvas. "How would you describe this painting, young lady?" he asked in a precise, clipped tone.

"Beautiful," Kat said.

"It is clear you are well acquainted with the concept of beauty," he said, his eyes searching her face. "However, this work is more than beautiful. Take a closer look," he encouraged. "It is very nice to say, 'Ah, what a pretty picture,' but how do you know it's real? What tells you it's real?"

Katerina, at a crossroads between fascination and confusion, stepped closer to the painting, Monet's *The Beach at Honfleur*. An oil on canvas, it depicted a craggy beach, sailboats on the water, and a brilliant sky with drifting, vibrant clouds. At least that's how she would describe it.

"Go on, my dear," he coaxed, "what tells you this is a Monet?"

"I have no idea," she said.

"An honest answer," he said, cocking his head to one side and gazing at her. "I once authenticated a Monet for a Rothschild, and do you know, he said the exact same thing." Lifting the umbrella, he pointed to a stroke of paint. "Monet was consumed with the depiction of light. See how he paints to render reflected light. Monet was quite fond of using lead white in order to realize the effect."

"You specialize in Impressionist paintings?" Katerina asked.

"All art and antiquity concerns me, young lady, especially what has been neglected, forged, forgotten, or subjugated for nefarious reasons."

"Are there any fakes here?" Kat whispered.

He laughed and gave a little swing of his umbrella. "Oh no, my dear, everything is as you see. And I would know. Once, as the esteemed guest of the Sultan of Brunei, I found myself surrounded by twenty armed men. The Sultan insisted the Rembrandt he had paid millions for be declared genuine. It would have been highly inconvenient to him, and to my person, if I had to be the bearer of bad tidings."

"What did you tell him?" Katerina asked, thoroughly drawn in by this strange imp of a man.

"I felt obliged to confirm the painting had been done in the *school* of Rembrandt and there existed every hope that the great man's hands had, at the very least, passed over the canvas," he said with a tiny, delighted chuckle.

Katerina smiled, then twitched in surprise at Winter suddenly appearing at her side. He slid his arm around her waist, and she turned her head, gazing up at him. A sudden, unexpected panic filled her. *I don't ever want to be without you.*

As if sensing her thoughts, Winter's arm tightened around her. "I'm sorry, I've been neglecting you," he said. "Introduce me to your friend?"

She opened her mouth to speak, catching herself. "Frederick, this is . . ." She looked at the little man.

"Arthur Penny, art historian and adviser at large of objet d'art," he said with a flourish, offering his card.

"A pleasure," Winter said with a polite nod, leaving it to Katerina to accept the card.

"Your charming lady has been a most willing student."

Winter pulled her closer. "Yes, she possesses a quite curious nature. What have you been teaching her?"

"We have been engaged in object-based learning to truly "see" a painting, to identify the parts that make the sum, allowing her to recognize what makes a real work rather than a forgery, and to determine its place in the larger world."

"I'm afraid I have a great deal to learn," Katerina said with a studied deference.

"I would like to see such an exercise," Winter said. "Do you mind?"

Arthur Penny gave an exaggerated nod of delight. "It would be my pleasure. I once did a demonstration for a descendant of the Habsburgs. It was quite simple, you know . . ."

Winter gestured to move off toward another painting, allowing Arthur Penny to lead the way as he chattered.

Standing in front of Winter's choice of canvas, Katerina had the sensation of everything falling away, as if the Los Angeles County Museum of Art had emptied and she stood alone before the painting in a vacuum of silence.

A Monet.

Water lilies.

"See how he uses the color contrasts, the yellow and the lilac," Arthur Penny said. "Observe the rough texture, almost like an application with a dry brush. The paint does not glide, oh no, it is very rough, as if it were pulled. You can easily imagine how the paint dried and then he began his work once again. Do you see?"

Katerina nodded, mesmerized by the intimate close up of the lilies in a pond. She had seen them before only in a different composition,

Bridge Over a Pond of Water Lilies. She had seen three paintings last year, all fakes, in Simon Marcus' apartment.

The painting before them was not a fake. This was the real thing.

"Claude Monet crafted over two hundred paintings of the lilies in his garden at Giverny," Arthur Penny was saying, "they have a special name."

"*Nympheas,*" Katerina said, uttering the name Winter had taught her.

"Very good, my young lady," Penny said.

As Arthur Penny continued his scholarly recitation, Katerina glanced up at Winter. He gave her a warm smile.

Katerina Mills understood they had come to the museum to see this painting.

Alexander Winter intended to steal it.

Chapter 60

They got into the BMW and closed the doors.

"So, it was Alexander Winter, in the museum, with the Monet," Katerina said.

Winter smiled and started the car.

***

When they reached her hotel, Winter parked the car and cut the engine.

"You're not going to tell me anything, are you?"

"No," he said.

Katerina pressed her lips together to keep the words she wanted to say from falling out. "Can you tell me where Penny fits into this?" she asked. "Why do you need an art expert to steal a genuine painting?"

"I don't," Winter answered. "That's today's unexpected lesson, the happy accident. Your Mr. Penny's presence may just have served a purpose."

"Bob . . ." Kat began, "Arthur Penny seems like a decent man. He's not going to get—hurt, is he?"

"No, I don't think so," Winter said. "Now, you've helped me with my business, let's talk about yours. What do you want to do?"

Her eyes moved over his face, taking him in. *Run away with you and never look back.* She lowered her gaze. "I wish I knew. I don't see how I get this done."

"Katerina, why are you staying with this agency?"

"I needed to stay in so I can stay a step ahead. You know, like the movie *The Godfather*?"

Winter shook his head.

"'You keep your friends close and your enemies closer?'"

Winter shook his head again. "Stay one step ahead of what?"

"It's—"

"Complicated," he finished. "All right, your business is your own. But Katie, consider this. If you did find a way to work this situation, to complete, or appear to complete the job, do you believe the agency will pay you?"

Katerina sat back in her seat, staring out the window. She shook her head, then turned to him. "I can't win," she said.

"I didn't say that. You have to look at it from the agency's point of view. That's what I'm trying to teach you, Katie. The opinion that matters the least is yours. What the other person thinks, what they want, what motivates them, what frightens them, is all that matters. Once you understand that, you can find your way forward."

Katerina thought of Angel's advice. *See as they see. It's the only way.*

"Take your Romanov, Mr. Zilinsky," Winter said. "Tell me again about the meeting, everything, word for word."

Katerina repeated the exchange until she finished with "so after we had a history lesson, he demanded I recover Mother Russia for him, calling it his 'birthright.' Then he told me Mikhailovich had what he needed, but he didn't say what *it* is, but I should get it from him."

"Birthright," Winter repeated. "That's interesting. And then you lost your temper."

"No, I had done that way before," Kat said. "If you were me, what would you do?"

"I'd go back to him. Shake the tree. Press him on what Mikhailovich has, ask him how once he gets it, whatever it is, he plans to ascend to the throne and take his rightful place. He'll either get annoyed or he'll play along and then—"

"Another happy accident?"

"Let's not make that standard procedure."

She shook her head. "Zilinsky was specifically hired to play a crazy Russian. He's waiting for me to fail so he can call the agency. He gets paid only when I get fired."

"Are you sure? If I'm right about this—this isn't his first rodeo. I think he's tipped his hand."

His tone came out matter-of-fact, without accusation or disapproval. Katerina waited for the lesson she knew she needed.

"Did you go to Sunday School?"

Katerina smiled. "Yes."

"Do you remember the story of Jacob and Esau?"

Kat nodded. "Older brother gives up the first-born benefits package in exchange for a bowl of Quaker Oats. So what?"

He grinned at her. "Let's not be quite so literal. What is a birthright, Katerina?"

"It's being the firstborn. It's being next in line for the throne."

"You have your phone. Get it out. Look it up."

She pulled the phone out of her purse and tapped the screen. After a moment, she held it up to him. "See? Any right or privilege to which a person is entitled by birth. Zilinsky's story is Mother Russia belongs to him. She should welcome her son home and hand him the crown."

The smile stayed firmly fixed on Winter's lips. "Scroll down for more definitions."

She did as he said. "The privileges—or possessions—of a firstborn son. Inheritance." When she glanced up, she found him studying her.

"I think he wants *something*. I think he believes it's possible you can get him what he wants. That's why he gave you Mikhailovich's name. Go shake the tree."

Katerina let out a sigh. "I'd rather shake something else," she muttered.

He leaned in close. "Are you being playful with me?" he asked, his voice low and inviting.

"I certainly hope so."

He kissed her. "I want that too, but now it's time for me to go back to work. Keep the tracking phone on."

Katerina gave another sigh and a nod. "By the way, I saw your shadow earlier today. He showed up at Fashion Island."

Winter gave her a mischievous smile as a comment.

"But of course, you knew that," Katerina said, annoyed she had missed the obvious. *Did you think he'd let you go without protection?* "Tell Keyes he's good at his job."

"He knows that, Katerina. What did Daniel want?"

"He pitched for me to trade in the original model," she said, tilting her head at Winter, "for an upgrade."

Winter raised an eyebrow. "And what did you say?"

She looked into his eyes. "I accept no substitutes. Are *you* going to see Daniel again?"

"I'm sure I will. In the meantime, he'll have to play with his own friends."

"When you do see him, you need to know I lied to him. I said I never told you the painting in Marcus' car was a fake. You think it's an original." She paused. "When will you tell me about Daniel?"

Winter gave her a sweet, gentle kiss on her lips. "When you can lie to everyone—the first time.*"*

She wanted to argue but couldn't. She hadn't lied to Daniel Clay. She had tried to cover her mistake. *God, I hope it worked.*

Chapter 61

In Central Park, under a frigid gray sky, men and women wore dripping raincoats as they trudged over the sodden grass, collecting evidence. Detectives Ryan Kellan and Walter Lashiver came up the path, then veered off into the secluded brush behind the statue of King Jagiello, seated on his horse, his sword raised for battle. They approached Detective Tommy Morse and a detective from the Central Park Precinct, Dennis O'Connoll. O'Connoll, a seasoned veteran with a weary look about him, accepted Lashiver's outstretched hand.

"Denny O, appreciate the call," Lashiver said.

O'Connoll nodded. "How you doin', hotshot?" he said to Ryan.

Ryan took the dig and let it pass.

The detectives moved closer and watched the techs perform their ritual over the body of Will Temple.

The technician crouching over the body glanced up at the detectives. "Do you want me to state the obvious or should I just skip to the bad news," he asked.

"No, please, Garcia, take your time and do the whole number," O'Connoll said. "I love standing out here looking up a horse's ass while heaven pisses on my head."

"Hey, there's always a bright side," a female tech named Zinetti, piped up. "There are coy wolves living in the park. You're lucky this guy wasn't lunch."

"What the hell is a coy wolf?" Garcia asked.

"It's an actual wolf," Zinetti said.

"I understand that. But what makes it a "coy" wolf?"

"It plays hard to get," she said.

Garcia gave a snicker.

"You think I'm kidding?" Zinetti asked. "There's been a coyote in Battery Park City, a tiger in Harlem, there was even a flying squirrel in Queens—"

"Hey, Bullwinkle, pause the Wild Kingdom episode," O'Connoll snapped as he squatted down next to Garcia. "You want to tell us how this guy died?"

"Entry wound is on the lower right, toward the back of the head," Garcia said, pointing with a gloved finger. "The bullet traveled to the front and the exit wound is on the left side, above the eye."

"Why the hell would he hold the gun toward the back of his head?" Ryan asked. "He could have just put it up against the side, above his ear."

Zinetti held up an evidence bag containing a crown. "Probably trying to avoid this, which was probably on his head."

"So we're looking at a suicide?" Lashiver said.

"This guy wanted to be up on the stage at the Delacorte," Morse said, glancing off in the direction of the theater.

"Yeah, well, if he wanted to take his final bow, he should have kept walking," Zinetti said.

"It's surprising he made it this far," Garcia said, pulling back the sheet to expose the naked body down to the midsection. He pointed toward the stomach and ribs. "Looks like he's been on a hunger strike."

"Any signs of sexual abuse?" Ryan asked.

He nodded. "Plus ligature marks on the body. It'll all be in the ME's report. With the storm, I wouldn't get my hopes up for DNA."

"What's the estimated time of death?" O'Connoll asked.

"Maybe six to eight hours ago. Again, with the storm, it's hard to tell."

"What about his clothes?" Ryan asked.

"Over there." Zinetti pointed toward technicians working by Turtle Pond.

Detective O'Connoll drew the sheet back over Will Temple and stood up. The detectives shared a solemn, silent moment over the body, then walked away.

"No way this is a suicide," Ryan said.

"If he's good for the killing of your vic, that's motive enough for him to do this," O'Connoll said.

"We've got no connection between him and the second victim," Lashiver said.

"The same person is responsible for all of them," Ryan said.

O'Connoll held up his hand. "Hold it. There were gunshot wounds on the first two victims?"

"No," Lashiver said.

"Temple would never have done this and never here," Ryan pressed. "A guy who wanted to be famous and his last performance is walking into the park, stripping naked by a pond, and killing himself in a secluded spot," he said, pointing back toward the statue, "looking up a horse's ass while heaven pisses on his head?" Ryan threw O'Connoll a pointed look. "No fuckin' way."

"He's right," Morse said.

"When the autopsy is finished, you're my first call," O'Connoll said.

"Appreciate it," Lashiver said.

The detectives exchanged handshakes in turn and walked away, each lost in his own thoughts.

Chapter 62

When Katerina arrived at the restaurant, she found Zilinsky fidgeting, eyes darting around the room. He did a double take at the sight of her in a short, blond wig.

"You have made progress already?" he asked.

"Of course, Mr. Zilinsky. But I have a few additional questions."

Zilinsky shook his head. "Another lie. Another disappointment. Perhaps I should call the agency now," he said, almost to himself.

He patted his jacket pockets as though he were about to reach for his phone. Katerina observed the pantomime and said, "On the contrary, Mr. Zilinsky, everything is in motion."

Zilinsky stopped. "Really? What could you have?" he baited, with a sneer of derision. "You have seen Mikhailovich?"

Katerina smiled and patted his hand. "Mr. Zilinsky, I have to make sure we're on the same page so I can bring you the exact item which will restore you to the throne. When do you plan to return to Russia?"

Zilinsky sat back, considering her.

C'mon Vlad, bite the bait. You know you want to.

Zilinsky began vigorous head shaking. "I don't know. I don't know." He pulled folded pieces of paper from his pocket and laid them out on the table. "Look, look how handsome he was as a boy."

Katerina glanced over the black and white photocopies of the Romanov children: Olga, Tatiana, Maria, Anastasia, and Alexei.

"'The Little One.' That's what my great-grandfather called him. His pet name for him."

Sure thing, Uncle Vanya.

"He was the apple of my great-great-grandmother's eye."

Katerina did a mental calculation of the family tree. "The Dowager Empress. Maria Feodorovna."

"Yes, yes," Zilinsky said, leaning forward. "Imagine, losing her son *and* her grandson. I don't know how she bore it. Forced to flee, she lost everything, even the keepsakes of a son's devotion. My grandfather would have been a fine ruler, keeping the traditions of his father. Now it falls to me."

Katerina listened to Zilinsky's bullshit with a better eye to what Winter had been trying to teach her. Zilinsky's part in scamming her didn't matter; regarding him as an enemy didn't matter. Understanding his thought process and staying one step ahead of him; that's all that mattered. She decided it was time to get back on track. "I will return the *Rodina* to you, Mr. Zilinsky. If you can tell me more about what Viktor Mikhailovich possesses, I can complete the assignment faster."

Zilinsky stared at her as if she had just beamed down from the mother ship. "The diadem."

Katerina desperately wanted to pull out her phone and look it up but didn't dare.

"No one places the crown on the Tsar's head. He does this himself. He crowns himself and then he rules all."

Katerina found herself at a loss, wondering if Zilinsky was only a liar, or a lunatic as well, or a combination of the two. "Where did Mikhailovich find it?"

Tears sprang to Zilinsky's eyes as he whispered, "Everywhere he has been looking for the crown jewels, from Siberia to the auction houses in London. Now, he has found it, I know. I tried with the others. So many others. But they could do nothing."

Others?

"You've hired consultants before?" Kat asked.

"Yes, yes. But it came to nothing."

Of course it did. They were sent to you for disposal.

Katerina had the distinct thought that Mr. Zilinsky had just become useful. "I'm sorry the previous consultants failed you. Believe me, Mr. Zilinsky, I will do whatever it takes to satisfy your request. How much did the other consultants achieve? For instance, what did Lisa accomplish?"

Zilinsky shook he head. "I don't know any Lisa. There was a Michelle, a Veronica, Isabella tried her best but, ah," he shrugged his shoulders, "she could do nothing."

"Anyone else?"

"There was another."

Katerina held her breath as Zilinsky struggled to remember.

"Sara, yes, it was Sara. She pushed, she pressed. She would not let go. She begged me to give her more time. One more day, one more day. She was out of her mind, desperate. But I see she cannot do anything. What can I do? I gave her many chances. How many chances do you need?"

"Only one. But I must have your assurance you will allow me the time I need to complete this assignment."

"How much time?" he asked.

"No more than two weeks. No matter how the agency pushes you to declare it a failure. Do I have your promise of two weeks? I assure you, Mr. Zilinsky, it will be well worth the wait."

Zilinsky considered her. "I look at you and I think maybe it is finally possible, maybe you will be able to do what the others could not. And I will have my birthright returned to me. I consider this the greatest purpose of my life. Yes, I agree. Do not fail me, Ekaterina. You must not fail me."

"Trust me, Mr. Zilinsky, I won't."

"Now, let me tell you how my great-great-grandmother barely escaped with her life..." As Zilinsky returned to babbling on about Maria Feodorovna's flight to freedom, and her loss of her royal riches, Katerina took stock of her predicament; she still had more questions than answers. She knew only three things: whatever Zilinsky was after, it was big, MJM had hired Zilinsky to work this scam in New York, and Sara had been the fixer who didn't make it out of MJM alive.

Chapter 63

Katerina followed Winter's instructions, taking a roundabout route to the meeting point in Irvine, making stops and switching vehicles. When she finally got the all-clear, she followed Winter's text message to the restaurant. She made her way to the bar, a New York newspaper under her arm. Settling on a stool at the end, she ordered a glass of rosé. She checked her voice mail, wincing at the sound of Philip's voice, alternating between cajoling and insisting she had to call him. She deleted the messages and opened the newspaper.

She read about the latest volleys being lobbed between the Mayor and the Governor. The photo showed Governor Haley announcing the new initiative for battling the opioid crisis in New York State. *Good luck with that.* She had no doubt that business was humming right along. *I wonder if my father is back in business.*

Katerina zeroed in on the young woman standing in the background, Destiny Haley. Cleaned up and covered in couture, it was the same young woman from the train, but it wasn't. She appeared stoic, a "Stepford Wife" expression on her face. All the life had gone out of her eyes. A fresh stab of guilt pierced Katerina's conscience.

When she forced herself to turn the page, her eyes fell on the caption at the bottom of the page; she froze.

Missing Actor Found Dead

Katerina scanned the article, struggling to focus through the tears stinging her eyes. A man out walking his dog had discovered the nude victim; a crown was found near the body. *Just like Felicia Reynolds, found naked with the wig on her head.*

What was it Will had said?
Someday I'll be tragic Hamlet.
The Prince is dead.

A detective from the Central Park Precinct, Dennis O'Connoll, was working the case. Katerina put the paper down on the bar.

She caught sight of Winter as he entered; he headed to a secluded table in the corner. Katerina slid off her chair and followed, taking the newspaper with her.

***

Winter ordered a scotch neat and another rosé for Katerina. They sat in silence until the server left. He watched her, head bowed, eyes cast down at the table.

"How was your day, dear?" he asked.

She gave a short, bitter laugh as tears began to trickle down her cheeks. "Swell," she said.

"What's for dinner, chicken or fish?" he asked.

She swiped her palms across her face. "Fish. Not for me. Someone else. He already ate the fish. One helluva fish."

"Tell me."

Kat held out the newspaper and Winter took it from her hand. She took up her glass while he read.

As Alexander Winter skimmed the article, his jaw set. He took Kat's hand in his own, his thumb massaging her fingers in a rhythmic motion. He folded the paper and put it aside. He turned to her.

"I work for MJM Consulting," Kat said. "I'm a B-girl."

"B-girl?"

"I do the bitch work no one else can."

He nodded at her frank statement.

"A man named John Reynolds was my first client. He hired me to follow his wife, Felicia, go everywhere she went, watch everything she did. To recommend a birthday gift, that's what he said."

"And the actor?"

"Felicia's lover. I followed her to his apartment. I saw her leave. I saw him lean out his window, watching her go." Tears threatened again and Kat pulled in a shaky breath. "Reynolds had—someone—a man in a blue Ford—follow me." Katerina nodded at the newspaper. "Reynolds is responsible for this. He had his wife killed. He had Will Temple killed. He had another socialite, Cheryl Penn, killed to muddy the investigation. He admitted it all to me, right before Christmas."

"The earrings, in your apartment," Winter said.

Kat nodded. "They belonged to Felicia. She gave them to me. Reynolds insisted I talk to her. So, I did."

"Where?" Winter pressed. "Where did this happen?"

"Saks."

"And Temple? Did you ever talk to him?"

Kat nodded. "One night he showed up at my apartment building. He said he was looking for a production company, Random Girl Films. He said he got a call to come for an audition for a movie, *Loves Fury*. He had my name. He was a nice guy, a young guy . . ." She shook her head and took another swallow of the wine.

"All of it, Katie, everything," Winter said, the muscles in his jaw working. "What happened in New York before you came out here?"

"I went to get the money from a safety deposit box. Reynolds ambushed me outside the bank. He took the cash, except what I had stashed in my coat and my purse. He demanded I start working for him again. I threatened him, said that I would finger the killer and then it would all come back on him. I tried to keep him away . . ."

Winter took Kat's wine glass from her and set it on the table. He wrapped his arm around her, pulling her close.

"He told me what happened to Will depended on me," Kat whispered. "If I hadn't threatened him, if I hadn't made that play . . ."

Winter kissed her forehead.

Katerina cast her eyes downward.

"What happened with Zilinsky?" Winter asked.

Katerina sat up. "Didn't you hear what I said?" she asked, her voice an angry whisper. "He killed them."

"I heard you," Winter said, his voice calm and even. "They were dead before you ever met John Reynolds. Nothing you said or did was ever going to change the end for them."

"Cheryl Penn didn't do anything to anybody."

"An innocent victim, an *unhappy* accident. It happens all the time, Katie. Reynolds already taught you that. Random Girl Films? If not you, it would have been some other consultant. I have one concern,

Katie," Winter said, giving her a pointed stare, "only one. What happened with Zilinsky?"

"He says Mikhailovich recovered the Tsar's lost crown from wherever it was buried, and he wants it. Is that even possible?"

Winter's eyes narrowed, a look of confusion crossing his face. "There are always stories about treasure hunts, like the search for the Nazi gold train. Anything's possible but this, this I'm not sure about."

"He'd have to be crazy to screw MJM."

"Unless the crown, or something else, makes it worth the risk. Occam's Razor, Katie."

"What—?"

"Occam's Razor says when there are two possible theories or explanations to choose from, the simpler of the two is probably the right one."

"Keep it simple."

"Always. For now, if he says Mikhailovich has a piece of the missing crown jewels, find out something more about them."

Exhaustion washed over Katerina and she slid into his embrace. They passed a few moments in silence. "So, I just forget them?" she finally said. "Like they were never here? Like they were nothing?"

"They are not nothing, Katie. But if you don't put them away, your head won't be clear. You'll make a mistake." He moved his head back so he could look into her eyes. "They're in the past now. You have to leave them there. Or they will take you down with them."

"Is that today's lesson?" she asked.

"Yes," he said.

"Will I ever graduate?" Kat asked.

Bending his head toward her, he gave her a soft kiss. "Yes."

"Will I be as good as you?"

"You will be better than me. The student always surpasses the teacher."

"And then what happens?"

"You told me what happens. She takes what she's earned, and she leaves."

Katerina swallowed hard and blinked quickly.

"But we're more than teacher and student. We're friends, aren't we?"

"Always," Kat said.

"When you're going to leave, promise me you won't just disappear. Promise you'll let me say a proper goodbye. Will you do that for a friend?"

"Yes," she said, knowing if she tried to say more, her emotions would come spilling out. She gazed up into his face, memorizing every feature, every line. *How will I ever walk away from you?*

"Do you have to go to work now?" she asked

Winter pulled her closer. "Not yet," he said, his voice gentle. "We have a little more time."

Chapter 64

Thomas Gallagher sat at his desk in his study. At the telltale clicking of high heels, he leaned back. Lisa sauntered into the room. She tossed her purse on the desk and settled into a chair, crossing one long, lithe leg over the other.

"This is an unexpected pleasure," he said.

"It shouldn't be," Lisa said. "But I think we should wait to start the meeting until everyone is here."

Gallagher's eyebrows quirked in an expression of innocence. "I wasn't aware of a scheduled conference."

"Your man should be here any minute with his update. You know you should never use men as consultants. They're not detail-oriented," she said with a tut-tut sound of disappointment. "And I thought we had an agreement."

"Believe me, my dear, we do. Our agreement is binding and final."

"And yet, you've been going behind my back, hiring someone else to bring in the princess, trying to cut me out." She made another tut-tut sound.

Gallagher smiled. "Not at all. He's been hired for a specific function—unless you're adding wet work to your résumé."

"No thanks. You might want to look for a replacement. Last I heard, he was bitch-slapped by a lady of the evening."

At the sound of footsteps, they turned to see Joseph Smith enter, looking as if he needed to recover from a rough night.

"Hello, Mr. Smith," Lisa said. "I'm so sorry Gal Friday couldn't help you with your need for an assistant."

She watched him register recognition of her voice. He gave her a cold stare.

Lisa turned to Gallagher. "If you wanted to find the owner of Gal Friday, Incorporated, all you had to do was ask me," she said.

***

"And all Katerina wanted you to do was answer the phone for Gal Friday because the detective would be calling to check on her," Gallagher said.

"That's it," Lisa said.

"Gal Friday is owned by a shell company, IGS Capital," Smith said.

"Well done, Inspector Clouseau," Lisa said, turning her attention to Smith. "I know that."

"Then let's discuss something you don't know," Smith snapped, turning back to Gallagher. "At your request, I located MJM's client. He's in California going under the name of Zilinsky. As you see," he said, handing over an iPad over to Gallagher, "she met with him recently."

Gallagher lingered over the photograph of Katerina, her chestnut hair covered by a short, blond wig, her eyes hidden behind a pair of oversized sunglasses. He tore himself away from the image and handed the iPad to Lisa.

She glanced at the picture. "My, my, Rapunzel has been busy," she said. "Your team is tracking her and this Zilinsky?"

Smith shot Lisa a look that could burn through her like battery acid. "It's a process," he said.

"For some people it is," Lisa said with an exaggerated sigh. "Let's hope that part of your "process" includes finding her again."

"I find it odd," Smith said to Gallagher, "that you knew so much about this client, considering MJM's impeccable reputation for confidentiality. They keep the secrets; they don't share them. Surely, you didn't get this information from them, did you?"

"I have no idea who MJM is," Gallagher said.

"Then this has something to do with the newspaper articles in the girl's apartment?" Smith continued.

Lisa's eyebrows quirked in interest; she looked to Gallagher. He sat silent, his poker-face firmly in place.

"If this is just a game," Smith said, "I should have been told up front."

"It's all a game. If you can't handle it, you should get out," Lisa said.

Gallagher took Smith's comment, with all its implications, in stride; playing with a young girl's life, a trifling of the rich and bored. It had been that way with his former partners; the young ladies had been appropriated and discarded at will. And all the women had acquiesced, willingly, gladly, out of blind love and devotion.

He did not conceive of himself as the same as those long dead men, no, not at all. The consultants he had brought to the apartment, that too, was different. Those women had come with greed and avarice as their agenda; they had received their just rewards. No, that was entirely different.

"I assure you Mr. Smith," Gallagher said, with a sharp look at Lisa, "I have my own ways of discovering secrets, and no one views this as a game. To return to the subject, who is the owner of IGS? What is his name?"

"We're working on it," Smith said.

"Because it's a process," Lisa said. "No, it isn't. It's a phone call." She gave Gallagher a smile. "One that only I can make."

***

Smith watched Thomas Gallagher dismiss Lisa with an almost imperceptible nod of his head, leaving the two men alone.

"What is the risk of exposure from the escort?" Gallagher asked.

"None," Smith lied.

"And if she contacts "W"?"

"She has nothing to tell him. There is no exposure," Smith said.

"I'm glad to hear it."

Smith got up and left, knowing his employer didn't believe a word of what he had said. He would have to find an insurance policy; from this moment, "W" wasn't the only one on Thomas Gallagher's target list.

Chapter 65

Katerina had the burner phone at her ear as she crossed the university campus. She flashed back to hustling across a New York college campus last October, waiting for her parents to answer the phone, already knowing something had gone terribly wrong.

She exhaled in relief, as she always did, when the call connected. "Mom," Kat said. "Where are you? Why did it take you so long to answer?"

"My girl, I'm visiting Sergei," Linda Mills said softly.

"Why are you whispering?"

"He's been working himself to death on his paintings. He's resting. Where are you?"

"I'm in . . . Iowa," Kat said, hating the lie.

"Iowa? All right my sweet girl. You sounded like you were rushing to a class."

Katerina glanced up at the brick and tile structure, built to resemble a basilica. "It's more like an independent study."

"What about, dear?"

Katerina pulled a flyer from her pocket. "The Rise of Modern Art Amid the Elegance of the Edwardian Era."

"That sounds nice, dear," her mother said. "I'll tell your uncle you're quite safe . . . in Iowa."

***

Inside the building, she found Arthur Penny standing on stage in front of a lectern, his slight frame dwarfed by the empty lecture hall. Using a small microphone pinned to his chest, he coordinated his speech with pressing a button to move to the next slide

Katerina had missed the rise of post-impressionism, modernism, and Dadaism but had arrived in time for Albert Edward—Bertie to his friends and family, King Edward VII to his subjects—to usher in a new age of elegance and industrialism during his ten-year reign. It was because of Edward VII that Katerina had come.

Arthur Penny brought his lecture to a close. At the sound of solitary clapping, he squinted and peered at the back of the lecture hall. Sitting in the last seat, in the last row, Katerina raised her hand.

"Yes, you have a question?"

Katerina lowered her hand. "Do you have Prince Albert in a can?"

Arthur Penny smiled. "Why, yes I do."

"Then you better let him out."

Penny gave a delighted laugh as Katerina rose from her seat and made her way down to the podium.

***

After a five-minute inspection of the restaurant and an in-depth discussion of the best location to avoid any excessive drafts, they chose a corner table.

"When did you know you wanted to make art your life?" Kat asked.

Arthur Penny jumped at the opportunity to tell the story of his life. "My grandfather came to this country as a young man and promptly struggled for the rest of his days. He ran a small, insignificant, secondhand shop of bric-a-brac, leftovers not suitable for estate sales, that sort of thing. I confess I never appreciated his sacrifices as I should have. But I was young and impetuous. I yearned for true beauty, antiquities, and artifacts."

"To restore them," she said.

"Yes, for many years I toiled faithfully in the bowels of a museum. Then I went on to teach, which is a kind of restoration. You are imparting wisdom and knowledge about these precious objects. In a way, that is what keeps them alive and safe."

"Safe. From who?" she asked.

"From *whom*," Penny corrected. "Art has been reduced to a commodity to be acquired and hidden away. Their significance in history has been obliterated by Philistines, degraded to being valuable only for what they can bring in trade."

Let's go Katerina. Game on.

"You're thinking of what became of the treasures of Edward's nephew, Tsar Nicholas the Second, the Royal Family's possessions, after the Revolution?"

Arthur Penny's eyes lit up. "You have the makings of a historian. Very good, young lady. Yes, I suppose that qualifies. The Royal Family's treasures were under siege from within and without. Bolsheviks sold them away to the highest bidder. Here at home, we had Armand Hammer, the good doctor. Why should an oil magnate have been allowed to remove a country's wealth, hawking items in department stores of all places? Unconscionable. He is not the only one to do this, of course. The world is filled with plunderers, Miss Mills. People who only know how to take without appreciating an item's value, and by value, I don't mean money."

"I understand some items are still waiting to be plundered."

Arthur Penny gave a laugh. "The billions in bullion, the baubles and trinkets, buried somewhere in Siberia. Tall tales. Besides, Russia has a history that is much more precious, items of religious significance. Icons were paraded and pedaled in the great loan exhibition in the nineteen thirties. They were sold away, absconded by those who don't deserve—" Arthur Penny halted, collecting himself. "What is your interest in all this?"

"I have Russian nationality in my background," Katerina lied without missing a beat. "My uncle encourages me to be more in touch with my heritage, to understand what has been lost. Are all the Tsar's riches just trinkets and baubles? Doesn't the royal diadem have any cultural meaning?"

Arthur Penny took out his phone, swiping and tapping his finger across the screen. Katerina tried to hide her surprise at his easy, deft touch working with the device. She imagined he still preferred a quill and an abacus. He held out the phone and she leaned in to see a black and white photograph; an elaborate necklace of rhombus shapes, each boasting a stone in the center and a teardrop jewel dangling at the bottom. Precious gems attached each shape together. "Not just a crown, young lady. The crown jewels. You've heard of the book?"

"No," she said, open and forthright. *But do tell.*

"The Russian Diamond Fund, a volume dated nineteen twenty-two. The United States Geological Survey has a copy. The inventory has three pieces that a later volume does not account for: the necklace, the bracelet, and a crown, all vanished."

"With all your travels, you've never once thought to go on the hunt? You're not even a little curious?"

He shrugged. "I am not Indiana Jones, though I do look rather dashing in a fedora."

Katerina gave him a smile. "You must have a theory."

"Young lady, I enjoy a ghost story as much as the next man, but these items are gone, along with a host of other items from the Tsar's vast fortune, daggers, sabres, and the infamous missing Eggs. They live on like the stories of the Royal Family's survival—mysticism and myth. Like Rasputin, the charlatan who duped the Tsarina, making her believe he alone had the power to heal her only son. It is smoke and shadows. There is nothing to any of it."

He took Kat's hands in his own and she noticed how they trembled. "Now, did I ever tell you about the time I authenticated a Vermeer for the Queen . . ."

Katerina wrestled with her disappointment as Arthur Penny launched into his story. A historian, restorer, and lecturer whom the world had passed by, Arthur Penny was a sweet man with nothing left to do but drop names and tell of adventures he never had.

Katerina listened with half an ear while she ruminated. She was not ready to concede defeat. She doubted Zilinsky's story more than ever but there was nothing to do but continue.

Chapter 66

"Letourneau."

"Monsieur, it's Katerina."

She heard a noise of agitation from the other end of the line. "Where are you?" he asked.

"Iowa," she said. "Any response?"

"*Rien*. What do you expect them to say, mademoiselle? They do not send thank you cards."

Katerina took the rebuke. *What did I expect? I expected James Sheridan to be dead by now. I expected them to let me go.*

"Katerina, do you like it in Iowa?"

"Yes," she said.

"*Bien*," Henri Letourneau said. "Stay there. Please, for your own sake, do not return."

The line went dead.

***

To put the call with Letourneau out of her mind, Katerina returned to the Los Angeles County Museum of Art. As she wandered the third floor of the Ahmanson building, Kat wrestled with the MJM dilemma. Zilinsky had given her a clue: Sara, the fixer who never made it out. What to do with this information? How to leverage it for the one hundred thousand dollars she desperately needed to escape and get her mother to safety?

The familiar pressure of confusion bloomed in her head. Katerina knew why: Alexander Winter. She wanted him today, tomorrow, and every day. She counted off the men standing in the way: Desucci, Massone, Sheridan, her father, and the drug dealers. But her greatest obstacles were the man in the blue Ford and John Reynolds.

Her stomach jumped and her heart pounded in her chest as a thought flashed like a lightning bolt across her mind.

Ivan.

The hit man who had gotten in her car by accident last year.

The hit man who had let her live on Anthony Desucci's say so.

The hit man who had needed money and she loaned it to him.

The hit man who in return for the favor said, "You paid me. I work for you."

The hit man who could stop John Reynolds.

That the thought had occurred to her, that it had always been lurking in the back of her mind, buried deep, terrified her. She found herself leaning into it, a siren's song calling to her, drawing her in; an act worthy of damnation that could be her salvation.

You paid me. I work for you.

Still, her mind tiptoed over the idea that she could contact him, like flipping a switch, engaging him to remove John Reynolds.

Then the terror rushed in, flooding her conscience as if she were a child again, imagining eternity, an endless infinity, a black hole impossible to escape.

The trepidation worked its magic and Katerina pulled back, dismissing the idea.

She stood before Monet's Water Lilies, *Nympheas,* and understood why she had come; she had expected to find Winter prepping for the theft.

"It is beautiful," she heard a voice say, a voice with a thick accent.

Katerina froze.

A Russian accent.

She pivoted toward the voice and laid eyes on Viktor Mikhailovich in the flesh, the oligarch, the plunderer, the dangerous man who knew dangerous people.

The wolf.

He was taller than she, but not as tall as Winter. He had a sturdy build; he still wore his hair in the same style as the picture she found on the internet, the short chop. His suit was expensive and tailored; he wore a dark tie.

Keep it together, Katerina. This is a stranger. You don't know him. Lie.

"This is treat for me," he said. "I have pleasure watching one beautiful thing looking at another beautiful thing."

Mikhailovich smiled and it sent a shiver through her. *It's not real.* "And which one of us is the treat?" she asked.

He laughed. "I think you are . . . student. Yes?"

Keep the lie as close to the truth. It's easier. "Sometimes," Kat said, giving nothing more.

He nodded, pleased with himself. "Of course, I am right."

Kat noted the two men behind him. Big, burly, and surly.

"Why does beautiful girl, who is sometime student, come to the museum when she is not studying?"

"I like to see—art—look at pretty things . . ." she paused to give him a coy look, ". . . and make new friends."

Mikhailovich put his finger to his lips, nodding his head, a detective in deep thought. "She is alone? She is not with man? She is not with boyfriend?"

Katerina searched her options. The fire pit lay open, the choice was hers to fall in. "I'm all by my lonesome. Why are you here all alone?"

"I am on the board of this museum."

"You must be a very important man," Kat said, her eyes lighting up on cue. "Do you choose the paintings that are here?"

She watched him travel the length of her with his eyes.

"This is right," he said. "Now you tell me, who is this stupid man, who would do this stupid thing to leave you alone?"

"He wasn't nice to me, so, I left."

Mikhailovich zeroed in on the faint yellow tinge, the last evidence of the Massone warehouse incident. "Ah," he said, without any sign of concern. "Tell me, how can a man be nice to you? What do you like?"

"I like to travel and see new places."

"What places?"

"Paris."

"Ah. You like to do the shopping, hmmm? You like to buy the pretty things?"

"Oh yes," Kat said, a kitten giving a purr.

Mikhailovich laughed. "I own many businesses in Paris," he said. "You could be model."

"No," Kat said, blushing.

"Is true. You come to work for me, you go to Paris and many more places. You would like this, I think."

His attention shifted for a split second, glancing behind her, then coming back. "I am having little party at my home, on Balboa Island. There will be many people there. This is good for young girl. I will have driver pick you up at your hotel."

Katerina gave her best performance of apprehension: eyes aflutter with a touch of anxiety, her body giving a slight recoil. "We . . . we just met. I don't even know your name."

Viktor put his hand to his chest. "I am Viktor. I am nice man, very nice to young girls. I only have nice people to my parties. So, we are new friends and now you come, okay? Okay."

"Yes," Kat said and gave him the name of her hotel.

He left abruptly, walking away with his bodyguards. Katerina watched him go, wondering why he had not attempted to whisk her away immediately. When she turned to leave, she saw a family, parents with precocious Mensa preteens carrying pads and pencils.

Witnesses.

Chapter 67

Heather settled into a backup location on the Upper West Side. Hunched over her laptop, she finished moving her money. She'd have to lay low for a little while. It wasn't the first time.

She knew the man Smith wanted. "W" used several different names to preserve his anonymity.

A big man, tall, trim, and strong, he had been visiting her for several years. The first time, she had found his careful manner charming, even sweet. She looked forward to his visits, never turning on the taping system when he came. Not that he talked much, she thought with a wry smile. Skilled and attentive, he knew how to make a woman feel beautiful—and breathless.

She typed out a text and attached pictures of the unconscious Smith and his driver's license.

I could leave him out in the cold, on his own, she thought, staring at the text. I haven't seen him in months.

She read the text again.

You're blown. H.

Just a hooker with a heart of gold, she thought, shaking her head. She hit send and put the cell phone away.

Chapter 68

"Are you listening to me?"

Winter read the text message, studiously keeping his face blank; he had been taught the skill long ago. Even the slightest twitch of an eyebrow would be a tell.

Winter raised his head to look at Daniel Clay. "Do I have to?" Winter typed out 'thank you' on his phone and tapped the send button. "What were you saying?"

Daniel Clay extracted a LACMA pamphlet from his pocket. He tapped it against the arm of the chair and dropped it on the coffee table. "I was saying we need to talk about when you're breaking into the museum to steal the Monet."

***

Entering the hotel, Katerina forced herself to take slow, measured strides. She didn't bother to glance at the check-in desk. *Always look like you're where you belong.* She made it across the lobby, stabbing the "up" button for the elevator, praying no one would come along to share.

When the doors opened, she let out a sigh of relief at seeing the empty car. Ducking inside, she tapped the "close" button in a rhythmic pattern. By the time she reached the floor and the doors opened, her breathing had become forced and shallow, perspiration oozing from her pores.

***

Winter sat on the couch, arms relaxed and open, watching Daniel Clay become more animated as he continued to plead his case.

"This is a perfect opportunity for you," Clay was saying.

"How do you figure?" Winter asked.

"We cover more ground with two people and make a larger profit."

"You're assuming I'm interested in this museum."

Clay gave a laugh. "C'mon man, after all we've been through."

"We rode in the same car."

"All the way upstate."

"We weren't climbing Kilimanjaro."

"We faced the FBI."

"Those men were not FBI," Winter said.

"No shit," Daniel said. "All I'm saying is a little trust wouldn't hurt."

"It might," Winter said, his voice turning low and cold.

"We make a great team. Like Batman and Robin."

"That's a tempting offer, Boy Wonder, but I'll pass."

Daniel Clay shifted forward to the edge of his chair. "Okay, Bob. I'm gonna level with you."

"No, you won't, but it's a nice thought."

Clay glanced around. "Can I get something to drink? You've got a fridge."

"Go take a look," Winter said.

"You can't offer me something?"

"Advice. Get to the point."

"Look, I know you were at the museum, casing the Monet."

"Yes, Daniel, I know," Winter said. "You have partners. They need to practice blending."

Daniel Clay laughed. "They're good guys. Look, I've worked a long time on these arrangements. If you go in first, it's gonna screw up my operation."

"I'm sorry to hear that."

"If we coordinated, that issue would be resolved. I think you owe me that. Can I get a freakin' drink?"

"Put your mouth under the sink tap."

"You don't appreciate what I bring to this operation."

"What operation?" Winter said.

Clay leaned in. "How are you going to do it?"

Winter smiled.

"What I've got is foolproof," Daniel Clay said. "No guards, no alarms, no nothing. Can you do better than that?"

"I certainly can," Winter said. He moved to say something but a knock at the door brought the conversation to a halt.

**

Katerina stood at the hotel room door, rapping out a chorus of urgent knocks.

Please be here. Please be here.

The door opened and her eyes widened in confusion.

Daniel Clay.

"Hey, beautiful," he said, a ready smile on his face.

She stood dumb.

"Beautiful? What's wrong?"

Her eyes went to Winter, standing in the middle of the room.

Clay turned to see Winter hold out his hand for her to come in; she rushed forward.

***

As Winter led Katerina to the couch, she had reached the point of hyperventilation, her body shaking. She registered the museum pamphlet on the coffee table. In her haze of panic, she realized she needed to help Winter, somehow, to find some way to get Daniel Clay out of the picture so Winter could complete his job.

"Katie," Winter said, holding her hands in his own.

Katerina's mind swirled, jumping from the pamphlet, to Winter, to Clay. Her eyes rested on this pest of an interloper. How to get rid of him? *Are you afraid of a man who might as well be a god, Daniel? Let's find out.*

Katerina fixed her gaze on Winter. "Mikhailovich showed at the museum," she lied, "just like you said."

Winter nodded. "And did everything go off as planned?" he asked, playing along.

"What plan?" Clay asked. "You met Viktor Mikhailovich?"

Katerina concentrated her attention on Winter. "Why is Yoko here?"

"Hey, we were discussing business," Clay shot back but his body language had shifted as he took a slight step back.

"He agreed to the terms?" Winter asked.

"What does Viktor Mikhailovich have to do with you stealing the Monet?" Clay asked.

Terms. Right. Terms of sale. Stealing the Monet and selling it to Mikhailovich. Keep up with him. "That's to be discussed. Tonight. He's having a party at his house on Balboa. He's sending a driver to pick me up at my hotel," she said.

This isn't your first rodeo either, Kat thought as she looked at Winter. It felt strange, acting out this play for an audience of one. The experience gave her a surreal feeling, as if she were standing outside the scene, watching, thinking, "Oh yes, I see. This is how it's done."

"The price is the price, nonnegotiable," Winter said.

"You gotta be kidding me," Clay said. "You're gonna steal a Monet from a museum and sell it to the guy who's on the board of directors?"

That's right. Now, let's convince you that you don't want any part of this. "He's anxious about getting this done as soon as possible," Katerina said, stunned at the words pouring out of her as if she'd done this a thousand times. "He's made arrangements and given assurances that he'll have the item by an agreed date."

"His buyers are not my problem," Winter said, satin smooth. "I'll explain that to him tonight."

Daniel Clay stood with his hands on his hips. "Mikhailovich is *paying* you to steal the Monet so he can sell it to someone else? You are seriously not getting into bed with this guy. Do you have any idea what he's into? He's connected all the way up to the top of the Kremlin."

Katerina concentrated on Winter. "He insists I come alone or no deal."

She watched Winter fall into a stony silence, his expression blank, impossible for anyone else to read. *Yes, I went off script. I won't have anything happen to you because of me.*

Clay stood in the center of the room, deep in thought, as if he had lost his way and found himself in a strange place.

"No hard feelings, Daniel. Catch you on the way back," Kat said.

Her words jolted Daniel Clay from his silence. "Hey, no, I'm a stand-up guy. I wouldn't bail on you. I can help. You know what? I'll order up a bottle of wine. This is gonna take a while."

While Daniel placed the order, Katerina gazed up at Winter and mouthed the words "I'm sorry."

Winter stroked Katerina's cheek. "You did good," he whispered, but his expression had darkened with anxiety.

***

There were three glasses but only Daniel drank.

Katerina locked into Winter as he spoke. The story was turning.

"He'll give you the tour," Winter was saying, "so you may not be left alone. Once you're in the house, you won't have much time to scope it out. Three minutes max. Maybe."

Katerina saw the switch. *Keep up. Follow his lead. Don't let him down.*

"What am I looking for?" she asked.

"That's right," Clay asked. "What is she looking for?"

"In each room, work clockwise, twelve, three, six, and nine," Winter said. "Make one full revolution—carefully. At each stop, take a photograph, so when you're done you have a visual record of the full layout of each room and everything in it."

"Isn't she negotiating for delivering the Monet?" Clay cut in.

Winter and Katerina zeroed in on each other. She watched him make his play, the tiniest of tells, a hint of a smile. Like a reflection, she mimicked what she saw.

"Wait a minute!" Clay said. "Wait a minute! Holy shit! You're going to double-cross Viktor Mikhailovich for the Monet *and* steal from him? Man, you have balls." He turned to Katerina. "You sure you don't have balls?"

"Are you still here?"

"Hey, you're lucky I'm here. You need all the help you can get. You're walking into the lion's den."

Katerina felt the jolt, the flush of fear at the reference.

Winter suddenly stood up. "He's right. This is too hot for you. You'll cancel, disappear, and I'll make arrangements to go in another night to take a look around."

Katerina stood up. "I'm staying," she said, ignoring Daniel. "If I leave now, he'll know something's wrong. You know it's better to be invited in. It's simple. Simple is best."

"She's right, you know," Clay said. "Hey, I'm a stand-up guy. I got just the thing to help you out. We're getting the band back together."

Winter didn't answer.

Chapter 69

Detectives O'Connoll, Kellan, and Lashiver followed the medical examiner into her office. She had an open file in her hand.

"Will Temple died of a single gunshot wound to the side of the head."

"And he was capable of doing it himself?" O'Connoll asked.

"We looked at the spread shot. The distance between the barrel and the victim was less than an inch, so technically, yes. But the point of entry and the angle of the bullet track make it highly unlikely."

"Did you get anything from his clothing?" Lashiver asked.

The medical examiner shook her head. "The rain washed everything away."

"Convenient," Ryan said.

"Isn't it though?" she said, scanning the report. "The deceased was malnourished, dehydrated, and exhibited signs of decreased muscle and tissue mass. He had bruising and contusions on his wrists and ankles."

"How old were those marks?" O'Connoll asked.

The medical examiner flipped through the pages. "Some of the ligature contusions were weeks old, others only a day or so. Wherever he was, Will Temple was bound and tortured."

"Can you go back and pull the details for Felicia Reynolds and Cheryl Penn and look for any similarities between all three?" Ryan Kellan asked.

The medical examiner closed the folder and nodded. "Give me a couple of days."

***

The detectives lingered in the lobby of the building.

"What if he was targeted?" Ryan asked.

"Go ahead," O'Connoll said.

"What if Felicia Reynolds was tailed to check out her routine. If the killer saw her, then the killer saw Will Temple. And maybe the killer thinks Will Temple saw him and can make an ID, so he's gotta take care of the loose end. If that's the case, couldn't the husband also be in danger?"

The veteran detectives listened and nodded.

"A woman's lover is found murdered," Ryan continued. "We have to inform the husband. Check his whereabouts. Strictly routine. But we also have to think of his safety. He could be a potential next victim."

"When we do it, I give him the bad news," O'Connoll said. "Let's see if it rattles his cage."

Chapter 70

Katerina came out of the bathroom and heard the low murmur of voices from the living room. She spied the outfit on the bed; an Emilio Pucci two-piece. She slipped into the outfit and glanced at herself in the mirror. The short-sleeved top had a barely-there black lace pattern and two strategically placed lace strips, leaving little to the imagination. The fabric ended one inch below the breasts, exposing an open midriff. The floor-length, sheer skirt with an asymmetrical lace pattern covered just what needed to be kept hidden.

She listened to the voices, stung by the idea of Winter and Daniel Clay talking without her. She suppressed her anger at the insult; Winter would give an explanation later. Whether it would be the whole story, she didn't know. *He's not sure I'm ready.*

She took one last look in the mirror.

I'm not sure, either.

***

When she emerged from the bedroom, she saw Winter's eyes open wide, then turn dark with desire, leaving her feeling as if she stood before him naked.

"Whoa, beautiful," she heard Daniel say.

Winter held out his hand and she crossed the room. The incessant buzzing of one of her cell phones cut through the silence. She opened her purse and tapped the phone to reject the call.

Winter turned to Daniel Clay, giving him a pointed look.

"Oh sure," he said. "I'll just wait outside."

After the door closed, Winter drew Katerina into his arms, enveloping her in an embrace.

"I'm sorry," she said. "I really thought Mikhailovich's name would scare him off."

"You took your best guess. You don't need to be sorry. He's turning out to be useful, for the moment." Winter pulled back to see her face.

"Katie, why did you say Mikhailovich insisted you come alone? Once you go into that house, I won't be able to come for you."

"I kept it simple," Kat said. "You know we can't both go and only have Daniel watching our backs."

Kat's phone buzzed again. Cursing softly, she grabbed the cell phone and rejected the call.

She watched Winter wrestle with the untenable situation until he let it go with a shake of his head.

"What did you tell Viktor?" he asked.

"I said I was alone. I had a bad boyfriend who didn't treat me right. So I left."

Winter handed her a phone while he mined her story for possibilities. "Use this phone to take the pictures. An email address is already loaded. Upload all the pictures, hit send, and you're done. The pictures will automatically erase."

Kat took the phone. "Got it." The look of concern in Winter's eyes sent a rush of panic through her. Kat's cell phone buzzed again. She cursed, pulled away from Winter, and went to reject the call a third time.

"Answer it," Winter said.

Kat checked the caller ID and clicked on the call. "Yeah?"

"What's up, buttercup?" Lisa's voice came through. "Sorry to be the pea beneath your mattress, but we've got a problem. Actually, you have a problem."

"Yes, I do" Kat said. "You have my money."

"That's right. And as soon as you get your shit together, you can have it. I'm calling about Gal Friday, Incorporated."

Kat held the sharp retort that danced on the edge of her tongue. "How often is the cop calling?"

"This time it's not the cop. Someone called asking for the owner, they mentioned IGS Capital. Whoever did you a favor has a problem."

Katerina's stomach somersaulted and she hit the mute button. "Lisa says someone called Gal Friday looking for you."

She watched Winter's face, stoic, unreadable. "Ask who and when," he said.

Katerina unmuted the phone. "When did this happen? Did they give a name?"

"Why do I have the feeling you're not all by your lonesome? Put the owner on the phone."

"Not here and never going to happen," Kat said.

"Listen, Rapunzel, I'm the one in shit now and I need to get paid for my part. Let me repeat myself because you know how I love to do that. Put the owner on the phone or I don't see any reason to continue sticking my neck out. Or maybe I'll just keep your fee as payment for being inconvenienced."

Katerina was about to open her mouth, the words "go ahead" on her tongue, when Winter hit the mute button and slipped the phone from her hand.

"I don't care, let her have the mon—"

Winter clicked the mute button again. "What's the name?" he asked.

"What do I call you?"

"Bob," he answered. "What's the name?"

"He didn't say. He said he needed to speak with you, and he would be back in touch. What now?"

Katerina observed Winter, his calm, controlled voice a contradiction to the fingers of his free hand tapping against the side of his leg in a nervous, rhythmic pattern. She snaked her hand within his and he held tight. "Leave an automated voice message on the phone that the business is closed," he said. "I'll take care of dissolving the company and disconnecting the number."

"Understood. Now what about my fee?"

"How much?"

Katerina moved to protest but Winter shifted away from her.

"Ten thousand."

"Text an account and swift number. I'll take care of it," he said, "*after* she gets paid."

"Understood," Lisa said.

Winter hung up the phone and slipped it into his inside jacket pocket. "It's done. No more interruptions."

Kat dropped the "Viktor" phone in her clutch purse.

"No, keep it out," Winter corrected. "Like most young ladies, you have an attachment to your phone."

Katerina extracted the phone, cradling it in her hand, watching Winter work through the details. "Good, that will make it easier for you to take pictures. You'll receive texts during the evening from "the boyfriend." I'm persistent and you will answer."

"Got it," Kat said.

"Deep breath," Winter instructed. "Put everything else away. *Everything*. Focus."

She leaned in for a kiss, stunned when he pulled back.

"He'll know you've been kissing someone else."

"How can you be sure?"

"Because I would know," he said. At the sound of insistent knocking, Winter went to open the door.

***

Lisa clicked off the phone and turned to Gallagher and Smith.

"It was your lucky day," she said.

"Well done," Gallagher said. "I will give you the account number to send to Bob." Gallagher addressed Joseph Smith. "Mr. Smith, stay at the ready, please. Once the transfer is made, I trust your IT group will begin the trace. I want to know everything about "W," every alias, every shell company, every account, every transaction, every penny he has. And I want his exact location."

"Of course," Smith said.

"You're welcome," Lisa said, throwing a shit-eating grin in Smith's direction.

Chapter 71

Emma Flynn tugged on the café door. Her compact, sturdy, five-foot-five body handled the vacuum between the heated interior and the vortex of frigid wind around the entrance with ease. Still, she cursed silently, her daily diatribe against the freezing weather that never seemed to end. God, give me an unbearable Southern heat wave, she thought. *Bring it on.*

She didn't want to come to this meeting. Your fiancé's best friend calls you for only two reasons: he wants to arrange something for your fiancé's birthday, or he wants to talk about his ex-girlfriend. Entering the eatery felt like returning to the scene of last year's crime, ambushing Katerina for Ryan so he could plead his case.

She spotted Ryan at a table, staring out of the window, his coffee forgotten. She wanted to open with the line, "You'd make a lousy criminal, returning to your old haunt," but she wouldn't say that. Her Southern upbringing had taught her not to kick a man when he was down, and Detective Ryan Kellan was plunging toward the basement.

He glanced in her direction, straightening up in anticipation as she approached; rising, he helped her off with her coat. Emma allowed the chivalry and they sat down across from each other. She smoothed her nurse's uniform and then her honey blond hair held back in a ponytail.

"Thanks for coming," Ryan said. "Look, I don't want you to tell Frank about this. I'm a little—it's not—"

"If he asks, I'll tell him. If he doesn't, I won't bring it up."

Ryan nodded. "Have you heard from her? Do you know if she's back?"

Emma shook her head. "No, and maybe you should just let things be for now. Ryan, Katerina's special. She's different. She's not like most girls."

Ryan leaned forward with a sudden anger flashing as his eyes. "What does that mean?"

Emma sat back, putting space between herself and Ryan's aggression.

Ryan's shoulders dropped.

"Look," Emma began, "she has something . . . a vibe, like a magnet. She gives off something, she attracts—"

"Men."

"And trouble," Emma said with a nod. "I swear, she could stand in the corner of a room facin' the wall with her head down and still they would come, like flies on shit. I saw it countless times when we shared a place. Good guys, yeah, but a lot of bad guys, too. They all wanted her."

Ryan turned his head to stare out of the window.

Emma noted the strain in his face, his pale pallor.

"Call her," Ryan said.

"Sugar, you're makin' a mistake" Emma said.

Ryan took a hold of her wrist. "Call her."

Emma's eyes widened, her face flushing crimson. Ryan jerked away, releasing her. "Sorry," he said. "I didn't mean that. It won't happen again."

Emma kept her arms tucked against herself. "What I was sayin' is you're makin' a mistake. The last time we saw her, we just about called her a prostitute. You think she's just gonna forgive that? If I haven't been able to work up the nerve to call her, why would I suddenly do it now?"

"Because I want her back," Ryan said. "I need her in my life. Emma, she's the one. I know it. We're meant to be together. She needs me, too. I'm the one who can stop all this crazy. I'm the one who can get her out of all that shit that's always happening to her. She just needs the right man to take a hand with her. I'm that guy."

Emma kept the space between them. "You can't force people to be what they're not."

"She doesn't know what she should be," Ryan pressed, his voice growing louder. He surveyed the eatery and then whispered, "She's confused. I'm telling you, without me, she will get into trouble that she can't get out of. Now, please, help me get her back. Call her. Explain the situation. Please."

The silence hung between them, an eternity. "I'll text her and see what happens," Emma said.

Ryan exhaled, his hands splayed palms down on the table. "Thank you," he said.

Chapter 72

The three-level Tuscan style home sparkled in the waning rays of the sun, twinkling like a diamond against the oncoming night. Gazing at it, Katerina's breath caught in her throat.

The chilly, damp breeze off the Pacific fell against her face and curled around the bare skin of her torso. She shivered.

The ride to Balboa Island had been quick and silent. The driver, a bull of a man, performed his duties without a word or a smile. He held the door open for her when entering and exiting the car, grasping her elbow, like Sergei's nephews. His ham-sized hand made her feel caught, trapped. She ran through one last mental pep talk, reviewing the questions Mikhailovich might ask, the answers she would have to give. But the phone call with Lisa kept invading her thoughts, an unwelcome diversion, demanding a place in the front of her mind, breaking her concentration. *Not now, Katerina. Remember where you are, right now. You cannot blow this.*

The driver escorted her to the patio. She glanced back across the water toward the Fun Zone, drawn to the lights of the Ferris wheel winking against an inky backdrop. Somewhere over there, Winter and Daniel Clay watched and waited. She turned back to the house, its wide-open pocket doors beckoning her to enter. The driver, his hand still at her elbow, guided her inside.

Katerina stepped out of Southern California and into the Italian Renaissance. Glancing down, she stepped across area rugs adorned with a zigzag pattern, accented by the two-headed eagle. Above her, frescoes of cherubic angels adorned the Great Room walls; she followed them to the curved latticework bannister and staircase.

The pressure vanished from her elbow as the driver drifted away. Guests milled through the house, men in tuxedos, women in elegant dresses, wearing obviously expensive jewelry. She saw young women, like herself, some on the arm of a man, others alone; girlfriends, lovers, ornaments; anonymous, they would come and go. *No one will remember they were here.*

Kat scanned the room for Mikhailovich. Nothing. She had a small window and she needed to get moving. Keeping to the periphery, her phone ever present, Kat snapped pictures on the sly until stealing away up the stairs.

***

Alexander Winter sat at the table on the deck, watching Daniel Clay dig into his meal with a hearty appetite.

"C'mon, man, eat something," Clay said, nodding toward Winter's full plate. "Don't worry about her. Everything's going to be fine. Didn't I promise I would help you out?"

Winter nodded, staring off across the bay. With Katerina out of his reach, unprotected, his nerves were stretching to the breaking point. His stomach clenched in hunger, but he had no appetite.

"So how come Katerina gets on so well with Viktor Mikhailovich?" Clay asked.

"They're both Leos," Winter said.

Clay laughed. "No shit, really. Think about it. Whatever you guys are looking for, he might keep it in the bedroom. Little Katerina might get to see it."

Winter glared at him, his hands curling into fists.

"Hey, man, I'm just kidding. Of course, that won't happen. My guys are keeping a close eye on her. While we're waiting, we can talk about our partnership," Clay said, taking a swig of wine.

"I already have a partner," Winter said, his eyes staring out across the inlet.

Clay nodded. "Yeah, but we have this whole Butch, Sundance, Etta Place thing going on. You know Etta felt torn between the two men. Should I ask Kat about it?"

"You shouldn't be asking her anything," Winter said.

"All right then, I'm asking you. What about the museum? What about the Monet?"

"I've already made my arrangements," Winter said, gazing across the bay as he slipped his phone out of his pocket. He checked his watch and typed into the phone.

Daniel Clay smiled.

***

Katerina crept up the stairs, the party noise below her fading away. She heard the buzzing of the phone and checked it. A text message flashed on the screen. One of the "boyfriend" texts, coming right on time. She texted back a quick retort and hit send.

She found herself standing in a loft-style office. She gave it a sweep, already disappointed at seeing nothing unusual. She was about to tuck her phone back into her purse but remembered Winter's admonition. *Don't jump to conclusions. Don't lose your temper.* She took snaps of the area including the desk and a decorative wood chest. A few more clicks, they uploaded and emailed.

The phone buzzed with another text from "the boyfriend." The words struck her as familiar and she realized why. Winter had appropriated Ryan's texts from her regular phone, re-sending them to the burner phone.

As Kat moved to continue her search, a panel door slid open; she found herself standing in front of the elevator and Viktor Mikhailovich.

"Oh," she managed.

"Why you are up here?" Viktor demanded. With his poker face, Kat couldn't tell if he was angry or suspicious.

"Looking for you," she said.

With a curt nod, he took her by the hand, giving her a head-to-toe examination.

"Exquisite," he said, pulling her towards him.

She slid out of his grasp, wandering the office area; his eyes followed her every move.

"You must conduct all your important business here," she said.

"No talk of business," Mikhailovich said. "I want to talk fun—games. Games for two. You like to play games?"

"I like to dress up and look pretty," Kat said, with a coy tip of her head.

"That can be game," he said.

"How?"

"I like to undress pretty things."

Kat stopped at the decorative wood chest. She leaned over, running her fingertips across the piece while she turned to look at him. "Maybe you like to *collect* pretty things," she said.

He gave a laugh as he came up behind her, curving himself against her, pressing close. Katerina fought the urge to run. *Hold on. It'll be over soon.*

"You are smart college girl. I like that. Yes, I enjoy to collect beautiful things. I am very—particular in what I choose. I chose all the things in this house myself."

"I would have thought you like new things," she said.

Mikhailovich shook his head. "Antiques, the old things, they are reliable."

Katerina gave a half-hearted pout, as if she had been insulted. He squeezed her tighter to placate her.

"They have witnessed many things, they hold many secrets. If they could talk . . . but I do not worry. They will never tell."

Chalking up the rambling to some obscure Russian wisdom, she turned around so they stood inches from each other. "I can keep a secret," she whispered.

Viktor smiled. Katerina's stomach turned.

The buzz of the cell phone sounded. He lifted the phone from her hand. She stood dumb as he tapped and scrolled through her messages, reading the emphatic, passionate pleadings. *What if the photos haven't uploaded? What if they didn't go through? What if they didn't erase? What if he sees them?*

She watched Mikhailovich's eyebrows lift as he read the text. "He is pest," he said, tucking her phone in his pocket.

Without warning, he leaned in and kissed her. Every muscle in her body froze. The kiss was restrained but she sensed the power behind it.

"I would be pest, too," he whispered. "I know what I like, I know right away. You are special girl. I want to treat you special. You believe me?"

Kat gazed up into his eyes, her lips slightly parted. *No chance.* "Oh, yes."

"Good. I will give you everything you like."

As she did her best to beam at him in delight, Katerina wondered what she looked like in the mirror. With his next word, she knew she had done her job well.

"Come," he said.

***

The chill in the night air snaked its way inside Alexander Winter, tormenting him as he pulled his phone from his pocket and scrolled. The raw need to tap on the arm of his chair gnawed at him. He continued to grip the phone with a light touch, paying studious attention to the texts.

"She done? Are the pictures in?"

Winter nodded. "He probably took her phone by now. They need to be deleted."

"Hey, that software will work, believe me. He won't find a thing. Hundred percent." Clay paused. "Look, I like you."

Winter chuckled.

"I don't want you to have a problem with Mikhailovich because I get into the museum first. Mikhailovich is a real bad guy. He's connected all the way up to the top in the Kremlin."

"So you told me," Winter said with a shrug.

Clay's cell phone buzzed. He connected the call and listened, and then turned his head, gazing out across the water into the distance.

"We have a little problem," Clay said to Winter.

Winter shot up in his seat, staring out across the bay.

"They've got her on the dock," Clay said. "She's being moved."

"Shit." Winter's jaw clenched so tight his teeth began to ache.

***

A bodyguard had hustled Katerina past the guests drifting in and out of the house, ushering her to the dock and onto a small boat. The engine revved and the vessel moved out of the channel.

Shivering in the night, the salty air clinging to her skin, Katerina spied two small yachts; and behind them a super yacht.

**

When they pulled up alongside, a bear of a man grasped Kat's hand, hoisting her on board. The chilled, whipping wind curled around her, making her teeth chatter. One of the men took her by the arm, hustling her inside.

Ushering her through an entry hall lined with gold leaf, a bodyguard deposited Katerina, without ceremony, in a large bedroom. *His bedroom.* She forced her most innocent smile and he left without a word, closing the door behind him. Standing in the center of the room, Kat sucked in deep gulps of air, trying in vain to quell the panic threatening to engulf her. She stared at the king-sized bed covered with a purple satin quilt and shimmery silk sheets. Winter's words echoed in her head as the bile rose in her throat. *I won't be able to come for you.*

There's no way out.

**

Winter watched as Daniel Clay listened on his cell phone, interjecting an "mmm" every few minutes.

"So?" Winter asked.

Clay held up a finger, listened, and then put his hand over the mouthpiece. "She's on board. They just took her to his room."

"What, no foreplay?" Winter seethed.

Clay uncovered the receiver and said, "What are the options?" He listened again, then put his hand over the mouthpiece again. "Give me all the details of the Monet job. The whole plan, everything."

Winter's eyes darkened. He shifted in his seat, ready to rise up and lunge forward.

Clay raised his free hand in a sign of surrender. "You know it's not just me in this. I gotta keep my guys happy. You don't give me the info, I can't help her. Do we have a deal?"

Alexander Winter rattled off the information without hesitation. "Now get her out of there," he said.

Clay uttered "we're good here" into the phone and hung up.

***

When the door opened, Katerina started. Viktor Mikhailovich said a few cursory words in Russian to the bodyguard standing outside the door. She saw the bodyguard move away as Viktor closed the door. At the click of the lock, her heart began to thud against her ribs. She fought to remain in full doe-eyed college girl mode gazing in wonder at her next sugar daddy.

"Everything is so beautiful," she gushed.

He didn't answer as he came to her and took her hands in his own, placing them on his shoulders. He ran his hands down the length of her torso, gliding over her hips and back again. Her stomach roiled. The polite foreplay was just that. A minor recoil, a mild rejection, any sign of resistance and the farce would end. What did Daniel say? *Don't do that. That'll get you a beating.* The smallest slight would result in pain, terrible pain. *And I can't stop it.* He tilted his head, his mouth moving to her neck. Katerina held stock still, until the loud grumble of the engines caused her to give a start. He smirked.

"Where are we going?" she asked.

"Do not worry," he said. "We take nice trip. I buy you presents. You like that, yes? You will swim in pool, you can lie on deck, and warm yourself in the sun."

"I don't have a bathing suit," Kat teased.

"No need for suit," he said.

"But the crew," she said.

"Ahh, you do not worry about them, they see nothing," he said, waving off the comment. "I want to see you," he whispered in her ear.

Taking hold of her, he grasped the waistband of her skirt, yanking it down in one sweeping move, revealing her barely there black lace bikini panties. Slipping his hand between her thighs, he grasped the soft, hidden space, his fingers giving a rough massage. Katerina closed her eyes, conscious of his scrutiny, remembering to plaster a smile on her face in spite of the pain of his touch.

Viktor took his hand away and stepped her out of the skirt.

A loud knock at the door and Kat swept up the skirt, crushing it against her body.

Viktor yanked the door open. A valet, wiry with straight black hair, and a face of sharp planes and angles, entered. He pushed a rolling cart brimming with food and a bottle of champagne.

The valet seemed not to notice Katerina as he peppered Viktor with questions in Russian. Katerina watched Viktor's annoyance grow with every query until he waved his arms. "Is enough, is enough," he said, his voice rising. "Get out now, get out." With an abundance of obsequious apologies, the valet backed out of the room.

Viktor took off his jacket and threw it on the bed. Grabbing the skirt from her, he tossed it aside. "Lift your arms," he ordered.

Katerina obeyed.

He took hold of the fabric and swept it over her head. Sitting down on the edge of the bed he took hold of her, pulling her over to straddle him, his hands exploring her breasts. As he put his mouth on her, Katerina felt a curious absence, as if she was watching it happen to someone else.

She felt him grow hard through his clothing and her mind went blank, entering a suspended state in space and time. Her body's movements did not belong to her; these were the actions of a stranger. In this vacuum, she endured each interminable moment, knowing it would grow worse, knowing there was nothing to do but wait for it to be over.

Hooking his thumbs in each side of her panties, he pulled to snap the fabric apart.

Sudden shouts and cursing from the hallway jarred them both. Footsteps thundered toward the stateroom; Katerina scrambled off Viktor's lap, snatching up his jacket to cover herself as a pounding began on the stateroom door.

Muttering in anger, Viktor pulled the door open. The bodyguard, eyes darkened like a thundercloud, spoke in hurried Russian. Viktor listened, said a few words and the bodyguard disappeared down the hallway. Viktor closed the door and turned to Katerina; she stood motionless, hugging the jacket against herself, fearful of what might happen next.

"Get dressed," Viktor ordered.

"What's wrong?" she asked, her voice shaking as she pulled on her clothes.

"You attract attention," he said.

"I . . . I'm so sorry, I didn't mean to," she said.

"I know you did not," he said as he took one last leer at her full, rounded breasts as they disappeared beneath her top. He held his arm out, beckoning for her to hurry, as if anxious to be rid of her.

***

The bodyguard escorted Katerina back on deck. She turned at the noises from behind her; the valet who had wheeled in the food cart. Flanked on both sides by Viktor's bodyguards, he appeared the worse for wear now, his face purpling and blood dripping from his chin. Viktor said something in Russian and the valet went sailing overboard. Katerina wondered if the crew would have found this amusing if not for the presence of their boss, who clearly didn't see the humor. The bodyguard produced a broken cell phone from his pocket and showed it to Viktor. Katerina was led down to a small boat, handed her purse, and ushered to a seat.

As the small vessel made its way back, Katerina shivered in the brisk night air, coaching herself, hearing Winter's voice in her head, the words he whispered upstate, in the storm. *Hang on. One more minute.* She kept her eyes peeled for that first sight of the dock, knowing every minute brought her closer to escape—and back to Winter.

Chapter 73

Two bodyguards walked Katerina into the hotel, flanking her in the elevator as it shot up to her floor.

"Thank you," Kat said as she drew her room key card out of her purse. "I think I'll be all right now."

They didn't move.

She passed the room key card over the sensor, waited for the green light and opened the door. One bodyguard placed an arm out, like a toll gate, to prevent her from entering. The other bodyguard entered the room. She heard the opening of doors and closets, hoping against hope Winter wasn't inside. After a few moments, he reappeared.

"Is okay for you," he said.

"Thank you, good night," she said with a nod.

She locked the door behind them.

Katerina sank onto the edge of the bed, her hands in her lap, trembling.

***

She peeled off her clothes, leaving them in a pile on the floor. In the shower, she scrubbed herself from head to toe under the pounding hot water, convincing herself that nothing had actually happened.

Forget it.

It could have been worse.

A lot worse.

Still, the mental images and imaginations brought a surge of bile from her belly up to her throat; she leaned against the tiled wall, waiting for the feeling to pass.

After the shower, Kat bundled into the hotel's plush terry robe and climbed into bed. She watched television, using mindless channel flipping to decompress, wondering when she would see the pictures she had taken, what the next step would be . . . when Winter would come to her. She closed her eyes, telling herself it would only be for a moment.

***

Katerina woke in the dark to a persistent buzzing sound. Disoriented, she lurched out of bed, stumbling toward the noise. She found the culprit in a zippered compartment of her suitcase.

A cell phone.

"Hello," Kat said.

"At any point this evening, were you *not* wearing your clothes?" Winter's voice came over the line.

Kat hesitated. "Yes."

She listened to the beat of silence.

"Are you hurt?" he asked.

"No," she said.

"Did anything happen?"

"No," she said.

"Then don't tell me," he said. "The pictures came through."

"He took the phone."

"Good," Winter said. "He'll have the texts from the boyfriend. Nothing else."

"Who was the guy who went overboard?"

"Just a guy who went overboard. He took heat for taking pictures of you and Viktor. Viktor thinks he was an investigator taking snaps for his wife to use in the divorce."

"Did you know Mikhailovich was going to take me on that yacht?"

"I suspected he might."

"Did you know Daniel could take care of it?"

"Yes."

"And what did this cost you?" Katerina asked.

"Nothing I wasn't prepared to pay."

Katerina took the news in silence. *I'm putting you at risk. And I don't want to let you go.*

Winter interrupted her thoughts. "You did good work tonight."

"Viktor had two other smaller yachts close by."

"Wealthy men often travel with an entourage."

"I would have wound up on one of them, wouldn't I?"

Winter didn't answer.

"Don't lie to me, Bob. Not about this."

"Possibly," he said. "I don't know."

"Do you think he had a buyer for me?" she asked.

"I doubt it," Winter said. "First, he was going to test you out himself."

"And then?" Kat asked.

"Keep you or pass you along."

"Then Daniel was telling the truth. That's how it works. In a second, I'm gone . . . where no one can find me."

"Katie," Winter said, his voice gentle. "You're safe now. I promise you no one is going to come to your hotel room and take you away."

Katerina didn't answer.

"Do you trust me?" he asked.

"You said trust is not a word we use."

"With *other* people," Winter said.

"Yes, I trust you," she said.

Katerina had a sudden urgent need to push the evening and Viktor Mikhailovich as far away from herself as she could. "When do I see the pictures?' she asked, changing the subject.

"We'll look at them together. But for now, tell me every word he said," Winter instructed.

Katerina repeated the evening's conversation verbatim, her face flushing when she skipped over Viktor's intimate comments. "What now?"

"I'm sure Viktor is already planning a reunion. He's going to come back for you. He was interrupted. That annoyed him."

"He could get any girl. What's so special about me?" she asked.

She heard his soft laugh through the phone line. "He'll be back. Next time, he'll make sure no one interrupts."

"Why haven't you come?" Kat asked, afraid because she suspected the answer.

"He's having you watched."

Katerina paced the floor. "So, what do I do?"

"Get some sleep. We have work to do and we'll get to it. I'll be in touch in the morning."

"Bob," she said, calling him back from hanging up. "I'm getting better at lying."

"I know you are, Katie. Soon. First things first. Tomorrow we set up your shell company and account."

The question "How?" sat on the edge of her lips but Katerina held it in check. If Winter said it would be done, she trusted he could get around Mikhailovich's watchers. *This is what I wanted. To disappear, get away from everyone. Everyone but you.*

"Do you know where you want to go?" he asked, as if reading her mind.

"Some place my mom will like. Some place quiet. Maybe a little village in France. I speak French."

"Really? Talk to me," he said.

Je t'aime.

"Bonjour, comment allez vous," she said.

"Beautiful," he said, the gravel sound of his voice warm and deep. "I don't speak French."

"Have you ever been to a foreign country?"

"Yes."

Kat opened her mouth. She calculated how many questions she would blow trying to determine which one.

"Can you speak the language of that country?"

"Yes," he said.

"Say something."

"It's better if I tell you in person."

"No," Katerina said, her heart skipping a beat. "Now, please."

"*Voglio fare l'amore con te ora,*" he whispered, lingering over the word *l'amore.*

Katerina's belly tumbled. *I know you'll be nice.*

"Would you like me to translate?" he asked.

"Does it have something to do with being together in your hotel room?"

"Yes, it does" he said.

"I get the idea," she said, suddenly sweltering in her robe. "Are we going to get back to that?"

"Would you like to?"

"Yes," she answered without hesitation.

"I'll keep that in mind," he said.

***

After clicking off the call, Katerina settled in for the remainder of a restless night. She lay in the dark, allowing her thoughts to drift unchecked. She thought of the part she had just played with Mikhailovich, the sugar baby. Katerina Mills had vanished. Her father had done it all those years, pretending to be someone else.

Am I my father's daughter?

Chapter 74

In a hotel room, Daniel Clay sat at the desk, poring over a campus map of the Los Angeles County Museum of Art.

His crew consisted of three others: Halliday, earnest, the worrier of the group; Burnett, medium height with a full head of hair and an easy smile, the roll of pudge hanging over his pants making him look like he should be driving an insurance desk; and Prescott, level-headed and steady. Except for Daniel, they all looked toward the bathroom as Nicholas emerged, a towel wrapped around his waist and another in hand, the sharp angles of his face marred by swollen bruises and angry cuts with clotted blood on his forehead and chin. He toweled off his wet hair, his damp neck and chest still glistening.

"You want to tell me why I had to take a beating for that little chickie," he said. "I had my own sweet setup going."

"It's not about the girl," Clay said, still intent on his study.

"We shouldn't be getting involved in this," Halliday said. "She probably told him that the idiot's painting hidden in the Porsche was a fake."

"She definitely did," Clay said. "But she did a decent job trying to convince me otherwise. She's learning."

"Halsy's got a point, Danny," Burnett said. "What the hell is it with the pictures she took in the Russian's house? We gotta know what we're into."

"Yeah, what is the story with Mikhailovich and the Monet?" Prescott asked. "Who is he selling the painting to?"

"I don't know yet," Clay said.

"You don't know?" Nicholas pressed. "Six months of work shot to shit and you don't know if the Golden Boy is worth all this trouble?"

"Oh, he's worth the trouble, believe me. I've been following his trail."

"And you never got anything solid, Danny, just a bunch of aliases," Halliday said. "He's a damn ghost."

"A ghost that disappeared until suddenly late last year he's back in business. Now I know why."

"You're obsessed, you know that?" Burnett said. "You're like that guy chasing the whale. Captain Queeg."

"No, no, no. Queeg had the fruit fetish," Prescott said. "The guy with the whale was Captain Bligh."

"It was Captain Ahab, assholes," Halliday said.

"Who gives a shit?" Nicholas said, throwing his hands in the air. "I had serious business going on until you geniuses came knocking on my door. How did I get so freakin' lucky?"

Daniel Clay glanced up, giving Nicholas a pointed look. "Because that's the way the Boss wanted it."

"Danny, we have no leverage if we don't know who Alexander Winter really is," Halliday said.

"I'm telling you, relax," Daniel Clay said. "It's gonna come. Alexander Winter, Bob, whatever his name is, he's pay dirt. He's done it all. Museums, private homes, shit, he takes jobs to steal what's already been stolen."

"You *think*," Prescott said. "Where's the proof?"

"Trust me. He's responsible for some of the biggest heists in the last decade. He's gonna give us names, dates, locations, an inventory of billions of dollars' worth of art. He's a goddamn walking treasure map and it's all gonna fall right in our lap."

Prescott shook his head. "And he's just going to give all of it to you."

"That's right. We're going to be very close."

"Really, sweetheart?" Nicholas said, his lip curling. "Let me know if he whispers any sweet nothings in your ear. Better yet, send me a postcard."

"I won't need to," Clay said. "From now on, you're gonna be here with us. That's the way the Boss wants it. We need to keep an eye on Katerina."

"You just said she doesn't matter," Burnett pointed out.

"She matters to Alexander Winter," Halliday said.

Clay pointed at Halliday with a nod.

"We should just squeeze the old guy she was talking to at the museum," Burnett said.

"Forget him," Clay said. "Winter's using him. He doesn't know anything."

"Doesn't mean he can't be useful," Prescott offered.

"Everybody relax, okay?" Clay said. "Payday is coming, don't you worry. We're going to arrange a little setup, a meeting for Mr. Winter with a potential new client. When he shows up, we reel him in. Whatever this shit is with Mikhailovich, Katerina is in way over her head. She's going to be very handy when it's time to play let's make a deal."

Mumbling an obscenity, Nicholas stormed back into the bathroom, slamming the door behind him.

"I don't know what he's griping about," Burnett said. "We fished him out of the water, didn't we?"

The group shared a laugh, but it soon died away.

"Danny . . . you sure the Boss is okay with this?" Halliday asked.

"Hundred percent," Daniel Clay said. "Don't worry about it." He returned his attention to the map of the museum. "The Boss is fine with everything. Alexander Winter is the gift that's going to keep on giving for a long, long time."

Chapter 75

Katerina settled behind the wheel and turned over the engine. Taking out her cell phone, she waited for the call. When the phone buzzed, she connected the call on the speaker.

"Good morning," came Winter's voice.

"Good morning, Mr. Phelps," Kat teased. "Where's the self-destructing tape?"

He didn't answer.

"Sorry," she said.

"Check the glove compartment," he said.

She popped the glove box and found an envelope. Peeking inside, she found a set of forms. Her heart skipped in anticipation and she almost didn't hear his instructions.

"Pull out of the parking lot and head for the freeway."

Kat stashed the papers on the passenger seat and did as she was told. "Where are you?"

"Close by as always."

Her stomach somersaulted as a realization set in. "Who's following me?"

"Mikhailovich has a two-man detail on you."

Kat's grip on the wheel tightened. The joke she had thought so clever a moment ago turned sour in her mouth. "Shit," she blurted.

"Relax, let's see if we can't throw them off that intoxicating vanilla scent. We have work to do today."

***

It took over an hour and a trip to two malls, but Winter finally gave Katerina the all-clear. She pulled into a hotel parking lot and cut the engine. The drive had frayed her nerves, a flash back to the previous month in New York, stealing the Porsche, bringing it to Desucci. The fear didn't fit with the sunshine, the palm trees, the daily mirage whispering to her that this place was safe, an escape from what she left behind. Shaking off the serpent's song, Kat checked her look in the rearview mirror, smoothed out her shoulder length, jet black wig, got out of the car, and headed inside.

Striding into the business center, Kat found Winter waiting for her. He was clean shaven, dressed in black slacks and a crisp white shirt. They completed the application forms and sent off the fax. Kat paid careful attention, committing the process to memory, ensuring she would be able to take care of it alone next time.

He whispered in her ear and she nodded and walked out, leaving him to his own business.

Back in the car she waited until the cell phone buzzed and then turned over the engine to pull out of the lot and follow instructions.

***

Winter led her back to an industrial complex of warehouses near LAX. The one-story buildings, low and flat, sat in the midst of car rental companies, their shuttle buses tooling in and out.

Katerina wondered why Winter had chosen this bustling place of activity at this hour of the day. *Wouldn't the dead of night, under the cover of darkness, be more suitable?*

Entering the warehouse, memories of Vito Massone flooded back to her. Even though this warehouse was a clean hospital white, the antiseptic space did nothing to quell her mental replay of the experience. Massone would be held in check for the time being, courtesy of Anthony Desucci. *Anthony Desucci, who didn't kill me for lying to him and deceiving him with a fake Porsche, even though I indirectly caused him to be left with a fake painting. Why didn't he kill me?*

Kat forced herself to let the train of thought go, spying the gym bag on the floor next to a table with two chairs. Winter sat on one of the chairs. She realized the sounds of life outside the warehouse had faded away.

As she approached Winter, Kat swept the wig off her head, revealing a tight braid pinned neatly to her head. A surge of excitement fluttered within her as his eyes, a fiery blue, fixed upon her.

Katerina's attention shifted to the series of photos spread out on the table; the interior of Mikhailovich's house.

"Are they worth anything?" Kat asked as she slid into her seat, doubt punctuating her words. "I never got to the bedroom. If he has a safe, it was probably in there."

Winter tapped the picture of the decorative wood chest. "This is the safe."

She studied the photo, shaking her head. "That's a wood chest."

"Herring and Farrel. Late eighteenth century. Painted to look like wood. The dial is concealed under the right-side door. It's a three number, combination lock. Did he say anything about it?"

"He said all antiques are reliable. He said they were witnesses to things and they knew secrets but they would never tell." Kat searched to find the sense in Mikhailovich's words. "Do you think he had a relocker or a booby trap installed?"

Winter's eyebrows quirked in surprise at her question. "For something this old, it would be pointless to do a retrofit. He's decided to be clever and hide something in plain sight."

Katerina picked up the photograph. "So, I'm breaking into a safe?"

"No, *I'm* breaking into a safe. But you're going to learn how."

Winter opened the gym bag, extracted an item, and placed it on the table. Katerina surveyed the combination lock mounted into a stand, the square piece of glass cut through the center of the lock, leaving the dial on one side and the mechanism on the other.

As if she had just been given a new toy, Katerina leaned in, examining it on both sides.

And I didn't get you anything, sat on the tip of her tongue. She clamped it down, her curiosity already working its wicked magic.

"Welcome to lock manipulation," Winter said. "Lesson one."

She met his eyes, her mouth slightly ajar, at a loss for a comeback. No shit, no bullshit, Katerina thought. *Playtime is over. This is happening.*

***

They worked in one-hour intervals with Winter calling for a break whenever he detected a glassy, far-away look creeping into her eyes. She absorbed everything into her flawless memory. He didn't need to repeat information because she wouldn't forget. He peppered her with review questions, and she fired off her answers in rapid succession.

He demonstrated the parts of the lock: the wheels, the fly, the pins, the fence, their uses and functions. It had been how he received his training and the instruction had served him well.

"The fly sits on the wheel," Winter said, pointing it out, "and the motion is transferred from the fly to the drive pins, they connect and drive the wheels. The object is to take readings in order to find the spot where each wheel's gate," he continued, indicating the square cut-out in each wheel, "is positioned under the fence." He ran his finger over a bar positioned above the wheels. "Once you get the gates lined up, the fence will fall, the bolt will retract, and the lock will open."

"Won't I just hear it?" she asked.

"Sound is the least important element," Winter said, "unless you're listening for someone coming up behind you while you're trying to do this. Your sense of touch is your closest friend."

He took her hand and placed it on the dial. "You must be consistent in touch when you do this. You need to find your rhythm and stick to it. Remember, you're trying to position the gate as close as you can to fall under the fence. You could be off by a fraction and that's the difference between success and disappointment."

The warmth of his touch made her breath catch and she understood why he had chosen the antiseptic, open space. *Because this is work time, not playtime. No fooling around.*

"Remember, your most important tool is your consistency of rhythm and touch," he repeated, his voice soft and patient. "Your movements in working the dial never vary."

She nodded.

He taught her how to do a wheel count, rotating the dial in order to tell whether a lock had three or four wheels. By the afternoon, he spread out the charts she would use to take contact readings, her first attempts to locate the magic number for one wheel.

"They never use charts in the movies," Kat said.

"*We* use charts, Sundance."

She followed him with her eyes as he got up from the table. "Was it something I said?"

"I'm getting lunch. I'll be back," Winter said and slipped out noiselessly. If she hadn't been watching him, she would never have heard him go.

***

Fifteen minutes later, Katerina's hands had broken out into a sweat as she scribbled numbers, erased them, and scribbled more numbers on the charts.

In a fit of frustration, she checked behind her for Winter. With the coast clear, Kat adjusted the cutaway, tilting it toward her, switching between observing the dial and the wheels behind.

"What are you doing?" a voice whispered in her ear. Kat started, letting out an involuntary yelp, the cutaway slipping out of her grasp and hitting the table, the loud *thud* reverberating in the open space. *Busted.*

She hazarded a glance at him out of the corner of her eye.

"Peeking," Kat admitted.

"There's no peeking," Winter whispered.

"Depends on what I'm working on," she said.

"Mmm," he said, the deep sound resonating in her core.

Winter put a plastic bag on the table and sat down next to her. "What were you thinking about?" he asked. "Tell me your exact train of thought while working through the process."

"First, I thought that I didn't know what was taking so long to get the right number and then how I was hungry and then how I couldn't figure out the number and then where the hell were you because I'm hungry and then I got annoyed because you picked the most unromantic place to have this lesson."

"At what point did you decide to tilt the cutaway and check the back."

"Oh, that was a while ago, before any of that other . . . stuff."

"I see," he said. "Do you know the *second* most important quality for lock manipulation?"

Her eyebrows arched. "Concentration?" she asked drily.

"You get an A," he said.

"Are you going to ask me what the first, most important quality is for lock manipulation?"

"I am," Winter said.

"Then my guess would be . . . patience?"

"A-plus," he answered, all the while considering her.

A deep sigh escaped her. With every exercise, the pressure increased, as if an actual physical weight continued bearing down on her: Winter working to reshape parts of her personality, pushing her to change out of a necessity that would not be denied. An involuntary reaction kept kicking in, a natural desire to push back, to resist. Yet, he continued to carve away, to remake her; two steps forward, three steps back, a painful process. She had succeeded with Zilinsky but failed here. She recalled Professor Schoeffling's lessons on Buddhism. Suffering comes from a lack of acceptance. *No shit, Sherlock.*

***

They ate in silence.

"Is it pleasant where you are?" Winter asked, seeing her faraway look.

Kat smiled at being caught and then said, "I just don't see Mikhailovich sending an exploration team to dig in Siberia. Do you really think it's possible he has the last Tsar's crown in that safe?"

"I don't know."

"I guess that was never your problem, not knowing, since you always steal to order."

Winter smiled. "Is that a question or a statement?"

Katerina reflected. "Statement. My question is, how do you deal with a situation when you don't know what you're dealing with?"

"Chickens and eggs, Katerina."

"What does that mean?"

"It means it doesn't pay to think about what you don't know or what you don't have."

"C'mon," she chided. "You don't ever let your imagination wander?"

A smile crept to Winter's lips. "I let my imagination wander about certain things," he said.

Kat nodded, a blush burning her cheeks, feeling the familiar rush of anxiety, the best kind of nervous excitement.

"All right," Winter began, "suppose we let our minds wander. Suppose he has one or all three of the missing Crown jewels in the safe. Suppose you get your hands on them. What are you going to do with them?"

She stopped in mid-chew.

"Possession is nine-tenths of the law, Katerina."

"Said the man who's a thief," she said.

"It is what it is," Winter said, without offense. "Find the truth and admit it. What would you do with them? Give them to your client, who's *not* a Romanov? Keep them? Sell them? Where? To who?"

Katerina felt like a target in a shooting gallery as he fired the options at her.

"What is Zilinsky going to do with them?" she deflected.

Winter shrugged. "He could make copies and sell them, keep the originals in reserve. He could probably do that for quite a while, if he's careful. You could do that as well."

"That's some con. You're a regular Henry Gondorff, aren't you?"

He gave her a blank stare.

"Oh, c'mon," she protested. "*The Sting?* The movie? Newman and Redford? Newman plays Henry Gondorff, training Redford's novice grifter Johnny Hooker to play the big con? Didn't you ever go the movies?" she asked.

"I prefer other activities in the dark," Winter said with a smile.

Kat's cheeks burned afresh but she couldn't argue that he had made his point. *I haven't thought of any of this. I'm completely unprepared.* Katerina glanced at the cutaway. "What now, Professor?"

"Keep researching, Katie. Remember, even liars leave clues, because the best lies are as close to the truth as possible. Something Zilinsky said will lead the way. Now, finish your lunch, Sundance. And then it's back to work."

"What happens tomorrow?" she asked.

"Tomorrow you return to playing your part. Go shopping, spend money, practice, and wait for Mikhailovich to call."

Kat nodded, knowing once again Winter withheld information. Her thoughts ran to the shell company that would soon be in place. If this situation worked out, somehow, she would be out and gone; MJM, Desucci, Massone, Sheridan, drug dealers, and John Reynolds would all be a memory.

She looked over at Alexander Winter.

I don't want you to be a memory.

Chapter 76

John Reynolds maintained a simple, efficient office in Midtown. The deep brown décor resulted in a utilitarian atmosphere, the exact opposite of the rich, colorful, modern ambiance of his apartment.

On the fiftieth floor, Reynolds' secretary, Elizabeth, a woman in her middle forties, who would have been described as "handsome" at the turn of the twentieth century, ushered Detectives O'Connoll, Kellan, and Lashiver into the stolid space.

The detectives took note of the beige panels behind the enormous desk, covering the windows.

"Mr. Reynolds avoids daylight, Elizabeth?" Detective Kellan asked.

"The panels are fully retractable," Elizabeth said in her customary efficient, humorless delivery. "I'm preparing for Mr. Reynolds' conference call. The panels cut the glare on his computer screen."

Lashiver wandered close to the desk, peering around the other side. "So, Mr. Reynolds takes all of his conference calls here?"

Elizabeth stood with hands folded one over the other. "Yes."

"And the computer has a web cam," Ryan said, maneuvering around the other side. "And everyone on the call can see him?"

Elizabeth eyed O'Connoll, who stood silent and watchful. "Participants with a laptop have a webcam. Others with a desktop may have a web cam installed," she answered with a deliberate patience. "If an executive is traveling, he, or she, will call in and listen."

The detectives nodded again.

"How long have you worked for Mr. Reynolds?" Detective O'Connoll asked.

Fifteen years," Elizabeth said. "I relocated when he moved his company from Illinois."

"What was Mr. Reynolds' business in Illinois?"

"He began in materials and construction and then expanded, adding holding companies and investing."

"What does he invest in?" Lashiver asked.

"He has a diversified portfolio, food processing, insurance, utilities, and technology."

The detectives nodded.

Ryan pointed to a closed door. "And what is in here?" he asked.

"That is Mr. Reynolds' private washroom," she said.

"Could I just use . . ." Ryan began, his hand on the doorknob.

"There are executive washrooms down the hall—"

"I'll just be a minute," Ryan said over her protests as he opened the door and backed into the private bathroom.

The door closed leaving Elizabeth, Lashiver, and O'Connoll standing in silence. Lashiver smiled. O'Connoll did not.

***

Inside the bathroom, Ryan searched for a sign of a false wall or panel, anything that would give an indication of a secret exit. After searching along the seams of the wall, he lowered his arms in frustration.

***

When Ryan emerged from the bathroom, he found John Reynolds standing in the middle of the office.

Reynolds took in Lashiver and Ryan. "Detectives. What a surprise." He eyes flickered over O'Connoll. "And you brought reinforcements. Long overdue, I should think."

Ryan gave his best smile.

***

John Reynolds sat at his desk, in front of his computer, glancing down at his cell phone. Behind him, Elizabeth crouched over his shoulder, tapping keys on the computer keyboard.

"I don't understand what I did here," Reynolds said to her.

"Mr. Reynolds, can we speak privately," Lashiver said.

"My assistant is my most trusted confidant, detectives, perhaps even more so than my attorney. She is aware of my late wife's failings, and you may speak freely."

"Mr. Reynolds," O'Connoll said.

Reynolds gave a curt nod and Elizabeth straightened and left the room.

"Mr. Reynolds, Will Temple has been found. He's dead."

Reynolds pressed the intercom button. "Elizabeth, let the others know the conference call will be delayed."

Reynolds slipped his cell phone into his pocket and sat back in his executive chair. "You gentlemen are under the impression that I don't keep up with the news."

Detective O'Connoll continued. "We think it's possible Will Temple was killed by the same person who killed your wife. The killer could have become aware of Mr. Temple while stalking Mrs. Reynolds."

Reynolds nodded his head. "I see. But why would the killer choose Mr. Temple? He chose two women as the first victims."

"He?" O'Connoll asked.

"A logical supposition," Reynolds said with a bored sigh. "The perpetrator of the crimes," he corrected, his voice clipped with annoyance.

"We haven't figured that out yet, sir," Lashiver said.

"How silly of me. Of course not," Reynolds said. "Detectives, why are you here?"

"Mr. Reynolds, we have reason to be concerned for your safety," Lashiver said.

"Will Temple had been abused prior to his death," Ryan said.

"How so?" Reynolds asked.

"I don't think we should get into that," O'Connoll said.

"No, I think Mr. Reynolds should be aware of the danger he's in," Ryan said. "The victim had been chained and subjected to sexual torture."

John Reynolds took out his cell phone and glanced down at it, then shifted it into his other pocket.

"We believe you may be at risk," O'Connoll said.

John Reynolds gave a snide chuckle as he rose from his chair. "Gentlemen, you may continue on with your theories, but I am convinced there is no danger here. As a matter of fact, I think we will find that this untimely death of Mr. Temple by his own hand—"

"No one said Will Temple killed himself," O'Connoll interrupted.

"According to the newspapers, it was a gunshot to the head," John Reynolds said.

"The newspapers didn't say he killed himself," O'Connoll said.

"It's not a difficult conclusion, gentlemen. My wife and the other victim—"

"Cheryl Penn," Lashiver said.

Reynolds nodded. "—were not killed by gun violence. Even though you don't see it, it is clear that Mr. Temple killed my wife, and killed—Ms. Penn—to cover his first crime. He then proceeded to harm himself, or allow himself to be harmed, undoubtedly from guilt and self-loathing, until he ultimately took his own life." He directed his attention to Lashiver and Ryan. "Finally, a crime simple enough for even you to solve. I'm so glad I could be of help."

"Then, I'm sure you won't mind telling us where you were during that twenty-four-hour period, just for our records," O'Connoll said.

"Not at all," Reynolds said, avoiding direct eye contact with O'Connoll. "Elizabeth can supply my schedule. That particular evening, I hosted a dinner party at my home. Several of my guests stayed over. My housekeeper lives in and can attest to my being at home all evening and waking me in the morning. My driver brought me to the office at six a.m. where I had a two-hour conference call with my Belgian counterparts. If you need any further documentation, Detectives, it can be provided."

"Thank you for your time," O'Connoll said.

***

The detectives didn't speak until they had walked out of the building.

"He did it," O'Connoll said.

"Yes, he did," Ryan said.

"How did he do it?" Lashiver said.

O'Connoll shook his head. He stopped and turned to Ryan. "Listen to me, hotshot. I know he's good for it." O'Connoll pointed to Lashiver and said, "He knows he's good for it, and you know he's good for it. But if we don't prove it, if we don't get it right the first time, 'cause we're only gonna get one chance, we're done, you understand me? No medal is gonna save you and we'll all be handing out parking tickets and lucky to collect our pension. There is no room for error here. We fuck up, we're finished."

"I got it," Ryan said.

"We need to get him for all three murders," Lashiver said.

"You see how excited he got over the details," Ryan said. "Sick bastard."

"He's digging a hole," O'Connoll said. "Eventually, he'll fall into it."

"I'm sure the wife cursed the day she met him," Ryan said. "She sealed her fate."

Chapter 77

Katerina spent the next two days shopping, the anxiety of waiting for what would happen next gnawing at her nerves. As she pulled the car into the hotel parking lot and cut the engine, the buzzing of the cell phone caught her attention. She checked the burners before realizing it was the regular phone. She recognized the number. After a hesitation, Katerina clicked the phone on.

"Yes, sir—Thomas," Kat said.

"Katerina, I hope you will forgive me for intruding upon you once again."

She listened to Thomas Gallagher's smooth, easy tone, the confirmed bachelor playboy, a voice without anger, sarcasm, or annoyance. A man with no place to go and all the time in the world to get there, she thought. Katerina realized she had no idea what he might ask or what she might say.

Just play along. You're not out yet. Everything has to appear normal.

"No. What I mean is, of course, it's fine." *Get your game on, Katerina.*

"Katerina, are you in New York? We did have an agreement that you would call when you arrived."

Katerina's heart thudded in her chest, struggling to find a way out.

"Yes, we did," Kat said. "I was in New York . . . I'm not anymore. I'm sorry. I had personal business to take care of," she said. *Like staying alive.* "It was urgent."

"I see," Gallagher said. "You know, Katerina, in the short time you've worked for me, I've come to regard you as more than a consultant."

"Oh," Kat said, blindsided by the sudden candor.

"You'll forgive me for being straightforward, won't you? That is how I do business. I confess I have been uneasy for you since before the holidays. You fell ill during our dinner and the last time we met you were clearly injured—"

"Thomas—"

"I am certain you are in need, Katerina. Would you do me the honor of allowing me to assist you with your situation, whatever it is?"

Katerina's mouth opened but nothing came out. She searched but came up empty. "Mr. Gallagher, Thomas, you are—very kind."

She thought she heard a small chuckle come through the line.

"Not at all. Where are you now? And how can I facilitate for us to meet?"

A stab of fear shot through her. *That cannot happen.* "I needed to go out to the Midwest, to visit relatives. I have—a friend helping me."

She heard silence from the other end of the phone. "I'm glad to hear that," he said finally. "As long as you have assistance, I am satisfied."

"Can you be patient with me a little longer?" Kat asked.

"Katerina, I will wait as long as necessary," Gallagher said. "I'm confident we'll see each other soon. But I want to extract another promise from you, with no excuses this time. You must promise me, and hold to your promise, that if you are in need of help, at any time, for any reason, you will contact me at once. Promise me," he ordered.

"Yes," Kat said. "I promise."

Kat clicked off the call, trying to process what had just happened. He had been kind and yet a sliver of suspicion snaked its way through her though she couldn't pinpoint why.

She forced herself to return to her present situation. She gathered the shopping bags from the trunk and went into the hotel, making her way to her room unmolested. Passing the key card over the sensor, she entered her room to find a large bouquet of flowers, a bottle of Russian vodka, and an invitation From Viktor Mikhailovich for dinner and an "adventure" at eight. Kat shuddered at the wording. She sent a text off to Winter. After a minute, she received an answer with instructions. She read them twice and began to prepare.

***

Gallagher stewed in his own thoughts. The account for Lisa to receive the professor's payment was in place. He could have just waited until Katerina had been brought to him. He found it disturbing that he couldn't wait; he struggled but then gave in to the need to hear her voice.

She had lied to him again. When this situation ended, she would have to be punished. Enough so she would know not to do it again. Then his anger would subside; her indiscretions would not be discussed again. He would forgive her. But she needed to understand the consequences.

Chapter 78

At seven o'clock, two bodyguards built like tanks waited in the hotel lobby, casing the area and checking their watches. At ten after seven, Katerina breezed into the hotel, her fingers entwined around the handles of shopping bags, her hair bouncing about her, loose and carefree.

"I just needed to get a few more things," Kat said, and in a one-breath monologue, chattered about her excursion, her purchases, and her perceived problems. The bodyguards took the diatribe with a studied, blank look as she finished with, "I just need to go up and put these in my case and I'm ready to go. I'll be right back." With that she moved toward the elevator, only to find herself hemmed in on each side.

"Please," one of the bodyguards said as he relieved her of the bags.

They crowded into the elevator and Kat beamed with practiced delight at being waited on hand and foot.

Ten floors up, they disembarked and made their way down the hall to her room. Katerina passed the key card over the sensor, waited for it to turn green, threw open the door and went inside.

A heavy hand clapped over her mouth while the other hand held her arm in a vise grip. She let out a muffled cry, her eyes flying open in terror as she struggled, kicking at the ankles of her captor.

Two men, as big as their prey, swarmed the bodyguards, placing guns against their temples and forcing them to the ground. Packages dropped as they sank to their knees.

The man holding Katerina laughed. "He told you, he doesn't like it when you wander."

In vain, she twisted against his grasp. Fear swarmed her. *He? Who? Massone? Desucci? Sheridan?*

The bodyguards jolted from the tasers and crumpled to the floor.

In a fit of panic, Katerina jammed her heel into her captor's foot while she bit into his finger.

She heard him curse as she struggled to escape his grasp. Instead, he shoved her down on the bed on her stomach. The air went out of her as he lodged his knee in her back. She strained, flailing as he caught her arms and yanked them behind her back, clasping a zip tie around her wrists. She shook her head as he forced a gag over her mouth and hauled her to her feet.

"Clean the room, boys," he said as he yanked her toward the door.

***

He shoved her out a side exit, into the darkness. A limousine idled, the tailpipe giving off faint puffs of smoke.

Katerina dug in, pressing her full weight against him, planting her feet as a wedge to keep from being propelled into the vehicle. Kicking out her legs from behind, he forced her forward toward the limousine. Katerina resisted, lifting her knee to brace against the limo but he half-carried her toward the door as it swung open. Pushing her head down, he thrust her inside, slamming the door. He rapped twice on the roof and the limo pulled away.

***

Katerina struggled even as she heard the electric locks click into place. Hands grasped her shoulders, forcing her still. She continued to scuffle even though she knew it was futile.

"Katie."

She went still.

Hands slipped the gag off and then moved to her wrists, cutting the zip tie.

Katerina whirled around to stare at Alexander Winter.

"I needed you to have an honest reaction," he said. "*They* had to believe it was real."

Winter began to draw her into his arms, but her anger, hot and fast, spiked like a sudden fever. Her hands balling into fists, she pounded at his arms, chest, and shoulders.

"Why don't you trust me?" she cried.

He allowed the blows in silence.

Suddenly, fear cut through her anger as she realized what she was doing; she let her arms drop to her sides. "I know how to do my job," she said. "I played my part with Richie. I got him to talk."

"You knew him. You knew how to manipulate him."

"I lied to Sheridan. I got him to chase Richie."

"You were acting out of survival."

"I lied to Daniel and he bought it."

"You were fixing what you did wrong."

Her hands curled into fists. "Why do you keep bringing that up?"

"So you won't forget and do it again," Winter said.

Katerina squeezed her eyes shut. "I made one mistake! One!"

"One is all it takes," Winter said in a quiet voice.

Katerina threw herself back against the seat. "You don't give me credit for the things I do right."

"I do give you credit, and I do tell you. But I also tell you when you must do better."

She shook her head, the agitation building again.

Kat turned to him. "I can play any part with you, any time. I can tell you anything I want to and make you believe it. I can lie to you right now," she challenged.

Winter's eyes softened with affection. He drew her close and she allowed him to take her into his arms. Kat felt the breath go out of her as if her entire body had exhaled. His lips, warm and tender, found hers. With each kiss, she could feel her anger ebbing away.

He drew his head back as she nestled in his embrace; their eyes locked.

"Tell me you *don't* love me," he said.

Chapter 79

"Not fair," Kat whispered.

"Everything is fair. That's what I'm trying to teach you, Katie. Identify your goal and plan for it. Identify your enemy, the one keeping you from your goal and plan for him, or her. Prepare in advance, play your part. You have to be on, before, during, and after."

Katerina recognized the instruction. Henry Gondorff. *He's trying to teach me and I'm blowing it.*

The argument lost, Katerina abandoned her objections. "Can everything be planned down to the last move?"

"Of course not. There will always be moments you don't anticipate. But for everything that can be controlled, know what you want to accomplish. Play your part."

Katerina sat up and settled back in the seat and kicked off her shoes. "What about Daniel?"

"What about him?"

"You said he was more dangerous than Sheridan. You didn't plan for him."

"We're not talking about me."

"But I want to be as good as you," she said.

"You will be better than me," Winter said.

"You treat him with contempt."

"I treat him that way because that's how I've decided to play it. When you size up your enemy, you have two choices. You can show deliberate weakness and your enemy will think he has you and he'll relax. Or you can come on strong. Your enemy will think you're unpredictable. That will put him on his heels, forcing him to be more cautious."

"What if your enemy really is stronger? What if he really does have you?" Kat asked. "I guess you wouldn't know anything about that. No one's ever caught you."

Winter kissed her forehead. "Not yet. Remember Katie, there will be moments when you feel everything is lost and you're boxed in. If you can walk out the door, you're not caught. If there's even one move left to make, it's not over."

"Then what do you do? You can't plan for that."

"No, you can't. Take your best guess. It's all you can do."

"Will you at least tell me who those men were?"

"Daniel's playmates," he said.

"Where are we going now?" she asked, looking out the window.

"LAX. Viktor Mikhailovich is about to be told you've been forcibly removed, by the boyfriend. You need to disappear for a few days until he's convinced you're out of the area."

"What happens while I'm gone?" Kat asked.

"I'll observe Mikhailovich's house, find out about the security system, get a sense of his schedule, and work on an entry plan."

"What about my things at the hotel?"

"The room has been cleaned. There's a packed bag for you in the trunk. The cutaway is in the bag. You're also the proud owner of a shell company, XLS Corporation. It's linked to an account and a balance of fifty thousand dollars. You've been paid for consulting services."

Katerina started. "I can't pay back all that money to you now."

Winter quieted her. "Consider it an incentive gift for opening the account... like a toaster."

"That's some top of the line toaster," she said, thinking of the bank of Pablo. "Thank you."

"Now, contact Lisa and take care of your business. Let me know when it's done, and I'll pay her. We'll take care of the job when you get back."

They came together in a kiss, the full weight of their desire, and frustration, heavy between them. They lingered close, as if afraid to be too far apart from each other.

"I'm sorry I hit you," Katerina said.

"I deserved it," Winter said. "But if you feel you need to make it up to me, I won't stop you."

They held on to each other, kissing until they were out of breath, until the lights of the approaching airport signaled they were out of time.

She couldn't help but smile as he cursed under his breath. He sat back and pulled an envelope from his pocket. "Today's lesson," Winter said, "is how to disappear. This is your ticket. Your name is Katherine Seymour. You have a driver's license, social security card, passport, and prepaid credit card. When you land at JFK, Luther will be waiting. He has the address of an apartment in the city."

"How do you do that?" she asked.

"That's the easy part, Katie. There's always someone to take cash and skip a credit check. I'll let you know when it's time to come back."

As the vehicle entered the maze of LAX, they held hands, feeling the pull as the limousine swerved into the sharp turns.

"Don't go anywhere you normally go," he coached her. "Do you have any holdover clients, through the agency?"

"Just one," she said, giving him a recap of Thomas Gallagher's phone calls.

"Is Thomas Gallagher the one who bought you the clothes?"

"You're the one who bought me the clothes. He was outfitting an employee."

"You spent the night at his apartment?"

"After I became ill and fainted, yes," Kat said, as tendrils of tension snaked their way into her head. "I spent the night at your apartment."

"That's different."

"Why?'

"Because it was *my* apartment."

"Actually, it was Steven Bartholomew's apartment."

"He doesn't like you spending time at this man's apartment, either."

"I spend a lot of time sleeping in men's apartments. I don't *sleep* with any of them."

"Who do you want to sleep with, Katerina?"

"No fair asking questions you already know the answer to. I didn't even get my full twenty questions."

"When you come back, you will. Katie, you'll be safe in New York. Reynolds won't find you."

"So I just sit around and do nothing?"

"You have work to do. You have research. Romanov research. Chickens and eggs."

She nodded but a nagging feeling began to bloom, telling her she needed to be somewhere else.

"Alex, I need to go to Florida. There's something I have to do there."

Winter took the news with his mouth pursed until he said, "This is necessary?"

"Unless the person who erased you can do the same for me, yes."

Winter shook his head. "I never needed to be erased."

She found that her hand had settled in his, their fingers entwined; she liked the feeling.

"I'll give Keyes his new instructions."

"I don't need anyone there. No one would be looking for me. I can make the flight arrangements on my own."

The limousine idled, the driver waiting for an open spot at the curbside drop off. A Town Car pulled away and the limousine slipped into the spot. The passion in the air had all but vanished, leaving anxiety in its wake.

"Let me have your cell phones," Winter said.

She turned them over without question, accepting a new burner phone in their place.

"Keep the tracking phone on at all times," he said.

"I will," she said.

"Look for a compartment sewn into your bag. It has an extra set of ID documents, just in case you need them. Plus cash."

He pulled her close for a last kiss. "It's a few days, no more," he said.

They held each other's gaze for a split second and then he kissed her, soft and sweet.

When they parted, she nodded her head and got out of the car.

***

Taking a seat by the gate, Katerina checked inside her bag, smiling at the sight of Rachel's necklace. Insight and clarity. Meaningful coincidences. Kat closed her purse and stared at the boarding pass in her hand, a ticket from LAX to BOC.

The sacred stone would be needed for this part of the trip.

Chapter 80

"You want to tell me what we're doing?" Halliday asked. "If she's important to him, why help her go? Plus, we had to bring in reinforcements. That shit costs money."

Daniel Clay detected the familiar anxious annoyance in Halliday's voice. "It didn't come out of your pocket," he answered. "This works out better for us."

"Really, how's that?" Nicholas piped up.

"We're gonna finish this up while she's gone," Burnett said.

"We're not ready yet," Prescott cautioned.

"We're gonna have to leave right away and he's gonna have to come with us," Burnett said.

"Why are we talking like it's a done deal that Mr. Winter is going to cooperate?" Halliday asked.

"He will," Clay said, "because little Katerina will be out of his reach and we will use it as leverage. He can't get to her. We can." Clay nodded in Prescott's direction. "We're ready. Let's wrap up Mr. Winter, put a bow on him, and deliver him to the Boss."

Chapter 81

Lester Callahan attempted his best macho maneuver as he placed his hands on the pool's edge and hoisted himself out. As the water cascaded away from his body, he had a vision of himself, an Adonis rising, like the bird that comes out of the ashes. *What the hell is the name of that bird?* After a few minutes of mental gymnastics, he gave up, annoyed he had interrupted his own fantasy. He tried to return to the moment, but it had flown the coop. Just like the bird. *Whatever the hell its name is.*

Lester straightened in a slow stretch, allowing the other bathers in the small, gated area a clear view of his physique. After moving in, the fantasy of a babe-laden pool at a luxury hotel soon faded like a film negative, leaving the reality of a low-rent motel with the middle-aged cleaning woman pushing her cart along the row of first floor rooms. He glanced at the families in the pool area; mothers stuffed into their bathing suits, yelling at their sniveling kids. No one paid him any attention.

Lester spotted two girls on the opposite side of the pool, maybe eighteen or nineteen years old, lounging on chairs, their heels digging against the white straps. He approached and struck a pose, hands on his hips.

"Hi," he said with a cockeyed smirk. "You ladies on school break?"

The girls took in the anemic-looking man standing before them, sharing sideways glances and smirks.

"Yeah," said one. Giggling as they got up, they slipped past him to jump into the pool.

Lester took a furtive look around. How many bathers had witnessed his humiliation?

None.

Retreating to his lounge chair, he toweled off and lay down; he could feel the sun burning his skin. He opened one eye every few minutes and scanned the area. Anyone watching? He gave up and swinging his legs over the side, he sat hunched over, elbows on his knees, surveying the D-list surroundings. Those guys wouldn't get on to him here. They wouldn't find him. He had been foolish to panic and dump his apartment and run. Boca was too freakin' hot. He didn't care about all the bullshit of being close to the ocean. His wife didn't like the heat. His girlfriend liked it. But his wife had a problem with it, and the humidity.

Lester interrupted his train of thought, switching to the idea of checking out a gym while he was here. The hotel had an exercise room, but it was a cheap shit setup with one freakin' stationary bike, a treadmill, and a few barbells. He wanted a real gym, fully loaded. Maybe after the thing with the condo was settled. No one knew where he was. No one was coming after him. His girlfriend wouldn't say anything to anybody. She wasn't like that. He decided he was worried for no reason.

Hoisting himself off the chair, he grabbed the towel, and headed indoors.

***

Lester padded along the worn, dull brown carpeted hallway. He noticed his pale legs and wondered if he shouldn't try tanning. He could use a little color.

Still lost in thought, he looked up, realizing he had reached his room. He stared at the open door, the safety latch keeping it ajar, the noise of the television drifting into the hallway.

Lester considered his options. *No, no way those guys got on to me.* The cold, clammy feeling of his shorts made him uncomfortable. Shit, he thought. *I want to get changed.* But he didn't move.

The door opened. After a moment of confusion, he saw past the blond hair and registered the familiar beautiful face of the girl standing in front of him, arms folded across her chest.

"Really, Lester," Katerina said. "How long are you going to stand out there? I haven't got all day."

***

Katerina leaned against the wall, watching Lester morph into masher mode in his damp, clinging bathing trunks, his hair askew. Smoothing the bedcover, he sat down, patting the spot next to him.

"Have a seat."

"No."

"Can I order a little room service for you?" he said with a wink.

"No."

Lester straightened up. "Then what are you here for? Hey, you're not supposed to be here. You're not supposed to do this."

"Do what?" Kat asked, crossing her arms.

"Use your position to take advantage of clients."

"Trust me, Lester. I have no intention of taking advantage of you."

"You know, you still got that nasty attitude," Lester complained.

Katerina took a deep breath thinking it might magically bring her patience. Maybe this wasn't a good idea, she thought. Glancing around the room, she realized all hotel rooms were basically the same once you got down to a certain price point. Staying above that magic number, that was the trick. Disappearing in style. *The way Winter does it.*

"What happened to the condo?" she asked.

"I'm workin' on it. Closing costs are a real bitch. You know real estate people are thieves."

"Imagine that," Kat said, pushing herself away from the wall.

Lester sulked at the comment. "So, what's the story with you?" he asked.

"I need to find Rebel One," she said.

He got up off the bed. "Why?"

"That's my business."

"Oh, listen, I don't know," he said, fidgeting. "You know, I need to get changed."

"No."

"It's not healthy to stay in a wet bathing suit. I could get chafed."

"Try baby powder. Where can I find Rebel One?"

"I don't know where to find the kid," Lester said. "You have to go into a special chat room on the internet and you buy a code for entry and that code is only good for so long and then it expires and then the kid's gone. I'm sorry I can't help you."

Katerina stepped forward until they were nose-to-nose. She gazed at the pale, sallow skin, the expression of earnest confession, feeling the faint hint of his sexual tension.

"Lester," Katerina whispered.

"Yes?"

"Cut the Keyser Söze bullshit and give me the contact info."

Lester took a step back as he said, "Awww, c'mon, this isn't right. You can't come here and do this. And no, I won't give you the information. You know why? Because you're not nice to me. Maybe you should be nice to me and show me some respect."

Katerina raised an eyebrow.

"That's right. I'm your client. You have to treat me right. You know, I don't know what other people think about you. Maybe they like you, but you're not a nice girl."

"That's right, I'm not," Kat said even as her heart fluttered in anxious discomfort.

"You think you're better than me. You think you're smarter than me. You're so much smarter, you go find the kid."

"What's the problem, Lester?"

"I can't have you interfering in my professional connections. I'm trying to keep a low profile."

"So, you're saying you came out here and got right up to your old tricks and now you're hiding out again. Isn't that it, Lester?"

"People operate at different levels, you know."

Katerina folded her arms. "I love what you've done with your basement."

"Hey, I have something big going on now. I'm in the middle of a very sensitive, very lucrative deal. I can't have my business interrupted."

"Lester, I promise not to disturb your hallowed place on the bottom rung of the criminal food chain, okay?"

"You're a bitter woman, you know that? What happened? You're not getting any?"

Katerina advanced; Lester backed up, flopping down onto the edge of the bed. He gazed up at her, mouth open.

"Now Lester, I helped you once and I can help you again. So, here's what I think you should do. Tell me what I need to know, and I'll tell you what you need to know, for your good health and long life. Where's the kid?"

Lester shook his head but without conviction.

"Tell me where to find Rebel One or I feed you to Vito Massone and Anthony Desucci. If they're not looking for you, I bet they know who is."

Lester blanched, the color draining from his face; he rattled off the information.

"Thanks, Lester," Kat said. She straightened up, pulling her purse strap onto her shoulder.

"I like the wig," he offered as an olive branch. "You look good as a blond."

"Thanks." Katerina stopped at the door and turned around. "By the way, you know a guy back in New York, a big, beefy knuckle-dragger, looks like he can crush a skull with one hand, tattoo of a black dagger, has a red snake wrapped around it, on his right arm?"

Lester swallowed, his Adam's apple bobbing. "Yeah . . . I know that guy, why?"

"He's living with your girlfriend."

"Oh," Lester said, his shoulders sagging. "She has a little trouble knowing who to trust."

"Get a new girlfriend, Lester. For five bucks and a cup of coffee, she'll tell anyone where you are."

He nodded. "Thanks."

Katerina walked out.

Chapter 82

"I hope you have a piece of paper and a pen handy," Katerina said as she walked through the terminal.

"Why? I don't take dictation," Lisa shot back. "Are you ready or what?"

Kat rattled off an account number. "Now you."

She listened to Lisa recite the account number, committing it to its eternal place in her mind, never to be forgotten.

"Fine," Kat said. "As soon as I get my money, I make a phone call. You get paid."

Lisa gave a chuckle. "Now, I *am* impressed," she said.

Kat clicked off the line.

***

At the gate, Kat found a quiet spot off in a corner, choosing a seat where she could see everyone coming and going. *Never have your back to people. You'll never know who's coming up behind you.* It was Winter's signature move. *I learned something.*

"Good afternoon, Professor," she said gamely. A hot flush of embarrassment suddenly rose to her cheeks, a delayed shock of realization at her outburst in the limo; and the fact that she had struck him. It dawned on her that maybe Winter had been thinking about it. What if he harbored anger, or worse, unforgiveness?

"Katie."

The steadfast sound of his kind, graveled voice in her ear made her pull an instinctive breath of relief.

"How did you find your trip?" Winter asked.

"Productive," she said.

"How reliable is your contact?" Winter asked.

Katerina had a visual of Lester in his bathing trunks, all righteous indignation. "He's a bit gamey."

"We're all a bit gamey," Winter said.

Katerina hesitated and then said, "He said I was mean." When she heard no answer, she said, "I'm not mean. Do you think I'm mean?"

"Do *you* think you're mean?"

"No," she reacted. "The guy's a schmuck."

"But it bothers you. You do realize you're in a profession where hurting people's feelings is not a concern," Winter said.

She could hear the amusement in his voice. "I did notice, yes."

"Katie, remember what I told you. You're going to have to come to a point where you make a decision—"

"I know. I can't live two lives. I have to decide if I accept all this."

"You have to decide if you accept yourself and the things you need to do. If you don't, you won't have to worry about one life destroying the other. *You* will be destroyed. Do you understand?"

"But it's not the same."

"What isn't the same?"

"Being with you. You're different from this man, all of these men. You're not like them."

"I take what doesn't belong to me. Just like they do."

I don't care.

"You want to dance with the devil in the pale moonlight—"

"I know, in the morning don't say it was dark and I didn't see who it was," Kat finished.

"Don't say it was dark and you didn't see who *I* was," he said. "It is what it is. Find the truth. Admit it."

"I saw the truth, who you really are, upstate, in the woods. You came for me. You would have done whatever was necessary—for me."

She heard him sigh. "That stubborn streak of innocence," he said. "I'll give you two questions."

Katerina switched gears, trying to think of questions that would give her more information when she remembered something. *Not his first rodeo.* "You work alone now. Have you ever worked with others?"

"Yes."

"Did you have a mentor, someone who taught you?"

"Yes."

"Is this person still living?"

"No."

"Did you trust this person?"

"Yes. And that was more than two questions."

"Then you should keep better count," Kat said. "How do you know who to trust?" she asked.

"Keep it simple," Winter answered. "It's the person you can't lie to."

Kat smiled.

"Where are you headed?" he asked.

"Long Island. I want to stay outside the city."

"Fine," he said. "I'll make arrangements."

"Did you have a chance to—if you didn't have time to check out the house—"

"I always have time, Katie. Did you receive your payment?"

"Yes," she said and gave Lisa's account number. "Thank you for helping me with the transfer," Kat said. "I'm grateful."

"Yes, Katie, I know."

Katerina heard the phone click off. He was gone.

***

Lisa stood before Gallagher and Smith. She handed a piece of paper to Gallagher. "His and her account numbers," Lisa said, "and she was in an airport."

Chapter 83

Katerina's plane touched down at Long Island MacArthur Airport by late afternoon. JFK and La Guardia don't need to worry about any competition, she thought. Only about fifty miles from Manhattan, this part of Long Island was akin to Shangri-La, something alien and far away from "the city."

As Katerina came into the terminal, she still felt that distance; her problems were "out there," somewhere else. A smile stole across her lips when she spotted him. Tall with an almond complexion, wearing a suit under a full-length dark coat, holding up a sign in one hand with her fake last name, a snow-white winter coat draped over his other arm.

"Hello, Luther," Katerina said, barely able to contain her joy at seeing a familiar face. "What do you know?"

Luther tucked the sign away in his pocket and held up the coat. Kat put her bag down and turned, feeling the delicious warmth as the coat enveloped her.

"Oh, you know, Miss Katerina, little of this, little of that. Nothing worthwhile to tell," he said, taking up her bag.

Smart man. "I take it you know where I'm going?"

"It's all taken care," Luther said. "The man gave me all the details."

"I'm sure he did," Kat said, hugging herself inside the coat as the sliding doors opened and the frosty January air flowed around them.

I'm back.

***

The quaint bed-and-breakfast was tucked away on the North Shore. The fluffy, cotton puffs of snow covering the property only added to its charms.

The host, a gregarious woman in her fifties, gave her the tour of the comfortable sitting room with warm, overstuffed couches and the kitchen, accented with pots and cooking utensils, along with an old-fashioned wood burning stove providing ambiance as well as heat. "I'll show you to your room," she said. "Your packages were delivered."

***

Upstairs, Katerina settled into a cozy room with its own fireplace. In one corner sat an inviting Queen bed covered with a country quilt in warm autumn colors. In front of the bed, packages were stacked in neat piles. Luther came in behind her, setting her bag down on the floor.

"What else can I do for you, Miss Katerina?"

"Thank you, Luther. You've already done more than enough," she said. "I'll catch you on the way back."

"I'm on call, twenty-four seven."

"This is way off your path. I don't expect you to come out here again," she said.

"The man paid me. I'm here twenty-four seven."

"He didn't expressly say I couldn't run errands on my own, did he?"

"Miss Katerina, the man is concerned for you."

"I know. But I'd like a separate car, just for one or two days. You wouldn't happen to know where I could get a car, no questions asked?"

Luther smiled. "I'll make a call. But I drive."

"No, but you can follow at a distance. Agreed?"

Luther nodded.

***

After Luther left, she gave him time to send Winter the all-clear message and the details of their conversation. She opened her gifts, laying out the warm winter outfits, bulky sweaters, and corduroy pants. She smiled. *Of course, he thought of everything.*

She smiled as the phone vibrated.

Do you like the room?

Kat typed.

Perfect. As always. Why this place?

Kat waited.

>Because you still need to do research.
>Can I ask why you need to drive yourself?

Kat hesitated.

>I don't want him involved.

She hit send and waited. The phone buzzed a minute later.

>Understood. But be off the grid as short a time as possible.
>Let him know where you will cross paths with him.
>That way he'll know something is wrong if you don't show.

Katerina texted back she understood. Before she could finish, the phone buzzed again.

>Have the pancakes for breakfast. They're delicious. W.

Katerina gave a half-hearted fume at his abrupt sign-off. *That's it? Not so fast, Mr. Winter.* On impulse, she typed again.

>Do you miss me?

She waited.

>We'll discuss when you return.
>It's better if I show you in person.

She flushed as she read the text and typed a response.

>Can't you tell me a little bit now?

She waited.

> Are you being playful with me?

She smiled at having him on his heels. She had a sneaking suspicion pillow talk via text was not Alexander Winter's style. She typed.

> Maybe. Want to continue?

She waited. And waited.

> Behave yourself. I'll check in on you later. W.

Blowing out a mouthful of air, she tossed the phone onto the bed.

***

After a few hours of practice with the cutaway lock, Katerina settled into bed for the night. She took out her cell phone and made a call.

"How are you my girl?" her mother said, sounding positively light-hearted, the happy lilt in her voice jarring in Katerina's ears.

"Making progress, Mom," Kat said. After a few pleasantries, the awkward silence settled in, eating away at Katerina. Why was there nothing to talk about? *How is it I lived with my mother for twenty years and know nothing about her?*

"I'm visiting with Uncle Sergei. Why don't you talk to him?"

Katerina spoke up before Linda Mills could hand off the phone. "Mom, I want to talk to you. I mean, I want to talk to Uncle Sergei but . . . don't you want to talk to me?"

She heard her mother bring the phone back to her ear. "Of course, I want to talk to you. What do you want to talk about?"

Katerina pursed her lips at the constricting question. "Well, I want to know what you like to do and . . . where you want to go. We should go where you want to go."

"Oh, Katerina, it doesn't matter to me. I'm sure wherever we go will be fine. I really don't have a preference."

"Mom, I want to make it up to you. I mean, you were unhappy with him for all that time."

"Katerina, it's in the past now. I don't want to talk about your father."

"Okay, Mom, fine," Kat said, her frustration bubbling to the surface.

"Don't be annoyed with me," her mother countered.

Katerina suppressed the urge to blow up, compounded by the sudden inspiration to cry. "I'm not annoyed. I just—never mind."

"How's your special friend?" Linda Mills asked.

"I think he'd be better off without me," Katerina said.

"I'm sure that isn't the case," Linda Mills said. "I'm sure he needs you."

"I don't bring much to the relationship. There's not much I can give him."

She heard her mother sigh through the phone. "They tell you it's about what you give, and what you get in return. Don't believe it, Katie. It's about what you'll do, what you'll live without, what you'll give up. But you won't give up on the person. You won't move on, because they are worth all of it, all the pain, all the suffering, all the waiting. They are worth more than your own life."

Katerina absorbed her mother's words and used her hand to swipe the tears away from her eyes. "I don't think I'm worth all that," she said.

"That's exactly why he knows you are," her mother said. "Katie, I want you to come back, but if he is the man who is worthy of you, then you need to go with him."

She barely spoke to her mother and yet Katerina couldn't fathom how Linda Mills knew exactly what she was thinking. Katerina said her goodbyes with a promise to call back to speak to Sergei. Hanging up the phone, she lay down to rest, her mind ready to go to war for another night, wrestling between what she should do and what she wanted to do.

And no idea how to get any of it done.

Chapter 84

"Mami." Moose's smooth, "come hither" voice came through the line.

"*Papi,* I need transportation," Kat said, "but it's out of your area."

"No te preocupes, mami. The Moose has branch locations in all five boroughs, Nassau and Suffolk counties, and parts of New Jersey. I'm—cómo se dice—"

"Diversified?" she said.

"Yeah, yeah, the Moose is very diversified. I got you covered. Where you at?"

Katerina hesitated out of habit. She shrugged off the familiar fear and gave the address.

"And you need something low-key, not something that says, 'I'm the trophy girlfriend of a midlife crisis.'"

Kat smiled at the echo of their first meeting. "Exactly."

"Give me an hour. I got the perfect ride for you."

"How much?" she asked.

"Goodwill," Moose said and hung up.

Katerina clicked off the cell phone. She would accept his goodwill. Since she never forgot anything, before all this ended, she would repay him.

Chapter 85

Katerina's cell phones lay next to each other on the desk, positioned in perfect alignment. Alexander Winter sat near the fireplace, the warmth of the crackling flames burning off the evening chill. One of phones buzzed; he allowed it to ring several times before he rose to answer.

"Hello, Katerina," the voice said.

"Miss Mills isn't available," Winter said.

A thick silence hung on the line. Alexander Winter imagined Thomas Gallagher taking in the sudden development, and recalculating.

"I see," Gallagher said. "How's our girl?"

"Miss Mills is fine," Winter said.

"I'm glad to hear it."

"Is there something I can help you with, Mr. Gallagher?"

Winter heard the anger in Gallagher's soft chuckle. "You have me at a disadvantage, Mr. . . . ?"

"I certainly hope so. What is your business with Katerina Mills?"

"I'm a client through the agency."

"What is your *business* with Miss Mills?" Winter repeated.

Another hollow chuckle came through the line. "A man who comes to the point. I appreciate that. I enjoy Katerina's company and have come to feel a personal claim upon her, for her benefit."

"No, but go on," Winter said.

"I sense Miss Mills is in the midst of some difficult circumstances, yes?"

"Go on," Winter said again.

"I am the person best equipped to provide for her needs. Perhaps we might come to a gentleman's agreement."

"I'm not a gentleman," Winter said, "so there will be no agreement. Let me be clear. Anything Miss Mills is in need of, I will provide. Goodbye, Mr. Gallagher."

"Goodbye."

Winter disconnected the call. In the void of enraged silence, he stood and crushed the phones under his heel. Picking at the pieces, he threw them into the crackling fire and sat down to watch them burn, a nervous anxiety beginning to gnaw at him. He suspected Gallagher had been behind the spyware but couldn't be certain. There were others out there: Smith, the MJM agency, and Reynolds. And of course, Daniel Clay.

He could be certain of only one thing: none of them, especially Thomas Gallagher, had any intention of giving up. He shifted in his seat as a raw fear began to snake its way through him.

Katerina had to be protected, no matter the cost.

Chapter 86

On Long Island's South Shore, Katerina drove down Montauk Highway. She passed through one town after another, each with its own Main Street stretching two, maybe three blocks. Whatever charms they held were hidden under the plowed piles of blackened snow from a recent storm. Katerina sighed. She missed California, the feel of the sun warming her skin, the sparkling Pacific. She missed Winter.

Kat rolled into a town where gentrification had screeched to a halt, leaving several blocks like a poor relation, ostracized and ignored. Parking the car, she trudged against the wind for half a block until she entered a rundown pawn shop.

A locked display case held an eclectic jumble of used computers, laptops, phones, and cameras. Behind the counter, two millennials dressed in rumpled shirts and jeans viewed her with interest. A third one, seated, briefly glanced up from his phone before returning to swiping his finger across the screen.

"Help you with something?" the taller one asked.

"You looking to buy or sell?" the other one, shorter, soft and doughy, chimed in.

"Looking for someone," Kat said. "I need to buy a service."

"Sorry," the taller one said. "We only sell what you see here."

"That's not what I heard," Kat said. "I heard you have a technician that provides extra services. Goes by Rebel One."

The taller one shook his head. "Don't know who you're talking about. Sorry."

"Can I leave a message?" Kat asked, already annoyed at a wasted trip.

"Look lady," the shorter one said. "We don't sell anything else but what you see here. You want a credit card, go to a bank."

"Rebel One doesn't come around here anymore," the seated one said, not looking up from the phone.

Kat stepped up to the counter and slid a fifty-dollar bill under his nose, placing it on the phone. His eyes slid up.

"Where's the new hangout? Kat asked.

***

A bell jingled as the door to the comic bookstore opened. An eighteen-year-old girl, wearing a boy's faded pea coat over a gray sweatshirt and baggy pants, skulked in. Her jet black, chin length hair, accented with shocks of red and purple, peeped out from under her navy blue wool cap. Small, round silver rings jutted out from her bottom lip and her left nostril; a heart with a corkscrew stuck out from the fascia of her ear. Her large, dark eyes darted around, checking the area.

The bright, inviting store boasted wire mesh racks for bobbleheads and action figures. Near the ceiling, a shelf held an elaborate parade of ceramic action figures.

Two young guys manning the shop smiled, giving her a friendly greeting while they wrestled with plastic sleeves, stuffing them with comic books. She nodded, settling at one end of a packed stand. Her eyes flicked over the only other customer, a young woman standing at the cash register, before returning to her search. She didn't hear the jangling of the bells when the woman left.

The girl thumbed through the comic books, eyeing the staff every few moments. Choosing several books, she held them against her chest as she wandered the store. After twenty minutes, she approached the register, placed the books on the counter, and put a credit card on top.

The cashier handed the card back.

The girl hesitated.

"It's all taken care of," the cashier said as he placed another book on the pile and said, "and this too. Do you want a bag?"

***

Outside, the girl pulled out the book, flipping through it until she came upon the piece of paper. She read the address and headed down toward Main Street.

***

Sayville's holiday decorations, oversized bells and angels, were still at their posts along Main Street as the girl entered Starbucks. Scanning the tables, she zeroed in on the woman seated in the corner, the table nestled next to a display of packaged coffees.

The woman sat with her back to the wall, a perfect location for an unobstructed view of the store-wide front window. The woman's eyes watched the sidewalk, never wavering.

The girl approached and dropped into the empty chair. She took a close look at the woman; young, with perfect features; she looked tired.

"Thank you for coming, April," the woman said. "I hope you like the comic books."

"What do you want, cop?"

The woman's eyebrows quirked. "Your boyfriend gave me your name. Why would your boyfriend give your name to a cop?"

"'Ex-boyfriend. 'Cause he's a moron."

"Lester gave me your code name and the pawn shop contact."

"What's the sich?"

"I need you to make someone disappear. But I don't know if you just got lucky with Lester. I was able to find him."

"Lester's an asshole. And you didn't find him by an online search, did you?"

The woman didn't answer.

"That's how good I am."

"Can you handle school records? Phone bills?"

"Do I look like a noob?" April asked as she surveyed the food case. "How come you bought me the comics?"

"Because you might have paid for them with a stolen credit card and in order to complete my job, I need you out of jail."

April shrugged. "I work better on a full stomach."

"What happened to the money Lester paid you?"

"That was over a month ago."

The woman pulled a twenty out of her purse.

***

April wolfed down a chocolate chunk muffin and gulped a large coffee while the woman considered her.

Why do call yourself Rebel One?"

"Anonymous was taken," April said around a mouthful of food. "So, who am I erasing?"

"Me," the woman said.

"Five thousand," April said.

The woman didn't flinch. "You charge five thousand dollars and you're gnawing that muffin like you've never seen food?"

"Tuition."

"Bullshit. You're not in school. What else do you do besides credit card theft and erasing people."

"Nothing. I've reached Nirvana," April said.

The woman pulled an envelope out of her purse. "You get one quarter now, the other three quarters when the job is done."

"I get half now or you can find someone else to erase you."

The woman leaned in. "You get one quarter now, or you can go back to your stolen credit cards and hope you get paroled before you're thirty."

April screwed up her face like a kid who's been had. "Fine." She waited, then rolled her eyes. "You want a drumroll?" She watched the woman hesitate, as if sensing the danger in uttering her own name.

"My name is Katerina Mills. Make sure I disappear."

Chapter 87

Winter placed the call, teeth clenched, listening to it ring. Finally, the phone clicked, and he heard her voice.

"And they say chivalry is dead," Heather said.

"I wanted to be sure," he said. "Did he hurt you?"

"He didn't get the chance," she said.

Winter rubbed the pain radiating along his jaw. "Full physical description."

Heather rattled off the information.

"I'll compensate you for the inconvenience."

"I appreciate the gesture," she said, "but it's not necessary. Are you squared away?"

"No problem," Winter lied.

"Do you know why he's after you?"

"It's under control. Thank you again."

"My pleasure for a favorite client," she said.

Winter caught himself smiling. "If you get into trouble, call me. I'll make arrangements."

"I know you will," Heather said. "Watch your back."

He clicked off.

Chapter 88

Katerina crept downstairs in her pajamas. Fixing a plate of eggs and toast, she tiptoed back up to her room. She practiced with the cutaway, forcing herself not to peek. Begrudgingly, she admitted Winter was correct: with tedious repetition, she had made progress. Her small victory did nothing to quell the growing restlessness deep within her. Winter would do anything for her, including the Balboa break in. But if every operation required planning, didn't that include planning for his absence? He had his own job to attend to. What if circumstances made it impossible for him to be with her? What then? In the end, the job was her responsibility alone. *I have to plan as if he won't be there. I have to get into the safe on my own. But how?* The buzzing of the cell phone made her start.

She heard the familiar, "*Que lo que,*" come through the line.

"*Ta to, papi, ta to,*" Kat said. "Thanks for the transportation."

"I thought I would check in personally, like one of those customer satisfaction surveys, you know what I'm sayin'? You got everything you need?"

"Not yet," she said.

"Dimelo, mami. Tell the Moose what you need. I make it happen."

Katerina swept up the cutaway from the bed, fiddling with the dial. She told Moose what she wanted.

"This kind of instruction, chica, it ain't free."

"I know," Kat said. "And I'll need a set of tools and equipment shipped and stored where I can get to them."

"Give me a few hours. If everything is go, Luther will bring you in."

"Thanks, Moose."

She was about to click off when Moose's voice caused her to pull back. "Chica, *if* we go, no phones. We off the grid for this, *entiende*?"

"Understood," she said and clicked off.

Kat sat on the bed, toying with the lock's dial, trying to convince herself she was doing the right thing. *I have to be prepared.*

Chapter 89

Daniel Clay sat on a couch in the hotel's lobby, a cell phone at his ear. He made sure not to check his watch too often or indulge any other obsessive tick that might make him memorable. He knew Alexander Winter had entered the hotel through a back entrance. He knew *Bob* was on his way up to room 420 to meet a potential client. The client had called with an urgent request for a stolen Matisse. When Alexander Winter entered the hotel room, he would be met by Prescott, Burnett, and Nicholas.

He would give the big man a few minutes to calm down; then he would go up and show Mr. Winter the real time surveillance on Katerina Mills. That should sew things up nicely, Daniel thought. Then they would all leave together. And Alexander Winter would be on someone else's schedule, permanently.

"What's the story?" Clay said into the phone.

"Maybe he took the stairs," Prescott said.

"He picked a great time to get his fuckin' cardio," Nicholas griped.

"Easy, Nicky," Clay said, in part because he knew Nicholas hated the nickname. "Remember to be nice to the newest member of our little club when he gets there."

They hung on the line in silence, an inkling of discomfort itching in Daniel's ear. *Why is he taking so long?*

"Halsy," Daniel said into the phone. "Anything by the exits?"

"No, man. He hasn't come back out. He's still inside. You sure this plan is gonna work?"

"It's the Boss' plan. It'll work."

"I'm going to look out into the hallway," Nicholas said.

"Stay where you are," Clay ordered.

"Well, where the fuck is he?" Nicholas asked.

Daniel Clay got up from the couch. He turned and found himself staring at Alexander Winter.

"Have a seat, Daniel."

***

Daniel Clay fidgeted as Alexander Winter settled next to him.

"I'm supposed to be meeting a client in room four twenty," Winter said. "There's no client in room four twenty, is there, Daniel."

Clay gave a short, mirthless laugh, turning his head to survey the lobby.

"Your man is still in the parking lot, watching the exits. Tell me Daniel, why would a stand-up guy lure me here to a fake meeting?" Winter asked.

"Because I am a stand-up guy, and this is for your own good, to protect you."

"I'm touched by your affection," Winter said without a smile, "but I like a kiss before I'm fucked."

"Hey, I bought you dinner. It's not my fault you didn't eat it."

Winter gave him a cold smile.

Clay glanced around again. "Listen, this isn't just about you, okay? You need to think about her, about protecting her."

Winter's eyes narrowed at the reference to Katerina.

Daniel Clay held out a second phone. He watched Alexander Winter view Katerina Mills in real time, getting out of a limousine in New York City.

As Clay talked, Winter kept his eyes on the video, watching Katerina.

"Look, from now on you're going to be working for my boss, on his schedule, to bring out the Monet."

Winter observed the driver getting back into the car. *Luther.*

"If you don't, she's collateral damage. My boss is gonna take her and I don't know what he'll do. But it's going to be unpleasant for her—and you."

On the phone, Katerina walked with a man of medium height, slender, with a face of sharp angles and dark hair, cut short. Winter zoomed in, his eyes narrowing at the teardrop tattoo on the man's face.

"You come in with us, she'll be okay," Clay said. "I promi—"

Daniel Clay made an involuntary noise at the sudden, sharp pain in his ribs. He looked down at the gun in Winter's hand. He saw the silencer.

"Hey, man," he said in a choked voice, "are you deaf? *You do this job or she's in deep shit.*"

"I heard you," Winter said, his voice low and hard. "Tell me Daniel, have you ever heard of synchronicity?"

Clay swallowed hard as he looked into Winter's eyes, cold with rage.

"Because I would say this is a meaningful coincidence, but I don't think you've learned what you need to," Winter said.

"Danny?" Prescott's voice came through the phone.

"I needed to get you on my schedule, understand?" Clay said. "I answer to someone."

"That's your problem," Winter said. "I don't kiss rings—or asses."

"Look, you already told me how you're going to do it. What difference does it make when you do it?"

"Danny," Burnett's voice sounded. "Something's wrong. Nicholas went to check the hall, but we can't get the fuckin' room door open. We're breakin' it."

"Tell them to stay where they are," Winter whispered, "they will never get to you in time. Understand?"

"Everybody relax," Clay said into the phone. "Halsy, stay at your post."

"Hands folded across your chest, Daniel," Winter said.

Clay complied. "Look, we can deal. We can go in on your schedule. But you gotta meet my guy."

"Daniel," Winter said with exaggerated patience.

"You can't blame a guy for trying," Clay said.

"Oh, but I can. Now listen carefully to your lesson."

Winter leaned in close. Clay stiffened at Winter's breath on his face.

"If at first you don't succeed . . . don't *ever fucking* do it again. Stay out of my way. And Daniel, if anything happens to her, anything, you will be the first to pay."

***

Daniel Clay sat alone on the couch, his breathing quick and shallow, beads of perspiration breaking on his forehead.

"You okay, man?" he heard Halliday say.

"Yeah," Clay said, feeling lightheaded, sweat rolling down his sides, soaking his shirt. "Do we know exactly where she is?"

"Yeah, heading into Washington Heights. They're standing by, waiting for a go signal."

Clay contemplated Winter's move, despite Katerina being vulnerable. He glanced at the surveillance again, the man walking with Katerina. She didn't look vulnerable at all. "No go," he said.

"The Boss is on the line," Prescott said. "He wants to talk."

"Who's gonna tell him he had a shitty plan?" Nicholas asked.

Daniel Clay closed his eyes. Pulling the cell phone away from his ear, he wiped his forehead with his sleeve, then lifted it back again. "Put him through," he said, steeling himself. He would explain that Alexander Winter would not be easy to get under control; he had a vicious, violent streak. Daniel Clay was certain this was not the first time. Any mention of the girl would bring it out. He was not in a hurry to see it again.

Chapter 90

Katerina didn't bother glancing around; Enrique was close, keeping the watch. Approaching the building, she recognized the young guy standing outside smoking a cigarette and scanning up and down the block like a metronome. *Déjà vu.*

"Another bank of Pablo?" Kat whispered. "What is this, a branch location?"

Moose gave a chuckle. "Yeah, yeah. Pablo has several branch locations. Listen, chica. This ain't a done deal, *entiende?* You're gonna have to negotiate."

She nodded. For a split second, Katerina had a fleeting fear that Winter was right. Trust was not a word she should be using; maybe this wasn't a good idea.

***

They found a brisk business going on in an apartment on the fourth floor. The inventory included clothing, shoes, jewelry, and electronics. Pablo sat in a corner, keeping an eye on it all.

"Imelda Marcos," Pablo said with a smile.

Katerina's gaze locked onto the gun in his hand as she said, "Moose told you what I wanted."

Pablo nodded. "This ain't a technical school. I don't give out diplomas."

"No, quizzes, no exams, no number two pencils. Just show me how to drill and supply the equipment. I'll pay you five thousand, includes everything."

Pablo shook his head.

Katerina's temper flared; she worked to keep it under control. "How much?"

Pablo held out his hands, palms up, as if pleading his case. "It's not about the cash, chica. My technician is giving you a valuable life skill. This skill has return on investment potential. If I provide these skills, and the tools, something should be coming back to me. It's like those incentive programs, you know? Like when someone pays your college, and you graduate, you like, give back, you know, using your skills to work for the community."

Kat's mouth dropped open. "You want me to do a job for you."

Pablo nodded. "What I want, when I say so."

Katerina realized the crew had been watching the situation develop. She calculated the cost of walking away. *I would have seen the flaw in the plan and done nothing to fix it. I'll be a growing burden on him.*

"One job, that's it," she countered. "I get the right to say no. We both have to agree on the job and the timing."

"The job and the schedule are negotiated only up to a point," Pablo said. "In the end, you do the job I need done when I need it done."

"One more thing. This is between us. He," Kat said, pointing to Moose, "is out of it."

"I agree," Pablo said. "Chica, this is what they call a binding agreement."

Kat nodded. "I understand. I agree."

Pablo broke out in a wide smile. "Okay, Imelda. I hope you got a good memory."

"Photographic," Kat said, shucking off her coat.

***

They worked at a dizzying pace. The safecracker, a small, humorless man, gave Katerina the information in Spanish mixed with broken English. She quickly noticed the difference in techniques. If lock manipulation was elegant and sophisticated, then drilling was its country cousin, requiring only brute force for entry. Lack of skill was not a deal-breaker. As long as you didn't care about being found out, neatness wasn't a necessity.

The safecracker explained the different drills and bits, demonstrating how to locate the various drill points; without ceremony, he got down to it. He stopped after a few minutes, extracted the bit, and handed the drill over to her. As she went to work, the feeling of handling the tool while working at the farm came back to her. She practiced drilling from the front, side, and back, as well as the equipment options available for each location to either manipulate the lock wheels or sidestep the fence to open the lock.

When she finished, she turned to find Moose and Pablo considering her.

"I want to come back tomorrow," she said.

Pablo nodded his head. "Hasta mañana."

Chapter 91

Kat picked up her cell phone from the nightstand. 3:00 a.m. Lying back down, she rearranged the blankets, and stared up at the ceiling. She was grateful Winter had her real phone; Philip would certainly still be leaving messages and she didn't want to hear them. The burner phone had one voicemail. She hesitated to dial the number even though the message said to call at any hour.

"*Moya malyshka*, Katya," came Sergei's voice. "What has happened that you cannot find your sleep?"

Where do I begin?

"Just can't, Uncle."

"Then your Uncle Sergei will tell a bedtime story. One I used to tell to you, when you were little. *Masha and the Bear*."

"Another Masha," Katerina said with a smile. As she listened to the deep, accented rumble of her uncle's voice, a sense of comfort and warmth began to flow through her.

"This Masha, she was clever little girl who lived with grandparents. One day, she went to the forest to collect mushrooms and berries. She lost her way and came upon a little hut. She went inside, but she stayed too long. The hut belonged to the bear and he came home to find her."

"And what happened?" Katerina prompted.

"The bear, he said to Masha she can never leave. She is to keep the house of the bear and cook for him. Every day he goes out and every day he says, 'If you go out, I will find you and I will eat you.'"

"What did Masha do?"

"At first, she cries and cries but one day she tells the bear she only wants to take to her grandparents some pies. The bear says, 'No, but I will take for you.'"

Katerina sat up in bed. "How did that help her if the bear would not let her go?"

"Ahhh, Masha is very clever girl. She makes the pies and put them in the basket. She says, 'I will climb tree and watch you go.' But Masha, she climbs into the basket. The bear takes basket and goes to Masha's grandparents."

"How did it all end?" Katerina asked.

"The bear talk to himself, saying he wants to sit and rest and eat a pie, but Masha calls out, 'I see you. You don't eat the pie. You take it to the grandparents.' Two times he does this, and two times Masha calls out. The bear, he thinks Masha is smart girl who can see and hear all. The bear comes to the house of the grandparents. He knocks on the door and calls out, 'I have something here for you from Masha.' But the dogs, the dogs smell the bear and frighten him. He runs away. The grandparents, they look in the basket and see their little Masha, she has come back. She is safe. They are happy their clever little girl is home."

"So the moral of the story is . . .?"

"Be careful, Katya," Sergei whispered. "Watch for the bear."

"I thought I had to watch out for the wolf," Kat said.

"Dangers are everywhere," Sergei said, his voice low and grave. "You must watch for bear and for wolf. Promise me this."

"Yes, Uncle," Katerina said.

"My little Katya," Sergei said. "You make me very happy. I hope you can find your sleep now. In the morning, do not forget Masha."

Chapter 92

Katerina crossed the open expanse of the university campus quad. The relentless wind attacked her clothes and the scarf wrapped around her mouth and neck. A numb sensation settled in her fingers, thighs, and feet. She tugged open the door to the library and stood in the main corridor. Her eyes skimmed the staircase off to her left and over to a set of doors straight ahead to a periodical room. Winter had thought of everything. *As usual.* The university was near the bed and breakfast. *And I have research to do. Romanov research.*

Kat spent the next few hours wandering the cavernous, deserted stacks searching call numbers, checking them against a slip of paper. Weighed down with books, she found a cubby to deposit her pile and start reading.

Hours later, her brain overflowed with details of the last Tsar and his long-suffering German wife, Alexandra. She had spent their marriage alienated, untrusted, and unaccepted by the Russian people, including her own mother-in-law, the Dowager Empress Maria Feodorovna.

Katerina sat up and stretched. *This is going nowhere. What now?* She recalled Winter's sage advice. Don't lose your temper. Inhaling a deep breath to gather patience, she mentally reviewed her conversations with Zilinsky again. The birthright. Siberia. London auction houses. The lost crown. The Tsar's mother, Maria Feodorovna. Zilinsky had babbled on about her specifically, how she had to flee, leaving behind the symbols of a son's love, the keepsakes of his devotion. *And what were the keepsakes of the Tsar's devotion?*

Katerina returned to her research, reading over the material one more time; every Easter the Tsar gifted his wife and mother with a delicate, decadent jewel in the shape of an egg. Each Fabergé egg contained a clever, surprise gift inside.

Arthur Penny said the bullion, the baubles, and the eggs, were gone, lost forever.

What if they're not?

Katerina grabbed another book from the pile, flipping the pages through Armand Hammer's travels to Russia, buying the Tsar's treasures from the Soviet agency, Antikvariat, and shipping them to the United States. Dr. Hammer might have been an astute businessman, but he had poor timing. In the wake of the crash of 1929, most people were not interested in a piece of the Romanov treasures; they were more concerned with daily survival. As a last resort, he had fallen upon the idea of exhibiting the Royal Family treasures in department stores.

Kat cross-referenced the list of Hammer's Fabergé egg purchases against the list of all the eggs and their current whereabouts. There had been fifty eggs; eight had been presumed lost—until one had been discovered just a few years ago. Katerina kept flipping pages. As she did, the filmy curtain of confusion parted, and a flash of clarity appeared.

Seven eggs were still missing.

All seven eggs had belonged to the Dowager Empress, Maria Feodorovna.

I want my birthright. Retrieve it for me.
What is a birthright, Katerina?
The privileges—or possessions—of a firstborn son.
Possessions.

Katerina spent the next hour at the copy machine, emailing copies to herself.

This is it. It has to be.

Chapter 93

Katerina spent the next two days reviewing her research, working with the cutaway, and traveling to the city for drilling practice. Despite the activity, everything had come to a halt. The longer she waited, the more her impatience grew. But she knew once things did move, the risk would return. *The woman at the hotel room door. She's still out there, somewhere. How do I go back to California and get the job done while I have to look over my shoulder? I stayed with MJM to stay one step ahead. I'm doing a lousy job.*

She questioned herself.

How do you stay one step ahead?

Her mind whispered the answer.

Hire an insider.

***

Katerina sat in a corner booth, facing the door. She breathed a sigh of relief when she saw him enter the diner. He had the beginnings of a smirk on his lips as he approached and slid into his seat.

"Lookin' good, baby," Angel said by way of a greeting.

Kat nodded. "I have a job. I need someone for specialized work. I'm willing to cut you in for twenty-five percent of the take."

"I'm going to need the rest of the numbers for this equation," Angel said.

Katerina hesitated, remembering Winter's first lesson. *The next time someone asks you what your cut is, it would be better if you didn't give the real amount.* "One hundred thousand," she said, lamenting that Winter was still right. She couldn't lie to everyone. She wouldn't be worthy of his secrets until she could.

Angel gave her a measured look. "Where and what?"

"California, Balboa Island. You watch my back while the job gets done. Anyone tries to interrupt me, you take care of it. I pay for your airfare, hotel, and transport, plus the twenty-five percent."

"You breaking the rules, baby," Angel said.

"Is that what Sara did?" Katerina asked. "Is that why she didn't make it? Because she broke the rules?"

Angel leaned forward. "She didn't make it because she didn't understand the game. She didn't want to understand. This ain't the end. This is a pit stop on the way to making something real. She wanted to hang on. She wanted *this* to be real." He gave her a smile. "You understand the game, don't you, baby? You take what you can get—and you go make something you can live with."

"Yes, I do," Katerina said, her voice cracking.

"You breaking the rules asking for my help."

Kat smiled. "The rules say I can't ask other consultants for help. You're not a consultant, and I'm not on probation. New rules. *No rules.*" She leaned across the table. "In or out, *baby*, I need to know. And if you say yes, someone comes at me or my partner—"

Angel smiled. "You with the man," he said.

"—I don't care who they work for, keep them off us."

Angel gave Kat a long, hard stare and then nodded his head. "Ain't nothing wrong with a little sunshine," he said.

Long after Angel had gone, Kat still ruminated on her latest discovery. MJM may own their consultants, but they didn't own Angel. He came and went as he pleased. *And there are no consultants on probation for him to babysit.* Katerina tucked away the useful information. She pulled out her cell phone and sent off a text.

Safe to come back now?

She waited.

Yes. Have you done your research?

Kat typed.

I'm an A student. Found what I was looking for.

She smiled, already knowing the response coming next.

> Anytime you want to tell me.

Katerina typed.

> Chickens and eggs, Professor. Actually, just the eggs.

She waited for the next message.

> Text your flight info when you have it.
> I'll tell you where to go when you land.
> Waiting for you.
> Hurry.

Chapter 94

John Reynolds sat at his desk in his office. He cradled his cell phone in his hands, holding it in his lap, situated beneath his keyboard. Watching a video, he smiled, a tiny, involuntary chuckle escaped his lips. In a flash, his mood soured in dissatisfaction; he wanted to show the video to someone, to share the experience. Annoyed, he chose a different one. Reclining in his chair, he watched young, beautiful Katerina Mills standing on a New York City sidewalk, talking to a handsome actor. *The formerly living Will Temple, now deceased.* He repeated the phrase to himself several times. He enjoyed it.

Reynolds closed the video and tapped open an email from retired Detective Timothy Green. He opened the attachments, photos taken in December at the northeast corner of University and Waverly Place. Katerina appeared lost and fragile. Swiping through the photos, Reynolds studied a healthy, strapping man getting out of a car. An interesting development, he thought, wondering where this mystery man had been hiding. The next photos showed Katerina Mills in this man's embrace. Interesting, indeed.

Oh, Katerina. So much to do, Reynolds thought, as he swiped through the photos again. *So much to do.*

Chapter 95

Crossing the airport terminal, Katerina carried her coat over her arm and basked in the rush of warmth. Stopping at an ATM, she pulled out her new offshore account card. She extracted the money and sank down into a nearby chair. Sidling up, Angel slid into the seat next to her. Kat rose, placing a newspaper down on the chair. It wasn't their usual cozy transfer, but it would do.

***

Katerina drove to Orange County and found the lounge joint off MacArthur Boulevard. The host greeted her with a toothy smile and led her to a private, curtained cabana. Slipping behind the curtain, she looked into the face of Alexander Winter. Her breath caught in her throat as it always did when she saw him, as if it were the first time. Rushing into his embrace, a wave of desire flooded through her. His arms tightened around her as his mouth closed over hers. A sudden desperation washed over her. *How will I say goodbye to you?*

He lifted his head, looking into her eyes. Her stomach tumbled at the raw desire in his gaze, and then she saw something else. Fear. *He's afraid.* She opened her mouth to question him, but a fresh, dizzying tide of his kisses overpowered her, drowning out her apprehension.

"Anytime you want to tell me," he murmured.

"There were fifty Fabergé eggs," she said in a whisper.

"Uh-hunh," he said, his mouth teasing hers.

"Forty-three are accounted for."

"Mmm," he said.

"The missing Third Imperial Egg, was found a few years ago—at a flea market."

Winter shifted, his lips exploring, leaving a scorching trail on her neck.

Kat's eyes closed, a soft sigh escaping her lips. "The seven remaining eggs all belonged to Maria Feodorovna. Zilinsky kept going on about great-great-grandma and how she had to leave them behind. He wouldn't shut up about it. He said he wanted the crown. What he wants is the eggs and he thinks Mikhailovich has one or more of them. Maybe all of them."

"My star student." Winter's eyes turned an inky black as they moved over her face.

Katerina wrapped her arms around him, pulling him close, surrendering to the intensity of his kiss, pushing reality to the recesses of her mind, pushing away the growing danger closing around them.

She pulled back and said, "Each egg could be worth thirty million."

Winter nodded.

Katerina glanced at their surroundings. "Why are we meeting here?" she asked.

"To avoid unwanted company," he said.

Kat pursed her lips in frustration. "Daniel's following me again?"

"No. He's following me, because of the job."

Katerina weighed her words before she said, "You know, I don't believe that's the only reason."

"That's why you're my star student."

"I'm your *only* student. We're not going to be able to shake him?" she asked, unable to keep the frustration out of her voice.

"I didn't say that." Winter pulled her close. "It's just going to take a little doing."

Katerina snaked her hands around his waist; she stiffened. "You have your gun with you."

"Yes."

"Would you ever use it on Daniel Clay?"

Winter smiled. "No."

"Have you ever used it?"

Winter hesitated. "Yes."

Katerina looked at him for a long moment. "Have you ever shot anyone?"

"Yes."

Katerina hesitated. "Have you ever killed anyone?"

"That was your twenty," Winter said.

The realization hit Katerina. "No fair," she said.

"Everything is fair, Katie. What have you learned from this exercise?"

"You're inflexible."

"No. Next time, keep better count."

Katerina nursed her annoyance with a brief pout.

He nuzzled her cheek with his nose. "By the way, Philip is desperate to talk to you."

She pulled back. "You broke into my phone?"

"I'm a thief. I break into everyone's phone."

She grimaced. "I'm going to need it back."

"I dropped it," he said, avoiding her eyes. "I'll replace it."

Kat's brows pinched in disbelief, but she decided to let it go. "Is Mikhailovich still here?"

"He is. The word is he'll be leaving soon. Being an oligarch is a hard job, Katie. Places to go, people to see, money to launder. He's going to have a large party on the super yacht tomorrow night. That's when we go in."

"So we have time tonight—for us . . ."

"Right now, we have a little time, and then we'll have tonight. No more talking," Winter said, taking her in his arms.

Chapter 96

Thomas Gallagher entered his office to find Smith and Lisa sitting in the guest chairs, permeating the office with the scent of hostility. A smirk began to curl on his lips as he crossed the room and stood behind his desk.

"She flew into LAX," Smith said. "I'm booked on the next flight."

"*We're* booked on the next flight," Lisa said.

Smith didn't look at her. "That isn't necessary. *You* aren't necessary."

"What I find amazing," Lisa began, "is how you neglected to think this through." She directed her attention to Gallagher. "If you want this done right, you need to do it without force."

"I will handle transport," Smith said. "She'll come willingly, believe me."

"Rapunzel needs to see a friendly face."

"I want a shock event," Gallagher said. "Make it appear as an ambush by an unknown assailant. It will throw her into a panic."

Lisa nodded her head and said, "Then I step in and spirit her to safety."

"Mr. Gallagher," Smith said. "This is why you brought me here. She'll jeopardize the goal."

Lisa gave a hollow laugh and crossed her arms. "As opposed to you getting tossed by a hooker?"

Gallagher ignored the bickering. He was used to static situations suddenly shifting. This felt different; there was anticipation, a sense of feeling alive, something he had not experienced in quite some time.

"Both of you will go," Gallagher said.

Smith rose from the chair and left without a word. With a crooked grin, Lisa got up and followed.

Thomas Gallagher took a few moments to collect himself. He had already decided on Katerina's punishment. It would be administered to the degree she could tolerate, and then longer, to break her spirit and her will. She would recuperate, of course, but she would never again be sure of his reaction. That would guarantee she would not commit such an infraction again.

Perhaps she's correct. Maybe formality is better. He decided she would refer to him as Mr. Gallagher and he would reciprocate . . . Mrs. Gallagher. He surprised himself but subconsciously he had known for some time this was where the road would lead. There was no other option: he must own her wholly and completely.

Chapter 97

Sitting at the table, Winter kept his hands in his pockets. He appeared calm and unperturbed. The man seated across from him, a middleman, Durant, sipped his espresso, dabbing his mouth with a napkin after each swallow. The waiting, and placating an antsy customer, grated on Winter's nerves.

"My client wants to know if we're on schedule," Durant said, his voice smooth, the words rolling off his tongue in his soft, French accent.

"We are," Winter said. "I'll go in at the optimum moment to retrieve the item. Not before."

Durant's eyebrows twitched. "Mr. Bartholomew, he cannot wait forever. There will never be a perfect time, unh?"

"Of course, there's a perfect time," Winter said with an air of serene confidence even as the anxiety squeezing his chest caused a physical pain to coil around his heart. Everything weighed on him: Daniel Clay, the Gallagher phone call, and above all, Katerina's safety, all crushing down upon him. "It's time when I say it's time. Not before. Having me followed isn't going to make the right time come any sooner."

Durant shrugged. "He is not the only one, hunh? He had, how do you say, a feeling," Durant continued, "that there is an issue. Do we have an issue?"

"Not at all," Winter lied. "Tell him if there's any more surveillance, I'll return the deposit and call it off."

Durant's expression conveyed his lack of concern. "He takes an interest in his employees, like a father with children."

"I'm an orphan—and an independent contractor. He should remember that."

Durant picked up his glass. "*Et voila,*" he said, taking a last swallow from his cup. "I will report back to him that all is well and soon we shall expect more good news."

Chapter 98

Katerina stood in front of a rack of party dresses, engrossed in examining each one. When she turned around, she let out a cry of surprise.

"Hey beautiful," Daniel Clay said. "Glad you're back."

***

Kat maneuvered around him, walking away. "Why is that?" she asked.

"Because Alexander Winter is a lot more fun when you're around."

"Oh goody. Let me know when the rave begins," she said.

Clay stayed in step with her. "C'mon, you know how these types are."

Kat gave a bored sigh. "Types? What types are we talking about?"

"Type A. They need something to take their mind off the pressure."

"What pressure?" she asked.

"Oh, c'mon, beautiful. Scamming Mikhailovich? That guy is connected all the way up to the top of the Kremlin."

"You told me that one already," Kat said.

"Yeah, I know. Everything is so efficient over there. In the Russian government, crime is regulated, like agriculture or education. You have the crime department."

"What does this have to do with Winter?"

Clay laughed. "Wow, tell me you haven't figured this out."

Kat walked away. Daniel Clay circled around to block her.

"Beautiful, how do you think Alexander Winter gets around? How do you think he manages to always be one step ahead? Yeah, we're Butch and Sundance and Etta but maybe one of us, *isn't*. Did you ever think about that?"

Katerina stared at him.

"Where do you think that fake ID in your purse came from?" Clay continued. "It's fool proof, untraceable. The only people who can do that are either really good criminals—or cops."

Kat broke out in a laugh. "Do you lie awake nights dreaming this shit up? Now he's what—a Fed?"

"You think cops, agents, can't commit crimes? How do you think those guys stay undercover? They get permission, Katerina."

Katerina crossed her arms. "Okay, so now he's a cop. Then I guess you're in the shit, aren't you?"

"Exactly. And you're right in it with me. We need to look out for each other."

"If you're so concerned, maybe you and your friends should be on the next plane out of here."

"My friends are your friends, remember? They helped you out."

Katerina pursed her lips, at a loss for a comeback.

"*I* am your friend. I wouldn't lie to you, Katerina."

"You lied about the painting in the trunk."

"Hey, I can't have him thinking I'm a fuck up, can I? I have to keep him close so I know what he's doing, so I can stay out of the line of fire."

Acutely aware that the entire argument sounded insane, Katerina made sure to keep her expression blank, even bored.

"What did he tell you about the museum job? What *really* happened when you met Mikhailovich?"

Katerina vacillated, looking everywhere except at Daniel Clay.

"C'mon beautiful, help a guy out here."

She appeared to be at war with herself until she said, "I did what he said. I took an inventory of everything." she hesitated. "And I delivered a message. Twenty-four, two point four."

Clay peered at her. "Do you know what it means?"

Katerina nodded. "He's going to do the job on the twenty fourth and he's charging two point four million for the theft."

Daniel Clay slipped his phone out of his pocket and swiped open the calendar app. He nodded and glanced up, staring out at nothing, lost in his own calculations. "Sure, the museum is closed on Mondays," he muttered, almost to himself. "Makes a good cover story. Have it removed, use it for the sting, have it back before it opens." He refocused on Katerina. "Do you know what he's after in Mikhailovich's house?"

Katerina shook her head. "He wouldn't tell me."

"Mikhailovich is a mega bust—if he can bring him down. You don't want to be in the mix if that happens. Shit, I don't want to be in the mix if that happens."

Glancing around, Katerina shifted her weight from one foot to the other.

"Let me see your phone."

"Get lost," Kat said.

"To give you my number, okay?"

"Just tell me."

"Will you remember it?"

"I remember everything."

Daniel Clay rattled off the number. "I'm telling you straight, beautiful, you're in trouble. Remember *Charade*, Cary Grant's *Alexander Dyle* turned out to be a Treasury cop. See? Meaningful coincidence. When you need me, and you will need me, call me. I'll help you. We'll help each other. Take care, beautiful. Be careful."

Katerina stood in the middle of the aisle, watching Daniel Clay disappear into the crowd of shoppers. Taking out her phone, she made a call. "He just made an appearance," Kat said. "I told him everything, exactly as you said." She listened and a smile crept across her lips. "See you soon."

Katerina clicked off the call. She punched in numbers and smiled when she heard the familiar voice say, "May I help you?"

"Hi Gertie, is my package on the way?"

"I already confirmed delivery. You made a fine choice if you don't mind me saying so."

"Are you sure it will fit?"

"Such a question, bite your tongue. I know my girls. Like a glove, darling. Enjoy yourself."

Katerina hung up the phone. *Right time, right moment. Finally.*

Chapter 99

Detectives Ryan Kellan and Walter Lashiver sat in the office of Gerald Manning, John Reynolds' attorney. Manning entered the office, carrying a manila envelope in one hand. Retired Detective Timothy Green followed behind him.

"Thank you for coming, gentlemen," Manning said. "Detective Green has uncovered something in his investigation that will hopefully be of some assistance to you."

Manning held out the manila envelope.

With a glance at retired Detective Green, Ryan took it and tore open the lip of the envelope. He withdrew a color photograph.

The detective examined the photo of a pretty, young socialite, a fresh-faced former chorus girl who had kicked in the line before a fortuitous marriage to a wealthy businessman in New York. A young woman who had been the victim of a brutal murder, tortured before her death.

Gerald Manning settled into the executive chair behind his desk while Green sat in a guest chair off to the side.

Ryan looked at Green.

"The earrings," Green said. "They were made special for her, quartz with diamonds."

Ryan passed the photograph to Lashiver. "And?"

Manning spoke up. "Detective Green—"

"Former Detective Green," Ryan pushed.

His jaw tightening, Green shifted as if shrugging away Ryan's statement.

"*Detective* Green," Manning persisted, "performed a review of the family photographs. During a consultation with Mr. Reynolds, it came to light that the earrings are missing."

"Maybe she sold them," Lashiver said.

"Unlikely, Detective," Manning said. "They were Mrs. Reynolds' most treasured gift from her husband. Detective Green thinks she could have been wearing them on the day of her death. If that is the case, they could still be in the possession of the killer right now."

"Mr. Reynolds already announced his belief that Will Temple murdered Mrs. Reynolds," Lashiver said. "We didn't find these earrings in Temple's belongings."

"So, I guess you and your boss are out of luck and everyone is still a suspect. But, hey, kudos to you," Ryan said to Green, taking the photograph from Lashiver. "You actually formulated a theory."

"I don't have to take your crap," Green said, bolting out of his chair and lunging for Ryan.

Ryan stood up, his body bracing.

Jumping up, Lashiver inserted himself between the two men as Manning rose from his chair.

"At least I know how to locate a fucking clue," Green said.

"Ryan—c'mon," Lashiver said.

"Yeah, you're a regular Miss Marple, if you're paid enough," Ryan continued. "You know all about getting paid, dontcha Timmy."

"Smart ass, I oughta . . ." Green went off, shoving Lashiver to reach Ryan.

"Gentlemen, enough," Manning broke in, his voice sharp with disgust.

Lashiver put his hand on Green's chest, pushing him away.

"Next time, Sherlock, do your job and I won't have to."

"Yeah, how's that?" Ryan taunted. "What'd you do, Inspector LeStrade?"

"Try looking at the photos and comparing them to her belongings, *Detective*," Green said.

"Detective, please," Manning said.

"Is that all it takes?" Ryan taunted. "How often does Reynolds look at his wife's stuff?"

"All the time, asshole. That's what a husband does when his wife dies," Green said. "They can't part with anything."

"Detective Green," Manning said, loud and insistent. With a black look at the attorney, Green backed off.

"My client may be mistaken. Perhaps his wife, foolishly, gave Mr. Temple the earrings to sell for cash, or sold them and gave him the cash. Either way, there is a third party out there somewhere with information. Perhaps this person may also have information about the murder of Mrs. Penn. It is imperative we find the person who has these earrings. Mr. Reynolds expects you to publicize this photo, immediately, or we will," Manning said, his voice tight. "Make no mistake. If this is left to us, we will have a talk with the police commissioner. I think you would find that less than ideal, correct?"

"We'll take care of it," Lashiver said.

***

Outside the office, Lashiver stood by as Ryan collected himself, smoothing out his coat.

The door opened and Green emerged.

"Let us know when you find Hoffa," Ryan said.

"Fuck you," Green said, heading for the stairwell.

The detectives rode the elevator in silence. When they left the building and settled into the privacy of their car, they turned to one another and smiled.

"Whatever Reynolds has on Green must be nuclear," Ryan said.

"Yeah, but the old man didn't count on him running his mouth. That's a gold star fuck up, right there. I'll call O'Connoll," Lashiver said, pulling out his cell phone as Ryan maneuvered the car into traffic. "This thing with the earrings is bullshit. But you might just get your wish."

Ryan turned to his partner. "How do you figure?"

"You said there's one person out there that's the key to pulling this whole case together. I'm beginning to think you're on to something. You know what else?"

Ryan broke out into a smile. "What?"

"I think Reynolds agrees with you. Whatever this is, the earrings may be the kick-start to get us there. We're gonna play along. We'll put this out today."

Chapter 100

Katerina slipped the cell phone out of her purse, made a face at the number, and tapped to accept the call. "What?" she asked.

"What are you doing?" April asked.

"Working. I hope you're doing the same," Kat snapped.

"I *was* working but it's a little tough to make you disappear when you're still enrolled in school. You're taking Shakespeare? Why?"

Katerina pulled in a deep breath. She had forgotten all about school.

"Hello? Earth to the Invisible Woman. When are you dropping out?"

"I'm out of town right now, but I'll take care of it in the next few days. Okay?"

"Whatever. I'm not the one who needs to get lost. But if you don't take care of it, I still get my money."

"Got it," Kat said, "I'll let you know when it's done."

"I'm holding my breath," April said.

The phone went dead.

Chapter 101

Arthur Penny finished his lecture shortly after five o'clock, thanking the university and the thirty people scattered throughout the lecture hall.

The audience gave respectful applause; several people approached the podium, eager to question the slight, odd little expert. He obliged while clutching his briefcase against his chest like a security blanket.

When the last attendee drifted away, Arthur Penny shrugged into his coat and shook hands with the faculty members. Checking for his cell phone in his jacket pocket, he headed for the exit, his briefcase in one hand and rental car key in the other.

***

Penny crossed the campus, the chilly late afternoon air curling around him. He approached his car, parked in a remote corner of a lot next to a cluster of woods. He pressed the button on the key; the passenger door clicked open. He deposited his briefcase on the seat. Hands grasped his shoulders, swinging him around. Letting out an audible gasp, the keys fell from his hand.

Chapter 102

Katerina passed the key card over the sensor. The light flashed green and she entered the room, wheeling her suitcase behind her. She took in the art deco suite and its seating area, done in pristine white, tempered by cream-colored carpeting; a small, well-stocked bar in walnut and chrome sat off to the side. Signature Winter, she thought; luxury bathed in crisp, clean lines. In the center of the coffee table, a thin-necked vase held two roses, a shock of red against a snow-white landscape.

Glancing in the direction of the bedroom, she kicked off her shoes, left her suitcase, and padded to the doorway.

The king bed with a gold and white duvet sat in the center of the room. Her heart skipped when she saw the clear plastic garment bag lying across the bed.

She unzipped the bag, her skin tingling as she extracted the white lace applique mermaid dress. Her mind hadn't played tricks; it was just as she remembered. She ran her fingers over the delicate lace, a secret smile touching her lips as she imagined Winter seeing her in the dress. She sighed at the flush of heat flaring within her, enjoying the sensation snaking its way through her body. A taste of things to come.

***

Katerina checked her look in the mirror; she had swept up her hair, allowing the dress to take center stage. The lace sheathed her arms, breasts and torso, concealing the barest minimum. The plunging neckline exposed her décolleté, creating the illusion of wearing nothing at all. Her legs, revealed through the sheer fabric, heightened the sense of seduction and desire.

She slipped on silver stilettos, snaking the thin cords around her feet and tying them at her ankles. The ringing of the hotel phone broke her thoughts.

"Your car has arrived," the efficient concierge said. "The driver is waiting for you."

"Thank you," Kat said.

***

The host ushered her into the restaurant's private dining room. Katerina spied him, seated in a secluded booth. Her skin warmed at the sight of him. The host escorted her to the table; Winter stood; he wore a tailored black jacket with a black and white pinstriped shirt and black pants. She spotted the telltale glint of onyx in his eyes.

A smile curved his lips before he bent to kiss her cheek. She closed her eyes, breathing in his clean, cool scent.

"Stunning," he whispered in her ear as his arm coiled around her waist.

***

The elegant room held several oval tables for two; strategically placed potted flora afforded privacy for each couple. Ecru linen tablecloths and napkins, crystal glasses, and fine silver settings added to the opulence. A few couples on the dance floor swayed to soft music. Katerina flushed at the touch of Winter's strong hand as he led her to floor, drawing her into his embrace.

I want to spend the rest of my life in your arms.

As if sensing her thoughts, Winter's embrace tightened.

The blowsy sound of the saxophone intermingling with the piano soothed Katerina and she rested a hand on his chest, following his lead.

Moving to the music, her imagination went to work; a vision of them together brought a rush of heat flowing through the deepest part of her. Suddenly, a thought fluttered through her mind . . . she could feel her body tense.

"Tell me," he said.

"The night does strange things," Kat said.

"In what way?"

"Everything is different in the morning."

"Only if you were with the wrong man the night before," he whispered, pulling her closer.

When Kat trusted herself to look at him, her anxieties fled, her excuses vanished. Unfettered relief flooded through her; she lay her head on his chest, relaxing against him.

"Katie, I—" he began.

She pulled back to see his eyes filled with concern.

"I wanted to make everything . . . special."

"You have . . . it is . . . it will be."

Pulling her in, he put his lips near her ear. "Are you hungry?" he murmured.

"Starving," she whispered, her lips against the warmth of his neck.

Winter took her by the hand and led her off the dance floor.

***

Winter closed the door to her bedroom and pulling her into his arms, eased her down onto the bed. Katerina could feel the surging power he held in check, restraining himself, going slow. With every touch of his hands, desire raced through her, spreading like a fever, her skin burning beneath the delicate fabric of the dress. She wanted it off, impatient to have him strip it away from her body. His mouth moved over her, leaving a trail of heat from her neck to the hollow between her breasts.

Desperate to touch him, her fingers fumbled with the buttons of his shirt. His hand moved over her, skimming the curves of her waist and hip; with maddening restraint, he began to peel the dress from her, caressing her skin, finally cupping her breast with the lightest of touches. Her breath came fast and ragged and her body trembled as he bent his head and his mouth moved over her skin, his tongue tasting and teasing. She heard her own voice let out a moan as her body arched and released, warm and wet.

Suddenly, buzzing noises sounded, competing with each other. Insistent, they stopped and then started in a round. Winter went still, waiting. When they began again, he let out a string of curses and rolled away from her.

Tears sprang to Katerina's eyes.

Grabbing his cell phone from the night table, he connected the call. "What," Winter said into the phone.

"Don't hang up on me or someone's gonna die."

Chapter 103

"Are you listening to me, man?"

Winter, his breathing still ragged, pushed off the bed as he listened to Daniel Clay's overwrought babbling. Standing over Katerina, Winter took hold of the dress and covered her.

"Yes," he said into the phone.

Katerina got out of bed, slipped back into the dress and retrieved her purse from the chair. She extracted her cell phone and connected the call.

"I told you there was going to be a fuckin' problem," Clay said.

"Get to the point," Winter snapped, his attention divided as he watched Katerina.

Kat said a few words into the phone, ending with "I'll call you back," and clicked off. She came to Winter, listening in.

"My boss got a little upset. He's got your man, the old guy you're using at the museum. He's got grandpa and he says he's gonna keep him until you take care of business."

Clay stopped speaking. Winter listened to the silence, acclimating to this new reality of a situation spiraled out of control. It wasn't a new experience.

"I need proof of life," Winter said. After a beat of dead air, the sound of the old man's recorded voice came over the line.

Winter watched Kat's body stiffen, every muscle tensing. Her hand slipped into his, gripping tight.

"You gotta get here. We have to get this done or that old man, he's gone, you get it? He's done."

Winter's mind began to spin, searching for a move he could make. But the inkling, the idea, like the tiniest of drums, had begun its familiar, steady beat in his brain. He thought of the instruction he had received long ago; she had drilled it into him. *Whatever you do, don't get caught.*

"Where are you?" Daniel Clay asked.

"Iowa," Winter deadpanned.

"That shit's not funny, man. We're fucked."

"Give me twenty minutes to get on the road and I'll call you with an ETA."

Winter listened to Daniel Clay's exhale of relief. "Okay, this is a plan. You're gonna let bygones be bygones, right? You'll call me back, right?"

"Twenty minutes," Winter said, ending the call.

Katerina held onto his hand as she sank down onto the bed.

He sat down next to her. "I won't let anything happen to him."

"A recorded message is worth nothing. He could already be . . ."

"He isn't."

"How do you know?" she asked.

"Because I know," he answered. "Who called you?"

"Angel."

Winter's eyes narrowed.

"I hired him. I thought we might need backup."

Winter nodded.

"He did a run on Mikhailovich's place. There must have been a change in plans. A large party of houseguests arrived, and they have big suitcases. Mikhailovich has taken them out for the evening. Angel said if we're going, we should go as soon as possible. Tonight," she said.

"Daniel is demanding the museum job for Penny's release," Winter said, giving her hand a gentle squeeze. "Things are going to happen fast now, Katie."

"I can keep up."

"We'll go to Balboa and then I'll go meet Daniel. I will make sure he releases Mr. Penny, unharmed."

"How can you be sure *you'll* get away unharmed?" she asked.

Winter drew her into his arms; the heat of her body against his caused an ache of longing to well up inside him. He held her, trying to ignore the voice in his head blaring like a siren, warning him of a nameless danger lurking, waiting to strike.

"No one's caught me yet," he whispered into her hair.

She crooked her head to look at him. "*We* go meet Daniel and get Penny back. Then you take care of your job and I'll go to Balboa alone. Angel will shadow me."

Winter shook his head. "Out of the question. You're not ready to crack a safe."

"I don't need to crack it. I can drill it."

"We didn't cover that lesson."

"*I* covered that lesson, in New York."

Winter, taken aback, took a moment to process the information. "I don't have any equipment here for you."

"I made arrangements. I have the equipment."

Winter's eyes widened; he fixed her with a stare, his mouth ajar; for once, at a loss for a piece of wisdom or an instruction.

Kat's cell phone buzzed again. When she connected the call, her eyes flew open, staring at Winter as she spoke.

"Arthur," she said into the phone. "Where are you?"

Chapter 104

"Young lady," came the cracked, breathless voice of Arthur Penny, "it is most fortunate that I found you. I seem to have been accosted and kidnapped."

Katerina reminded herself to act as if she were ignorant of everything. "Arthur, my God, I'm so sorry. What happened? Who attacked you? Where are you? Is someone still there?"

"I did not see them. The philistines wore masks and no, I'm not with them."

Katerina closed her eyes, zeroing in on the sound of Penny's voice, concentrating on his every word.

"Thank goodness they did not take my briefcase. I have rather copious notes for my next lecture on Byzantine Art and Religion. It would have been most inconvenient—"

"Arthur, Arthur," Katerina soothed. "Can you tell me where you are?"

"Well, my dear, I am in . . . the trunk."

Katerina looked to Winter, watching his eyebrows pinch in confusion. "You're in the trunk of your car?" she repeated

"I deposited my bag on the passenger seat and then they came up behind me. They made me talk into a cell phone. Most curious. They absconded with my keys and my phone and then dispatched me to the trunk with my briefcase."

"But, how are you calling me?"

"Well, my dear young lady, like the Boy Scouts, I am always prepared. I keep an extra cell phone in my briefcase in case of emergencies, which this certainly qualifies."

Katerina watched Winter scribble on a piece of paper and hold it out to her.

"I must tell you that I do dislike small, dark spaces—"

"Arthur," Katerina interrupted as she took the paper from Winter's hand, scanned it, and nodded her head. "Arthur, I am coming to get you, you understand? I'm coming. Where did you park your car?"

"I do prefer a well-lit corner of a parking lot, but it was quite crowded on the campus today—"

"Arthur, I know you're scared," Kat said. "Believe me, I do. But, please, try to concentrate and describe exactly where your car is parked."

Arthur Penny gave the location. "I am like Odysseus, my dear young lady, I am simply trying to find my way safely back to home."

"Arthur, hang on, I'm coming. I promise."

Katerina clicked off the phone. "You really believe they won't hurt him."

"Yes," Winter said.

"Is that a hard yes or a soft yes?"

"That's a yes."

A knock sounded at the door and they both whirled around.

***

"We go in three separate cars," Winter said.

"What do you tell your little brother?" Katerina asked, alluding to Daniel Clay.

"He's going to have to amuse himself for a while. He'll wait."

"Someone's watching that car," Angel said.

"But no one expects *us* to be there," Katerina said.

"You're both right," Winter said. "There is someone babysitting the car, just to be sure drunken frat boys don't boost it. And there will be more than one person at different vantage points to cover all the bases."

"Then I should approach the car," Kat said. "That will get at least one person's attention and divide them up. Then you can split up and take care of them."

Winter pursed his lips. "Fine."

"Penny said they took his keys. The doors are probably locked."

"I can't teach you to break into a car in ten minutes," Winter said.

"You don't have to. I just have to look like I'm breaking in. I'm sure you have something I can use."

Angel gave a soft chuckle of appreciation.

Winter nodded. "Okay. We get your man, then we go to Balboa."

"I told you, I'm going to Balboa alone."

"And *I* told *you*, that is out of the question," Winter said in a tone that brooked no rebellion. "We go together or not at all."

Angel took a step back, reverting to the position of spectator.

"I have to be able to do this alone," Katerina said. "For now, quick and dirty will do."

"Not when Mikhailovich comes home and sees a hole in his safe."

Katerina considered his words. "It is what it is," she said, parroting his favorite expression. "This is the truth. Admit it. This is what we're dealing with. I'm not being stubborn, Bob. I'm not. This is the simplest thing to do and my one chance to do it. This I can do. I'm more concerned about you. How are you going to deal with Daniel?"

"It's taken care of," Winter snapped. The room fell into a tense silence as Winter struggled and lost. He turned to Angel. "You cover her, every minute, every second."

"Understood," Angel said.

"We'll be down in a few minutes," Katerina said to Angel; he left the room.

Katerina retreated to the bathroom. She gave herself one last look in the mirror, then stripped down and changed into jeans, t-shirt and jacket. When she came out, she had a short, blond wig on her head with a cap over it, pulled down low.

They packed up and cleaned the room in silence. Katerina burned the slip of paper with Winter's handwriting. She stood off to the side, watching him perform his ritual checks, once, then again. He fell into deep concentration, each cycle sucking him further into the compulsion.

Katerina went to his side and took his hands in her own. "You did it. It's done. It's done right."

Winter nodded, abandoning the exercise.

"So, they lock Arthur Penny in the trunk of a car so you have to break into a museum to save a total stranger. How did they know you wouldn't just say to get rid of him? How did they know that?" she asked.

"Because that might dampen *our* relationship. It was a smart move on Daniel's part."

"Would you have let them hurt Arthur Penny?"

Winter looked her in the eye as he took her in his arms. "No."

Katerina took him at his word as she squeezed him tighter, inhaling his scent, desperate to preserve the sensation and commit him to memory.

***

Smith sat in a car parked at the far end of the hotel lot. He had weighed and discarded making his move while they were in the room. That would have raised too many questions, created too much of a mess. If Gallagher's prize got poked by someone else that wasn't his problem.

He observed the tall gentleman with the bald head he had seen going into the hotel making his way out to his car. Smith congratulated himself that he had made the right call. Smart girl, he thought, hiring a bodyguard to watch her back. Smart indeed.

Smith's thoughts turned to Lisa. Knowing that bitch was somewhere in the parking lot, sitting in her car, waiting, soured his mood. She had made him look bad. He had decided she would get hers before this situation was taken care of. He had figured out the perfect time to do it, too.

Smith snapped to attention when a woman with short blond hair emerged from the side entrance, walking with a tall man, his head down.

Smith started his car and watched the man and woman split off into two separate cars. The third vehicle with the bald-headed man pulled in behind them and they headed out single file.

Smith moved to follow at a safe distance. This looks promising, he thought. His cell phone rang. *Lisa.* He ignored it and rolled out of the lot. *You go ahead and keep up, bitch. Bob isn't the only one who's going to fall victim to a shock event. I'll be bringing the girl home by myself.*

Chapter 105

The sun had long slipped below the horizon as the cars took the 405 Freeway to Los Angeles. In her own car, Katerina could feel the pressure she lived with in New York rush back in like the tide. She tried deep breathing to tamp down her nerves and calm her pounding heart. She resisted the urge to call Winter, knowing he would be consumed with his own thoughts and anxiety, preparing in his own way. Maybe he was calling Daniel Clay, putting his own plan in motion. *Now you're thinking like a professional, Katerina. It's about time.*

She had her own call to make. She dialed, put the speaker on, and listened to the ringing and the connecting click.

"Yo."

"Papi," she said.

Moose's voice dropped down, low and smooth. "*Que lo que?*"

"*Ta to*," she said. "Necesito ayuda, papi."

"Dimelo. What can the Moose do for you?"

Katerina took a breath. "Suppose someone needs to break into a car using a slim jim to open the door lock. How is it done?"

"Uh, chica, you don't just *do* that, entiende? It takes skill that's, como se dice—"

"Specialized?"

"Yeah, yeah. The Moose recommends a short, intense training for this specialized skill. Is this person, you know, good with mechanics?"

Kat smiled. "A little. Talk to me, Moose. Talk me through it. I've got the tools and I need to look like I've got those specialized skills. Tell me how to do that."

"All right, mami. I got you."

Katerina tooled down the highway, the sound of Moose's voice filling the car.

***

Katerina parked on campus and killed the lights. She exited the car with the tools tucked away inside her jacket. When her eyes had adjusted to the darkness, she spotted Arthur Penny's vehicle exactly where he said it would be, a copse of trees and shrubs nestled behind the car. There could be no one lurking in those trees, or one person, or two. No matter who was out there, Angel and Winter had them in their sights. She was not alone and the text on her phone, the one she had been waiting for, finally came in.

We're in place.

Katerina took a deep breath and stepped out onto the pavement.

The car, at first far away, grew larger with every step she took.

***

Smith scanned the scene, blinking a few times to be sure he was seeing correctly. *What the hell?* He realized that Thomas Gallagher's prize appeared to be in the process of breaking into a car, and the two men were concealed somewhere, watching her do it.

He shook his head, considering the unwanted publicity of Bob's dead body being found on a college campus. Whatever this shit was, now was not the optimum moment to insert himself into the situation. He made a sound of disgust and sat back in his seat. Retrieving Katerina Mills was becoming infinitely more complicated.

***

Burnett and Prescott cooled their heels in a car affording an ample view of Arthur Penny's vehicle. Burnett, in the driver's seat, had his arms folded across his chest, head down, eyes closed.

Prescott scanned with his binoculars. "You gotta be fucking kidding me." He elbowed his partner. "Wake up, dumb-ass. You're not going to believe this," he said, holding out the binoculars.

Burnett roused himself and took the binoculars. Focusing on the car, he watched the figure wearing a cap pulled down over short blond hair wander over to the car and test the locked door.

Without a word, they scrambled out of the car.

***

Katerina, planted at the passenger door of the car, turned and glanced at the woods behind her. Nothing. Returning her focus to the car, she took out a jam and wedged it between the car window and the weather stripping; then she withdrew the slim jim from inside her coat, threading it inside the window, down to the door lock.

***

Burnett crept noiselessly through the darkened woods, threading his way through brambles scratching at his arms and face. He came out where he could sneak up behind the woman trying to break into the car.

Crouching low, he crept to the edge of the woods, ready to pounce, when an electric current knocked the wind out of his lungs; he sank to the ground.

Alexander Winter bent over the inert body and tugged it back into the brush. He rifled the man's pockets, extracting a cell phone and tucking it away in his own pocket. He searched again, looking for keys. In frustration, he rolled the body over and patted him down. Nothing. He had gotten the wrong one. The other one had the keys.

***

This isn't moving fast enough.

Katerina decided to pull out the slim jim and move from the passenger door to the trunk, an invitation for someone to jump her from behind. Shaking, she took a screwdriver out of her jacket and inserted the tool into the trunk lock. The voice of Arthur Perry called out, "Are you there? Young lady? Is anyone there?"

Katerina's nerves shredded in trepidation as she anticipated someone coming up behind her at any moment. The sound of a man's grunt made her whirl around, one arm up in self-defense; she found herself staring into the empty darkness.

Muffled scuffling sounds made her squint, trying to see into the shrubbery. A rustling from the trees followed; she stiffened, poised for flight.

Angel emerged; Katerina remembered to breathe.

He tossed her the keys. Inserting the key, she popped the trunk.

***

Looking through night vision binoculars, Smith focused on the car and the figures in green. He saw Katerina, the man with the bald head, and a small, older man, sitting up in the trunk. The elusive "W" was nowhere to be seen. "Some shit," Smith mumbled under his breath.

He shifted in his seat, scanning the area again. This time, he spotted another car, the same one he had picked up since he left the hotel. It wasn't Lisa, the bitch. He dialed Gallagher's number, shaking his head. *Rich people playing games.*

***

"Oh, my dear," Arthur Penny said. "I am so pleased to see you." He rambled on as Angel hoisted the frazzled little man out of the trunk. "I cannot tell you how I appreciate this. This could have been quite a bit more unpleasant. Thank goodness the trunk was very clean."

"Put that on your customer satisfaction survey," Angel said.

Arthur Penny chuckled. "Oh, indeed," he said.

Katerina handed Penny his briefcase and the little man clutched it to his chest, his hair askew in the night breeze.

"I can't imagine what they wanted," Penny mused. "Most mystifying."

"Probably a college frat prank," Kat said. "I'm so sorry this happened to you," she said as she opened the car door and settled him in behind the wheel.

"It is a brutal world my dear Juliet, brutal indeed."

Katerina kneeled down at his side. "Arthur, will you be able to drive?"

"Oh, yes . . . yes to be sure, young lady."

"You could call the police to report this . . . but I believe it might be more . . . prudent to let it go and be on your way. Do you understand, Arthur?"

Arthur Penny took Kat's hand. "I agree completely. And thank you. And to you as well my good man," he said to Angel.

Katerina smiled, stood up, and stepped back to allow Arthur Penny to close the door and start the car. She watched the vehicle pull out. She didn't look for Winter. They had already said their goodbyes in the hotel room.

"I need to make one stop on the way for the equipment bag."

"Let's fly, baby," Angel said.

Katerina nodded; she fell into step with Angel, hustling to get back to their cars. It was time. *This is what I wanted. This is the way it has to be.*

***

Thomas Gallagher hung up the phone and sent off a text message to MJM.

> I know what you're doing.
> Call it off.

He waited. The phone buzzed.

> No. The situation must be taken care of.

Flushing crimson, Gallagher sucked in a long breath to stem the rage boiling up from his chest into his throat. He typed again.

> Leave KM to me.
> MJM's hands will be clean.
> I will recompense you. Name your price.

He waited.

> MJM's hands will be clean.
> This is the second time the agency has had to handle your mess.
> There is no price.

Gallagher typed another message but after a moment of silence, he placed the phone down on the table with a ginger touch so as not to break it. When he had sufficiently calmed down, he picked it up again to make a call.

Chapter 106

Winter drove off of the campus. He abandoned any attempt to prepare for the job; it would be a meaningless exercise. His thoughts were fixed on a beautiful, young woman, her hair tucked away under a short blond wig, on her way to complete a job, her first job on her own. The thought of her alone, exposed, made a cool sweat break out on his forehead. He visualized each step she might take to get the job done. *There should have been another way, instead of her breaking into the safe alone—*

Katerina's voice sounded into his head.

Antiques are reliable.

They hold many secrets.

They will never tell.

Do you think he had a relocker or a booby trap installed?

They will never tell.

"Shit," he said, making a sudden, wild U-turn. He lead footed the accelerator and raced back to the 405. He needed to get to Katerina . . . before it was too late.

Chapter 107

Daniel Clay sat parked where he could see "the lamps," a light installation that served as a defining hallmark of the museum. When the cell phone buzzed, he hesitated at the number. He didn't recognize it.

"Who's this?" Clay asked.

"Who the fuck do you think it is," Burnett yelled into the phone. "It was an ambush."

Clay started. "What? How?"

"How the fuck should I know?"

"Did you see who it was?" Clay asked.

"No, I didn't see *them*. The little princess was in a blond wig. She was the bait."

"Let me guess, they got your cell phones and your keys."

"Oh yeah, Dick fuckin' Tracy," Burnett yelled.

"How the hell did they find out?" Clay mumbled.

"How should I know?" Burnett said.

Daniel Clay made a face. "That was rhetorical, asshole. Where are you?"

"We're at a fuckin' frat party," Burnett said and gave the address. "Send someone to come and get us."

Clay hung up the phone and checked his watch.

A voice from the passenger seat of the car shook him out of his thoughts. "Is he coming?" Halliday asked.

Daniel Clay looked out at the museum. He didn't answer.

Chapter 108

Katerina pulled into a small shopping center, the bridge to cross over onto Balboa Island in the near distance. She parked the car and left it. Grabbing a gym bag from the trunk, she set out to cross the bridge on foot.

The town had closed up for the night. Katerina shivered in the chill air as she stole along the quiet, empty streets and the hodgepodge of homes clinging close to each other. When she knew she was close to her destination, she ducked into an alley, taking light steps, alert for any noise that would indicate someone close by.

Slipping out of the alley, she glanced to her left and right, then stepped up to the front door. She entered the code into the keypad with a gloved hand. Applying pressure on the door handle, she felt it turning under the weight of her hand. Perspiration broke out under her clothes, cold and clammy, as she slipped inside. She didn't want to know how Winter had obtained the passcode. That was a lesson for another day.

Inside the house, the pocket doors to the patio were closed up tight. Katerina stood like a sentry at a post, straining her eyes to adjust to the darkness. The words Winter had spoken before they left the hotel whispered to her. *There will be a moment. You will be in the house, and you will say to yourself, this is insane. I am doing this, and it is insane. You must put that thought out of your mind—or you will fail.* Katerina nodded and moved.

Remembering the layout, she took careful steps until her hand rested on the bannister at the foot of the staircase. She took every step as if she were about to levitate off the floor. It was the house in the Hamptons all over again. Kat had the surreal sensation that if she closed her eyes and opened them, she would find herself back in that house, taking those steps up to the bonus room, only this time, there was no Alexander Winter to take her by the hand and lead her out.

Chapter 109

Sitting in the car, Daniel Clay's annoyance rose with each passing moment. When the cell phone rang, he jabbed his finger on the green button.

"Yo." Prescott's voice filled the car.

"Don't give me yo," Clay snapped. "Where the hell are you?"

"We're having tea and scones," Prescott said. "Is he there yet?"

"No."

"You know where he went, right? Where *they* went?"

Clay stared out at the museum, rejecting every option that floated through his mind. "Yeah, I know."

"Burnsey wants to go down there," Prescott said. "Threaten to turn them over to Mikhailovich and get 'em on the hook that way."

Clay ran through the scenario. "No, too dangerous. We can't be found in that house."

"We used Nicholas on the boat. What's the difference?"

"The difference is he was set up and established. Here we got nothing. We get found in that house, we're screwed, you understand? We're not going in there."

Prescott's voice muffled as he spoke away from the phone. Rustling noises told Clay the cell phone was being passed. Burnett's voice came back on the line. "What now?"

"Get back here. We wait. Maybe he's going to take care of Balboa first and then he'll come here. He's never missed a delivery. Never."

Daniel Clay disconnected the call. He checked his watch. Only a few hours of darkness left. Once the sun came up, the party was over.

Chapter 110

Katerina reached the top of the stairs. By memory she took careful steps until she put out a hand and found the chest. Placing the bag on the floor, she got down on her knees and snapped on the penlight. She opened the right cabinet door, revealing the dial on the combination lock. White hot fear caused her breath to come faster, making her heart thud in her chest. She ran an arm across her forehead to wipe away the sweat.

Remember what he told you.
Survey the workspace.
Zero in on the drill point.
Get to work.

With a slow, methodic pace, Kat extracted a drill and a punch rod. She took out a head strap and connected the penlight.

She calculated the drill point, hoping to God she was right. Picking up the drill, she placed the bit, and went to work, hoping this wouldn't be the one night a neighbor heard an unusual noise and called the police.

***

Outside the house, Angel took his post, keeping a laser gaze fixed on the dock and the walkway. A boat cruised through the channel. On its third rotation, it docked four houses away.

Angel straightened to attention. There were two men, dressed in black.

***

Katerina stopped and lowered the drill. She didn't know how long she'd been at it, but her arms ached and it was taking too long. Doubt snaked its way through her mind like tentacles.

Suddenly, she froze, her senses on high alert. *Someone's here.* She listened, willing her body to hold still. Her fingers reached for the punch rod next to her feet and grasped it.

Rising up, she raised the punch rod as she whirled around. The penlight blinded the intruder. She brought the rod down. It caught something solid.

***

A deep grunt and a curse sent a spasm of shock through her. She threw off the head strap, focusing the penlight.

Katerina's breath caught in her throat as she let out a cry.

Winter.

"Oh God," she let out as she reached for Winter's injured hand.

He snatched it away from her grasp.

"I'm so sorry," Katerina said, her voice thick with oncoming tears.

"Put the drill away," Winter ordered, his voice tight.

"But I'm almost through."

"No," he ordered. "Manipulation only."

He used his left hand to take his own penlight out of his pocket as he moved to the chest. He crouched down to inspect the drilled hole.

Katerina's senses drowned in panic; with shaking hands, she tucked the drill back into the bag. She focused the light on his swollen hand; the bruised skin had bloomed an angry red. She blinked back tears.

"Please let me finish," Kat said.

"It's booby-trapped," Winter said.

Kat halted, shocked into silence until she said, "How can you be sure?"

"Because he told you."

Katerina's mind raced back through the conversation with Mikhailovich but came up empty. She thought to protest but held her tongue. *The professor knows best.*

Katerina focused the penlight, castigating herself as she watched Winter struggle to turn the dial and line up the wheels.

With every twist to take a reading, she knew the distress in his face revealed a fresh burst of pain. She watched as he struggled to keep his hand steady while he tried to locate the contact points. He stopped, started, and stopped again, straining to establish a reliable sense of touch as over and over his concentration broke.

Katerina clipped the penlight to the head strap and tilted her head to focus while propping her hands underneath Winter's arm and wrist.

She watched a rivulet of sweat roll down his temple, his jaw muscles working, clenching against the pain.

Kat's arms ached; she realized that however much time had been spent, it had been long past time.

It's over.

"Bob," Kat whispered.

Winter let his hand drop away from the lock. He held it against himself, cradling it. "You have to get the last number," he said.

A thunderbolt of fear pierced her. "Are you sure about the trap? Maybe—"

"Katie, you have to get the third number."

Katerina nodded.

They switched places.

***

With silent footsteps, Angel followed the two men, waiting to see which path they would take. When they went for the alley, he hung back until they were shrouded in the darkness of the narrow space. He would have only one chance at this.

***

Katerina placed her fingers on the dial, spinning the wheel four times until she sensed she had picked up all the wheels.

"First two numbers are thirty-eight and four," Winter said.

"You sure?"

"Pretty sure," he said.

The silence hung thick between them as Katerina wished she could do this one thing.

Just one number. Not three. Just one. Next time you'll do more. You'll be better.

She turned the wheel with a feather touch, taking her readings.

"How long have we been here?" she asked.

"Longer than we should and not as long as you think. Concentrate."

"I didn't realize—I didn't sense it was you."

"Obviously."

"I'm so—"

"You'll make it up to me later. Concentrate."

Kat let it drop and returned to her task, desperate for that sensation of pure concentration. That magical moment when the mind clears, and like a curtain falling away, everything else disappears. She had no idea how many minutes had passed.

She turned by half, quarter, and eighth inches—until she stopped.

"Twenty-two," she said.

"Do it," Winter said.

Katerina spun the dial several times.

She turned the dial.

Thirty-eight.

She turned the dial in the opposite direction several times.

Four.

Katerina turned the dial the other way until she stopped.

Twenty-two.

Her sense of touch told her the wheels had aligned. The gates were open. The fence had dropped.

Katerina pulled the handle. It resisted for a moment; her heart sank. She gave another tug.

The door opened.

***

The young woman crept her way to the entrance to the house. Stepping up to the etched glass doors, she manipulated the keypad, clicked the latch down, and silently opened the door.

***

In a state of expectant trepidation, Katerina swung open the safe door. She focused the penlight, illuminating three vials attached over the housing for the lock.

"Shit," Katerina uttered. "What is it?"

"Some kind of gas," Winter said.

"Bob—"

"You'll thank me later."

You have no idea.

She shined the light on the velvet-lined shelves. Empty. Katerina clamped her eyes closed, watching each fantasy she had entertained dispel and disintegrate.

When she opened her eyes, she pulled out each drawer. In the last drawer, she found sheets of yellowed paper. She scanned one, a list with descriptions with dollar amounts. She shoved the papers her jacket pocket.

Katerina packed up the tools in her bag. She and Winter stood in unison and she switched off the penlight.

As Winter went for the stairs, a buzzing sound and two electric currents cut through the darkness as the taser jammed into his chest.

Chapter 111

Katerina heard Winter's groan and the heavy thud as he fell to the floor. Lunging for him, a figure charged into her, tackling her to the floor. Katerina punched and clawed at her assailant, struggling to gain control. She heard a high-pitched cry.

A woman.
The housekeeper.
The killer.

She heard the metallic sound of an object hitting the floor.
Gun.

Panic shot through her as they rolled on the floor in the dark, fighting for supremacy, groping between blows to find the gun. The woman drove a fist into Kat's side. Katerina grunted, lifting her knee and jamming it upward, finding a soft landing in the woman's abdomen. Then, the attacker was pulled away.

***

In the alley, Angel took aim and emptied the rubber bullets in quick succession, hoping he hit both marks. He heard grunts, then silence.

Creeping forward, he laid a hand on one inert body. He turned to check the other body, but a hand closed on his wrist and the man rose up, pushing Angel back against the wall.

***

Katerina heard Winter's guttural noises of pain as he struggled with the attacker.

Free, Katerina scrambled to her knees, her arms outstretched, hands sweeping wide, hoping to find the gun. She heard the buzzing sound and saw the crackle of light.

A blast of hot rage erupted within her.
Bitch.

Kat heard the killer coming up behind her. Balling up her fist, Katerina turned and struck out with all her strength; her fist contacted something solid. She heard a cracking sound and the woman cried out.

Katerina heard a mechanical sound. She turned as the elevator door opened.

A flash of blinding light made Kat raise her hands to shield her eyes. Silhouetted in the open elevator, a man stood, his arm outstretched, his hand holding a gun.

"Angel?" Kat said.

She heard a female voice cry out and then the sound of a body hitting the floor.

***

Angel took the first blow but shifted in time for the fist to fly past his head and into the wall. A string of curses followed. The man turned and attempted to land a blow with his other hand. Angel ducked and drove into the man's chest, forcing him down to the ground. Angel tried to reach for his gun. His assailant landed punches to jar the weapon loose. They rolled in a struggle; Angel underneath, his arm wrapped around the man's neck. The man squirmed, striking at Angel's arm. At the first sign of faltering, Angel's grip tightened. He reached out his other arm, laying his hand on his gun. Jamming it into the assailant's side, he discharged another rubber bullet. The assailant lay still, a dead weight.

Angel rolled the man over. He got to his feet and tasered both men for good measure, then set about binding their hands and legs.

He shot up straight, standing in the darkness, listening to the stillness. He turned. Creeping to the end of the alley, he waited, waited for the sense of another body to crystallize. One second too long and he would lose the advantage.

He held still.

Reaching out, he pulled the person into the alley, clasping a hand over the mouth. At the muted protest, he stopped and pushed the person up against the wall. He held up a light, illuminating the face.

Lisa.

***

As Katerina grasped Winter's shoulders, she said, "He's hurt."

She squinted at the glaring light. "Angel, turn that off, you're blinding us."

Kat watched the arm rise again, the gun pointing at Winter. Katerina threw herself over him.

A popping noise sounded, and the light fell away; Kat heard a body collapse to the floor.

Katerina, still clinging to Winter, lifted her head as a soft, diffused light filled the room.

"Easy now," a man's voice said, smooth and soft. "The bad dream is over. You're ok."

Katerina remembered to breathe as Keyes came forward. He took Winter's hand and heaved him to his feet. Carter the younger, Kat thought. Just in time.

***

"What's the story," Angel said to Lisa.

"MJM sent a contractor to take care of the princess. I don't know what she did, but she's been marked for removal."

Angel said nothing, his expression a cipher.

"These guys are his backup. He's inside the house right now. We've got to go in and you're gonna need more than rubber bullets to take him out. Don't worry about an exit strategy. I have one."

Angel eyed Lisa. "The cavalry's already in the house. Baby went in with a way out."

"Glad to hear it," Lisa said. "She's good, isn't she?"

Angel kept space between them, his hand at rest near the gun in his waistband, watchful and wary. "As good as you," he said. "What's your way out?"

Lisa gave a tiny, hard smile.

***

Winter's ragged breathing echoed the pain etched into his pale face.

"Who's who?" Keyes asked.

Winter pointed. "The woman was for her."

Keyes shined a light as Katerina crouched down over the young woman. She checked the jacket and pants pockets, even taking off the shoes to look for a hidden ID. "Nothing," Kat said.

Keyes flashed the light over the inert man, a pool of blood spreading underneath his left shoulder. Winter looked at the face. *Mr. Smith.*

***

Keyes led the way through the side alley, gripping his gun. Behind him, Kat supported Winter, her arm around his waist. Keyes put out a hand to hold them back.

Angel appeared.

"Where have you been?" Kat demanded.

Angel motioned for them to step around the two unconscious shapes slumped over each other. "It takes a village, baby," he said.

"I believe you," Kat said.

Without another word, they stole away.

Chapter 112

After a while, Winter stopped sweating, his pale complexion regained its color, and his breathing returned to normal.

Angel and Keyes stood out of earshot, giving the couple a wide berth.

Katerina held an ice bag to his injured hand. They leaned against the car and each other, as if holding each other in balance. Winter winced as he shifted to look at her. "You did it," he said with a soft smile.

She pulled the bag away, her heart squeezing at the sight of his swollen hand. "Yeah . . . I did."

He shrugged away her comment. "You covered me," he said.

"Every day, every time," Kat said, caressing his face. "I will always protect you."

As her hand stroked his cheek, his lips caught her fingertips.

"You need Doc and you haven't got him."

"I've got it covered," he said, parroting her favorite phrase.

Kat glanced over her shoulder at Angel, then turned back to Winter. "I'm sorry MJM got on to you because of me."

"I'm not sure who Smith is working for," Winter said.

Katerina shook her head. "Lisa called MJM's contractor "him." He was sent for both of us. I don't know who sent the woman."

Winter shrugged. "What about Lisa? Why would she come to your rescue?" he asked.

Kat gave a snarky laugh. "Mother Theresa of Manhattan? I'm sure it was out of the goodness of her pure heart."

Winter's chuckle turned to a grimace as he turned his wrist to check his watch. "It's my turn."

Katerina shifted, ready to join him.

Winter answered with a raised eyebrow.

Kat shook her head. "No. No way you're going alone."

"You still have a plan to follow."

"This is the new plan. Now, I help you."

"Stick to the plan," he said.

Katerina shook her head. "The plan's shot to shit. And even if it wasn't—"

"Patience," Winter chided. "Mikhailovich had those papers in a booby-trapped safe. They're worth something. Do you still have a move to make?"

"Yes," she said, resisting the urge to add "I think so." Winter didn't deal in "I think so." You either knew or you didn't.

"Then stick to the plan. Think of every possible thing Zilinsky could say, MJM could say, and come up with a response. Think like they think. Remember Katie, at this moment, MJM thinks you're dead."

Winter pulled himself up. "When you're done, check into a hotel near LAX. If I can't get to you—"

Katerina started in protest.

"Katie, if I can't get to you, book a flight to anywhere but New York. Once MJM makes the transfer payment, immediately move the money as I taught you, new shell companies, new accounts. Keep the money moving so it can't be found."

She wrapped her arms around him.

"Take Angel with you, or Keyes," she said.

"I'm going alone."

"What if you get there and you can't do the job?"

Winter smiled, planting a tender kiss on her lips. "I've never missed a delivery."

Katerina opened her mouth to speak but let the words go. She stayed close as Winter gingerly settled in behind the wheel and turned over the engine. She stepped back as he closed the door and pulled out of the parking lot. Katerina watched him go, her heart thudding in her chest.

Chapter 113

The woman entered the house, canvasing each room quickly, methodically. When she finished searching the main floor, she moved up the stairs with cautious urgency. She scanned the rooms with the penlight, finding two large bloodstains on the carpet.

Descending the stairs, she stood still, thinking, unsure of what to do; suddenly she turned. Reaching out a gloved finger, she pressed the button on the elevator. The door opened to reveal the wounded girl lying on the floor, eyes half-closed, her breathing shallow and uneven.

Looking up, the girl's face lit up in recognition. "I'm sorry," she said, struggling for breath, "there was another one . . . I didn't see him . . . why didn't you come?"

"Shhh," the woman soothed, placing a finger on her lips. "I'm here now. I would never leave you. Don't you know that?"

"It hurts so bad," the girl said, pain darkening her eyes.

"I'm going to make it better," the woman reassured. "I'm going to fix it."

***

The woman worked with cool efficiency, removing the girl from the house without hesitation or delay. The house belonged to a Russian; he would object to returning home to find a wounded young girl bleeding to death on his expensive carpet.

The woman maneuvered the girl onto the boat and guided it out of the channel and into open water.

The young girl shivered under a blanket, a sticky wetness spreading over one side of her body. Her face had taken on a sickly, sallow color, her hair matted with sweat and salt air. She labored for every breath.

"I need a doctor, Meg," the girl cried, "why aren't we going to the doctor?"

***

Out in open water, the woman cut the engine and came to the shivering girl.

"I tried," the girl gasped. "I tried."

"Shhh," the woman whispered, stroking the girl's face with a loving touch, wiping away the perspiration. "I know."

"I hurt, Meg," the girl whimpered. "I hurt."

The woman took the girl in her arms. "I'm going to make it better," she said, rocking the girl like a baby. "Don't I always make it good for you?"

The girl tried to smile as she struggled for breath. "I love you," she said, her voice a hoarse whisper.

Smiling down on the girl, the woman reached into her jacket pocket and extracted a gun with a silencer attached. She pulled the trigger and the girl went still, her eyes open, her mouth ajar.

The woman leaned over, placing a soft kiss on the girl's lips. "I love you, too," she whispered.

She laid the body down and got to her feet. This one had lasted a bit longer than the others. She had been twenty-two. Old enough to know better, as far as she was concerned. She was glad she didn't have to listen to the crying anymore. The woman maneuvered the boat further out.

She should have enjoyed a peaceful evening, but the Katerina Mills business now irritated her. It had become a time suck. First there was the mysterious boyfriend hanging around, the other contractor, and the other hired gun yammering at Katerina in the mall. She didn't like complications—or marks that seemed to find a way to stay alive. That brought bad karma to a job. She remembered the advice of her mentor many years ago: if you have to force something to get it done, it isn't right.

She glanced over at the body in the boat and grimaced in annoyance. She would have kept this one for a while longer. The kid had been eager to learn and eager to please, especially at night. She would have thrown the girl away as she had the others, of course, but she hadn't planned on it being so soon. She brooded about it some more but then gave it up. "Meg" would have to pick up a new "apprentice." Meg. She hated the name; she didn't know why she chose it. She would have to come up with something better next time.

She returned to concentrating on her course. There had been shark sightings in the waters off Newport Beach and Corona del Mar. That would work. *Throw some blood in the water and they all come running.* The sharks would take care of everything.

Chapter 114

Daniel Clay crept through the darkened exhibit rooms, his stomach in knots as he turned a corner. The penlight revealed the Monet, *Nympheas,* in its place.

Two other penlights cut jagged swaths of light through the room. Nicholas and Burnett stopped when they saw him; they hung back.

Clay approached the painting to stand before it. He held up the light, illuminating the water lilies.

Leaning over, he examined each side of the painting in turn, running the light along the length the frame. He paused.

Focusing the light on one area, he crept closer, squinting into the space between the canvas and the wall. Reaching out, he extracted a slip of folded paper.

Training the light on the paper, he slid it open and read the typed message.

I DON'T LIKE MUSEUM JOBS. W.

Nicholas sidled up and peered over Daniel Clay's shoulder. He gave a low, bitter chuckle, and walked away.

Chapter 115

Winter slipped onto the darkened property. The family had left, as expected, to visit with relatives in Europe.

He crept along the side of the house to the back entrance used for deliveries. Entering the security code, he slipped inside. He kept his wrapped hand cradled against his chest. Pain medication would have to wait, there was no time for it now.

Winter made his way along the darkened hallway to the study. Entering the room, he crept over to the wall where a glass enclosed display sat. He cursed under his breath.

Empty.

He stared at the barren case where an icon of the Madonna and Child, painted on wood, should have been. Three years ago, the owner of the house had commissioned the theft to spirit it out of Russia to the West. Now, someone else had gotten to it first.

Alexander Winter lowered his head.

For the first time, he would fail to make delivery.

Chapter 116

Katerina breezed into the hotel and stopped at the front desk for directions to the business center.

She extracted the flimsy, delicate papers from her purse. The first was an original sheet from a 1934 Lord and Taylor catalogue. Their New York store had hosted an Armand Hammer exhibition of the Royal Family's treasures. The description read "miniature silver armour holding wheelbarrow with Easter Egg, made by Fabergé, court jeweler." The missing Cherub with Chariot Egg.

The handwriting on the second, antiquated paper was little more than a scrawl. With difficulty, she made out "egg," the same description, and the names on the receipt. Tavis and Florence Middleton, buyers; Dr. Armand Hammer, seller.

Katerina made a set of photocopies, realizing how much of Philip's instructions she had absorbed. Photocopies were old school. *The original ways are always the best.*

Returning to the front desk, Katerina handed over a sealed, stamped envelope for the outbound mail. Thanking the courteous staff, she left the hotel.

As she crossed the parking lot, she spied Keyes in his car, keeping watch. She wondered about Winter, tormenting herself with anxieties and imaginings. Forcing herself to focus, she called Zilinsky. She gave him an address and instructions. "Be there in an hour," she said and hung up.

Chapter 117

Zilinsky found Katerina sitting at a table in the corner of the bar. He sat down across from her. He found himself feeling a little sorry for her; not his style at all. After all, he'd been through this several times. But this one had personality, something the others had lacked. Maybe he had even been holding out hope while ducking MJM, giving her extra time. It was a shame. Whatever she thought she had . . . too bad. It was all a waste of time, just to turn her down and get rid of her. But he had his own problems; who thought he'd wind up doing this shit for a living, just to get by? He'd had plans for something big, something important, not becoming a crappy shill, like a boxer you pay to go down in the fourth. What a goddamn cliché. He remembered to call up his accent.

"All right, Ekaterina, what have you brought me to secure my birthright."

"Hands behind your back," Kat ordered.

He laughed. Seeing her stony expression, his smile slipped away. His attention traveled from her to the man crossing the room to sit at the table behind him. He looked like a businessman . . . an unpleasant businessman. Zilinsky complied.

Katerina took out the fragile sheets of paper from her purse and placed them in the center of the table.

Zilinsky stared at them. How long had he been playing this game? He looked up at Katerina. Was it even possible this girl had done what no one else could?

He moved to reach for them, but her hand shot out and snatched them up out of his reach.

"No," he protested, and in his excitement, the accent wavered. He put his arms behind him again. "Please," he said.

Katerina returned the papers to their place.

Zilinsky scanned the documents, the catalogue page, the bill of sale. *My God. The real thing.* He stared at the girl in wonder. *She did it. How?*

"Mr. Zilinsky," Kat said, "I present your birthright. This is what you wanted, yes?"

No more grifting and scamming, he thought. *This is my ticket to the big time.* He'd have to get out of California and go underground. Mikhailovich hadn't found the egg yet. If he could get to the prize first, he could disappear for good. No one would find him.

"Mr. Zilinsky?"

"Yes," Zilinsky said. "Yes."

"Fine," Kat said, pulling out her cell phone. "I'm going to place a call to my office. You will report that I completed the assignment. I will wait to receive confirmation that the wire transfer is complete. And then you may take your birthright and leave."

Zilinsky went to open his mouth but halted.

"Is there a problem?" Katerina asked.

Zilinsky, perspiring now, shook his head.

***

Katerina punched the numbers into the new burner phone and waited until she heard Jasmine's familiar voice say, "MJM."

Katerina handed the phone to Zilinsky.

She watched him lick his lips as fresh beads of sweat broke out on his forehead.

"This is Zilinsky," he said in a halting voice, his eyes glued to Katerina as he spoke. "The job is done."

Kat watched Zilinsky with the phone at his ear, listening, a slight wince his only tell. She leaned over and snatched the phone away. "Hello, Jasmine, this is Katerina." A wave of silence followed. *That's right, bitch. Go tell MJM I'm not dead.* "On second thought, don't worry about paying me in cash. I have an account number for a wire transfer. You can do that right now."

"We're going to need incontrovertible proof that you have established the client as a Romanov," Jasmine said.

Katerina's face burned as anger boiled up within her. "Proof to the agency was not stipulated in the assignment."

"It's stipulated now. That's the joy of being off probation," Jasmine said. "There are no rules. Send proof that he's a Romanov."

"Is that what you demanded of Sara?"

Jasmine went silent.

Play your part. Go in for the kill.

"Whatever happened to Sara? Oh, right. I remember now."

"Are you sure you know what you think you know?" Jasmine asked.

"Don't pay me. Find out," Katerina said.

A pregnant silence hung between them.

"Please hold," Jasmine said.

Katerina held her breath, watching Zilinsky's eyes transfixed on the papers beneath her hand.

Jasmine came back on the line. "Confirmation accepted."

"I'm sending the account information," Kat said. "Make the transfer now."

The phone went dead.

Katerina and Zilinsky sat at the table; the silence broken only by the buzz of her phone. Katerina tapped and swiped. She stared at the screen, at the confirmation of one hundred thousand dollars now in her account.

It's over. MJM just paid for my escape.

Zilinsky watched her nod at the man seated behind him.

With slow, deliberate precision, Katerina shifted the papers toward Zilinsky. She leaned in and said, "*Dasvidaniya*," and took her hand away.

***

Zilinsky snatched the papers, holding them with shaking hands. He lifted his head, tears in his eyes, but only saw Katerina's back as she walked out, the man following behind.

He had to get on the road. She had outsmarted them. MJM would never believe he wasn't in on it.

He had to run.

Chapter 118

Katerina checked into a hotel near LAX and tried to crash without success. Giving it up as a lost cause, she sat on the couch to watch television. Only when her eyes opened did she realize she had dozed off. She found Alexander Winter sitting in a chair next to the couch.

Kat bounded up, stumbling into his waiting arms. Curling into his embrace, they shared a deep, sweet kiss. She traced a finger over the bandage on his hand.

He kissed her forehead. "My flight leaves in two hours."

"You got it," she said, dizzy with relief. "What are you going to do, put it in the overhead luggage bin?"

He answered with a soft smile.

She narrowed her eyes. "What?"

"Katie, who said I was after a Monet?" he asked.

She pushed off his chest to sit up. "We went to the museum."

"Yes."

Katerina scrambled to her feet. "We stood in front of the painting."

"We did."

Winter rose out of the chair.

Katerina shook her head and crossed her arms, a half-hearted fume at the misdirection. "What were you here for?"

He kissed her forehead. "The job is over. Everything is under control. What happened with Zilinsky?"

She gave him the recap, watching his eyebrows quirk as she explained MJM transferred the money.

"Do you know what happened to this consultant?" he asked.

"Only that she died and MJM was responsible. I took a chance."

"A-plus," he said, appearing more than a little surprised at her maneuver.

"Almost as good as you," Kat said.

He took her into his arms, crushing her to him. "And what now?" he whispered.

Katerina glanced away.

"I thought we were friends," he said.

"We are . . . always."

"And don't friends keep promises?" he said.

She nodded.

"You promised me you would tell me when you were leaving and where you were going."

"I promised you I would let you say a proper goodbye," she corrected, "and I promised I would protect you. Look what I've already caused. It's better if you don't know where I'm going. It's dangerous for you to be around me."

"No one's caught me yet," Winter said.

She gazed up at him, his six-foot frame overshadowing her. Katerina couldn't say the words spinning in her head, how she wanted to keep him, possess him, belong to him.

"Do you have housing?"

"Not yet," she said.

"Do you have ID's and a passport for your mother?"

"No."

"Have you decided where you'll go?"

"No," she said, breaking away from him. "I don't want to play twenty questions."

"The game has already started," Winter said, his voice light. "Would you cheat me?"

"Never," Kat said.

"Has your hacker erased you?"

"No."

"Why not?' he asked.

"She can't finish. I haven't dropped out of school yet. I haven't cancelled my cell phone, my credit cards . . . I've been a little busy."

Winter pulled her into his arms, rubbing her back, a hypnotic, soothing motion. "Katerina, did you go to Sunday School?"

She shot him a narrow-eyed look. "Yes. What is today's lesson, Professor?"

"Do you remember the story of Esther?"

Kat nodded. "Pretty woman becomes concubine, catches a lucky break because the King is into her, in more ways than one."

"Let's not be so literal," Winter said. "Let's say she's very special to him."

"Are you asking me to be your girlfriend?" she asked.

"No," he said softly. "I had something else in mind. What does he tell her, Katie?"

She caressed his face, running one finger along the edge of his bottom lip. Before she finished, he caught the tip of her finger in a kiss.

"He said, 'And what is your request? Whatever you want, even to half the kingdom, will be given to you.'" Winter's eyes flashed soft and warm. "Half of all I have, Katie. It's yours."

"And what about you?" Kat asked.

He hesitated, then reached into his pocket and drew out a ring of delicately sculpted silver, its single diamond winking in the light. She gave an audible gasp of surprise. When she looked up, she found his eyes a darkened, fiery onyx.

"Will you take me?" he whispered. "All of me?"

"Yes," she whispered, "the answer for you is always yes."

His mouth closed over hers as the circle of his arms tightened around her. When they parted, a laugh escaped her lips. Her heart beat a frenetic rhythm as he slipped the ring on her finger. A perfect fit. She held out her hand to admire it. Simple and elegant, she thought, signature Winter.

"My right jacket pocket," Winter said.

Katerina extracted an envelope. Inside, she found a ticket to Paris, a driver's license, and a passport. She read the name, a shiver of excitement running up her spine.

"I should come with you now," she said, snaking her arms around him and pulling him close. "Then we can go on to Paris together."

"The client would see you and it's best you remain anonymous. I'll meet you in two days."

She nodded. "Where am I going in Paris?"

He kissed her forehead. "Somewhere I think you'll like. Relax, enjoy yourself. When I get there, we finish all the arrangements for your mother. Check in with your hacker and do what you need to do. I'll show you everything I'm doing. Everything I know, you'll know."

"And then I'll be better than you," she teased.

He chuckled, giving her a kiss. "You know," he said, a twinkle in his eye, "it's different when I say it."

She nodded, making a note to remember that professors have egos.

"What happened to the extremely dangerous Daniel Clay?"

"He's still around," Winter said. "One day, he might even come in handy again."

Katerina lay her head on his chest, inhaling his warm, clean scent. She raised her head and leaned up, giving him a deep, slow kiss. "I know you have to go," she murmured, "but I wanted one more."

"Two days," he said. "Only two days."

They forced themselves to break away. Giving her one last kiss on the forehead, Winter moved to the door.

"Wait," she called.

Kat went for her purse and pulled something out. She came to him, Rachel's sacred stone necklace dangling from her hand. "It helps to maintain connection, and provides protection," she said, slipping it around his neck.

He looked at it, nodding in recognition. "You can't be too careful."

Alexander Winter gave her a kiss. Then he was gone.

Chapter 119

The guests were removed from the house and taken back to the yacht. A cleaning crew, private, discreet, was called in to clean up the mess of blood and fluid. They fell silent when the owner of the house entered.

Viktor Mikhailovich paused at the open elevator to survey the sprawling blood stains. He took the stairs, stopping on the landing. His eyes moved over the area, resting on the ruined safe, the door hanging open, marred by a drilled hole. The bottom drawer lay open . . . empty.

His wife? Perhaps. One of the guests? Maybe. A rival? Possible. Mikhailovich gave instructions to make inquiries at once and find the one responsible. His staff nodded and hurried off to obey.

Standing over the safe, a thought drifted through his mind; a beautiful young woman who had appeared out of nowhere, and just as suddenly, disappeared, vanishing into thin air.

Chapter 120

Katerina checked in at LAX without incident, passing through the security screening with ease. She slipped her shoes back on, planning to call her mother and Sergei after she settled in at the gate. Passing a kiosk, she performed her usual ritual, buying a newspaper, a drink, and snacks.

At the gate, Kat found a chair at the end of an unoccupied row and sat down. Ripping open a bag of chocolate, she popped a few in her mouth, letting them melt on her tongue. She let out a deep exhale; for the first time, the dense, dull pressure that had sat on her chest like a crushing weight had vanished. *Free. Of everything.*

Sitting back, she opened the newspaper, giving the headlines a cursory glance, skimming the news, politics, and gossip.

Flipping a page, she found herself staring at a picture of Felicia Reynolds wearing an evening gown and a pair of quartz, shell-shaped diamond crusted earrings. Katerina sat up, hovering over the newspaper, racing through the words.

A private investigator, hired by the family, had discovered the earrings were not among her belongings.

The NYPD detectives assigned to the case, Walter Lashiver and Ryan Kellan, were seeking information leading to the whereabouts of the earrings in connection with the socialite's brutal murder.

Katerina stared at the photo, her heart thudding against her ribs, the chocolate turning to ashes in her mouth.

The desperate need to put distance between herself and this new situation rushed back with a vengeance. What to do?

Why do anything?

She reasoned with herself in an attempt to tamp down the panic taking off like a runaway train. *Why would the police get on to me?* With Ryan Kellan out of the picture, nothing would lead them to her door.

But he's not out of the picture. He keeps calling.

I disappear.

Gal Friday is closed.
He'll look for me.
He won't give up.
He'll search everywhere.
He'll find them.
Call Winter. Tell him. He'll know what to do.

Katerina wrestled in the quicksand of her panic, sinking in a suspended state of indecision. Whether she called Winter or not, the end result would be the same. The earrings had to be retrieved and destroyed.

I can't involve him.

Haven't I done enough to him? The least I can do is come to him with a clean slate.

I will always protect you. Isn't that what I told him?

Don't call him. The simplest thing to do is get the earrings, get rid of them, and when I meet Winter it's done and over with.

I'm a grown woman.

I took care of Zilinsky.

I took care of MJM.

I can take care of this myself.

Still, Katerina didn't move to get up out of her seat.

With each beat of her pounding heart, her fear grew to a fever spike. Katerina stood up, gathered her belongings, and headed for the desk at the gate.

"Excuse me," Katerina said to the ticket agent as she handed over her passport and boarding pass, "I've had a business emergency and I need to change my flight to go back to New York."

The agent examined the documents. "Of course, Mrs. Winter," the agent said.

Chapter 121

The frigid chill of the New York winter greeted Katerina as she deplaned. At the baggage claim area, she waited eternal moments to retrieve her suitcase from the carousel. She turned and spotted Luther standing with a sign.

Eyes darting left and right, Katerina closed the gap between them, pulling the suitcase behind her. She greeted him with a nod and nothing more.

Luther tucked the sign into his pocket and took hold of the suitcase. He gave her a sideways glance as he quickened his pace to keep up.

"Everything all right with you, Miss Katerina?"

"Fine," she said.

"You don't have any more projects, do you?"

"One more, Luther. Last one."

***

Luther stowed the suitcase in the trunk of the limo and settled behind the wheel, eyeing his passenger in the rearview mirror.

"Where to, Miss Katerina?" he asked.

"You tell me," she said. "I was supposed to come back here a week ago. He had made arrangements and you were going to pick me up. Take me there."

As Luther put the car in gear, Katerina took out her burner phone. "Papi," she said, when the phone clicked on. "I'm local. I need a car. What's the price?"

"No te preocupes, mami. Dime la dirección. Tell me where and when you want to pick up the car."

Katerina rattled off an address in Soho and a time. "Papi, I need to make something disappear."

"You want to break it up?"

"Break it up, melt it down, I don't care."

"Bueno. When you're done with the car, you call me. I got you, mami. I got you."

Katerina hung up and sat back. She stared out the window at the gray landscape, wishing the day away. Every passing minute would feel like an hour. The cover of darkness couldn't come fast enough.

She turned off Winter's tracking phone. When she glanced at the rearview mirror, she found Luther studying her. "Don't even think about calling him, Luther."

"The man would want to know, Miss Katerina. If you're not okay, it won't be right with him. Never. You understand?"

"Do not call him, Luther. It won't make a difference. By the time he gets here, it'll be over."

Chapter 122

Winter sat poolside, his right hand tucked away in his pocket. In the midst of the warm temperature he craved, the perspiration gathering from the heat of the sun beating down on the back of his neck made him shift in discomfort.

Durant sat across from him, staring at the class of novice scuba divers practicing in the deep end of the pool. He picked up his drink, something orange with an umbrella, and took a sip.

"I was clear with the instructions," he said.

"I was clear there would be no guarantees," Winter said.

Durant's eyebrows quirked. "My client will be very disappointed."

"Cost of doing business," Winter said.

Durant focused like a laser on Winter's pocket, on the hand hidden from view. "Perhaps, not the only cost." He made a soft, *tsk-tsk* sound and sighed. "To be so misguided in one's choice of professional. *Eh voila*. This is very sad. What do I tell my employer?"

Winter didn't bother to protest. The theatrics were part of the plan, to test for intimidation, to elicit a response.

"Tell him it's the cost of doing business. But not his cost. The two and half million has been wired back."

"*Et voila*? No, it is not. Someone else has the item. Cost is not only money, *monsieur*. It is time and missed opportunity and these things cannot be repaid. Very disappointing."

Durant returned to watching the amateur scuba divers, ending the conversation. Winter got up and left the table. As he made his way out through the lobby of the hotel, his eyes scoured the area for a tail. He would have to dump his ID's before he got on the plane. The name Steven Bartholomew could never be used again. The knot in the pit of his stomach twisted at the thought of this client following him.

He checked his cell phone. Katerina's tracking phone had gone off. He tapped and swiped at a notification of the flight change. He checked his voicemail and made a call. When the line connected, he asked, "Where the hell is she?"

Chapter 123

A deserted street. In the sky, the man in the moon glowered down on everyone, his mouth set in a scowl. He does not approve, Katerina thought.

After picking up the car, she had zigzagged around the city to be sure Moose had not been followed. A run-in with Massone was a disaster she didn't need.

She had parked the car down the block from her apartment and watched. Katerina hunched forward, her hands gripping the steering wheel, as if it were a lifeline, her only means of survival.

I go in, get the earrings, get out, get rid of them.
Then we can get away, clean.

She hesitated, scanning again for any sign of an unmarked police car; Ryan's car.

Clear.

Katerina pulled up the collar on her coat and slid out of the car, stepping lightly across the street. Pushing the ghost of Will Temple back into the recesses of her mind, she hustled up the front steps of her building. *Leave them in the past or they will take you with them.* She thought only of the next moment in front of her. Entering the building, she went to her apartment door, turned the key in the lock, and slipped inside.

In the dark, Katerina made a beeline into her tiny bedroom and went to the dresser. Pulling out the top drawer, she reached her hand underneath and felt around until she stopped. With a firm grasp she pulled, and brought out the earrings, the tape still attached. Clasping them in the palm of her hand, she turned and fled the room.

Heading for the front door, the lights flicked on.

With a gasp, Katerina stopped short, the earrings dropping from her hands with a small plunk as they hit the floor.

She stared into the face of a killer.

Felicia Reynolds' killer.

"Pick them up," she heard from behind her.

She knew the voice. Her eyes fixed on the killer, she crouched down, scooping up the earrings with shaking hands.

Katerina stood rooted to the spot. She heard rustling sounds, footsteps as he approached, coming around to stand before her, lips drawn back in a wide, maniacal smile.

"Miss Katerina," John Reynolds said.

Chapter 124

Waiting at the baggage claim, Luther almost missed him. The strong, strapping man he expected looked different. He appeared weak, his pallor gray, the strain wearing on him, visible now. Luther spotted the bandage on the right hand. Now it made sense; he'd been in pain.

Winter allowed Luther to take his bag.

Winter nodded. "Did she say anything?"

"She made a call to the Moose. Said she needed a car and then she had to get rid of something. She told me not to call you because by the time you got here, whatever it was, would be over."

"Take me to the apartment," Winter said, his good hand tapping against his side in a rhythmic motion, three times, then a pause, then again.

Chapter 125

John Reynolds opened Katerina's fingers one by one to reveal the earrings.

"Mmm," he said, maneuvering her hand to view them from different angles. "'She seems to enjoy jewelry items that are specialty designs.' If my memory serves correctly, that is what you said, isn't it?" He sighed. "I must confess my surprise at her giving them up to you so easily, vain, selfish creature that she was." He glanced up, staring into Katerina's terror-filled eyes. "You must have had quite an effect on her when you spoke in the department store that day, Saks I believe it was."

Reynolds pulled out his phone. Kat's head tilted in horrified fascination as she watched video of herself talking with Felicia Reynolds. Then the video spliced and changed. Now, she was chatting with Will Temple outside her apartment.

"A young college student, pre-law, has an affair with a feckless actor, only to discover he's cheating on her with a wealthy, married woman. She cannot accept this, this young, pretty girl. She becomes unstable."

Katerina's eyes flickered away from the screen to the killer standing just a few feet away. His vacant, dead eyes stared through her.

"She begins trailing the married woman. The woman does everything she can to hide from this obsessed, unstable girl. She has an idea, she goes to a theater where she offers financial support. She borrows costumes to disguise herself. But this young girl, she is relentless. Even the lover, the actor, comes to the young girl's apartment late one night, begging her to stop. But this college student doesn't listen. When she follows the married woman to a department store, the woman doesn't realize how dangerous the girl is. She thinks she will get rid of the girl with a trifling payoff, and gives the pretty, young thing her earrings. The wealthy wife doesn't know this young girl will keep them as a trophy after killing her, believing she will now have the lover all to herself."

Reynolds gave a chuckle and a satisfied shake of his head. "This story gets better every time I practice it. I'm sure the police will find it interesting," he held up his phone, "as well as the video evidence that will come to light. You will be brought in for questioning, accused, and charged. You could decide to be honest with them, tell them everything, thinking you will save yourself. Of course, MJM will not be happy you placed them in jeopardy, exposed their secrets."

Katerina shook in trepidation.

"What will your policeman boyfriend say about all this? Oh, I forgot, he's not the boyfriend now, is he? There's someone else."

Oh God. Not Winter.

Reynolds held up the phone and Katerina stared at the photos of herself, taken near the university; Winter putting his arms around her, comforting her, guiding her into his car.

Reynolds nodded his head. "My wife had an appetite for more than one man as well. She received the just desserts she craved." He swiped through his phone and pulled up another video.

He held out the phone.

Katerina felt a jolt of shock course through her as she watched a bloodied Felicia Reynolds, her mouth open in silent screams, as the killer performed his gruesome violations. Katerina let out a cry and turned her head.

"Look or he will make you look."

The killer stepped forward, hovering over her. Shrinking away, Katerina stared at the suffering of Felicia Reynolds, a wave of nausea rising up in her throat.

"She loved her body. She stared at it in the mirror, so proud of those feminine curves. He carried out my instructions exactly. He ruined those curves, marked them, cut them, burned them. And that was only what could be seen. My wife was so fond of *penetration*," Reynolds sighed. "Be careful what you wish for."

Tears slid down Katerina's cheeks.

Reynolds leaned in, holding the phone inches from her eyes. "I made sure she was *penetrated,*" he whispered.

Reynolds moved to a chair and sat down. Katerina stared straight ahead, feeling the heat of the killer's body, his sharp scent of sweat stinging her nostrils.

She heard Reynolds soft, dull monotone voice. "I was so disappointed with our last discussion," he said. "To think we would not be together. We are connected Katerina, you and I. I told you, we have work to do."

The room weaved, the ground beneath her feet giving way. Somewhere through the terror, the realization set in. *Wrong. I had gotten it all wrong.*

"We are joined together, married in blood, if you will."

That first phone call from Joe Lessing. Katerina, I need some help. Be a good girl and come over here and I'll make it worth your while.

If I had never picked up the phone.

"Look at him, Katerina," Reynolds ordered.

Katerina stared into the dead eyes of the killer.

"See how he stands, obedient, waiting for his next instruction. So, you must make your choice."

Even though she had heard every word, Katerina couldn't process the information. "What choice?"

"Come, come, Miss Katerina. All decisions have consequences. It must be this way. Someone must pay for your refusal to follow instructions," Reynolds said with a smile.

Now, who is your choice, the lover, or your dear mother?"

One move to make.

"I'll do whatever you want," Katerina blurted, unable to tear her eyes from the monster. The face, a soulless mask, made it seem as if the body was a shell; the inhabitant in the shell was no longer human. Inside her head, hysteria grew, a seeping madness enveloping her whole being.

"Yes, yes, all creatures, when cornered, give their useless platitudes of love and loyalty. All lies." Reynolds rose out of the chair and approached her. "Choose, or I choose for you. But one will suffer and pay. That is a certainty. Infractions have consequences, and punishments."

"You have me—"

"You're not listening." Reynolds said, grasping her wrist with surprising strength. His grip tightened.

Katerina, sharp, shooting pain bringing tears to her eyes, felt her legs buckle.

"Please—" she began, sinking to her knees.

"Beg all you want. Beg for death, but it will not come. It will never come. He will never touch you. Those are my instructions. You will live to bear witness to the suffering of those you love. How much they suffer depends on you. But remember this: you will live knowing all that befalls them is because of you, your decisions, your actions. That is your punishment. Now choose, or I choose for you."

"You have what you want," Katerina cried, hands extended, pleading.

"Very well," Reynolds said, looking at the monster. "Take care of—"

"Don't hurt my mother!" Katerina begged. "Please, don't hurt her."

Reynolds bent his head close to hers. "That is not good enough. Say it. Say 'I choose my lover. Take him.' Go on. Say it."

Katerina, tears streaming down her cheeks, whispered the words.

"Very good. Now, call him. I've been keeping an eye on your driver. He made a second pick up."

Oh God. Luther.

Reynolds released her wrist from his grasp; Katerina struggled to her feet as her cell phone buzzed in her purse.

Reynolds' eyes lit up with a childish delight. "I bet I know who that is. Even better. Tell him you're coming home. I want him to be nice and relaxed. And remember Katerina, be sincere."

Katerina swallowed her tears and the burning, sour taste in her throat. With trembling hands, she took out her phone. Reynolds stood glued to her side, listening.

"How was your day, dear?" she said before Winter could speak.

She heard a beat of silence.

"Swell," he said, keeping his voice light. "Where are you?" he asked.

"Out, getting something special for you."

Reynolds' iron grip dug into her arm, bringing a fresh burst of pain.

"Mmm," he said. "You're going to cook for me, aren't you? What's for dinner, chicken or fish?"

"Filet of sole," Kat said, "your favorite."

"Sounds perfect. I'm waiting for you. Hurry."

Katerina clicked off the call.

Reynolds gave the killer a nod and he left the apartment.

"Tape the earrings back under the drawer," Reynolds ordered.

Dazed, Katerina tottered into the bedroom. Stumbling against the edge of the bed, she fell.

"Hurry, Katerina," she heard Reynolds say.

Kat forced herself to rise and going to the dresser, pressed the earrings back up under the drawer, struggling to get the tape to stick. It finally held and she pushed the drawer back in its place.

She returned to the living room.

"If you attempt to remove them again, I will know, and he will bear the consequences for your actions." Reynolds studied her for a moment and then waived his hand. "Go into the bathroom if you must. Leave the door open."

Katerina rushed into the bathroom. Reynolds sat there, legs crossed, tapping his gloves on his knees, listening to the sounds of Katerina's retching.

***

When the cell phone buzzed, Katerina jumped in fright. Reynolds clicked to take the call and listened. "Go ahead," he said and hung up.

"Your lover wasn't at the apartment. I did figure as much. As you are predictable with your little code words and clues, so am I. So is *he*. I understand him. I know what he needs. He finds the exercise more satisfying when there's a hunt. And so, he has begun his pursuit. He will find your lover, and you will be the witness," Reynolds said, holding up the phone. "Remember Katerina, how you perform your assignments will determine how much he suffers." Reynolds stood up and came to her. "At the right moment, he will know you chose him."

The words were muted in Katerina's ears, drowned by the white noise blaring in her head.

"Look at me, Katerina."

Katerina raised her head.

"You will remain at the ready. I will call you at the hour I choose with your first instruction and you will carry it out immediately. Do you understand?"

Katerina nodded.

"Perhaps, if you are a good girl, your mother will be fine. Who knows? We'll see."

Katerina closed her eyes at his words.

Reynolds glanced around. "So nice to have you back at home where you belong. I almost forgot." Reynolds removed a small book from his pocket. "The new semester starts soon. I took the liberty of reviewing your schedule and getting you a little gift."

He held out the book for her to take. *Macbeth.* Katerina stared at it.

"No?" he said in artless innocence, and with a cock of his head, he left it on the table on his way out.

***

On her knees, Katerina hunched over the cell phone cradled in her hand. She dialed the number, listening to the repeated ringing, over and over, her body rocking back and forth, her cries desperate and deep.

Chapter 126

"Katerina, my God, calm down. I can't understand you."

Katerina babbled, the words swallowed by halting bursts of breath. "Mom, you have to leave. Right now. You have to pack up and go. I'm so sorry. You have to go now!"

"Katie, what's happened?"

It's not about what you give or what you get. It's about what you'll do. What you'll give up. What you'll sacrifice. What did you sacrifice for me?

"Tell Ethel to keep the shotgun ready, for protection, until you leave. You have to do that? Okay? You have to."

She heard her mother speaking away from the phone. After a rustling, she heard, "Katya, what has happened?"

"Take my mom and take her away. Now. Tonight. The man watching her, Carter. He can't protect her alone. He's not enough. Not against this. Not against him."

"Katya," Sergei broke in, more insistent now. "Tell me."

"I got caught by the bear, Uncle," Katerina cried. "I got caught by the bear and I can't get away."

Through her cries, Katerina heard Sergei make soft sounds of comfort, as if she were a child.

"Katya, listen to me. Listen very carefully. We will help you—we will come to you—"

"No! Uncle, stay away from here, both of you. It's too dangerous. Promise me you'll go away, promise me."

He soothed her until she quieted. "Is there nothing I can do for you?"

"No, *dyadya*."

She heard him give an exhale of frustration.

"Katya, listen to me. I will never let anyone hurt your mother again. Believe me in this. We will not leave you, Katya. You must be very brave. You must watch, watch for that moment. You will trick this bear, and then you escape. And we will wait, wait for you to return home."

Katerina cried.

Chapter 127

Days later, Thomas Gallagher still struggled to understand how the situation had gone awry. He watched the video again, then returned to the live feed.

Strange it should turn out like this, he thought. No doubt, Reynolds' lunatic would find the "Professor" and kill him. One obstacle removed but another one to take its place, he thought as he turned his attention to Mr. Smith.

Smith, his features tired and drawn from his recent wound, sat in a guest chair, his arm in a sling. The bullet had just missed a major artery.

Pity, Gallagher thought.

"You realize you are now an accessory after the fact to murder," Smith was saying, "not that anyone will ever discover you know about this, of course."

"Of course," Gallagher said. "You're a keeper of secrets."

"Absolutely," Smith said. "I have an extra copy of these videos, tucked away safe and sound. Just in case something happens to me. For your protection, of course."

"Always thinking of the client," Gallagher said with a tight smile.

"I'm not a two-bit contractor standing in a snowstorm."

"Of course not," Gallagher said, glancing down again at Katerina Mills, weakened, helpless—broken. At least she was isolated, so he could work on her. He looked up. "Anything else?" he asked.

"You have good taste," Smith said, nodding toward the video feed. "She impressed me. She threw herself over the professor to save his life, no hesitation."

Gallagher gave a tight smile at Smith's twist of the knife and glanced away for a moment. "Anything else?" he repeated.

"Yeah. Keep that bitch, Lisa, out of my way."

Gallagher nodded.

Chapter 128

Katerina sat on an exam table in a small room outfitted as a makeshift doctor's office, babbling between gulps of air. Doc, his six-foot frame struggling under his excess weight, didn't answer her as he went about his work taking her temperature, checking her pulse, and listening to her heart.

Gertie entered, a cup of water in her hand.

"I wanted to come right away, but I was afraid. I had to wait, I had to make sure I was clear and no one was following me. When did he come? When did you see him? He did come here, didn't he?"

Doc shook his head. "No doll," he said with a raspy, labored breath, "I haven't heard from him."

"He had to come. He's hurt, he hurt his hand, and it was all my fault, I did it, I did it . . ."

Doc took a pill bottle from his pocket. Popping the cap off, he extracted a pill and held it out to her. "Miss Kitty, take this. You hear me? Take this now and you'll stay here until you calm down. You need to calm down."

With a shaking hand, Katerina slipped the burner phone from her pocket and held it out to him. "You see, I keep calling him, but he doesn't answer. He doesn't pick up. Doc, he's hurt and he's out there all alone. I made one mistake, one mistake . . . and one was all it took." She began to weep.

Doc held up the pill. "Take this," he ordered. "Now."

Doc gave Gertie a nod and the older woman came to Kat's side. Taking the phone, she slipped it back in Kat's pocket.

"Come, darling," Gertie coaxed, "deep breaths. In and out. You have to think with a clear head. You have to do it for him."

Katerina placed the pill on her tongue and gulped a swallow of water. Gertie rubbed Kat's back and watched her breathing slow, even as the tears kept sliding down her cheeks.

Doc and Gertie helped Kat off the table and shepherded her to the couch, covering her with her coat. As Katerina closed her eyes, Gertie's words floated in her head. *Things to do . . . for him . . .*

***

It was after ten o'clock when Katerina exited the subway. A light snow had begun to fall. Making her way home, she meandered through a park, the medication's effects making everything appear off balance. Her problems floated through her mind; she could see them but couldn't react or respond.

Tripping, she lurched forward. Throwing out her arms to break her fall, Kat landed on hands and knees. Her purse landed a few feet away, her belongings tumbled out.

Dazed, she registered the pain, the skin burning from the scrapes on her palms, blood oozing from the cuts.

Crawling forward, she began scooping her things into her bag.

Sensing a presence, she looked up and saw it. The fox had a rusty coat that lightened under its neck and chest, turning to snow white; its long, bushy tail had a white tip. It considered her with soft, soulful eyes, as if they were the only two in the world, alone together.

The fox began to trot away, then stopped and turned its head back, waiting.

Katerina rose to her feet, slow and careful, and pulled her purse strap onto her shoulder. The fox padded forward a few steps, then paused, waiting until she kept astride.

They walked together in the darkness, side by side.

Chapter 129

Thomas Gallagher came out of the bathroom, his naked, toned body toweled off, feeling freshened. His breathing had returned to normal, his heart rate settled back down.

He dressed with slow, measured movements. While he buttoned his shirt, fixing each cuff in turn, he crossed the room to the left side of the bed.

Lisa lay in the bed, her arms above her head, her wrists shackled to the bedpost, her flushed complexion stained with tears. She tucked her knees up against her belly; a line of blood trailed from between her thighs, staining the sheets.

Gallagher leaned over and stroked her cheek; he smirked as she recoiled from him.

"This wasn't part of the agreement," she said, her voice thick from crying.

He caressed her hair. "It was implied."

The door opened and Mrs. Shields entered.

Gallagher placed his lips close to Lisa's ear. "Perhaps it would have been better if I had just called her *again*," he whispered.

Lisa closed her eyes as her own taunt was repeated back to her.

Gallagher ushered Mrs. Shields out of the room. "Let her stay that way for a while," he ordered and closed the door behind him.

Chapter 130

One last move.
If there is one move to make, you're not caught.
I will always protect you.

The cell phone buzzed, jarring Katerina from the torment of her own words. She answered the phone and exhaled at the sound of the voice. The guardian angel. She gave a concise update on Winter's situation.

"You understand the risk?" she asked.

"I understand," Keyes answered.

One last move to make. Winter wouldn't be able to take on the killer alone, but if there were two . . .

"You can find him?"

"I can track him," Keyes said. "Two hundred thousand."

"Send me the account number. I'll transfer half now. Half when the job is done. Find him, help him, whatever it takes, and bring him home."

"Understood," Keyes said, and the line clicked off.

Katerina put the cell phone away. She needed more money. A lot more. She had an idea of where and how to get it.

Chapter 131

April was about to tell Katerina she looked like shit, but then she took a closer look, beyond the red-rimmed, bloodshot eyes. The girl was hurting; April let it go.

Katerina handed April an envelope. Flipping the lip open, April peeked inside. "This is more than we said. I didn't even finish."

"What else can you do with computers?"

"What, you mean fix them?"

"No, I mean hack them."

April glanced around to check for listeners. She shrugged. "I got skills. What's the sich?"

"If I give you a laptop, can you get into the email, the online banking accounts?"

April thought it over. "I'm good but I don't promise. If I get it done, you pay me. If not, then don't."

"This could get ugly. Law enforcement ugly. If you don't want any part of it, I understand. I'm hot and you have a right to know."

April nodded. At their last meeting, Katerina had been calm and in control. April wondered what could have happened to take that all away. "I'm in," she said.

Katerina nodded. "As soon as I get the laptop, I'll be in touch," she said, and got up and walked out.

April watched Katerina leave; shoulders slumped, she walked as if an invisible weight were crushing the life out of her. This girl's life is totally screwed up, she thought.

I'm right where I belong.

Chapter 132

Moose settled behind the wheel and felt around underneath the seat until he put his hand on the cell phone. He turned it on, checking for a text. He found one with a phone number and a message.

Call me.

When the call connected, he listened to the strained voice struggling to get the words out.

"Thank you for the car," Katerina said.

"No te preocupes, mami," Moose said. "Whatever you need, I come to you."

"No, you stay away now," she said. "This is no good for you."

"What about the bag, mami? That could help you."

"Not now. I'll need the laptop, but I have to work it out. There's a luggage storage place on Thirty-seventh street. They hold packages. I'll call you when it's clear to check it there so I can come get it. Give me a price for everything and I'll get the money to you."

"You pay me when we see each other. We gonna see each other, mami. I know this. *Recuerdes chica*, no matter what, the Moose got you covered. I got a lot of that goodwill for the right person."

Moose thought he heard her say 'thank you' before the line went dead. Whatever shit went down, it went bad, he thought. Real bad.

Chapter 133

Katerina found the restaurant empty save for a few patrons, sitting in pairs. She spotted Philip Castle, alone at a table all the way in the back. He had called every day, leaving messages, begging, pleading for her to meet him. With a knot twisting in her stomach, Kat knew she couldn't put it off anymore. What had he told her? There were two bullies fighting over the photo negatives. She had seen Massone. If she didn't see this new enemy face to face, she would never see it coming. Better to know all the players.

She barely glanced at the few patrons she passed, consumed by the mental merry-go-round beginning one of the thousands of daily revolutions. *I will always protect you. Where are you? Are you alive?*

Philip stood up as she approached the table, ready to hold out her chair.

"Save it," Kat said, and sat down.

"I wanted to tell you how sorry I am, really, about everything," he said as he took his seat.

Katerina caught her expression in the mirror-paneled walls. She appeared the picture of calm, while inside she trembled, waiting for the inevitable disaster.

As Philip babbled, she watched his eyes. They darted back and forth, like a metronome. *Like Richie.*

She glanced at the mirrored wall panels.

The tables had emptied.

Philip's words died away; he fell silent.

Katerina watched men, bodyguards, enforcers, soldiers, take seats at the tables on either side of them. One man, separate from the others, approached their table.

He was medium height with coal black hair and a sharp nose. She guessed his age as early forties. Casually dressed in a fitted shirt and a dark pair of pants, he wore a ring on his pinky finger. He had tattoo marks on the tops of his hands, snaking up his wrists, disappearing under his shirt sleeves.

"Ekaterina," he said. "I am Grigory Federov."

Russian.

He went to take her hand, but Katerina moved it away.

Grigory smiled and shrugged. "We need to talk about photo negatives."

"I don't have any negatives," Kat said.

He shrugged again. "So? You get them."

Kat looked over at Federov. "This is his deal," she said, nodding at Philip. "I don't have anything to do with it."

Grigory shook his head. "No, no, no. You agreed to hold negatives. Philip already tells me this."

Kat shot Philip an angry stare.

"So, you are involved. Even if you do not have negatives now, you had them. Now you must get them back. This is what you do, yes? You get things, things that people want."

Katerina didn't bother searching for an answer. That wasn't the point of the exercise. She needed to see her enemy and now she had.

"I need you to say 'Yes, Grigory, I get this thing for you. I bring to you. Not Vito Massone.'"

"I'll get them for you and only you," Katerina said.

Grigory nodded. "Very good, Ekaterina. Very good."

***

Katerina fought the biting wind as she walked away from the restaurant. She heard Philip's voice behind her, calling her name. They said New York hadn't seen a winter like this in ten years. They said it would only take thirty minutes of exposure before frostbite began. She wished it wouldn't take that long; maybe Philip would freeze while walking and talking. Maybe he would become a part of the city landscape, silenced and gone.

He caught up to her and said, "Kid, I'm sorry, what can I say?"

Katerina whirled around, striking out with her fists. Philip raised his arms as shields, struggling to stay on his feet.

"What can you say? What can you say?" she yelled. "You can say 'I'm a fucking moron who's trying to ruin my ex-girlfriend's life.'"

He tried to grab her arms, but she wrenched away from his grasp and landed a punch to his cheek; Philip lost his footing and fell.

Katerina, exhausted, stood in the middle of the sidewalk, taking great heaving breaths, sending white puffs of oxygen out into the air.

"Kat, I'm sorry. Just let me talk to you," Philip said. "Just for a minute."

***

Katerina huddled over the untouched cup of soup, her hands wrapped around the bowl, allowing the heat to seep into her chapped fingers. She stared into the yellow, gelatinous liquid, pieces of chicken and carrots breaking the surface.

Philip leaned forward over the table. "It was supposed to be simple," he whispered, his voice cracking in panic.

"It always is with you," Kat said, taking in the bent pinky finger on his hand. *Massone's handiwork.* "Quick, simple, and lucrative. Who's in the negatives?"

"Look, I started networking and helping individuals, wealthy individuals, set up corporations, for a fee. It's a relatively simple—"

"Yeah, I got it Philip. You act as the agent. You send over a fax with a copy of a passport and then every time a bell rings, a criminal gets his own shell company in Belize."

Philip sat back, taking her in as if seeing her for the first time. "Okay, yes," he said, "but then I thought, there are other services I could provide. I could become a major player."

"I've already seen this movie," she said, flashing back to Richie. *Synchronicity.* "Since everything you told me last time was a lie, why don't we just start over."

"C'mon, kid, that's harsh."

"You were helping to clear up a little real estate dispute? What real estate are we talking about? Upper East Side, Upper West Side?"

"Bigger than that," he said.

"Brooklyn? Staten Island? All five boroughs?"

"The whole state, maybe even bigger than that," Philip said, leaning over the table towards her.

"And you were *hired* by Massone or Federov to get the pictures? Why do I think no one hired you?"

"Okay, well, I thought, okay, no, no one hired me. I'm doing this corporate work and I'm thinking, what if I had something that could be licensed, you know, where certain individuals get limited use for a fee."

"You wanted to license out blackmail photographs to organized crime?"

"Hey, I would be a major player."

"And you thought they were going to go along with paying you indefinitely?" Katerina shook her head. "Who's in the pictures?"

Philip moved in close. "The Governor. Look, he's got a future in national politics—but he has a little problem. He has a soft spot for young ladies under the age of eighteen."

"Don't you mean a hard spot?" Kat said, keeping her face neutral, giving no indication he was telling her something she knew.

"Yeah, exactly. So, I got an in, where I could meet him at a fundraiser. You have no idea how easy it is to infiltrate certain circles. It's ridiculously simple."

"Boring," Kat said, down to her last tether of patience.

"Okay, so I did a few little favors for him, gained his trust, you know what I mean. And then I got on to how he makes his arrangements. He's pretty smart. I mean how many guys have gotten screwed using a service. The service gets caught, the records get subpoenaed—"

"Completely bored now," Katerina said.

Philip raised his hands in surrender. "I get the details, I put the photographer in place—"

"The *dead* photographer," Kat said, her voice low.

Philip's face drained of color at the reminder.

"And there's only one set of negatives," Kat said.

"That's it. The old ways are the best."

"So, if it's so fucking foolproof, what the hell happened?"

Philip gave a furtive look around. "I don't know. I had you hold on to them while I finished setting up my office in Boston. The day you gave me the negatives, I put 'em right in the mail. You remember? You set it up so that once it gets to the mailbox store—"

"You have instructions to keep sending it to the next mailbox store. So the negatives are on the move and tough to trace until finally it has to land somewhere. Yes, Philip, I worked for you. I remember."

"It was delivered to my office in Boston. The secretary signed for it. Then it disappeared. She doesn't know what happened."

"Who is she working for?" Katerina asked.

"It's not her. Trust me."

"Trust is not a word I use," Katerina said.

"Federov thinks I'm holding out on him."

"Imagine that."

"He feels there has been a breach of—"

"Implied contract? What about Massone? What'd you do? Blow him off? Brilliant. But not before you told him I had the negatives."

"No, no, I didn't do that, I swear. He must have been following me when I went to your apartment, or when I met you in the park."

"Cut the bullshit. I was the buffer," Kat said. "In case something went wrong, something like this, you'd pawn it off on me. I never gave you the negatives, I sold them, I made a set of prints."

"No, kid—"

"You're a miserable piece of shit, Philip, a rotten, miserable piece of shit."

"Listen, we have to get them back."

"We?" she snorted. "There is no *we*."

"There is now," he said, his voice hoarse. "They're gonna kill me."

"Don't hold your breath waiting for me to care."

Philip nodded. "Okay, okay. You hate me. I get it. You think you're gonna go back to them and explain all this and they're gonna say okay, no problem Katerina? Those guys, Federov, they're Vor, you understand? You know what that means? They go into the Russian prisons, the gulags, and when they come out, they're members of a great big, fucking family. You see those tattoos on his hands? They go all the way up his arms and all over his body. I'm telling you kid, you see one of these guys with stars tattooed on their knees, that means they bow to no one. You see stars on their shoulders, you can run but you'll never escape, you understand?"

Katerina watched Philip's mind catch up to his mouth, the full weight of all he had said, of all he had brought her into, settling on him.

She couldn't catch her breath. How many nights had passed already? Winter was out there. Somewhere. Alone. *Where are you? Are you alive?*

Katerina gathered her purse and slid out of the seat. "You can get the check," she said.

Philip caught her arm with a light touch. "Kid—"

"Leave it alone, Philip," she said, shifting out of his grasp. "Just leave it."

Chapter 134

The cell phone buzzed. Katerina held the phone in her hand, staring at the number. She clicked on the phone and brought it to her ear.

"Return to the policeman," John Reynolds said. "Tonight. Rekindle the relationship. Open your legs and allow him to *penetrate* you as often as he likes. Report his progress on the case to me."

The thick silence on the open phone line hung between them.

"Do you understand?"

"Yes," she said.

"Good. And Katerina, remember to appear to enjoy yourself."

The call clicked off.

Katerina sat with the phone at her ear, feeling as if everything within her had been scraped away, leaving nothing more than raw, ruined skin.

***

Emma got the text after ten o'clock. Frank, sitting on the couch and channel surfing, turned to her for an explanation.

"Katerina," Emma said, pushing off the couch. "She wants to talk."

Frank turned back to the television, his expression sour, his mouth set in a grimace. He heard his fiancé talking softly into the phone until the bedroom door closed.

***

Detective Ryan Kellan made a beeline into his apartment building and up the stairs as if he were chasing a suspect. Nearly stumbling as he took the last steps, he threw open the door to his floor. When he rounded the corner, he found Katerina Mills leaning against the wall next to his apartment door.

He took in the flushed complexion, her sheepish look of awkward, shy embarrassment.

Ryan took halting steps but after a moment's hesitation, he swept Katerina into his arms, tasting the salty stream of her tears mingling with the kiss. As she broke down, he unlocked the door and ushered her inside the apartment.

Chapter 135

Daniel Clay grabbed his bag from the rotating carousel. Scanning the terminal, he spotted Nicholas and they fell into step with each other.

"What no uniform? No sign?" Clay asked.

"Fuck you," Nicholas said.

They pulled up their collars in unison as they stepped out into the frigid night air.

"This is a waste of time," Nicholas said.

"Not a chance," Clay said. "My boy goes missing, that's news."

"She's back with the cop."

Clay stopped short. "No shit?"

"No shit," Nicholas said. "You clear this with the Boss?"

"Yeah, yeah, he knows," Clay said as he started walking again. "He's fine with it. Trust me, wherever Mr. Winter is, he's coming back for her."

"Uh hunh," Nicholas said.

They walked for a minute in silence. "So you're not going to carry my bag?"

"Fuck you," Nicholas said.

Chapter 136

Katerina answered her cell phone. "Monsieur Letourneau," she said.

"They called," he said. "They know you are in New York. Why did you not stay in Iowa?"

"I wish I could have. It was beautiful there," Katerina said.

"They have sent a message," Letourneau said. "They want the name. Now."

Agent James Sheridan. Now, she would have to deal not only with him, but the drug dealers as well.

"Did they say anything else?"

They said you have fifty thousand reasons to give it to them."

Katerina closed her eyes. *They know about Richie's money.* "Thank you for your help, monsieur," she said.

"Listen to me, Katerina. They are coming for you," he said. "Do you hear me? They're coming."

"*Merci, monsieur,*" Kat managed. "Thank you for your kindness." She hung up before he could say anymore.

Chapter 137

In the middle of the night, Alexander Winter sat up, wide awake. The Gideon Bible lay open on the other side of the bed. He got up and moved to the motel window. Shielded by the curtain, he watched the street, one hand tapping a relentless rhythm on his thigh. The ritual didn't comfort him. In his other hand, he gripped the sacred stone, massaging its smooth edges.

His cell phone buzzed. He picked it up, staring at the number. He tapped the green button and held the phone to his ear as he looked out of the window.

"Good evening, Professor," Thomas Gallagher's voice came through the line. "I heard you had to leave your student unexpectedly. Pity."

Winter's teeth clenched, radiating pain in his jaw. He smelled the sharp scent of his own perspiration, anger mixed with fear.

"Are you still there, Professor?"

"Yes," Winter said. "I'm still here."

"You should have let my two operatives take hold of her upstate. All of this could have been avoided. Now, look what's happened. Now she's all alone."

Winter listened to Gallagher sigh through the line.

"Let me comfort you in your last hours. Have no anxiety about our girl, *Bob*. I'm going to rescue her. She'll be in good hands, no one will get to her. No one."

Winter heard the line click. He put the phone down. His mind floundered in a swirling eddy of panic. Desperate to quell the storm, his hand played a frenetic tapping rhythm against the side of his leg. He went to the desk, arranging items: key, bottle of water, phone, pencil, pen. He lined them up, then started again until he clamped his eyes shut, forcing himself to stop and stand very still.

Winter heard Katerina's voice in his head, the pep talk in the van, before their first job in the Hamptons.

Bob, I am in deep shit.

If you could pull yourself together and help me get through this.
She's out there, alone.
She's not ready.
I have to get back to her.

Winter assessed the situation. It was impossible to be sure how much Gallagher knew. He had to assume the accounts, identifications, everything was compromised. He would have to go back to the beginning and do this old school. The way he had learned years ago.

The way she taught me.

Chapter 138

Linda Mills sat at the table, the scent of cigar smoke hanging in the air. A bottle of vodka stood on the table next to an empty cup of tea. In the fireplace, the flames crackled, warming up the small, comfortable living area.

Sergei brought the envelope to the table and extracted the photocopies. His shirt sleeves, rolled up past the elbow, exposed the mosaics of tattoo ink snaking up his strong arms. He examined the ledger and the bill of sale, passing them over, one at a time, to Linda Mills.

She reviewed the papers and passed them back, watching Sergei fold and tuck them back in the envelope. Finally, he handed her a handwritten note. Linda Mills fingered the scrap of paper. Struggling to focus her tired, red-rimmed eyes, she read the words several times.

> Dyadya, please keep these safe for me.
> Katya

She handed it back to Sergei, letting her fingers rest on his forearm. "How can this help her? she asked.

Sergei placed his hand over hers. "I do not know. But she is clever girl, little Katya. We have to wait and see."

Chapter 139

A self-described romantic, Professor Evans, tall, trim though not athletic, had sensitive eyes and a mop of unruly dark hair that fell over his forehead. He had a reputation for being considerate of student opinions; he preferred lively discussion, rather than lecture, to explore the text.

"Now, we come to what I think is the crux of Macbeth," he was saying, "the matter of his guilt. Does it truly make a difference that Macbeth is conflicted over what he has done? What he is doing? Clearly the visions he sees in Act Two are an expression of his discomfort with his own deeds."

A young woman, Bethany, raised her hand. Katerina knew her from other English classes. Bethany was also on the pre-law track. Katerina had pegged her as a competent, driven person, wholly unimaginative, convinced of her own black and white view of the world. Kat disliked Bethany for no other reason than her disdain for the girl's spotless mind.

"You think, yeah, the guy feels bad, sure, but he's still doing it, so good for him that he's self-aware. So what?"

"Well, it is good for him," piped up another student, a girl Kat didn't know. "It does matter that he cares. We've all done things."

"Killed people?" Bethany said. "I don't think so."

"Okay, not killed people, but we've all done things, fooled around on someone, told a lie, stolen something. No one's perfect. Even a monster has a piece of humanity."

Killed people. Katerina remembered her question to Winter. *Have you ever shot anyone? Have you ever killed anyone?* The sickening panic, the crushing guilt, her constant companions, squeezed her heart until she felt the physical pain. *I promised I would always protect you. Where are you? Are you still alive?*

"Mmm, mmm," Professor Evans interjected, "humanity within the monster. That's a fascinating point."

Katerina glanced around at the other students while the screaming sounded in her head. *How can you sit here listening to this? Don't you know what's happened?* Still, she continued to play the part of the interested student, carrying on as if all was normal. Her nerves would not cooperate; like sparkplugs, they tormented her with the urge to get up and run out of the room. *I was supposed to be gone. We were supposed to disappear together.*

Professor Evans nodded his head in approval. "I think these are fascinating questions to consider, especially when we look at the circumstances. Macbeth was a fine soldier and an honorable man, but at the mere suggestion that he could be King, we watch a man's natural inclinations, the human conditions we all suffer from, curiosity, vanity, greed, and desire, begin to lead him on the path to destruction."

"But he wasn't really ever good," Bethany said. "Look at what he said. 'I'm up to my ass in blood but if I stopped killing, it would be tedious?' The guy is saying he'd find it boring to stop committing murder, as boring as if he kept doing it. What's that about?"

"You are a little loose on the accuracy of the quote," Professor Evans began, to a collective laugh from the class, "but that is a fascinating question. This, I think, is one of Shakespeare's most misunderstood passages. What does Macbeth really mean by this?"

"His personality won't be different if he stops," another student piped up. "He'll still be greedy. He'll still want the kingdom."

"I think it means he doesn't give a damn," Bethany said. "He doesn't care."

"It won't change anything," Katerina said.

"Uh, something will change. Someone else won't die," Bethany challenged.

The class went quiet.

"What do you mean, Katerina?" Professor Evans asked.

"What he's done, he can never make it right," Katerina said. "It'll never be right again. So what's the point?"

"Oh, so he's bored by that?" Bethany said. "It's *tedious* to him?"

Katerina looked Bethany in the eye. "Tedious has other meanings. You have your phone. Look it up. It means unrelieved. He'll never have relief from what he's done. There's no forgiveness, anywhere, ever. There's nothing to do but keep going and take it to the end."

"This is fascinating, just fascinating," Professor Evans said. "Excellent work, Katerina. Excellent."

***

After class, Katerina headed for the subway. She got off in Midtown and walked over to Rockefeller Center. Wandering over to the railing, she stared down at the ice-skating rink, watching while she waited. Then she felt it, the change in the air as he came alongside her.

"*Mishka*," Ivan said.

Katerina continued to gaze down on the skaters making their gentle curves and turns. "You remember what you said the last time we saw each other."

"*Da.*"

"You said, 'Someday, you will have despair.' You said, 'Do not despair. You paid me. I work for you.' Did you mean what you said?"

"*Da.*"

Katerina Mills opened her purse, extracted a newspaper clipping with a photo, and passed it to him. He examined the picture and glanced over at her.

"That's John Reynolds," Katerina said. "Kill him."

Coming Next

Katerina Mills Will Return In:

The Fixer: The Good Criminal - Part One

ABOUT THE AUTHOR

Jill Amy Rosenblatt is the author of *Project Jennifer* and *For Better or Worse*, published by Kensington Press. She has a master's degree in creative writing and literature from Burlington College. The Fixer series is Jill's first adventure in self-publishing. The first two books in the series are available in e-book and paperback formats. She is currently at work on Part Two of the fourth book in the series, *The Good Criminal*.

She lives on Long Island.

You can visit her at her website, https://www.jillamyrosenblattbooks.com

www.ingramcontent.com/pod-product-compliance
Ingram Content Group UK Ltd.
Pitfield, Milton Keynes, MK11 3LW, UK
UKHW021028100125
453365UK00013B/693